The Falcon of Siam

AXEL AYLWEN

The Falcon of Siam

METHUEN

Acknowledgements

I would like to acknowledge my gratitude to Tony Koltz for pointing me in the right direction, to Trish Garibaldi and Susan King for hours of deciphering my hieroglyphics, and above all to the patience and tireless counsel of Elsbeth Lindner – editor extraordinaire.

First published in Great Britain 1988
by Methuen London Ltd
11 New Fetter Lane, London EC4P 4EE

Copyright © INTERSAF CO. (ASIA) LTD. 1988

Printed and bound in Great Britain

British Library Cataloguing in Publication Data
Aylwen, Axel
The falcon of Siam.
I. Title
823'.914[F]

ISBN 0-413-16340-7

To my loving family,
Mother, Bennie, Sasha and Christopher

This book is drawn from history, but makes no claim to adhere to it. The Siamese records were all destroyed in the eighteenth century when the invading Burmese sacked their capital city of Ayudhya, while contemporary accounts of foreigners – Jesuits, missionaries and adventurers – are for the most part conflicting. So who, 300 years later, is to say what really happened . . .?

One

─────────────

It was the sudden glint of steel that saved him, a flash of sunlight that reflected off the deadly blade and shot across his closed pupils, jerking him instantly awake. Briefly he glimpsed the tip of the curved Malay dagger shimmering behind the teakwood mast and in the next instant his assailant was lunging for him.

Phaulkon had been prepared for a general mutiny but not this solo attack; he was dozing on deck with his back to the second mast and his legs spread. Instinctively he rolled to the left just before the Malay flew past him like a hurtled spear and buried his kris into the mast, in the very spot where a split second ago the Greek's head had been resting.

Now Phaulkon scrambled to his feet and spun round to face his cursing opponent. Thirty years old, Constantine Phaulkon, skipper of the 120-ton Siamese junk *Royal Lotus*, stood a good head taller than the wiry Malay deck hand who was frantically trying to extract his kris from the solid teak in which it was embedded. With a cry of frustration he abandoned the attempt and whirled angrily round on Phaulkon.

For a moment the two men faced each other, unarmed, each sizing the other up. They were alone on deck. Around them lay a flat coastal sea, and in the distance the mountainous outline of the shore was visible through the morning haze.

Both men were barechested. Phaulkon wore the black, baggy pyjama-like trousers of the Chinese while the Malay, Faisal, was clad only in a loincloth. In the deceptive early light of dawn they could almost have passed for kinsmen, so similar were their jet-black hair and deep brown complexions – the one from birth and the other from years of sun and sea. Then the sun emerged from a cloud and shattered the illusion as an oblique ray picked out the high cheekbones and the recessed nose of the Malay in contrast to the sharply defined Mediterranean features of the Greek.

I

Warily they circled each other in the free space between the masts. Phaulkon considered shouting for his colleagues, the two Englishmen below decks, but thought better of it. What if the other Malays awoke first? There were three more of them below and they would outnumber the Europeans four to three. Suddenly it struck him as odd that Faisal had not called on the others himself.

'I'm surprised you're acting alone, you cur,' Phaulkon said in fluent Malay, as cautiously they gauged each other like two boxers in a ring before the first exchange of blows.

'Why, pig-eater? I won't need help to spill your infidel blood.' Faisal turned his head to one side and spat contemptuously on deck.

'I'll have you strung up before the day is out,' growled Phaulkon, throwing his head back to keep the hair out of his eyes.

'If you're alive to do the hanging, Captain.' The Malay's laugh was scornful and his black, semi-slanted eyes flashed defiance.

Phaulkon's instinct was to smash this dog to pulp. But first he needed to know why Faisal was attacking now, and attacking alone. There was too much at stake in the hold. If the Malays knew about the hidden cargo . . .

'Why aren't your friends with you?' he demanded.

'What good will it do you to know,' retorted Faisal, 'when you're rotting in hell with the rest of the infidels?'

Spurred by his own words the Malay charged, aiming a vicious kick at Phaulkon's groin. The Greek twisted sideways and moved his hands to protect himself but only partly cushioned the blow. Wincing with pain, he grabbed the Malay's foot and jerked it with all his strength to one side. Faisal let out a squeal but with acrobatic agility cartwheeled his whole body round in a full circle, wrenching his foot free. As he stood unsteadily before Phaulkon, his right foot clearly injured, the Greek moved in. He aimed a massive blow at Faisal's solar plexus but though the Malay was not reacting with his usual speed he managed to sidestep and the Greek's fist glanced off his ribcage instead.

It was just enough to wind him and, as Faisal fought for air, Phaulkon ducked under his shoulder and swung his right arm over the Malay's head, locking him in a grip of iron. The vice

2

contracted and Faisal's initial cries quickly turned to muffled chokes.

'If you want to stay alive you'd better speak now,' barked Phaulkon. 'Why the attack?' Phaulkon's grip tightened until the Malay's eyes bulged. Then slowly he released the pressure to allow the man to speak.

'*Berhenti disitu! Jengan dekat!* Stay where you are!'

The shouts had come from behind. Phaulkon wheeled round, dragging Faisal with him. Standing a few feet away at the top of the companionway were Achmed and Mohammed, their krises drawn.

They hesitated a moment, then a look of concern came over Achmed's face and he thrust the kris back into his loincloth, nudging his companion to do the same.

'Tuan Kapten, you are all right?' he inquired obsequiously. 'We heard cries and came running. Has this dog been misbehaving?' He pointed a finger at Faisal.

Phaulkon stared hard at Achmed, the first mate and leader of the crew. As tortuous a devil as ever drew breath, but a canny sailor by Malay standards. Were you behind this, you squat-nosed vermin? he wondered. And why?

'Your mate tried to kill me while I was dozing, if that's what you call misbehaving,' retorted Phaulkon drily.

Achmed flared. 'Leave him to me, Tuan Kapten, if you please. This dog has dishonoured us.' He moved closer and Phaulkon braced himself for some treachery.

'Stay where you are, Achmed. I will question him myself.'

'He is a member of my crew, Tuan. I am responsible for him, and I must punish him to restore our honour.' Achmed continued to advance, an expression of apology on his face.

'Don't move,' snapped Phaulkon. 'You will have him when I have finished with him.'

At that moment there was the stamp of bare feet and the gangling form of Richard Burnaby, dressed in an ankle-length white nightshirt and armed with a musket, appeared at the top of the companionway. Behind him scrambled Thomas Ivatt, a diminutive Englishman with a thick crop of woolly brown hair. Both men were out of breath. They stood, an incongruous pair, staring in confusion at the scene.

'What the hell is going on?' demanded Burnaby, cocking his

3

musket at the Malays. Achmed stopped just short of Phaulkon. 'Are you all right, Constant?' called Burnaby.

'Yes, Richard. A little misunderstanding with Faisal, that's all.' The Greek's English was accentless, the product of twenty years in the service of His Britannic Majesty's merchant marine. He had joined in 1658, a stowaway child of nine.

'Please explain to His Excellency that we cannot endure such dishonour,' said Achmed pleadingly to Phaulkon. He could not communicate directly with Burnaby, as the honourable chief of the East India Company in Siam understood no word of Malay.

'Achmed is very anxious to administer justice himself, Richard,' said Phaulkon. 'Keep him covered.'

'Tuan Kapten,' said Achmed addressing Phaulkon, 'Faisal here, to my eternal shame, is my blood brother. Allow me to question him in your presence. He will tell me what he would never tell you, even under torture.'

'What is he saying?' demanded Burnaby.

'He wants to interrogate Faisal himself,' said Phaulkon. 'Claims the vermin wouldn't reveal anything to me anyway. Keep them all covered, Richard, and you too, Thomas, but don't shoot unless you have to. We need every one of this festering, two-faced crew to man the junk, God curse our luck.'

It was true that Faisal would not squeal, thought Phaulkon. These Malays might be outwardly fawning but they had guts of iron. Perhaps he would read between the lines of Achmed's interrogation. He pushed Faisal towards the first mate.

Achmed grabbed Faisal by the arm and led him out of Phaulkon's reach. Then he whispered something in Faisal's ear and pointed skywards. As Faisal looked up, Achmed's kris flashed and Faisal sank to the deck, the blood gushing in torrents from his throat. He did not even have time to scream.

'Good God, man!' exclaimed Ivatt, steadying himself against the ship's railing.

'Forgive me, Excellency,' said Achmed, bowing to Phaulkon. 'But whoever insults the Tuan, insults me too. It was the will of Allah. May his name be for ever praised.'

'Goddamn you,' cursed Phaulkon, starting towards him.

'It's no use, Constant,' cautioned Burnaby. 'We'll never know the truth now.' With difficulty Phaulkon restrained himself. The old man was right. For once his proverbial caution was justified.

4

'No risk' Burnaby they called him. There was no point in punishing Achmed. The blackguard was the only one of the Malays who knew anything about sailing a ship anyway. But had they found out about the cargo? he wondered. His stomach clutched at the thought.

Achmed now motioned to his companion, and together he and Mohammed raised Faisal's body and carried it, dripping blood, to the ship's side. 'Allah's will be done,' pronounced Achmed, as they swung the body overboard. In that instant, as if he had been an invisible witness to the proceedings all along, Abdul the massive cook appeared silently on deck with a bassinet of water and a short rattan brush. His narrow eyes, almost disappearing into the copious folds of his cheeks, took in the scene impassively. He squatted down and with casual movements began to wash the blood off the deck. Then he walked over to the stern and took up his customary position behind the giant black cauldron which he stirred at frequent intervals from dawn to dusk. There was a perpetual smell of curry about him.

'All right,' said Phaulkon, glancing at the sky and gratefully sniffing the wind, 'we're moving on.'

They had been anchored for the night off the coast of Ligor and he was suddenly anxious to leave this stretch of coastline behind him. It was here that the Malays had begun to act suspiciously, culminating in Faisal's attack. 'Achmed, Mohammed, let's make sail and weigh anchor. You'll have to handle the work of three men now.' Next he turned to Ivatt, who was still leaning against the rail staring at the Malays. 'How are you faring, Thomas? You can go below and rest if you like.'

'Thanks, but I think I'll stay here.' He smiled thinly. 'I'd hate to miss more of the action. I've led such a quiet and retiring life up to now. It's time for a change.' Phaulkon smiled. He liked the little man, even though he had known him only a short time, and he knew that Ivatt's life had been anything but quiet and retiring.

Thomas Ivatt had had more than his share of excitement, and horror. Born into a performing family in Yorkshire, he had watched his grandfather mauled by a tiger in a menagerie when he was only nine. When his partner on the trapeze, John Matthews, had slipped and fallen to his death before his eyes, he had quit the travelling theatre and joined the East India Company, hoping, at the age of twenty-two, to start a new life and

5

obliterate the memory. At this moment Ivatt wondered whether he had been wise to give up the dangers of the high wire for the 'quieter' life of Asia.

'What the devil happened with Faisal?' asked Burnaby, ambling up to Phaulkon, still holding his musket cocked in front of him. Strands of his straw-coloured hair ran wild over his normally well-coiffed head. There had been no time for toiletries this morning. As befitted his rank, to which he had risen slowly, the chief factor in Siam prided himself on being fastidiously groomed at all times. Now, at the age of forty-eight, it had become an obsession.

'He waited for me to doze off and then tried to kill me, Richard. I should have wrung a confession from him, while I had the chance,' said Phaulkon bitterly.

'Were the others in on the attack too?' asked Burnaby, shaken.

'It's hard to say. They were below decks when it happened. But my guess is they were waiting to rush you and Thomas as soon as they got the signal from Faisal.'

'So they know about the merchandise, then?'

Phaulkon avoided the question. 'Let's get underway before we discuss this further. This particular stretch of coastline makes me uneasy.'

He pointed to the shore some ten miles away, at the white ribbon of beach and the fringe of jungle. In the far distance were mountains where the late monsoon clouds were beginning to spill their rain. Somewhere in there, he reflected with disquiet, was the river of Ligor.

'I want you to mark each of the Malays,' continued Phaulkon. 'Don't let the bastards out of your sight at any time. Even the cook. I don't trust him any more than the dung he throws into that damned cauldron.'

There was a flurry of activity now, as the *Royal Lotus*'s great sails, beautiful pieces of work woven out of palm rushes, were hoisted, caught the wind and bellied. Built of sturdy teakwood in the boatyards of Ayudhya, Venice of the East and fabled capital of Siam, the ship was modelled after the junks of the Middle Kingdom whose traders had for centuries brought tea and silks and porcelains to Siam, and sailed back to Canton with bulging cargoes of sapanwood and rhinoceros horn, spices and tigers' bones.

6

The wooden anchor weighted with stone was hoisted into place and in a few moments *Royal Lotus* was underway. The two-masted Siamese coastal trading junk, duck-bellied, flat-bottomed, her enormous sails bamboo-ribbed like bat wings, her brown hull sleekly varnished in tung oil, was heading due south down the Gulf of Siam.

'So, Constant, you still maintain they know nothing about the merchandise?' They had been deliberating for some minutes over the reasons for the attack and there was a note of exasperation in Burnaby's voice. He was sure Phaulkon was wrong for once, but the pleasure Burnaby might normally have felt at proving his canny deputy fallible was somewhat marred by the thought of what the consequences might be if the Malays did know about the hidden cargo. Burnaby took his hands off the wooden deck rail and clasped them firmly behind his back. Next to him, Ivatt listened in silence, one eye on the Malays.

Phaulkon looked across at them from the helm and casually took in the positions of the crew. Next to the lanky chief of station, Ivatt looked even more diminutive than usual. Mohammed was scrubbing the deck, Abdul stirring the cauldron and Achmed surveying the coastline.

'I took every precaution, Richard,' he replied. 'The Malays were given the day off during the loading and I had every one of them followed.'

'Why did that dago try to kill you then?' persisted Burnaby.

Phaulkon shrugged. 'Perhaps I offended him in some way. You know how sensitive these Malays can be.'

'Do you think it might be time to let me know what's going on?' asked Ivatt, grinning. 'It might help me decide whether to side with you fellows or the Malays.'

Burnaby glanced at Phaulkon but the Greek discreetly shook his head. It was not that he did not trust Ivatt, but the less people knew about the contents of the hold the better.

Ivatt glanced from one to the other, awaiting an explanation. This was not the first time he had noticed that the Greek had the last word. Though he seemed to pay lip-service to his chief, it was increasingly evident that it was Phaulkon who was in command. He certainly looked the part, mused Ivatt, observing the athletic frame and the strong, self-assured bearing. The large

7

hazel eyes reflected amusement and defiance in ready succession, and the smile could charm a raging buffalo.

'There is nothing to tell you really, Thomas.' It was Burnaby who spoke. 'We are not sure of the position ourselves. You know as much as we do. One of the Malays attacked Constant this morning and we are obviously going to have to be alert. Unfortunately we need the rest of them to man the ship.' It was an unusually casual statement for Burnaby.

Out of the corner of his eye Phaulkon saw Achmed and Mohammed slip down the companionway and he nodded quickly to Burnaby and Ivatt. They turned and followed the Malays below decks.

Phaulkon tugged at the line that held the tiller to straighten his course and glanced up at the sky. Though it was barely past the hour of nine in the morning the sun was already high in the heavens and as usual at this time he put on his white muslin shirt over his baggy trousers to shield him from the tropical onslaught. He was alone on deck now but for Abdul the cook who continued to stir his pot impassively, and he was grateful for the solitude. They were sailing parallel to the coast down the narrow isthmus that separated the Gulf of Siam from the Bay of Bengal, or more broadly the Pacific from the Indian Oceans.

With one eye on Abdul and the other on the expanse of ocean before him, he let his mind range over the events of the previous day that had led to this morning's attack, seeking the clue that eluded him.

The junk had been ten days down from the mouth of the Menam Chao Phraya, the Noble River, or River of Kings, which to the Kingdom of Siam was what the Nile was to Egypt or the Ganges to India, the mother of life and civilization. A sweet northerly breeze had held steady for the first nine days but then had died during the night. The burning sun had risen on limp sails and glassy sea; no cloud intruded into the brilliant sky, no breeze stirred. The junk wallowed in still waters within sight of shore, its Malay crew listless, its cargo silent. Even the ever-present creaking of the timbers was noticeably absent. Nothing seemed capable of trespassing on the surrounding peace.

Nothing, that is, except Phaulkon's own instincts. Two things gnawed at him. One was the awesome stillness of the ocean which lay hushed as if gathering strength for some terrible

8

purpose, and the other was a subtle shift, barely perceptible, in the manner of the crew, ever since they had sighted the point of Ligor at dawn that morning.

Phaulkon expected Malays to be obsequious. It was an attitude they adopted with masterful guile, but Achmed had slipped up to him at first light grinning considerably more unctuously than usual.

'We must be approaching Ligor, Tuan?' Achmed's final inflection had suggested a question.

'Why do you ask?' Phaulkon had inquired in his fluent Malay. 'We're putting in at Songkhla, not Ligor.'

The Malay had glanced up at the sky and Phaulkon had followed his gaze. Everywhere, as far as the eye could see, the heavens were the colour of an Aegean summer and the ocean, like a vast shimmering lake, stretched out unruffled to the horizon.

'With the weather so calm, Tuan, would it not be wise to put in to Ligor? We are not making any headway as it is, and we could at least replenish our provisions.'

'Our papers authorize Songkhla not Ligor. Songkhla is only two days away and we have ample provisions.'

According to their official papers, embossed with the august seal of the Barcalon, the First Minister of the great King Narai of Siam, *Royal Lotus* was granted passage from the capital of Ayudhya to the Malay States south of the Siamese frontiers. En route she was permitted to put in at Songkhla, a southern Siamese port, for trade and provisions. Besides the Malay crew of four, the register bore the names of three farangs, as white foreigners in Siam were known; Richard Burnaby, chief of the English East India Company's trading post at Ayudhya; Constantine Phaulkon, his deputy and the ship's captain; and Thomas Ivatt, a new recruit from the Company's headquarters in London.

The cargo's manifest indicated superior English broadcloth of the finest vermilion dyes, much prized by the ceremony-hungry rajahs and sultans of Malaya, many of whom owed allegiance to the powerful monarch of Siam. Their official cargo was not, however, all that *Royal Lotus* carried. For concealed within the great bales of cloth – and known only to Phaulkon, Burnaby and one Captain Alvarez – were five of the finest Dutch cannon, priceless items of merchandise, cast in Amsterdam by de Groot

9

himself. The East India Company's regional headquarters in Madras had no more knowledge of their presence on board than the Siamese authorities in Ayudhya. Together, these cannon were powerful enough to destroy – or create – a kingdom, and in Pattani, their ultimate destination just ten leagues south of Songkhla, their value was beyond price. To the Muslim Queen who ruled that state, they were to be the means of defence against, and even deliverance from, the Buddhist Kingdom of Siam. The Queen of Pattani had refused to send the annual tribute of a flower of gold to Ayudhya, which was required of every vassal state, and it was only a matter of time before the royal regiments of war elephants arrived from Siam to chastise her. Just two months ago, Captain Alvarez, Phaulkon's secret emissary to the court of Pattani, had sent word that . . .

Phaulkon laughed out loud. The recollection of Alvarez's plight still convulsed him. In the stern, Abdul the cook looked up from behind the large black pot that partially hid his expansive frame and glanced quizzically at Phaulkon before resuming his endless stirring.

Poor Alvarez! He had boasted of his amorous conquests once too often. Phaulkon smiled again. The imperious Queen of Pattani, whose lusts were vastly larger than her tiny kingdom, had taken a fancy to the handsome Portuguese mariner, sent to her by Phaulkon to arrange terms for this dangerous enterprise, and forced him to remain with her as part of the exchange. In the desperate message carried to Ayudhya by a travelling Jesuit, Father Coelho, Alvarez had bemoaned his fate: the Queen kept him naked in her bedroom on a leash like a dog and ordered him to be fed huge quantities of blood meat to keep him virile, and measures of opium to dull his resistance. Alvarez had been so wrapped up in his tale of woe that he had almost omitted to mention the prodigious sum the rebellious Queen had agreed to pay for the cannon.

More than enough to put my cherished plan into action, mused Phaulkon. There were only four months left before the rendezvous with Samuel White at Mergui, Siam's great western port on the Bay of Bengal. When Samuel, buccaneer and private trader par excellence, reached Mergui with a large merchantman 'borrowed' from the East India Company in Madras, Phaulkon would have to be ready with the merchandise that would make their fortune in Persia: Chinese silks and potteries, Japanese screens, and Siamese scented woods and precious stones – the kind of merchandise that was in heavy demand at the opulent court of the Shahs. The sale of the smuggled cannon to the eccentric Queen of Pattani would provide the gold to purchase the goods for Sam White's boat.

Time was of the essence, for Sam's arrival and departure at Mergui was linked to the tides that prevailed across the Bay of Bengal and his ship would be able to put in to port only briefly.

'And how long will it be before the Siamese army comes to punish the Queen?' Burnaby, ever sceptical, asked as soon as Phaulkon had translated Alvarez's message to him. 'And when they do, don't you think they'll be curious to find out where she got her cannon from?'

But Phaulkon's plan was thorough. 'From me, Jan Federman, the free Dutch trader from Bantam. This is the name that Alvarez has given the Queen. And when the Siamese identify the Dutch markings, they will never for a moment doubt that anyone but the treacherous Dutch were involved.' It was common knowledge that the Siamese authorities had watched with growing alarm as the Dutch, hungry for colonies, swallowed whole tracts of Java and Sumatra, the rich spice islands of the Moluccas, the fertile Celebes Islands, and now, ever closer to home, the province of Malacca at the south-western end of the Malay archipelago. Nobody in government circles in Ayudhya doubted that the acquisitive Hollanders had their sights on Siam. What protection would 100,000 of His Siamese Majesty's war elephants be against the cannon and warships of Holland? Precious little, thought Phaulkon. Only diplomacy and canny political manoeuvring could outfox the Dutch at this stage. It was in keeping with the politics of the day that Jan Federman, fictitious Dutch trader, should supply cannon to the Pattani rebels; Constantine Phaulkon, deputy chief of the English East India Company, would never be suspected. It was a dangerous plan but one whose successful outcome would make him wealthy beyond dreams and enable him to set his political plans in motion – 'If the Gods and the weather and the devil-cursed Malays allow it,' he growled inwardly.

He had smuggled the cannon in from Bantam a year ago when he had first arrived in Siam as Burnaby's deputy to open the

English trading post there. While Burnaby fretted over the presence of such dangerous contraband in the East India Company's official warehouse, Phaulkon had waited patiently for the moment to use the weapons to their best advantage, and exploit their Dutch markings. The Siamese might be adept at making splendid multi-jewelled halters for their war elephants, but casting cannon was another matter. The homemade weapons produced by this highly artistic and largely agricultural people would as likely explode in their own ranks as decimate the enemy.

Phaulkon sniffed the air now, and turned his thoughts to the present. He tasted a changing wind. Thin high clouds raced across the sky and in the distance dark belts were blanketing the horizon. The ship's timbers were beginning to creak and groan ominously. There will be a storm, he thought, the one he had feared since yesterday. He gripped the tiller line and damned the gods of this place for the fickle weather. He wanted a steady wind to take them to Pattani, not a blasted gale. An early storm could force them into port at Ligor, and without papers to land there, the cargo might be searched.

Mohammed appeared on deck closely followed by Burnaby. As the Malay wandered casually over to Abdul, Burnaby approached Phaulkon. As always, the Englishman was dressed in European clothes, grey knee-breeches and a white laced coat. He was craning his neck skyward and shielding his eyes from the glare.

'What do you make of the weather, Constant?' he asked, with a note of sarcasm. 'I thought the monsoons had ended.' Burnaby had been against setting out so near to the end of the monsoon season, but Phaulkon, worried by the rumour that the recalcitrant Queen of Pattani had ignored a reminder to pay the mandatory tribute of gold to the court of Ayudhya, was anxious to close the deal before the Siamese army intervened. He had assured Burnaby that the monsoons would be over by the end of October. It was now 25 November 1679, and there was mounting evidence that a monsoon was in the making.

'Perhaps I was wrong, Richard. The rains are not always punctual. But this is a sturdy vessel and the shoreline is visible . . .' At times Phaulkon found it difficult to stomach Burnaby's constant fretting. If things had been left up to him they would never have ventured anywhere in their year in Siam.

12

'I think we should sail closer to shore anyway. No point in risking our skins out here,' fussed Burnaby.

Phaulkon laughed. 'Nearer to the shore we'd be at even greater risk. Here at least we're safe from inspection. No Siamese will put far out to sea in this weather.'

Out of the corner of his eye Phaulkon watched Achmed appear on deck and slip silently by them to join Abdul in the stern. Ivatt was close behind him. The Malay leader squatted down on his haunches beside the cook and chatted to him in rapid tones.

'We should be level with Ligor soon, Richard,' Phaulkon said, raising his voice so the Malays could hear him, though he knew they spoke no English. 'If things turn bad, we'll have time enough to pull into port.' He watched as Mohammed who was on his haunches scrubbing the rear deck glanced over at Achmed. The first mate lowered his eyes briefly to indicate that he too had heard 'Ligor'.

Ligor? Phaulkon wondered. Why are they so damned interested in the place? Ligor was a port, a river and a first-class province of Siam. No Siamese would have identified it by that name. Nakhon Si Thammarat, however, had been too difficult to pronounce for the early Portuguese – those master mariners who had discovered half of Asia and who for a century and a half had roamed the Eastern seas unchallenged. So they had named it Ligor, and all farangs still called it thus today; even the cursed Dutch, thought Phaulkon.

'Ligor, Constant?' Burnaby said. 'Never! The devilish Dutch have a factory there. They are already fuming that the Siamese have invited us back to trade in Ayudhya. They would be sure to instigate a thorough search. And when we are found with cannon—'

'I have no more desire to put into Ligor than you do,' interrupted Phaulkon. 'But the Malays seem very keen on the idea.'

'They must know about the cannon,' Burnaby muttered bitterly. As chief of station he would of course be the one to answer questions if the cannon were ever discovered.

'They are behaving almost as if they did, but I can't see how they could know.' In Ayudhya Phaulkon had hand-picked the men who had toiled to hoist the overweight crates from the Company's riverside warehouse into the hold of the *Royal Lotus*.

13

The labourers had all been Siamese, he had known every man among them and trusted them, and he had paid them well. The Malay crew had only been allowed on board after the crates had been thoroughly sealed and the hold barred.

'If Faisal was acting alone when he attacked you, what was his motive then?' persisted Burnaby.

'I did not say he was acting alone.' Phaulkon glanced round at the three Malays. 'But I have a feeling we may know the answer to that soon. These motherless mutineers are planning something right here, off Ligor. If we didn't need the extra deck hands I'd be for blasting them off the face of this ship here and now.'

Phaulkon would have preferred a Siamese crew, but that was impossible. Though they might be the pleasantest and most friendly people in the world, the Siamese were surely its worse sailors. They were only at home on the myriad canals and waterways that criss-crossed their beautiful land. They saw no point in tempting fate on storm-swollen seas where monsters and wrathful gods abounded. Only very high pay could tempt a Siamese to leave his tranquil waterways. Looking at his crew of cut-throats, Phaulkon mused that it might have been well worth the money. Yet there was one advantage to the Malays: like the subjects of the rebel Queen of Pattani, the Malays were Muslims, as fervent as any of the Arab traders who had come out of the Western seas four centuries ago to conquer and convert, driven by the will of Allah. If anything were to go wrong, they would be less likely to co-operate with the Buddhist authorities of Siam.

His senses sharpened. The three Malays were heading towards him and Ivatt and Burnaby were glancing at Phaulkon for guidance. Achmed stopped in front of Phaulkon and bowed. Mohammed and Abdul remained a respectful distance behind their leader. Burnaby and Ivatt stood behind them.

'Tuan Kapten, Your Excellency,' began Achmed, 'I am not afraid of the sea, but my men here' – he indicated the other two with a sweep of his hand – 'are unwilling to sail into this approaching storm. They fear the wrath of Allah is upon them for the cowardly behaviour of their brother Faisal. They want to be put ashore in Ligor before it is too late. I believe we are near Ligor, no, Tuan? They are sufficiently worried that they are even prepared to forgo their pay. But Allah is all-merciful, Kapten, because it happens I have a cousin in Ligor and can find you a

14

replacement crew in no time. I will of course sail on with you myself.' He bowed again. 'There is nowhere on this ocean I would not venture with the Tuan Kapten.'

Phaulkon stared him firmly in the eye for a moment.

'Your men were hired to do a job, Achmed, and you were hired to supervise them. They should not go to sea if they do not like storms. They will be put ashore when and where I say.'

'As you command, Tuan Kapten.' Achmed inclined his head submissively. Then he turned abruptly on the other two. 'You soft-bellied sons of whores!' he bellowed. 'You see how you have angered the Tuan and made a fool of me.' He drew his kris and raised it above his head. 'Get back to your work before you share Faisal's fate.' He turned briefly to Phaulkon. 'Forgive me, Tuan. Their shame is my own.'

He strode off, driving the other two in front of him, past Ivatt and Burnaby whose musket was already cocked.

'What was all that about?' inquired Burnaby anxiously.

Phaulkon considered for a moment and then looked up at the darkening sky. 'I think they are probably—'

A scream came from below. Phaulkon's eye skimmed the deck. There was no one there but the cook, squatting behind his pot as if nothing had happened. Fumes billowed skywards from the steaming cauldron. 'Quick, go and check below!' Phaulkon shouted to the two Englishmen.

They bounded down the companionway, Ivatt close on Burnaby's heels. There was another scream, a different pitch this time. Then muffled cries and, finally, silence. Phaulkon felt a cold shiver run down his spine. He edged forward, glancing sideways at Abdul all the while, and peered cautiously over the hatch. The lower deck was in shadow.

'Richard? Are you there? Thomas?' He heard nothing but the pounding of his heart.

With every nerve taut, Phaulkon inched his way down the gangway, pausing at each step to listen. A rat scurried in the shadows below him. At last his feet met the lower deck. Warily he held his arms in front of him, ready to lash out. He could hear breathing now, close by, but his eyes, fresh from the outside glare, were not yet accustomed to the semi-darkness. The ship's timbers groaned eerily. To his right, he knew, was the small

15

two-bunk cabin where the Englishmen slept, and on the left the large sliding door that led into the hold where the cannon were stored.

As the darkness dissolved, he made out a form lying not more than a few feet in front of him. The body was too short to be Burnaby's but it could be Ivatt's or either of the Malays'. Then the light grew dim again and he looked up to see the cook squatting above him, his huge form obstructing the light from the hatch. He was holding the boiling black cauldron by both handles, tipped slightly towards Phaulkon's head.

Suddenly the silence was shattered as the door of the hold slid open, screeching noisily. Phaulkon swung round. In the doorway, on his knees, was Burnaby, held firmly in place by the two Malays. His wrists were tightly bound in front of him – and a rope was wound about his chest and arms. Two nasty curved krises pointed at each side of his throat. Burnaby started to speak but Achmed immediately jerked his knife and blood seeped from the Englishman's neck. Even in the half-light Phaulkon could see Burnaby's eyes grow wide with fear.

Phaulkon checked his urge to lunge. He had been outman-oeuvred. The razor-sharp points of the krises would take only an instant to enter Burnaby's gullet. Was Ivatt alive? he wondered.

As Mohammed held Burnaby back at the point of his kris, Achmed advanced on Phaulkon.

'If you co-operate, your friends will live,' he said. All trace of his obsequiousness had vanished. In his hand he held a thick cord. Though neither the Siamese nor the Malays had any hemp, Phaulkon knew that the fibres of the coconut tree could be twisted into as tough a rope as anyone could ask for. He restrained his rage as Achmed tied the cord, first round his arms and chest, then about his wrists and feet, and shoved him roughly to the floor.

'Achmed!' came the cook's voice from above. 'The sky is closing in. It's getting very dark. You'd better take a look!'

Phaulkon could hear the splash of rain now, and *Royal Lotus* was beginning to roll and pitch with increasing violence.

Achmed bent over Phaulkon, his black eyes glaring. 'Now, Tuan Kapten, tell us how to steer for Ligor.'

'It's your ship now, do what you like with it,' said Phaulkon.

Achmed spat in Phaulkon's face. 'Infidel swine-eater, your

16

friend will pay for your insolence. Mohammed! Help the Kapten find his tongue.'

Mohammed jerked his knife roughly and Burnaby screamed. The chilling sound pierced Phaulkon.

'Constant!' gasped Burnaby, feeling the blood flowing slowly from his neck down his chest and arms. 'What are they asking you to do?'

Phaulkon ignored the question and with an effort controlled his voice. 'If you touch my friend one more time, you motherless savage, I will give you no help at all and the monsoon will carry you and your stinking crew down to a Mecca-less grave.'

'What monsoon?' scoffed Achmed. 'The monsoons are over.'

Despite the arrogance, Phaulkon detected a note of nervousness in the Malay's tone.

'The one that's about to engulf this ship and take us all down with it.' As if in confirmation, the boat rocked threateningly and Achmed put a hand on the gangway to steady himself.

'We will steer for Ligor. Now!' he barked.

'First get that savage off my friend.'

'Mohammed, throw him back in the hold. And the other one, too.' Achmed jerked a finger towards the motionless body of Ivatt.

'Is he alive?' demanded Phaulkon.

'Maybe,' shrugged Achmed.

'He'd better be,' Phaulkon said bitterly. 'And you'd better head for shore while there's still time.' The boat lurched more violently this time. '*If* there is still time,' he added.

Achmed forced a laugh. 'You think you're indispensable, eh, Kapten, and that I, Achmed, can't steer a ship? Well, you'll have plenty of time to contemplate your importance in the hold.'

Achmed and Mohammed half kicked and half dragged Phaulkon to the entrance of the hold and threw him roughly inside.

The door slid to, and the thick ironwood bolt ground shut behind them.

It was dark and cramped in the hold, but cracks of light appeared at brief intervals through the teak gratings, flashes of lightning that lit up the heavy, angular forms of the crates that occupied most of the space. The wind howled relentlessly and at increasingly brief intervals thunder struck with a shattering roar. Above

17

the prisoners' heads was the large trap door that opened directly on to the deck and through which merchandise was loaded; in front of them was the sliding door that led out into the lower passageway.

As soon as the bolt had slipped shut, Phaulkon wormed his way painstakingly over to Ivatt, bending over the little man until his ear rested on his chest.

'Is he all right?' Burnaby asked.

'He's just unconscious, thank God. What happened?'

'The bastards were waiting for us in the shadows at the bottom of the gangway. They were at our throats before we could even see them. Ivatt resisted and Achmed smashed him over the head with a belaying pin. They searched me and took the keys of the hold.' He paused. 'How bad is the storm?'

'Serious.'

'And those curs can't navigate worth a damn. I knew those blasted cannon would be our undoing,' said Burnaby bitterly.

'But you approved of them anyway,' countered Phaulkon.

Yes, thought Burnaby, thanks to that slick, persuasive tongue of yours. 'The Malays have clearly been tipped off,' he said aloud.

Phaulkon remained silent.

Burnaby grunted, 'Do you know why or by whom?'

'I can't answer that yet.'

The boat lurched wildly. 'We may never find out,' reproached Burnaby. There was a crescendo of grinding timbers. In the confined space, the men's bodies butted against each other. Flashes of light flared with increasing frequency and the sound of pelting rain grew in intensity.

'Are we going to lie here like pigs in a market cart?' demanded Burnaby irritably. 'Can't we do something?' The blood was still flowing from the cuts in his neck, though less steadily than before.

Phaulkon stopped tugging at the cords on his wrist, and considered Burnaby's question.

'Not as quickly as the storm can. When it's as black as night up there, the Malays'll think the world is coming to an end. Achmed'll stick it out but the others will plague him to fetch us. They'll come running for help soon enough, I'll wager.'

'Let's hope it happens before we founder and—'

18

The boat rolled and pitched wildly, cutting Burnaby off in mid-sentence and hurling him against the others. He swore. Then amidst the creaking and the rattling, came another sound, a series of low moans. Ivatt was stirring.

'Oh, Christ almighty, my head!' he groaned. 'Where am I?' He blinked and searched around him in the darkness.

'Thank God, Thomas,' Burnaby said. 'We were worried.'

'Thank you,' the little man said, turning towards the voice. 'This is not at all what they promised me at the interview.'

'Are you missing the submissive women?' Phaulkon asked with a tight smile, aware of the rosy picture the East India Company in London would have painted of life in the tropics. 'Or the cool sherbets?'

'At this moment, just the women actually.'

The boat lurched severely and then seemed to crash down on its nose. The three bodies tumbled against each other.

'Who the hell is steering this craft anyway?' asked Ivatt. 'The curry-stained cook?'

'At this point just the tide and the storm, I should think,' commented Phaulkon, struggling to sound calm as the boat heeled more massively than before. His mind was groping for alternatives if the Malays did not release them soon.

There was a groan from Burnaby who twisted his head to one side and retched. Then his body rolled with the next pitch and he cried out as his face plunged into his own vomit.

'Oh sweet Jesus,' moaned Ivatt. 'I was better off unconscious.'

The bolt above them snapped and the hatch was raised a little. There was a sudden shaft of grey light, and the rain-drenched face of Achmed peered down at them. His soaking turban dripped steadily into the hold. 'All right, Tuan Kapten,' he growled. 'Come up.' The hatch closed on them again. None of the three men spoke but their minds were all weighing the possibilities of escape. A moment later the lower door of the hold creaked open and Achmed steadied himself in the doorway, one hand on the frame, the other wielding his kris menacingly in front of him. He moved to cut Phaulkon's bonds.

'I'll need the others with me as well,' said Phaulkon firmly. 'We'll need every hand on deck if we're to survive this turmoil.'

'The others will stay here,' Achmed barked. With a deft

19

movement he slit Phaulkon's cords. Then he pointed up the gangway. 'You first. Move!'

Phaulkon stood still. 'Whose orders are you following?'

'I said, move!'

Phaulkon stared at him, gauging the distance. 'Whose orders?' he repeated firmly.

The Malay kept his smouldering eyes riveted on Phaulkon and readied his kris for the lunge. Then the ship heeled violently and the first seawater cascaded down the gangway. From above came a loud crash. It sounded like one of the masts. The Malay was thrown off balance and flung on to his side. He scrambled to his feet again and stared at Phaulkon.

The Greek had not moved, his sea legs holding him steady.

'Infidel son of a whore,' Achmed blurted out, 'your warehouse keeper sold you to the Dutch farangs at Ayudhya. They are waiting for you at Ligor. Now move!'

Phaulkon stepped on to the ladder, his brain spinning. So that was it. The Malays had been bribed to bring them to Ligor, to the Dutch factory on the coast. He climbed slowly, waiting for the right moment. His hands gripped the gangway firmly as the ship tossed and rolled like a wild stallion trying to throw its rider. The wind screeched and the monsoon rain pelted down on his head, and he lost his footing as a torrent of seawater fell across his shoulders with unexpected force. But his hands held on and his feet groped their way back on to the rung. Out of the corner of his eye he saw Burnaby being flung helplessly across the floor of the hold. Without the use of their limbs, he and Ivatt were at the mercy of the swell.

'Move!' shrieked Achmed from just below him. There was a growing note of panic in the Malay's voice. Phaulkon edged up one more rung, ostensibly seeking a foothold in the increasing sway. As his foot found the rung, a shaft of pain drove through his sole, and seconds later another piercing jab tore at the skin of his calf. The motherless cur was lunging upwards with his kris, prodding him on. He started to move again when there was a rousing cry, and the trussed-up form of Ivatt rolled towards the gangway, gathering speed as it went. Achmed twisted round to look and in that instant Phaulkon's foot smashed into his head. Both men lost their balance and pitched over backwards.

The Malay, still clutching his kris, landed squarely on Ivatt,

20

momentarily winding him. Then Phaulkon toppled down on both of them. The ship lurched and they were all thrown into a corner together. The Malay's arm came to rest an inch from Ivatt's face and he readied to plunge the dagger between the Englishman's eyes. But Ivatt's reflexes, conditioned by years of acrobatics, were instantaneous. He sank his teeth into the Malay's wrist and snapped his jaws shut with all his strength. Achmed screamed and struggled to free the arm that held the kris, but Ivatt hung on until he was forced to come up for air. In that instant Phaulkon grabbed the kris, swung it round and buried it deep into the Malay's heart. Achmed's body convulsed several times and then went limp.

Phaulkon jerked the bloody dagger free and cut Ivatt's ropes loose. The little man spat out a mouthful of blood. 'Tasteless,' he muttered.

'Well done, lad. But that's only the first course. Here, take the knife and free Richard. I'm going on deck.'

He climbed the ladder quickly now and peered over the top. The sky was almost black despite the noon hour, and the pelting rain stung his face. The main mast had crashed across the deck, leaving a trail of splintered wood and tangled rigging, and the sea was breaking over the ship with an angry roar. Glancing around the debris, he spotted Mohammed and Abdul cowering in the stern, clinging to the rail for dear life.

Ignoring them he groped his way to the helm and grabbed it. The sea and the wind tore at him as he exerted all his strength to swing the helm over. But the ship, now in the grip of a more powerful master, barely shuddered at the human effort and did not answer the helm. Phaulkon's anger mounted at the storm and the cursed Malays who had waited too long. He thought of his cannon and shouted himself hoarse at the elements – first in English, then in Greek, Italian and Portuguese. Remembering it was a God-cursed local storm, he bawled at it in Siamese and Malay too, his raging voice lost in the thunder around him.

If only he could work the ship closer to shore. At least they might try and swim for it. Each time the bow plunged into the depths, Phaulkon vaguely discerned the shore's outline, but then it disappeared as the bow soared up out of the water and rushed to meet the howling heavens. Was it fifty, a hundred yards away? He was not that far off course. With help he might just nudge

21

the vessel a few more degrees to port. Clinging desperately to the helm he craned his neck, searching for the others. The monsoon rain lashed his face, and his eyes smarted with the pain. Then a large wave pounded the stern, lifting the vessel into the air like a raised chalice and flinging it down into the swirling trough below. He almost lost his grip; his hands felt numb from the effort of hanging on to the helm. He yelled now for Ivatt and Burnaby, doubting that his voice would carry above the roar. But just then he caught sight of the tall Englishman groping his way to the head of the companionway.

'Hold on,' Phaulkon yelled, as another wave hurtled down on them and the ship reeled from the blow. Between onslaughts he raised an arm to wave the Englishmen over to him. The pressure on his other arm was intolerable. Quickly he thrust his hand firmly back on the helm. Mohammed and the cook, whose eyes were glued to Phaulkon, mistook the signal for them and, trusting in the wisdom of this raging seaman, made a run towards him. But the hungry sea ambushed them and swept them off their feet, carrying them to the side, screaming. Mohammed was dashed against the solid teak railings and his guts spewed across the deck. Abdul was cruelly lifted on the crest of a wave to give the shrieking cook a bird's eye view of his colleague's fate, before being plunged mercilessly into the swirling waters below.

Momentarily spellbound by the fate of the Malays, Burnaby and Ivatt groped their way painstakingly towards the helm and then made a dash for Phaulkon's outstretched arm. 'Help me to swing to port,' he yelled. 'Every degree counts.'

They struggled with the helm, while the sea seemed to grow more furious and resentful with their every effort. But the ship inched round and gained precious moments as each great wave propelled her a little closer to shore. Then Burnaby lost his grip and the helm swung back. Phaulkon locked his arm round it and both he and Ivatt hung on to Burnaby, struggling to pluck him back from the clutches of the ravenous sea.

The ship was off course again now and taking in water fast. The storm had reached a peak of fury and the towering ocean was cascading down the hatch in torrents. Phaulkon could feel the increase in the ship's weight and knew that it would be only moments before the sea engulfed her for the last time.

There was nothing for it, he realized with a sinking heart. They would have to abandon ship – and its cargo, too – and swim for it.

'We're going to have to swim ashore,' Phaulkon cried above the roar. 'I'll go first. You follow me. Try to ride the crest of a wave. We're less than fifty yards away. Can you swim, Thomas?'

'Yes, though I don't go out much in this weather,' he shouted back, grinning even now.

Would to God Burnaby were fifteen years younger, Phaulkon thought, as he wrenched a half-loosened plank from under himself and thrust it towards the older man. 'You'll stand a better chance with this, Richard.'

Phaulkon took one last look around him and held on as another angry wave roared across the deck. Then he muttered a quick prayer to the Almighty, climbed over the rail and jumped into the boiling water. Burnaby and Ivatt plunged in after him and the very next instant another huge roller descended on the wounded ship and tore it apart. With the thundering crack of a thousand timbers the hull caved in; from every direction the waves moved in for the kill, flinging themselves against the dying ship, swamping and smothering it, pushing it ever downwards: first the bow, then the masts . . . For a while the stern held its head up proudly above the swirl until it too gave up and slid down to its ocean grave.

Only vaguely aware of the destruction around him, Phaulkon was carried off by the mountainous sea and sucked up to the crest of a wave. After the biting chill of the monsoon rain, the water below seemed warm and with an effort he forced himself on to his stomach and flailed frantically in the direction of the shore. If only he could cover enough distance before exhaustion set in, his mind kept telling him, the undertow might be less severe close to shore.

Then the folly of such speculation came home to him as the giant wave he was riding crashed with a deafening roar and bore him down with it, hurling him helplessly out of control. His knees knocked into his chin and his limbs were jerked out of their sockets; he felt as if his whole body were being ripped apart, like his ship before him. For a split second he thought he glimpsed the shoreline, even imagining there were people there – hands straining towards him. He fought to get a closer look but his

23

strength was failing. The sea took advantage and thrust itself down his throat, choking him with its nauseating saltiness.

Then the covetous ocean claimed him back and swept him out on a powerful riptide. He knew the helplessness of a child once more and felt a brief exhilaration at the thought of surrender. Peace. No more struggle. To yield to the force of the sea and let it draw him where it would.

As if reading his mind, the undertow dragged him further off, resigned to his fate, and prepared him for the final sacrifice. Then he spotted a huge roller heading towards him, growing ever taller as it fed on the waters in its path. With a flash of defiance his anger returned and the will to live surged desperately in him. He could not die here, not now, with so much still to accomplish. Not now, when his life's course was taking shape and his ambitions were within his grasp. The suction caused by the giant wave was terrifying but he allowed himself to be drawn towards it at breakneck speed before he swung up and around, brilliantly judging the moment, and soared towards the shore, like a low swooping bird, on the peak of the mountainous wave. Closer and closer it bore him until he realized that if there were rocks further in, he would be dashed to bits against them. But to give up now was certain death. He had to ride the giant till the end.

Without warning the wave broke and threw him on to something hard; the roar in his ears was shattering and he thought he had died.

Hands clutched him and lost him, and he swallowed huge quantities of water. Like a great hooked fish he rose one last time and was flipped over and slammed face first on to the sand. He knew no more.

Two

Bantam, Java 1676

It was a sultry morning in the crowded, noisy streets of Bantam. Lithe, Sumatran peasant women balancing earthenware jugs on their heads mingled with lighter skinned hawkers in Chinese coolie hats carrying poles across their naked shoulders, twin jars of rice and tea water hanging at either end. Noblemen in formal dress of multi-hued batik were followed by dark-skinned, scantily clad Javanese slaves, holding umbrellas over their masters' heads to shield them from the scorching sun or the pelting rain – whichever prevailed. Pale oxen with nostalgic eyes were driven through the mud-baked streets by willow-legged herdsmen who spurred them on with sharp sticks and rested a sinewy hand on their fly-covered rumps to guide them through the throng. Diffident, mangy dogs sniffed the ground and scampered about for any form of sustenance.

In a small side alley, oblivious to the teeming life around them, two men sat on a wooden verandah huddled in earnest conversation. One, obviously the elder of the two, ebullient, large-bellied and curly-bearded, was arguably the greatest trader in Asia, while the other, an ardent, strong-featured youth in his mid-twenties with lively eyes and a Mediterranean complexion, sat forward in his rattan chair, hanging on the older man's every word. Both men had removed their shirts in the heat, and an unlit cheroot hung casually from the older man's lips.

There, on the creaking, canopied verandah of the single-storeyed house on stilts, they had talked through the night and past the dawn, sipping brandy from delicate Venetian glasses. It was the finest black market brandy available in cosmopolitan Bantam, offloaded from the Spanish galleons that called there to discharge a discreet portion of their rich cargo bound for Manila. It had been a year since the two men had last met and they had much to catch up on – women, Company gossip, dreams and failures.

The expression on the older man's face suddenly changed and he pulled himself up in his chair, extracting at the same time the unlit cheroot from his mouth. For a moment he observed his apprentice thoughtfully as if to reassure himself one final time that the younger man was worthy of his confidence. Then he spoke.

'We will shortly be receiving a visit from a Spaniard of noble birth who is in financial difficulties. He claims to have five superlative cannon for sale.'

'Cannon?' asked Phaulkon, taken aback.

'That's right, lad. And I'm thinking of buying them.' George White paused. 'For you to take to Siam.'

'Siam!' Constantine Phaulkon whistled through his teeth. The very mention of the place had always instilled awe in him. More, he sensed his destiny to be linked to that exotic, virginal, semi-forbidden land whose vast resources lay untapped and whose door to the outside world was barely open.

He had listened avidly to travellers' tales of diamond-caparisoned royal elephants feeding off the breasts of voluptuous maidens, and marvelled at the wealth of exotic stories brought back by the handful of traders who had been there. However disparate and conflicting the rumours about Siam appeared to be, one element bound them together. There was not one visitor who had not professed to be fascinated by all he had seen. Phaulkon longed to learn the truth for himself.

Then, almost six months to this day, here in Bantam, he had encountered his first Siamese. An ambassador and his secretary, wearing conical hats with varying numbers of rings of gold, their fingers bedecked with rubies and diamonds, had disembarked from a Dutch ship. They had attracted considerable attention, walking with studied grace and smiling constantly, and during their entire audience with the Governor they had remained prostrate, lying respectfully on their bellies like glittering lizards. They had remained but a short while in Bantam but the sight of them had left an indelible mark on Phaulkon's mind.

Now George White, the brilliant, unorthodox trader to whom he had been apprenticed for most of his seafaring life, had unexpectedly appeared from a secret visit to that very place, bringing a sudden sense of possibility to Phaulkon's dreams.

26

'Siam!' he repeated, unable to contain his excitement. 'When? How soon?'

'Very soon, if all goes well in London,' said George White, his blue-green eyes still full of lustre despite the lack of sleep. 'The great King Narai himself has invited the English traders back.'

'Through you, George?' Phaulkon's heart beat a little faster. Fabulous stories circulated the foreign trading posts about the King of Siam and his retinue.

George smiled and lit his cheroot. 'You might say that. Casually, unofficially, you know. It wouldn't do for His Majesty to appear too eager. First he sent feelers to Madras. I was there at the time and I wagered His Siamese Majesty was a bloody sight more perturbed than his silk-coated emissaries would allow.' He lowered his voice. 'It's those arrogant Hollanders who are the cause. They actually had the gall to blockade the estuary of his holy river, the Menam, and demand concessions.' White slapped his knee. 'And by Jove, they got 'em! That must have put the fire of Hades into His Majesty's veins. The Dutch bastards now have a monopoly in the trade of hides from Siam to the Japans. Worth a bloody mint, I should say!'

Phaulkon had heard of this episode. He sought out whatever scanty information was available on Siam, though the contradictory reports made it difficult to separate truth from myth.

Small wonder, he thought, that George had lowered his tone. They were, after all, in Bantam, until a year ago the territory of the Sultan of that name, now a fully fledged Dutch colony administered, officially at least, from Holland.

George read his thoughts: 'It's only by the grace of God and a little help we gave the Dutch against Catholic Spain that the English are still allowed to maintain a trading post here. But for how long? We're no safer here than they would be under us. They're too much like us, the truth is. Clever, cunning, thorough, good traders. But they're just not English, that's their—' George's voice broke off and he looked over the wooden rail into the street. Phaulkon followed his gaze. A shrunken beggar, barely in his teens, was crawling up to them on hands and knees and holding out a withered arm. One of his emaciated legs was half the length of the other. 'In Madras they mutilate the poor devils at birth to arouse greater sympathy,' said George despondently. 'I suppose it's the same here.'

'I'm afraid so,' said Phaulkon. 'When a family can't afford to feed another mouth . . .'

'Well, there are no beggars in Siam, thank God! Except for the King and all his courtiers.'

Phaulkon looked perplexed. 'What do you mean?'

George threw a coin to the skeletal boy and smiled. 'It's some nation, I tell you, lad. They're all Buddhists there and, to learn humility, every one of them from the King down shaves his head and spends half a year of his life in a temple. During that time he goes out at dawn every morning with a little wooden bowl and begs for his food.' George shook his head. 'There's a lot some of our English aristocrats could learn from these Siamers, starting with the board of our own honourable Company.'

The beggar stared at the coin for a moment, transfixed. Then he beamed a toothless smile at George and hopped deftly in and out of a group of naked children, who were scooping water from the puddles and dousing each other with shouts of delight. They stopped for a moment to let the beggar pass and he disappeared jubilantly into the crowds.

'So the King of Siam has invited the English to open a factory in Ayudhya,' said Phaulkon, eager to renew the conversation. 'But how will a few traders counter the Dutch menace?'

'It's more than a few traders, lad. It's a symbol. As a branch office of Madras, in turn a branch of London, in turn a part of the royal monopoly, why, those few traders in Siam will be the tip of the fingers on the long arm of His Majesty King Charles of England, long may he reign.' George winked. 'Despite the treasonous behaviour of some of its employees, the Company does represent good King Charlie, and anyone tangling with it must reckon with that.'

The Company, mused Phaulkon. So vast and all-embracing, no one even bothered to use its full name: The English East India Company, the most powerful trading monopoly ever created. In 1661 King Charles II had laid down the latest charter. Ten years ago Phaulkon had learned it by heart. It was required reading for all employees.

'We of our ample and abundant Grace have granted the Company of Merchants trading in the East Indies that they and their successors shall for ever hereafter have the *WHOLE ENTIRE* and *ONLY* trade and the *WHOLE ENTIRE* and

28

ONLY liberty use and privilege of trading to the East Indies. And *ALL OTHER* of our Subjects we prohibit to visit or trade in the East Indies by virtue of our Prerogative Royal . . .'

Yet enforcing such royal edicts on the high seas of seventeenth-century Asia was easier said than done and a host of private traders, more buccaneer than gentleman, plied the waters from Persia to the Japans, lured by the smell of ample profit and as ready to line their own pockets as those of His Britannic Majesty. The Company chiefs themselves, snug in their headquarters at Madras on India's eastern seaboard – and far from the scrutiny of London – often overlooked the rules and traded for themselves on the side, branding as 'interlopers' lesser mortals who did the same. For rare was the Englishman in these parts, of whatever standing, who had not come East to seek his fortune.

'And *is* the Company going to open up in Siam?' asked Phaulkon, his heart quickening.

George gestured for him to be silent. 'I'm coming to that. Don't be so impatient, lad. You Mediterraneans have got to learn to exercise control.' He shook his head despondently. 'And after all the years I've tried to make a proper Englishman out of you.' George wore the expression of a teacher whose favourite pupil had just let him down and Phaulkon could see that he was amusing himself. 'The art of control, my boy, is essential to getting along in Siam. You don't shout and rant and rave, God forbid, or even raise your voice. You smile whenever you're angry or hurt or embarrassed and you swallow your frustration. You never let the other person know your feelings. You show courtesy – and more of it – at every occasion.

'In order to get it right, you unlearn all you've ever learned and start all over again, like a newborn babe.' George leaned forward. 'Why, when I was there I saw a poor devil flogged almost to death in the public square. No sooner had he recovered, by the grace of God, than he sent lavish gifts to His Majesty, thanking him for pointing out his failings and ordering his chastisement. The poor blighter never once cried out, despite the harshness of the punishment, for to do so would denote protest at the justice of his sentence and earn him double the penalty.' George paused and stared down the alleyway in front of him. He sighed. 'Ah, the sounds and smells of Asia! How I shall miss them in England.'

29

A bullock cart drawn by two grey-white oxen with mournful eyes had just turned into their alleyway and was heading down the muddy street towards them. Bells round the beasts' necks announced the cart's passage, its over-sized wheels sinking into the rain-soaked ruts and clattering noisily as they were dragged out again. In the cart was a profusion of tropical fruits – bananas, mangoes, mangosteens, pomelos and jackfruits. Their pleasant aromas, mixed with the more pungent stench of the toiling oxen, wafted up to the verandah.

And how I shall miss you, thought Phaulkon. For in his heart he knew that once George was back in England he would be too old to return. Asia without him would never be the same.

The old man had been like a father to Phaulkon, the father he had not seen since the day he had stowed away on the English merchantman that had lain in harbour in Cephalonia. He was nine years old and already fired with a hunger to see the world and make a place for himself. His life at sea had begun that day as he had hidden, trembling, in the hold, praying that the ship would leave before he was discovered. He had tried not to think of his mother who doted on him but only of his father's beatings and of the dreariness and confinement of the little island; its whitewashed houses and its whitewashed walls and its interminable gossip.

His father thrashed him regularly with his thick leather belt, usually on the flimsiest of excuses, especially when he was drinking, which was often. Young Phaulkon sensed that his father was unhappy because he had come down in the world and people still talked about it, about how the great Andreas, Constant's grandfather, had once been the Governor of the island while his son had gambled away the family money and prestige and been reduced to running an inn on the waterfront.

'You know why, of course?' the sniggering villagers would say. 'Because the drinks are free there!'

The young boy had overheard the gossip and it had cut him to the quick. He had sworn never to be a failure himself and one day to restore the family fortunes. The image of his grandfather, tall and proud, whom he had never known, had remained his guiding light; he pestered his mother to tell the same stories about him again and again. His good, kind mother. How she had suffered for his beatings.

30

In those breathless, interminable moments of waiting in the hold, the tearful image of his mother kept returning to haunt him and stamp his soul with guilt . . .

'What have we here, then?' The bearded sailor who had discovered him behind some crates had looked down at him with a combination of amusement, surprise and irritation. 'The youngest mariner I ever did see, by Jesus. You'd better come with me, lad. The captain's going to have a few words to say to you.' Young Phaulkon had followed the straw-haired giant with a sinking heart, but as they climbed the gangway to the upper deck, he noticed with a surge of hope that the shoreline was out of sight. Perhaps they would be too far out for the captain to turn back now.

'Begging your pardon, Captain, sir, but I discovered this young mariner hiding in the hold. Shivering like a newborn pup he was, behind some crates.'

Before the stern man in the smart blue uniform, standing with his hands behind his back, could answer, the boy had fallen on his knees and reeled off the string of English words he had painstakingly translated from Greek and committed to memory. It had been his first exercise in persuasion.

'Sir, please sir, I am small but strong. I look like a boy but I work like a man. I work like a man but you can pay me like a boy.' A curious crew had gathered round and, encouraged by their laughter, Phaulkon continued boldly, 'And when your crew is hungry, Sir Captain, I can make the best Greek stew. I learned from my aunt who is famous all over the islands.' When the laughter had subsided, the captain issued an order which Phaulkon did not understand. The extent of his English was limited to the words he had memorized. At the age of nine he spoke only Greek and Italian: Greek from his parents and Italian from the Venetians who ruled Cephalonia.

The captain was asking him a lot of questions now and he just knelt there with his head bowed repeating over and over: 'Forgive me, Sir Captain, I cannot yet understand. But I will learn to speak your language. Please give me a chance.'

He looked around him. One man was smiling at him kindly and Phaulkon smiled back, beaming gratefully at him, aware from his mother that his smile was a pleasing one. Then he smiled up at the captain and looked at each of the crew in turn.

He saw more friendly faces than not. He waited till he felt the moment was ripe, then he stood up and removed his shirt. There was a gasp from the audience. Across his shoulders and back were a series of nasty welts.

'My father . . .' he said. The meaning was all too clear. 'Please, Sir Captain, help me to stay with good people.' A tear rolled down his cheek and he saw from the expression on the captain's face that he had won.

'What is your name, boy?' asked the captain, in a gentler tone.

That much the young lad understood. 'Constantine Gerakis, Sir Captain.'

'Gerakis? That means a falcon,' observed the first officer, a keen student of ancient Greek.

'We'll never remember that. We'll call him Constantine Falcon,' announced the captain.

In no time he had become the ship's pet and the spelling of his name had changed from Falcon to the more Greek-seeming Phaulkon. After serving on a variety of merchantmen for six long years as a cabin boy, he had finally been apprenticed to Captain White of the East India Company. For the next ten years – the happiest of his life – he had roamed the Mediterranean, the Barbary Coast and Asia with his effusive master, gleaning the wisdom that would help him pursue his ambition and – like his mentor – following the rules only when they were fair. Phaulkon had never loved another man as much.

At the age of twenty-six, his life had changed. Through his own diligence and George's recommendations, he had been promoted to senior clerk at the East India Company's Java office, at Bantam. Here were the headquarters of the Dutch East Indies empire, the greatest empire in Asia. There was much to be learned.

'You've seen enough of the ocean for one lifetime, lad,' George had said. 'And you won't get much further than captain on the water. Now on land that's a different story. There's room for the likes of you to manoeuvre.'

The old man had recently begun to feel his age. He was fifty-five and though his mind was unimpaired, his body felt increasingly tired. It took a greater effort to achieve the same things as before. But he still had plans to fulfil and matters to resolve and it was young Phaulkon whom he had chosen to see them through.

He loved the lad like a son and knew that if he could channel the youth's enormous energies and talents in the direction he wanted, and curb his tendency to leap before looking, the chances of success were more than even.

George was convinced that for the English, Siam was the key that would determine whether they would dominate Asia or not, because if Siam fell into Dutch hands, the overall grip of the Netherlands would be too strong to crack. Moreover, time was running out. Those peabrains in Madras could not see beyond the end of their grog-reddened noses. That was why he would go straight to the board in London . . .

George had stayed only three months in Bantam and during that time he had casually instilled the notion of Siam into his protégé until he could see that the lad's appetite was whetted.

Phaulkon was at first desolate when George was called away on a 'special mission', especially as the old man was not at liberty to disclose any details; worse still, he did not even know when George might be back. Phaulkon had been with George without interruption for ten years and it was like losing both a father and a best friend. Phaulkon reacted by immersing himself in his work – accounting, warehousing and filing – and in mastering the Malay and Dutch languages, gleaning at the same time what information he could about Siam, though unfortunately no books on the language were available.

It was the Dutch who controlled trade with Siam, and his increasing knowledge of the Dutch language allowed Phaulkon to devour every paper on the subject. Thus engrossed in his studies, he had awaited news of the old man.

Now, a whole year later, George was back, and from Siam of all places! Instinctively Phaulkon sensed this was a turning point in his life. He looked at the old man now.

'And in Siam, George, did you meet the King?' It was a question he had been longing to ask. The wealthy potentate, around whom so many legends were woven, had always fascinated him.

'Meet the king?' replied George with a short laugh. 'Why, in his realm the King of Siam has more power than even the Sun King old Louis of France. At the mere mention of his name people fall flat on their faces. Nobody has ever gazed upon His Majesty's countenance, except perhaps the girls in his harem when they lie with him, or the Bishop of Heliopolis who brought letters from the Pope and King Louis.' He leaned forward confidentially, enjoying Phaulkon's excitement. He knew full well he was not telling the lad anything new, but Phaulkon listened avidly as if every word were a pearl. 'I hear negotiations dragged on for six whole months before the Bishop was finally given clearance to stand in His Majesty's presence. It was the first time any human being had not lain flat on his stomach before the King of Siam, and it caused a sensation at court.' George chortled. 'The old ecclesiastic was rushed off to China before he had time to disclose his impressions!

'It's a society that's bound with rules like hoops of iron, with the King on top and everyone else beneath in clearly defined ranks and orders, like our own navy. I tell you,' he sighed, 'there is no more splendour this side of Cathay. When His Majesty leaves his palace, twenty thousand slaves are in attendance, and the mandarins of the court bow low on their bejewelled elephants and vie for his attention.

'No one meets the King, my boy. Why, a person has to be raised to the rank of the nobility before protocol allows His Majesty even to address him.' He chuckled. 'A wise precaution on his part. Though his ancestors have followed the Buddhist faith for two thousand years, the French Jesuits are trying to make him a Catholic, the Persian ambassador a Muslim, and the Dutch traders a Protestant.' With a decisive movement George extracted from his mouth the Manila cheroot and brought his face nearer to Phaulkon's. 'And *you*, me lad, must make him a fleet!'

'A fleet?' exclaimed Phaulkon.

George's eyes flashed defiantly. 'That's right, boy. He has none of his own. That great country has none,' he repeated as if amazed by his own statement. 'The Siamese are an agricultural people. They don't travel and they don't trade.'

'What do they do, then?'

'They live, lad. That's just it. They know how to enjoy themselves. Food, women – the pleasantest in the world – games, dancing, festivals, it's a *rich* country, boy.' He shrugged. 'When there's more than enough food, loving and shelter for all, why bother with toil and commerce?'

'And that's why the Moors run the country's foreign trade,'

34

muttered Phaulkon, mostly to himself. It had always amazed him how no ethnic Siamese were seen in Bantam, or anywhere else in the trading world for that matter. The Moors, all Muslims, were descendants of Indian and Persian traders who had settled in Siam generations ago. Some had intermarried with the Siamese but most still bore the distinct features of their Aryan race. The representatives of Siam abroad looked like any other Indian merchant.

'The Moors have commerce in their blood, lad,' elaborated George. 'From Siam's western port of Mergui they trade across the Bay of Bengal with their cousins in India and Persia. It's a bloodsucking monopoly. And they rob the King blind.'

'But why does His Majesty allow it?' demanded Phaulkon. He had often asked himself the question. He was especially curious now that George was confirming the rumour.

George shrugged. 'Because it's always been that way, and traditions die hard in Siam. And because his own people are not interested in the job. But there are others who could fill the role.' He paused. 'They could give His Majesty a better return and still have plenty to fill their own pockets. Anyone come to mind, Constant?'

'You and I again, George?' Phaulkon laughed happily. 'The old team!'

George smiled. 'Now you're talking, lad.'

'But how, George?'

The older man leaned forward. 'I have it on good authority that these Mecca worshippers are getting too big for their bootstraps, that they're beginning to look more to the Persian ambassador than to the King of Siam for direction. I've even heard that a great conspiracy of the faithful is underway to bring Siam under the wing of the Prophet, like Acheem and Golconda and Java and Malaya and Borneo and the southern Philippines—'

'Who is backing the Moors?' broke in Phaulkon eagerly.

'Quite a team, lad. The Shah of Persia in Isfahan, the Great Mogul in Delhi and the Grand Turk in Istanbul.'

Phaulkon whistled. He was quiet for a moment, then his eyes lit up. 'Couldn't we get the Company to supply the ships?'

George shook his head sadly. 'If they even had the sense of newborn babes we could. But those halfwits in Madras are so busy lining their own pockets, they can't take the time off to think. And they're scared brainless of starting a war with Holland, especially without London's authority.'

'Why haven't the Portuguese offered their services? I hear there are still some four thousand of them in Siam.'

George brought up phlegm and spat over the wooden rail. 'The Portuguese are washed out, lad. No sea legs left in 'em.' For a moment a shadow came over his face and he looked almost sad. 'And to think they were once the finest seafarers in the world. Let it be a lesson to us all. Those poor devils up in Siam are intoxicated with opium, wine and sirens' calls.'

'Not a bad way to go,' smiled Phaulkon. 'They say the women are the finest in Asia.'

'The women, lad?' The old man's turquoise eyes danced. 'I had to drag these old bones away before they made a fool of me.' He winked. 'They're the fairest creatures on God's earth. Slender, graceful, for ever smiling. With your appetite, you'll love 'em all. God save the poor wenches!' He turned his eyes to heaven. Then he closed them for a moment and settled deeper into his chair, his cheroot back in his mouth. There was a smile on his lips and Phaulkon wondered whether he was dreaming of some recent encounter. With difficulty he restrained himself from disturbing the old man's reverie.

His own mind crowded with thoughts, of the Portuguese, the Dutch, the Moors, the women of Siam, the King and his fleet. He had read with fascination the accounts of the early Portuguese travellers, De Barros and De Couto, who had first described Siam and the beautiful island capital of Ayudhya, a metropolis larger than Paris. Its maze of bustling canals had given rise to its name, 'Venice of the East', and its three hundred golden pagoda spires were said to glisten like flaming jewels against the sky. All the early travellers had been captivated by it, as instinctively he knew he too would be.

In 1511, when the envoys of Don Alfonso d'Albuquerque had first sailed up from the Portuguese settlement of Malacca and set foot on Siamese soil, they had been received by King Ramatipodi II with lavish hospitality – and boundless curiosity at the sight of the first Europeans. A friendly and profitable relationship had blossomed between the two countries. In exchange for trading posts and lucrative concessions in sapanwood, gold leaf, saltpetre,

36

buffalo hides, birds' nests and rhinoceros horns, Portuguese mercenaries served as officers in the armies of Siam, when 250,000 foot soldiers and 20,000 war elephants marched on the arch-enemy Burma.

But now, with only a viceroy still in place at Goa and a couple of governors in Macau and Timor, Portugal was but a name – though a glorious one on the roster of history: first to sail round Cape Horn, first round the Cape of Good Hope, first to circumnavigate the globe. Phaulkon was fond of the Portuguese. He had been to Lisbon and traded with them in North Africa; he had studied their language and perfected it in Asia – it was still the lingua franca of Asian trade – and he admired their gallantry and good humour. They were honourable people, mostly. After 150 years in the saddle they were clinging desperately to their special relationship with the Siamese crown and attempting by every means to stem the advance of the Dutch, calling them sea gypsies with no fixed abode.

How transitory were the reins of power, reflected Phaulkon, how soon the players of history dethroned. As a child he had learned of the glories of ancient Greece, even while the Venetian invaders ruled his island home. And now, the great Buddhist Kingdom of Siam, with its many tributary states and its vast wealth, was at the mercy of new predators: the Moors from within, the Dutch from without.

But how could he build His Majesty a fleet? For a moment he wondered if George had gone soft in the head. No, he decided. The old man was as sane and canny as ever. The idea was brilliant. The fact that the English had been asked back to trade in Siam suggested that the shrewd King Narai was looking for a buffer against the Dutch. If the English could ingratiate themselves and capitalize on the King's immediate needs, it was not beyond the realms of possibility that they might be asked to build and run a trading fleet for him across the Bay of Bengal – especially since the Moors were robbing him blind. Someone with experience of Asian trading and conversant with Asian languages could be put in charge . . .

Phaulkon looked over at George. The sly devil, he's planted the seed and now he's leaving me to digest. Typical! That was how the old man had always taught him and that was how Phaulkon had learned to think things out for himself.

But build His Majesty a fleet without the help of the Company? George had ruled out their co-operation. Why would the motherless Company not help anyway? 'Damn it,' he burst out aloud, 'it was Madras who sent you to Siam to investigate in the first place!'

'Aye, they wanted an old dog to perform a last trick.' The old man smiled. 'Well, lad, I'm going to do more than that. I'm going to circumvent Madras and go straight to the board in London. I still have a little influence there and old Sir Joshua sits up pretty straight when I talk. And I'm going to see to it, before I retire, that Siam is fully opened to English trade and that *you*,' he wagged a finger in front of Phaulkon's nose, 'are the one to oversee it.'

Phaulkon for once was speechless. 'But . . . the Company would never . . . I'm only twenty-seven, too young . . .'

'To be promoted to chief factor?' broke in George. 'True enough. And it wouldn't look right for me to suggest it either. That's why I'm going to recommend Richard Burnaby, with you as his second.' He winked. 'You can handle him.'

Phaulkon's mind was spinning. If anyone could manage it, George could. Some of the bureaucrats on the board in London might despise George for his unorthodox tactics, but others who had a little vision secretly admired him, and the president, Sir Joshua Childe, was a man of action.

'Now just remember this,' continued George, emphasizing every word, 'the Siamers are looking for someone to counter the power of the Dutch. That someone must be us, because the soul-thirsty Jesuits are already pushing for France. "La grand alliance" and all that Gallic extravagance. And the cunning Jesuits are the only ones who have mastered the tongue-twisting lingo. Now with your gift for language . . .'

Phaulkon smiled. George had touched a nerve again. Phaulkon had been longing to learn Siamese but there was not a teacher available anywhere or a book on the subject. The more rumours he heard about the impossibility of the language, the more determined he was to master it at the first opportunity.

'Learn it fast, lad. And then teach yourself a brand new set of manners.' He smiled. 'Forget those of the English gentry I've tried so hard to instil in you, and embrace those of the Siamese aristocracy instead. You never point at someone's head, or show

38

him the soles of your feet, or cross a bridge when a gent of rank happens to be passing below.'

'But the fleet, George, will you get the board in London to finance the fleet?'

'No,' replied George, firmly. 'Too much red tape. There's a better way. *I'll* send you your first ship, captained by my brother Samuel, who's joined the Company in Madras. He'll get lost somewhere in a storm in the Bay of Bengal and seek shelter at Mergui on Siam's west coast. You find a way to buy the cargo to fill that ship – and you will. Once I've got you to Siam.'

'And the rest of the fleet?'

'It'll take no more than one shipment to show the Siamese Treasury how much the Moors are pocketing. The Siamese themselves will jump to finance the rest. All you have to do is purchase – officially, mind you, from the Siamese Treasury – a full complement of goods for Persia and load it on Sam's ship. Then you sail it to Persia, instead of the Moors, and devote half the profits from that single journey to the Siamese crown. I tell you, lad, it's more than they'll have seen from the Moors in a lifetime.' George suddenly laughed. 'Why, you might even be the first commoner to be addressed by the King!'

George stood up and walked over to Phaulkon. He put an arm affectionately round him. 'I want my schemes for Asia to live on in you, my lad. So make yourself as indispensable to those Siamers as you were to me throughout the years—'

There was a flurry of movement in the street below and an irrepressible voice broke in on them.

'Ola, señores!'

White and Phaulkon looked down over the verandah. A large Spanish-style hat was doffed and a broad grin was beamed up at them.

'This must be the man whose intermediary came to offer me the five cannon,' said George quickly. 'I've never met him but I'm intrigued. I asked him to come here rather than to the office.' Phaulkon knew George well enough to be aware that if an offer 'intrigued' him, it probably meant he had a definite plan in mind already.

'This is the aristocrat fallen on hard times?' whispered Phaulkon, barely concealing his surprise.

'It could happen to any of us,' chuckled George.

39

The tall, one-eyed Spaniard was standing below the verandah gazing up at them. Apart from the black eyepatch, he wore half a week's stubble on his cheeks and his hair was unkempt and matted. His ruffled lace blouse and black breeches were covered in dust. A skull and crossbone pennant flying above him was all that was missing to complete the picture.

'Do come up, señor,' said George. 'You must be the Marquis de Alcatraz?'

The Spaniard's grin widened even further and he hobbled up the wooden steps that led to the verandah. He had a noticeable limp and he seemed grateful to sink into the rattan chair offered him.

'That is one of my names, señor,' he said grinning. 'It is easier to meet people that way.'

Phaulkon glanced at George. His face remained impassive.

The Spaniard mopped his brow with a dirty kerchief and looked around him importantly. His single eye settled greedily on the half-empty bottle of brandy that stood on a wicker table in one corner of the verandah.

'A glass of brandy, señor?' asked George politely.

'Why not?' The Spaniard's eye remained fixed on the bottle as if he feared the contents might evaporate if he turned away.

George carefully poured three glasses. The verandah was open to the elements on three sides yet the air was hot and muggy. A bamboo awning kept the overhead sun out, and only an occasional ray penetrated here and there through slits in the lattice-work. Flies buzzed about but the mosquitoes had mercifully gone into hiding for the day.

'*Salud*, señores.' The Spaniard drained his glass and handed it back to George for more. 'We are very fortunate to make our acquaintances.' His one eye roamed from one to the other of the men. 'You are with the English Company, no?'

George nodded.

'Sorry, my English is not so good,' continued the Spaniard.

'You're doing fine, señor. By the way, my name is Constantine Phaulkon.'

The Spaniard inclined his head slightly. 'Don Pedro de Alcatraz y Mendoza is at your service. Ah, señores, mine is a long history.' He cast his arms tragically up to the heavens as witness. 'You see before you an officer of the Imperial Spanish Navy. I served on the great ship *Santa Cruz* when we carry fortunes in gold from New Spain to Manila. And now . . .' He shrugged and pointed to his leg. 'After the accident, I am, er, you say, retired, no? But I have connections, señores, many connections—'

'Connections to special merchandise, I understand,' prompted George.

'Ah, *si, muy especial*.' He handed his glass out again as if requiring sustenance before proceeding. He waited for the glass to be filled and then drained it again in one go. 'I have, for sale,' he said leaning forward confidentially, 'five of the finest Dutch cannon. Originals from de Groto.' He kissed the tips of his fingers appreciatively. '*Preciosos!*'

White and Phaulkon exchanged glances.

'Cannon from *whom*?' asked Phaulkon.

'De Groto, señor. *El numero uno* in Amsterdam.'

'He must mean de Groot!' exclaimed George, impressed.

'Si, si, de Groto,' confirmed the Spaniard, seemingly delighted that they were familiar with the exclusiveness of his merchandise. He looked at them conspiratorially. 'Because of special circumstances, I can sell at special price.'

Phaulkon wondered how this cut-throat could possibly have acquired such a priceless commodity, probably the finest cast cannon in the world. And not one, but five of them!

'How did you come by these cannon?' asked George.

'*Perdon*. Come by?'

'Er, how did you find them?'

'Ah, señor, in my business discretion is everything. My reputation, you understand. I cannot say where I buy just like I cannot say where I sell.' He spread his palms out. 'Fair, no?'

'I am afraid we're not interested, señor,' said George.

The Spaniard looked downcast. He was silent for a moment. 'If I tell the señor more, can I count on his discretion?'

'Possibly,' answered George.

'*Bueno*.' His one eye shone with pride. 'I buy from Prince Dai before he escape to Siam. His followers capture the cannon from the Dutch, but when he escape he need gold not cannon.'

It was just conceivable, reflected Phaulkon. Prince Dai, leader of the notorious Macassars, a fanatical Muslim tribe from the Celebes Islands who swallowed opium before battle and routinely fought to the last man, was the subject of endless speculation in

41

Bantam. His people had been slaughtered by the Dutch in their advance on the Celebes and the Prince had finally fled into exile with what remained of his men. He had sailed for Siam where the King was reputed to grant ready asylum to political or religious refugees.

The germ of an idea was forming. Phaulkon turned suddenly to George, switching into a Scottish brogue he had picked up in the navy. 'There are still a number of vassal states owing allegiance to the Siamese crown, are there not?' Phaulkon saw from the bewildered expression on the Spaniard's face that he found the accent unintelligible.

'Quite a few, lad. Why?'

'Are any of them in a state of rebellion just now?'

George considered for a moment. 'I heard that the Queen of Pattani is becoming hostile, though I don't think she can be said to be in open rebellion yet. Her subjects are Muslims and have periodically resented owing allegiance to a Buddhist king.'

Phaulkon seemed pleased. 'Pattani is one of the wealthier vassal states, isn't it?'

'Very much so. Her Majesty's small kingdom has huge reserves of tin.'

Phaulkon looked intrigued. He turned to the Spaniard. 'How much for the cannon?' he asked, speaking normally.

'Fifty gold sovereigns, señor. A real bargain? No?'

'I'll give you twenty.' Phaulkon switched into Spanish for the first time. 'With twenty per cent commission. We can split it between us.' He winked. 'We Latins must stick together. We are brothers, after all. The old man here is the only one with the authority to buy. Maybe I can talk him into it. It depends . . .' He smiled engagingly at the Spaniard.

'You are Portuguese?' asked the Spaniard suspiciously. Phaulkon nodded. They eyed each other for a while, each man seeming to take the measure of the other. Then the bargaining began in earnest.

George watched fascinated as his protégé, the young man he had always joked about bringing up in the mould of an English gentleman, set all decorum aside and embarked – with obvious relish, on a gesticulating free-for-all, a boisterous haggling session in which ruined families, dying mothers and destitute children played dominant roles. The two men tore at their hair, threw

42

their arms up in the air, appealed to the Holy Virgin and swore that they were ruined, the one for paying more than he could afford and the other for receiving less than he had bought the cannon for. Eventually they settled for twenty-seven gold sovereigns and embraced.

'We have agreed to examine the goods this evening after dark,' said Phaulkon turning to George. 'We can always find fault with the merchandise,' he added in an undertone.

George was grinning broadly.

'What's the matter?' asked Phaulkon.

'Oh nothing, lad. You seem to have ruffled our friend here. Why don't you show him where to wash. He looks as if he could do with a douse.'

As he helped the Spaniard out of his chair, Phaulkon fancied he saw George wink at him. The Spaniard hobbled off, smiling effusively, and turned at the door to bow in their direction.

'Well, what was all that about?' asked George as soon as the pirate was out of earshot. 'You looked like a couple of rabid crones in a Barbary Coast souk.'

'Twenty-seven gold sovereigns with a commission of two for me. That leaves twenty-five,' beamed Phaulkon. 'Just five gold sovereigns per cannon. If they really are original de Groots, that's the bargain of the decade. What do you say, George?'

'And how would you be planning to pay for them, my boy?' There was an amused twinkle in George's eye.

'From Company funds, George. On your personal authority. As chief bookkeeper here, I'll be glad to record the transaction.' Phaulkon smiled. Even George was taken aback.

'And why would the Company be buying cannon in the first place? Not to mention foreign brands?'

'For the protection of the new factory in Ayudhya. The Siamese authorities, should they inquire, will be told that the English always install cannon in their compounds as a symbol of the prestige that benefits such a great nation. Strictly for defensive purposes, of course.'

George nodded approvingly. 'They might swallow that,' he agreed. 'But Dutch cannon? Since when do the English not have good enough cannon of their own?'

'True enough, George. But since the Dutch are threatening Siam, what if we were to supply a rebellious vassal with their

43

own cannon? Would it not look as if the treacherous Dutch were arming the rebels? And while the cannon would hardly be enough to threaten the extinction of Siam, the money from their sale might be enough to fill Sam's ship.'

'By Jove, lad. I think you're ready to run Siam.' George slapped him affectionately across the back. 'It's strange how we see eye to eye, you and I. You're a rascal. Too much like me for your own good. That's probably why you've always meant so much to me.'

'And you to me, George. But will you help me read the markings on these cannon? Don't forget the future of the Dutch empire is at stake,' he said laughing.

'I've already read them, lad. They're genuine de Groot all right.'

'What?'

'And I've already bought them. With the same idea as you in mind.'

Phaulkon was speechless.

'There's only one problem,' continued George. 'I offered thirty sovereigns for them and you agreed to twenty-five.' He roared with laughter.

Phaulkon was about to find his voice when Don Pedro de Alcatraz y Mendoza appeared in the doorway again. Phaulkon stared at him open-mouthed. Gone was the Spaniard's eyepatch, his hair was properly coiffed, his breeches were free of dust and there were only a couple of small cuts where he had shaved off his stubble in a hurry. He was a tall, proud figure who looked as if he belonged in the salon of an ancient castle in Andalucia.

He stretched out his arms to George. 'How wonderful that we meet after all these years, my friend.' His English was flawless.

'Twelve isn't it, Don Pedro? I am sure Manila has never been the same since.'

'They still talk about you there, my friend, especially in—' He looked at Phaulkon and thought better of it.

Phaulkon stared in amazement as the two men embraced warmly.

Don Pedro turned to Phaulkon. 'And the moral of the story, señor? Never judge by appearances. But allow me, please.' He held out his arms and embraced Phaulkon in turn.

'Do you always have two identities, señor?' asked Phaulkon finding his voice at last.

'Such precautions are necessary when you are selling, er, delicate merchandise, señor. If the Dutch were to hear about it, they would be looking for a one-eyed pirate, not the Marquis de Alcatraz, friend of the Governor. I am also a friend of Prince Dai. It was I who persuaded him to flee to Siam to save his race from extinction and I who bought the cannon from him to pay for his passage. You see, they were not worth much to Prince Dai. Though he had captured them from the Dutch, not one of his men was willing to stoop to such a degrading form of combat. There is no honour to a Macassar in fighting with anything but the kris. But the cannon, I can assure you, are beautiful – and genuine. If I didn't need . . . If I didn't need the money I'd take them home with me. But since gambling away my estates in Spain, I have been reduced to earning a living. And speaking of money, señor, you certainly drive a hard bargain. And not even in your mother tongue.'

'Thank you. But with a Portuguese accent.'

'Perhaps,' smiled Don Pedro, 'but your Scottish brogue is perfect.'

'You Spaniards are incorrigible,' said George, 'selling the same merchandise twice over. No wonder you lost the armada. I think I'll withdraw my offer.'

Don Pedro laughed. 'Ah, but I prefer your offer, George, to your friend's.'

'How shall we resolve it then?' asked George.

'There's only one fair way,' said Phaulkon. 'We'll pay twenty-seven and a half sovereigns for them.'

'Ah, my friend, I can see you are a worthy successor to the famous George White. It is just as he said. I am honoured to make your acquaintance, sir.' He shook Phaulkon warmly by the hand. 'Now, señores, there is a story attached to the cannon which I feel it my duty to tell you. You see, many years ago in Sevilla a gypsy palmist told me I would one day sell weapons of war to two foreigners in a distant country. It was a strange and unlikely prophecy to make to a Spanish nobleman who had never yet left his country. But the interesting point,' Don Pedro paused and eyed them carefully, 'is that she insisted that it was not I who would make my fortune from the sale, but they.'

'I'll drink to that,' said George. He poured out three glasses and raised his own high. 'To the Falcon of Siam,' he toasted.

Three

Prostrate, Phaulkon glanced up in awe at the powerful man, the man who could destroy him. He was the King of Siam's First Minister, in charge of the Treasury and foreign affairs, and to all farangs he was known as the Great Barcalon.

The Barcalon was reclining in the manner of the Siamese aristocracy, leaning forward on one vertical arm with both legs swept elegantly to one side beneath him. From a distance he appeared encased in his raised, palanquin-like dais of black lacquered wood covered with a trellised canopy, which stood at the end of the spacious wood-pannelled audience hall. The elaborately carved arms of his dais ended in sculpted mythical garuda birds and the slender fingers of the potentate's free hand, glittering with jewels, drummed gently on one of the bird's crested heads.

The nails of his little fingers had never been cut and even at that distance the long unpared growth was plainly visible. It was the sign of a ruling class and a visible reminder that he had never indulged in menial chores.

The Great Barcalon appeared tall for a Siamese, and regally elegant. He had a mole on his right cheek out of which grew a single long hair which had been allowed to grow unmolested. His nose was straight and aristocratic and his nostrils were only slightly flared. His hair was dark and shiny and his ears were larger than those of a European. His complexion, a smooth, hairless brown, was lighter than that of an Indian but deeper and less sallow than that of a Chinese. His keen eyes observed Phaulkon with a feverish glow and hinted at ruthless reprisals for those found guilty.

He was dressed in a panung, the Siamese knee-length cotton cloth that was wrapped between the thighs and tied in front. Above it he wore a richly brocaded collarless coat with flowing, three-quarter-length sleeves and gold filigree buttons all the way up the front. Its gold-edged embroidery indicated a gift from His Majesty the King, to be worn only by royal permission and when conducting official business.

46

Rich Persian carpets adorned the floor around him and an elaborate brass spitoon lay by his side. In one corner of the room stood a gold-lacquered manuscript chest whose door panels were covered in sculpted figures of ancient deities and heroes of the Ramayana epic.

In the shadows behind the Barcalon, a retinue of slaves cowered expectantly, awaiting a sign from their master. The heat was oppressive and whenever the Barcalon raised his hand, they shuffled forward on their knees and elbows and circulated the air around him with long fan-shaped sticks. Others crawled forward to present him abjectly with his diamond-encrusted betel box and others still brought his tall, brass hookah and, prostrate, raised it to his mouth.

An involuntary shiver swept through Phaulkon. In England this man would be known as the Prime Minister. The Barcalon reported twice a day on affairs of state to His Majesty, careful not to omit the slightest detail. He was directly responsible for every farang in the land and a legion of spies reported to him on the activities of anyone of consequence.

For the moment the terrible loss of his five cannon was forgotten, overshadowed by the fear of the present. What if even one of the crates had been washed ashore? With no trace of authorization to transport weapons of war in Siamese waters, the penalty would be certain death. His Excellency was reported to be extremely shrewd and there were even rumours that he did not accept bribes, though Phaulkon had yet to come across such honesty among the potentates of Asia. But what if it were true? And what money was left to him for a bribe anyway?

At the Great Barcalon's side a dark-haired farang priest – Portuguese no doubt – sat cross-legged in the flowing robes of a Jesuit. Prostrate at His Excellency's other flank two muscular retainers, dressed only in loincloths, awaited the order to begin. They reminded Phaulkon of panting dogs, eager for the call that would release them.

The Barcalon now gave an order, and the two retainers at his side rose and advanced towards Phaulkon. The muscles of their brown, hardened bodies rippled as they walked. Their black slanted eyes showed little emotion. They carried the sinister instruments of their trade: the iron hoop that slowly crushed the temples and, oh sweet Jesus, the long, razor-sharp slivers of bamboo that were inserted into, and out of, the most sensitive areas of the body, like so many threading needles. They took up their positions on either side of Phaulkon and the interrogation began in Siamese.

'Mr Phaulkon, you are captain of the junk, *Royal Lotus*, chartered by the English Trading Company on the ninth day of the moon's decrease in the eleventh month of the year of the Great Mare, are you not?' The Barcalon's voice was deep and resonant and the rich Siamese tones, like so many sharps and flats of a keyboard, pealed across the room. The voice of the Jesuit interpreter that followed sounded flat and reedy by comparison.

The Barcalon emitted a discreet cough and leaned forward to listen to the reply of the accused.

Phaulkon heard himself say: 'I am, Your Excellency.'

'As such you are responsible for its movements? And its cargo as well?' The Barcalon leaned over and sucked expansively on his hookah which a servant had just placed on the floor by his side. Blue smoke rose and hovered like a cloud above his head, mingling with the thin trails that rose upwards from a number of scattered mosquito coils. The sweet smell of camphor pervaded the room. Then he resumed his contemplation of Phaulkon.

'I am, Your Excellency.'

'What exactly were you transporting on your ship when you ran aground?'

'Broadcloth, Your Excellency, for the Malay States in the south.' Phaulkon's voice felt hollow even to his own ears.

'Indeed?' The Barcalon turned again and sucked deeply on the Moorish water pipe; the instrument emitted a pleasant, gurgling sound as if it were pleased to be of service to its master. The potentate pensively fingered the single uncut hair that grew out of the mole on his cheek. 'I understand your ship ran aground not far from Pattani. Do you know Pattani, Mr Phaulkon?'

'I've heard of it, Your Excellency. Isn't the ruler there a queen?'

'Indeed she is. An ambitious lady with two passions: farang men and farang weapons of war.' The Barcalon grinned suddenly. 'She would pay handsomely for either. And if she ever managed to lay her hands on both at the same time, why, her munificence would know no bounds.'

48

'Is that so, Your Excellency?' responded Phaulkon, trying to sound matter-of-fact.

'It is indeed, Mr Phaulkon. So much so that when our fishermen discovered some crates at low tide off the coast of Ligor, we were naturally curious as to their contents.' Phaulkon's heart beat faster and he felt suddenly sick to his stomach. 'It appears that they were from your ship, Mr Phaulkon. Would you care to divulge their contents? Or would you like me to assist you?'

Phaulkon swallowed hard. 'If the crates were from our ship, Your Excellency, the contents could only have been broadcloth.' Phaulkon was surprised at the firmness of his voice.

The Barcalon looked at him impassively. 'Try again, Mr Phaulkon.'

'I can only repeat, Your Excellency,' said Phaulkon resolutely, 'if the contents were anything other than broadcloth, they were not from my ship.'

A look of irritation creased the Barcalon's smooth brow. 'No doubt your traumatic experience has temporarily impaired your memory.' The Barcalon gave a signal and, like chained beasts suddenly let loose, the torturers sprang to life. In the Buddhist manner, they respectfully joined the palms of their hands in front of their foreheads and inclined their heads to Phaulkon as if asking his forgiveness for the pain they were about to inflict. Then one of them pinned Phaulkon's arms down while the other unfolded a cloth and spread an array of sharp bamboo slivers of varying sizes on the Persian carpet in front of him. Carefully he selected one and tested the point for sharpness. Then he rose and turned towards Phaulkon, leisurely running the bamboo needle in front of his victim's eyes as if seeking his approval first.

His heart pounding savagely, Phaulkon looked across at the Barcalon. The figure of the potentate appeared distorted, alternately advancing and receding, and when he turned to suck on his hookah, the loud gurgling sound reverberated across the room as if bouncing from wall to wall.

Now the second torturer crawled prostrate towards the Barcalon and presented him with the sliver of bamboo for his inspection. The Barcalon examined it, felt the tip with his finger and smiled his approval. Behind him, crouching servants took up

49

their master's cue and smiled; the smiles grew to laughter and soon a chorus of mirth boomed across the room.

The torturer crawled backwards and turned to bow one last time to Phaulkon. Then, holding his neck fast with one hand, he pierced the skin of the nape and slowly inserted the bamboo needle.

Though Phaulkon remembered George White telling him that one never cried out under torture in Siam, he could not stifle the piercing scream that rose to his throat.

Phaulkon sat up with a start and blinked, every nerve in his body taut, the sweat pouring in rivulets down his face and neck. Thank God it had only been a dream. Yet the vague shape of the torturer still loomed above him and seemed to be preparing to insert a sliver of bamboo into his groin. Phaulkon's head pounded viciously as he prepared to strike. Then he stopped, perplexed, as his adversary swam into focus. The features of a young girl, bent over his private parts and nervously tying on his panung again, gradually became clear. She must have been overcome by curiosity. She smiled sheepishly at being discovered, displaying a row of fine straight teeth blackened by the constant chewing of betel nut and the application of burnt coconut. She wore her thick black hair cropped short in the manner of the Siamese peasantry. There was not a wrinkle in her face and her skin was a beautiful shade of light teak. She wore a plain blue panung, and her upper body was bare except for a bright coloured sash that hung loosely over her breasts – not out of modesty, he knew. Most of the peasantry went bare-breasted. It was the love of colours, turquoises, pinks and saffrons, that prompted some to wear the additional garment. As often as not the women draped it round the shoulders without even bothering to cover their nipples.

Her long slim fingers touched his shoulder blades gently, pushing him back on to the cushions. His torso, groin and the inside of his thighs felt soaked. She began to sponge his moist body. A wave of relief engulfed him.

Now a flood of memories returned. He felt the waves flinging him about and dashing him against the ocean floor, and he saw hands stretched out towards him.

He sat up again painfully and one by one raised his arms and legs until he had tested each limb. Miraculously, despite the multiple bruises and dull pain, nothing seemed broken.

50

The girl pointed now to little porcelain salvers of vegetables, rice, salted fish and an assortment of fresh fruits – pineapple, custard apple, miniature bananas and papaya. But he shook his head and glanced painfully around him.

The room came slowly into focus. It was sparsely furnished: a small bamboo screen, a large brown clay water urn with dragon designs, a thin mat of rushes and the cushions he was lying on. The walls were of wood and the two panels which served as a door were open, allowing a pleasant breeze to drift through. The sun streamed in and the sounds of children playing outside came through the open doorway. On one side of his straw mat fresh flowers, gardenias and small wreaths of jasmine, were arranged in an elegant white vase, and on the other side a pot of Chinese tea stood on a tray on the floor, next to the food.

The girl was fanning him now, using a bamboo fan lined with rice paper, and he lay down again relishing the cool air and trying to gather his thoughts.

He was anxious to know whether the others had survived and what had happened to the cannon. Then he remembered the rendezvous with Samuel White and his heart sank. How was he ever going to obtain the goods to fill Sam's boat now? The rendezvous was only three months away and here he was penniless in some provincial backwater, probably in custody, with the authorities no doubt waiting to question him. Though the cannon might once have been his ticket to success, under the circumstances he could only pray that they were drowned deep in the ocean. It was essential to find out where he was, where the cannon were and whether his friends had survived, but he was hesitant how best to establish this.

He weighed the alternatives. The Malays who could testify to his knowledge of Siamese were all dead. Assuming he was now in provincial Ligor, where no one was likely to speak a word of English, would he be better off talking to the authorities in Siamese and risking having to answer embarrassing questions? Or should he pretend ignorance and perhaps overhear the authorities discussing his fate? The Siamese spoke quite unguardedly in front of farangs, whose ignorance of the language they took for granted. He might be in a better position to manipulate them if he had advance knowledge of their intentions. Moreover,

51

the Siamese were less likely to use torture if they could not understand the language of the confession!

He gestured to the girl. 'Farang,' he said, pointing to himself and outlining with his arms two more such beings. She smiled back at him happily but he knew that could mean anything. The Siamese smiled when they were happy, confused, embarrassed or even angry. But then she pointed to him and repeated his gesture, raising two fingers.

'*Farang yu noon*,' she said happily. He pretended to look puzzled, but his heart leapt with joy. They were 'over there' she had said. She pointed outside and then closed her eyes to show that they were asleep. He laughed with relief and she laughed too.

Though his body felt like jelly, he struggled to his feet and, despite her repeated protestations, inched his way painfully over to the open doorway. When he tried to step outside, however, she physically restrained him and when he persisted, a retainer stepped out of the shadows beyond the doorway and blocked his passage. He smiled courteously, but there was no mistaking his meaning. Phaulkon gestured in the direction of the air and sunlight, but the man shook his head and pointed back to Phaulkon's bed. '*Nai ja thong pai pop Puwa Rajatkan prungnee. Thong norn korn.*'

Phaulkon shrugged his shoulders uncomprehendingly, and went back into his room. The guard returned to his post outside. So he was to rest before his meeting with the Governor tomorrow. It was sound advice, he reflected. He needed time to regain his strength and time to think. He would certainly need all his wits about him when he came before the Governor.

He walked unsteadily over to his bed but not before he had taken in the scene outside. His room gave on to a small, grass-covered courtyard surrounded by a thick bamboo hedge. A path led through it to a large edifice whose multi-tiered roofs of orange tile were visible in the distance. Presumably the Governor's palace. In the other direction green, waterlogged paddy fields glistened in the sunlight, and, beyond them, lush banana trees and stately palms dotted the landscape.

He lay back on his quilted rush mat and indicated to the girl that he would like a drink. She seemed relieved that he was behaving reasonably again and smiled warmly as she raised the small cup of lukewarm tea to his lips. The liquid tasted bitter but refreshing and he drank gratefully. Then he pretended to grope for the Siamese word to thank her: korb, korb . . .

'*Korb jai*,' she finished for him, beaming with pleasure. She was young, not more than sixteen perhaps, with a pretty face. The black teeth were not unbecoming. Most of the women blackened them. It put them on a plane above the wild beasts of the forest whose white fangs were used to kill. Humans, on the other hand, did not kill. The black colour came naturally from the constant chewing of the betel nut, which cleansed the mouth and kept the breath sweet. The aristocracy went a step further and rubbed their teeth with scented twigs.

Phaulkon waved his arms about and pretended to rack his brain for the Siamese name for Ligor. 'Nakorn . . . ?'

'Nakhon Si Thammarat,' she exclaimed, thrilled to get his meaning. '*Ban pu Rajatkan*.'

So they were in the Governor of Ligor's guest house. Rajatkan referred to His Excellency the Governor. Names were of secondary importance to rank in Siam. Thus the Governor was known only by his rank and title.

The girl now mixed a piece of salted fish with some rice and vegetables and, handing him a small shell spoon, held the bowl up to his mouth.

His appetite grew with the first mouthful and despite the pain of using his jaws he managed to swallow everything. The plain rice tempered the saltiness of the dried fish and the green bean-like vegetables tasted fresh and wholesome.

She seemed pleased with his performance and cupped her hands in front of her forehead before rising to fetch more food. He lay back feeling pleasantly sated and increasingly drowsy. The sounds of the children wafted through the open doorway. They must be playing in a nearby courtyard, though not his own. He had not seen any there. His eyes closed and his mind drifted back to his own childhood . . .

He was eight years old. He ran excitedly up to the great rock, as he had done every day for as long as he could remember. He clambered to the top and gazed across the blue expanse of the Mediterranean, shielding his eyes from the glare. Anxiously he waited. Then gradually the great seascape began to open up and pockets of mythical islands rose up out of the ocean. Shorelines

53

with white Moorish palaces and red Chinese pagodas and brown crenellated fortresses grew before his eyes. He waited a little longer, feasting his eyes on the sight, before the vision of the islands receded into the ocean once more and the sea resumed its former expanse. Not till tomorrow at the same hour would the islands show themselves again – only to him and his imagination.

He climbed back down the rock. It would soon be the evening hour when the seafarers came ashore to tell their tales over endless glasses of ouzo at his father's tavern on the waterfront. He listened avidly, with a growing conviction that life for him lay far from this little island of Cephalonia that already stifled him. He made his way along the maze of narrow, whitewashed alleyways past sad-eyed donkeys and black-shrouded grandmothers gossiping interminably. Emerging at the harbour, he stood still for a moment and gazed at the neat little row of identical whitewashed houses that lined the waterfront. Then he glanced up at the room above the tavern which he shared with his two sisters and a baby brother, and sighed. Out of the corner of his eye he saw a bearded Orthodox priest in black flowing robes and black hat enter the white-domed chapel on the hill. Nothing ever changed in this place, nothing except the seasons.

There was an autumn chill in the air as he opened the door and stepped gingerly into the noisy tavern. He glanced around him nervously. His father had forbidden him to enter here and he would be soundly thrashed if he were seen. But for the moment his father was out. The din was even louder than usual and the tables were filled to capacity despite the early hour. He followed the revellers' gaze and spotted the source of the commotion. A withered old crone shrouded in the mandatory black and with more lines on her face than a cobweb stood at the centre of the crowd, telling fortunes.

A group of regulars spotted the lad's arrival. 'Hey look, it's little Costas, the old man's son. Let the old bird tell the young man's future.' They all laughed. 'What do you say we all chip in?' shouted one of them, a bearded man in a blue sailor's cap. Several people voiced their approval and soon the crowd had taken up the idea.

'All right, granny,' said the bearded sailor, raising his hand for silence. 'Tell the boy what the world has in store for him. But you'd better make it worth our while, because we're all paying your fee!'

The revellers roared with laughter while Costas looked in vain for a place to hide. If his father came to hear of this . . . Suddenly a hand grabbed him by the collar and Costa's heart sank into his boots. But is was only the bearded sailor swooping him up and standing him on a table in the centre of the room. 'Make way, make way, clear the decks,' he bellowed.

As the mugs and glasses were cleared from the table, Costas was steered unwillingly along it, feeling nervous and self-conscious. Silence descended on the room as the old gypsy took his trembling palm in both her bony hands and stared at it intently for a while. Then she sucked in her breath and traced a course over it with a shaking finger. Gradually her black eyes grew wide and she pursed her shrivelled lips in surprise. Finally she glanced around with a hint of disdain at her eager audience as if to say that next to this young lad they were but scum.

'Mark my words,' she began in a hollow tone, 'this lad has a great destiny before him, albeit far from these shores. He will one day be chief of state of a distant land, wielding enormous power and wealth. Power such as you dunces have never dreamed of. But he must take care . . .'

The roar of the crowd drowned out the rest of her sentence as Costas' ears turned pink. 'That was a good one!' shouted one. 'Well worth the fee!' cried another. 'Tell us some more!' coaxed a third. 'Long live little Costas, the Prime Minister!' The crowd liked this one best and immediately took up the refrain, raising their glasses again and again to the mortified lad . . .

Phaulkon sat up, furious at the mockery. He winced with pain and frowned, perplexed not to find himself in the tavern. Instead a beautiful, bare-breasted maiden smiled down at him sympathetically and offered him more food. He declined, mopping his brow and politely attempting to mime the pain in his jaw.

She produced a small bamboo phial and began to rub an ointment gently into his bruises. It smelled of coconut and stung slightly, but it brought relief. The Siamese, he knew, had a remarkable knowledge of herbs.

She rubbed it gently into his chest and across his stomach and then unwound his panung and applied it to the area around his genitals. He felt a slight, ever so gradual stirring, and he smiled with relief. It was a step in the right direction. He was going to be whole again. She noticed it too and smiled coquettishly. '*Ik noi kong ja tham dai*,' she said, assuming that he could not understand. 'Soon you'll be able to enjoy.'

It was at that moment that he decided he definitely would not admit that he spoke Siamese.

Four

'You're quite sure the farangs haven't communicated with each other, Your Excellency?' asked Joop van Risling, the Dutch factor at Ligor, for the second time. He spoke in Malay, addressing himself to the young, slight Malay interpreter from the Dutch factory, who, prostrate, translated into Siamese for the Governor.

The portly mandarin raised his black eyebrows fractionally and tried to keep the irritation out of his voice. His dark, semi-slanted eyes, sunk behind high cheek-bones, flickered for an instant before resuming their air of polite inscrutability.

One did not ask the Lord of the Province, a man with no less than ten thousand dignity marks, the same question twice. These farangs might have great ships of war and powerful weapons, but they had no manners, and no dignity or patience either for that matter. He would not exchange all their power for such execrable gracelessness.

'They haven't spoken to each other, Mr Lidrim,' replied the mandarin courteously. Even though the farang had been in his province eleven months already, he was still unable to pronounce the impossible name. The Dutchman was fortunately unaware of the corruption of his name, since he spoke no Siamese, and by the time the interpreter had rendered it back into Malay, it had almost resumed its legitimate sound. Joop van Risling understood Malay perfectly. He had been stationed as a trader at Batavia in Java long before the Dutch had colonized the place.

'They have been housed separately, Mr Lidrim,' added His Excellency.

'And none of them speaks Siamese?' the Dutchman asked again.

The mandarin stared impassively ahead of him and discreetly observed the farang's ears. How ugly and ignoble to have such small ears. His own were genuinely large, and not unnaturally stretched from childhood like those of the Laotians, the tips of

57

which sometimes reached down to the shoulders. His Majesty himself had once complimented him on the size of his ears.

'I'm told one of them speaks Siamese,' the Dutchman was saying, shaking his head in frustration.

The Governor of Ligor Province, a mandarin of the first grade, surveyed the farang briefly. It would be bad manners to stare too openly at him, which was fortunate in this instance, he reflected, since the sight was most ungainly. The large, florid Dutchman was perspiring profusely, the sweat trickling from the top of his bald pate through his orange beard, down the inside of his ridiculous farang apparel into his foul-smelling stockings. If custom did not forbid a man wearing shoes indoors, he would almost have preferred him to cover those feet with his strange-looking boots. Even the water buffalo after a hard day's plough-ing did not emit so unpleasant an odour. Thank the Lord Buddha, he was the only farang living in Ligor.

No. There was one other, he remembered, a priest from the Portugals who smelled almost as bad; but in accord with Siam's long tradition of religious tolerance, the Governor permitted him to carry on his work unmolested and had little to do with him.

'My female slaves have reported that the newcomers speak hardly three words of Siamese between them,' responded the mandarin graciously. They were in the teak-panelled audience chamber of the Governor's palace, and the bare-chested Malay interpreter, whose mother was Siamese, crouched next to the mandarin's chief aide, the Palat. Both rested permanently on their knees and elbows at the Governor's foot, while servants squatted abjectly in the corners. The mandarin and the Dutch-man were both standing, a position adopted through compro-mise. The Dutchman found it uncomfortable to sit cross-legged like a tailor for any length of time. Instead of chairs, which were not in use in Siam, the audience chamber contained straw mats and cushions, as well as fine Persian rugs and exquisite pieces of Ming porcelain which for the most part were gifts from His Majesty the King to the worthiest of his courtiers.

Under normal circumstances His Excellency would be sitting comfortably with his legs folded under him and spread to one side, as befitted a man of his rank, with all those present lying prostrate before him, their heads well below the level of his. Yet here he was, he reflected distastefully, forced to stand awkwardly

58

next to the oversized farang. This gross-featured, evil-smelling boor was a whole head taller than he was, causing him offence and vexation. What would his own people think? The farang merchant's head should never be higher than his.

'I must repeat, Your Excellency, that I received an urgent dispatch four days ago from Ayudhya informing me that members of the English Trading Company have been usurping the beneficence of your gracious King . . .'

At the mention of His Majesty, the Governor prostrated himself, and the Palat, interpreter and servants grovelled still lower, while the Dutchman, abandoned in mid-sentence, waited irritably for the Governor to rise.

'. . . and that these Englishmen have been transporting cannon illegally down the coast of Siam,' he finished.

'We would not think of questioning the accuracy of your reports, Mr Lidrim,' responded the Governor amiably, while carefully adjusting the gold brocade of his silk panung, 'but unfortunately our laws require proof.'

'But their own warehouse keeper saw them being loaded on to the boat!' exclaimed the Dutchman. The apathy of these Siamese exasperated him. There was no doubt about the accuracy of his information. His superior in Ayudhya, the Opperhoofd himself, had signed the dispatch and it had been sent by elephant courier to stress its urgency. There were cannon on board the English junk, it advised, and his orders were to intercept the ship at all costs off the coast of Ligor and expose the English for what they were: frauds and smugglers. Van Risling clenched his fists. This was the opportunity he had long been waiting for, the chance to crush the God-cursed English and throw them out of Siam by their backsides as he knew they soon would be out of Bantam. What satisfaction to see that upstart little empire crumble, those impudent intruders who imagined they could challenge the might of the Netherlands.

The Governor pursed his lips at the unseemly outburst and waited for the Dutchman to recover his dignity. 'But the boat, I understand, Mr Lidrim, together with her cargo, is no longer available for inspection.' The mandarin fingered one of the beautiful filigree buttons that ran down the front of his gold-embroidered silk coat.

Van Risling controlled himself with difficulty and considered the situation. These buffoons would not see the tiger till their head was in its jaws.

'I'll find the proof you need, Your Excellency, and when I do, your country will be pleased to be rid of the English traitors, once and for all. And regarding the one who speaks fluent Siamese, I have sent an urgent dispatch to my head office requisitioning a description of the man. The Siamese warehouse keeper couldn't pronounce any of the names, so the report only mentions that one of the three spoke the language. I am expecting an answer from Ayudhya within three weeks, Your Excellency.' It infuriated Joop van Risling to have to wait that long; in the meantime he would at least ensure the farangs did not leave Ligor.

'Good. We shall await it with interest.' The Governor paused. 'But do tell me, Mr Lidrim, I am curious. If, as you suggest, there were cannon on board the English boat, where do you suppose they were taking them?'

The Dutchman hesitated just a fraction. 'I wouldn't be surprised if it were to the rebels in Pattani, Your Excellency. They would fetch a good price there.'

'Indeed, I am sure. But wouldn't their markings have made them readily traceable to the English? Would that be a wise move on the part of a nation that has been soliciting to re-open trading posts on our shores?'

The Governor was aware, as were possibly a dozen of the highest-ranking mandarins in the land, that it was in fact the Siamese King who had solicited the English. But official policy had it that the English had been the supplicants. Of course if the English were guilty of smuggling cannon, as this Dutch farang contended, there would be a heavy price to pay. It would be within his jurisdiction as Governor of the province to have them all executed for treason, and he would not hesitate to do so if they were found guilty. But first he needed the proof, which the Dutch farang claimed was on its way.

Van Risling admitted to himself that he was stumped by this evident lack of logic. Why would the English jeopardize their welcome by supplying cannon to the rebels? Not even the English were as stupid as that. He avoided the mandarin's question.

'So, Your Excellency, we put our little plan into effect, eh? The three Englishmen will be brought together for the first time since the accident here in your audience chamber. They will have

60

much to say to each other, and we will no doubt learn a lot. Then your deputy will arrive and inform them solemnly that a part of their cargo has been washed ashore . . .' The Dutchman smiled in anticipation. Siamese houses were all built on teakwood stilts to avoid flooding during the monsoon season, and the lower floor was raised some four or five feet off the ground. There would be plenty of space for concealment under the timber flooring. Van Risling would be sitting directly underneath the Englishmen, listening to their every word.

'You speak their language, do you?' inquired the mandarin politely. He wondered how far he would be able to trust this Dutchman's translation. Still, there was no one else to verify it. His most able spy, Snit, would of course be positioned out of sight, to observe the Dutchman's reactions. If his face reflected pleasure, it was likely to mean that he was hearing what he had hoped to hear. If not . . .

'Well enough for the purpose,' replied the Dutchman. He too was wondering how the mandarin would be able to check the accuracy of his translation. 'And they will not be allowed into the town or even out of their houses until after our test, Your Excellency?'

How tiresome he was, this farang, with his constant repetitions. 'Correct, Mr Lidrim, they will remain separately in their guest houses until then. They should be well enough by tomorrow. It is the fourth day now since the shipwreck and they have recovered well, all except the tall one, I am told. He has a foot injury. And you have my assurance, Mr Lidrim, that they will remain in Ligor until I am satisfied that the truth has been established,' added the Governor, anticipating the Dutchman's next question.

Van Risling forced a smile. 'Very good then, I'll be here tomorrow morning, Your Excellency.'

He bowed his head briefly and the mandarin shuddered at his lack of breeding. The farang never even observed the most basic forms of respect. Would the English farangs prove to be as ill-mannered? Though he had never met one of their breed before, he did not doubt it.

There was certainly little love lost between these two farang nations, he reflected. That was why the truth would have to be sifted carefully. But he had his methods. A sudden thought struck him. Might their countries have been at war for centuries

61

over the possession of each others' white elephants and slaves, or some similar prize, as his own country and the Burmese had been? The Dutchman's hatred was so painfully obvious. Were all farangs as childishly open about their feelings? If the English farangs reacted like that too, it would be the most unsubtle confrontation. He chuckled. Just by observing them he should be able to get some indication of the truth. And if not, the Palat's more subtle methods of interrogation would soon unearth it. One thing was certain. The Dutch farang had been so determined to expose the English, in the belief that that would result in their wholesale expulsion from Siam, that he had helped to save their lives. Indeed, the Governor doubted that they would all have survived if the orange-bearded devil had not been by the shore directing operations. He must have been waiting for the boat to arrive. It was he who had organized the fishermen in a human chain out to sea.

'Kling!' summoned the mandarin. The crouching deputy shuffled forward on his hands and knees towards his master. His nose was short and flared and seemed expressly designed to follow any trail.

'Mighty Lord, the dust of your feet awaits your orders,' the Palat intoned, using the prescribed form of address to a mandarin of the first rank.

'Send a slave to the boxing terrain. Chai or Wan, one of the more reliable ones. I want a report on its condition.'

'I receive your orders, mighty Lord.'

'It is now four days since the great storm. I want to know exactly how wet the ground is and what the chances are of holding the tournament the day after tomorrow.'

'I receive your orders, mighty Lord.' The Palat knew how much the tournament meant to the Lord of the Province. The Governor adored kickboxing. The report would have to be detailed and accurate.

'And Kling, I will want a thorough investigation of these farangs. In particular I wish to ascertain the precise nature of the cargo they were carrying. I will leave the finer details to you, after we have examined the Dutch farang's evidence.'

The deputy beamed with pleasure. 'Mighty Lord, I receive your orders.' He crawled out backwards, not wishing to offend the Lord with the sight of his hindquarters.

62

Five

The Palat entered the small, wooden guesthouse on stilts where Phaulkon was staying. He was barefoot, as were almost all Siamese both in and out of doors. Only mandarins wore curved Muslim slippers when they travelled outside. He wai'd politely to Phaulkon, an inclination of the head with the palms joined together above the forehead, the traditional form of greeting among equals.

Phaulkon returned the greeting. The Palat's nose was particularly flat, even for a Siamese, but otherwise he exhibited the normal features of his race: dark, slanted eyes, straight black hair, high cheekbones, a light brown complexion, and a fine physique, slighter than that of the European.

'Choen, chiao,' the Palat said politely. Phaulkon assumed a perplexed expression. The Palat then beckoned him to follow. Every now and then the Governor's deputy turned as if to ensure that Phaulkon were still behind him, but the Greek had the distinct impression that he was being sized up.

It was afternoon, but Phaulkon did not know what day it was, for he had lost count of the time he had slept. He felt immeasurably better. The herbs and ointments had done wonders for his bruises, and he felt alert and fit again. He had been given clothes, a panung to cover his loins, a muslin shirt, and even a formal brocade coat though it was not clear for what occasion. Several times now he had tried to see the others or slip out to check the shore for any debris that might have been washed up from their boat. But each time guards had blocked his passage. He had not been allowed beyond the little grass courtyard outside his single-storeyed guesthouse. He sensed his companions were nearby, but it would have been rude to shout or to insist and there was no point in antagonizing his hosts. He had spent the time eating, sleeping, and exercising.

Now he followed the Palat through an opening in the thick bamboo hedge that surrounded his courtyard and entered another courtyard, large and rectangular, in the middle of which stood a magnificent old banyan tree, its huge frame surrounded by a maze of intertwining trunks, like serpents. The courtyard was covered in grass and its borders planted with evergreen gardenia trees. It was a pleasant and shady spot. He was greeted by the festive sounds of naked children, brown as berries, playing around the huge tree. Most of them wore silver bracelets and anklets; the faces of the younger ones were covered in yellow turmeric paste which kept the mosquitoes and other insects at bay. The kind-hearted Buddhist Siamese also applied the powder to dogs and cats, and it was not uncommon to see yellow-faced children playing with equally yellow domestic animals. The older children were supposed to fend for themselves and did without it. Some, not more than six or seven years old, were smoking tobacco wrapped in enormous palm leaves. They all stopped to stare at him. He obviously presented an even greater diversion than their favourite banyan tree. The children of Siam, Phaulkon mused, though as playful as any in the world, had a reverence for authority that would have been the envy of any parent in Europe.

Phaulkon and his guide were now on a busier part of the grounds. Barefoot servants in loincloths came and went, bowing low to them as they passed. Some prostrated themselves on the spot, while others leaned far forward, seemingly defying the laws of gravity, as they hurried by.

On the far side of the courtyard stood the Governor's mansion, a palatial residence by Siamese standards, built on twenty-four foundation pillars instead of the customary four. It was a sturdy structure of teak and ironwood, with attractive multi-tiered roofs that curved upwards into triangles at the corners. The whole edifice was raised on a multitude of stilts, and a series of steps like a broad ladder led up to the main entrance, which consisted of two thick teakwood panels opening inwards and serving as a door.

They mounted the steps and entered a spacious, wood-panelled room, tastefully furnished with Japanese lacquered screens, vases and bowls of Ming porcelain, fine Persian rugs and a large silver spittoon. Suddenly there was a yelp of delight and a figure sprang out of the shadows at the far end of the room.

'Thomas!' shouted Phaulkon holding his arms out delightedly to the little man. Ivatt ran up, took a flying leap, and landed in Phaulkon's arms, his legs firmly astride Phaulkon's waist. His panung came off with the effort, exposing his bare buttocks. They both roared with laughter.

'You look unscathed, Thomas,' said Phaulkon.

'Oh, we used to simulate shipwrecks in the theatre,' responded Ivatt. 'I thought it was just another rehearsal!'

'Were you conscious when you reached shore? Did you see what happened?' asked Phaulkon.

'I am afraid I was in another world,' responded Ivatt.

'So was I.'

The Palat had now discreetly withdrawn and they were alone in the large antechamber. Phaulkon showed Ivatt how to tie his panung on by winding it round his waist and between his legs and knotting the two ends in front. It was a simple yet practical apparel, not inelegant and well suited to the warm climate. The Greek put his arm round Ivatt and steered him past an ornate gold-lacquered cabinet of the early Ayudhya period to the other side of the room. He had grown fond of this man, whose height was just under five feet, making him about equal in size to most Siamese men, which did wonders for a self-esteem long diminished by years of living in a nation where most of the men were considerably taller than he was. The little man was as cheerful and eager as a sparrow.

'Be very careful what you say,' Phaulkon whispered in Ivatt's ear.

'About the broadcloth you mean?' Ivatt whispered back.

Phaulkon smiled despite himself. The little man knew.

'About anything,' muttered Phaulkon. 'The walls may have ears. Have you seen Richard?' he inquired in a normal tone.

'No, but my slave indicated in sign language that there was a giant in the vicinity. It has to be him.'

'You are housed separately as well?'

Ivatt nodded. 'Just me and my slave. She seems more interested in my anatomy than anything else. Especially the less public parts.'

Phaulkon laughed. 'I had the same experience. Farangs are obviously a novelty around here.' He paused. 'I suppose you didn't hear whether any of our broadcloth was saved, did you?'

'Only about half of it, I understand,' quipped Ivatt, and then felt immediately contrite as he watched the blood drain from Phaulkon's face. 'Forgive me, Constant. A poor joke. I am just happy to be alive.'

Phaulkon forced a smile. At that moment there was a hobbling noise outside and they turned towards the door. The figure of Burnaby, stooped and leaning heavily on a bamboo cane, appeared in the doorway.

'Richard!' they both cried, running over to him.

His left foot was greatly swollen and was swathed in a cotton cloth. His whole leg exuded a strong smell of coconut oil. Burnaby smiled weakly and for a moment they looked at each other in silence, each thinking of his narrow brush with death.

'What happened to your foot?' asked Phaulkon, as they arranged a pile of cushions on the floor and gently eased him on to them.

'I think it's sprained. I must have bashed it against a rock or something. I don't have a very clear recollection of events. But thank God we're all alive. I'd like to get back to Ayudhya to have it seen to. The damned physicians here tried to apply some remedy of vulture or eagle bile. Thank Christ I managed to stop them, and show them how to tie a bandage instead.'

'Well, as you say, Richard, we're lucky to be alive,' said Phaulkon, 'and to have landed among such genial hosts. It's a pity that none of us speaks the language to thank them.'

'What do you m—?' began Burnaby, but Phaulkon cut him short.

'We'll just have to do the best we can with sign language, Richard.'

'Have you gone mad? We need to get out of—'

'It's funny,' interrupted Ivatt, 'I don't remember much about our swimming outing, either. Except, strangely, I kept fancying there was a red-bearded monster stretching his arms out to me from the shore.'

'Hands outstretched?' exclaimed Phaulkon. 'That's what I remember too.'

'Maybe we were all helped ashore,' suggested Burnaby. 'You haven't been down to see if any of our goods were washed up, have you, Constant?' He had also not been allowed beyond his room.

'No, but I'm sure we've lost all the broadcloth. Even if the tide washed it up, it would be unsaleable now. That's a pile of treasure down the drain.'

'It was your idea,' grunted Burnaby. 'Where do we go from here, eh, Constant, you with the bright ideas?'

66

'First we thank God for keeping us alive,' replied Phaulkon. 'Then we ascertain our situation.'

'And how do we do that when none of us speaks the language?' asked Burnaby drily.

'We'll find ways, Richard,' said Phaulkon making an effort to stay calm. 'And then we'll see how else we can fill Sam's boat.'

Burnaby scoffed. 'With what? Mannah from heaven? Raise another fortune in three months, I suppose? I should never have listened to you in the first place.'

'Who is this Sam anyway?' asked Ivatt. 'Do I know him?'

'He's due at Mergui in three months and at this rate he's going to be a very disappointed man,' said Burnaby bitterly. 'We may still be rotting in prison by then.'

'But at least we're alive,' insisted Ivatt. 'Besides, I like this place. It must belong to some bigwig. The house is standing on more legs than a centipede.'

Phaulkon chuckled. 'It's the Governor's palace, I imagine. He's probably a mandarin of the first grade, with maybe eight or ten thousand *sakdina*.'

'With what?' exclaimed Ivatt.

'Dignity marks,' replied Phaulkon. 'Every official in Siam has dignity marks which go with his position. It serves to let every man know precisely where he stands in the hierarchy.'

'How many dignity marks do I have?' Ivatt asked.

'Too few to count,' replied Phaulkon. 'And by the way, Thomas, what have you done to your hair?' He noticed for the first time that Ivatt's mop of curly brown hair was looking very shiny.

'My slave oiled and scented it for me,' he replied, mimicking an upper-class accent.

'You lie, Thomas Ivatt. No Siamese woman would touch a man's head, least of all yours,' said Phaulkon.

'Why not?' laughed Ivatt. 'She touched everything else. What's wrong with my head, anyway? It's not as bald as Richard's.'

'It's your sacred extremity, Thomas,' said Phaulkon.

'Is it? I would have given the award elsewhere.'

Even Burnaby attempted a smile.

Whoever's listening to this exchange, thought Phaulkon, isn't going to be much the wiser about our intentions.

'Are we going to meet the Governor, do you think? And how do we address him if we do?' asked Ivatt.

'You don't. You just lie prostrate and keep quiet.'

'Doesn't he have a name?'

'Officials are known by their rank and not by their name.'

'But how can you tell a man from his predecessor then?' asked Ivatt.

'That's the whole point. The system helps prevent the making of heroes – apart from the King, of course. The personalities of the Barcalons, for example, as well as their accomplishments, are soon forgotten when all those before and after bear the same name.'

'You might say the system helps them *not* to make a name for themselves,' quipped Ivatt.

'Why, after all these days, have we been brought together for the first time?' asked Burnaby, turning to Phaulkon as if he were responsible.

'Our hosts are obviously considerate people, allowing us first the time to recover and then to come together before we meet the Governor,' replied Phaulkon. 'What could be more reasonable?'

'And what time would the Governor's reception be?' asked Burnaby drily.

'Judging from your dress, Richard, I don't think you've even been invited,' teased Ivatt.

Phaulkon looked at Burnaby. It was true. He had not been given even a muslin shirt, just a sash round the shoulders, the kind usually worn by women. And then he understood. Burnaby was over six feet tall; they just had not been able to find large enough clothing for him. 'Never mind,' Phaulkon said, 'you'll come with us. We'll explain that you lost your baggage.'

'It's going to be a dazzling affair, too,' said Ivatt. 'Somebody lent me their gold-embroidered coat. He's exactly my size too. I must get his address. I wanted to wear it right away, but my slave wouldn't let me. It must be for later.' He stood up suddenly. 'All this talk of parties and dignity marks is giving me the urge to relieve myself. Where would you suggest?' Phaulkon noticed him eyeing one of the Governor's Ming vases and quickly directed him outside. There was still no sign of servants anywhere.

Ivatt descended the steps, and without even having to bend,

walked under the raised floor of the audience hall where they had been sitting, and untied his panung.

At that moment the Palat strode up accompanied by the young Malay interpreter. He paused in front of the steps and was about to climb them when he noticed Ivatt standing under the floorboards, naked from the waist down. He watched in amazement as the little man looked up, jumped and emitted a fearsome yell. Within seconds servants appeared out of the woodwork, slaves came pouring across the courtyard and Phaulkon bounded down the steps, almost colliding with the Palat. Burnaby hobbled along after him.

At the sight of the Palat the servants and slaves prostrated themselves on the ground and all eyes turned on Ivatt.

The little man, still half undressed, was pointing a finger in front of him and exclaiming over and over: 'It's the red-bearded giant! The monster I saw in the water with his hands outstretched!'

Ivatt looked around now, and seeing all eyes on him, turned away and fumbled with his panung, while the vision with the red beard crawled out of its hiding place and stretched itself to its full height, visibly flustered.

'Joop van Risling, chief factor of de Royal Dutch Company en Ligor. At your service, mijn heeren,' he said in heavily accented English to the assembly in general. 'I vait for my turn with His Excellency to talk.'

Phaulkon burst out laughing, the Palat politely followed suit and the rest of the slaves, taking their cue from this exalted official, with three thousand dignity marks, joined in boisterously.

'Well, spit on a Dutchman!' came Ivatt's voice from behind, as he finally managed to negotiate his panung.

At this moment the Lord of the Province, the Pu Samrec Rajakara Meuang, appeared on the scene, and, with the exception of the Dutchman, those who were not yet prostrate became so instantly, and everyone froze in place.

The mandarin looked slowly around him and focused his gaze on the newcomers. One of them was prostrate in the correct position with his forehead touching the ground. This both surprised and pleased him. He noticed too that this man had normal, straight black hair. Another, an older yellow-haired giant, was

69

also prostrate, though a little more awkwardly than the first. He was the one who had hurt his foot. And a third man, normal in stature, was making a ridiculous attempt to put a simple panung on, and in his haste to prostrate himself he had tied the piece of cloth over his heavenly parts like a sash. Ludicrous! But at least he was attempting some manners. The Governor caught the Dutchman's eye and swung his gaze round to the other farangs as if to indicate there were some who could behave like civilized people.

Phaulkon glanced around him from his supine position and noticed that the Governor was looking uncomfortable. He wondered what was causing his distress when he perceived that the tall Dutchman was still standing, towering over the mandarin's head. There were more Siamese than Europeans in the courtyard, and their distaste at this gross discourtesy was almost tangible.

Although he knew that he should not speak ahead of the Lord of the Province, Phaulkon decided to risk a breach of protocol. 'Heer van Risling,' he said quickly in Dutch, 'my chief, Mr Burnaby, from the English East India Company is honoured to meet his celebrated Dutch counterpart. He has unfortunately injured his foot and is unable to stand, but he would be grateful if you would sit down and speak with him.' Whether it was the flattering tone or the unexpected fluency of Phaulkon's Dutch, the ploy had its desired effect. The florid Dutchman lowered himself on to the grass next to Burnaby, and though he was not prostrate, at least his head was now below that of the mandarin's. The tension in the courtyard diffused. Decorum had been restored.

The mandarin glanced over at the farang with the straight dark hair like his own, and saw that he was smiling. Had this farang whose manners were surprisingly good spoken words that caused the red-beard to sit down? The mandarin was intrigued.

'Kling!' he addressed his supine Palat.

'Mighty Lord, the sole of your foot awaits your orders.'

'Explain what happened.'

'Mighty Lord, I receive your orders. The farang who cannot tie his panung came down to answer the call of nature and discovered the red-beard spying on him. He cried out—'

'Who cried out?'

70

'Mighty Lord, I receive your orders. The farang who cannot tie his panung cried out.'

'Good, we will call him the short farang. The one with the normal hair we will call the medium farang, and the old long-limbed one will be the tall farang. Red-beard will remain as before. What happened then?'

'Mighty Lord, I receive your orders. After that the farang who cannot t . . . the short farang forgot the reason for which he had come down and tried to tie his panung again because of the audience.'

'What audience?'

'Mighty Lord, I receive your orders. The audience which heard his cry and gathered here: the medium farang, the tall farang, the red-beard, the dust of your feet, and the august Lord himself, as well as some slaves.'

'Good. And how is the odour of the small, medium, and tall farangs? Is it similar to that of red-beard?'

'I, a hair of your head, have found it not as strong. But I, a hair, think that the slaves of the mighty Lord may have been scrubbing them earlier.'

'Good. Then gather them together in my audience chamber while they are still fresh. The new farangs and red-beard. Send for the Malay interpreter so I can talk to them, and order food, musicians and dancers.'

'Mighty Lord, I receive your orders.'

At that the great mandarin smiled graciously at the assembly and solemnly walked away. All then rose from the ground except the slaves while the Palat was still there, and Phaulkon pondered whether he had been right to conceal his knowledge of the language. He had been familiar with every form of address he had heard. Still, the Governor had referred to the Dutchman in very unflattering terms and that was worth knowing. If he could just give Ivatt a few lessons in proper behaviour and make sure that he and Burnaby washed with greater frequency . . . Though Phaulkon's knowledge of etiquette might arouse the suspicions of the Siamese, they would have no proof that he spoke their language. Further situations were bound to develop to justify concealing his knowledge of the language, he reflected optimistically, as the Palat led them round to another side of the palace where a further series of steps led up to the main audience hall.

71

Six

'So you speak Dutch,' said van Risling, eyeing Phaulkon with a mixture of suspicion and respect. He sounded relieved to be conversing in his mother tongue again. He knew little English and his conversation with the chief English factor on the way to the audience hall had been stilted and brief.

'A little,' replied Phaulkon modestly. 'I was two years in Bantam before coming to Siam.'

They were sitting on the teakwood floor of the hall waiting for the Governor to appear and for the Palat and the interpreter to return. Rich Persian carpets covered all but the teak borders of the room. The four farangs had the place to themselves apart from the usual bevy of silent, crouching servants. The Dutchman sat clumsily cross-legged next to Phaulkon. He was heavyset and florid, and his untrimmed red beard must have seemed the height of devilry to the superstitious Siamese, thought Phaulkon. He was dressed in the European style, breeches and a blouse, but he had removed his long boots outside, in deference to the local custom. Phaulkon could well understand the mandarin's preoccupation with the odour of the newcomers. Three more such additions to the room could have made life unbearable. The Siamese were an obsessively clean people, bathing several times a day, and he often felt shamed by the stench of his fellow Europeans whose habit of not bathing was particularly offensive in the torrid climate of the tropics. 'The English used to have a trading post there,' he added.

'So I remember. But that was in the old days. Now of course the whole area belongs to Holland.' Van Risling smiled smugly.

'Indeed, I recall how one minute you were trading with the King of Bantam and the next he was your vassal.'

The Hollanders' elaborate network of trading posts was unsurpassed, and no other European nation was capable of thwarting them. The Spanish, weakened by Drake's defeat of their armada, were occupied with the Philippines, Portuguese power was on the wane, the British were busy expanding Indian trade, and the French had so far concentrated their efforts on Africa.

'And did you also learn Malay while you were there?' asked the Dutchman, ignoring the jibe.

'Not more than two words,' lied Phaulkon. 'Most of my friends were European.' When the mandarin arrived, Phaulkon knew that the conversation would go from Siamese to Malay and back, and he wanted to appear ignorant of both.

'But you are not English, are you, Heer, er . . . Phaulkon, I believe you said?' The Dutchman observed him. He did not look English, more the Mediterranean type, clean-shaven and easily tanned by the climate. He was a little taller perhaps than the average southerner. The bastard had an engaging smile, he had to admit.

'No, I'm Greek. But I've worked for the English since I was nine so I'm probably more like one of them by now,' he said with a smile.

'A Greek? You're the first I've heard of in these parts. And the other two?' he asked, turning his head towards Ivatt and Burnaby. 'They're both English?'

'Now you two,' said Ivatt, noticing the stare, 'I hope you're saying pleasant things about us.' Neither he nor Burnaby, who were sitting to one side chatting, understood Dutch.

'Yes,' Phaulkon replied to the Dutchman's question, 'we're all with the East India Company, Heer van Risling.'

'You mean the English one? You should specify, Heer Phaulkon. There is a Dutch East India Company, as you know, and a French one too. In these parts *the* East India Company is the Dutch one. We are, after all . . . shall we say, this is our trading area?'

'For the moment perhaps, mijn heer. But nothing lasts for ever. Look at what happened to the Portuguese. One hundred and fifty years ago who would not have thought them invincible?'

It was true. The industrious Dutch had turned the tide. By 1630 the Dutch were in virtual control of Siam's foreign trade and the Portuguese reduced to the role of bodyguards and mercenaries.

'So enjoy youself while you may, mijn heer,' said Phaulkon.

'Who is there to stop us?' the Dutchman snapped. 'A few English pirates from Madras? Godverdomme, Heer Phaulkon, you English are wasting your time in Siam. Better go back to Madras and trade with your Indians.'

'Since when do you have a monopoly on Siamese trade then, mijn heer? You'd be wise to get used to our presence.'

'I doubt you'll be here long enough for that to be necessary, Heer Phaulkon,' retorted the Dutchman. 'Contraband is not tolerated by the Siamese authorities.'

Phaulkon's heart lost a beat but his face showed no emotion. 'What do you mean?' he inquired casually.

'I mean that shipping arms without permission is a crime against the state. As for supplying cannon to the rebels, Heer Phaulkon,' the Dutchman paused to observe Phaulkon's reaction, 'why, the authorities here have interesting forms of chastise-ment in such cases, always linked to the nature of the crime, you understand. Do you know that in the case of conspirators, the less important of the two is beheaded first and his severed head attached to that of the living leader, so that he can carry it about with him for a few days and contemplate his guilt at leisure.' The Dutchman chortled. 'I wonder who would be considered the chief conspirator, you or the Queen of Pattani? And to think she always wanted a farang round her neck. Ha, ha!' Van Risling shook with laughter, the perspiration emerging in streams below his red beard.

'You have been too long in this distant outpost, Heer van Risling, and I fear the sun has affected your imagination,' observed Phaulkon.

His mind was racing. If van Risling had the proof he required, then why had he found it necessary to eavesdrop on their conversation earlier? But how the devil could he know about the Queen? That swine of a warehouse keeper in Ayudhya might have betrayed the presence of the cannon but he knew nothing of their destination. He could not possibly know. Only Phaulkon, Burnaby and Alvarez knew, and Alvarez was still in Pattani. Van Risling must be guessing. A chilling enough bluff, he had to admit.

'You are perhaps wondering about my proof, Heer Phaulkon? Do not fear, it is on its way. And in the meantime you and your friends are to be detained here. So enjoy yourself while you may, mijn heer.'

'I hardly think the Siamese authorities will detain us at the whim of a Dutchman, when they have invited us back to curb your very arrogance. You see, Heer van Risling, we have been asked to redress the balance of power.'

'You'd better not cross the path of Holland,' said the Dutchman, his voice rising. 'And remember, we officially control the trade in hides.' He banged his fist on the floor in front of him.

'Do I detect heat in the conversation?' interrupted Ivatt, turning towards them.

'Ja, ja, heat,' said the Dutchman in English, turning on the other two. 'And you,' he pointed at Burnaby, 'vhy you lie down to de natives? You are chief tradesman. Not good impression, even for Englishman. Farang must to stand up to de Siamezen. Cannot be like slave.' He waved his arms in the direction of the grovelling servants. 'You are animals or you are trading chief, Godverdomme?' His mounting anger was feeding on itself. 'Vhy you verdomme Engelsen come back to Siam anyvay?' he demanded of Burnaby.

'Constant, what have you been saying to this nice man? You've got him all riled up,' said Ivatt.

'We've come to take over from the Dutch,' said Burnaby with icy cool. 'First it was Portugal's turn, then yours. Now it's ours.'

'Zwijn!' exploded the Dutchman. At that moment, the Lord of the Province, preceded by his sword bearer, his betel box carrier and four semi-naked slaves, appeared in the doorway. 'You vill go to de prisons, you Engelsen,' pursued the Dutchman undaunted, 'and then to de grave, you vill see.' He made a sign of slitting his throat, in a graphic gesture.

The mandarin's eyes narrowed. Whose rasping tones were disturbing the harmony of his household? It was the Dutch farang again. He had turned the same colour as when he drank spirits, and his hands were shaking.

At the sight of the mandarin, Phaulkon immediately prostrated himself. Burnaby and Ivatt followed suit. The Dutchman remained seated, breathing heavily. The mandarin smiled graciously, then sat folding his legs under him, and spreading them over to one side. One hand rested on his thigh and the other was placed on the floor, propping up the bulk of his body. This was his usual position – comfortable for him, but excruciating for the farangs, who rather than attempt to adopt it, preferred to lie prostrate in the manner of his subordinates. The jewels on the

75

Governor's fingers and the gold of his expansive brocade coat sparkled in the sunlight that filtered through the open shutters. He was clearly not in the habit of stinting himself, thought Phaulkon. The Siamese peasantry for the most part had spare and athletic builds, but the Governor's stomach billowed, and more than one roll of fat hung below his chin. He appeared fortyish, but Phaulkon had long ago given up guessing Siamese ages. Their skins seemed to stay smooth and unwrinkled far longer than Europeans'.

On his head the Governor wore a conically shaped white hat attached under his chin with a string. It was only worn on ceremonial occasions or during official business, and never doffed; it had a golden ring round it to indicate the rank of mandarin first grade. There were five ranks in the mandarinate, the first being the highest.

There were also four classes of province. As a first-class province, Ligor would probably have under its jurisdiction a score of other provinces. The Governor of Ligor was, without question, the most important Siamese Phaulkon had ever met.

A servant carrying his master's betel box, gold with diamond encrustations, another indication of his exalted rank, shuffled forward and placed it on the ground by his Lord's side, while his ceremonial sword bearer knelt behind him, resting his Lord's bejewelled sword over his left shoulder. Semi-naked servants clustered prostrate in every corner.

The Palat now appeared with the Dutchman's Malay interpreter. They prostrated themselves immediately at the entrance, and as they advanced across the length of the room on all fours, Ivatt was reminded of a couple of hunters approaching their game unobserved. He was sorely tempted to give voice to his observations, when he remembered his promise to Phaulkon to keep silent at all times in the presence of the mandarin.

The Governor now opened the proceedings: 'We are pleased to note that you have had time to become acquainted,' he said, looking first at the Dutchman and then at the other three. An air of amusement crossed His Excellency's face. 'We welcome our new arrivals and thank the Lord Buddha that this life's cycle did not end prematurely for them. And we thank, of course, Mr Lidrim for his efforts in saving them.' He nodded courteously to the Dutchman.

76

So Ivatt was right, thought Phaulkon.

Merciful Lord, make this speech brief, prayed Ivatt, unaccustomed to the painful posture. He had copied Phaulkon in every detail and was now resting on his knees and elbows with his forehead just above the ground and his palms joined together in an attitude of prayer.

Burnaby was wondering how soon their stay at Ligor would be over and they could get back to Ayudhya. Apart from the pain in his foot, he was desperate to return to the safety of the English factory. There were too many unknowns here. What if one of the crates were suddenly washed up on shore? He wished he could understand what was being said. Although he had spent over a year in Siam, he spoke hardly a word of the language. He had never regretted his ignorance as much as now. But it was so damned difficult – all those sing-song tones and subtle nuances, impossible unless of course you had Constant's gifts. Even the Jesuits admitted he had mastered the idiom more thoroughly than any foreigner before him. Burnaby felt a sudden yearning for the peace of his garden in Ayudhya – the tuberoses and jasmine and the wondrous kadung flower that only gave out its perfume at night, when the heat of the day no longer subdued its spirit. How he longed to be away from this treacherous place.

Van Risling was looking pleased with himself. He would trap and expose the Greek. The tall Englishman might be the official leader, but he sensed it was the Greek who was the true head. The Englishman had no ear for languages, whereas this Greek . . .

He glanced at him now, lying prostrate and servile. Typical Mediterranean, he thought, smooth and unctuous. He had to be the one who spoke Siamese. In less than two weeks he would have the answer, but meanwhile he just might catch him out anyway. Or perhaps it would be easier to trip up the tall Englishman, a more ready prey.

He turned now to Burnaby, translating directly from the Malay into English: 'His Excellency says you verdommed lucky being alive.'

'Tell His Excellency that it is thanks to him and to his physicians,' replied Burnaby. 'Please thank him for his gracious hospitality and tell him that we are now well enough to travel to

77

Ayudhya. If he would again be so obliging as to lend us a boat and crew, we will entirely repay him on arrival in Ayudhya.'

'The chief of the English factory says they are well now. They want a boat, a full crew, provisions, and money,' translated the Dutchman.

Phaulkon bristled, and the mandarin, on hearing the Malay's translation, blinked. Could the tall farang really have said that? the Governor wondered. He seemed to have said much more. How much was the Dutch farang really translating? He addressed the Dutchman again.

'Tell the chief of the English farangs that we unfortunately have no boat available for the present but that as soon as we do, one will be provided.' The mandarin inclined his head gracefully towards Burnaby.

Phaulkon knew that this was nonsense. The Lord of the Province could rustle up ten boats in as many minutes.

The Dutchman delivered his latest translation. 'De Governor say no boat. You stay here until you confess.'

'Confess?' asked Burnaby.

'Ja. About what cargo you carry. Better you confess now. Everybody here know it.'

Burnaby's stomach turned. 'Knows what?' he said, blandly. 'I don't understand.'

'You want me speak more? All right. Confess about de cannon.' He paused. 'You understand, de cannon which washing up before mijn factory. On de beach. Better you confess now. I tell mandarin no torture, good? You confess now, I tell him no torture. Much better for you.'

Burnaby's heart missed a beat. The pain in his foot was temporarily forgotten. Out of the corner of his eye he sought out Phaulkon. But the Greek stared back at him impassively.

'I don't know what you're talking about,' said Burnaby, looking perplexed.

Behind the expressionless façade, Phaulkon's mind was churning. He turned now and spoke to the Dutchman in a tone that would sound courteous to the mandarin. 'Now hear this, Dutchman, it is obvious that you are scared to death of the English. And you have every right to be. We are cleverer, more honest, and better traders than you.' The Dutchman bristled, but Phaulkon continued to smile affably at him, aware that the mandarin

78

was watching. 'The policy of the English government,' he carried on in Dutch pleasantly, 'is to have every blood-sucking, putrid son of Erasmus out of Siam within six months. And we three have been given that task. And as for the cannon . . . yes, we had cannon on board.' He paused. The Dutchman gaped, scrambled to his feet, and burst into Malay.

'He says there were cannon on board! Tell His Excellency! He's confessed!' he shrieked, pointing at Phaulkon. Burnaby and Ivatt looked from Phaulkon to the Dutchman in confusion.

The Governor, displaying obvious displeasure, was forced to rise too. After hearing the interpreter out, he turned directly to Phaulkon. 'Ask the medium farang whether he was transporting cannon on his boat,' he ordered.

The interpreter translated the Governor's question into Malay and the Dutchman turned gleefully to Phaulkon.

'Were you transporting cannon on the *Royal Lotus*?' he asked officially in Dutch.

Phaulkon looked towards the Governor and then shook his head emphatically from side to side.

'Absolutely not,' he said. 'Whatever gave you that idea?' he asked the Dutchman, perplexed.

The Dutchman leapt into the air and stamped his foot angrily. 'Godverdomme, you two-faced son of a Greek whore,' he raged. 'You castrated slave of the Turk, you just admitted you had cannon on board. I'll order the mandarin to put you in chains until you repeat what you said.'

'You'll order the mandarin?' Phaulkon would have given anything to translate this. 'So you're already behaving as if you own the place, eh, Dutchman? This is Siamese territory and we will see to it that it remains that way. I saw how you Dutch in Java helped one Sultan defeat another and then swallowed up the winner.'

But the Dutchman was barely listening. He was shaking his head like an angler who had just lost a prize fish. 'Godverdomme, but you just admitted . . .'

The mandarin turned now to the interpreter with an expression of obvious distaste.

'Would you explain to me what is going on?'

'Mighty Lord, though I cannot speak their language, it seems

79

that Heer Risling believes the *Royal Lotus* was transporting cannon while their leader denies it.'

'Ask the medium farang then exactly what he was transporting on board, where he was heading for and whether he has any papers to prove it.'

The Dutchman put the question to Phaulkon.

'We were transporting English broadcloth, Your Excellency, to the Malay states south of your borders,' replied Phaulkon, smiling amiably at the Governor. 'Our official papers are still locked in the strong box. The box is virtually watertight, so if the wreck could be found . . .'

The Governor surveyed Phaulkon as he listened to the translation. Then he addressed him once again through the interpreter. 'Your ship has unfortunately not yet been found, Mr Forcon, but our coast guards are watching for anything they can salvage. You may rest assured that we will keep you fully informed.' Van Risling's final rendering of the translation sounded more ominous than the Governor had intended.

'Thank you, Your Excellency.'

The mandarin eyed Phaulkon carefully. Perhaps you are telling the truth, he thought. Perhaps the Dutch farang's hatred of your nation is such that he must incriminate you at all costs. We will find out. The contents of your ship may lie on the ocean floor but if Ayudhya confirms that you or any one of your team speaks our language, then we will know that you are not telling the truth and that you are not to be trusted. And you will be tortured until you reveal all. But why hide your knowledge of our language in the first place? Is it that you fear our methods of interrogation? You do not look like a coward. Perhaps it is the tall one. He does not look so resistant. Or perhaps again the Dutch farang is making the whole thing up. We shall see. For your sake I hope it is not true. You have manners, more than I thought possible in a farang.

Phaulkon now turned to Burnaby. 'Unfortunately, Richard, none of the contents of the *Royal Lotus* has been recovered, but His Excellency has graciously consented to continue searching for them.'

Burnaby smiled for the first time, while the Dutchman shook his head once more.

'Zwijn, but you admitted only a while ago—'

80

'Perhaps I did,' said Phaulkon calmly, 'but if I were in your shoes I would take the knowledge quietly with you to the grave. Because the cannon were all Dutch, mijn heer, and if they were discovered you would have as much to explain as I. Mr Burnaby was merely paid a large sum of money by your factory in Ayudhya to transport *your* contraband weapons on an English-owned ship. How would Englishmen otherwise be in possession of Dutch cannon? The English have perfectly good cannon of their own.'

The Dutchman exploded. 'You're lying!'

'You're a fool to think so, mijn heer,' said Phaulkon with quiet composure.

'You're not even a clever liar, Greek. What about the dispatches I received from my head office to apprehend you and your cannon?'

'That was just a precaution of theirs in case we were caught. You would obviously show your dispatch and deny our story.'

'And what about the markings?'

'The Siamese couldn't read them anyway.'

The mandarin had had enough. The atmosphere was defiled. The Dutchman not only remained upright but his contemptible lack of self-control had become intolerable. The medium farang, on the other hand, had retained his composure throughout. He was clearly the actual leader of their group, not the tall one. He wondered how many dignity marks the middle farang might have in his own country. And he wondered for the first time whether there could be other farangs from other countries with more nobility than the crude specimens that traded along his shores. Farangs more like the middle farang. And if there were, perhaps they could balance the power of the Dutch and prevent a recurrence of that ignominious day when the Dutch had blockaded the mouth of the Menam Chao Phraya and demanded a monopoly in the trade of hides. Though His Majesty was outraged, Dutch cannon had forced him to concede. It had been the first time a farang power had dared to challenge the sovereignty of Siam. Although the whole affair had been carefully downplayed, it had been a lasting loss of face. He squirmed at the recollection and tried to put it out of his mind.

'Kling!'

'Mighty Lord, the dust of your feet awaits your orders.'

81

'Have you prepared the entertainment?'

'Mighty Lord, I receive your orders. The musicians await outside.'

'Good. We will eat and be entertained.'

'Mighty Lord, I receive your orders.' The Palat understood only too well that his master should wish to end the proceedings. He was surprised that his august self had allowed the barbarity to continue for as long as it had.

Seven

The Europeans were ushered into a neighbouring room and invited to sit cross-legged on rush mats, a position they all found considerably more comfortable than the one they had just endured. The room, with wood-panelled walls, was roughly the size and shape of the audience hall except that one half of it was on a raised platform about two feet from the ground. In the section where they sat were Persian rugs and blue and white porcelain; but the other half clearly served as a stage. Presently a most peculiar collection of musical instruments was set up on one side of this stage.

Ivatt had been placed like a buffer between the Dutchman and Phaulkon and he was relieved to note that with the imminent arrival of food, the Dutch bear had found a new distraction. A period of calm appeared to be in store. Barnaby sat on the other side of the Dutchman, and then the mandarin, resting in that peculiar position he seemed to find so comfortable.

The sword bearer and betel box carrier had disappeared and only the Palat and the interpreter now remained. They were in their favourite grovelling position at the foot of their master. There was no single dining table but each guest had a round wooden stand placed before him laden with gold vessels, into which serving girls now placed the contents of a variety of steaming dishes.

Ivatt wondered where the wife or wives of the mandarin were, but presumably women did not attend official functions in Siam. Instead, a bare-breasted young slave girl knelt at every guest's side mixing his food and filling his drinking cup.

He was examining the contents of his dishes when an interpretation of the culinary delicacies came down the long line of translators. 'You will inform the guests,' said the Governor to the Malay interpreter prostrate at his feet, 'of the contents of each dish.' The interpreter then rattled off a string of Malay sounds to the Dutchman, who was reluctantly obliged to pause from devouring a large prawn.

'His Excellency vants you to know vhat you eat,' he said

83

pointing hurriedly to each dish. 'Dis is de baby turtles, de garlic eels, de crocodile eggs, de curried prawns, de fresh river fish soup wit de lemon grass, de broiled lizards, de fried locusts, and de skinned bats. *Smakelyk eten, mijn heeren!*'

'What was that last one?' asked Ivatt. 'A snakelike herring?'

'Huh?' said the Dutchman.

Phaulkon laughed. '*Smakelyk eten* means good appetite.'

The farangs watched in awe as the Dutchman resumed his attack on the array of dishes before him, indiscriminately thrusting his shell spoon first into one and then another of them, stuffing the contents into his gaping mouth. His nose, chin, and cheeks were soon covered with sauces. Even the skinned bats failed to deter him.

Ivatt's slave smiled coyly at him and pointed encouragingly at his rice bowl and a little round dish containing a pungent but tasty sauce made from fish roe. Then she raised a small gold cup to his lips and tipped a vitriolic rice brandy down his throat, which instantly set fire to his insides.

No sooner was it empty than she replenished the cup from a large blue and white jug with a pale blue spout.

He was just pushing what he took to be the crocodile eggs to one side, to ensure that he was not asked to swallow one, when the Governor noticed the gesture.

'Crocodile eggs are much prized,' he said, smiling graciously at Ivatt.

The Dutchman listened to the Malay's translation and groaned. 'I don't know de English for dat,' he said.

'Say it in Dutch,' offered Phaulkon, 'and I'll render the English.'

The Governor resumed, 'The eggs are prized because they are so costly to gather. Many a collector has left his arm in the jaws of an irate mother. The female crocodile is quite opposed to the abduction of her young. The men who return to tell the tale all speak of the same techniques to obtain the eggs, and to survive: a fast horse, a low swoop, and an excellent balance. But I see you are saving this great delicacy for the last,' he said appreciatively to Ivatt. 'Mr Lidrim,' he added, turning to the Dutchman, 'you must insist that our young friend taste the eggs first before the other sauces contaminate his palate.'

The Dutchman turned to Ivatt. 'You must eat de crocodile

eggs now. Governor's orders,' he said, briefly lifting his face from a large plate of curry.

Ivatt glanced at Phaulkon, but the Greek's face registered only amusement. Barnaby, too, was barely suppressing a grin. Van Risling was too busy chewing even to notice. He wouldn't get much sympathy out of this group, thought Ivatt. Even the Palat was observing him slyly from his recumbent position.

At the Governor's insistence, Ivatt's slave now placed the rare delicacy in front of him, and he found himself staring down at a huge raw egg. Then she divided it into four equal parts and added a dark brown sauce from a little dish. He braced himself and swallowed his first piece of crocodile egg. With the Governor looking on, he did his best to maintain an expression of ecstasy, and as the final piece slid down his throat, he wondered whether eating crocodile eggs was the reason why the Siamese crawled about on their stomachs half the time.

'Delicious,' he sighed, licking his lips and washing the slimy, gelatinous contents down with a liberal measure of rice brandy. Oddly enough, the rest of the food tasted much better after that.

Phaulkon stole an amused glance at Burnaby and then turned to observe the mandarin, who was beaming his approval across his little table. Accustomed to wielding power and authority since childhood and unfamiliar with argument or contradiction, the Governor was not a man to be thwarted, thought Phaulkon. His was probably a hereditary appointment. If the truth of the *Royal Lotus*'s activities were to emerge, this seemingly amiable man, with his ever-present concern for his guests, more courteous and refined than most 'gentlemen' Phaulkon had come across in his life, would become the most vindictive, implacable foe.

The thought of the cannon's discovery descended on Phaulkon like a dark cloud, blotting out the festive air of the banquet. What had the Dutchman meant when he said that proof was on its way? What proof? It was obviously true, reflected Phaulkon, that they were being held prisoner, albeit with an outward show of hospitality, else why would the Governor have denied Burnaby's request for a boat? One word from the mandarin would have sufficed to send them in comfort back to Ayudhya. They were obviously waiting for something. With an effort he forced himself to concentrate on the proceedings and join in the jollity.

85

'Yes, we respect the crocodile,' the Governor was saying, 'and we do not harm him unless he comes to a village and carries off one of our people. And then a special ceremony occurs, presided over by a crocodile charmer, a man well versed in tracking the culprit. Accompanied by a number of men in boats and armed with spears, he goes in search of the animal. When he locates it he springs deftly on to its back and skilfully stubs its eyes with his fingers, while his attendants fasten its throat and legs with ropes and drag it back to the village. Here it is bound to one of the pillars of the headman's house in expiation of its crimes.

'In other parts of the country I have heard that they bind the guilty crocodile with ropes and cut a slice off the beast's tail. Then it suffers a cruel end.' The mandarin looked around at his guests and lowered his voice slightly. 'They insert a long, sharp bamboo sliver slowly along its spine from the sliced end of the tail as far as the brain, until the animal expires.' There was a momentary silence, and Phaulkon felt a shudder go through him.

It was at this point in the narrative that Ivatt bit into a well-camouflaged chili. He choked and gagged, turning quite crimson in the face. Interrupted by the noise, the Dutchman glanced up from the culinary debris in front of him, diagnosed the problem instantly and slammed a bear-like paw across Ivatt's back. The little fellow was catapulted nose first into the curry.

'Ha, ha! Getting right down to de food, eh?' The Dutchman burst into laughter, shaking like a jelly and looking around the room for approval. Confronted with the polite smile of the mandarin, he turned his attentions to the other two. 'Come, come, Heer Phaulkon, you must enjoy yourself while you can. Life is short. Especially yours. Ha, ha!'

Phaulkon had glanced across at the mandarin during Ivatt's predicament, observed the potentate's unamused expression and checked his own urge to laugh. The Siamese loved to laugh, but they did not always share the farang's sense of humour. They were more attuned to the puns to which their tonal language so readily lent itself. He had seen them holding their sides with laughter over the attempts of the French Jesuits to illustrate to their pupils the tonal differences of the Siamese language in a single sentence. Any farang attempting to make a study of the idiom would be given a table of tones to master: 'Khai khai kai khai na khai' which meant 'Is anybody selling eggs in the city?'

86

To the newcomer, of course, this sounded like a repetition of the same word five times, but to the Siamese ear the correct inflection and tone of each word altered its meaning entirely. The endless pitfalls attending this exercise were a constant source of amusement to the Siamese.

Joop van Risling's laughter was now finally subsiding and as a slave washed the last of the curry from Ivatt's face, the Dutchman turned to the Governor and bowed his head slightly, coming as close as he was capable to a moment of courtesy.

'Very good, ja? Your Excellency's cooks are first class.' He rubbed his hands together, then swilled another glass of rice brandy. 'And now what about the dancing girls?'

The Governor inclined his head and gave an order to the Palat. Immediately the servants cleared away the little sauce dishes that lent such exquisite flavours to Siamese cuisine: garlic, saffron, ginger, nutmeg, lemon grass, and pepper. For these were substituted a splendid assortment of fruits: figs, durian, tamarind, guava, pomelo, jackfruit and the diminutive bananas known as elephants' teeth.

At the sight of so fitting a finale to the great feast, Phaulkon turned to the Governor and expressed his appreciation by smacking his lips and inclining himself profoundly. The mandarin acknowledged the compliment with a slight obeisance and moments later the dances began.

Mastery of the Siamese classical dance required training from early childhood, and this training was evident from the moment the female dancers entered gracefully on to the stage. As an admirer of the dance himself, Phaulkon was curious to see his first provincial troupe in action. He was not disappointed.

First the instruments played a lengthy introduction, with each musician giving a solo rendition extolling the virtues of his particular instrument. There was the Khong-Bong, a kind of semi-circular xylophone, which practically surrounded the seated musician and which was played by two hammers; the Saw-an, a type of sitar or violin, whose value was enhanced by the difficulties of procuring a coconut shell of the precise semi-circular curve required to form the body; the Klui, an enchanting nose flute; and the Takhe, something like a guitar, resting on the floor and plucked by a female musician with artificial nails made of copper.

These were several inches long and affixed to the tips of her fingers with an adhesive paste. To the Western ear, the music, with a scale of five notes instead of seven, was discordant, at times vibrant, at others mournful, but always somehow hypnotic.

Following a crescendo of the entire orchestra, the female dancers entered the stage from behind a curtain. Wearing tall, pointed hats glittering with gold leaf, and flowers in their hair and elaborate costumes of rich greens, reds and blues, the girls swayed gently to the mesmerizing music of the small orchestra. Their supple fingers bent to touch their wrists, their eyes flickered coquettishly from side to side, their necks undulated like charmed cobras, and their feet rose backwards like birds in flight. It was a flawless co-ordination of the entire body.

Soon the tempo changed and the girls vanished behind the curtain, to be replaced moments later by a warrior monkey who leapt on to the stage to the roll of drums and placed a hand across the front of his hideous mask to scan the forest for the enemies of the Princess in distress. Phaulkon recognized scenes from the classical Hindu epic, the Ramayana, complete with kings, ogres and abducted princesses. Then the music softened and the nostalgic nose flute dominated as the Princess herself made her entrance. It was the first time this dancer had appeared on stage and it was soon evident that she was foremost among them. She was a girl of striking beauty, noticeably taller than the rest of the troupe and her presence commanded instant attention. She had large, innocent eyes, broad though feminine shoulders which accentuated the smallness of her waist, and light, honey-coloured skin as smooth as the finest silk from China.

The hypnotic, undulating movements of her arms resembled the statues of Hindu deities come to life and the rhythmic flicker of her eyes as she shyly thanked the warrior monkey for his help left the audience entranced. Her long slender fingers bent back so effortlessly to rest upon her wrists that the farangs were unaware of the extent of the tortuous feat. Whether she danced the part of a frolicsome deer in the forest or a princess fleeing the advances of the evil king, her movements were exquisite and her timing flawless. Phaulkon, aided by a good quantity of rice brandy, was finding it increasingly difficult to disguise his admiration. It would be rude, he knew, to stare too blatantly at the girl and he was almost relieved when she disappeared off stage.

The orchestra now continued on its own, and to its haunting tones was now added a most unclassical sound: a loud and irregular snoring. Van Risling was deeply asleep, his chin collapsed on to his chest, and his body jerking spasmodically. Phaulkon glanced at the mandarin and their eyes met briefly. The Greek shook his head apologetically, and the mandarin lowered his eyes in acknowledgement. Phaulkon noticed that the Governor himself was not partaking of any rice brandy.

Once more the tempo increased, with an earthenware drum, covered with buffalo hide, taking over as the dominant instrument. The Dutchman woke briefly with a start as suddenly two very lithe and athletic men, both wearing frightening masks, one of a monkey and the other of a devil, leapt on to the stage and started duelling with real swords in a frenzied acrobatic whirl that required utter precision. The dancers struck at each other in cadence with the rhythm of the instruments; and it seemed a miracle that they avoided injuring each other. This was the famous sword dance. Phaulkon had seen it once before in Ayudhya, but never quite as audaciously performed as this. The sharp-edged swords swung so close to the ears and noses of the contestants that it seemed as if they were actually bent on mutilating each other.

As the bare-chested, muscular sword dancers whirled about the stage, the Governor engaged for the first time that evening in conversation with his deputy. 'You know, Kling, that medium farang has a good build. I believe he'd make a fine boxer. He reminds me of the sword dancer on the left. See the one? What a pity farangs don't box. Wouldn't it be exciting to train one, though, and send him round the country representing our province? What a sensation!' The Governor chuckled at the thought.

'My Lord,' replied the Palat. Simple repetition of the honorary title indicated the affirmative. There was no word for 'yes' in Siamese, nor was there one for 'no' as it was considered offensive to contradict someone directly. When it became absolutely necessary for the Palat to express an opinion, phrases like 'I think it may not be so' could be used to indicate the negative.

'Do you think the middle farang would be fast off his feet like the tokay lizard, or cumbersome and strong like the buffalo?' pursued the Governor.

'Mighty Lord, I receive your orders. I, a hair, believe he would

89

be more like the tiger, both swift and strong.' The mandarin's eyes glowed. 'But August Lord, would he not be larger and heavier than his opponents? And would such a fight be fair?'

'Does the little elephant scorpion not cause intolerable pain to the mighty pachyderm?' The elephant scorpion was the largest of the scorpion family. Its sting caused elephants to roar in agony. The mandarin sighed, 'I suppose we shall never know.'

Though he was seemingly engrossed in the performance, the Governor's remarks were not lost on Phaulkon. He stored the knowledge and watched as the exquisite dancers left the stage for a change of costume.

As the orchestra droned on discordantly, he turned away, closed his eyes for a moment and thought of these people whom he loved. The Siamese were so much more graceful than the Europeans. Not just their dancing but even their boxing shows were an art form compared to the usual slugging match in the West. It was true that their social and political system, based on rank and despotic authority, was strict and rigid, but this was tempered by other traits: by the natural fun-loving quality of the people themselves and by Buddhist generosity, the same generosity that inspired people to place food and water outside their homes so that anonymous passers-by could partake without having to ask.

The Buddhist ethic taught not only generosity but humility. For even the all-powerful Governor, whose every utterance was law, would at one time in his life have shaved his head, donned the saffron robe, and completed his span at the temple. Like every man in the nation, from the richest prince to the humblest beggar, this potentate would have abandoned all wordly possessions and lived for a time the life of a simple monk, meditating, venturing out alone at dawn with his empty begging bowl, and eating no food from noon until sunrise the next day. Had he forgotten the meaning of humility and charity, it would have been brought back to him then, as a generous people, eager to gain merit by good deeds, filled his bowl with rice. And he would have recalled that everything in life was transient, as was life itself.

So was his seemingly unshakeable authority. Who would have guessed that the rule of this aristocratic despot had its system of curbs and controls too? The King who had appointed him would also spy on him. To all the provinces came royal spies, hand-picked by His Majesty. Disguised as ordinary travellers, the spies asked discreet questions and determined whether the people were satisfied with the Governor's rule. If too many complaints were registered against him, the commissioner was empowered to identify himself and try the Governor on the spot, and in extreme circumstances even to have him executed. Being far from the seat of central power was no licence for the abuse of authority. And heaven help the governor who was not found at his post. Apart from the twice-yearly summons to the royal court to drink the water of allegiance with His Majesty and to report on the situation in his province, no governor was permitted to leave his post without the express consent of the King. For the governor was the King's servant, appointed by him from among his mandarins and responsible to him alone.

A grunt from the Dutchman brought Phaulkon out of his reverie. He turned and saw that the bear was wide awake now, swilling rice brandy with renewed vigour, his face the colour of a ripe tomato. His eyes glowed with intoxication, and he stared at the girls lasciviously as they returned, wearing charming rice farmers' outfits for a dance depicting rural life.

The tall one in the centre now looked more stunning than ever. Her loose, three-quarter-length trousers, the colour of the tropical sky, were tied round her waist with a white sash, and a collarless cotton shirt of matching blue followed faithfully the contours of her shapely body. A silver pendant in the shape of a pear hung down from her neck and accentuated the well-rounded curves of her breasts. Phaulkon could not keep his eyes off her. Neither could the bear. They both smiled at her simultaneously, and she smiled back graciously at them; and each man was sure the smile was meant for him. Ivatt was staring at a little girl who did not look a day older than thirteen, and she too smiled sheepishly back at him. Burnaby could not make up his mind which one he wanted most. All of them really.

The tall dancer, who looked about sixteen, now led the others in rhythmic mimes that described the preparing and ploughing of the soil and the sowing of the seeds. Her long, slender fingers distributed the imaginary seeds in the furrows, and her dazzling black eyes shot glances of fire at Phaulkon and van Risling, as each of them imagined. Phaulkon's heart was beating faster now and there was a distinct stirring in his loins. It was a joyful dance and the tempo increased during harvest time as the girls laughed and gyrated and gathered the rice. The Dutchman began to clap in rhythm, 'Wondershoon!' he cheered. Soon the other farangs were joining in, clapping boisterously and making obvious signs at the dancers.

Suddenly Ivatt jumped up, quite carried away, and announced to the little thirteen-year-old: 'I'll take you back to England with me. You'll be an actress!' Phaulkon glared at him, but Ivatt gave him a look that told him to mind his own business. The rice brandy had taken its toll, and Phaulkon, himself somewhat unsteady, watched helplessly as Ivatt leapt on to the stage shouting, 'Better still, we'll entertain the Governor together!'

Hardly daring to look across at the mandarin, Phaulkon kept his eyes riveted on the stage, determined to restore decorum at the first opportunity. This was a classical dance show at a provincial palace, not some street theatre in London.

The bewildered dancers abruptly ended their performance and the little girl only just escaped Ivatt's clutches as he bowed to the Governor and embarked on an impromptu display of acrobatics, interspersed with clowning, gleaned from his years with the menagerie. Phaulkon glanced apprehensively at the mandarin and saw that His Excellency's expression remained unchanged, as if the whole agenda were proceeding according to plan. Phaulkon sensed it might be futile to fight the situation. He relaxed and waited to see what would happen next.

Ivatt finally sat down and another round of rice brandy materialized. The Dutchman raised his glass to the already embarrassed lead dancer. 'Proost!' he toasted boisterously.

The five dancers were more embarrassed than flattered by the attention being lavished on them. Not knowing what to do, they just smiled back at one and all. Now, anxious to leave the stage, they joined their palms in front of their foreheads and bowed deeply to the audience. This unwittingly released a torrent of enthusiasm from the appreciative Europeans. As one they rose to their feet and clapped and cheered and whooped and roared. Amidst the splendid revelry, Phaulkon vaguely wondered how much damage this performance was causing, but the thought dissolved as quickly as it had intruded.

When the rumpus had finally died down, the Dutchman

announced to all in English, 'De tall one, she is mine.' As if to stress the point, he extended his arms towards her. 'Kom mijn kleine schat, come to Uncle Joop.' He already had two Siamese girls living in his European-style brick house by the factory, the only brick house in the province, as he constantly informed anyone who bothered to listen, and this beautiful dancer would make a fine addition to his harem. How strange he thought, that he had not seen her before, though it was true he had not often attended the Governor's dances. He would surely have remembered her, if he had.

The leader now bent her body forward, almost double, to walk respectfully round the backs of the farangs and prostrate herself before the Governor. His Excellency muttered something to the Palat who in turn spoke to the girl. She nodded discreetly in the direction of Phaulkon. He caught the gesture and turned to the Dutchman. 'I think,' he said in Dutch, 'that the lady you refer to is already spoken for.'

'Ja, ja, I know. I have taken her,' the Dutchman responded with conviction. 'I will add her to my household.'

'Heer van Risling, I don't think you understand. The lady is engaged elsewhere.' Phaulkon's blood was beginning to boil.

'Elsewhere? Who would dare . . . ?' The Dutchman looked belligerently around him. The little thirteen-year-old was now nestling shyly by Ivatt, while another, somewhat older dancer, had sat down by the chief of the English factory. Godverdomme, that fawning Greek must mean himself. Van Risling turned heatedly on Phaulkon. 'Are you blind? Can't you see she has been smiling at *me* all this time?' She was in fact smiling at that moment, as all Siamese did when embarrassed.

Phaulkon was in a predicament. He could hardly insult the Governor in his own house by causing a commotion over his lead dancer. On the other hand, he was damned if he was going to let this bear of a Dutchman have his way.

With an effort, he made his voice resume its earlier dulcet tones. 'We will discuss this outside,' he said in Dutch, forcing himself to smile.

'Discuss what?' challenged van Risling. 'There is nothing to discuss. She is mine.'

Phaulkon's mind churned. Women in Siam, despite appearances, were remarkably independent. They were free to accept a

93

man, or leave him, according to their choice. He recalled how, just before he had left Ayudhya, one young lady had caused a stir by divorcing her husband, a prominent judge, on the grounds that he had smelly feet. He looked at the dancer now. He doubted that she would leave with the Dutchman against her will, unless perhaps the Governor specifically requested her to, which he felt was unlikely. He had seen His Excellency muttering something to her through the Palat, but he would count on the girl asserting her rights before he created a scene. Decorum at all costs had to be preserved. He would first pretend to withdraw.

'Heer van Risling, I stand down,' he said politely in Dutch, indicating the girl with a sweep of his hand, and turning his back on the Dutchman as if he were giving up the contest. The mandarin appeared to be impressed by the gesture and smiled at Phaulkon. The Dutchman, however, took Phaulkon's withdrawal for granted. The Greek obviously knew when he was beaten. Van Risling advanced towards the girl to claim his prize. As he put his hands on her shoulders she glanced at Phaulkon and then turned a pleading eye on the Palat, a look which told the deputy she did not want to offend the distinguished guest of her master but there were limits to indignity.

Phaulkon started to rise. The mandarin now whispered something to the Palat and the official hurriedly left the room. His Excellency inclined himself politely to the Dutchman while Phaulkon, on one knee, paused with his fists clenched. 'Mr Lidrim, though it is clear that my lead dancer is most anxious to escort you, it is our custom in Siam when more than one guest covets the same prize to decide the outcome by a game of chance.' This was the first Phaulkon had heard of such a custom. The Dutchman appeared annoyed as the words were translated, but the Governor did not give him time to object.

'Mr Lidrim, as the senior in rank, it would be fitting if you would be the one to make the first guess. My Palat has a strange quirk of birth. One of his ears is larger than the other. He himself believes that it is the result of a last-minute indecision of the gods whether he should return to earth in this cycle as an elephant or a human. And it is a fact that no man in this province understands elephants better than he does. Well now, Mr Lidrim, perhaps you have already noticed that one of my Palat's ears is larger?'

94

Van Risling shook his head irritably. 'No? Well then, let that be the deciding factor. Please guess which one it is, Mr Lidrim.'

The Dutchman muttered something about childish games and replied brusquely, 'The left one.' The Governor then summoned a slave and told him to fetch the Palat. An awkward silence settled over the room.

'What's going on?' asked Ivatt, who had been watching the proceedings with one eye on his little girl.

'The Palat apparently has different-sized ears. If the left one is bigger, our Dutch friend claims the dancer. If not, I do,' replied Phaulkon curtly.

'I never noticed that about squat-nose,' remarked Ivatt tipsily. 'He must have been quite a sinner in his last life to deserve so many defects.'

'I must say I never noticed it either,' put in Burnaby. 'Which one is it?'

'I don't know,' admitted Phaulkon. 'But we'll find out soon enough.'

At that moment the Palat returned and they all stared at him. It was true. One of his ears was actually considerably larger than the other . . . The right one. How strange, thought Phaulkon, that no one had noticed it before.

Van Risling cursed and looked aggressively around him.

'Mr Lidrim,' said the mandarin, pretending not to notice the Dutchman's frustration, 'I am hoping to preside over a boxing tournament tomorrow, depending on the weather. I do hope you will do me the honour of attending. I myself am a great enthusiast.'

The Dutchman bowed curtly and briefly thanked the mandarin for his hospitality. Then he scowled at the others and turned on his heel, taking the Malay interpreter with him.

Bending low, and wordlessly, the lead dancer walked across to Phaulkon. She knelt and took her place by his side, smiling up at him coyly.

Phaulkon, followed by Burnaby and Ivatt, prostrated himself before the mandarin, who smiled courteously.

'Kling!'

'Mighty Lord, the sole of your feet awaits your orders.'

'Escort the farangs back to their rooms. And at first light tomorrow morning I want you to check the condition of the boxing terrain. If the ground is still wet, bear in mind that another day of sunshine may make the difference. And invite the farangs to attend with red-beard. They seem to have struck up such a special friendship.'

'Mighty Lord, I receive your orders.'

The candles flickered and threw playful shadows on the ceiling. The gold leaf of the lacquered cabinet shone wanly in the artificial light. Fresh flowers and warm Chinese tea stood on either side of the quilted rush mattress. The silk coverlets had been turned down.

With gentle movements, and smiling shyly, the lead dancer began to undress Phaulkon. She felt a powerful thrill mixed with fear at the imminent intimacy with this farang, the first she had ever known. It was not just curiosity; ever since she had noticed him smiling up at her on stage, she had felt strangely drawn to him. He had such an engaging smile.

She caressed his skin as she removed his muslin shirt and felt a stirring inside her. He was so well built – such broad shoulders! He smiled at her warmly. There was a desire in his eyes which infused her and when he rested his hand lightly on her panung, a shiver went through her body. She longed to inhale him, but it was too soon yet. She had first to oil and massage him, to relax and prepare him for the final pleasures. There was plenty of time. She had heard some amazing rumour that farangs did not inhale each other but sucked on each other's lips instead. How grotesque! And how sad not to know the ecstasy of placing one's nose against a lover's cheek and inhaling the delicate aromas of his skin. How else could one truly dwell inside another person? She hoped he would not ask her to put her mouth on his, the same mouth that God had given them to swallow foods!

She touched his shoulder blades, pushing him gently on to the mattress, and looked down at him now. He was not fat, but his bones were obviously bigger than those of her people. He had a few hairs on his chest, which she would rather not have noticed, but he was certainly less ape-like than the red devil farang who had stared at her shamelessly during the dances. Never would she have accepted intimacy with that vile one, even for curiosity's sake. He stank. This one was at least clean – except for his breath, which smelled of those terrible intoxicating spirits the farangs like to dirnk. She was aching to open his panung, but everything had its time.

He sighed as she caressed him, and stared up at her with that wonderful smile that made her want to inhale him more than ever. She longed to tell him how His Excellency had manipulated the guessing game, because the Palat's ears were of course identical, and the slave who had fetched him had been able to tell him which one to cover with the false one. Sarit the maskmaker was a true craftsman. She had once seen a whole face which he had carved of the mighty Lord himself, and the likeness was so great that when Chang the mischievous sword dancer had worn it as a joke, they had all prostrated themselves as before the great Lord himself.

His Excellency had clearly taken a liking to this farang. She had noticed it and had even overheard him saying what a great boxer he would make. Imagine a farang in the ring! She laughed to herself. The mighty Lord was so keen on the sport, he would envision anything.

She let the sash that loosely covered her breasts slip to the floor. His eyes devoured her, and she saw his panung stir. It must be the fairness of her skin that excited him. Her breasts were a shade lighter than the skin around them, which had suffered more from exposure to the sunlight.

It could not be her breasts themselves. She had always felt awkward about their large size and her long limbs, which were more developed than those of her friends. She was grateful at least that they did not seem to offend or repel him.

He was asking her something now, pointing to himself and saying something she did not understand. Then he pointed to her with a questioning look. After another attempt, she grasped his meaning.

'Sunida!' she said happily. 'My name is Sunida!' But his name, if that was what he was repeating, was unpronouncable. Kosa-tanat, or something.

What a pity he did not understand her language. There was so much she would have liked to ask him. He was courteous and well-mannered, and she sensed she had nothing to fear from this farang. She opened a little bamboo phial and poured scented oil over his chest and stomach and gently rubbed it into him. She applied her most beguiling touch, then probed and kneaded and

97

pressed her long fingers into his stomach. After that, she lightly brushed his flesh beneath the panung. And she saw with pride that he was aroused. His pleasure stimulated her in turn. She smiled warmly at him and her touch became more sensuous still. He would soon be bursting out of his panung, she thought, and anyway she could hardly contain her curiosity any longer. She untied it and then was still, gaping. Lord Buddha save us! Were all farangs like this? More like horses than humans. And so much hair everywhere! She was wondering with trepidation how painful his love lance would be if it entered her, when there was a commotion outside the door, and a distressed voice begged to be admitted.

She barely had time to cover him up before little Maew rushed in, tears streaming down her cheeks. 'I just couldn't, elder sister,' she sobbed, using the term of respect to an older girl. Sunida was twenty. 'His love lance was so . . . large. It hurt me.' Her tears intensified at the mention of it. Poor Maew, thought Sunida. She had just turned fourteen. Even though the other farang was smaller than this one, perhaps their love lances were all the same.

'Oh elder sister,' whimpered Maew, 'what will the mighty Lord say when he finds out? He wanted to know all about their love lances and their love habits.'

'I will prime you, little mouse, don't you worry. You just listen and nod and say that your experience was exactly like mine.'

'Oh thank you, elder sister,' she replied gratefully.

Ivatt now appeared in the doorway looking very abashed. He started to speak when Phaulkon cut him off.

'Don't worry, Thomas,' he said, rising and putting an arm round the little man. 'It isn't that she doesn't like you. You just frightened her, that's all. She's very young.'

'Constant, she actually screamed when she undid my panung. How do you think I felt? Anyone would think it was festering with maggots.'

Phaulkon laughed, pleased to note that Ivatt's sense of humour was still intact.

'Listen, Thomas, I'm having the same problem myself.'

'Did she scream too?' asked Ivatt, sounding almost relieved.

'She was about to when your girl came in. Europeans are just built differently, that's all. And we're a great deal hairier than the Siamese. What a sight we must present. I can't say I blame them. Look, go back to your room and be gentle. Don't insist if she doesn't want to. She'll get used to you. Let it be gradual. If it isn't today, it'll be tomorrow. She has to report to the Governor on your attributes anyway.'

'Good God!' exclaimed Ivatt. 'I could be arrested on the description alone!'

Phaulkon laughed. 'You're already under arrest, Thomas. We all are. But your sentence could be doubled, it's true.'

'Oh well,' said Ivatt philosophically. 'I suppose there are worse prisons than this one.'

Phaulkon smiled now at Sunida who was chatting quietly with little Maew in a corner. He went up to them and put his arm round Ivatt's frightened child, cradling her gently in his shoulder. He smiled reassuringly at her and held her for a moment until eventually she stopped sobbing. Sunida observed him gratefully. Little Maew was smiling sheepishly now and Phaulkon took her by the arm and led her over to Ivatt, patting her shoulder as he went.

'Now you look after her, Thomas. And remember what I told you.'

'If you hear any more screams,' smiled Thomas, 'it'll be me, being chased around the room! Good night.'

As Phaulkon turned back from the door, Sunida stood in front of him, her arms outstretched. She moved closer to him and pressed her whole body into his, snuggling her face into the nape of his neck. He held her tight for a long while, savouring the moment, and then led her slowly back to the mattress. He lay her down by his side and pulled her body against his, the passion welling up inside him. She was statuesque for a Siamese, he thought, long limbs and full breasts forming an almost European build, enriched by the delicate features and the silk-like skin of a Siamese. Her body fitted into his like a glove, as if a sculptor had moulded them to the exact size. Her thighs pressed against his and he felt a surge of passion, with a craving at the same time to be gentle. Slowly she unwound his panung and seeing the strength of his desire she put a finger to her lips and gave him the most glorious smile, as if to promise there would be no screaming this time.

Slowly, with infinite gentleness, he eased himself into her,

99

while she dug her fingers into his back to distract her from the pain. When he thought he was hurting her too much and tried to withdraw, she shook her head vehemently and, her face still contorted, urged him on with her eyes. And then at last he was there and she closed her eyes, a smile of relief playing on her full lips. He put his nose to her cheeks now and inhaled them deeply, one after the other. Her eyes opened and shone with pleasure and gratitude. He was honouring her customs.

Now she pushed him over and, still pinned to him, climbed hungrily on top. She held his arms above his head and voluptuously inhaled his face and chest and stomach until the heat of her passion surged through his limbs. He surrendered himself completely to her warmth until in the series of explosions that followed, he knew that this was no ordinary emotion. The stunning dancer from the court of Ligor had reached down to the innermost recesses of his soul.

Eight

There was not a cloud in the sky as the procession made its way out of the palace gates and along the narrow alleyways – some paved, some mud-baked – that led through the town to the arena. It was shortly after dawn on the first day of December 1679, and the cool dry season had settled in firmly after the unseasonal monsoon that had almost cost Phaulkon, Burnaby, and Ivatt their lives. Phaulkon glanced up at the brilliant sky and inhaled the pleasant, balmy air, savouring it.

The Siamese called it the cool season only by contrast with the torrid, humid days that stretched from March to May before the monsoons returned in June to cool and irrigate the parched earth and replenish the stagnant waterways. The cool season was the most pleasant, idyllic part of the year, a cloudless succession of balmy days akin to a European summer with no rainfall.

The Governor's golden palanquin was borne by eight bare-shouldered men, while a further four stood by to relieve them. The silk curtains were drawn open to reveal His Excellency sitting cross-legged on a raised dais, viewing with interest the crowds that surged towards the arena. He was dressed in his gold brocade robes and wore his conical hat and curving Muslim slippers.

Alongside him but slightly to the rear walked the Palat. Behind him and also to the right marched three senior aides with 1,600 dignity marks each. These were in charge of court, military and civil divisions. They were followed by eight officials of 1,400 dignity marks apiece, who were responsible for the management of the Governor's palace and the supervision of the staff and household retinue: physicians, scribes, astrologers, law-court officials, bodyguards, craftsmen, monks, pages, dancers, cooks, servants and slaves.

A score of slaves ran ahead of the procession, brushing the crowds aside and clearing the way for the Lord of the Province, while the farangs, with two slaves each, clustered around another palanquin which brought up the rear. Phaulkon walked just ahead of this sedan, much smaller than the Governor's and borne by only four men. Inside was Richard Burnaby, who was unable to walk because of his injured foot. Ivatt trotted alongside.

There was a carnival atmosphere that day in Ligor as hundreds of barefoot peasants, clad only in loincloths, spilled out of their little wooden houses built on stilts and headed down the alley-ways past the market place into the broader, tree-lined thorough-fares and finally on to the outskirts of the town where the arena and their fortune – or their fate – awaited them. It would be a great day for gambling, Phaulkon mused.

Saffron-robed monks, their heads shaved, government officials with scarf-like sashes draped over their shoulders, dark-skinned slaves and finely apparelled freemen all headed in one direction. Women came too, some bare-breasted, others wearing a sash, some balancing infants at the hip, others leading naked children by the hand.

Mangy pariah dogs tried to insinuate themselves into the Governor's procession but were quickly shooed away by the slaves, while naked, brown children, taught from the earliest age to respect their elders, ceased their activities and fell prostrate by the wayside to honour the procession. As the parade passed there were shouts of farang! farang! and the astonished onlookers gaped till the last moment before falling on their faces.

They now passed the marketplace, which looked strangely deserted. Most of the wooden stalls had been abandoned and only the pungent smell of the durian fruit, like ripe cheese, still hovered in the air. For the hub of commercial activity had shifted to the neighbourhood of the arena. Everyone there would be spending. Those presently on their way had money in their purses for both food and gambling; and later, the winners would come to purchase food offerings for the temples.

'The whole town must be attending!' exclaimed Ivatt, catching up with Phaulkon. 'And I love the way the boys are clearing a path for us. It makes me feel like a regular squire!'

Phaulkon smiled wanly. If only they really were visiting squires, he thought, honoured guests of the Governor, invited to share his favourite pastime, instead of prisoners on borrowed time with a death sentence hanging over their heads. It was essential that he gain some hold on the Governor, that he somehow ingratiate himself and predispose the potentate in his favour.

He glanced past the rows of minor palace officials towards the Governor's palanquin. A regal arm protruded from the window, magisterially acknowledging the crowd, while slaves in front sounded gongs to announce His Excellency's passage. Thin clouds of dust rose up from both sides of the road where the people fell flat to wait for the procession to pass. Phaulkon felt a certain rapport with the mandarin, and he was sure that was the key to their early release providing, of course, the cannon did not turn up.

He was painfully aware that he had to return to Ayudhya as soon as possible to take on the gargantuan task of seeking alternative means to fill Sam White's boat. Though at this stage he was not sure where to begin, every day spent in Ligor was one day less in which to accomplish it. Yesterday there had been ninety days left before the rendezvous in Mergui. Today there were only eighty-nine, and Sam's boat would not wait. Neither could it be allowed to leave empty.

Phaulkon watched, deep in thought, as elderly matrons with white, close-cropped hair and sagging breasts, less vigorous than the rest of the crowd, knelt first before prostrating themselves, and for a moment he wondered how many of them might have been Sunidas in their time. The tall dancer from the night before still preyed on his mind. He had tried to find out whether she would be at the arena but she had been unable to fathom his meaning. He hoped he might see her there. To his knowledge, women spectators sometimes attended boxing matches, though only from the furthest rows in the back. Tradition excluded their presence at the ringside where they might impair a fighter's attention and where their female aura would certainly upset the atmosphere of the ring. Yet Phaulkon had heard that in some remote provinces women entered the ring themselves, playing by the same rules as men, and sometimes even knocking their female opponents out cold. He smiled. They were quite something, the women of Siam: proud and independent, yet loyal and feminine at the same time. They owned houses and boats and slaves like men, they divorced like men, they wore almost the same clothes as men, they had the same legal rights as men and even when a rich man owned more than one wife, it was the woman, his first wife, who ruled over the rest of them and ran his household, minor wives, slaves and all. In the families of the common people too, while the men were in the mandatory service of the King for six months of every year, it was the wives who ran their affairs.

He wondered now about Sunida's background, where she might have come from and how she had been inducted into the Governor's service. She must have been sent to dancing school at a very early age because classical dancers began their training almost as soon as they could walk. Had the Governor picked her out at random from some poor village blessed with the Lord of the Province's munificence, or had her parents been wealthy nobles who had destined her for a respectable dancing career? It was hard to tell her background. The women of Siam were all invested with such natural grace and bearing.

'How did you get on with your little girl in the end, Thomas?' he asked, recalling the events of last night.

'I took your advice, Constant, and nothing much happened.' The little man's face assumed a sudden expression of despair. 'Tell me, am I doomed to eternal celibacy in this country on account of the inordinate size of my love lance?' he inquired, only half in jest.

Phaulkon laughed. 'We'll surely be able to find someone to accommodate you, Thomas. In Ayudhya perhaps. As soon as we get back I'll ask my Portuguese friends for some recommendations.'

'And will we in fact be getting back to Ayudhya, Constant?' Ivatt's tone was for once serious, almost melancholy. He had not once asked about the merchandise, though Phaulkon was sure he knew. He appreciated the little man's discretion very much.

'I have every intention of seeing to it, Thomas, especially as, of all of us, you are the innocent party.' Phaulkon smiled reassuringly at him and dropped back beside Burnaby's sedan. 'How's the leg, Richard?'

'Not too bad, thanks. I'm glad I'm not doing this on foot though. When do you think I might visit my physician in Ayudhya?'

'Not for a while, I am afraid, Richard. Not until they believe we're innocent. And if we push it too hard, they'll only become suspicious. Just relax and enjoy yourself. The company's not half bad, and you're in no condition to travel anyway.'

'How can I relax when I know we're being held here? And why are they detaining us anyway if the cannon haven't been discovered?'

Phaulkon had not yet told Burnaby about the proof of their complicity which the Dutchman had claimed was on its way. Burnaby would only fret and ask him over and over what that proof might be. Phaulkon did not know the answer himself at this stage and it was enough that he should have to worry about it.

'They're probably detaining us because they want to make sure of our innocence first.'

'And how are they going to do that?'

'By default. If the cannon don't turn up, they have no reason to suspect us any more. They're just waiting a little longer.'

'What if they do turn up?'

Phaulkon restrained his annoyance. 'If they do, Richard, we have quite a problem. I'd rather cross that bridge when we come to it.'

'How long do you think it will be before they abandon the search for our goods?'

'Not more than a few days, I shouldn't think. Just the amount of time you need for your foot to get better.'

Burnaby scoffed. 'My foot would heal quickly enough if it were resting on the deck of a boat bound for Ayudhya.'

'If we can stay in the Governor's good graces and impress him with our manners – remember, Richard, that manners are everything to the Siamese – I think we could speed up our release. It certainly doesn't help that you look glum and worried all the time, you know.'

'Aren't you worried, for God's sake?' asked Burnaby irritably.

'Of course I'm worried. But I'm not about to show it. It doesn't go with the face of innocence.'

The boxing arena now came in sight in the centre of a large field on the outskirts of town. It was slightly elevated, and its confines were marked by four bamboo posts joined by ropes made of coconut bark. Its surface was grass, which meant that it had needed five days of constant sunshine after the storm to render it dry enough to hold the contest. In the sport of kickboxing it would not do to churn up mud and send it flying in an adversary's face.

The arena was packed with squatting spectators, and the Dutchman was awaiting them by the raised dais that was the Governor's place of honour on a wooden platform above the crowd. He came forward to greet them and paid his respects to the Governor. Then he turned to Phaulkon and bowed stiffly. 'I trust you had a pleasant evening with the dancer,' he said with bile in his voice.

'Most enjoyable, thank you. In fact she entertained us all,' Phaulkon said ambiguously, unable to resist it.

The Dutchman stiffened and the blood rushed to his face. But before he could speak, there was a clash of cymbals, a gong sounded, and all activity suddenly ceased. Thousands fell prostrate to the ground. The Lord of the Province had shown himself to the people and was taking his place on his throne-like chair.

Now he invited his retinue to occupy their rightful places in descending order of rank by his side, and only when they were seated did the huge crowd settle back and the noise resume once more.

A ripple of excitement swept through the assembly and thousands of curious eyes turned towards van Risling, Phaulkon, Burnaby and Ivatt as they took their places, cross-legged, to the left and below the Governor. Farangs! Hardly anybody had set eyes on a farang before. Even after they had stared their fill, Phaulkon noticed their glances returning again and again, as if they expected this strange sight to disappear at any moment.

Several dignitaries, high-ranking officials from the town, tax collectors, lay judges, and senior members of the boxing commission now came over to pay homage to the Governor, and he chatted briefly with each of them as they lay prostrate. Meanwhile, the Dutchman turned his back conspicuously on the other farangs and did his best to ignore them. Burnaby, heeding Phaulkon's advice on good manners, made repeated attempts to carry on a conversation with him.

The hordes of spectators, the majority barechested and barefooted, sat cross-legged in neat rows, or squatted on their haunches, exchanging bets and arguing over the merits of each contestant. Vendors hawked dishes of steaming noodles, fried insects, rice dumplings, fish and fruit, all served on platters of palm leaves, and the air was thick with the aroma of dried fish and the stench of durian.

'Is that money I see?' asked Ivatt. He was staring fascinated at the crowds and had noticed some cylindrical objects changing hands.

'Yes, it is,' replied Phaulkon, 'and you'll probably see lots of coris shells too. They use those for small change.'

There were five kinds of silver money in use in Siam. The tael was the largest. The baht, or tical, a cylindrical silver coin with a cleft in the middle and the double imprints of a heart and a small circle below the cleft, was a quarter of a tael. The salung, inferior in size, was itself worth a quarter of a tical, the fouang was worth half a salung, and the sompai half a fouang. Small money was counted in coris shells, a small sea shell of which it took eight hundred to make up a fouang, a sign of the inexpensiveness of life in Siam, where the basic staples were in abundance. Phaulkon recalled the words of the esteemed thirteenth-century monarch, King Naresuan the Great: 'There is rice in the fields and fish in the waters. The people are content.' Little had changed, Phaulkon reflected.

'Are the gambling stakes high?' asked Ivatt.

'High? They bet far beyond their means. By sundown most of these fellows will be pawned to their creditors as slaves. And they will probably have thrown their wives and families into the deal too. They're inveterate gamblers.'

'Whole families pawned as slaves?'

'Oh yes. If they lose, the entire family will enter into the service of the creditor tomorrow morning.'

'But can they free themselves again?' Ivatt was clearly amazed.

'As soon as they pay their debts back, yes. It's not as bad as it sounds, you know. A redeemable slave retains five dignity marks and keeps most of his rights. There's no shame attached to it. He can even marry and have children, and his second, fourth and all even-numbered offspring are born free.'

'What happens to the odd numbers then? Are they strangled at birth?'

'No, the first, third and fifth become the property of the master, and as most Buddhists treat their slaves with charity, they're well taken care of. Some even choose to remain on after they've paid off their debts, especially as slavery exonerates them from the annual six months' royal service.'

'And are all slaves redeemable?'

'No, not those purchased outright, or those captured in war. As opposed to debt slaves, they and their children remain slaves for ever and depend entirely on the good will of the master.'

'So if I bet against one of these blokes and win, I can keep him for life?'

'If he can't pay his debt, yes.' Phaulkon smiled. 'But if you lose, the poor blighter would be stuck with you. What a fate! To be landed with an untrainable slave like you!'

Ivatt chuckled. 'It might start a new fashion. To own a farang slave could become the ultimate form of prestige! I wish we could place a bet or two,' he added wistfully, 'but I'm penniless. Come to think of it, we all are. Do you think squat-nose might give us some credit? He could take half of our winnings.'

'It might amuse him,' put in Burnaby, who had finally given up trying to make polite conversation with the Dutchman, 'to see a farang lose his shirt. Though perhaps not with his money.'

'If I'd known shells were used for money here, I'd have brought some from home. The Yorkshire coast is teeming with them. I'd be as rich as a mandarin,' quipped Ivatt.

Phaulkon laughed. 'I'm afraid you'd be arrested for counterfeiting, Thomas. They use a special type of shell here, imported from the Maldives and the Philippines.'

'I'll go mad watching everyone else place bets. Imagine going to the races in England without a penny in your pcoket. How many bouts are there anyway?'

'I don't know,' Phaulkon said, 'but in Ayudhya the top fighters come on at the end and take on the winners of the earlier bouts. Sometimes outsiders even jump into the ring and challenge a winner. It all adds to the excitement and unpredictability.'

Their conversation was interrupted by the appearance of a stocky, powerfully built man with a square head and close-cropped hair who stared at the farangs rudely before brushing roughly past them. It was rare for a Siamese to show discourtesy to strangers, especially foreigners, and Phaulkon was struck by such unusual behaviour. There was an aura of menace about the man, a haughty, chilling presence that sent an involuntary shudder through the Greek. The man's physical appearance only added to this impression. He was built like a bull, with a thick, squat neck, and arms and legs bulging with muscles that practically disfigured them. For a moment his narrow, venomous eyes locked onto Phaulkon's and a contemptuous smile played across his lips. He looked steadily from one to the other of the farangs before his gaze returned to Phaulkon again. It was as if he had decided that this was the one most deserving of his disdain. He stared as if he were appraising some fish at the morning market.

'I wouldn't like to tangle with this bull,' observed Ivatt. 'Thank God he's got it in for you, and not me, Const—'

The thug whirled round on Ivatt with such force that the words froze in the little man's mouth. He looked about him sheepishly, suddenly fearful that he might have been understood. With a final glare the man turned on his heel and strode off. They watched in silence as he slowly merged into the crowd.

'What was all that about?' asked Ivatt, still shaken.

'Perhaps he's the one in charge of the search for our ship,' suggested Burnaby, equally unnerved.

'Let's hope we've seen the last of him,' added Phaulkon. He was glad when a gong sounded and he could turn his attention back to the arena.

A four-piece orchestra had now begun playing: a reedy-sounding Java flute, two drums of identical size but of different pitches and a pair of brass cymbals. The excitement of the crowd increased.

Then at a signal from the Governor's aide, two athletic-looking youths strutted up to the ring and a hush fell on the crowd. The men were barefoot, dressed only in loincloths, and with a length of cord wrapped round each fist. They ducked under the ropes and swung nimbly into the ring, prostrating themselves towards the Governor and remaining abjectly prone for a few moments. Then they turned in the direction of their home or birthplace and, raising their hands to their faces, touched their heads three times to the ground in homage to the teachers and parents who had imparted their knowledge to them. After a short prayer they returned to their corners to perform the pre-fight ritual, a series of slow-motion steps like a dance, swaying on their haunches and imploring the powers that be to come to their aid. Next they walked once round the ring, glaring defiantly about them as the cymbals and drums rose to a crescendo. At each corner they

109

stopped to lower their heads on to the ropes and stamp their feet angrily, to ward off any evil spirits that might be lurking in the ring. Finally, they wai'd to each other and returned to their corners. As soon as they had squatted down, a number of spectators converged on the ring, shouting furiously at both contestants.

'What is going on?' asked Ivatt.

'It's all part of the betting,' explained Phaulkon. 'The spectators are promising one of the contestants a portion of their winnings if he beats his opponent. They hope it will give him an added incentive. In some cases spectators even call in a witch doctor to weaken the opponent.'

Phaulkon enjoyed the sport and had often been to matches in Ayudhya. He had explained to Ivatt and Burnaby that in Siamese boxing you could punch or kick your opponent and use your knees and elbows as well, and any part of the body could be attacked. The cord which was wrapped three or four times round the hand served as protection. No other protection was allowed, apart from the sea shell which covered the groin. Every time a boxer connected with any part of his opponent's body, he scored a point. The match ended when one of the contestants was knocked out or simply collapsed from exhaustion. There were two judges today sitting by the ring to keep score.

A referee, barefoot and wearing only a loincloth, now strode into the arena and brought the contestants into the centre. He spoke to each of them in turn, reminding them of the rules and exhorting them to do their best in front of the Governor. Then he wai'd to them and stepped back.

A gong sounded and the fighters were at each other in a flash, swinging their legs round and up to kick at their opponent's head or straight out into his stomach. A jab and a flick of the elbow, and one or the other would twist or leap aside. It was lovely to see. The tempo of the music changed in accordance with the action in the ring as the versatile musicians followed the combat closely.

Ivatt had watched plenty of bare-knuckle boxing matches in England, but by comparison those now seemed brutal, hard-slugging affairs. At home one of the contestants inevitably lost his teeth or cracked a jaw, and the match always ended in a knockout. What he now witnessed was also a fight to the end but an artistic cross between boxing and acrobatics, which required more speed and skill than brute strength. The fighters darted in and out of reach and jabbed at each other instead of delivering heavy punches.

Yet Phaulkon had warned him not to underestimate the impact of the kicks. The boxers' feet were lethal weapons, conditioned and forged by months of pounding against the solid trunks of banana trees. By the end of the training period the fighters' shins and insteps were rock hard. Their speed and agility was honed to the limit by maintaining a log of wood in the air for several minutes with a rapid succession of left and right kicks.

They were in fact incredibly nimble on their feet, and their balance was remarkable. At times they pivoted on one leg; at others both feet left the ground as they swung their bodies round for a kick. The legs were used more frequently than the hands, though both were legal. The contestants were as lithe as monkeys, and their legs shot out like the tongues of the gekko lizards Ivatt had watched snatching insects on the ceiling of his room. He glanced around and saw Phaulkon strangely pensive, a distant look on his face. Next to him sat the red-faced Dutchman, silently sweating in his European clothing, and above him the Governor, wearing a fixed expression of unmistakable delight. On Ivatt's left, Burnaby watched with a frown as though his thoughts were on the cannon more than the ring.

Ivatt found the crowd as fascinating as the fighters. They roared their approval every time a kick connected, and egged on the contestants with shouts and exhortations. The noise was ceaseless and he could see money changing hands constantly. At times spectators would stand and shout bets across the arena to those on the other side, offering or accepting a challenge. Excitement was at fever pitch. Women squatted in the back rows, shouting as eagerly as the men, but there was no sign of the dancers from the Governor's court.

When finally one of the boys was barely able to stand, his opponent was declared the winner. A roar went up from those in the crowd who had bet on him and all the others fell silent.

There followed three more bouts and Ivatt was beginning to discern the finer points of the sport when the judges called a halt to the last fight and huddled together to declare a champion from among the winners of the four bouts. This champion would now have to stand in the middle of the ring and accept any challenges, but if no challenger came forward he would be declared the final winner.

The judges chose the winner of the third bout, a brilliant, stylish fighter with lightning reflexes who had knocked his opponent out cold, and a roar went up from the crowd. He was known as the 'Young Lion' and Ivatt was pleased to note that he would have been his choice too. The Young Lion stood in the middle of the ring and wai'd to the crowd, acknowledging their enthusiastic cheers. He waited but no one got up to challenge him. Ivatt restrained his urge to clap, which was obviously not the form in Siam, and glanced round at the others.

The Governor was cheering ecstatically as was his entire retinue, while Phaulkon sat there as if in a dream. Something about his expression worried Ivatt.

As Ivatt turned to face the ring again, the roar of the crowd abruptly ceased and a deathly hush descended on the arena. It was as if His Majesty the King himself had suddenly made an appearance.

Phaulkon had removed his shirt and without a word was making his way towards the ring. Ivatt and Burnaby looked at one another in disbelief.

Phaulkon was gesturing to the champion now to remain where he was and a moment later he was climbing over the ropes into the ring. The silence was awesome. The champion stared at him nonplussed, unsure how to react. Then Phaulkon turned to the equally stunned referee and cupped his hands expressively over his groin. He was requesting the authorized protection. The referee gaped at him for a moment and then sprang to life. A gasp rose from the crowd now as the realization of what was really happening sunk in.

The referee ducked under the ropes and delved into his cloth bag which he had left in the care of the judges. In a moment he produced a fair-sized sea shell and a length of cotton cloth with a string attached. He returned to the arena and offered the shell to Phaulkon, wai-ing to him as he did so. Phaulkon examined the shell, turned it over in his hand and shook his head. Then he pointed to his groin and described a considerably larger shell with his hands. A roar of laughter broke out from the crowd and when Phaulkon smiled in return they cheered him on wildly.

Delighted shouts of: 'The farang wants a larger one! The farang needs a bigger one!' could be heard above the clamour. The Governor must be loving this, thought Phaulkon with satisfaction, and if I don't get killed in the process, I should be able to ask him a favour or two. He felt weak to his stomach but he kept telling himself that it was his best chance of inclining the Governor in his favour. Anyway, it was too late to back out now.

He wondered with apprehension how far his fighting experience in the navy would serve him against these athletic wizards. True, he had won a couple of championships in the merchant marine, and against some pretty tough cases, but this was a different kind of exercise altogether. These boxers were more like acrobats with the kick of a horse. He was much taller and heavier than his opponent, he could see, but much would depend on whether he could land enough solid punches.

The referee now returned with a considerably larger sea shell and the crowd shouted its approval as Phaulkon placed it over his groin and nodded, satisfied. The referee covered the shell with the piece of cotton cloth he had brought and tied it firmly in place with a string. Then he wound some cord round Phaulkon's wrists and with a respectful bow retired.

Phaulkon now raised his hands to his forehead and, turning in the direction of the Governor, prostrated himself deeply in the Siamese manner. The crowd murmured. The Governor cupped his hands in front of his face and returned the greeting, smiling broadly. The mandarin's raised throne-seat was not more than twenty feet from the ring and the space before him was empty so that nothing would hamper his view. Even at that distance Phaulkon fancied he saw an expression of delight written over His Excellency's face. Ivatt and Burnaby were cheering and waving frantically in his direction, while the Dutchman appeared silent and sullen.

Phaulkon turned now to each section of the crowd and wai'd. They responded with a burst of enthusiasm, cheering, roaring and stamping their feet. Then he noticed something unusual. All betting had come to a standstill. The odds were impossible to gauge and no one dared risk the outcome. They would be cured of their hesitation soon enough, he thought with a wry smile, just as soon as they saw him fight.

Briefly he glimpsed the mandarin muttering to the Palat who

113

then walked over to the farangs and pressed something into their hands. Money! They were being given money to bet! Who are you going to put it on, you bastards? he wondered. And you, van Risling? I bet I know who you'll back. Then he saw the mandarin delve into his purse and hand a heap of coins to the Palat, whispering something in his ear. Phaulkon would have given anything to know what was being said at that moment.

Phaulkon went down on his knees now and made the sign of the cross three times. The sight of the farang ritual seemed to please the crowd. The throng murmured again as if the strange ritual were just what it had hoped and expected to see. The Young Lion, who had been squatting silently in his corner all this time, went once more through his own ritual, still looking bemused by the proceedings.

Now the referee brought the contestants into the middle of the ring and wai'd to them, omitting to deliver the usual exhortations. The gong sounded. Phaulkon's stomach churned. A hush fell over the assembly.

The Siamese came in cautiously and skipped around Phaulkon for a while. He appeared short and wiry next to the farang, but he was muscular and Phaulkon knew just how frighteningly agile. His naked torso glistened with the recent application of coconut oil. His black hair was closely cropped, and he wore a white band across his forehead. Phaulkon must have seemed a giant to him: broad-shouldered, with a long reach, and a good head and a half taller.

Phaulkon watched him carefully, moving his hands in small circles in front of him with the left arm leading the right. This appeared to puzzle his opponent, who decided to move in and try a kick. His left leg flicked out and wrapped itself round Phaulkon's waist. Phaulkon felt the hardness of the man's foot in his ribs, but the Young Lion did not follow it up. He was staying well out of range of Phaulkon's long reach. It would be harder, thought Phaulkon, for the man to kick him in the face because of his unaccustomed height. Sure enough, Young Lion came in lower now. He kicked hard with his left foot and connected with Phaulkon's thigh. Phaulkon kept watching him attentively, still weaving his arms around in front of him, waiting for him to come within reach. Slowly the Siamese grew bolder. He came in closer this time and landed several kicks in rapid succession to Phaulkon's legs and ribs. There was still no response from Phaulkon.

Then suddenly it happened. The Siamese came in like lightning, jerking his knee up into Phaulkon's solar plexus. But a fist shot out and connected with a thud to the attacker's jaw. He was catapulted backwards and landed on the grass, his head swimming. The crowd gasped. Phaulkon too was winded, bent over and clutching his stomach. Suddenly the betting fever resumed in full fury, as if seeking to make up for lost time. The referee ordered Phaulkon to stand back as the stunned Siamese tried to rise. A spectator jumped into the ring and volunteered to rub Phaulkon's legs down with coconut oil. Then Ivatt rushed up, took the bottle from the bewildered man's hand and started to apply it himself to Phaulkon.

'Well done, Constant,' he said, rubbing the liquid into his legs, 'we're with you all the way. But for God's sake be careful. We've got money on you. The Governor's as excited as a child in a sweet shop. I think he's planning to decorate you. You're doing brilliantly. Keep it up.'

The referee ordered Ivatt out of the ring and Phaulkon called after him. 'I'm going to have to try a kick or two. For appearance's sake. Don't let them laugh at me if I fall over.'

'I'll take them on myself if they do,' shouted Ivatt, climbing out of the ring.

Bets were being hurled in all directions now and Phaulkon could not help wondering which way the tide of opinion was going. Young Lion had raised himself up and the music grew to a crescendo as he skipped from one foot to the other, finding his balance again. Without warning he came in like a bullet, ducking as he went. A series of kicks rained in on Phaulkon and jabs of pain pierced his body. No sooner had Phaulkon parried one blow than his opponent was striking at another part of his anatomy, darting off like a fly every time he tried to swat him. Determined to stop the onslaught, Phaulkon took a huge sweep with his right leg, lost his balance, and landed squarely on his backside. At first the audience was quiet, then a few in the crowd began to laugh and soon the whole arena was engulfed in unbridled mirth. But, to their credit, no sooner had Phaulkon, looking sheepish but chastened, risen to his feet, than the crowd urged him on once more.

Young Lion was on to him again in a flash, but this time Phaulkon was wise to not using his feet. The blows stung him sharply and he cushioned as many as he could. The man was using his feet instead of his hands because of Phaulkon's superior reach and Phaulkon knew if he was to have a chance he had to lure him closer in. Suddenly Young Lion twisted his body as if to swing his leg round from the side but at the last minute he changed course and flicked his foot forwards, straight into Phaulkon's groin. The force of the impact thrust the sea shell backwards, cutting painfully into Phaulkon's crotch. The Greek grew angry.

Throwing caution to the winds, he charged, ducking and feinting, past the kick blows and under the man's cover. A powerful left hook rammed into his opponent's head. As the Siamese reeled to one side, a mammoth right uppercut connected with his jaw and sent him flying off his feet. He lay gasping for air, vainly trying to pull himself up.

Phaulkon stood over him like a raging bull, and the sight of him must have been daunting indeed; the Siamese made a last effort to lift his head and then collapsed on to the grass. The referee called a halt to the fight and pronounced Phaulkon the winner.

A roar went up from the crowd and an agile spectator leapt into the ring and placed a garland of jasmine round Phaulkon's neck. Money changed hands rapidly as people settled their debts and Phaulkon wondered how many families might have been pawned into slavery on his account that day. Two men helped lift Young Lion, dazed but conscious, out of the ring.

Phaulkon now climbed over the ropes and walked slowly past the cheering throng towards the Governor. Though his heart was thumping with joy, he tried to keep the triumph from his face and show only the modesty that was deemed proper. He had not finished with the Governor yet. There was more entertainment in store for him. He stopped before the Governor and prostrated himself. The mandarin was bubbling over with excitement. He smiled exuberantly at Phaulkon and let loose a jumble of questions through the interpreter and van Risling. 'Tell the farang . . . amazing. Has he ever boxed before? In his own country? Is that where he learned? I never . . . not for a moment . . . wonderful . . . what a performance!'

Phaulkon now moved a pace to the left and stood in front of the Dutchman, while apparently awaiting the translation. 'His Excellency says it is not proper boxing when you do not use de feet. He asks you to sit.' Van Risling spoke in English.

Phaulkon listened politely to van Risling's words.

'But first will you do me the honour, mijn heer?' he asked, pointing to the ring with a smile.

The Dutchman gaped.

'What, me?'

'Yes, you, mijn heer.'

Before van Risling had time to protest, Phaulkon turned to the Governor and described with gestures what he had in mind. He saw the Governor's eyes widen, and then, as the full potential of the situation came home to him, a look of delight spread over His Excellency's face. He nodded instant approval and looked expectantly at the Dutchman. Phaulkon heard him muttering over and over: 'Red-beard in the ring with the boxing farang. What a day! What a day! Kling!'

'Mighty Lord, the dust of your feet awaits your orders.'

'Note the precise hour. We will give special offerings at the temple this evening.'

'Mighty Lord, I receive your orders.'

The Dutchman meanwhile had turned crimson and was stuttering 'I . . . am . . . am not a boxer, sir. I tell you, I am not.'

'But surely, Heer van Risling, you will demonstrate to our host how brave you Dutchmen are, not cowards like the English? His Excellency has already taken your valour for granted and is urging you into the ring.'

The Dutchman avoided the Governor's eyes and looked the other way. Burnaby and Ivatt, interpreting the situation, began to jeer and boo and soon the crowd, though oblivious to the meaning, took up the sound. In no time the entire assembly was jeering, and the Dutchman sat red-faced with his head buried in his hands waiting for the noise to subside.

At that moment a familiar bull-like figure strode up to Phaulkon, wai'd formally and pointed first at him and then at the ring. There was no mistaking his meaning. Phaulkon took one look at the man and knew that this was trouble. With the same expression of contempt that he had worn earlier in the day, the Siamese stood staring at Phaulkon, his arms folded across his chest.

117

He gestured again and then turned towards the ring as if to say he could wait no longer. Some of the crowd had spotted the challenge and began to chant encouragement. Others took up the refrain. 'Let the farang champion fight again!' Soon the entire crowd was urging them on. For Phaulkon it was too late to back down now.

The Dutchman's face switched from the humiliation of a moment ago to undisguised relief. 'I'll bet fifty ticals on the bull!' he cried, delving once again into his purse, despite his earlier loss. It was the second time he would bet against Phaulkon.

'And we'll put all our winnings on Constant,' Burnaby and Ivatt shouted together. They glanced over at the mandarin. He was already engrossed in the latest turn of events – having seemingly forgotten the Dutchman's failure to take up the earlier challenge.

The bull now led the way into the ring and without preamble went into his pre-fight ritual. His was a briefer ceremony than that of his predecessors, as if he was anxious to proceed with the fight.

Phaulkon crossed himself once more; his prayer this time was more fervent than he could remember. All the while his mind was reeling. He could not allow himself a defeat, least of all an easy one. But this brute looked like a serious boxer and if his speed turned out to match his brawn, then Phaulkon was in trouble. He would have to use every artifice to outfox and outmanoeuvre him and try to tire him out.

The referee brought them into the centre of the ring and made them bow to each other. For a moment their eyes met and a shiver passed through Phaulkon. What he saw in the other's face was sheer venom. The bull was not fighting simply for the sport. His eyes seemed to reveal a hatred for farangs, embodied now in the person of Phaulkon. Had this Siamese been insulted by some farang before, or did he perhaps abhor the Jesuits' attempts to entice his people away from their religious traditions? There were some, Phaulkon knew, who thought the King of Siam's liberality to outsiders had gone too far.

They separated on the gong. The bull flashed towards Phaulkon, his whole body surging up to power his kicks. Any hopes Phaulkon had had that the man was slow on his feet were soon shattered. He was as swift as a panther, and he was all muscle.

Although a head shorter than Phaulkon, he weighed at least the same as the Greek. Immediately after his first savage attack, he was on to Phaulkon again with a left kick and a right and another left, his body twirling like a sabre.

Phaulkon, every nerve taut, parried the hail of blows, absorbing some, dodging others and though his attacker's arms and legs were striking in lightning succession, Phaulkon was in good control of his defences, deliberately inciting his opponent to use up his strength.

Seeing he was not achieving the desired effect with his feet and arms alone, the bull now came in closer to use his knees and elbows. With its short range and speed, the elbow attack was the most difficult to defend against. The combatants' bodies locked together and Phaulkon winced as the bull pounded his ribs repeatedly with his powerful knees. Closing his mind to the pain, Phaulkon grabbed his attacker's thigh and hoisted him off balance. The bull fell on one knee, momentarily bewildered, catching his breath. Like thunder in the distance, Phaulkon heard the crowd roar. He charged, ramming the bull's face with a fierce right swing. The bull crashed backwards.

He lay there writhing for a moment, then shook himself like a dazed terrier and sprang to his feet again. Quickly he wiped an arm across his forehead, his black eyes smouldering. Then with a chilling cry he lunged. Twisting his body to the left as if to prepare a kick with his right, incredibly he changed course in mid-flight, spinning the other way and crashing his foot into Phaulkon's temple. It was the dreaded jump kick.

Phauldon's vision grew blurred. Instinctively he retreated, leaning backwards out of range with split-second timing, and the bull's follow-up fell just short of him. As his attacker's head dropped forward with the impetus, Phaulkon dashed the crown with a downward thrust of his elbow, stunning his opponent and sending a shaft of pain through his own arm in the process.

The Siamese toppled forward, grimacing horribly and gasping for air. Though Phaulkon knew there was not a moment to lose, his right arm felt limp; the power had gone out of it. Quickly he rammed the ball of his foot into the prostrate bull's spine, provoking a cry of pain before the Siamese rolled over deftly out of range. Phaulkon chased after him but the bull rolled all the way to the corner, turning and springing suddenly to his feet to face him. As the Greek lunged forward, the Siamese ducked and grabbed his neck, jerking it downwards while his knee shot up into Phaulkon's face. There was a shattering crunch and Phaulkon fell backwards on to the grass clutching his face with his hands. The arena receded before him and when the figure of the bull swam into focus again, he was standing over the Greek, angry, confident now, lusting for the kill. Phaulkon saw that the bull was bleeding profusely from the nose and running his tongue steadily over his lips to stem the flow. If only he could muster the strength, thought Phaulkon.

With a supreme effort he buried his fear and his fatigue and rose unsteadily to his feet. In the next instant an elbow slammed into his jaw and a blinding series of kicks to his ribs and kidneys sent spasms of pain through his body.

Everything started to grow dim. With a final exertion he flung his fists wildly in the direction of the blows, connecting with some but merely cutting the air with others. Vaguely he heard the roar of the crowd. He no longer had the stamina to put up his defences to meet the shattering kicks and elbow jabs that rained on him from all directions. Then a sledgehammer blow caught him in the solar plexus and cut his wind. The arena swam and he was down. He never heard the referee call the end of the fight.

Ivatt and Burnaby rushed up to Phaulkon while the Governor ordered his personal physician to attend to him immediately. The two Englishmen listened anxiously to the translation as van Risling, barely masking his satisfaction, pronounced Phaulkon badly bruised, with a lacerated lip, two black eyes and a sprained elbow. Bearers laid him carefully out on a bamboo stretcher and carried him off, under the Governor's orders, to the palace. Ivatt and Burnaby followed.

The bull walked over to the Governor and prostrated himself briefly. Before His Excellency could even ask him where he came from, he had slipped away in the confusion and was gone.

As the stretcher was carried away, the crowd gave it a rousing cheer and both the Dutchman and the Governor rose to their feet, the one to stare with malicious pleasure and the other to pay homage to the farang who had fought like a tiger.

Nine

When Phaulkon awoke it was pitch black around him. His body ached, his head pounded and the slightest movement caused him pain. As his eyes adjusted somewhat to the darkness, he twisted his head slowly round, and made out a silhouette curled up at the foot of his straw mat. He stared at it for a while but it did not move. He could not recall any piece of furniture so close to his bed, so it was probably human, perhaps a guard or a physician who had fallen asleep. He forced himself to concentrate, despite the throbbing in his head. The events of the last few hours – he was not exactly sure how long ago – came back to him by degrees. The boxing arena, his initial victory, then defeat at the hands of that thug. The image of the bull-necked boxer rose vividly before him. Once more he saw the viciousness of the stare, and the cold, narrow eyes without a flicker of humanity in them.

Whatever pain he was now suffering, he knew instinctively that his efforts in the ring had been worthwhile. He had seen beyond doubt the look of pleasure in the mandarin's eyes. His performance could only stand him in good stead. Somehow he had to make it the harbinger of his return to Ayudhya.

The loss of his cannon was a disaster, of course. Two whole years of waiting and planning – for nothing. His stomach felt sick at the thought. But what if he had drowned? What if the cannon had been discovered instead? Or what if he had been tortured mercilessly, until he was forced to reveal the truth anyway? For a moment at least he had gained the attention of the Governor. If the potentate was now more favourably disposed towards the farangs, he might even consent to their early release. Once Phaulkon had obtained that, it was only a short step to requesting some form of introduction – recommendation even – to those in high office in Ayudhya, the friends and colleagues of His Excellency – the Barcalon, for instance.

A trickle of light seeped in beneath the doorway, and the shape at the foot of the bed stirred. Then it raised itself on what

121

appeared to be an elbow and turned towards him. In the gradual light of dawn, Phaulkon recognized the warm smile of his favourite dancer, Sunida. He felt a surge of pleasure, despite the pain.

She glided to her feet and walked over to the window, pushing the bottom of the wooden shutter outwards and inserting the bamboo stick that held it in place. As the light filtered through, she returned to his side and examined his bruises, frowning solicitously at every new discovery. '*Pai ha mor*,' she explained, pointing first outside and then at his sores.

Too weak to argue, he watched her rise and adjust the ends of her panung before she slipped gracefully out of the room. So she was going to fetch the physician. He wondered with apprehension what sort of a cure he might be subjected to. He hoped that the doctor would not walk all over his body, as he had seen many of them do, in an attempt to distribute more equitably the body's forces. Though the Siamese had a profound knowledge of local herbs and their healing powers, there were aspects of their medicine that leaned entirely on myth and superstition.

When they saw his weakened condition, they would no doubt diagnose it as an imbalance in the four elements that composed the human body: fire, earth, wind and water. For ill health was caused by any disturbance in this delicate balance. His fever would be ascribed to the preponderance of fire in his body and the pounding in his head to an excess of wind rushing upwards. He remembered a doctor in Ayudhya once explaining to him, when he had complained of a severe stomach upset, that it was an excess of water in the body that caused the bowels to burst open.

The wrinkled, white-haired physician who now entered the room with Sunida was fortunately too weak to trample all over Phaulkon's body. Instead he knelt by his side and opened a large travelling box. His eyes shone kindly as he gently felt Phaulkon's wounds. He examined the patient's swollen eye and professed himself satisfied that there would be no permanent damage. But when he probed his right elbow and snapped the dislocated bone into place without warning Phaulkon screamed with pain and Sunida cried out too, as if the anguish had been her own. The doctor explained to her that the elbow bone was broken, that he had just set it and that the patient's arm should be kept bound tightly in a cloth. The bruises would eventually go away. He prescribed an ointment with a base of lemon grass herbs and coconut oil and told her to rub it gently into his wounds every six hours. Finally, he confirmed that the patient was feeling faint because the balance of his body's properties was upset. There was insufficient wind in the body, which caused faintness, just as it might do on a listless summer's day. Sunida was to keep the patient well aired at all times, with open windows and constant fanning, to restore the correct level of wind in his system.

Sunida thanked the doctor and whispered something to him but he frowned and shook his head. 'Honourable doctor,' she persisted anxiously, 'His Excellency and all the court are waiting.' The doctor considered for a moment but shook his head again.

'If you want him to be cured, he must not be moved. Besides, any movement will cause him great pain. Surely His Excellency will understand that the farang is simply not well enough?'

Sunida looked distressed. 'I agree, honourable Doctor, but His Excellency was so insistent – determined even – to have the farang attend. It would after all reveal the whole truth about his shipwreck.'

Phaulkon understood and his stomach turned. Of course. What else could be so pressing that he had to be moved immediately? *Royal Lotus* had been found. Or perhaps the cannon discovered. Or both. He shuddered. What a condition to be in to have to face further interrogation. He glanced at Sunida. She looked so concerned. Was it his painful condition that furrowed her smooth brow or was it the knowledge of the fate that awaited him outside?

It was best to get it over with. Delays would only aggravate the Governor more. At least his execution would put an end to the terrible pain, he reflected bitterly. With a sinking heart he forced himself to his feet. But the movement seemed to bring every bruise in his body alive at the same time, and he felt suddenly faint. Sunida and the doctor rushed to his aid but it was too late. He collapsed back on to the straw mat, unconscious.

The breathless messenger fell prostrate at the entrance to the courtyard. The man, whose loincloth was covered in dust and whose chest and back were streaming with sweat, crawled forward, panting, and stopped a short distance from the

123

Governor's feet. His whole frame heaved fitfully as he struggled for breath. The entire court leaned forward expectantly, while at a sign from the Governor the peasants whose performance had just finished, crawled backwards out of the courtyard like an army of retreating crocodiles. Burnaby and Ivatt glanced at each other uneasily, their worst fears rekindled. This was surely the messenger bringing the tidings of *Royal Lotus*'s discovery. Would it be just the ship or the cannon as well?

'Oh great and mighty Lord,' the messenger began, gasping for air, 'the dust of your feet brings great tidings. Your Excellency has been thrice blessed. In the forests to the south, some farmers have captured a white elephant.' There was an awed silence as the messenger paused for breath. The assembly sat enraptured. 'The noble beast is on its way here now, mighty Lord. The crowds are swelling with every village it passes. Fame and honour are upon your Excellency.'

A murmur of joy went up from the assembly and the Governor looked quite ecstatic. The whole court turned and made a spontaneous obeisance in his direction. Ivatt and Burnaby appeared perplexed, as they too followed the others and bowed low to the mandarin. Then the whole court rose, each man speaking volubly with his neighbour, as he retired to prepare for the magnificent omen. Each person would don his finest apparel for the great ceremony that was to follow. The Governor glanced briefly at the farangs as if he wished there were some way he could communicate the enormity of the news he had just received, but the barrier proved too daunting. In the absence of the Dutch farang, who had pleaded indisposition when invited to observe the peasants' performance, the Malay interpreter was not in attendance. With a resigned shrug the Governor ordered the Palat to accompany the farangs to their quarters and try his hand at explaining the wondrous event.

Cautiously Burnaby and Ivatt peered through the window of the guesthouse containing Phaulkon. Seeing that he was awake, they entered.

'Thank God you're still alive, boys,' said Phaulkon, relieved to find his two companions in one piece. 'I thought we were being summoned to our execution.'

'So did we, Constant,' admitted Burnaby. 'But how are you faring?'

'I feel I've been run over by a herd of cattle, but the pain tells me I'm alive.'

'Remind me never to step in the ring with you, Constant,' said Ivatt, jovial as ever.

'What happened out there?' asked Phaulkon.

'A strange ceremony was held in the courtyard, performed by thirty-odd peasants,' explained Burnaby. 'At first when they turned and bowed to us I thought the brawny peasants might be our executioners but instead they formed two rows and tied a long piece of hemp round each other's waists, securing one man to the next. Then they turned sideways and clasped hands. Finally they formed two rows of fifteen men each while the front man in each row stretched his hands out towards us in a human chain. They were apparently enacting our rescue at sea.'

'Really? Very decent of the Governor to go to the trouble,' observed Phaulkon. 'I hope you thanked them at least.'

'We bowed and smiled and generally made asses of ourselves, if that's what you mean,' commented Ivatt. 'But at least we understood that part of it. Because the next bit was totally baffling. A messenger crawled in on all fours uttering something so momentous that the whole court just swooned. Every man looked as if he had died and been given the keys to heaven.'

'The Governor kept glancing at us as if he wished he could explain,' said Burnaby. 'I got the distinct impression he wanted us to share in their joy.'

Phaulkon was intrigued. 'Can you give me any clue? What happened next?'

'The squat-nose Palat accompanied us home and made an utter fool of himself,' said Ivatt. 'At one point he took us to see an elephant and then pointed at Richard's arm. He kept doing that over and over as if he had suddenly discovered the two of them were related. Richard kept smiling and bowing, not knowing what else to do. But the elephant took a different view of things. It raised its tail and made an awful mess on the stable floor.'

Phaulkon laughed. 'How strange that the Palat only pointed at Richard and not at you, Thomas.'

Ivatt lowered his head. 'I'm too small to be related.'

'Shush! Quiet!' whispered Phaulkon. 'I hear voices.'

Ivatt and Burnaby lapsed into silence as Sunida and the doctor approached the guesthouse, chatting excitedly.

Phaulkon strained his ears. He caught Sunida's voice.

'. . . no way of explaining. The Governor is so anxious to tell them. Do you think there could be any connection, honourable doctor?'

'Between the white farangs and the white elephant? It's possible. The Lord Buddha often gives us signs. It certainly is curious that the farangs should have appeared at the same time as the noble animal was discovered.'

'How wonderful for our province,' exclaimed Sunida, excitedly. 'But we must be quiet in case he's still asleep.'

'I heard voices a moment ago,' said the doctor.

They peered in and looked at Phaulkon. His eyes were closed. Ivatt put his finger in front of his lips to indicate that they were sitting quietly until Phaulkon awoke.

The doctor seemed to understand and nodded, beckoning Sunida to leave with him.

As soon as they were out of earshot, Phaulkon opened his eyes and Burnaby and Ivatt converged on him.

'Oh my God,' said Ivatt, observing Phaulkon, 'he's wearing that same expression of ecstasy as the courtiers a while ago. It must be contagious.'

Phaulkon's mind was in a whirl, his aches briefly forgotten as the infinite possibilities of the event unfurled before him.

'What did you overhear?' asked Burnaby, leaning forward anxiously on his cane.

'Enlighten us, O oracle,' pleaded Ivatt.

Phaulkon raised himself painfully on one elbow and gazed at his companions.

'A rare white elephant seems to have been found in the forests of Ligor,' he began. 'It is one of the most auspicious omens that can occur in any monarch's reign. The animal must immediately be presented to the King, bringing honour and privilege to the province of its discovery.'

'And could this be of benefit to us?' asked Burnaby in one of his rare moments of optimism.

'It certainly could,' replied Phaulkon. He smiled as a sudden thought struck him.

126

'Will it bring honour personally to the Governor?' asked Ivatt, beginning to see the potential himself.

'Indeed it will,' replied Phaulkon. 'The discovery will reflect directly on him. You have no idea how seriously the Siamese view such an event. A monarch's greatness is often measured by the number of white elephants in his stables. Whole wars have been fought over the beasts. They say the soul of a former prince resides in them and that they are one of the incarnations of a future Buddha.'

'How rare are they?' asked Ivatt, more and more interested. He began to imagine bringing a white elephant to a menagerie in England.

'I understand there is only one such beast at the court of the present King and I have heard that it is attended day and night by forty-eight slaves. It only eats and drinks out of bowls of solid gold.'

'Good God. I'll change places with it any time,' chuckled Ivatt. 'But is it really white?'

'It's an albino, I believe. I've never actually seen one, but it looks as if we may have the opportunity soon.'

Burnaby was unusually cheerful. 'This should put the mandarin in a good mood,' he remarked. 'It has got to be the moment to ask him about our departure, Constant.'

'Indeed, Richard.' Phaulkon's mind was churning. There had to be some way of playing on the superstitions of the Siamese. If only he could somehow equate his presence here with the discovery of the white elephant. Then the idea that had vaguely suggested itself to him took substance. He turned to Ivatt.

'Were there any elephants in your menagerie, Thomas?'

'Yes, there were two from India. A male and a female. But they were just your average greys, I'm afraid.'

'And were you involved at all in training them?'

'I was a trapeze artist. But I spent a lot of time with the trainers and the animals.' He smiled. 'The animals, in particular, were very fond of me.'

'Would you know how to make an elephant kneel?' asked Phaulkon, restraining his excitement.

'I expect so, if he were reasonably tame. But this isn't a further manifestation of your megalomania is it, Constant?' The little

127

man was tickled. 'The great white elephant kneeling before the great white boxer!' He laughed at the image.

'That's precisely it,' replied Phaulkon. 'Could you manage it?'

'Oh my God, no!' moaned Ivatt. 'You're actually serious?'

'I most certainly am,' replied Phaulkon.

It was early evening in the courtyard. The Governor was dressed in full ceremonial attire. His white conical hat with its single golden hoop was held in place by a string round his chin, and he wore his gold brocade coat with wide flowing sleeves and a splendid silken panung embroidered with a border of gold. It was made from those beautiful hand-painted cloths of the Indies, known as Chit of Masulipatam. Having been presented to him by His Majesty the King, it was reserved strictly for ceremonial occasions. On his feet he wore his flat, Muslim-style slippers, upturned at the ends like boats. His sword bearer carried his ceremonial sword embossed with diamonds, while another slave bore his golden betel box containing the betel nut and areca, wrapped up and ready to be chewed whenever His Excellency felt the urge.

His court was equally resplendent, though none but the Governor wore the silk panung with the border of gold. On this most auspicious occasion, the ladies of the court, the wives, daughters, and nieces of the palace officials, as well as their female slaves, appeared for the first time, wearing somewhat more flowing panungs than the men. Sunida was there too, striking in a black panung. Black, enhanced by gold or silver embroidery, was clearly the prevailing colour, and Phaulkon wondered whether it was the fashion of the day or simply the ladies' favourite colour. Their complexion was somewhat paler than that of the average peasant woman, as they spent less time outdoors. But unlike the men, their torsos were bare, covered only by the sash of plain white muslin cloth that was draped casually across their breasts. Pear-shaped earrings of silver or gold hung from each of their ears and the last three fingers of each hand were heavily adorned with a multitude of diamond rings and other precious stones. Their fingernails remained excessively long, having never been cut, as was the custom with aristocracy, and the little fingernail of each hand was painted red. Their dark hair glistened with sweet-smelling oils and their lips

128

were made paler by the application of perfumed pomatum. White chalk marks above their breasts indicated that they had just partaken of long bathing rites and were ready to make a visit of consequence, such as this one. The ladies were spotlessly clean, perfumed all over and most alluring.

A murmur of approval greeted the three farangs as they arrived fully attired in their formal coats of brocade. Burnaby's coat was absurdly short for him, but nobody seemed to mind. The Governor motioned them towards some cushions next to the Palat. The Dutchman was conspicuously absent.

As soon as the assembly was seated, cross-legged, a string of twelve bare-breasted maidens, in the full bloom of youth, their black hair sleekly cropped and oiled, was led into the courtyard and placed in the front row. Their plain white panungs contrasted vividly with the predominantly black attire of the ladies of the court.

A blare of trumpets and a clash of cymbals now announced the arrival of the great white beast outside the palace walls. The gates were flung open, the guardsmen fell to the ground, and the holy animal, garlanded with wreaths of jasmine and preceded by six chanting Brahmin priests, clad only in white, entered the palace compound. A huge red parasol was held over the young elephant to shield it, and four mahouts marched deferentially by its side to guide it. Any other beast would have been ridden by its mahout, but not even the King himself would think of sitting astride a former prince, perhaps one of his very own ancestors.

The whole assembly now lay prone, and out of the corner of his eye Phaulkon watched as the twelve beautiful maidens, chosen from the host of volunteers in the villages surrounding the elephant's place of discovery, stepped forward and prostrated themselves in its path. The animal stood about eight feet tall and its skin was of a creamy-white colour, while its toenails and the edges of its ears appeared whiter still. It came to a halt in front of the silent array of maidens and surveyed them out of pinkish eyes, as if contemplating their various merits. The maidens rose to their knees and bowed their heads expectantly. Then, unerringly, it headed towards a pretty one in the centre and lifted its trunk to her exposed breasts.

The young maiden offered herself gladly, thrilled at the honour of being chosen. She closed her eyes and joined her hands respectfully above her head, giving herself up wholeheartedly to the animal's playful advances. She remained motionless as it ran its trunk over her breasts and navel and sniffed her bare shoulders. When it had seemingly had its fill of her, the royal beast gazed briefly at the others and then passed them by. The lucky girl who had had the honour of being fondled would now be singled out as a consort for His Majesty the King.

Guided by the mahout, the elephant made its way towards the Governor. The crouching Palat handed his master a golden salver laden with sugar cane, cakes and fruits. The Governor himself knelt in the elephant's path and held the offering out in front of him. The animal greedily devoured the contents, sweeping them up in two swift forays of its trunk, and the salvers were immediately replenished by attendant slaves.

The Governor retired, crawling away backwards, for the first time in the eyes of his court, in deference to the elevated rank of this prince of beasts. It was now the Palat's turn to make the offering. To the consternation of the crowd, however, Ivatt suddenly shuffled forward, apparently seeking for himself the honour of serving the next helping. The perplexed Palat looked round at the retreating Governor for guidance, while, at this unexpected breach of protocol, two guards stepped forward, their hands on the hilts of their swords. The whole court tensed.

Ivatt smiled reassuringly at the guards before prostrating himself at the feet of the elephant in an attitude of prayer. Then he began mimicking the mating calls he had so often heard in the menagerie. Politely he edged the golden bowl away from the still flustered Palat, and crawled further forward until he was practically under the belly of the great beast. One of the guards drew his sword and advanced on Ivatt. But incredibly, the elephant turned on the guard and the superstitious soldier stopped in his tracks, bewildered and uncertain. The Governor, by now upright again, stood motionless, his eyes fixed on Ivatt.

With his free arm, Ivatt began to stroke the area behind the elephant's right knee with a stick of sugar cane, while with his other hand he positioned the bunch of bananas low enough for the elephant to have to reach down for them. Then abruptly he whacked the great beast behind the knee with the stick of sugar cane.

Right on cue, Phaulkon stepped forward. He bowed to the

130

Governor and fell prostrate before the elephant, touching his head three times to the ground, in the royal salute. At that very moment the animal sank to its knees and gathered the bunch of bananas in its trunk. An awed hush descended on the superstitious assembly as it watched, transfixed, while Phaulkon and the royal beast apparently paid homage to each other.

The Governor, momentarily bemused by the turn of events, now attempted to restore order to the proceedings. Gesturing to Phaulkon and Ivatt to resume their places, His Excellency called for the young farmer who had discovered the beast to be brought before him. In accordance with age-old tradition, the lucky peasant was exempted, together with his entire progeny, from any further payment of taxes to the crown. At the same time he was absolved from the six-monthly service to the King. He had already served another prince, by bringing him out of the forest into a more comfortable and befitting way of life. Following the bestowal of these honours, His Excellency gave orders for the roads through which the royal pachyderm would pass on its way out of the city to be thoroughly swept and sprinkled with holy water; and he assigned several persons of rank the privilege of fanning the animal through the night. Finally, he ordered the elephant to be housed in his finest stables with priests and slaves in attendance, in preparation for its month-long journey to the capital.

The governor was now satisfied that he had completed all honours which were within his authority. It would be up to His Majesty now, he reflected, to confer a rank of nobility on the royal beast, to give it a great name, such as 'Glory of the Land' or 'Radiance of the World', and to place a diamond diadem on its head and encircle the royal tusks with rings of gold.

The mandarin smiled with satisfaction as he thought of the honour that had befallen his province and the rewards that he personally would reap. His Majesty would no doubt confer on him the Order of the White Elephant first class, and Ligor would almost certainly be named province of the year. There might even be an increase in his *sakdina*. His pleasure doubled. With twelve thousand dignity marks he would not only be the highest-ranking provincial governor, he would be second only to the Barcalon in the entire kingdom.

Yet he could not help wondering about the medium farang.

Could this man from a distant land who boxed and prostrated himself and behaved almost with the dignity of a Siamese have anything to do with these auspicious events? Was he some kind of emissary? For a moment it had actually seemed as if the white visitor and the great white beast were revering each other.

As he watched the royal elephant being led away to its stables and the prostrate assembly disperse, he determined to consult his foremost astrologers. Then he gave orders for Phaulkon to rest for a day and to be brought to his audience chamber the following evening before sundown.

The last rays of the tropical sun danced through the foliage of the great banyan tree and a soft evening light tempered the skies as Phaulkon followed the Palat through the courtyard to the Governor's audience hall. He had slept, albeit intermittently, through almost an entire night and day, and his pain, though still acute, felt less severe.

He had been summoned alone and he wondered whether there might be any connection with the performance of the white elephant on the previous day. The Siamese were probably more familiar with elephants than any other nation, he reflected, and they had more than likely seen through Ivatt's trick of making the beast kneel before him. Yet, so influenced were they by signs and portents, they might have looked beyond the simple truth in search of a more complex interpretation. When it came to the legendary white elephant, Siamese superstition knew no bounds.

As he made his way painstakingly across the Governor's courtyard, Phaulkon remembered Père le Morin running along beside him that night in the Portuguese quarter of Ayudhya, his short, stumpy legs barely able to keep up. They had both just dined at the house of their mutual friend, Mestre Phanik, the Japanese trader, and the little Jesuit was volubly pursuing the conversation that had dominated the dinner table. 'Mon cher Constance,' he was saying, as he gesticulated to the heavens in frustration, 'how can you teach the ways of the Lord to a people who believe that truth lies in entering a temple and putting your questions to the image of the Buddha?' The father shook his head despondently. 'And do you know how you get an answer? Why, you simply ask your question, pray for a moment and then go outside to listen for the first words uttered by the first passerby

132

you run across. And in those words lies the answer to your question! The truth!'

He shrugged his hunched shoulders and shook his head again. 'Bon dieu, if life were only that simple! But it is impossible to convince the Siamese otherwise. They are instilled since early childhood with these kinds of superstitions and nothing can shake the belief later on. You know, of course, the story of the former King who inquired about his future?'

'I don't believe I do, Father,' replied Phaulkon.

'Oh come now, Monsieur Constance. Every child knows it.'

'Ah, but I am not a child, Father.'

'Well then, my young man, I will tell it to you as a perfect illustration of the problems I face. You see, this former King sent his messenger to the temple to inquire about the royal future on his behalf, because only commoners would go themselves on such a mission. When the messenger emerged from the temple he encountered an old man plucking hairs from his face with a pair of tweezers. "Look at that great one on the ground!" the old man exclaimed, as a large whisker floated to the earth. The King then interpreted this as a sign of his own body lying on the ground and, though not advanced in years, he fell ill and died shortly after. And it is impossible to convince the Siamese that this is not pure coincidence. To them, the temple oracle had spoken.' He raised his arms in a hopeless gesture. 'Everyone from the King down continues to consult the astrologers at every moment and regulates his life according to their predictions.'

Phaulkon had to sympathize with the Jesuit. It could not be easy for him. But then why try to convert these happy people in the first place?

A young Malay boy awaited Phaulkon now at the entrance to the Governor's audience chamber. On seeing him the boy bowed and addressed him in halting but understandable Dutch.

'At request of His Excellency, the Governor, I been ordered here from Dutch factory to interpret you, sir. My master, Mr Joop, send his regrets to Governor that he himself not able attend. He not feeling so well.' The boy bowed again and preceded Phaulkon into the audience chamber.

Phaulkon climbed the outer steps and paused at the massive teakwood panels that formed the doorway. He prayed that the powerful superstitions that Père le Morin had so bitterly

133

complained about might stand him in good stead on this occasion. He drew a deep breath, tried to master the pain within him and entered. He stood still in the doorway, staring in front of him. The whole court was present again, glittering with jewels and adorned in full ceremonial attire. He spotted Sunida, looking towards him, a proud expression on her face. In these surroundings, seated cross-legged on fine Persian carpets and ringed by His Excellency's exquisite collection of Ming porcelain, the assembly looked even more dazzling than the one that had gathered the day before in the courtyard to receive the white elephant.

Phaulkon prostrated himself in the open doorway and crawled forward painstakingly on his knees and one elbow towards the Governor, who was seated as usual above the rest and who observed him for a while in silence, until seemingly satisfied, he addressed himself to the interpreter.

'It has not escaped our notice, Mr Forcon, that your visit here has brought much honour to my province. My astrologers have further assured me that your arrival here was no mere accident. The discovery of the noblest of animals soon after my people had saved you from death is an omen that cannot be disregarded.' The mandarin paused.

'Apart from such auspices, your bravery in the ring has personally gratified me. There was no shame in your defeat. On the contrary, you did remarkably well against one of the finest boxers I have seen. I have tried to ascertain who he was but he vanished as discreetly as he arrived. He was not from these parts.' A slight smile parted the Governor's lips. 'If you will permit me to say so, you should practise your kick.'

Phaulkon was about to respond, when the Governor continued.

'It is in my power to grant certain honours to those who have served my province well. And though you are a farang, I see no reason why that should render you ineligible. My country has always honoured those who benefited her, regardless of their origins.

'I have today prepared a dispatch to His Excellency the Pra Klang in Ayudhya, and a full report of your activities has just now been sent to him.' The Governor paused to allow the Malay to interpret, but Phaulkon was not even listening to the

134

translation. A dispatch to the Barcalon! A recommendation perhaps to the highest official in the land! He might have lost his precious cannon, but had he just conceivably been presented with an alternative means of achieving his goal? Could he obtain through open exhortation what he had failed to gain through smuggling? Was there a chance of filling Sam White's boat after all? There were still almost three months to go. The Governor's voice, his tone more formal than ever, interrupted his thoughts.

'In my capacity as Governor and chief representative of His Most Gracious Majesty in the first-class royal province of Nakhon Si Thammarat, I hereby bestow on Mr Kosatanin Forcon the Order of the White Elephant, third class.'

A murmur went up from the assembled court at the announcement of so exalted an honour. Phaulkon was speechless. The Order of the White Elephant, third class! This was the highest award a provincial governor was empowered to confer. Only His Majesty could grant those of the first and second class. Might this now give him the prestige to deal directly with the Barcalon, the chance tactfully to expose the duplicity of the Moors and ask for the opportunity to lead one trade mission to Persia himself?

'I suggest that it would be appropriate for you and your friends to serve as part of the escort that will accompany the noble white elephant on his journey to Ayudhya. Under normal circumstances he should depart immediately, but I am prepared to delay his departure by one day to allow you to recuperate further from your wounds.'

It was a while before Phaulkon could find his voice. 'The extraordinary honour Your Excellency bestows upon your humble servant overwhelms me. My heart is filled with gratitude and my absolute pleasure is marred only by the sadness I feel at leaving the province of so distinguished and enlightened a governor.'

The mandarin inclined his head as the interpreter translated Phaulkon's words and while the entire assembly looked on, the Palat draped a silver pendant round Phaulkon's neck, a glittering medal embossed with the image of a white elephant and inscribed with the name of the province in gold letters at the bottom.

The Palat had just returned to his place at his master's foot when there was a commotion outside and all eyes turned towards the door. A flustered guard prostrated himself in the entrance, begging His Excellency's forgiveness.

'Mighty Lord, a messenger from the Dutch factory forced his way into the palace, insisting on seeing Your Excellency personally. The guards would have killed him if he had not continuously asserted that the message was of great consquence to Your Excellency.' The guard shook with fear, uncertain whether he and his colleagues had acted correctly.

'Where is he now?' demanded the Governor irritably. How unseemly to be interruped like this in the middle of a ceremony.

'Mighty Lord, he is being held outside.'

'Send him in!'

'Mighty Lord, I receive your orders.'

A young messenger, half Dutch, half Siamese, appeared now in the doorway, nervously eyeing the glittering assembly. A pair of stark blue eyes looked out implausibly from his Oriental face.

He prostrated himself in the direction of the Governor and spoke in fluent Siamese.

'Mighty Lord, my master, Mr Joop, has asked me to inform your Excellency that he has received an important letter from Ayudhya. He is not well enough to come to see Your Excellency himself but begs you to meet with him urgently at the Dutch factory. It concerns the English farangs.' He paused for effect, as his master had instructed him to do. 'My master now has all the proof you require.'

Phaulkon listened with trepidation to the messenger's words. Was this the proof the Dutchman had claimed he was awaiting? But what could it be? Phaulkon felt his stomach turn. Would he be thwarted now at the last minute just when the tide seemed to be turning in his favour? But how could a letter from Ayudhya have arrived so quickly? Even the fastest sea transport would take fourteen days, and only nine had elapsed since the shipwreck. Or was it perhaps a letter sent before the shipwreck and containing some information damaging to himself?

He saw the Governor glance ill-humouredly at the messenger while the whole court leaned forward expectantly.

'We are busy now. You will inform your master that we will attempt to see him in the morning.'

'Mighty Lord, I receive your orders.'

The messenger was about to depart when he spotted the

136

decoration hanging from Phaulkon's neck. He remembered the message his master had given him for the farang if he should run into him. He turned to him and said in Dutch, 'My master knows now that you are the one who speaks perfect Siamese. He said to tell you that your time has come, Mr Phaulkon.'

The Governor dismissed the assembly and turned away, leaving Phaulkon to reflect upon the extent of the mandarin's fury once the potentate discovered that he had been thoroughly duped.

Ten

Van Risling's young clerk, Pieter, the same Eurasian interpreter who had been sent to the palace the day before to deliver the Dutch message, walked down the stark corridor of the great brick factory that was the Dutch empire's outpost in Ligor, and knocked on the door of his chief's office. He was visibly excited. It was not every day that the Governor of the province, the Pu Samrec Rajakara Meuang, with ten thousand dignity marks, paid them a visit. Pieter's mother, a Siamese from the village of Ban Seri near Ligor, had instilled in him a respect since childhood for the hierarchy of officialdom, and the thought of lying prostrate in the reception committee for the great Governor left him breathless. Already the previous day he had felt awed when, due to the indisposition of Hassan, the Malay interpreter, he had been sent to the palace for the first time. He had tried to overcome his fear by pushing his way in and acting haughtily like he had seen his master do, but inside his stomach had felt as soft as an overripe banana fruit. It amazed and frightened him that his master, Heer Joop, seemed to display an almost open disdain for the Siamese, even for the mighty Governor, and Pieter had often wondered whether his own father, an itinerant Dutch trader who had died when he was only a child, had had the same attitude. He doubted it. He had never seen anyone behave quite like Heer Joop. The truth was, his master's manners were appalling. Even the English farangs behaved with greater dignity. But it was also true that Heer Joop paid well, and the money enabled Pieter to take care of his widowed mother with whom he lived. There were some pecuniary advantages to being the only Dutch speaker in Ligor, he reflected, although he was aware his Dutch was far from perfect.

Young Pieter sighed. How he wished he were like everybody else and not half farang. He felt so much more Siamese inside and the Siamese had more dignity than the farangs. He knew little of Dutch ways other than those of his crude master and the

138

kind old surgeon – now dead – who had taught him all he knew of the language.

'Come in!' His master's gruff voice interrupted his thoughts.

Heer Joop had been extremely sullen and irritable of late, ever since the boxing match in which the tiger farang had so excelled himself. Since yesterday, when reports of the great honour conferred on the fighting farang had reached the factory, his mood had become even worse. The Order of the White Elephant, third class! Heer Joop had quite simply exploded. Pieter had watched him through the keyhole, pacing up and down his office, staring vacantly at the maps on the wall, cursing and muttering to himself.

He opened the great wooden door of his master's office – the door that had only one panel and opened outwards like no other door – and peered in.

'Yes, what is it, Pieter?'

'Excuse me, sir, but His Excellency the Governor is on his way. A slave has come ahead to announce his arrival.'

Van Risling's face lit up and his corpulent frame spread across the wooden desk as he leaned forward. His fingers drummed excitedly on the varnished surface.

'Good, see to it that His Excellency is received with full honours, and let me know the minute he appears.' The Dutchman was delighted with the Governor's visit. It showed at least that the mandarin was interested enough in the Dutch revelations to come and see for himself. It would not have been the same, reflected van Risling, if he himself had paid the Governor a visit. He wanted him here on home ground and so he had feigned indisposition.

'Very well, sir,' replied Pieter, hiding his surprise. It was not like his master to show such respect.

'Have you made sure that the entrance hall is properly swept?' the older man asked. His Excellency would have to pass that way.

'I have, sir. All the employees are lined up prostrate on either side of the hall now, awaiting His Excellency's arrival.'

'Good. Now bring me my white brocade jacket, the formal one,' ordered van Risling.

There was the sound of a trumpet outside and Pieter bowed and hurriedly left the room.

139

'Hurry up,' came van Risling's voice from behind.

Moments later, as Pieter returned with his master's ceremonial jacket, the same collarless, puffy-sleeved vest with the gold trim that high-ranking dignitaries in Siam wore for official visits, His Excellency the Governor strode magisterially through the entrance of the only brick edifice in Ligor and the awed employees buried their faces in the ground on either side of his path.

Thrusting his arms hurriedly through the sleeves of his coat, the Dutch factor stood up importantly behind his desk, smiling congenially as the Governor appeared in the doorway. Then he executed a low bow. Lower, it seemed to Pieter, than he had ever seen his master perform before.

'Pieter, the chair!' ordered van Risling, straightening himself up. Pieter scrambled to his feet from his prostrate position and drew up a rattan chair, placing it gingerly behind the Governor.

'The cushions, Pieter. Bring more cushions, you fool. You know His Excellency likes to sit higher than anyone else.'

His Excellency did not in fact like to sit at all in these excrutiatingly uncomfortable contraptions the farangs used. They were so impractical. You could neither squat nor sit cross-legged in them because the wretched arm rests got in the way. You were forced to maintain a ridiculous position with your legs dangling down in front of you like some monkey hanging from a branch. Especially when the seat of the chair was so high that your feet were not even able to reach the round. Of course the farangs, with their outsize legs, managed to plant them on firm ground, but even so they looked ridiculous.

His Excellency lowered himself distastefully into his chair while his betel box carrier and the Palat sank to the ground on either side of him. Half a dozen slaves crouched at a respectful distance behind their master. His sword bearer was conspicuously absent, a sign that His Excellency considered this an informal visit.

'Welcome, Your Excellency, to our humble factory,' said van Risling with uncharacteristic modesty. 'May I offer you some refreshment?' Young Pieter rendered the translation, relieved that for once etiquette was being observed. Until now he had been under the impression that his master knew no better.

'Not for the moment, thank you, Mr Lidrim.' The mandarin observed the Dutchman and wondered what he was so nervous about. 'I have many matters to attend to and only the urgency of

140

your message persuaded me to interrupt those commitments. My visit, I am afraid, can only be brief.'

'Of course, Your Excellency, I understand, and I am most grateful that you should have honoured me at all. I will come straight to the point.' He leaned forward importantly. 'Your Excellency, it is my duty to inform you that despite the continuous pretence to the contrary, one of the members of the English Company speaks fluent Siamese.' He paused. 'And we now know who it is. It pains me to have to reveal such treachery when I have seen with my own eyes the great courtesy with which Your Excellency has received this person. But it is better that Your Excellency should learn the truth before it is too late.'

The Governor pursed his lips. 'Indeed? And what proof do you have of this accusation, Mr Lidrim?'

The Dutchman opened the drawer of his desk and produced a letter. It bore the official seal of the Netherlands East India Company and was dated Ayudhya, 4 December 1679. Sixteen days ago. The contents were in Dutch.

'Pieter,' he said, turning to the young clerk, 'would you translate for His Excellency, please.'

Pieter held out a nervous hand and took the letter. Remaining prostrate on his knees and elbows he began to read out the translation which he had spent the better part of the night preparing.

My dear van Risling,

Further to my recent urgent dispatch regarding the clandestine activities of the English Company, I have now completed extensive inquiries and can confirm beyond any doubt that one of their factors speaks excellent Siamese. It is the young man, Thomas Ivatt by name, who is masquerading as a new recruit. He is an accomplished linguist and his extensive knowledge of the Siamese language has been corroborated by several sources: two French Jesuits, three Portuguese traders, his entire domestic staff at his home and a ranking official at the Ministry of Trade, Nai Prasert, with whom Heer Ivatt has had dealings.

You will no doubt want to pass this information on to His Excellency the Governor of Ligor who, in his wisdom, will wish to take appropriate measures. Heer Ivatt will undoubtedly deny his knowledge of the language, but I am sure that His Excellency, in whom I have every confidence, will find means of extracting the truth.

We now know beyond any doubt that the junk *Royal Lotus* was transporting contraband cannon down the coast of Siam and we are of the firm opinion that these weapons were destined for the rebels in Pattani.

We are gratified to have discovered this act of treason in time and to be of service to our old friend and ally, Siam, with whom we have always shared such a special relationship.

You are requested therefore to act immediately upon this information and if necessary you are authorized to show this letter, bearing our official seal, to His Excellency the Governor, whom we know by reputation to be a worthy and capable man.

Pieter looked up: 'The letter is signed Aarnout Faa, Chief Factor of the Honourable Dutch East India Company in Ayudhya.'

The Governor's expression had remained grave throughout the reading.

'And this letter has just arrived? Did it come in answer to one of your own, Mr Lidrim?'

'No, Your Excellency,' replied the Dutchman, carefully avoiding the trap. 'The report I sent after the shipwreck would hardly have reached Ayudhya yet.'

'May I see the letter, Mr Lidrim?'

'Of course, Your Excellency,' replied van Risling. 'I have taken the liberty of including a Siamese translation on the reverse side, which Pieter here was reading from.' He bowed respectfully and handed it to the mandarin across the table.

'Most helpful, Mr Lidrim.' The Governor perused the letter and continued staring at it for a while. 'Ah yes, I recognize the seal of your honourable Company. I should like to take this document away with me as evidence, Mr Lidrim, with your permission of course.'

The Dutchman beamed. 'But of course, Your Excellency.' The mention of 'evidence' was most promising. 'And if I can be of any further assistance, Your Excellency, do not hesitate to call upon me.'

'I will, I will, Mr Lidrim. In the meantime perhaps you would be good enough to send me your interpreter this evening to the palace?'

'With pleasure, Your Excellency,' responded van Risling eagerly.

'Very well, then, I will leave you now. It has been most instructive, Mr Lidrim. Thank you.'

'Your Excellency is most gracious. It is I who thank Your Excellency for taking time off from your many commitments.'

The Governor rose and, from his supine position, young Pieter watched in wonder as Heer Joop, bowing obsequiously, showed the Governor to the door.

When, a moment later, the Dutchman returned to his desk, there was an expression of deep satisfaction imprinted on his features, as if he had just won a great victory. The young man, Ivatt, would more readily succumb under interrogation than that devil Phaulkon. The tension and anxiety that had seemed to pursue him these past two days fell from him like a ripe mango from a tree.

Phaulkon lay on his bed, his mind in a whirl. Just when it looked as if the danger was over, van Risling had come back to haunt him. What did the cursed Dutchman really know? Could he be bluffing? What new information had come to light? Could he, seeing the way the tide was turning and foreseeing Phaulkon's imminent release, have made a last desperate attempt not to allow him to slip from his grasp? One thing was certain. Whatever information had come from Ayudhya, it could not have been in response to any letter sent by van Risling since the shipwreck. There would have been no time for an answer to reach Ligor.

Phaulkon knew that the Governor could not delay the departure of the white elephant any longer. Not even one more day. The princely beast should have been sent to His Majesty immediately following capture. Tomorrow at sunrise the procession would depart. And he had to be part of it.

Sunida had peered in twice already to check on his condition and tiptoed out when he had pretended to be asleep.

He had wanted to appear relaxed and resting, rather than nervous and awake, as he was sure she would be reporting back on his condition to the Governor. He had longed to ask her whether His Excellency had paid a visit to the Dutch factory, but it would have been too difficult to express in sign language, and a suspicious sort of question anyway. How was he supposed to know about the visit in the first place?

At one point she had knelt by his side and gently stroked his temples to increase the depth of his sleep and he had heard her murmur. 'How my heart will grieve when you are gone, my handsome farang. Will I ever see you again?' He had longed to make love to her then as he had yesterday but he was supposed to be asleep. The sorrow in her voice had torn at his heart, and in that moment he had cursed his decision not to speak the language. There was so much he wanted to tell her. He was amazed to discover that his eagerness to reach Ayudhya was actually tempered by the thought of leaving her behind. Could he not take her with him? he wondered. But was she even free to go? And what would the Governor say? He knew so little about her.

He lifted his head off the cushions and peered across at the open window. The door too, was open, no doubt in accordance with the doctor's instructions to restore the balance of air in the patient's body. A bamboo fan lay by his bed ready to be used as soon as he awoke. He could see from the sun's angle that it was late afternoon. Only one more night to get through and then he could be on his way to Ayudhya, safe for the time being. Tonight Ivatt was preparing a farewell acrobatic show to the keep the Governor distracted.

Phaulkon fingered the decoration that hung from his neck. Would this award earn him a face-to-face interview with the potentates of Ayudhya? Was this his entrée to the Barcalon? he wondered. His stomach heaved as a thought suddenly struck him. How could he speak Siamese to the Barcalon after denying his knowledge of the language all this time? But the question was academic, Phaulkon realized. Now that he had been so prominently honoured, the powerful Barcalon would be bound to make inquiries about him, and with his horde of spies, he would discover the farang's knowledge of the language. Phaulkon would have to come up with a damn good explanation.

The shapely form of Sunida dressed in a flowing blue panung peered in again. Finding him awake this time, she smiled happily

144

at him and lowered herself gracefully down by his side, sweeping the folds of her panung underneath her.

Bubbling with gentle laughter she produced a letter from her pocket and pointed gaily to it. Then she spread her arms out wide and outlined an imaginary beard on her cheeks, puffing them out deliberately as she did so. It was not difficult to recognize the corpulent form of van Risling. A letter to Sunida from the Dutchman! Phaulkon took the letter from her and pretending to read the signature in Dutch he ran his eyes briefly over the Siamese script above it. His expression remained unchanged as he read the Dutchman's invitation to become his consort and live at the Dutch factory with him. The letter was written in Siamese, presumably by the interpreter, and signed by van Risling.

He pointed to the large child-like scrawl that was the signature and said laughing: 'Mr Lidrim!' She nodded affirmatively and tried to indicate with signs that he had asked her to become his minor wife. Then she screwed up her face in an expression of distaste and shook her head categorically from side to side.

He laughed but, inside, his blood was rising and he felt a sudden urge to possess her himself and take her away from here. He waved in her general direction, for it was rude to point, and then indicated himself and said, 'You and me, Ayudhya?'

She contemplated him for a moment in silence, as if she were trying to make out his meaning and then she repeated, '*Nai leh dichan? Pai Ayudhya?*' He nodded happily and her face lit up. '*Pai! Pai duey!*' Yes, yes I'll go with you!

Instinctively he held his arms out to her but the sudden movement caused him pain, and seeing him wince she put his arms back by his side for him. She looked at him lovingly and placed a finger across his lips for silence. '*Ja mee okat,*' she said warmly. There will be plenty of opportunity. '*Pai, pai Ayudhya!*' she said again happily. He smiled just as a servant entered announcing the Palat.

The deputy wai'd briefly to Phaulkon in the doorway, before turning to Sunida. 'His Excellency wishes to see the farang immediately,' he said.

Something in the Palat's tone sent a shiver down Phaulkon's spine.

*

145

Phaulkon lay prostrate before the Governor. How strange, he thought, that no interpreter was present. The mandarin greeted him curtly and then turned to the Palat.

'Kling!'

'Mighty Lord, I receive your orders.'

'Kling, we have received startling news. The Dutch factory has just furnished me with irrefutable proof that one of the farangs – the small one – speaks our language fluently.' The mandarin produced a folded letter from his cotton purse and waved it over the Palat's prone body. 'How extraordinary that he should have wanted to keep his knowledge secret all this time. He must have had something important to hide. It will be your duty, Kling, to find out exactly what that is.'

The Palat beamed at the prospect of rendering his master service, especially in ways in which he excelled. 'Mighty Lord, I receive your orders.'

'As a start, you will fetch the small farang and take him to the dungeons.' The Governor paused and curled his lips distastefully. 'Make sure the door is well sealed. You know I dislike those sounds.'

'Mighty Lord, I receive your orders.'

'You will address the small farang in Siamese and if after several attempts he still refuses to answer, you will slice off his tongue, as a reward for his insolence. If it is silence he seeks, we will see to it that he never speaks again in any language. You will then bring me the tongue so that we may show it to his friend here.' The Governor gestured towards Phaulkon. 'Perhaps Mr Forcon will then be able to throw some light on the situation and explain to us why his friend attempted to deceive us all this time. Go now, Kling. And send the interpreter in, so that I can converse with Mr Forcon in the meantime.'

'Mighty Lord, I receive your orders.' The Palat crawled out backwards.

The Governor turned his attentions now to Phaulkon and smiled amiably. With a great effort Phaulkon returned the smile. He felt quite sick to his stomach. Poor Thomas! He could not allow this to happen to him. The little man was innocent, after all. But how to stop it without owning up himself? His mind reeled. Even the stupid Dutch could not have concluded that it was Ivatt who spoke Siamese. Ayudhya must know that he had only just arrived in Siam, though the Governor would not be aware of that. It was obviously a trap set by van Risling. But if the Governor believed it, Ivatt was in trouble.

The Eurasian interpreter now crawled into the room and took up his position near the mandarin.

'I summoned you here to inquire about your bruises, Mr Forcon,' said the Governor genially through the interpreter. 'Do you think you will be well enough to travel tomorrow?'

'I think so, Your Excellency, thank you. I still have another night's rest before me which I shall take full advantage of. I am only sorry that I shall miss the entertainment that Mr Ivatt, our youngest colleague, is preparing for Your Excellency. The children of the palace are with him now, watching enthralled as he practises. I saw them as I crossed the courtyard. They won't leave him alone.'

'How delightful, Mr Forcon. I look forward to the performance.' The mandarin paused. 'By the way, Mr Forcon, the Dutch factory has received some extraordinary news from Ayudhya.' He surveyed Phaulkon steadily for a moment. 'It seems that a member of the English Company speaks our language with absolute fluency.' He waved the letter again through the air.

Phaulkon swallowed hard and made an effort to sound casual. 'Indeed, Your Excellency? I only wish it were so. The Dutch farangs, unfortunately, will stop at nothing to throw suspicion on us, their rivals. No doubt they have fabricated yet another story to incriminate us. Would Your Excellency allow me to see the letter?' He listened to the interpreter and was surprised at the honesty of the translation. The young Eurasian was not yet corrupted by politics.

'I see no reason why not, Mr Forcon. In our country the accused always has the right to speak for himself.' The mandarin smiled pleasantly as a slave carried the letter over to Phaulkon.

There was a sudden scream from below and the sound of a door banging. The mandarin pursed his lips at the unseemly noise. 'Snit,' he ordered, 'see that these sounds are shut out.'

'Mighty Lord, I receive your orders.' Snit the slave crawled rapidly backwards out of sight.

Beads of perspiration were forming on Phaulkon's upper lip and his heart pounded fiercely. He would have to own up now. It was all over. He could not let them do this to Thomas. He

147

glanced briefly at the letter and was about to confess when something on the page struck him. His brain reeled. There was something odd or familiar about it. And suddenly he saw it, staring up at him.

'Sunida! Get me Sunida!' He shouted in Dutch. 'Your Excellency, these are lies, all lies, and I will prove it.' There was such outrage in his voice that the governor could not fail to notice it. Oh Thomas, Thomas give me a few moments more. All I need is time. Resist, Thomas, please resist. He heard the Governor give an order and a slave disappeared to look for Sunida.

Phaulkon scanned the letter again. You bastard, van Risling, he thought, if Ivatt has been harmed, I'll pull you apart limb from limb. Where was Sunida, damn it?

'Your Excellency,' continued Phaulkon, forcing himself to stay calm. 'I heard screams. Is anyone in pain?'

'I heard it too,' replied the Governor. 'I have just sent Snit to investigate. He should be returning shortly. But you were saying, Mr Forcon? Oh yes, that the Dutch accusations were all unfounded, I believe?'

'That is so, Your Excellency. And I know that in Siam you would never condemn an innocent man without proof.' He looked pointedly at the Governor. 'This letter did not come from Ayudhya, Your Excellency. It was written right here in Ligor and by none other than the Dutch factor himself, Heer van Risling.'

'Indeed? And how do you surmise that, Mr Forcon?' inquired the mandarin intrigued.

'I will show you, Your Excellency.' Where the devil was Sunida? What was taking her so long? And why did the Governor not order someone to release Ivatt or at least to hold off the torture? Phaulkon's heart was hammering. He felt on the point of screaming at the mandarin in Siamese. But just then Sunida appeared in the doorway, prostrating herself reverently.

The mandarin turned to her. 'Sunida, Mr Forcon has requested your presence. It seems he has something to say to you.'

Sunida looked across nervously at Phaulkon and managed a shy smile. Was he going to ask His Excellency's permission to take her to Ayudhya now? Her heart beat faster.

'Sunida,' began Phaulkon through the interpreter, 'you showed me a letter earlier on. Do you still have it with you?' It took

148

every effort for him to stay calm, while the hammering in his heart continued unabated.

'You mean the letter from the Dutch farang?' she asked in surprise.

'Yes, yes,' said Phaulkon abruptly. 'Please may I see it.'

Sunida was nonplussed. This was not what she had expected. She had shown him the letter in confidence. The expression on Phaulkon's face, however, drove her to action. She extracted the letter from her cotton bag and handed it hurriedly across to him.

He glanced at the letter. Then he crawled rapidly over to the Governor, masking the driving pain in his elbow.

'With your permission, Your Excellency.' He spread both letters on the floor in front of the Governor. Though the signature on the supposed letter from Ayhudhya read 'Aarnout Faa' and that on the letter to Sunida read 'Joop van Risling' they were undoubtedly written by the same person. The ink and the quill were identical and the sprawling child-like characters were the same. Even to the Governor, who could read no Dutch, it was obvious that the letter had not come from Aarnout Faa, the head of the Dutch Company in Ayudhya.

The Governor nodded his head in acknowledgement and seemed almost relieved at the discovery.

'Very convincing, Mr Forcon. It would appear that the Dutch farang has abused you. Such false accusations will not go unpunished. Ah, but here comes Kling.' He turned to the Palat who was just prostrating himself.

'Well, Kling, have you dealt with the prisoner?'

'Mighty Lord, I have.'

'And where is he now?'

'Mighty Lord, he is back in his quarters. I put a young coconut in his mouth to stop the bleeding.'

'Good then, that will be all.' He turned to the interpreter. 'You may tell your master that he will be hearing from me. Have a good rest, Mr Forcon.'

Phaulkon was so distraught about Ivatt that he did not even notice the look of disappointment on Sunida's face. Oh Thomas, Thomas, what have I done to you? How could I have been the cause of your suffering? I will never forgive myself. Furious and wretched, Phaulkon accepted Sunida's arm and hobbled off as fast as his wounds would take him. He had to find Ivatt quickly.

Oh God! When Sunida tried to slow him down he turned angrily on her and she lowered her eyes to hide a silent tear.

The laughter of children grew louder as, breathless and aching all over, Phaulkon neared the edge of the courtyard that surrounded Ivatt's house. He stood still, gaping at the scene before him.

Ivatt was standing on his head, surrounded by screaming children who were trying to balance themselves on the soles of his upturned feet. On seeing Phaulkon they jumped down and stepped aside and Ivatt somersaulted back on to his feet.

Phaulkon stared at him wide-eyed.

'Impressed by the quality of the performance, eh, Constant? Richard and I came over to see you a moment ago, but you were out. Aren't you supposed to be resting?'

'Thomas, your tongue . . . ?'

'What about it? Do you think I should paint it blue for the show?'

A curse on that crafty, triple-faced mandarin, Phaulkon swore again and again. He buried his head in Sunida's shoulder and collapsed.

Eleven

They set off at dawn. There were in all sixteen elephants and fifty men, generally three men per beast, not counting the baggage animals. One man sat astride the elephant's neck, directing it with a sharp iron goad, another across its rump, and a third rode in the middle. Howdahs were provided for the farangs and the nai in charge of the expedition. The others rode bareback. Phaulkon's howdah was a broad, elaborately carved wooden chair, strapped round the elephant's underbelly. It had a wooden roof to protect him from the sun and afforded an excellent view of the countryside. He had never ridden an elephant for any length of time before, and the fitful rhythm was at first unpleasant. Then gradually he grew accustomed to the rolling motion, not unlike a small boat in a mildy tossing sea.

The three farangs each rode on separate animals with a mahout perched between the enormous ears to guide them. They rode in single file, affording little chance for conversation, but the novelty and the view were sustenance enough to keep them occupied.

The journey began through flat coastal country, with the sea to one side and shimmering green paddies to the other. The road, a mud-baked surface of deep red clay, ran along the edge of the paddy fields and was barely wide enough for two elephants to pass. Water buffaloes stared indolently at the passers-by and small boys jumped off their backs and ran excitedly towards them. Sun-browned peasants in round, sloping hats looked up from their waterlogged rice fields and stared mutely at the procession. Then, suddenly divining the meaning of it all – for word of the white elephant had spread like wildfire through the countryside – they fell instantly to the ground, immersing themselves in the waters of the paddy fields where they had been standing.

To the modest farmers, the great procession must indeed have appeared imposing. Two of the elephants were fully laden with lavish gifts from the Governor to His Majesty the King and His

Excellency the Barcalon: local rubies, spices from Dutch-ruled Batavia, jewelled krises from the Malay States further south, and well-preserved Chinese porcelains, recently unearthed near Ligor. But the greatest gift of all was the white elephant which travelled, free of any load, in the centre of the procession. A dozen slaves attended it, two mahouts walked on either side, and it was accompanied by a young female playmate to distract it on the journey. Whenever the company dismounted for food or a brief rest, each man turned towards the white beast with the pink eyes and made his obeisance.

A few clouds sprinkled an otherwise clear sky and the men wound lengths of cloth about their heads, like kerchiefs, to shield them from the sun. Only the occasional rain tree spread its shady leaves across the road. Clusters of bamboo and banana trees dotted the landscape and palm trees fringed the nearby shore.

Though Phaulkon felt an intense relief at their departure, the trauma of the previous day still haunted him, and the absence of Sunida was an emotional thorn in his side. Once, when the procession had come to a sudden halt, he had dismounted and rushed over to Ivatt, desperate to inquire about the little man's tongue.

'You have the strangest obsession with my tongue, Constant,' replied Ivatt, mystified. 'And how is yours?' Phaulkon had not been able to bring himself to repeat the tongue incident to Ivatt or Burnaby, the first because he was ashamed to admit he could ever have let such a thing happen and the second because Burnaby would only have fretted the more. But now that Phaulkon had assured himself one last time that the whole episode had just been a ploy by the Governor, he determined to erase it from his mind.

Several of the men had now dismounted and made their way to the front of the column where a huge python blocked the road. It had swallowed a pig whole and they could clearly see the animal's outline in the snake's belly. The snake's skin was stretched to breaking point and it looked unable to move.

'It won't take kindly to being disturbed when it's digesting,' remarked Phaulkon to Ivatt. Both men had joined the babble of excited voices at the head of the procession.

'Just like my father after a Sunday lunch,' chuckled the little man.

'I'd get back on your mounts,' called Burnaby's voice from the back. 'It's the safest place. The area is teeming with scorpions and there are small snakes, too, that look remarkably like their surroundings.'

'There goes Auntie Richard, again,' observed Ivatt.

'He's right though,' said Phaulkon. 'Watch where you tread.'

After repeated attempts to coax the python off the road, the lead elephant was now brought to the rescue. Guided by two mahouts, it wrapped its trunk round the twenty-foot python and hoisted it off the road like a crane. The python lay motionless by the side of the road, indignantly regarding the long train of grey mammals as the men remounted and the procession once more got underway.

Birds of extraordinary colours, golden-green, bright yellow and ruby red, flew across their path, and monkeys sported with them along the way. Now they passed rows of cotton trees from which the Siamese made their ubiquitous cloth panungs. Cotton was the most popular fabric not only on account of its cheapness and ready availability, but because when drenched with human perspiration, it did not turn cold and cling to the skin like linen or silk.

Phaulkon's mind turned to Sunida again as he thought of the beautiful turquoise and azure cotton panungs she loved to wear, and how well they became her.

He had gone to see the Governor early that morning to ask him for permission to take Sunida with him. The mandarin had sent a messenger to the Dutch factory to fetch the interpreter but the messenger had returned empty-handed. The interpreter was nowhere to be found. Phaulkon suspected that van Risling had forbidden the man to return to the palace after hearing the account of the previous day's events.

In the absence of the interpreter it had been difficult to fathom the exact reasons for the Governor's refusal. Phaulkon was sure that the Governor must have understood his request because at first he had hesitated, but then, as if he had decided against it, he had shaken his head and pretended not to understand. Phaulkon had had the distinct impression that, for whatever reason, it had suited the Governor not to understand.

Sunida had lain by his side throughout the night, gently caressing his forehead and temples and carefully avoiding his

153

bruises. He was sure she had not slept. Every so often she had rubbed the ointment the physician had prescribed into his sores and brought tea to his lips. He had awoken and touched her too and inhaled her profoundly, feeling a new ecstasy in the gentle touching and caressing and comforting.

At first light he had tried to convince her to come with him to the governor to request her departure to Ayudhya but she had refused and indicated that he should go alone. Was she shy to tell the Governor she wanted to leave his service and go off with the farang? It had seemed so to Phaulkon. At any rate she was insistent that he do the asking. Perhaps she thought that would imply that the idea had come from him and not from her. He could see she was clearly willing, anxious even, to accompany him.

When he had returned to inform her of the Governor's refusal, she had lowered her eyes sadly and held tightly on to his arm. He had explained to her as best he could that though this was the wrong time to lock horns with the Governor, he would not soon forget her and he would return for her at the first opportunity.

She seemed to understand and pointed to herself and went through a series of dancing motions to indicate that this is where she would be, waiting for him, for as long as it would take. He had almost cried and he knew then that the absence of this ravishing dancer would be as great a loss to him as his cannon. He would strive to regain them both.

She had accompanied him as far as the edge of the town and smiled proudly when the Governor had ceremoniously handed him a letter for the Barcalon.

Phaulkon thought now about the letter in his pocket and wondered how it was worded. A letter to the great Barcalon! He was being given a reprieve in life, another chance to achieve his goal. With luck and a lot of carefully chosen words he might still be able to persuade the Barcalon to fill Sam White's boat with Treasury goods – on credit. There was no money with which to buy them. In one month he would be in Ayudhya and, taking into account a further two weeks to transport the goods from Ayudhya to the coast, that would leave him only a month and a half to accomplish his mission: to expose the Moors and convince the Barcalon. There was no time to lose.

The day passed quickly, filled with thoughts of Sunida and

154

Persian fortunes. The terrain now became wilder and the road narrowed. The paddy fields were replaced by scrub, and mountains loomed up in the distance. Dusk was approaching and they soon halted and set up camp in a clearing at the foot of some forested lower slopes. Tomorrow they would be entering thick jungle and the journey would begin in earnest.

Fires were lit, a main one in the centre of the camp and three more on the perimeter, to keep the wild beasts out. This was tiger and rhinoceros country, as the nai politely explained by drawing a rough sketch of the beasts in the ground with his stick. They were not to leave the vicinity of the camp. He smiled courteously at the farangs and handed them mattresses filled with kapok, and muslin nettings to keep the mosquitoes out. Any moment now, Phaulkon knew, swarms of them would appear from nowhere to gorge themselves on this unexpected feast. For some reason which he had never fathomed, farangs seemed an even greater delicacy to those bloodsuckers than the natives.

The cooks were just setting about preparing the evening meal and slaves were fanning and sprinkling the holy elephant with water when a shout was heard in the distance and a group of riders, their horses streaming with sweat, came into view. There were half a dozen of them and they had three extra horses in tow. The riders were heavily armed with swords and fork-like harpoons of the type which were dipped in poison, and one of them carried a musket.

How strange to see horses in a place like this, thought Phaulkon. Though the animals were plentiful in Siam, the nature of the terrain and the climate made elephants by far the more suitable form of overland transport. Only they had the strength and bulk to negotiate the thick jungles which covered a good half of Siam's surface. Even the King was said to own not more than two thousand horses, Persians, gifts for the most part from the Shah of that country. The often torrid heat and the lack of grass left the horses short of stamina and they were only good for short spurts on relatively open terrain. Phaulkon wondered where this particular group was headed.

The horsemen dismounted and wai'd to the captain of the expedition. They glanced briefly at the farangs before prostrating themselves in front of the white elephant. The horsemen were some distance away and Phaulkon could not hear what was being said but it looked as if they were planning to stay, because they now tethered their horses and joined the nai around the main fire.

The Europeans were stiff and tired from the unaccustomed hours of elephant riding and both Phaulkon's bruises and Burnaby's foot were far from healed. Although it could not have been more than seven in the evening when they finished their meal of rice and vegetables and salted fish washed down with tea, they were nevertheless ready for sleep. The endless droning of the mosquitoes kept them awake a while longer until, eventually, even that could not keep them awake.

Phaulkon slept fitfully and woke long before dawn. An uneasy feeling had crept over him. His mind returned to the horsemen. Why had they not come to salute him? he wondered. Were they not aware that he was the recipient of the province's highest honour, the Order of the White Elephant, third class? Perhaps they were shy of approaching him, knowing there was no communication between them.

He looked around him now. The whole troop slept, but for the watchmen keeping the fires alive. The sounds of a thousand cicadas competed with the crackling of the firewood.

Several times that night he had awoken and observed the horsemen chatting far into the night with the nai. He had strained to overhear their conversation but the sounds of the jungle and the fire had drowned out the words. If he approached them now, they would simply stop talking, he was sure. Then he chided himself for being so suspicious. Why should the arrival of these horsemen have anything to do with him anyway? The fact that they were armed was normal. Bandits and highwaymen might be rare in Siam but the danger of wild animals more than explained the need for weapons. No wonder the population had all settled along the river banks and stuck to river travel, he reflected. But why the three extra horses? a voice persisted. Obviously for a change of mount, another voice replied.

He dozed off, he did not know for how long, and then instinctively he was awake again. One of the horsemen had got up and walked over to the main fire. He said something to the watchmen and they glanced over in Phaulkon's direction. This time he was not dreaming. He squinted at them through half-closed eyes.

One of the horses neighed. And then a sound came from behind.

It was faint – a rustling of leaves and the snap of a twig. Something was approaching from the other side, as well. He glanced at Burnaby and Ivatt. They were sound asleep. Burnaby's long legs were stretched full length and his injured foot rested on a log. Ivatt was curled up in a ball like a cat.

Phaulkon pretended to shift about in his sleep. He turned on his back and rolled his head to the other side. He lay still and squinted into the darkness. Holding his breath he listened intently. Beyond the sounds of the night, there was silence. Then he heard it again. He strained his ears. Something was moving out there. Was it a wild animal? Or someone creeping stealthily towards him?

He peered through the blackness in the direction of the sound. Gradually he made out a contour, barely visible in the obscurity, only a short distance away. It rose to a great height – a tree. And something behind the trunk was shifting. He stared at the moving shadow. It was upright. A human being, not an animal.

A muffled cry came from the direction of the shadow. Phaulkon rose on one elbow and strained towards the sound, now a series of low moans. He made out a figure bent double, both hands clutching an ankle. He swung under the muslin netting and approached cautiously. The figure looked up. '*Maengpong!*' it whispered in anguish, not knowing who was approaching. A scorpion, poor devil! thought Phaulkon.

Phaulkon turned to summon the watchmen, but the words froze in his throat. Burnaby was sitting up, blinking. One of the horsemen was standing over his head, holding a sword. Ivatt was staring into the muzzle of a cocked musket. Three more men now pointed their poisoned harpoons at Phaulkon. A vague glow was lighting up the sky. The camp was stirring.

'Sombat has been bitten by a scorpion!' shouted someone in the background.

'Those bites are almost always fatal,' said another voice.

'I think he's dead,' said a third.

'Cremate him,' ordered the leader of the horsemen, his musket still fixed on Ivatt. 'Then let's be on our way.' He pointed to the bundles that lay on the ground, the few items of clothing that the

Governor had given the farangs for their journey. 'Pick them up,' he ordered, looking at Phaulkon, his meaning unmistakable.

Phaulkon slowly gathered them together as he watched the body of the now dead man being carried over to the fire. In the glow of the flames, Phaulkon caught the nai's eye but the captain turned away, silently acknowledging his complicity. So he was in on this too, thought Phaulkon, with a sinking heart. There was little chance of taking on an army of fifty men.

'What the devil's going on, Constant?' asked Burnaby, now thoroughly awake.

'Shall we go for them, Constant?' called Ivatt. 'Just give the word.'

'Not now,' replied Phaulkon. 'We're heavily outnumbered. The captain is in on it too, I'm afraid.'

'In on what?' demanded Burnaby.

'I'm damned if I know,' replied Phaulkon. 'But if these horses have come from Ligor, they could have left half a day later than us and still have caught up with us by nightfall. Maybe van Risling has come up with something new.'

'You mean these thugs might be here on official business?' asked Burnaby anxiously.

Several men looked round at them angrily, gesturing for them to be silent. The leader of the horsemen was chanting a prayer and moments later the body of his companion was thrown into the flames. The whole camp watched as the body was consumed by the fire. Then the leader mounted his horse and beckoned to the farangs to follow.

Phaulkon glanced around him. The whole camp was awake now, observing their plight with strange indifference. There was little point in appealing for help from that quarter, he mused. Once more he stared questioningly at the nai but the captain again avoided his glance.

The whole thing had obviously been planned, or at least agreed to. But why?

'Where are they taking us?' asked Burnaby. 'We must demand an explanation.'

'In what language?' said Phaulkon.

'Isn't it about time you broke into Siamese?' asked Burnaby bitterly. 'What is the point of learning the bloody language if you're never going to use it? I can't understand why you didn't use it in the first place. Might have saved us all a hell of a lot of trouble.'

'Constant's done pretty well so far,' put in Ivatt. 'Let's find out where we're going first.'

The horses started neighing as the leader detached them. The three spare animals were led over to the farangs and they were ordered to mount. The armed horsemen were not discourteous but they looked as if they were not prepared to stand for any nonsense.

'Just follow orders for the present,' said Phaulkon to the others. 'Half the camp is armed.' It was true. Every second man carried a weapon against wild beasts. He and Ivatt helped Burnaby on to his little mount, avoiding any pressure on the wounded foot. The lanky Englishman's legs hung over the sides almost to the ground.

The odour of charred flesh filled the camp as they rode off in the same direction as they had come. Orange streaks began to dot the horizon and the dawn sky opened up above them through gaps in the trees. The leader rode in front with one of his companions while the other three brought up the rear, with the farangs in between. As the day grew lighter, their pace increased and soon they were galloping through the forest, covering ground at twice the speed of the previous day. The air was cool and fresh at this early hour and under any other circumstances the experience would have been a thoroughly pleasant one. Phaulkon considered the chances of escape but the leader had passed the musket to one of the riders in the rear and he did not relish being shot at close range from the back. Besides, Burnaby was wounded and he himself was in no great shape either to fight or to run.

As they emerged from the forest, a great orange sky opened up before them in a rare display of majesty and they settled down to a walk to give their perspiring mounts a rest. Phaulkon spoke for the first time since they had left the camp.

'We are covering the same ground as yesterday. It seems we are returning to Ligor. I see little point in running for it. Even if we could get away in our present condition we'd soon be lost. I don't think they plan to do away with us yet or they would have left us to the wild animals.'

'I bet the bloody Dutch are behind this,' muttered Burnaby.

159

'Carrot-beard said we hadn't heard the last of him.' The frustrated Dutchman, on hearing of their departure, had sent a note to that effect. He had not been there to see them off.

'Do you think the Governor's in on this?' asked Ivatt. 'He seemed like such a decent bloke in the end.'

'Who else?' replied Phaulkon. 'These people wouldn't dare take us back to Ligor without instructions. We're in some sort of trouble, I'm afraid.'

'Our best bet really is to run into another white elephant,' remarked Ivatt, and despite their predicament they all laughed. The horsemen turned to look at them suspiciously.

Around noon they halted under the shade of a sprawling banyan tree and dismounted. The horsemen lit a fire and boiled some rice in a black cauldron. They sprinkled bamboo shoots over it and offered some to the farangs in small bowls. There were no spoons and they all ate with their fingers.

Phaulkon was hoping to glean some information from their conversation but the horsemen hardly spoke two words. At one point he considered breaking into Siamese and asking them what this was all about, but then he thought better of it. They were unlikely to tell him much anyway, especially as he had nothing to bribe them with, so he might as well keep his knowledge of the language up his sleeve a little longer. They rested a while after the meal and when they rode on, the sun was high overhead. The farangs wound lengths of cloth round their heads to shield them.

Burnaby recognized a fork in the road where yesterday he had seen a black, foot-long venomous centipede which he knew to be as deadly as a scorpion, and he reckoned they were now not more than an hour or two from Ligor. They rode on in silence until they came upon a few scattered peasant huts with farm animals – chickens, pigs and water buffaloes – and then they knew they were approaching the outskirts of the town.

In the distance, three horsemen came into view, blocking the road with their mounts. Two of the riders were barechested while a third wore a white muslin shirt with three-quarter-length sleeves. A senior official with two slaves, thought Phaulkon. None of them appeared to be armed.

As they drew nearer, the Europeans recognized the man in the shirt. He was one of the Governor's aides, subordinate to the Palat, and he had a particularly snub, squat nose which was hard to mistake. Phaulkon remembered Ivatt questioning how the man could possibly breathe through it.

The aide saluted the farangs with the minimum of decorum and gave an order to the escort. The five horsemen handed over the musket, swords and poisoned arrows to the two shirtless newcomers who rode off with them. Then the Governor's aide beckoned to the farangs to follow him, and the original escort, now disarmed, dropped back some fifty paces to the rear. They continued to follow at a distance while the aide, alone with the farangs, took a seemingly circuitous route, avoiding both the Governor's palace and the centre of town.

It now occurred to Phaulkon that their party was meant to appear as unobtrusive as possible. That would explain the distant escort and the dropping of the arms. For some reason they were not to attract undue attention. They turned left towards the shore and soon reached a wide stretch of beach that extended as far as the eye could see. They rode in silence at a casual pace along the palm-fringed shore, until eventually the aide stopped and dismounted at the top of a hilly sandbank which afforded an extended view of the ocean. He beckoned to the others to do the same. Phaulkon glanced back and saw the escort still following at a distance. The aide shielded his eyes and stared out to sea. They followed his gaze. A nasty suspicion crept up on all of them. With mounting anxiety they watched and waited. The tide was far out and in the distance a couple of small waves broke and receded again. Then for a while the sea was flat.

Suddenly they saw it. A second or two later it was submerged again by an incoming wave, but the sight left a chill in their hearts. They stared, transfixed, hoping somehow that it had been an illusion which would never reappear. But it did, and for a much longer while this time.

Jutting out clearly from the ocean floor was the mouth of a cannon. One of the five from the master caster de Groot that might have made their fortune with the rebel Queen of Pattani.

Twelve

'You, the criminal, stand forward!' The Siamese, paralysed with fear, stood rooted to the spot. He was dressed only in a loincloth and on his right arm was a tatoo of Hanuman, the monkey god.

'Forward, I said!'

The prisoner edged forward.

'Stick out your tongue!'

The tongue rolled slowly out. The prisoner's frame began to shake spasmodically. His eyes opened and shut as if he could not decide whether he wanted to watch or not.

'On your knees!' The prisoner sank haltingly to the ground. Two burly men stepped forward and held the whimpering criminal fast. One steadied the head while the other yanked the jaw open and wedged a bamboo stick vertically against the roof of the mouth, holding it open.

The executioner now advanced wielding a sharp pointed knife. The prisoner's eyes stared at the curved blade, transfixed. With an abrupt movement the executioner raised his arm and thrust the blade deep inside the victim's mouth beyond the bamboo stick. With one swift slash he severed the tongue.

There was a shrill, muffled cry and the executioner held up the tongue briefly towards the Palat before handing it to a crouching slave. A second attendant proffered a young coconut and the executioner took it and thrust it firmly into the criminal's mouth. The flow of blood was temporarily stemmed and the man was led away.

The wiry Governor's deputy now turned his attention to the farangs. The three of them were lined up in full view of the proceedings. He eyed each of them carefully as if trying to make up his mind. Finally his gaze settled on Ivatt.

'This one first!' he barked.

They were in the Governor's courtyard by the great banyan tree. Armed guards were stationed at every exit. The Governor himself had not yet appeared and the Palat was overseeing the sentences. Apart from the executioner and his team, only two of

162

the Palat's assistants and a dozen slaves were present. It was not a public affair.

Ivatt was led towards the spot where the criminal had stood just in front of the great tree. The same brawny hands gripped the little man's head and his jaw was wrenched open and another bamboo stick inserted. A crouching slave held a young coconut ready. Ivatt glanced forlornly at Phaulkon.

The Greek's mind was reeling and his face and body were drenched in sweat. If Ivatt resisted or any of them made a run for it, he knew their punishment would be twice as harsh. It would be deemed the greatest insult to question the Governor's justice. Furthermore, with every exit blocked and armed guards outnumbering them four to one, there was no reasonable chance of escape. Nonetheless, he decided, if Ivatt struggled, they would have to make a run for it and take their chances. If not . . .

The expression on Ivatt's face was like a knife in Phaulkon's heart. The little man had become a friend as well as a completely trustworthy colleague, and for the first time since Phaulkon had known him the twinkle had entirely disappeared from Ivatt's eyes. Without turning his head, Phaulkon heard Burnaby retch beside him.

The massive teak doors of the audience chamber now swung open and the Governor emerged in ceremonial dress, his conical hat at a slight angle. He was closely followed by Sunida, looking haggard and distraught.

The mandarin sucked in his breath and contemplated the scene for a moment from the top of the steps, his hands crossed in front of his portly belly. His usual air of courtesy was absent and he eyed the farangs coldly, without so much as an acknowledgement. It was the first time the farangs had seen him since their return to Ligor some three hours earlier. Sunida glanced timorously at Phaulkon. Her eyes shone with fear and her lips were parted in a slight tremor.

The Governor descended the steps. 'Remove his tongue!' he boomed.

The two burly men pushed Ivatt to his knees. The executioner stepped forward. There was a deathly hush in the courtyard. He raised his knife.

'*Yoooot! Mai tong!*' The words shattered the silence. The executioner's knife stood poised in mid-air. Phaulkon threw

163

himself at the Governor's feet. 'Stop!' he repeated in Siamese, 'I beg you, Your Excellency. I will explain everything. Do not harm this man.' The form of address was impeccable, the Siamese word perfect. The audience, and the mandarin, were stunned.

'I am an envoy of His Most Gracious Majesty the King.' At the realization that His Majesty's name had just been spoken, every man except Burnaby fell on his face to the ground. Only Ivatt remained kneeling, his eyes blinking in the confusion.

At that moment, Joop van Risling, followed by the Malay interpreter, emerged from the Governor's audience chamber, breathing excitedly. 'What did I tell you?' he blurted triumphantly. 'I knew it was him.' He glanced gleefully from Phaulkon to the prostrate Governor. Then he turned to the interpreter. 'We will not be requiring your services for the time being, eh, Pieter? Ha, ha!'

The Governor was the first to rise and Phaulkon, still prone, quickly addressed him. 'I, a worthless slave, beg the honour of speaking with Your Excellency alone. About matters of great importance.' Despite his obvious fury, the Governor could not help but register astonishment at the fluency of Phaulkon's language. This farang was using precisely the correct forms of address to one of his rank, which even his own minions sometimes got wrong.

The Governor hesitated barely a fraction of a second then nodded curtly and moved towards his audience chamber. At the top of the steps he dismissed Sunida and turned to the Palat.

'The executioner will wait here with the prisoner. No one is to leave the courtyard until authorized. And see that the tall farang's mess is cleaned up.'

Phaulkon followed the Governor up the steps with the Dutchman close on his heels, dragging the Malay interpreter with him. At the entrance to the chamber Phaulkon wheeled round on the Dutchman.

'Your presence is not needed here, van Risling,' he said in Dutch. 'I have private matters to discuss with His Excellency.'

'We'll see about that!' the Dutchman exploded. 'Who are you to give orders anyway? You will soon have no tongue to give them with.' He turned to the interpreter. 'Tell the Governor I must attend this meeting. This devil here is not to be trusted. Absolutely not.'

Before the Malay could render the translation, Phaulkon had spoken to the Governor. 'Your Excellency, I, a speck of dust, have sensitive matters of state to reveal to the mighty Lord. They can be for Your Excellency's ears only.'

They were now standing at the threshold of the audience chamber and the Governor considered a moment before turning to the interpreter.

'Ask Mr Lidrim to wait outside.' As the words were translated from Malay, the Dutchman's face turned purple. He opened his mouth as if to speak and then thought better of it. Muttering repeated obscenities he stormed out into the courtyard. He looked venomously back at Phaulkon.

'I may not be present at this meeting, slave of the Turk, or even in the boxing ring with you, but Godverdomme, I promise to be there at your funeral.'

Ignoring the outburst, Phaulkon followed the Governor inside. He prostrated himself on the Persian rug while the mandarin, quietly fuming, ordered his guards to remain outside on full alert. He turned contemptuously on Phaulkon. 'You have a lot of explaining to do and very little time in which to do it. Begin.'

'Your Excellency, I, a hair, know how you must feel, and I cannot tell you how difficult this has been for me all along. Your unrivalled hospitality, your generous nature, your great wisdom and your sense of justice have made my task the more unpleasant. And if it had not been assigned to me by the Lord of Life himself through His Excellency the Pra Klang, I would surely have declined this mission in the first place.' He paused. 'You see, Your Excellency, I have been sent to spy on you.' There was a momentary silence before the mandarin burst out laughing.

'Considering what little time you have before you, you'd be well advised to employ it more intelligently.' He leaned forward: 'Because that is the most preposterous suggestion I have ever heard.' His laughter rose again and then died abruptly. His eyes narrowed. 'It is also treasonous.'

Despite the menacing tone, and the Governor's furious indignation, Phaulkon thought he sensed the barest hesitation. He was fighting for his life now and, however slim, this was his only chance. He would have to pursue it to the end. 'I was chosen, Your Excellency, as no one would ever suspect a farang of, er . . . playing the role of commissioner.'

165

In the event of being caught out on the language question, this was the strategy Phaulkon had decided on, and he had rehearsed it a dozen times. His friend, Mestre Phanik, who knew more about the hierarchy of power in Siam than any outsider alive, had once told him that the fear of royal spies was the Achilles heel of every provincial governor.

'If you will excuse me, Your Excellency,' continued Phaulkon, 'no farang is expected to have much knowledge of your language. Thus no honourable governor would be likely to guard himself in the presence of a mere hair such as I. His Most Gracious Majesty personally conceived of the scheme,' he added in a confidential tone, 'and I could be executed for having revealed it.'

'Come now,' scoffed the Governor, 'what do you take me for? You are wasting everybody's time, including the executioner's. What about the cannon then?' The mandarin was growing visibly angry. 'Why did you deny their existence?'

'I was transporting them to Songkhla, on the orders of His Excellency the Pra Klang,' replied Phaulkon without hesitation, 'I was under oath not to reveal their existence.'

'*Their* existence? There was more than one?'

'There were five, Your Excellency.'

'And why were you under oath?'

'To ensure complete surprise. As Your Excellency knows, the people of Songkhla are loyal subjects of His Majesty. I was ordered to teach them to operate the cannon so they could deal a quick death blow to the Pattani rebels who have dared to defy the Lord of Life.'

'You have, of course, a letter of authorization to that effect?'

'Unfortunately, Your Excellency, it is at the bottom of the sea, along with the rest of my possessions.'

'How convenient,' observed the Governor with undisguised sarcasm. He leaned forward and casually extracted a nut from his golden betel box. He chewed on it thoughtfully. He had not been having an easy time, he reflected, since those fishermen had reported sighting a strange object protruding from the ocean. Having to execute a man he had only just honoured with the highest decoration in the province would make him a laughing stock. The people might not know a cannon from an eyeglass but every last peasant would have heard of the honours he had bestowed on the farang boxer. Worse than that, he had sent a

166

glowing report to the Pra Klang in Ayudhya, not only extolling the farang's virutes but even suggesting the Government might be able to use his services in some way. Damn this glib, two-faced farang. And to think he had even liked him! The report had left two days ago by elephant courier and there was no way of intercepting it now. The whole affair was a severe embarrassment, and potentially dangerous for him. How could he expect to retain his position as Governor when the Pra Klang discovered that he had conferred his province's highest honour on a smuggler? Even if he tried to suppress news of the matter, the Dutch farang, who was seeking the removal from his country of these English, would be bound to draw attention to the cannon and spread the word all over Ayudhya.

Already he had had to disarm the escort that had brought the farangs back to Ligor, for fear of starting rumours. All the guards had been sworn to secrecy on pain of death for themselves and their families. Now there was the added question of all those who had heard the farang speak Siamese in the courtyard. They would have to be silenced too.

Was this farang's fantastic tale even remotely possible? he wondered. One part of him almost began to wish it were. It would certainly save a great deal of embarrassment. But a farang working in internal security? The notion was ridiculous. His Majesty would never stoop to such things, even if this farang did speak the language like a native. Although that in itself, he had to admit, was astounding.

The farang seemed to read his thoughts. 'Your Excellency, I, a speck of dust, understand full well your reasons for doubting my explanations. I have no letter of authorization for the cannon and no identification to prove my status as commissioner. I kept my knowledge of Siamese from you and only revealed it when you threatened to torture my colleague. If you will forgive the presumption, I would not have felt any differently in Your Excellency's place.' He paused. 'There is perhaps only one way for me to prove my innocence, though it will be awkward to explain to His Excellency the Pra Klang later on.' He hesitated, while the mandarin observed him impassively.

'Your Excellency, I offer to remain in your custody while you send to Ayudhya for confirmation of my status. I would, however, entreat you to restrict your inquiries to the cannon only, for if it were known that I had revealed my role as commissioner, I will surely be executed. Perhaps when the truth of the cannon is confirmed, Your Excellency will accept the truth of my other role as well.' Phaulkon was well aware of the tremendous risk he was running but the executioner was still awaiting orders outside. He needed above all to gain time. The mandarin's fury at the deception as well as his mortifying loss of face could result at any moment in the order for Phaulkon's execution.

The Governor's lips parted in a wry smile. 'So, if I understand you correctly, Mr Forcon, you were ordered to deliver the cannon to Songkhla, two days' travel south of here, and to spy on my province at the same time? You are indeed a remarkable man.'

'Your Excellency, I was to put into Ligor for provisions en route to Songkhla. What could be more natural? And I was to remain here a few days to make my report. If you had insisted on a search of my cargo, my documents would have been perfectly in order. I might add, Your Excellency, that my report would have contained nothing but praise for your wise and just rule.'

Once more the Governor's expression resumed its usual inscrutability. He helped himself to another betel nut. The farang's suggestion to remain in Ligor as hostage might do more than just keep the man's head on his shoulders a little longer, he reflected. It might also present him, the Governor, with a face-saving solution. He could send the tall farang back to Ayudhya to obtain a new set of documents – if they existed – and keep the boxer here as hostage. If he sent the small farang to Ayudhya as well, it would not look as if anyone were being held prisoner. He would find a reasonable public excuse for retaining the boxer a while longer in his province, as his guest of course. He smiled to himself. He would send the other two back by boat. That could explain why they had not continued overland in the first place. Not being accustomed to elephants, the farangs had been taken violently ill. At the same time he would send a new dispatch to the Pra Klang, advising him of the discovery of the cannon, requesting confirmation of the medium farang's story and explaining his own precaution in retaining him hostage. He looked at Phaulkon and smiled for the first time.

'Your suggestion seems to me a sound one, Mr Forcon. I shall
168

send your friends back to Ayudhya in my boat. You will no longer be allowed to communicate with them until they return with the proper documents proving this mission of yours. You will be my "guest" here until that time, and quarters will be prepared for you in the main house. Sunida may keep you company if you wish.' It would be useful to have that loyal, alert girl spying on him, now that they could converse with each other, reflected the mandarin with satisfaction.

'Ah, and one more thing. That report you were preparing on my province. Would you complete it by dawn tomorrow? We will dispatch it to Ayudhya by the same boat.' It had always been the Siamese way, to keep all one's options open.

'Of course, Your Excellency,' replied Phaulkon, unsure how far to count his blessings. But at least for the time being he and the others would remain alive.

The Governor rose to his feet. 'Kling!' he summoned. The Palat crawled in noiselessly from the adjacent room. 'I want every man in the courtyard brought to me here, every last slave who witnessed the recent proceedings. And send the other farangs back to their quarters. The boxer will remain in the main house. He will be allowed no communication with the others.'

'Mighty Lord, I receive your orders.'

The evening sun shone through the open window, revealing a channel of dust across the low table on which Phaulkon was writing. He was in the main palace now, in a room almost identical to the one in the guest house.

He was writing his report to the Pra Klang, the great Barcalon, a man he had never even met. The only thing he was sure of was the correct form of address. The rest would have to be concocted with the help perhaps, willing or unwitting, of Sunida. But what if the report were really sent to the Barcalon? He was merely staying his execution, he knew. Yet if he did not write the report he would be admitting his deceit and this time the Governor would not hesitate. Better to be executed later than now. In the back of his mind, there was always the meagre chance, the distant hope that if he phrased it perfectly, the report would never reach the Barcalon.

He felt her presence in the room now, though his back was turned to her. She coughed lightly and he looked round. 'Sunida!

169

How glad I am to see you.' She had completely disappeared since the dreadful experience in the courtyard that afternoon.

'My Lord,' she replied simply. She lowered herself on to her haunches not to be higher than him. Then her face assumed a pained expression. 'Forgive me,' she began apprehensively. 'But why did my Lord not tell me he spoke our language?'

Phaulkon had been prepared for the question. 'I am afraid I am not at liberty to explain. Suffice it to say that it has nothing to do with the great respect I have for you.'

Sunida inclined her head: 'Perhaps my Lord wanted to discover things that he would otherwise not have discovered?' Phaulkon ignored the remark, impressed at the same time by her intuition.

'I requested permission to take you with me, Sunida. I would have spoken Siamese to you as soon as we had reached Ayudhya.'

Sunida appeared to cheer up somewhat. 'His Excellency asked me whether I would have accepted to accompany you,' she said coyly.

'And what did you reply?'

'I said it would be up to His Excellency, of course.'

'Because His Excellency is your patron?'

Sunida hesitated. 'Because he is my uncle.'

Phaulkon was caught unawares. 'Your uncle?'

Sunida nodded. 'He is the younger brother of my father who . . . was killed by the farangs . . . the Dutch farangs I mean, during the blockade of the Menam Chao Phraya.'

Phaulkon was completely taken aback. 'You mean twenty years ago when the Dutch blockaded the river to demand concessions?'

'That is right, my Lord.' She lowered her head sadly. 'I was only just born and my honourable father was the general in charge of our troops.'

'How terrible. You must hate the Dutch and all farangs for that matter,' said Phaulkon, with genuine feeling.

'I do not hate anybody, my Lord. There are good and bad people everywhere, in my country too.'

'And your mother, Sunida, what happened to her?'

'She married again, a Burmese mandarin, when I was very young. My uncle did not want me to be brought up in Ava, among the Burmese – they are our rivals, you know – so he kept

170

me here. My uncle's wife died in childbirth so I have been like a daughter to him. Beneath his stern appearance, he is a kind and generous man.'

'And a lucky one, too, to have you, Sunida.' In the light of these revelations Phaulkon wanted to ask her why her uncle ever allowed her to consort with him, a farang of all people, but he felt it was not an appropriate question at this time.

Sunida looked at him steadily. 'In case my Lord is wondering why His Excellency allowed me to spend time with you, it is because he has taken a great liking to you personally. He abhors the Dutch and thinks our country is increasingly at their beck and call. He feels strongly that perhaps you or your countrymen can help us restore our dignity.'

Phaulkon thought of the discovery of the cannon and doubly cursed his luck. What could he not have achieved with the good will of such a powerful mandarin behind him?

'And did His Excellency give a reason for his refusal to let you accompany me?' asked Phaulkon.

Sunida lowered her head modestly. 'His Excellency was most gracious. He said I was irreplacable in his dance troupe.'

As well as in his heart, Phaulkon almost wanted to say. He looked at her now. She was beautiful beyond measure, as well as clever and wise. In typical Siamese fashion, he sensed that behind the natural coyness and the outward submissiveness lay a strong will that knew just how and when to have its way. She was the personification of Siamese womanhood. He wondered now whether she had been sent to spy on him. Why else would the Governor have allowed her to keep him company? He would have to be careful what he said to her but at the same time he needed more information for his report. And he loved being with her.

He observed her quietly. Would this gentle, sensitive creature really betray him? He felt a sudden pang at the thought of losing her. Somehow he had to escape from here, and the Governor, her uncle, might never release her. It saddened him to think how he must have hurt her – even ridiculed her – by concealing his knowledge of the language from her. He remembered how she had struggled to express herself in sign language. And now, graciously and without apparent rancour, she seemed to accept his explanation. Or rather his lack of it. Smiling demurely, she met his gaze and he felt a craving to hold her – and to apologize to her for everything.

'I am sorry for the terrible things you witnessed today,' he said, with genuine feeling.

'I was very frightened, my Lord. For the little farang and for you.' She hesitated. 'His Excellency ordered me to forget all I have seen and never to speak of it again. I must obey.'

'It was all a terrible misunderstanding,' said Phaulkon.

'My Lord,' replied Sunida. She looked up at him. 'Will my Lord be staying long?' There was both hope and fear in her voice.

Phaulkon hesitated. 'A while longer, anyway.'

'My Lord.'

'I still have matters to discuss with His Excellency.' He appeared to consider the question. 'His Excellency is such a fine man. I imagine he is well liked in the province.'

'Oh yes, my Lord. He is just and the people love him. He is like a father to us all. Even the poorest farmer can bring his complaint to him.' A cloud came over her face. 'I have heard this is not always the case in other provinces. The Lord Buddha has indeed blessed us.'

'Have you ever visited other provinces?' asked Phaulkon.

'Oh no, my Lord. But perhaps someday I will see Ayudhya. Who knows.' She sighed. 'They say it is the greatest city in the whole world. But you, my Lord, who have seen everything, tell me, is it true?'

'It is indeed, Sunida; there is no finer place. And one day, by the grace of God, I will take you there.'

Sunida inclined her head. 'If it pleases my Lord.'

'Perhaps if you learn to dance a little less well, His Excellency will release you.'

She laughed. 'Oh, I could not do that, my Lord.' She looked mischievously across at him. 'But perhaps there are other ways.'

'And what might they be?' he asked, with genuine interest.

'I am afraid I am not at liberty to explain.' She laughed delightedly like a child. Phaulkon laughed too. He longed again to hold her. But his body ached so terribly and there were pressing matters to attend to.

'Tell me more about this wonderful province, and its kind and just Governor. I must have something to tell my friends when I return.' It must appear that there was no doubt in his mind that as soon as the new set of documents arrived to vindicate his story, he would be returning to Ayudhya.

Sunida considered for a moment. 'I don't know whether I should tell you this. It is really a secret. But I so much want His Excellency and you . . . not to have any more "misunderstandings".' She paused. 'You see, His Excellency really loves you. It was he who saved you.'

'What do you mean?'

'During the big storm, some fishermen ran to inform His Excelllency that a ship was in trouble. His Excellency came down to the shore with the big-eye.'

'The big-eye?'

'Yes, you know, the thing the Dutch farangs hold in front of their eye to make things look bigger.'

'A telescope!' muttered Phaulkon in English.

'Well, the Dutch farangs gave a big-eye to His Excellency for his birthday. When His Excellency arrived at the shore, the Dutch farang was already looking through his own big-eye. He told His Excellency the boat was flying the English flag and that he had received a report it was carrying contraband. It should be left to sink with all the men aboard.'

'How do you know all this?' asked Phaulkon, surprised.

'The Palat . . .' She hesitated.

'What about the Palat?'

'He was . . . interested in me,' said Sunida, bashfully.

Phaulkon felt an unexpected twinge of jealousy. 'And so he told you all these things to impress you?'

Sunida inclined her head. 'My Lord.'

'Go on,' said Phaulkon, his voice suddenly harsh. He knew he was not the first in Sunida's life, but it was the first time he had been obliged to confront the thought. And it troubled him.

'His Excellency needed the special rope the Dutch farangs keep in their warehouse. My uncle is a devout Buddhist with great respect for human life. He convinced the Dutch farang that if he helped save the English ship and there really was contraband aboard, all the English farangs in Siam would be asked to leave. After that the Dutch farang could not do enough to save the drowning men.'

Phaulkon was listening with half an ear. His mind kept

173

returning to the Palat. What had Sunida meant when she said he was interested in her? Did that mean . . . His eyes narrowed.

Sunida noticed the change in his expression. 'Forgive me, my Lord, if I have offended you,' she said, prostrating herself.

Phaulkon pulled himself together. What was happening to him? Why was he affected so? He could not recall his emotions running away with him like this before. Then he saw the expression of woe on her face and his heart melted.

Despite his aching body, he took her in his arms. Discreetly he inhaled the skin of her cheeks and shoulders. 'Oh my Lord,' she murmured sweetly. He pulled her down on to the mattress and she slipped out of her panung and lay beside him. She closed her eyes and gave herself up entirely to him. He took her and made love to her, with more tenderness and gentle passion than he had ever known in his life.

The prostrate Palat handed Phaulkon's report up to the Governor.

'You are sure it can be sealed again without it being noticed?' inquired His Excellency.

'Quite sure, Your Excellency.'

'Good, you may leave now.'

'Mighty Lord, I receive your orders,' said Kling, crawling discreetly backwards out of sight.

Attached to the report, which was written on rice parchment, was a letter of introduction. The Governor began to peruse it and his eyes grew wider with every line. It was addressed to His Most Exalted Excellency, the Pra Klang, Royal Minister for Foreign Affairs and the Treasury, Ayudhya, and was dated this twelfth month on the twentieth day after the full moon in the Year of the Great Mare. The report was marked 'Confidential'.

Your Excellency, I, a hair, have the honour to present the report of my findings in the Royal Province of Ligor.

I, a speck of dust, must regrettably begin by informing Your Excellency that due to an unfortunate misunderstanding, the Governor of this province has seen fit to detain me here so that I will be unable to resume my duties at the Ministry until such time as Your Excellency will be kind enough to set the record straight. I, the dust of your feet, very much regret this

174

enforced absence, and beg Your Excellency to understand the circumstances.

On Your Excellency's explicit instructions, I denied the existence of the cannon after the shipwreck. But upon their subsequent discovery, Your Excellency will appreciate that I had little choice but to disclose the truth. Despite my admission and notwithstanding the fact that he had just awarded me the highest honour in his province, the Governor was not disposed to believe me.

The Governor blanched and read on.

The Honourable Governor is in every other respect so wise and benevolent a ruler that I must confess to being confused at so blatant a misjudgement. Despite my detention, however, I bear the Governor no rancour and, if Your Excellency will forgive this slave's presumptuousness, I have even considered presenting the Governor with the cannon as a gift. This, I believe, Your Excellency would appreciate on two counts. In the first place, the single cannon would, on its own, not be sufficient to destroy the Pattani rebels and secondly, by presenting it to the Governor as a gift from the English Company, the over-confident Dutch might take heed.

Finally, Your Excellency, I, a speck of dust on your foot, enclose a report of my findings in the province, while assuring Your Excellency that my overriding desire is to return to my post as quickly as possible and serve the country I love so well. May the Lord Buddha, and Your Most Exalted Excellency, forgive the Governor his error of judgement.

The Governor had grown noticeably agitated. The written forms of address to one so exalted in rank were flawless. How could a farang possibly be familiar with them if he were not in the habit of addressing him? he wondered nervously.

He now turned to the actual report. It contained an account of the shipwreck and the discovery of the cannon and was followed by a remarkably detailed description of all the farang had observed in Ligor since his arrival: the state of contentment of the population, the condition of the marketplace, the extent of gambling at the boxing match and the general level of respect for the Governor.

The mandarin gripped the page more firmly now and went over the previous paragraph again. It could not be! Oh Lord Buddha, had the farang been somehow able to elicit this information from the Palat? Because only the Palat knew. But how?

Following the description of the ceremony in the courtyard in which the fishermen had re-enacted the farangs' rescue, there was an accurate rendition of the argument which had ensued between the Dutchman and the Governor over the fate of the Englishmen. While the Dutch farang had advocated leaving them to drown, the Governor had objected to this course. The report disclosed unequivocally that it was the Governor who had insisted on saving the lives of the English farangs. Amazing! The Governor began for the first time seriously to believe in Phaulkon's story. Besides, the cannon would look most imposing in his courtyard. No other province would be able to lay claim to such prestige. 'Kling!' he summoned.

The Palat hurried in on all fours. 'Mighty Lord, I receive your orders.'

'Have you been speaking to any of the farangs?'

'The dust of your feet is not able to converse in their tongue, Your Excellency.'

'But what about the one who speaks Siamese?'

'I, a hair, have not had the opportunity of addressing him since his knowledge of our language was discovered, Your Excellency.'

'Then how could he know the details of the rescue on the beach?' The Governor tapped the report with his fingers.

The Palat looked uncomfortable. 'I, a speck of dust, cannot explain, Mighty Lord.'

The Governor grunted, dissatisfied, and handed the report back to the Palat. 'See that it is properly sealed, and keep it in a safe place. Send the farang to me immediately!'

'Mighty Lord, I receive your orders.'

The two men sat opposite each other, observing all the outward forms of decorum, but with their minds working furiously.

'So, Mr Forcon, you have completed your report. It will leave with your friends shortly. As I said, you will remain in my custody until their return.' He paused. 'And your cannon too.'

176

This was the opening Phaulkon had been waiting for. The Governor would, of course, have read his report, though he would never admit to having opened so confidential a document. 'I would beg to have the honour of presenting the cannon to Your Excellency as a gift from the English Company. If I may say so, it would look splendid in the courtyard of your palace. A reminder to all who enter of the omnipotence of this great province.'

The Governor stared at him for a moment. 'And you would be able to move it here?'

'That should be possible, Your Excellency.'

'Good, then. It should be done today before the other farangs leave, in case their help is needed.'

Phaulkon paused. 'Your Excellency?'

'Yes, Mr Forcon?'

'While I was writing my report to His Excellency the Pra Klang, I could not help thinking how angry the exalted Minister will be at my not returning immediately to Ayudhya to report the loss of the cannon. He will surely want to take alternative action to crush the rebels in Pattani, now that his troops in Songkhla will no longer be supplied with the guns.'

'All that will be in my report, Mr Forcon, so His Excellency will be adequately informed.'

'Of course, Your Excellency. But I will not be there to answer any questions in person or to receive his commands. Suppose the Royal Minister wants to send me straight back to Songkhla with an alternative plan?'

'What exactly are you driving at, Mr Forcon?' asked the Governor, a slight smile on his lips.

'Only that, in fairness, Your Excellency, I feel I should be exonerated. I humbly request that you write a letter explaining my position: that I am being held here on your orders and that my requests to report for duty in person to Ayudhya have been refused. That way the Royal Minister's undoubted anger can no longer be directed at me. That is all I ask, Your Excellency.'

The Governor made an effort to hide his discomfort. What if by some chance this farang's mission were really genuine? The rebels in Pattani had indeed risen up and Ayudhya was preparing to crush them, he knew. What if this farang had secretly been chosen as the key to it all? It was just conceivable. He was

177

talented enough, that was obvious. And Ayudhya would have wanted to keep the Dutch out of this at all costs. On the other hand, what if the farang were an imposter, a scheming rogue with a highly developed sense of theatre? It was a nasty predicament. Was there an alternative, a compromise, a way once again of keeping all his options open? he wondered. An idea struck him.

'You are not the Chief of the English Company yourself, are you, Mr Forcon?'

'No, Your Excellency, Mr Burnaby is.'

'H'm.' The Governor paused. 'Perhaps it would be more appropriate for the head of station to remain hostage here, rather than his second-in-command. He would, of course, be released as soon as his deputy returned with copies of the appropriate authorizations.'

Phaulkon's heart leapt, even though he could already imagine the dismay on Burnaby's face. But of the two of them, he would have by far the better chance in Ayudhya of extricating them from this mess.

'As you command, Your Excellency. Mr Burnaby is, as you say, the officer in charge. But could I request that Mr Ivatt leave with me too? His presence is sorely needed at the English factory.'

'I think Mr Burnaby's need for company during this period will be greater than yours, Mr Forcon,' said the mandarin slyly.

'As you wish, Your Excellency,' said Phaulkon, not wishing to prejudice his existing gains. 'May I ask then that you kindly return to me the copy of my report to His Excellency the Pra Klang. I will need to present it to the Royal Minister on arrival.'

'Do not concern yourself with that, Mr Forcon. The report will be sent ahead by special courier.'

Phaulkon was silent for a moment. Damn. He might have known the wily governor would not return it that easily. But would he really send it on ahead? If he did, what kind of a reception would he find in Ayudhya? Phaulkon shuddered at the thought.

'And how long will my colleagues remain here, Your Excellency?' he asked, trying to get his mind off the consequences of the report.

'Until their departure is authorized by Ayudhya.'

178

'And may I consult with them before leaving?'

'There can be no communication.'

'May Sunida come with me?'

'Not now. Perhaps later, when the dust has settled.'

'Definitely then?'

'Possibly.'

'But will she be entirely free here?'

'As before your arrival. She is the leader of my dance troupe.'

'May I use your boat to return to Ayudhya?'

'I will need it back of course.'

'May I leave immediately?'

'As soon as you have moved the cannon to the palace.'

'Your Excellency is most gracious.'

The two men bowed deeply to each other, palms joined respectfully above their foreheads. Phaulkon knew that once verbally agreed, a deal was as good as sealed. In Siam one never needed to count one's change at the market place. The new farang arrivals who inadvertently did so caused irreparable offence to the Siamese.

That afternoon at low tide, with the help of three bull elephants, six lengths of double-thickness cord made from the green bark of the coconut tree, and an army of peasants with shovels and prayers, the cannon was pulled from the sea and hoisted on to a reinforced cart drawn by water buffalo.

In a grand ceremony attended by the court and every dignitary in the town, the cannon was officially presented to His Excellency the Governor by Constantine Phaulkon in the name of the English Company. The services of two Malay interpreters were used throughout. Burnaby and Ivatt were declared absent on account of indisposition. They had been taken seriously ill following their elephant ride and would be unable to travel to Ayudhya for the time being. Also indisposed was the Dutch factor. He was, in fact, busily writing a furious report to his superior in Ayudhya. It strongly recommended that a dispatch be sent to English headquarters in Madras detailing the clandestine activities of their factors in Siam. It ended by urging their immediate expulsion from the country.

*

179

The Governor and the court were at the jetty to see Phaulkon off. The Governor's boat, proudly flying the blue and white flag of Ligor, gently swayed with the swell as slaves, dextrously balancing sacks of provisions on their heads, mounted the steep bamboo steps to the deck.

The events of the previous day had been carefully suppressed and news of Phaulkon's departure brought everyone of consequence to the jetty, bearing gifts for His Excellency the Pra Klang. The honoured farang, recipient of the Order of the White Elephant third class, was leaving the province. It was furthermore rumoured that he was carrying a letter of introduction to the exalted Pra Klang from their noble Governor.

The ladies of the court were unexpectedly present, bejewelled and barefoot, and dressed again in their becoming black panungs. Sunida, radiant as usual among them, strove to catch Phaulkon's eye. They had spent the last night together, both with a heavy heart at parting. He turned frequently in her direction and the looks that passed between them spoke louder than any words. 'I will be back for you,' his eyes were saying. 'And I will be waiting,' hers responded.

Conspicuously absent again were van Risling, Burnaby and Ivatt. The Dutchman had sent an angry note to Phaulkon saying that though he might have fooled the Siamese, the Dutch had certainly not laid this episode to rest. Nor would they until every last Englishman and their Mediterranean lackeys had been buried or expelled from Siam.

Phaulkon had been forbidden any further communication with Burnaby so that he had been spared Burnaby's undoubted recriminations. He was sure that the older man would think he had somehow traded his freedom for his chief's. Phaulkon regretted not having had the opportunity of assuring both him and Ivatt that their release from Ligor would be his primary objective in Ayudhya. He felt sure that Ivatt would know that, but Burnaby's fretting would probably cloud his judgement.

The Governor now approached him with his interpreter. It was Pieter again, and Phaulkon smiled at him, knowing instinctively that the young man had taken a liking to him. Phaulkon would not forget the Eurasian's role in translating word for word what he had said yesterday, however unflattering to the Dutch. The young man glanced at Phaulkon and observed with admiration the decoration round his neck. He thought again of Phaulkon's quick mind and his fine manners. Perhaps his own father, reflected Pieter nostalgically, had been such a farang.

'So, Mr Forcon,' said the mandarin, addressing himself through the interpreter, 'your stay with us has come to an end. It has been a fruitful and eventful one and we have been honoured by your visit. I might add that some of our boxers here will be studying new techniques in preparation for your return.' There was pleasant laughter from the crowd. 'We trust you will be back soon,' he added pointedly. 'In the meantime, may the Lord Buddha and your own gods guide you safely on this journey.'

Phaulkon prostrated himself one last time.

'Your Excellency's hospitality has been most lavish and I am only sorry to further burden you with my colleagues' indisposition. I hope they will be able to make the journey soon.'

'We all hope so, Mr Forcon.'

The great bat-winged sail was hoisted, the weighted wooden anchor raised and Phaulkon climbed on board, casting a final glance in the direction of Sunida. Then the junk moved sleekly out into the blue waters of the Gulf of Siam.

Thirteen

The little slave girl, Lek, sat cross-legged in the royal kitchens, finishing her morning meal of rice and fish. She added a final touch of fish-roe sauce to what remained and mixed it with her fingers in the little bowl. Holding the bowl in one hand, she scooped the contents into her mouth with the thumb and fore-fingers of the other.

Around her, a score of other slaves were finishing their meals too, all sitting cross-legged at one end of the extensive kitchens while at the other, white-gloved cooks were busy plucking whole chickens and placing them in steaming black cauldrons. The gloves indicated that they were destined for the royal apartments, for no food prepared for the royal palate could be touched by human hands. Lek placed the empty bowl in a large basin full of water, wai'd to the cooks and left.

Crouching low as she walked, she made her way as unobtrusively as possible along the ever-ascending corridors to the apartments of her mistress, the Princess Queen. At the end of each corridor she climbed another set of steps to the next level, for there were seven levels of corridors in the Inner Palace and the closer one ventured to the royal apartments, the more elevated was the level. The Princess Queen's apartments were situated off the sixth corridor and only the Lord of Life himself was higher.

She had now reached the fifth elevation and already the corridors were more spacious and the decor more awesome. The wooden statues that lined the lower corridors were here of blue and white porcelain, the plain white walls replaced by lacquered panels and the wood floor covered in soft Persian rugs which muted the sounds of the constant traffic of Outer Pages, slaves and eunuchs. An occasional window now looked out on to the glistening streams and ponds of the manicured gardens below, and the late morning sunlight poured in to relieve the austere brass lanterns of the lower corridors.

One more set of steps and she would reach the sixth corridor, along both sides of which stretched the extensive quarters of the Princess Queen. Lek always felt a flurry of apprehension as she approached these venerable surroundings. The Princess Queen was strict and exacting, but especially recently, since her love for Prince Chao Fa Noi, the Lord of Life's younger brother, consumed her. Her moods were unpredictable, and now more than ever she had turned to her books, seeking solace and counsel from the adventures of Sita, that other princess from the pages of the Ramayana.

Lek was the Princess Queen's chief reader, and though she knew that she performed her task well, it was not until she had passed the first few pages and seen that her mistress was quite engrossed that Lek was able to relax. For the next few hours the Princess Queen would be absorbed in the world that Lek's skilful and versatile tones would recreate for her.

Gingerly the slave girl nudged open the carved teakwood panels of the first door on the right and entered the antechamber. She glanced up at the great gilded mirror that the farang priests had presented to her mistress. It stood above the ancient manuscript chest that the diminutive Lek could hardly see over. She looked around her surreptitiously and then briefly stood on her toes to catch her vision in the mirror. The plain brown face framed by short cropped hair stared back at her. How different to the well-groomed visage of the Princess Queen, she reflected, with its large black eyes, its thick hair sleekly oiled and scented, the lips painted with white pommade, and the sparkling rubies hanging from her ears. The tall, imposing Princess Queen did not have to stand on *her* toes to catch her reflection in the mirror. But then the noblest blood in the land ran through her veins, for her mother, the late Queen Achamalisee, was after all her father's own sister. Since the death of the Queen, the Lord of Life had seen fit to elevate her to the rank of Princess Queen, investing in her all the duties of her late mother. So now, at the age of twenty-one, the King's only daughter was sovereign Queen, holding sway over the five hundred women of the palace – consorts, eunuchs and slaves – and sometimes even accompanying the Lord of Life on his travels.

It was Her Majesty's duty to mete out punishment to the deserving, shaving the heads of some and slicing the lips of others. The little girl trembled at the memory of her brother,

183

Tawee . . . Lek's mistress had been troubled of late and the slave girl feared that the Princess's judgement had become impaired. All the women around Her Majesty knew the cause, though none dared speak it aloud before her. The Princess Queen was in love with the wrong one of her two uncles, for Chao Fa Noi was the younger of the Lord of Life's two brothers, and it was the elder, Chao Fa Apai Tot, the one nearest in age to the ruler, who would traditionally succeed to the throne. The Lord of Life would expect his only daughter to marry Chao Fa Apai Tot, his legal successor, and uphold tradition.

As she traversed the anteroom and approached the door that led into her mistress's chamber, an involuntary quiver shook Lek again. She wished she did not have to enter today. It had become so easy to displease the mistress. Lek's friend Kalaya, her fellow slave girl, who applied the red dye to the little nails of the mistress's fifth fingers and daubed the royal neck with the mistress's favourite aromatic scent made from aloe wood, had just been punished for spreading treasonous gossip and all the slave girls had been obliged to witness the sentence, as a warning to each of them.

The brave Kalaya had not cried out but her features had contorted with pain and terror as they threaded the needle through her lips up and down from one end of her mouth to the other, until they were sewn together in a symbol of silence. Of course Kalaya was a gossip-monger and it was not unlike her to spread such stories. But had she really accused the Lord of Life's favourite concubine of consorting with a farang? It seemed so far-fetched. How could that be when no concubine was allowed outside the palace walls and no farang within them?

Lek could not help wondering whether perhaps anything remotely connected with forbidden trysts set the Princess Queen off into a rage.

'Lek, is that you?' The austere voice called from the other side of the door. 'What are you waiting for? Come in immediately.'

Princess Yotatep put down her favourite episode from the Ramayana and, like her heroine Sita before her, emitted a long sigh. Who would ever believe that the only daughter of the great King Narai could feel so wretched? For she, who since the death of her mother had been elevated to the rank of Princess Queen

184

and whom many now addressed as 'Your Majesty' – she, in short, who had everything, was pining away for love.

'Lek!' she summoned again. The little slave girl with the large nervous eyes crawled forward and deferentially awaited her mistress's orders.

'Read on, and don't stop until I tell you,' commanded Yotatep, carefully handing her the large, disintegrating volume which her grandmother had bequeathed to her on her deathbed. Though the rice paper was worn and the beautiful characters occasionally faded, the Princess preferred this ancient volume to any of the newer editions. The sanctity of age and the love of the scribe seemed to emanate from every page.

It would be easier to gather her thoughts, she reflected, with the soothing voice of Lek in the background. The little girl was a natural reader, remaining tirelessly prostrate on her knees and elbows, reciting for three or four hours at a stretch.

Lek, she knew, was especially anxious to please her mistress, the more so since the little slave girl's brother, Tawee, one of His Majesty's Outer Pages, had brought disgrace on the family by pointing a finger at a sumptuous dish as it emerged from the royal kitchens on its way to the Lord of Life's table. Although the offending finger had been duly cut off, in Lek's mind the shame still lingered. Young Tawee might well have been awed by the sight of the steaming river tiger, no larger than a dog, lying sprawled across the huge golden platter, but he should have known better than to point at anything destined for the royal table.

The Princess glanced at Lek and smiled. The lesson taught her brother would ensure that this little slave at least would never point her finger at anything belonging to the Princess Queen or handle any article of hers directly, as that fool, Som, had done. Imagine having the effrontery to hand her ivory-toothed comb straight into her royal hands, without first placing it in the cup with the long golden handle and holding it up at a proper distance.

Yotatep sighed as Lek's voice continued to intone the familiar stories. How comforting the Ramayana could be and how full of wisdom. Here, too, was a troubled princess, someone who on the surface seemed to have everything, like herself. Did this

185

other heroine, in her exalted state, know true friendship? Or was it, too, mere adulation and flattery?

Yotatep took comfort in tracing again the purity of her bloodline. As the daughter of her father's very own sister, hers was an impeccable pedigree acknowledged by all, through an exclusively royal prerogative. Because incest, of course, was not permitted among the people, and rightly so. What need did the common people have of preserving an untarnished bloodline as the Chakravatin did, those God Kings descended from the Heavens? Whichever of her relatives she married, reflected the Princess, her husband's claim to the throne would be that much more strengthened by a union with herself, the Lord of Life's only daughter. Inevitably her thoughts turned to Prince Chao Fa Noi. If only her father was not so conservative, a characteristic increasingly evident as he aged. At fifty-four he was almost halfway through his fourth cycle. Should she take the plunge and appeal to him, she asked herself, as she had done so many times before? She adored her father. She respected his intellect and admired his sense of justice. Even with all the affairs of state that burdened him, he managed to find time for her. Sometimes he even summoned her to help choose a consort from among the high-born women who were sent to the palace as gifts. Together they had decided which girls were more suited to palace life, for once recruited, they would never know life outside the palace walls again. However her father invariably allowed the less eager ones to be ransomed by their parents and returned to their homes. It was a most convenient way of raising taxes.

Should she turn, then, to her compassionate father? No, she had not the courage. It frightened her even to think of suggesting to him that he should defy the laws of succession. She knew how fierce he could be when thwarted, and she did not want to risk losing his esteem. But how could she marry the brother of the man she loved? If only Siamese tradition did not insist on the succession passing from the King to his first brother. Her father had once told her that the Kings of Europe were succeeded by their sons instead of their brothers, but that was absurd. A royal son was too young and invariably immature, and anyway a brother was of a purer bloodline than a son. Only in the absence of a brother should a son be considered for the throne.

What strange creatures indeed were the farangs. It had amazed

186

her to hear that the King of France, whom her father spoke of as a grand monarch, had only one wife and apparently not a single elephant! How very sad. And though his country was supposed to be rich, she had heard that his fields bore him no rice! There were things in life that were hard to comprehend, not least that her father, whom the whole world revered, should secretly admire another: this same farang king. She had caught him on more than one occasion gazing at the portrait of the farang – Rouee the fourteenth or something – which the French Jesuit priests had given him as a present. Could there really have been thirteen of them before him, bearing the same name? And did they all have a head of hair like a woman's and a nose like a gorged lizard?

Yotatep tried to bring her mind back to Lek's reading, to find solace in the ancient tale, but she could not concentrate on the words. She had been having difficulty in recent times concentrating on anything other than her predicament.

Her depression deepened at the thought that her loved one might be sewn in a velvet sack and clubbed to death, the royal way. In bygone days, and recently too, most succeeding monarchs had done away with all the living male relatives of the previous King, and married every one of his surviving female relatives to ensure a firm hold on the throne. Chao Fa Apai Tot, who swallowed those intoxicating spirits which made his already fragile temper unmanageable, was more than likely to revive the old practice and remove his brother, as long as he was properly put to death in a crimson sack and no drop of royal blood was allowed to touch the ground. The people, mourn as they might, would be satisfied that tradition at least had been upheld.

Would she be forced, then, to lie with Chao Fa Apai Tot? He was old and physically deformed, and he would beat her if she displeased him, which was bound to happen when the very sight of him repulsed her.

This last thought roused her. If she could not risk confronting her father herself, she could at least test his feelings through another source. She resolved to speak to Yupin, to seek her advice, perhaps even suggest she raise the matter – however obliquely – with the King.

Of all the women in her father's harem none was more voluptuous than Yupin, a sister of General Petraja, Commander in Chief of the Royal Regiment of Elephants. She was as wise as she was beautiful and she commanded the ear of the King to a degree which no other concubine could rival. She was his undisputed favourite, but also a valued friend of the Princess Queen. Yes, Yotatep would draw on her old friendship with her father's favourite concubine and ask her for a service. She would have to be careful of course not to make it appear as if she were asking a favour. A Royal Princess could not be seen to beg, not from a simple concubine anyway, however much in the King's graces. But, Yupin was the one to help her.

Abruptly, Yotatep dismissed Lek. When the girl had gone, the Princess adjusted her gold-brocaded panung, tucking the ends firmly in at the sides, and did up the top two filigree buttons of her white silk blouse. She whitened her lips with pommade, primped her hair and added a spot of turmeric powder to her cheeks and forehead. Then she set off for the women's quarters in search of Yupin.

Slowly, her head held high, the tall figure of the Princess with the rounded shoulders descended towards the lower apartments that housed the concubines and slaves and eunuchs of the greatest palace in the land. The Princess's bare feet trod silently on soft Persian rugs, while on either side of her slaves and eunuchs, dressed exactly like women, in flowing panungs and with sashes draped about their shoulders, fell flat on their faces, remaining respectfully supine for several moments after Her Majesty had passed. At last she descended a final series of steps to the lowest level and entered the concubines' quarters. Here the rooms were simple and sparsely furnished – a few cushions, a Burmese tapestry or two, a lacquered wardrobe, a water urn for dousing and one or two images in wood or bronze of the Lord Buddha.

As she approached the door of Yupin's room, the Princess considered her best approach. She would be polite but firm. How absurd, she reflected, that the only daughter of the King, the most eligible woman in the land, should have to suffer like this, uncertain even if her love were reciprocated. Every man in the Kingdom should be at her feet.

At the door of Yupin's room a young slave girl prostrated herself nervously before the Princess. Her hair was cropped short in the peasant style and she was bare-breasted, clad only in a simple panung.

188

'I have come to see your msitress, little mouse.' The Princess used '*Noo*', or 'little mouse', the appropriate form of address to a young girl of low rank.

The slave girl shook slightly with fear. 'Great Majesty, I receive your orders. My mistress has been summoned by the Lord of Life himself.' Despite her nervousness, there was a trace of pride in the slave girl's voice at the mention of her mistress's whereabouts.

'Tell your mistress I wish to see her on an urgent matter, little mouse. She should come to my apartments as soon as she returns.'

'Great Majesty, the dust of your feet receives your orders.' The Princess turned and left.

The favourite concubine of King Narai the Great left the Lord of Life's chambers in high spirits. This was indeed a novel and exciting prospect! But how frustrating that she had been sworn to secrecy. What a story it would otherwise have made! Why, she could have extracted any amount of tribute from the gossip-hungry courtesans with this one. There had been nothing like it, she reflected, since the Circassian concubine from Persia, the one with the green eyes, had seduced the eleven-year-old second page of the royal bedchamber, and the two of them had been roasted on the spit for their trouble.

But now she was under oath, on pain of death for her and her next of kin, to breathe not a word and, in matters of such consequence, the Lord of Life's threats had always to be taken seriously.

Instinctively Yupin touched her hips as she walked, feeling their rhythmic swing, savouring the hint of seduction.

The pleasure she derived from the constant stares of the women she passed was undiminished with the years; at thirty-two she knew that there was hardly a female in the palace who would not part with her most precious belongings to lie with her. As she made her way back to her quarters, along the ever-descending corridors, she brushed her hand across her narrow waist, tracing the shapely contours downwards to the still firm thighs, and thought about her new assignment.

What an honour His Majesty had just bestowed upon her: to train a woman in the arts of love, in the accomplishment of

189

exquisite manners and in the more refined techniques of seduction. Her thoughts returned to the royal chamber as, prostrate, she had listened to the royal command.

'We are told this girl has natural grace and fire. But she is from the southern provinces and has never been initiated into the ways of the big city. You will develop that natural grace and kindle that fire until its flame is white-hot. You will impart all your knowledge to her, omitting nothing, and teach her every artifice you know. The man she turns her attentions to must be caught in a web from which there can be no escape.' The Lord of Life had paused. 'Like we ourselves, when we first encountered you, Yupin.' Though it was not permitted to look up, she could almost feel His Majesty's smile upon her. The Lord of Life was so gracious.

It was true, she reflected now, as she passed the last sentry post, manned by eunuchs, at the entrance to the royal apartments. She, Yupin, had no rival. It was no mean feat to have become the favourite of the Lord of Life and to have maintained that position for nearly twenty years, not only against the many women of fine breeding who were sent to him from the fifteen major provinces and thirty-four minor ones, but against all those sirens from Queda and Jambi and Laos and Pattani and Cambodia, and the numerous vassal states whose princes sought to please him. Just as she herself had striven to do from the beginning. Of course, she had been blessed with unusual attributes. It had not taken her long to discover that her face, with its high cheekbones and its delicately pointed nose and chin was of a perfect symmetry and that the dark, seductive eyes promised a world of pleasure to the onlooker. She smiled to herself as she recalled an early admirer who had told her that when she opened her mouth he expected her to purr instead of to speak. The Gods, he had insisted, had surely become confused between a human and a feline incarnation.

Without a line on her face and with firm breasts that still refused to sag, Yupin was well aware that even now, at an age when most women were considered old, she could turn a man's head sooner than any of the young puppies who thought the world was for their taking. His Majesty, well into his fourth cycle, still summoned her regularly, though often, it was true, just to discuss a point of courtly politics or some other matter of interest. She smiled deliciously. His Majesty's favour always aroused the envy and frustration of the younger courtesans.

How had the Lord of Life just put it? 'Though we are no longer in the prime of our youth, we wish to ensure that your talents, Yupin, shall not go wasted. They shall continue to render service to the nation.'

Then His Majesty had revealed the most amazing part of her mission. The unexpected twist that had added such spice to the assignment.

'And Yupin, take special heed. This girl you will train is destined to serve a farang. You will keep this knowledge strictly to yourself. But you will attempt to discover if these Europeans have any peculiar tendencies. Make inquiries. There are bound to be rumours.'

Yupin had blushed deeply and thanked the Lord Buddha that her face was well hidden behind her hands, away from His Majesty's gaze. A farang, she repeated to herself in amazement. Who on earth could it be? And why? Unprecedented! For even if a farang were important enough to be spied upon, how could anyone carry out such a mission without understanding a word of their language? Least of all some greenhorn from the south!

As she approached her quarters, her little slave girl, Nong, came running out to meet her, prostrating herself in the passageway. 'Forgive your little mouse, my Lady, but Her Majesty the Princess Queen was here in person. She wishes to see you urgently.'

Yupin's heart quickened. 'Did she look as if she needed something? A service perhaps, or a favour?' This could be the moment she had been waiting for.

'Little mouse wouldn't know such things, my Lady, but Her Majesty certainly seemed anxious.'

'Then go and fetch a sharp knife from the kitchen, Nong. And hurry back to my chamber. Say nothing to anyone. Hurry, I said.'

Oh no, thought little mouse, running off. Not again. How I hate this. It's been months since . . . and I thought my Lady had stopped . . .

Trembling, she sneaked through an open door of the nearby kitchens and, choosing a moment when the cooks' backs were turned, grabbed a knife and slipped it into the folds of her

191

panung. Then, reluctantly, she returned to her mistress's chambers. Yupin had already lifted her panung above her knee and was sitting cross-legged, holding her left knee out with both hands.

'Bring the knife,' she ordered. Gingerly Nong approached her. 'Now, little mouse, you don't want to inflict more pain on me than is necessary, do you?'

'Oh no, my Lady,' said Nong, wiping a bead of perspiration from her forehead.

'Then remember, make a deep gash the first time and you won't have to do it again. The more you have to repeat it, the more it will hurt me. So be brave. And do it in the same spot as last time.'

'Yes, my Lady,' whimpered Nong. Dimly she noted that the previous wound had almost entirely healed and she tried to console herself with the thought that this one would too. Then she placed the sharp point of the knife just below the knee where the slight scar remained, closed her eyes tight, and jerked the blade sideways, applying as much pressure as her failing heart would allow.

There was a sharp cry and the blood spurted from the open wound, running down Yupin's leg and covering her foot. Soon a deep stain was spreading across the wooden floor around her. Nong felt faint.

'Quick, the cloth,' cried her mistress. Nong, her head spinning, ran to fetch a cotton cloth from the bamboo rail attached to the wall. Then with trembling hands she tied it round her mistress's knee. The cloth quickly soaked up the blood and the little slave girl wondered in her anguish whether she might have applied too much pressure on the knife this time. She ran to fetch another cloth and this one too soon turned a bright vermilion. Not until she had applied six of them was the flow of blood eventually stemmed. Nong felt quite nauseous now and it took every effort on her part not to retch in her mistress's presence.

'Thank you, little mouse. I know it's not pleasant for you but I don't trust anyone else, and I don't have the courage to do it myself. Just forget what you've seen and you will be well rewarded. I'm going to visit the Princess now.'

'Shall I come with you, my Lady? Will you be all right?' asked

Nong anxiously. Yupin was touched, sensing the genuineness of the little girl's concern.

'I will be fine. Remember last time? It was all over in a few days. Just forget what you've seen. That's all I command.'

Yupin left the distressed girl to clean up the floor and hobbled off in the direction of the Princess Queen's apartments. Though she wondered exactly why she had been summond, she suspected it might have something to do with Chao Fa Noi. The whole palace had heard rumours that the Princess was madly in love with the wrong uncle. Perhaps she needed advice. Yupin smiled, despite her pain. Perhaps she needed a favour also. There were few in the palace who did not turn to Yupin when it came to problems of the heart – her smile broadened – or of the body, for that matter.

At the elaborately carved teakwood door of the Princess's apartments, a eunuch wearing a black, female-type panung stopped her, and then, recognizing her, bowed and escorted her as far as an antechamber. Though armed soldiers guarded the Outer Palace, none was allowed near the Inner, and unarmed eunuchs took their place, for no man could carry a weapon into the royal apartments.

The Princess Queen's apartments, festooned with bright Persian rugs, Ming porcelain vases of the finest blue and white, and delicately woven Japanese silk screens, were lavish. There were several teakwood doors leading off the main corridor, and in the anteroom into which Yupin was ushered were gold-lacquered chests, a bookcase filled with volumes of Buddhist literature, painstakingly inscribed by devoted monks, and several low-lying oval tables intricately carved by the greatest artisans in Ayudhya.

The Princess soon entered the room and Yupin immediately prostrated herself. The Princess stared at her for a moment. As always she was awed by the looks of this concubine. It was a while since she had seen her. There was still not a wrinkle on Yupin's face though she must be approaching her third cycle. How did she manage it?

'I am glad to see you, Pi,' said the Princess, smiling.

Although superior in rank, the Princess was younger in age and addressed Yupin politely as 'Pi' or elder sister.

'But what has happened to your knee?' she asked in alarm. 'Are you badly hurt?' Blood was oozing from the wound and trickling down Yupin's shapely brown leg. At least my skin is fairer than yours, thought Yotatep, suddenly wondering what her beloved Prince Chao Fa Noi might think of Yupin's looks.

'It's nothing, Your Highness. I tripped and fell against a sharp stone in the garden. I was about to call a physician when I learned of Your Highness's summons.'

'Oh, my dear,' said Yotatep, feeling guilty. She turned hurriedly to a servant who was squatting in the passageway. 'Plern, fetch me some coconut balm and a clean cloth. Run!'

'I, a speck of dust, receive your orders, Great Majesty.' Plern crawled quickly backwards out of sight.

The Princess's large black eyes examined Yupin again.

'I will not detain you long, elder sister, because I can see you are in pain and your wound must be properly attended.'

'I await your orders, Royal Highness,' replied Yupin deferentially.

The Princess hesitated. 'I understand you were with the Lord of Life. How is my esteemed father?'

'The Master of Life is well, Your Highness. And most gracious to me, his worthless slave, as always.'

The Princess smiled. It was true, her father was gracious. And very fond of Yupin too, fond enough to listen to her suggestions.

'I know you are his favourite consort, Yupin.' She paused. 'Justly so.' There was just the right amount of flattery in her tone. 'I also know he confides in you more than he does in any other.' Yupin remained silent. 'Does he,' continued Yotatep haltingly, 'did His Majesty mention any marriage plans for his successor?' She felt better now that she had said it. It was not easy for a Princess Queen to preface a favour.

'Marriage plans for the Lord of Life's successor, Your Royal Highness? I, a hair, always assumed that Your Royal Highness would marry His Majesty's successor. Who else would be worthy enough of you?' Any other response, Yupin knew, would have offended the Princess.

Was Chao Fa Noi really in love with the Princess? she wondered. The palace was hotly divided over the issue. Some said that the young Prince was only interested in the marriage for political reasons, as it would greatly enhance his claim to the throne, especially in view of his brother's frail health. Others insisted he was resigned to the legitimate succession of his elder brother and was genuinely in love with the Princess. Yupin looked at Yotatep now. She could not be called beautiful. She was too tall, almost clumsily so, and her shoulders were hunched forward as if to reduce her height. But she had some of her father's charm and she could hardly be said to be lacking in wealth and rank. Yupin had only seen Chao Fa Noi once, as he was emerging from His Majesty's apartments. He was handsome enough, and he had certainly responded to the sight of her. But then what man did not?

'Indeed,' replied Yotatep, 'but has His Majesty not just confined Chao Fa Apai Tot to the grounds of the royal palace on account of his rowdiness and disorderly conduct? And does my father still expect such a man to be his heir?'

Before Yupin could answer, Plern returned with the ointment and a clean cloth. The Princess dismissed her, saying she would administer the medicine herself.

She removed the bandage from Yupin's knee and winced at the sight of the deep gash. Perhaps she had been rash to offer her services, she thought. The wound looked more serious than she had imagined. A doctor was definitely needed.

Yupin's face contorted with pain as Yotatep applied the ointment, and the Princess resolved – with much regret – to postpone the audience until she had summoned the palace physician. But Yupin anticipated her intentions.

'The Lord of Life is, I know, most distressed over his rightful heir's health as well as his unbecoming conduct,' ventured Yupin, mastering her pain. 'He will, I feel sure, weigh the situation carefully. In his wisdom he may find it necessary – given such special circumstances – to break with tradition and appoint his youngest brother Chao Fa Noi as his successor. Of course,' she added slyly, 'Chao Fa Noi's choice of a wife could also make a difference to any claim of his.'

Yotatep's heart leaped though she did her best to conceal it. She appeared to consider for a moment.

'I think for the good of the country, Pi, I will become Chao Fa Noi's wife. It would greatly consolidate his claim to the throne, as you say.'

'If you will permit me, Royal Highness, for the good of the country I think it is an absolute necessity.'

'Would you then air these views with His Majesty, Pi?' she asked hiding her excitement.

'I would be honoured to,' replied Yupin. 'Perhaps I could bring the matter up the very next time the Lord of Life is gracious enough to summon me.' Yupin winced and clutched her knee. 'If only my wound would heal quickly. I feel too unworthy to appear before His Majesty in this state.'

'Let me call the palace doctor at once.' The Princess was about to give the order when Yupin politely forestalled her.

'Your Royal Highness, I know the palace surgeon. He's a very good man, of course, but . . .' She pretended to search for the right word.

'I know what you mean,' interrupted Yotatep sympathetically, 'but he's the best we have. Unless you'd rather summon one of those farang Jesuits?'

Yupin paused. 'I have another idea, Your Highness. I know of a Dutch surgeon. One of the palace guards told me about him. He is apparently expert at healing cuts quickly with the use of some new herbs from Europe. It is a pity I am not allowed to leave the palace. Otherwise . . .'

She looked up suddenly at the Princess. 'Unless, of course, Your Royal Highness would make an exception and authorize the guards to let me visit him briefly. I am sure the cure would not take long. And I would be ready to visit His Majesty the moment I returned . . .'

The Princess's enthusiasm overrode her concern for the stringent rules of the palace. No concubine was allowed outside its gates.

'I will do so immediately,' she said. 'Furthermore I will instruct Captain Somsak to allow you two outings.' She smiled conspiratorially. 'You may need to visit the surgeon once more to ensure the wound is properly healed.'

'Oh thank you, Your Highness,' said Yupin gratefully. The skin of her body had already begun to tingle. She prostrated herself and insisted on crawling out backwards, despite the Princess's protestations that she would do more damage to her knee.

Later that day, though in theory it was next to impossible for a royal consort to leave the confines of the palace walls during her lifetime, a limping Yupin presented a note, embossed with the royal seal of Her Majesty the Princess Queen, to the surprised Captain of the Guard. A moment later she was hobbling out of the main gate in the direction of the Dutch quarter. Once out of sight, her limp diminished and her direction changed. With quickening heart she turned towards the Portuguese encampment which lay outside the city walls. Her whole body began to perspire and she wondered how much of her excitement was fear and how much burning desire. It had been so long since she had seen him – not in fact since the old Captain of the Guard had been dismissed for accepting bribes, her own among them. And now they said her lover was back. She prayed with all her might that the rumours of his return were true.

After what seemed an eternity of alleys and turnings, she emerged into a side street where the houses were all of brick and of that strange farang architecture. It was his street and the hammering in her heart grew to thunder. She approached and saw lights in the house. With aching limbs she pounded on her lover's door.

As she waited feverishly on the porch, a thousand thoughts crowded her mind. She could be devoured by tigers for this. No, that was a royal concubine's punishment for adultery with a Siamese. The palace had a punishment for every form of offence, linked to the nature of the crime itself. She had witnessed death by tiger once, an ordeal reserved only for the severest crimes. The guards had tied the prisoners to posts in a field and placed the hungry beasts in cages without food for days, feeding the prisoners regularly in front of them. The famished brutes had howled throughout the night, driven mad by the scent. Then, at break of day, the guards had released them, securing them with chains just long enough to reach the extremities of the prisoners. The ravenous beasts had first devoured the hands and feet of the victims until, given by degrees a little more chain, they had gradually eaten them alive. For adultery with a farang there was surely no precedent. They might tie her to a spit and roast her with her lover over a slow fire. Was it really worth it? Oh yes, she acknowledged, for she had never known such transports as with this brute. She managed a cynical smile. The Lord of Life had, after all, commanded her to make inquiries about farangs. If she survived she would at least be able to tell that girl from the

197

south – what was her name? Sunida, the Lord of Life had said –
at first hand all about their erotic cravings.

Then she heard the deep, familiar voice. It was true, her
Captain Alvarez was back from Pattani!

Fourteen

At dawn on the eleventh day the Governor of Ligor's boat entered the majestic estuary of the Menam, the Siamese word for river, literally 'mother of waters', fully three miles across from shore to shore. A thrill went through Phaulkon as he leant over the wooden rail and stared at the exhilarating sight. The boat was sailing into the eastern and most navigable of the three estuaries, heading towards the very heart of Siam. For ten days they had followed the coastline of the narrow southern isthmus upwards from Ligor; now they were entering the vast expanse of land that spread northwards through Laos and China, westwards to Ava and Pegu and eastwards to Cambodia and Cochin China.

The 50-ton vessel had no trouble negotiating the sandbank, known as the bar, which was not more than a dozen feet deep, unlike larger vessels which were forced to wait, sometimes for months on end, for a favourable flood tide at the entrance to the estuary. When favourable, however, 400-ton trading ships could journey up the river all the way to Ayudhya, the glittering capital, a distance of some sixty miles from the river's mouth.

As the boat headed into the Menam itself, Phaulkon's heart beat a little faster. Along these ancient banks throbbed the heart of Siamese life. This was the essence of the country he knew and loved, a kingdom as large as France and England put together.

The river was huge, three times broader than the Thames, and when the annual rains came, it flooded with a vengeance, destroying vermin and fertilizing the land. The rice crops grew abundantly, and the rich land gave out sustenance enough to feed the population twice over and still have room for export, except for those times when the the gods were truly displeased. Then the floodwaters rose ten feet high and the fish were flung far into the countryside, and the rice seeds that needed to keep their ears above water were submerged and died.

Once a year, from time immemorial, when the end of the rains was approaching, the Kings ventured out in their glittering royal barges and in a grand ceremony commanded the waters to recede. Woe betide the unfortunate astrologers who had predicted incorrectly and advised the Kings of the wrong dates.

Houses came into view now along the banks, all built on stilts and of a uniform wooden construction. Except for the roofs, which were tiled, they resembled the houses in Ligor. Six round, thick, ironwood pillars sunk into the riverbed served as foundations, and a ladder led up to the raised floor of the single-storeyed dwellings, a few feet above the water, safe from all but the worst inundations. Phaulkon smiled at the recollection of how the houses could not be taller than one storey, in deference to the height of the royal barges. In the event that His Gracious Majesty, raised high on a dais in the centre of his royal barge and driven by 120 oarsmen clad in red, happened to pass by, no inhabitant would inadvertently find himself above the level of the royal head.

A canoe-like boat was tethered to each house, and men could be seen idly fishing from the doorways of their homes. In the rainy season in particular, from May to October, there was such an abundance of fish that half a morning's work would suffice for a man to provide for his family for a whole week without even stirring from his threshold. The Siamese were a truly amphibious people, reflected Phaulkon, thanks to the great river and the maze of canals and tributaries that criss-crossed the fertile central plain, the rice bowl where the majority of the population was concentrated. Their goods were bartered by boat as often as in the squares and marketplaces, and the paddle was as integral a part of the people as their legs.

The water was becoming less clear now, a swiftly flowing current of light brown, and along the banks a group of peasants, standing knee-deep, washed and rinsed their hair, while children leapt joyfully into the water from the thresholds of their houses, shouting with delight. The men and women bathed together, both barechested and wearing only cotton panungs to cover their lower regions. They bathed three or four times a day, despite the dangers of the dreaded moonfish which inflated itself as round as a ball and, though toothless, sank its jaws into the thighs and calves of the bathers, carrying off great chunks of flesh.

The boat had passed the little Dutch outpost of Little Amsterdam with its brick houses, where the Hollanders had another factory and several of their nation resided. Fully laden ships from their colony at Batavia in Java unloaded there, leaving with a cargo of rice and lumber, wax and gittagum, and paying their dues in both directions to the Siamese crown. The cluster of houses had looked peaceful enough, but Phaulkon recalled how only three months ago six Dutch sailors, dozing on the grass, had been dragged off by tigers and never heard of again.

The great river meandered round pretty little islands sending its offshoots into the countryside like so many shimmering arms. Jasmine shrubs and gardenia trees, their white flowers in full bloom, dotted the shore, mingling brightly with the flaming red of the bougainvillaea. Soon they would pass the small port of Bangkok with its wooden fort, famous for its variety of colourful fruit orchards visible along the shore: banana plantations, jack-fruits, papayas, guava, the pungent durian, mangoes, mangus-teens, tamarinds, sugar cane, pineapple and coconut groves. And now, as they sailed past settlements on either side of the riverbank, shouts of farang! farang! resounded from the more observant children on the shore, and small boats paddled by as smiling, bare-breasted women, laden with market produce, rushed to intercept them. Even when they arrived too late, the still smiling boatwomen threw flowers in the ship's wake and shouted friendly greetings after them. Nothing had changed. It might have been his first visit all over again.

Phaulkon had loved Siam from the moment he had set eyes on it. He felt he must have known it in another life, so strangely familiar and so dear it seemed to him. It was the very same scenes along this majestic waterway that had first captivated him. In Ayudhya he had spent the first six months immersed in mastering the difficult language, meeting and talking with traders from all parts, seeking a discreet outlet for his priceless cannon, and helping Burnaby re-establish the English warehouse. George White had omitted to tell him the whole truth about the English presence in Siam. It had been a Company secret. An English factory had in fact existed on and off for a number of years but had opened and closed down with such frequency and under such dubious circumstances that the many incidents had been glossed over and its existence conveniently 'forgotten'. The trading post had lain for the most part semi-dormant while its quarrelsome factors bickered among themselves, drank themselves into obliv-ion, gambled irredeemably, pawned the Company's assets and even borrowed money from the King. Some had actually spent time in a local prison before being expelled from the country. Now that the canny Siamese were anxious to see the English back, they too had conveniently overlooked the past and the Company was able to announce it had been invited to 'open up a post in Siam'.

It was around the fifth month after his arrival, just after his friend Pedro Alvarez had left to investigate a promising outlet for the cannon in Pattani, that Phaulkon himself, like his bickering predecessors, had almost come to blows with his chief. Burnaby had received Phaulkon in the living room of his house, in which, typically, the Englishman had tried to re-create the drawing room of a little Hampshire cottage: tables, chairs, a sofa and chintz curtains. Phaulkon, who from the very beginning had opted for a Siamese life style, had struggled to ignore the incongruous furnishings and had come straight to the point. Burnaby had listened in stunned silence.

'You want time off to go into a Buddhist temple?' he had eventually inquired, incredulously. 'Whatever for?'

'Richard, I need to feel more Siamese. It's a spiritual experience.'

'You're employed by the East India Company, Constant, and you are not paid to indulge in spiritual fantasies. How do you think I will explain your absence to Madras? The Company has had enough trouble here in the past as it is. Besides, I need you here.'

That part of it was true. Phaulkon knew that his early mastery of the language was already proving of invaluable assistance to his chief.

'I will only be gone three months, and I assure you it will pay great dividends.'

'You mean to tell me that shaving your head and donning a yellow robe will be of lasting benefit to the Company?' scoffed Burnaby. 'Or make you feel more Siamese, as you suggest? Why, you've already bought three slaves and talk like one of them, and keep a harem like any mandarin. How much more Siamese do you want to become?'

It was true that Phaulkon's purchase of Nid and Ut and Noi had caused quite a stir in the foreign community. But the transaction had been legal – and relatively inexpensive – and he lived sufficiently well on his Company earnings to treat his slaves kindly. They were more than content, he knew.

'These are material questions, Richard. I need to know the way their minds are formed from childhood. All life begins in the temple. It serves as a school and as a spiritual home. There is no other education as we know it and the monks are the only teachers. In three months I will know more about Siam than any farang before me. And that can only benefit the Company.'

Burnaby was adamant. 'No, Constant, I am sorry, you will remain at your post. I have indulged your whims long enough.'

'In that case, Richard, you leave me no choice, I must resign my commission.'

Burnaby was stunned. 'Resign your English commission to enter some foreign monkhood? Have you taken leave of your senses? Constant . . . why don't you get a good night's rest and we'll talk again in the morning.'

They had left it at that, but in the morning Phaulkon's mind was unchanged, and Burnaby ranted and raved and turned purple in the face and threatened to cut his salary completely, while Phaulkon calmly agreed that it would be only fair to do so. In the end a grudging Burnaby was forced to concede that it was better to have Phaulkon back in three months than not at all. The thought of dispensing with his services altogether had quite shaken him.

'But what about Captain Alvarez and the cannon?' he had asked in a last effort to deter Phaulkon from his plan.

'I'll be back before Alvarez returns from Pattani, I promise. It'll take him a good three months to complete his mission. That's why I've got to leave now.'

Reluctantly, Burnaby had granted him three months' leave without pay, and it was agreed that officially Phaulkon would be described as recuperating from a particularly severe bout of malaria in a safe place in the country, far from any contact with the rest of the community.

Phaulkon smiled now at the recollection of those days. What a wonderful three months they had been!

It was partly true that he had wanted to feel more Siamese, to undergo that intrinsically Siamese experience of being ordained as a monk and entering the temple for a few months of one's life. Yet beyond the strong sense of destiny that tied him to this land, there were specific motives that embraced his overall plan. He needed to study the Bali tongue, the ancient language of Sanskrit origin which differed widely from the Siamese and was the idiom of the Buddhist temple just as Latin was the idiom of the Christian Church. For the Bali tongue had many similar roots with royal Siamese, the lofty language of the court. It was in that language alone that His Majesty the King could be addressed by his courtiers. No farang had ever mastered it.

Ignoring Burnaby's final exhortations, Phaulkon had slipped out quietly one morning and taken a boat north. He had travelled deep into the provinces and eventually settled outside the walled city of Kamphaeng Phet where there was a small monastery whose fame had spread with that of its learned chief abbot. He had been well received by the kindly abbot who seemed as curious to learn of the ways of the farang as Phaulkon was to discover the ways of the Siamese. He had spent three unforgettable months in the company of the wise and scholarly man.

Phaulkon had been ordained as a novice and had sworn to abide by the ten commandments which differed little from those revealed to Moses but included as well interdictions covering the killing of any kind of animal or insect, losing one's temper or drinking intoxicating spirits. And he was strongly cautioned, once he had donned the yellow robe, against having relations with a woman, which crime incurred the penalty of being roasted alive over a slow fire. He had been given a Siamese name, Pra Somboon, and he had shaved his head and lain on a hard floor at night, rising with the great bell before dawn to go out and beg for his food. He had not eaten between noon and the following sunrise of each day and covered his tea with a cloth strainer to avoid killing the smallest insect life. He had learned humility and charity and seen the generosity of the Siamese, who were amazed at the sight of a farang monk, yet eager to fill his begging bowl and gain merit by their good deeds.

He had learned to love and respect all living things, sharing his very rice bowl with the birds and not offending the trees by cutting their branches, but bringing earth and sustenance instead to any that had suffered in a storm.

On certain days he had swept the temple inside and out and cleaned the latrines, and on others he had offered flowers and fruits to the golden images of the Buddha and fed grain to the fish that swam in the temple ponds. He had lived in the simplest cell of bamboo and leaves and learned to receive alms for today while keeping nothing back for the morrow.

In his second month he had learned to make medicine by compounding oil with a yellow powder from a local herb, while in his third and final month he had learned the secret, through intense meditation, of locating hidden objects.

Finally, studying several hours a day with his great *acharn*, or master, he had achieved his foremost goal: a fluency in royal Siamese, the mandatory form of speech at court with which hardly a soul outside His Majesty's immediate entourage was familiar.

'You ask to study the royal tongue as well?' The abbot had raised his shaven eyebrows in surprise. It was the first day of his apprenticeship and they were sitting cross-legged in the reception hall of the monastery, a bare, six-pillared wooden edifice with a roof of orange tiles. It was surrounded by grass courtyards and fish ponds, and adjoined the main temple whose golden stupas and glittering images and general opulence contrasted strangely with the spartan austerity of the monastic buildings.

Scattered about the temple complex were tall, graceful stone stupas and alongside the main temple stood two rows of box-like monk cells. The whole compound, two or more acres in size, was enclosed by a thick bamboo hedge, beyond which lay primitive forest. It was there that the 'solitary' monks repaired for one month of the year to meditate alone, far from the world of men.

Phaulkon remained silent, his head hung respectfully below that of the abbot.

'You are very ambitious for a novice,' pursued the holy monk, 'but what use can such learning be to you? Besides, we study the holy scriptures here, and in the Bali not the royal tongue.' The abbot's eyes twinkled. 'Surely you do not envisage entering into conversation with His Majesty the King?'

Phaulkon's heart quickened. 'Every aspect of this great country interests me, Your Holiness, and I feel sure a brief study of the royal language should be part of it.'

The gentle abbot screwed up his eyes and surveyed the farang quizzically. 'You are not one of those Christian priests in disguise?' he asked, only half jokingly. 'I hear they are most anxious to show His Majesty the "true path". Perhaps by learning the royal language . . .' The abbot held his fan over his eyes and squinted across at Phaulkon. Every monk carried a fan attached to a long stick to shield him from the sight of women.

Phaulkon laughed. 'No, Your Holiness. My life has been anything but virtuous. I would not make a good priest.'

'And yet you are studying to be a Buddhist monk. Are our standards so much lower?'

'Far from it, Your Holiness. But in your wisdom you allow outsiders to enter your temple and remain there to improve themselves. I am merely availing myself of this wise and liberal custom.'

The abbot thoughtfully fingered the edge of his saffron robe, the colour that most resembled gold, the symbol of the highest reverence for the Buddha. 'And it is for this reason that your Christian religion will not take root in our country,' he observed gravely.

'How is that, Your Holiness?'

'You are too dogmatic, and too self-important. And,' he smiled, 'too specific. You define your God and give names to his son. We cannot define anything so immense, so . . . inscrutable. That is why Buddha is but a guide, a teacher to show the righteous path. For there are many paths to God, my son. It is human arrogance to think otherwise.'

'But what you teach, Your Holiness, is it not ultimately rejection? The annihilation of emotion and feelings, an escape from the wheel of life?'

'Yes, but it will take millions of cycles to achieve such a condition and only a chosen few will ever do so.' The abbot smiled. 'And think of all the emotions you can enjoy in the meantime.' A film came over his eyes. 'Nirvana is man's ultimate state of serenity.'

'But is it not also human arrogance to believe that we are constantly re-born? Are we that important, Your Holiness?' asked Phaulkon.

'We are of little significance, my son, for life is but an endless cycle. Like the phases of the moon or the movements of the stars. Everything is born and dies and is born again. Look at the flowers and trees and everything that surrounds you. Why should we be any different? No, what is human arrogance is to believe that one brief life can determine all eternity! That is what our people will find impossible to accept in your doctrines. For it is not comforting to think that we are given but a single chance. But you, my son,' said the abbot suddenly rising, 'are retarding my own progress to serenity with your interesting chatter.' He turned to go. 'Nevertheless, I shall help you, and we shall speak together often. There is an old and venerable monk here, who was close to the former King. He lived at one time in the palace grounds. He has, of course, a perfect command of the royal tongue. I will see what I can do . . .'

A great shout brought Phaulkon out of his reverie. They had just rounded a large bend in the river with a forested island in the middle. The noise grew louder, and crowds which had begun to line the banks grew thicker as they progressed. Then the people started gesticulating towards them, unmistakably waving them ashore. When the cause of the commotion became apparent, the swarthy captain from Ligor quickly tugged at the tiller and headed away from the mainstream.

Hurtling towards them and devouring the distance at a seemingly impossible pace were five sleek racing boats. Powered by sixty oarsmen apiece, the boats were propelled forward to the sound of drums and wild encouragement from the spectators ashore, who had placed their bets on a favourite contestant. The rowers, seated on benches one behind the other, each crew dressed in a different colour, thrust their oars into the water in cadence with the beat of a long bamboo stick. The captain, the only one standing, bellowed exhortations from the stern, in time to the clanking of his cane. The crowds on shore now clapped their hands in unison and the shouts grew to fever pitch as two of the boats drew ahead of the others, neck and neck. At the last second, one of them surged forwards and hurtled past the two large canoes containing the judges. A great roar went up from the crowd. In the next instant scores of little canoes materialized and headed into the middle of the stream to garland the winner and offer refreshments to the contestants. It was one of those great boat races, a popular gambling event that invariably accompanied a festival or holy day, especially if the temple being honoured was situated by the river's edge.

With the race over, the inhabitants now turned their attentions to Phaulkon. They converged on his boat, chatting volubly. He must indeed have presented a strange sight, he realized, clad only in the panung which the Governor of Ligor had given him. Farangs were expected to wear farang clothes. With the ever-present smile of their race, the Siamese did little to conceal their curiosity. They threw jasmine and tuberoses on to the deck and as the ship set sail once more, a score of canoes followed them and escorted them past the racing boats. They passed alongside the winner boat and Phaulkon observed the sleek craft with admiration. Both ends of the long boat rose out of the water in a sweeping semi-arc, and the poop and prow, raised high in the shape of mythical garuda birds in brilliant gold and green lacquers, jutted majestically over the water. The hull was hollowed out of a single tree trunk.

As they sailed away into quieter waters and the journey resumed its normal pattern, another wave of anxiety swept over Phaulkon, as it had done periodically throughout the ten-day journey. He had only exchanged the occasional smile with the thickset captain and his dark-skinned crew of two, and they, oblivious to his knowledge of their language, had left him alone to his thoughts. He had dined on his own and spent hours brooding on deck, or hidden away in his box-like cabin.

He worried constantly about Burnaby and Ivatt, and the fact that he had been unable to explain his departure to them haunted him. Would they at least be well treated? How would he ever obtain their release if they were being held hostage against a new set of documents which did not exist? And Sunida – how he missed her! How much more bearable the journey would have been with her by his side, to take his mind off the constant worry. At times he wished the endless days would pass by quickly, while at others he was grateful that it was not yet time to face up to the consequences in Ayudhya.

He sensed that he had never been so close – or so far – from his goal. The knowledge that all he had worked for, the years of planning, the successes and the reversals, could be destroyed in the next few days filled him with apprehension. He was both thrilled to return to his beloved Ayudhya and wary of the reception the city would give him.

One thing alone buoyed him. As far as he could make out, the mandarin had sent no dispatches along with this boat. Phaulkon had carefully observed the movements of the captain at the quayside in Ligor and no documents had been handed to him.

Only yesterday he had overheard the crew grumbling that they would not even have time to disembark in Ayudhya. They had been ordered to turn round and head immediately for home. So what about the threatened remittance of his 'report' to the Pra Klang? The Governor had said it would be sent ahead by special courier. But the fastest method of transport to Ayudhya was by sea, and although the Governor possessed several small boats, there was only one, as far as Phaulkon could ascertain, sturdy enough to undertake the long coastal journey to the capital, and that was the boat he was on. This would explain why the mandarin had requested its immediate return. Sunida had disclosed to him that His Excellency had no cause to undertake such journeys to the capital other than the bi-annual visit to report on his province and to drink the water of allegiance with the King.

But what if his 'report', together with a new letter to the Barcalon, had left by elephant courier? It might not reach Ayudhya until after him, but that was sparse comfort. He would undoubtedly be executed for high treason once the Barcalon was apprised of his brazen claim to being a royal spy. What unparalleled insolence!

In his moments of deepest despair, Phaulkon forced himself to reflect on the initial glowing report – too late for the Governor to retrieve now – which the mandarin had sent to the Pra Klang before the appearance of the cannon, in which he had described Phaulkon's performance at the boxing match, the discovery of the white elephant and the conferring of the Order of the White Elephant upon him. Would the Governor really want to risk ridicule by first honouring and then reviling him? It would show poor judgement, not to mention the severe loss of face. Perhaps the two reports, the one praising him and the other condemning him, would reach the Barcalon at the same time, reflected Phaulkon bitterly.

But even if his sentence were commuted, with the cannon gone what chance had he of filling Sam White's boat? There were seventy-nine days left before the rendezvous, by his reckoning, though it was impossible to gauge it exactly. Sam's boat could be a few days early or late, according to the tides. The only man who could supply the cargo in time now was the same man who would most likely order Phaulkon's execution – the Barcalon. Somehow Phaulkon would have to bluff and outfox possibly the shrewdest man in the kingdom. Yet despite the odds, hope surged in him again, as it seemed to do whenever he had sunk to the lowest depths. He *would* outwit this man and he *would* liberate his colleagues in Ligor and fill Sam White's boat and send for Sunida. He would achieve his ambition to become a force in his adopted land, an intermediary between East and West, a foreign potentate in an Eastern world. He banged his fist angrily on the wooden rail and then turned to observe the crew, suddenly mindful that he was not alone and that he had been talking out loud and cursing noisily.

But none of the crew was paying any attention to him. Instead their eyes were riveted in front of them. He followed the direction of their gaze.

The boat had rounded a bend and there before them, in the distance, like some majestic fairyland, rose the spires of Ayudhya, three hundred golden steeples blinking in the sunlight. Whatever beauty in life might have touched Phaulkon before was as nothing against this sudden vision of splendour. Ayudhya, City of Paradise! How appropriately it had been named, he thought.

The island capital was as great a metropolis as London and even larger than Paris. The brick walls that entirely surrounded it were six miles in circumference, massive ramparts that every now and then were pierced by sentried gates at points where the city's canals fed into the main river. Round the whole city flowed the Menam, the same mother river that, forgetting its humble origins in the mountainous jungles of the distant north, swept majestically down through the great central plain and embraced the city of Ayudhya on all sides before winding its way into the Gulf of Siam. On the island city itself, broad, tree-lined streets paved in brick ran alongside endless canals dotted with humped bridges. It was not for nothing that the Portuguese had named it the Venice of the East. Phaulkon's island home of Cephalonia had been under the rule of the Venetians; Venice, not Athens, had been his capital. He had visited it as a young apprentice seaman and now, like Venice before it, Ayudhya had taken his breath away again. Here, in place of gondolas, great gilded barges propelled by vermilion-coated oarsmen plied the canals, and everywhere temples and spires, in lieu of domes and belfries, rose glistening to a stark blue sky.

Phaulkon loved the contrast of the glittering pagodas and the simplicity of the wooden structures on stilts that housed the people, and he revelled in the bustle and smells of the market-places and the activity along the canals that stretched as far as the eye could see. To the north of the city lay another walled city, a city within a city, some fourteen acres in area, from which rose the most magnificent spires of all, those of the Grand Palace – where His Majesty and all his court resided and wherein no commoner, on pain of death, could enter.

Standing alone on the deck, he was filled again with a hunger for power in this fabled city and a hunger to make Ayudhya, like the Venice of his youth, the greatest trading city on earth. For at present it was but a middleman, an entrepot between Near and Far East, where Chinese and Japanese merchants brought tea, porcelain and silks and carried back cargoes of birds' nests, pepper and scented woods. The Siamese, through the intermediary of the Moors, sold the same tea, porcelain and silks to the Indian and Persian merchants who shipped them westwards to their former homelands.

Why, Phaulkon asked himself again, as he had done countless times, should all the goods be transported by outsiders? With a merchant fleet of his own, the King of Siam could double his revenues. Because others traded on the King's behalf – and squandered the majority of his profits – the crown had imposed a mandatory option to make up for the shortfall. Whenever a trading vessel called at Ayudhya, it was first boarded by the King's officers and an option to buy all the goods on board – at prices determined by the crown – was exercised. It was hardly conducive to trade, reflected Phaulkon. Only whatever remained was free to be sold on the open market. While the Treasury's coffers might be temporarily bulging, the process was gradually eroding the number of ships calling at Ayudhya.

It was mid-afternoon when they moored at the port, a wide basin outside the city walls where ships could put in for repairs and where the duck-bellied hulls of new teakwood vessels were presently under construction. In this vicinity, outside the city, all foreigners were housed in camps or suburbs, for after nightfall the entire walled city closed its gates to outsiders and no foreigner was allowed to reside within them. The tiny English sector where

Phaulkon had lived was next to the extensive Portuguese one and very near the port. Anxious to be home again, Phaulkon wai'd to the captain and crew, gathered his meagre belongings and clambered over the rows of moored vessels that formed a bridge to the shore.

Almost immediately he was in the European sector where most of the houses were of brick and many had spacious gardens and broad, tree-lined alleyways that connected one sector to another. As he passed through the gate that marked the entrance to the Portuguese quarter, Phaulkon marvelled once more at the sagacity of the Siamese system and the monarch who had devised it. By forbidding the foreigners from residing in the city itself the King ensured that they did not mix too freely with his own people and corrupt them with their ways. By allowing them to govern themselves, he was relieved of the burden of doing so himself. Thus each nation was provided with its own suburb and was allowed to practise its own religion and live by its own customs, providing these did not come into conflict with the laws of Siam.

A Siamese mandarin was attached to each national sector. Although he was nominally in charge on behalf of the crown, it was more a position of protocol. Matters of any significance were always referred to the Barcalon, for that most powerful minister was responsible for every foreigner in the land, and without his consent none could enter or leave the kingdom.

Phaulkon's heart quickened as he caught sight of his home in the distance. It was in the Siamese style, wooden, single-storeyed, and on stilts. It was divided into three spacious rooms, a reception room and two bedrooms, while a smaller structure adjacent to it housed his cook, a servant girl, and the three female slaves he had purchased for life. A small garden separated it from the roadway and a wooden gate marked its entrance. It was unpretentious but adequate.

Sorn, the cook, was the first to spot him. As she saw him approaching, she shouted excitedly to the others and soon cries of 'The master is back, the master is back!' resounded from all over the house. Within moments the servants were running down the steps and prostrating themselves on the lawn in front of the gate: Sorn, Tip the housemaid, and Nid, Ut and Noi the slave girls, chosen for their exceptional massaging skills.

'Lord Master, we thought you would never return,' said Sorn, privileged, as the senior in rank, to speak first. 'A month is far too long.'

'How could I not return, when I knew you would only get lazy in my absence,' bantered Phaulkon. 'I am longing for a feast, a good bath and an endless massage. I hope you've all been keeping in practice.' Phaulkon loved Sorn's cooking, and his masseuses' skilled fingers were second to none.

'We have been expecting you every day, Lord Master,' said Sorn again. 'A messenger called three times this past week to see if you were back. He left a note. Tip, fetch it for the Lord Master.'

Tip ran off, crouching low, and returned a moment later with a folded sheet of rice paper.

Phaulkon opened it and a smile spread across his face. How fortuitous that he had returned today. He had been planning to visit Mestre Phanik at the earliest opportunity anyway. There were few people with a greater knowledge of Siamese politics than the 'Doutor', as he was known to everyone in the Portuguese sector. Had there been any universities in Siam, he reflected, the Doutor would certainly have held the Chair in Siamese affairs. And now, this very night, he was invited to a party in honour of Mestre Phanik's niece, Maria, whose sixteenth birthday it was.

'What else has happened in my absence?' asked Phaulkon.

'Nothing much, Lord, except that we all missed you,' replied Sorn. She was a large, exuberant woman, who looked as if she must have at least a dozen children tucked away somewhere.

'And I have missed you,' said Phaulkon with genuine warmth as he made his way up the steps into the house.

He entered the living room, strewn with artifacts of the early Ayudhya period: manuscript chests, book cabinets, a temple gong, wooden votive tablets covered in gold leaf, ancient musical instruments and a necklace of bronze bells that encircled a horse's neck.

He threw himself down on a pile of cushions in the corner and closed his eyes. Oh well, he would have to forego Sorn's cooking for one more day. There would just be time for a bath and a good massage before he set off for Mestre Phanik's house. The thought had barely entered his mind when Nid was silently at his feet, unwinding his panung, and Ut's expert fingers had come from behind to kneed his temples soothingly.

How well they understood his needs, he thought. And how good it was to be back.

Fifteen

Numerous slaves squatted in the broad courtyard and a number of sedan chairs stood in line with their porters standing by. Mestre Phanik's house was in the hub of the Portuguese quarter where lived some four thousand of their nationals, many from Goa. Mestre Phanik's house, unlike those of many of his neighbours, was in the Siamese style, raised on stilts, with a curving, triangular roof. Though Siamese houses were generally built of timber and bamboo, simple to construct and even easier to dismantle if the owner wanted to move to another location, this one, apart from its greater size, was of solid teak; and the difference was immediately evident in its appearance of permanence and the beautifully aged quality of the wood.

Phaulkon removed his sandals and climbed the steps to the front door. He had always considered it a most civilized custom to remove one's shoes before entering a house, the more so in the rainy season when the earth was turned to mud by the monsoons. A liveried servant stood bowing at the door and Phaulkon was ushered into an anteroom hung with wooden crucifixes and enclosed at one end by a beautiful Japanese lacquered screen.

Mestre Phanik himself came in to greet him, jovial as ever, his round Japanese face, with a touch of the European, lighting up at the sight of his friend. His story was a miracle; Phaulkon had heard it from Phanik's own lips. One of his fore-fathers had been the first Japanese to be baptized by St Francis in Japan in 1549. Following the wave of xenophobia that had swept across Japan shortly after that, thousands of Christian converts had been put to death by fire. But the courageous manner in which these martyrs, Phanik's great-great-grandfather among them, had succumbed, refusing unto death to recant their adopted faith, had only served to inspire new converts.

Following the Emperor's edict in 1614 banishing all Christians from Japan and confiscating their property, his grandparents had been deported to Nagasaki. In a country where the brave

215

disembowelled themselves in ritual suicide, the public torture of unrepenting men and women caused widespread sympathy for the victims, and the Emperor was forced to revert to a policy of minimal publicity. So it was decreed that all those banished into exile would be sewn into sacks, indistinguishable from cargoes of rice. Thus prevented from haranguing the populace, they were taken to the nearest port. Phanik's grandparents had been shipped out of Nagasaki and after a sojourn in China about which little was known, they had come to settle in Siam. The family had been engaged in trade with the Far East ever since. The yellow plague had struck down Phanik's brother when his daughter Maria was only two, and Phanik had apparently adopted her and asked the Portuguese Jesuits to baptize her. They had given her a Portuguese name and in honour of the family history the Jesuits had relaxed their rules and brought her up – a girl – in accordance with the holy scriptures. Phaulkon had met her only briefly when she was home one day from convent school, but she had made an impression on him as a lively child with a mind of her own.

'*Senhor Constant, que prazer*,' said Mestre Phanik exuberantly, engulfing his friend in a warm embrace. '*Tudo bom?*'

'*Tudo bom*,' replied Phaulkon in Portuguese. He was very fond of the spirited Mestre Phanik, and full of respect for his intellect. He had missed the jovial face which always reminded him of a moon drawn by children; a full, almost hairless circle with smiling eyes, prominent ears and a snub nose. Phanik was in his early forties, a good ten years older than Phaulkon.

'How fortunate that you are back. I sent a messenger three times to your home. How I have missed you! But come this way, amigo, you must meet some of my friends. Oh no, first let me take you to Maria. This is her occasion and you mustn't talk to anyone else before her or I'll be in trouble. She has been asking me about you. "Will he be coming? Do you think he's coming?"' he mimicked. 'She says you're the only man who doesn't bore her. And she hardly knows you! I tell you, that child . . . . !' Mestre Phanik shook his head and tried to look resigned.

He took Phaulkon by the arm and led him across the large living room, through clusters of guests sitting cross-legged on cushions like tailors. The chairs had all been removed. The Siamese did not sit in chairs and to invite them to do so would

216

create an insurmountable problem of protocol. Everybody would have to be seated slightly higher or lower than his neighbour, according to rank. Phaulkon had been carefully observing the faces around him, wondering which celebrities – for Phanik, as chief adviser to the Treasury on Japanese affairs, was well connected – might be present. Suddenly he caught his breath, staring nonplussed before him. Could this mature beauty coming to meet him be the same little girl he had hugged like a child barely a year ago?

In answer to his question, she beamed a dazzling smile and threw her arms round his neck, exclaiming: 'Uncle Constant, how wonderful to see you! I told my uncle you would be coming but he kept fretting: "Will he come? Will he return in time?"' She laughed and threw her head back.

'And how wonderful to see you on such an auspicious occasion, my dear,' replied Phaulkon in Portuguese, returning her embrace somewhat abashedly. She might well refer to him as uncle, but she aroused no avuncular feelings in him whatsoever, he reflected with a tinge of guilt. 'So today you come of age. You certainly look the part.' He was not flattering her. She was quite striking. Her skin was fair like a Japanese and beautifully offset by her black hair which, unlike that of many local women, had been left long and was drawn up in a chignon. When loose, he reflected, it would fall at least to her waist. She was petite, barely above five feet, and her nose was pointed and refined without the flatness of many Siamese. Her eyes were large and dark and slightly slanted and her full figure, exquisitely proportioned, ended in a pair of the most perfectly chiselled feet.

He racked his brains to think whom she reminded him of. Of course, the statue of Diana, the Goddess of the Hunt. This favourite statue of his childhood, chiselled in white marble, had stood in the fountain of the little square behind the tavern. How he had loved that statue, though it had been draped in a white toga, while Maria was dressed in a becoming dark blue panung, her upper body buttoned to the neck in a beautiful turquoise blouse with a mandarin collar. No doubt the influence of convent school, mused Phaulkon. Her whole personality exuded verve and resolve.

'But I can see my uncle is longing to move you on,' she said, flickering her eyelids coquettishly, 'so I will not detain you, Uncle

217

Constant. But I will expect you to come and find me when the other guests have sufficiently bored you.'

'I will,' said Phaulkon, amazed at her self-assurance at so young an age. 'Besides, I haven't even wished you a happy birthday yet.' He smiled back at her.

Mestre Phanik took him by the arm once again and led him across the room. 'That little girl of mine is going to be quite a headache. I've already had six requests for her hand since she came out of convent school last month. And she's still a child!'

'A very mature one, by the looks of it, Doutor. She's quite transformed since I last saw her. I would prepare yourself for a lot of trouble,' said Phaulkon honestly.

'Do you think so? Oh well, I suppose it had to happen sometime,' he remarked ruefully. 'But come, you must meet our guest of honour. And don't you dare leave early. If the Siamese slip out first, as usual, we can have a long chat. It's ages since I've seen you.'

'And I have much to discuss with you, Doutor.' He could hardly tell Mestre Phanik about the cannon but he planned to explain that his colleagues had been detained at Ligor for lack of papers. He needed to draw on Mestre Phanik's knowledge and above all he needed to find out all he could about the Barcalon. If luck were with him, his friend might even have met him.

His host now led him out on to a terrace overlooking a beautiful garden enclosed by a bamboo hedge. The yellow gladioli and the green lawn were illuminated by brass lanterns. Groups of Siamese were greeting each other silently, cupping their hands in front of their foreheads and inclining their heads slightly. Gestures and not words were exchanged in Siamese introductions. Most of the guests were dressed in puff-sleeved, collarless blouses, though a few were barechested.

A waiter crawled in on his knees, balancing a tray of drinks in one hand like a performing seal, and offered one subserviently to Phaulkon. There was *lau*, a local rice brandy, Spanish red wine, plain water or fresh lime juice. The Siamese, in deference to Buddhist moderation, were generally abstemious, but Phaulkon helped himself to a glass of sparkling Spanish red wine. The Spanish galleons often called at Ayudhya en route to Manila and the officers of the Siamese crown, thanks to the indifference of the royal palate, seldom depleted their stock.

218

Mestre Phanik and Phaulkon descended some wooden steps, with elaborately carved balustrades, into the beautifully illuminated garden. Phanik led his friend over to a distinguished-looking Siamese man with a thick head of cropped grey hair who sat with his legs folded under him and slightly to one side. Around him crouched a group of admirers reverently absorbing his every word. Mestre Phanik joined the circle and prostrated himself before the speaker. Phaulkon followed suit. The grey-haired man ended his discourse and smiled courteously at his host.

'Your Excellency,' said Phanik, 'permit me to introduce you to an old friend of mine who has fallen in love with your country and who has learned to speak the language better than I.' This was indeed an exaggerated compliment as Mestre Phanik was born in Siam, and Siamese was as much his mother tongue as Portuguese or Japanese or Latin. 'Mr Constantine Phaulkon, His Excellency General Petraja. His Excellency, I am sure, needs no further introduction.'

Indeed he did not. Phaulkon was impressed. General Petraja was the hero of the Burmese campaigns, Commander in Chief of His Majesty's Royal Regiment of Elephants, with twenty thousand war elephants under his command, and just recently appointed Chairman of the King's Privy Council. The general was the most decorated soldier in the land. Phaulkon remained prostrate.

Petraja smiled affably. He was a good-looking man, vigorous and in fine health. He did not appear very tall, but he was noticeably strong and his fine athletic build belied his fifty years. 'I am honoured to hear that you have mastered our language, sir. It can be said of very few outsiders,' he remarked.

'Your Excellency is too gracious,' replied Phaulkon, using the correct form of address due a mandarin of the first grade. 'This humble slave's efforts to speak your language have been motivated by a desire to communicate with the very kind and hospitable inhabitants of your country.'

The general was visibly impressed. 'And what good fortune brings you among us, sir?' he inquired, with obvious interest.

'I am employed by the English Trading Company, Your Excellency, and I hope to have the privilege of being of service to Siam some day as well.'

'Siam has always welcomed outsiders and rewarded them well for their services,' declared the general. 'We have allowed them to spread their own faith and live by their own laws. We have imposed little on them and asked little in return. But woe betide any who misinterpret our generosity and mistake our natural hospitality for weakness. We have always been free and we shall remain a free nation.' The circle of devotees murmured their approval.

Phaulkon assumed this was a reference to the Dutch, and was about to concur when a thought seemed to strike the old soldier.

'And how does your English Majesty view the Dutch, sir?' the general inquired.

Phaulkon appeared to hesitate. 'Your Excellency, we are wary of their intentions, their, er . . . ambitions.'

The general nodded, as if it were just what he had suspected. 'What precisely is His English Majesty doing about it?'

'The English Company is planning to put a check to their power, Your Excellency.'

'How?'

'By co-operating closely with His Siamese Majesty's government, Your Excellency.'

'So that any resulting conflict could extend to our shores?' The general eyed Phaulkon suspiciously.

'That would not be the objective, Your Excellency. We would merely strive to maintain the balance of power. And only of course if we were requested to do so by the government of your great sovereign nation.'

The general was interested in the subject as well as clearly impressed by the fluency of Phaulkon's Siamese. He looked around him irritatedly, as if he would have liked the circle of listeners to disappear.

'We must discuss this matter further. Do you hunt elephants?'

The general's skill in that field was proverbial, but it was one Siamese occupation Phaulkon had not endeavoured to master.

'I have never had the pleasure, Your Excellency.'

'Then I shall extend you an invitation.' General Petraja smiled. 'As a spectator of course.'

'This slave can think of no greater honour than to attend his first hunt in the presence of the foremost expert in the field.'

The general inclined his head modestly. 'It is true, I have

learned much about elephants over the last forty years.' The general's expertise in battle was legendary. When the armies of Siam and Burma clashed with twenty thousand elephants per side and three men on each beast, it might be expected that thousands would lie dead on the battlefield by dusk. But both antagonists were Buddhists, and the primary objective was not so much to kill as to capture and bring back slaves to increase each country's wealth. After a fierce battle had raged all day, it was not uncommon to find no more than thirty or forty corpses on the field. It was the skill in manoeuvring the giant beasts that eventually determined the victors and General Petraja's prowess was next to none.

'Ah well, it is time for these old bones to retire,' said the general, rising to leave, while the respectful audience around him – Phaulkon included – remained duly prostrate. He glanced down at Phaulkon.

'I've enjoyed our little talk. I will arrange for the invitation to next month's royal hunt to be sent to you at the English Company.'

'Your Excellency is too gracious,' replied Phaulkon, inwardly thrilled. The general's retinue now rose also, walking with a crouch and maintaining a respectful distance behind him. Petraja thanked his host graciously and as he passed Maria on the stairs he inclined his head to her and remarked gallantly how she made him wish he were young once more.

The indefatigable Mestre Phanik was instantly at Phaulkon's side. 'An impressive man, eh? He likes to pretend to be just a simple old soldier, but he's as cunning as a fox with three heads, and a true patriot.' Mestre Phanik lowered his voice. 'Between you and me, I don't think he likes farangs. But I must tell you the latest.' Mestre Phanik babbled on, draping an arm over Phaulkon's shoulder and wheeling him towards a quieter corner of the garden. 'The general's sister is His Majesty's chief concubine, no less. She has been the doyenne of the royal harem for years.' He lowered his tone further. 'Her name is Yupin and she has been cavorting with a Portuguese officer right here in the Portuguese quarter. Can you imagine, a royal concubine? Our musicians have already started composing bawdy songs about her. Just wait till the general finds out. Especially if my suspicion that he doesn't like farangs is true . . . But here comes Rashid,'

221

said Mestre Phanik, quickly changing the subject as a tall Indian-looking man with a heavy black beard headed towards them. 'I wouldn't have invited him, but these Moors are becoming a little too powerful to be ignored.'

'Mestre Phanik, what a delightful evening,' said Rashid, in Siamese, coming up to them. His dark, rounded eyes switched from his host to Phaulkon.

'You are most generous,' said Mestre Phanik. 'But allow me to introduce an old friend, Mr Constantine Phaulkon. This is Luang Mohammed Rashid. Luang Mohammed is a dangerous man to invite to one's party because he is Chief of His Majesty's Banqueting Department and he is able to judge too well the quality of one's cuisine.' Luang Mohammed laughed. 'Luang', Phaulkon knew, was a title of nobility, like Lord, which could only be conferred by the King.

Rashid was far from being the only Moor to have been thus honoured. These Muslims, so named after the Portuguese 'Mouros', the Barbary Coast faithful who had occupied the southern Iberian peninsula for centuries and built the Alhambra in Granada, were solidly entrenched in all aspects of government and some even lived within the palace walls as advisers to the King. Some four thousand strong, they had no suburb of their own like the Portuguese, the Japanese or the Malays.

'I assure you, Doutor, you have nothing to fear. One of the reasons I gladly accepted your invitation was in the hope of stealing one of your cooks. Especially as we have had news of the arrival of a distinguished ambassador from the Grand Sophy. His Majesty has requested full honours to be extended to him.'

Phaulkon looked puzzled, and the learned doctor came to his aid. 'You know him of course as the Shah of Persia, Constant. Correct me if I am wrong, Luang Mohammed, but is not Sophy a corruption of the word Sufi, the great dynasty that has ruled over Persia for the last twenty years?'

'Indeed it is, Doutor. I see that your reputation for scholarship is indeed well founded. The Great Shah Suleiman now reigns in the two hundred and forty-second year of the Sufi dynasty.'

'I remember when I was in India the King of Delhi was known as the Great Moghul,' remarked Phaulkon, pursuing the conversation in Siamese.

'Precisely,' nodded the Moor, observing him attentively. 'And to complete the trilogy we have the Sultan of Turkey known as the Grand Turk. What illustrious rulers, chosen of Allah, hold sway from the shores of Europe to the borders of Siam,' he asserted.

'Would that the Great King of Siam himself were to join the ranks of the faithful,' observed a short man who had just joined them. He was south Indian in appearance, darker than any Siamese, and with several rolls of fat under his chin. 'The word of God would then extend from the Mediterranean to the China Sea. May Allah bless His Majesty and guide him into the fold of Islam.'

Next to the newcomer, Luang Mohammed, who was tall and light-skinned and probably of Persian extraction, looked almost European. Yet despite the difference in colouring, both Moors had the same predominantly Aryan features. Either they were recent arrivals or their ancestors had inter-married little with the Siamese.

'Allow me to introduce Mr Abbas Malipatam,' said Luang Rashid. 'I took the liberty of bringing him with me. He is my new assistant in the Royal Banqueting Department. This is your host, Mestre Phanik and Mr . . . I'm sorry, I did not catch your name?'

'Constantine Phaulkon, at your service, sir.' The newcomer raised his hand to his heart in the Muslim greeting and Phaulkon wai'd to him in the Siamese fashion.

Over the short man's shoulder, Phaulkon caught sight of the unmistakable hook nose and windmill arms of his friend, Père le Morin. The little French Jesuit, gesticulating wildly, was obviously engaged in one of his harangues. He had not spotted Phaulkon yet.

'So, gentlemen,' said Mestre Phanik, 'His Majesty's Banqueting Department is here in full force tonight. You put me to shame.' As if to test his statement, a liveried waiter, bent almost double, held up a silver platter laden with small delicacies: garlic shrimps and canapé-sized Portuguese pastries much in favour with the Siamese aristocracy.

'Delicious,' observed Luang Mohammed, tasting one. 'Perhaps, Mestre Phanik, you would agree to hire your cooks out, if you steadfastly refuse to have them stolen.'

'Ah, but would they ever return once they had worked for the royal banquets, Luang Mohammed?' retorted Mestre Phanik, smiling.

'When is His Excellency the Persian ambassador arriving?' asked Phaulkon, his curiosity aroused. Was the ambassador's visit part of the great Muslim scheme to turn the Siamese King towards Allah, he wondered, or had the ambassador been invited by King Narai as a show of Asian solidarity against Dutch expansion?

'We are expecting him any time now,' replied the tall Moor. 'His Majesty has expressed great interest in the teachings of the Prophet,' he added pointedly.

A great burst of laughter came from a rowdy group nearby. They were farang traders, well into their drink, and all eyes, some showing undisguised disapproval, turned on them. In that instant Father le Morin's eyes met Phaulkon's and with a squeak of recognition he headed towards him.

'Mon cher Constant,' he said, embracing Phaulkon warmly. 'So you are back from your travels. What a surprise. We must pursue our little mission to restore you to your old faith.' For some time now the Jesuits had been trying to convert Phaulkon back to the Catholic faith of his childhood, although his indifference to matters of religious dogma gave them little scope for success. Yet despite the unrelenting attempts, Phaulkon liked them, especially the little Jesuit standing before him now.

Mestre Phanik introduced Father le Morin all round and then, with a knavish grin, spoke quickly to the priest in Portuguese: 'These gentlemen have just been expressing the hope that Allah will soon show His Majesty the true light.' As expected, the Jesuit bristled and his rounded shoulders almost straightened out as he rose to his limited height. Turning contentiously on the Moors, he spoke in heavily accented Siamese.

'Gentlemen, I must inform you that the Bishop of Beryte who not long ago was granted an audience by His Siamese Majesty while on his way to China, imparted to us the joyful news that His Majesty of Siam is most happily disposed to the Christian religion.'

'That is indeed a coincidence, sir,' replied Luang Mohammed, looking down his nose at le Morin, 'as we understand His Majesty is favourably inclined towards Islam. He has in fact written to the Great Shah Suleiman who has responded by sending his ambassador. The illustrious envoy is on his way now and I have the honour, sir, of being in charge of the welcoming festivities. My instructions,' added the Moor pointedly, 'have been to prepare a reception matched only by the welcome accorded ambassadors from the Emperor of China.' No ambassadors were received with greater fanfare than those from the mighty Middle Kingdom to the north.

'His Majesty's hospitality is proverbial,' responded the Jesuit with a slight bow. 'It may interest you to know, sir, that a portrait of His Majesty King Louis XIV of France, the defender of the Catholic faith, hangs in His Siamese Majesty's private apartments.' Phaulkon pricked his ears at this. 'His Majesty is a great admirer of our noble King.'

'How long have you been in our country?' inquired Abbas of the priest.

'Six years, sir.'

'Then you cannot have failed to notice that the administration of this country is in the hands of the faithful of Allah. His Majesty in his wisdom has seen fit to appoint the true followers, and no others, to positions of responsibility throughout the realm. The followers of Christ, I understand, are more concerned with profit.'

The Jesuit bristled again. 'Your people have been entrenched here a long time,' he said, struggling to contain his indignation, 'but the true word of God is spreading, nevertheless.'

'The Portuguese followers of Christ were here even before my great-grandfather's day,' asserted Abbas, his dark eyes flashing, 'but I am not aware that His Majesty ever appointed them to high posts in government, sir.'

'Gentlemen,' interrupted Mestre Phanik, 'you must excuse me from this fascinating discussion. But it appears some of my guests are leaving.'

'We will be leaving too,' said Luang Mohammed, turning abruptly to go. The two Moors saluted Phaulkon courteously and nodded curtly to the priest.

'A most illuminating exchange, Father,' said Phaulkon, reverting to Portuguese as soon as the others had left. Le Morin was fluent in both French and Portuguese. 'Is it true what you said about the portrait of Louis XIV?'

'Indeed it is. His Majesty of France is depicted on horseback.

Unfortunately I cannot reveal how I know of His Siamese Majesty's great interest in our Sun King. Suffice it to say we Jesuits have our sources,' said le Morin proudly.

They were, Phaulkon knew, a remarkably capable – and determined – order. In the 150 years since their foundation by St Ignatius Loyola and their approval by the Pope, the Jesuits had built up the largest missionary order in the world. The rigorous and thorough training of their recruits had produced some of the most disciplined, determined and intellectually able minds in the service of God. Le Morin himself had undergone nine years of training in the humanities and the scriptures before taking his vows of poverty, chastity and obedience. Once ordained, he had been appointed a school teacher for three years in a small Gascon town to gain practical experience in communicating knowledge. Then finally, to round off his training, he had spent a year in total isolation, meditating upon the scriptures and all matters spiritual.

In Siam he and his fellow Jesuits studied the language, spread the word of God, taught the gospel at the Seminary and assumed the roles of physicians and even engineers. They comforted tortured prisoners in their cells and rescued sick babies from an early death. Unlike other orders, as le Morin loved to point out, they did not expend valuable time in solemn liturgies or penitential practices. They dressed simply, in plain, clerical garb, spurned titles and honours and got down to the business at hand.

Now, after six years in Siam, Father le Morin was driven by one overriding ambition: to achieve the conversion of the Great King Narai of Siam.

'But tell me, Constant, Maria has informed me that she thought you might have abandoned for ever your Catholic faith?' The Jesuit sounded bemused. 'Surely that cannot be so.'

'I am afraid she is right, Father. I became a Protestant when I was a young lad at sea. My English masters persuaded me to adopt their faith.' There was a pause.

'Well, fortunately it isn't too late to put things right, Constant. I hope you will come and see me about it. And I am sure it would give Maria great pleasure to know we were discussing the topic. She made a point of mentioning it to me.'

'How has her schooling progressed?' asked Phaulkon, surprised to learn of Maria's interest in his beliefs.

226

Le Morin considered for a moment. 'She is of course highly intelligent but though devoted to her studies, she is by no means ready to accept all that we teach. She requires reasons and explanations for everything and they must satisfy her. It has certainly been a challenge to instruct her. You know we Jesuits do not as a rule instruct women, but we obtained special exemption from the Bishop in honour of the family's exemplary past.'

Phaulkon accepted another glass of red wine and out of the corner of his eye noticed that most of the Siamese had now left. He glimpsed Mestre Phanik at the top of the steps, bidding farewell to his departing guests. General Petraja had obviously been the most important of them. Phaulkon had spotted a few familiar faces among the Siamese – mostly junior officials from the Ministry of Trade – but he did not think he had missed anyone of consequence.

A large, gruff French trader with an unpleasant body odour now came over and introduced himself to Père le Morin. Phaulkon made a point of avoiding an introduction, grateful for a few moments to himself. He glanced around him. Several young Siamese girls – for in the all-male trading world of Ayudhya no farang women were permitted – were chatting excitedly to Maria in one corner of the large garden. Not far from them the same rowdy group of farang traders was still laughing, occasionally even cheering and some, Phaulkon noticed, were beginning to appear very unsteady on their feet. Waiters, no longer crawling so abjectly now that the Siamese dignitaries had departed, still wound in and out of the thinning crowds, offering savouries and crouching low as they passed.

Phaulkon noticed one farang, obviously a newcomer to the country, extending his hand in greeting to a perplexed Siamese. To extend only one hand was considered rude, as if you meant to give only a part of yourself, so the Siamese responded by placing both his hands under the farang's to indicate that he was putting himself entirely in that person's power.

'Farangs, farangs! You can meet them later.' Mestre Phanik was back at Phaulkon's side. 'They always stay till the last to finish off my liquor anyway. And we'll never get them to leave while there is a drop of brandy left. I've been trying to push everyone out so we can have a long talk. I'm dying to hear all about your travels. Why don't we just disappear to my study? There's no one of consequence left anyway.' They went upstairs and were soon comfortably settled in two armchairs.

'Maria asked me to ensure that you do not leave,' said Mestre Phanik to Phaulkon. 'She will be joining us in a little while.' He chuckled. 'She thought we might have things to discuss "unseemly for a woman's ears".' Pride in the girl was written all over his face.

'How can we justify her suspicions then?' asked Phaulkon, smiling. 'For a start I must tell you that our ship foundered off the coast of Ligor, that I fought in a boxing match there and that the sport-loving Governor awarded me the Order of the White Elephant, third class.'

The Doutor was at first incredulous, but seeing his friend was serious he clapped his hands in the air and roared with delight. 'That's the best bit of news I've heard all year. And you certainly chose the right Governor. He's one of the King's favourites. But come on, just to be sure, show me the medal.' Phaulkon produced it from the leather pouch round his neck. The Doutor stared at it in awe. 'The worst rogues have all the luck,' he said, shaking his head. Phaulkon then told him the whole story, omitting only the matter of the cannon, and Mestre Phanik continued shaking his head from side to side. 'Such things as fables are made of,' he repeated. 'So where to now, amigo?'

'Into government service, I hope,' replied Phaulkon. 'This may just be the opportunity I have been waiting for. I have a feeling that the Barcalon will be summoning me soon.'

'The Barcalon, eh?' Mestre Phanik whistled through his teeth. 'But where would they put a farang to work?' he asked, more to himself than anyone. He sat up in his chair. 'Although with your knowledge of Siamese it would have to be in the Minstry of Trade. That's it, by Jove.' The Doutor slapped his knee. 'You speak half the trading languages in Ayudhya. If you could just get a foot in the door, you could make yourself indispensable to them. What an opportunity!'

Phaulkon was silent for a moment. Then he leaned forward confidentially. 'What chance would I have of exposing the corrupt practices of the Moors?' he asked. 'In trade for instance? We know their methods.'

'We do; but exposing them?' The Doutor was aghast. 'You're

not serious? It's true that with the death of Aqa Muhammad they are without a real leader. But you would have to tread very carefully. Your life would be in God's hands.' Aqa Muhammad was the former Barcalon, a Moor of Persian extraction, whose family had been settled in Siam since the fourteenth century. By favouring other Moors and placing them in high positions, he had created a Muslim power elite which it was said the Siamese mandarins were now bent on dismantling. But it would need careful handling. The Moors would not easily relinquish that power.

'The present Barcalon is of pure Siamese stock, is he not?' asked Phaulkon.

'As all others have been before him, with the exception of Aqa. And though I'm sure you could gain the new Barcalon's support, I don't know how far he could protect you from the Moors' assassins.' He paused. 'Why would you want to expose them anyway?'

'Because I need to conduct a trade mission to Persia myself, and they have the monopoly. Given the chance I'm sure I could increase the Siamese Treasury's revenues threefold. I just need the opportunity to prove their embezzlement.'

Mestre Phanik was thoughtful. 'The one thing in your favour is that they have grown lazy from lack of supervision, ever since their brother Moors became the supervisors. They overcharge as a matter of course now and you might well catch them unawares.'

'You mean in areas other than Persian trade?' asked Phaulkon, his excitement growing.

'Oh yes. Banqueting for instance. They have a catering monopoly for all the royal banquets. That fellow Rahsid you met tonight is in charge. You don't think he pads the bills? Prodigiously, I should wager.'

'Why isn't anything done about it?'

'Because he's in charge and because authority is respected in Siam. But there is no doubt that the Siamese mandarins have begun to balk at the abuse by the powerful Moors and to look for an excuse to unseat them. From that point of view your timing is perfect.' Mestre Phanik's brow furrowed. 'The proof you need is right there, I'm sure, buried in the maze of files at the Ministry of Trade. But how to unearth it, that is the question.'

'There's only one way,' asserted Phaulkon. 'By obtaining a

post there and ploughing through those files until I eventually come across something.'

'But that could take a lifetime, Constant. And even if you could land yourself the job, how would Burnaby react to your being employed by the Siamese? You are, after all, an official of the English East India Company.'

Unwilling to disclose the matter of the cannon, Phaulkon had had to explain that Ivatt and Burnaby were to be released as soon as the ministry had sent a copy to Ligor of their original authorization to trade with the Malay States. The Doutor was thus unaware of Ivatt and Burnaby's present predicament.

'Burnaby will grumble as usual,' replied Phaulkon, 'until I show him the benefits to be derived from having someone planted in the heart of the ministry whose country we serve in.'

Mestre Phanik considered for a moment. 'But is that not precisely what the Barcalon – assuming he were to employ you in the first place – would suspect? Where would your loyalties lie?'

'I would need time to prove that they lay with Siam, of course.' Phaulkon looked Mestre Phanik straight in the eye. 'But you know, Doutor, they actually would.'

'I believe you, Constant. You love this country, I have always felt it.'

'I feel strangely drawn to it. Almost as if it were my own, and it were calling me.' He paused, his heart quickening as he thought of the one man who could destroy him – or give him the chance he needed. 'Have you ever met the Barcalon?'

'Once,' said Mestre Phanik slowly. 'And I can tell you that he's the shrewdest man I've ever met. Like most Siamese, he is immaculately courteous, while all along he is sizing you up, setting little traps for you, and before you are even aware of it, he has found out exactly what he wanted to know. It is even said that he does not accept bribes, though I still have doubts on that score. It is such an accepted way of life here.'

'But do you think he would object in principle to employing a farang in his ministry?'

'Probably not, even though it's never happened before. The Siamese are remarkably broad-minded in that respect. They don't care who you are as long as you do a good job. Look at the Moors. They're no more Siamese in origin than I am. Yet they're

230

in every type of government service. It's more a question of proving your loyalty. You'd be at a disadvantage initially, of course, working as you have been for the farangs. At least the Moors have always worked for Siam – and their own pockets. But in time you could overcome that.' Mestre Phanik paused. 'What makes you think you are going to be offered a job there in the first place?'

'I'm going to ask for one without pay. At least until my new employer is satisfied of my intentions.'

'Without pay, eh?' Mestre Phanik was impressed. 'That sounds tempting enough. But what would you live on?'

'I'll convince Burnaby to continue paying my wage, while I feed information back to the English from the heart of Siam's Ministry of Trade.'

Phanik slapped his knee and roared with laughter. 'I like that! If I didn't know you better, Constant, I'd say you were an unprincipled rogue. As it is, you probably just qualify as a principled one.'

'And what are my two wicked uncles plotting?' Both men turned round. Maria stood in the doorway, looking radiant. She had all of her uncle's effervescence, reflected Phaulkon, and considerably better looks. He found himself staring at her curiously. How self-possessed she had suddenly become. The shyness of a year ago had vanished.

'We were discussing Mohammedanism and Christianity and the King of Siam, my dear,' said Mestre Phanik. 'Are you going to join us?'

'I would be honoured to,' she said, settling in a chair next to her uncle. 'Unfortunately the King of Siam will never adopt the Christian faith,' she said. 'I keep telling the good fathers that they are deluding themselves, but they hang on to this great hope of theirs. It is an unattainable goal.'

'Why do you say that, my dear?' asked Mestre Phanik, intrigued. Phaulkon found himself leaning forward too.

'Why should he abandon the faith his ancestors have held – and thrived on – for two thousand years? To what purpose? To please a few visiting Jesuits? Would the King of France abandon his faith at the behest of a Buddhist delegation to Versailles?'

'My dear, you must not speak so frivolously,' said Mestre

231

Phanik, not a little shocked. 'Think of what our ancestors suffered.'

'They suffered bravely for their beliefs, Uncle, but that was in Japan where their right of worship was denied them. In Siam we are free to worship whomever we will.'

'But you are a believer, are you not, my child?' The Doutor sounded perturbed.

'Of course I am, Uncle. But that should not make me blind to the truth.'

'What if His Majesty's conversion were to mean saving his kingdom from the clutches of the Dutch?' asked Phaulkon, testing her.

'That would be a political conversion, and of no spiritual value,' responded Maria. 'And besides, the King of Siam is far too clever for that. He would simply give the impression of preparing to convert. But he would never go through with it.' The two men looked at each other.

'Anyway, let's not talk about religion, I have that all day long,' laughed Maria. 'What about some other exciting topic like Luang Sorasak, for instance.' She glanced mischievously at her uncle. He immediately rose to the bait.

'Why, that presumptuous scoundrel, just wait till I meet him,' huffed the Doutor.

'You'd be as warm and courteous as you are with everyone, Uncle,' teased Maria. 'But can I tell Uncle Constant?'

'I suppose so,' answered Phanik grudgingly.

'Well,' she began playfully, 'Luang Sorasak – none other than the son of General Petraja who was here this evening – wrote a letter to my uncle, from the palace, what's more, offering me the position of consort in his harem. You should have seen Uncle's face! The few remaining hairs on his head flew up as if they were readying for battle!'

Phaulkon laughed. He found himself quite taken by Maria's style, her startling combination of vivacity and acute observation.

'What?' she continued, mimicking her uncle. 'Are we thus to be treated, one of the oldest and most respected Catholic families in the kingdom? Do they not know that Catholic girls do not join harems?'

'Where did you meet this Luang Sorasak?' inquired Phaulkon.

'That's the strange part, I never even noticed him. Apparently

232

he spotted me at a reception where I was accompanying my uncle, and I don't even know which one he was. How frustrating!'

'She loves to tease me,' said Mestre Phanik, 'but in fact I was quite outraged.'

'You were an absolute killjoy, Uncle.' She turned to Phaulkon. 'He's so jovial and open-minded with everybody else,' she complained, 'but when it comes to his little niece . . . it's one law for poor Maria and another for the rest of the world.'

Phaulkon, too, had noticed a complete transformation in his friend wherever Maria was concerned.

'Uncle,' she continued, not letting him go, 'will you admit, now that a whole month has gone by, that his offer was quite honourably intentioned? After all, in Siamese eyes a minor wife is a respectable position to hold. And I am told that all minor wives must be treated equally. Whatever gifts are made to one must be made to the other. That's fair, isn't it?' She made one final attempt to provoke him. 'Why, even the children born of minor wives are considered perfectly legitimate. The truth is,' she added turning back to Phaulkon, 'that my uncle is just annoyed because Luang Sorasak didn't offer me the position of major wife.'

Both men laughed this time, and she got up and hugged them one after the other.

'So how did you turn him down?' asked Phaulkon.

She smiled impishly. 'I haven't yet.'

It was getting late, and Phaulkon rose to take his leave. As he did so, he felt Maria's gaze on him. She was exceptionally mature for her age, he reflected again. She had obviously learned a lot from her uncle, while retaining very definite views of her own. He promised himself to return to see them both soon.

Maria, for her part, watched Phaulkon with curiosity. Now she knew why his image had kept returning to disturb her ever since their first encounter. He understood, as she did, both sides of the world, the West and the East. He was at heart unconventional and ambitious, as was she. And he was very handsome. She smiled warmly at him, sensing within herself a growing excitement about this man, and a curious new awareness of her own body. Today she was sixteen, and a woman at last. Maria felt herself to be on the brink of something wonderful.

233

Sixteen

For the second consecutive day Yupin presented her pass and limped past the surprised palace guards. She slipped a few coris shells into the captain's palm for good measure and saw him smile. It was always wise to make a friend.

As the distance between herself and the palace increased, once again her limp became less prominent and soon she was striding through the archway that marked the entrance to the Portuguese quarter. Her thoughts filled with lust for Pedro Alvarez and her limbs longed for his brutal love-making. She knew that in the muscular Portuguese officer she had met her sexual match.

Her heart quickened at the thought of yesterday's encounter. The two of them had barely exchanged civilities before he had dragged her into his bedchamber and she, just as willing, had torn hungrily at his tunic and buried her lips in the thick matted hair of his chest. These farangs were like apes, she thought, and Lord Buddha they smelled like them too, no matter how they tried to conceal it with their perfumes. Yet the more pungent the stench, the more it seemed to drive her on. She had worked herself into a frenzy around his brawny body, until, unable to bear it any longer, she had taken hold of his huge love lance and thrust it deep within her, bracing herself for the inevitable pain. For he was like a horse and it never ceased to hurt her. She felt as if her body were being cleft apart, until she could no longer determine which was the more exquisite: the pleasure or the pain.

As she swung her hips beguilingly through the narrow cobbled streets of the Portuguese quarter, past the strange, whitewashed houses that had no stilts, she saw with pride that every passer-by turned her way: dark-skinned Goanese lackeys with European features, strutting Portuguese soldiers in handsome tunics, and even thin, half-caste women balancing earthenware jugs on their heads. All seemed to glance in her direction. Was it her beauty alone? Or had her effusive lover, despite assurances to the contrary, been boasting of his conquest of the royal concubine, even though he himself would share the same fate if they were discovered? Whichever it was, she revelled in the attentions of the passers-by, despite the risks involved. For a moment she again contemplated the terrible consequences of discovery, then dismissed them from her mind. These moments of ecstasy with her brutal lover were rare and unforgettable, and what was life without a man to satisfy her cravings?

She turned the corner now towards the narrow row of houses where her lover lived. And then she froze. For a moment she stood there paralysed. Could her eyes be playing tricks on her? She blinked them but the image did not go away. At the very door of her captain's house were two men, dressed in the red uniforms of the palace guard. They were talking animatedly to his servant. Finally her legs came to life. She retraced her steps, trying to walk as casually as possible. Then, turning into the first side street, she broke into a run. She ran, oblivious of direction and the pain in her leg, until she had completely lost her bearings. Eventually, noticing the curious stares of the passers-by and realizing the attention she was attracting, she slowed her pace to a walk. She turned into a broad, side alley where she was sure no one had yet seen her.

The alleyway was lined with trees, and large, spacious, brick houses with bamboo-enclosed gardens stood on either side of it. It was obviously the residential quarter of the well-to-do. One house, unlike most of the others around it, was in the Siamese style, but of wood with a great curving roof of orange tiles, and she felt there was a good chance its occupants would speak Siamese.

Desperate, she mounted the wooden steps, pulled the bell cord and waited breathlessly outside the house, longing for the safety of its walls. A servant answered and Yupin asked for the lady of the house. She was still breathing heavily, and her face and neck were beaded with sweat. The servant eyed her suspiciously. He was very dark, with Indian features.

'Is my Lady expecting you?' he asked in accented Siamese.

'Please tell her I must see her. It's urgent. I am a Christian,' she lied. It was a reasonable assumption that in the middle of the Portuguese quarter the lady of the house would herself be Christian.

The servant hesitated. 'Wait here, please,' he said, closing the

235

door on her. Yupin remained outside, glancing anxiously to either side of her, up and down the street. She huddled close to the doorway. Her mind was in turmoil. They were looking for her now, it was clear. Someone must have seen her yesterday. It could all be over soon. She shuddered at the thought of what they would do to her.

In this moment it struck her as amazing that she had allowed her lust to eclipse her fear of discovery, especially when she had known the consequences all along.

She recoiled as the door suddenly swung open again. Then a gentle voice said: 'Come in please and sit down. You look distressed. How can I be of service to you?'

Yupin slid quickly through the door, at the same time sizing up her potential saviour. She was a young woman, probably not more than sixteen or seventeen. She did not look Portuguese, but neither did she look Siamese, though she wore Siamese dress and spoke Siamese fluently. In any event she was decidedly pretty and she had a determined and self-assured air. Yupin would have somehow to manoeuvre her into summoning the Dutch surgeon here. It was her only hope. It would be too risky to venture out into the streets now without him, and only he could escort her back to the palace. She had used his offices twice before, just before her lover had left for Pattani, and she knew at least that he was amenable to bribes. He might help her again. She followed the lady into an anteroom and sat in the chair that was offered to her.

'You look flustered, Pi. You should rest a while,' said the lady of the house. 'What happened to your knee?'

'I had an accident, my Lady. I fell on a sharp stone.'

'You should see a doctor.'

'I will, my Lady. Please don't concern yourself.'

'Let me order some refreshments.'

'Thank you, my Lady.' Yupin was glad that the girl had called her Pi, or elder sister. It was at least a sign of respect. She glanced self-consciously at her attire. Her white blouse was soaked and clung to her skin, accentuating the heave of her breasts, while the ends of her panung had come loose.

She rose and adjusted them. Then she pulled up her blouse as best she could and smiled across at the girl, as she returned from ordering the refreshments.

236

'Would you like me to get you some clean clothes?' inquired her hostess. 'I think I have something that will fit you.'

'That is very kind of you. I will gladly accept. It is so hot outside,' explained Yupin. She needed time to think and the girl's departure would provide her with at least a moment's respite.

'Of course, Pi. I'll be back in a moment.'

Yupin followed the young woman with her eyes as she left the room. She had a graceful walk and one which the royal concubine could soon have refined into a most alluring gait. Yupin wondered now what kind of mixture the girl was. Her exotic looks and the exquisite paleness of her skin would at any rate have made her a fine addition to the palace harem.

What would be her best approach to the girl? she wondered. Flattery? A show of repentance, which the Christians seemed to relish?

A servant brought in refreshments now, tea and the famous Portuguese kanom cakes that had become so popular with the Siamese, just like the hot chili spices they had introduced earlier and which had become a staple of Siamese cuisine. Though Yupin had little appetite, it would be best to make every effort to please her hostess.

The girl now returned, bearing a clean blouse and a fresh panung. Yupin thanked her and slid the sash slowly off her shoulders, exposing her beautifully formed breasts. To her amazement, the girl actually lowered her eyes. How delicious, thought Yupin. She must be a farang at heart. Only farangs found shame in breasts. The girl's primness excited her and when the girl pointed to a Japanese screen at the end of the room, as if she were fearful that Yupin might now remove her panung in front of her as well, Yupin was delighted. What a joy to seduce this one!

'You can change over there, Pi,' said the girl, quickly.

'Thank you, my Lady.' As Yupin crossed the room, her eye alighted on a wooden crucifix hanging from the far wall and the sight of it determined her in the approach she would use.

She would speak in confidence to this young thing, confessing her sins to her with a solemn air of repentance and invoking her silence on the matter, as she had heard from her lover that the

237

Christians did when they confessed to their priests. Yes, that was it, she would appeal to her as a reformed sinner.

Yupin smiled as she slipped behind the screen, putting on the clean panung and buttoning up the blouse the girl had given her. Her breasts felt confined and imprisoned in this unaccustomed clothing and she had half a mind to remove the blouse again. But it was best to humour this Christian girl, especially if it were to result in Dr Daniel's summons.

'How can I help you?' asked her hostess as Yupin settled back in the chair opposite her.

Yupin appeared to hesitate. 'I can see you are a good Christian, my Lady. And I have sinned terribly. I don't know that God will ever forgive me.'

'There is nothing that Almighty God does not forgive the truly repentant,' replied the girl with obvious conviction.

'But even if God were to forgive me, my Lady, I doubt the palace executioner would.' Yupin lowered her eyes and began to sob gently.

The girl rose and placed a comforting hand on her shoulder. 'Are you employed at the palace, then?'

'Yes, my Lady, I am.' It was the moment to take the plunge. 'May I confess to you in total confidence?'

'That depends on what you have to tell me.'

It was not quite the answer Yupin had been expecting. Nevertheless, she would not alter her tactic now. 'I am in love with a Portuguese captain and I escaped to be with him. The palace guards are looking for me now. My fate is in your hands, my Lady.' She glanced disconsolately at her hostess.

The girl observed her in silence, as if she were trying to recall something.

'What is your position at the palace?' she asked.

Yupin paused. 'I am one of His Majesty's concubines.' She lowered her head in acknowledgement of the severity of her crime.

The girl stiffened. 'And what is your name?' she asked.

'Yupin, my lady.'

The girl now stared at her with increasing curiosity. 'And mine is Maria de Guimar.' It was all coming back to Maria now. Of course, Yupin. Rumours of this scandalous affair had been circulating in the Portuguese quarter for some time. A few months ago her name had been on everyone's lips. Then abruptly the rumours had subsided. It was presumed she had been executed. Yet here she was, resurrected once more. How exciting! And what a welcome change from the pious tedium of convent school. The whole affair, she reflected, only showed how separate the Siamese and Portuguese communities kept themselves. His Majesty was obviously unaware of the behaviour of this notorious concubine of his. But what if she were discovered in this house? A feeling of uneasiness crept over Maria as the implications of such a discovery dawned on her. Yupin was lucky that her Uncle Phanik was not in. He would have sent her back to the palace under escort without further ado. A voice told Maria that perhaps she should do the same.

'Hadn't you better return to the palace before you're discovered here?' she said, half hoping the woman would turn down her suggestion. When would another exciting opportunity like this present itself?

'I'd like to, my Lady, but it is too dangerous. The guards are out looking for me now. I saw them only a moment ago.'

'Where?'

'Outside Captain Alvarez's house.'

'Are you sure they didn't see you entering here?'

'Quite sure, my Lady.'

'Then you had better stay a while. Now I want to hear all about life at the palace. How long have you been a royal consort?'

'All my adult life, my Lady, since I was fourteen.'

'And when did you start seeing this captain of yours?'

'I met him almost a year ago, my Lady, but I have not seen him more than half a dozen times. It is very difficult to leave the palace.'

'I thought royal consorts could *never* go outside its walls.'

'They cannot officially,' said Yupin smiling. 'But a few of us manage.' Then remembering her strategy, she looked immediately penitent. 'But I will not be seeing him again, my Lady. I want to reform my ways.' She glanced pleadingly at Maria. 'Will you give this sinner another chance?'

Maria smiled. Who was this woman trying to fool? She had not the slightest intention of reforming, any more than Maria

239

intended to enter a nunnery. 'Perhaps I will, Pi, if you tell me all I want to know.'

'I will keep no secrets from you, my Lady.'

'Very well, then. For a start you can tell me all you know about Luang Sorasak. Who is he and is he handsome?'

Yupin hesitated. 'He is . . . my nephew, my Lady. I am afraid, though, that he can hardly be called handsome.' Yupin decided to omit any further details. It hardly seemed the time to go into his evil, vindictive nature, or his craving for power and his incognito boxing forays into the countryside.

Maria's eyes widened. 'You are related to General Petraja, then?' This was becoming interesting.

'He is my brother, my Lady.'

Meu Deus, thought Maria. If the songwriters in the Portuguese quarter could get hold of this one! And to think that all along they had been composing verses about a simple palace concubine. This was indeed news. She wondered if her uncle even knew.

She turned to Yupin. 'But tell me, Pi, where does Luang Sorasak live?'

'In a wing of the palace, my Lady.'

'In the palace?' Maria was not aware of that. To think that she too, like Yupin, could have been shut up with the rest of them, never to see the outside world again, lying there, perhaps plotting the occasional escape to meet her Portuguese lover. Of course, she would never have accepted Sorasak's offer anyway. No wonder her uncle had been so incensed at Sorasak's suggestion. 'The palace!' she repeated. 'But how does he come to live there?'

Yupin hesitated. It would be high treason to divulge such palace secrets. Yet this girl seemed ready to help her, and if she enjoyed these revelations as much as she seemed to, she might be disposed to repay her by summoning Dr Daniel.

'Luang Sorasak, my Lady, is officially my nephew. But in truth he is the son of the Lord of Life himself, born of a northern woman who lay with His Majesty during the Burmese campaigns. She was of too lowly a birth to be recognized as the mother so the child was given to my brother to bring up as his own. You will appreciate of course, my Lady, that I am telling you this in full confidence. I could be executed for such revelations.'

Maria clapped her hands delightedly as she had often seen her uncle do. 'You may rest assured on that score, Pi. I will divulge nothing.' She smiled broadly at Yupin. What an interesting afternoon. It was almost making up for all those monotonous days at convent school. She prayed that her uncle would not return to spoil it.

'But tell me, Pi, how do you spend your day at the palace?' Maria always imagined that everybody else's life was more glamorous and exciting than her own, even those imprisoned palace ladies.

Yupin considered for a moment. Should she divulge her mission to train Sunida? She thought better of it. She was, after all, under oath not to reveal any part of her assignment. Even though it might make this inquisitive girl more disposed to help her.

Maria noticed the hesitation. 'One more piece of information,' she coaxed, 'and you have my word that I will help you. You'll have to make it really interesting though.'

Yupin decided to take a chance. 'Will you summon Dr Daniel here, if I tell you?'

'The Dutch surgeon?'

'Yes. He is authorized to dress my wound and I have a pass from the palace to see him. It would be dangerous for me to leave this house without him.' She glanced out of the window. 'It will soon be dark.'

'Very well, Pi. I will do that. But you must say that you became lost and rang my bell for directions. Dr Daniel is a friend of the family and he'll be wondering how you came to be in this house in the first place. I'll send a messenger to him right away. The Dutch quarter is fortunately not far.'

'Oh thank you, my Lady.' Yupin was genuinely grateful. 'I am deeply indebted to you. You may ask me any favour in this life and I shall not refuse you.'

As Maria's prostrate servant received his instructions, Yupin considered one more time whether she should really reveal her mission to train Sunida. Yet she doubted she could make up another story quickly enough, and it was obviously the kind of disclosure this girl would relish. Besides, if she mentioned no names, the information would be harmless enough and a small price to pay for saving her from the palace guards.

'Now tell me, Pi,' said Maria eagerly, as soon as the servant had left the room, 'what dark intrigue are you going to reveal?'

Yupin observed Maria carefully. She sensed that though the

241

girl was young and full of the inquisitiveness of youth, she was trustworthy enough.

'I have been selected to train a new girl in the arts of seduction.'

'Really!' Maria seemed instantly curious. 'How do you go about that?'

Yupin looked at her speculatively. 'Ah, my Lady, such matters cannot be explained in words. They must be experienced. Perhaps on another occasion, I could—'

Maria quickly interrupted her. 'But I want to know everything. Who have you been selected to train? Is she beautiful? Where does she come from?' It was just as she had always suspected. Even life in the confines of a harem was more exciting than hers.

'I have never seen her, my Lady. She has not arrived yet. But I know she's from the south and I have heard she is exceptionally beautiful.' Yupin almost purred with delight as she thought again of the beautiful provincial novice.

'Is she destined for His Majesty's harem?'

'No, my Lady, strangely enough she is destined for some farang. To spy on him. It is most unusual.' There were thousands of farangs of all nationalities in Ayudhya so Yupin hardly felt she was revealing any great secret.

'A farang? Strange indeed. I wonder who it could be?' He would have to be important for the palace to want to spy on him, reflected Maria. 'You mentioned that I could call upon you for any favour?'

'Indeed, my Lady.'

'Then I would like to know the name of this farang. Can you find that out for me?'

'I will try my best, my Lady.'

'And what is the name of this girl you have been assigned to train?'

Yupin hesitated. That would be going too far. 'I do not know, my Lady.'

'How is that?'

'I have not met her yet.'

'Have you heard speak of any farangs at the palace?'

'I did hear the Lord of Life speak to my brother, General Petraja, about some farang who had been honoured by the Governor of . . . one of the southern provinces, I believe.'

'Nakhon Si Thammarat?' prompted Maria, trying to suppress her mounting excitement. Her uncle had revealed to her the great honour bestowed on Constant by that Governor.

'That's it!' exclaimed Yupin. 'I believe you're right. How did you know?'

Maria ignored the question. 'And what did the Lord of Life say about him?'

'I only overheard fragments of their conversation, my Lady, but the Lord of Life sounded quite intrigued. I heard His Majesty say that he was going to order the Barcalon to summon this farang to an audience.'

'Will you promise to keep me informed? This farang is a family friend and we are interested in his progress.'

'Of course, my Lady. Now that I know of your interest I will find out what I can about him.'

There was the sound of a bell outside and both Maria and Yupin rose expectantly. That would be Dr Daniel. He had not wasted any time. The door swung open and in walked Mestre Phanik, hat in hand.

'Hello, who have we here?' he asked jovially in Portuguese, embracing Maria and turning inquiringly towards Yupin.

The courtesan primped her hair and beamed her most beguiling smile.

'Er, this lady, Uncle, lost her way looking for Dr Daniel. So I sent Kowit out to fetch him. I hope you don't mind?'

'Not at all. You did the right thing.' Mestre Phanik turned to Yupin in Siamese. 'You certainly have come far out of your way, madam. May I ask where you live?'

'Near the palace, my Lord, but I am afraid I became lost. I am not too familiar with the European quarters.'

Maria gave Yupin a quick look which told her to be on her guard.

Mestre Phanik surveyed the visitor's bandaged knee. 'Are you badly hurt, madam?'

'Just a little fall, my Lord, but nothing Dr Daniel cannot cure, I'm sure.'

'Yes, he's very competent. He's an old friend as well. Do you know him, then?'

'I met him once, a long time ago,' replied Yupin, putting on her most serious air. Mestre Phanik observed her curiously.

243

'Isn't that my niece's blouse you are wearing?' he inquired.

'Indeed it is,' replied Yupin. 'I'm so sorry. I was about to run away with it. This kind lady lent it to me when she saw how I was perspiring after my long detour.' Before Maria or her uncle could stop her, Yupin had removed the blouse. They both turned away but Yupin did not miss the fleeting look of admiration on Mestre Phanik's face as her shapely bosom was revealed.

The doorbell chimed again and Yupin turned quickly to Maria. 'I must go now. I am so late. Thank you for all your kindness, my Lady.' She wai'd to Mestre Phanik and moved towards the door.

'Oh, do ask Dr Daniel in for a moment, if that's him,' insisted Mestre Phanik. 'I haven't seen him for ages. I won't keep either of you, I promise.'

'But Uncle, the lady is in a hurry,' said Maria, anxious to avoid a confrontation.

Before Yupin was through the door, a servant had ushered the Dutch surgeon in. He removed his hat, revealing a shock of blond hair and a face deeply reddened by the tropical sun.

'*Bom dia*,' he said, in heavily accented Portuguese. Then catching sight of Yupin he stared at her for a moment in confusion.

'*Godverdorie*,' he muttered in Dutch under his breath, 'you again! Are you going to get me killed this time?'

Mestre Phanik looked quizzically from one to the other.

'You two have met before?' he asked in Portuguese to the doctor.

Though Yupin understood nothing of farang tongues, it was clear from the expressions around her that she was in trouble.

The surgeon was about to reply when she extracted a piece of paper from a small cotton purse and handed it to Maria. 'Please inform the doctor that I have permission to visit him.' She pointed to her knee. 'Could you ask him to examine me as soon as possible, as I have to return before sundown. It is getting late.'

Maria read the document and translated it into Portuguese for the doctor, who spoke little or no Siamese. She omitted only that the order came from the palace. She had promised to return Yupin safely to the palace and she could not let her uncle spoil everything now. She began to usher the surgeon towards the door.

244

'Let me see that paper,' said Mestre Phanik, recognizing the lofty phrases of royal Siamese in the translation.

Before Maria could prevent it, he had taken the document from her hand and was perusing it. 'I thought the lady said she lived near the palace, not in it,' he said, turning suspiciously to Maria.

'That's what I understood too, Uncle. Perhaps she didn't want to intimidate us.'

Mestre Phanik looked increasingly doubtful. Maria prayed only that he would not recognize Yupin's name.

She turned to Dr Daniel. 'The order is signed in person by Her Royal Highness the Princess Yotatep,' she said pointedly. 'And it's getting dark outside, Doctor.'

Hearing the sound of Yotatep's name, Yupin extracted two gold coins from her purse, specially prepared for the occasion.

'Her Royal Highness asked me to give these to the honourable doctor for his services,' she explained to Maria.

The surgeon eyed the coins covetously as he listened to the translation. It was a great deal more than the examination was worth.

Mestre Phanik was about to request further explanations when the surgeon turned on his heel, beckoning to Yupin to follow him.

'We must be on our way, if we're to return by sunset,' he said, bowing quickly to Mestre Phanik and Maria. Yupin wai'd deeply to Maria and followed the doctor straight out, leaving a frustrated Mestre Phanik attempting to summon them back.

The young guard at the palace gate spotted her first. 'Sir Captain,' he called out excitedly. 'I see a lady coming. There is a farang with her. It must be the one.' The captain came running up.

'You're right. It's her. Go and fetch her.'

The young guard ran off and accosted Yupin.

'Is anything wrong?' she asked, masking her fear.

'You'd better speak to the Lord Captain yourself, my Lady. Follow me, please.' Yupin turned quickly to the surgeon and wai'd to him.

The doctor strode off, only too pleased to be on his way. He had cleansed the wound, bound it and despite the gold coins he had sworn it would be his last encounter with Yupin. The risks were just too great.

The Captain of the Guard was waiting for Yupin at the gate. He wai'd to her. 'The Lord of Life has ordered that you proceed to the royal chambers immediately.' Yupin's heart stood still. 'Messengers have come twice to look for you,' he added ominously.

With an effort Yupin held her head high and made her way across the myriad courtyards that led to the royal apartments. What a trick fate had played on her, just when she thought she was safely home. Would she have the strength, she wondered, to put on an act of outraged innocence, demanding angrily to know the name of the enemy who had falsely maligned her? Or would she simply beg for mercy, pointing to her years of service and asking only for a sudden, painless death?

She stopped short. Whichever it was to be, she was certainly not going to her fate looking the way she was. She had spent most of her life as the foremost courtesan at the court of the great King Narai and she would leave looking the part. She changed direction and headed instead for her chamber, to put on her finest apparel for her last encounter with the Master of Life.

A royal page in smart red uniform accosted Yupin at the entrance to the royal apartments and informed her that His Majesty was busy judging a poetry contest and would not now be able to receive her till later. She was to carry on with her duties in the meantime. There was a young lady waiting for her in the anteroom.

The page opened the door and ushered her in. Yupin stood still in the doorway, transfixed. For there, standing demurely by the window, was a vision of such feminine perfection that she could not recall anything quite like it in twenty years of palace service. The girl was exceptionally tall and long-limbed for a Siamese and she had high cheekbones and large almond eyes set in a face of stunning beauty. She smiled coyly at Yupin.

'Honourable teacher?' she ventured modestly, and receiving no denial from the speechless Yupin, she fell to the ground with the grace of a deer lowering itself into a shady spot.

'What is your name?' asked Yupin, struggling to recover her composure.

'Sunida, honourable teacher. The Divine Lord of Life commanded me to wait for you here. The messengers of His Most Infinite Majesty have been searching for you everywhere. I did not mean to be the cause of any trouble,' she added, looking suddenly anxious.

A wave of hope swept over Yupin. Was this perhaps the reason for the royal summons? The girl from the south had arrived. Faint with relief, Yupin leaned against the door.

Sunida's face registered instant concern. 'Are you not well, honourable teacher?'

'I am well, thank you. It is just the heat and the end of an exhausting day.'

There was a rustling sound from above. It seemed to emanate from somewhere high in the panelled wall to the left. Yupin wondered whether it was one of His Majesty's spies or perhaps even the Lord of Life himself, watching the proceedings through a small peephole. From the beginning, the Master of Life had shown unusual interest in this whole affair.

With an effort she pulled herself together.

'You have been chosen, Sunida, for a royal mission,' she began importantly. 'The Lord of Life himself, the greatest King on earth, has asked to be kept informed of the details. I need hardly tell you what an honour has befallen you.'

Sunida sank still lower on her haunches and her voice quivered. 'The Lord of Life himself has already addressed this speck of dust, honourable teacher. His Infinite Majesty told me that I had been chosen to serve the nation. If I do not appear as grateful as I should, it is only through bewilderment that so great an honour has befallen the worthless slave you see before you. But please know, honourable teacher, that my life, my loyalty and my love belong to my liege.'

Yupin smiled and walked over to her. 'Come then, little mouse,' she said, taking her by the hand, 'let us make a courtesan out of you.'

247

Seventeen

It was warm in the room and the water shimmered in the light of the open window as Yupin lifted the wooden lid off the large earthenware jar whose sides were covered in dragon designs. In the heat of the day the water looked the more inviting. Yupin bent down, picked up a silver bowl and scooped the water up, dousing herself copiously. She sighed luxuriously as the cool liquid cascaded over her naked body, reviving her with each ladle. For fully ten minutes she cleansed herself, then rubbed scented oil into her skin, and by the time she had finished she felt purified, absolved at last from the trials of the previous day.

Out of the corner of her eye she observed Sunida, standing by the plain lacquered cabinet at the far end of the room, shyly averting her eyes from the recessed corner that served as a bathing area.

'Come, little mouse, it is your turn now. You must learn how to bathe a man. Men love to be pampered, you know.' Sunida edged demurely forward. She stood by the earthenware jar in her panung, wondering when Yupin was going to move away and leave her the privacy to disrobe. It was not the idea of bare breasts that troubled Sunida – it was normal for breasts to be uncovered. It was the lower, secret regions that should always remain concealed under the panung, even when bathing. Unless, of course, one was entirely alone. A girl's entire modesty lay in her nether regions.

'Take off your panung, little mouse. You must not be shy with your teacher. We have so much to experience together.' Yupin smiled, and a slight tremor passed through her body as she watched Sunida dutifully begin to unwind her panung.

Glancing shyly across at Yupin all the while, as if she hoped her teacher might still change her mind and leave her alone, Sunida disrobed. But Yupin just stood there calmly gazing at her, until the panung had slipped to the floor and Sunida stood naked before her, her head lowered.

'You must learn to use shyness only as a weapon, little mouse.

248

In moments of intimacy, a man likes a woman to be without shame. You will learn to live without your panung.'

Yupin's eyes now feasted on her at leisure. The smooth, honey-coloured skin had not a blemish or a birthmark on it, and the strong sculpted curves of her waist and breasts, like those of a Khmer statue, wound perfectly into the long sensuous limbs and the soft thin fluff that covered her heavenly garden. She was a perfect specimen of womanhood, flawless and inviting.

Yupin felt a stirring inside her at the thought of the days of training that were to follow, with herself in command. She had let Sunida rest the first night after her long journey, the more readily since Yupin herself needed to recover from the emotions of the day before. But today the training would begin in earnest and she had summoned Sunida from the little room adjoining hers shortly after daybreak. Later, as the training progressed, reflected Yupin happily, she would not need to summon her any more, for Sunida would be sharing her quarters in final preparation for the farang for whom she was destined.

Her pupil stepped gingerly into the little washing cubicle and began pouring great streams of water over herself. After a while she grew accustomed to Yupin's stare and her mind, more relaxed now, began to wander. She thought again of her fate and heard the divine voice from above that still rang momentously in her ears. To think that the Lord of Life had actually addressed her! What strange, exciting things had happened to her since that wonderful man from another world had come briefly into her life. She wondered if she would ever see him again. She thought of her uncle's summons, almost immediately after her beloved farang had left, and of the secret trip under escort to Ayudhya and of her terror as she lay prostrate throughout the royal audience. Now this teacher also frightened her a little. It was all so daunting yet exciting at the same time.

Who was she being trained to serve? she wondered. She, a humble dancer, to serve the nation? And why so far from home? It was not for her to question, she told herself. It was enough that the Lord of Life had commanded.

She luxuriated in the cool splashes of water for a while longer and then, gingerly, took the bottle of scented oil that lay on a shelf. The sweet aroma of jasmine rose to her nostrils. She was

249

about to rub it into her skin, as she had seen her teacher do, when a hand took the bottle from her.

A moment later two hands came from behind and gently, with a soothing circular motion, began to smooth the oil into her body, first into the back of her neck, then across her shoulders and slowly down her spine, detouring to take in her ribs and waist as well. Though she felt her teacher's presence just behind her at no point did any part of her body touch hers other than her fingertips, and Sunida was induced to concentrate on the power in them. She shivered as they progressed still lower, brushing across her buttocks and probing the backs of her thighs. Then from behind her ankles they moved gradually upwards again, pursuing the same route in reverse. But this time she could feel Yupin's breath on her, a wisp of warm air climbing deliciously up her body and sending currents of desire through it.

Then, without warning, Yupin's whole body fused into hers and she felt her teacher's swollen nipples against her back. A pair of caressing hands came round to enfold her breasts and fondle them sensuously.

To Sunida's embarrassment, her nipples too became erect. But her teacher barely heeded them and in the next instant she had retracted her hands and pulled her whole body away. Suddenly she was gone and Sunida heard the door of the room close behind her. She felt strangely abandoned – and deprived. She did not want to be alone in this moment. She experienced a longing for her lover. If only he were here now. How she wanted him.

Unusually despondent she took a cloth towel from the shelf above her and began to dry herself. Then, resisting the urge to put her panung on again, she lay down naked on her thin quilt of rush mats and thought about her teacher. Why had she left so suddenly, without even a word? Where had she gone?

The Lord of Life had told her that she should feel no shame in being trained by a woman and that the Lady Yupin was the finest teacher there was. She certainly had a wonderful touch, reflected Sunida. It was difficult to obey the Lord of Life's command entirely and to feel no shame, especially when she realized she had not really wanted her teacher to stop. Better to take her mind off such considerations. She looked around her, impressed as always by the decor: the beautiful Ayudhya cabinet, the exotic tapestry from Burma, the silk screen from Japan. Her teacher's room was almost as grand as the Governor of Ligor's ante-chamber! As for the audience hall of the Lord of Life . . . she trembled at the recollection. Never had she imagined that anything so beautiful could exist, especially after seeing the golden spires of Ayudhya. Yet while she had kept her head buried in the soft carpets, hardly daring to look up, she had vaguely discerned the beautiful panelled walls with the glittering strips of red and gold lacquer and the tiers of golden parasols. Such unparalleled beauty.

The door opened and instinctively Yupin covered herself with her hands.

Her teacher entered carrying an assortment of ointments and liquids. In one hand she also held three short bamboo canes, to the ends of which were attached feathers of varying shapes and sizes. Sunida quivered. Were these going to be part of the training? she wondered.

Yupin smiled at her warmly. 'Stay where you are, little mouse. Whatever happens now I want you to relax. It may all be new to you, but nothing is going to hurt you. On the contrary . . .'

Sunida smiled shyly and kept silent.

Yupin knelt down beside her, naked except for her panung.

'Are you with knowledge of man, little mouse?'

Sunida hesitated. 'I am, honourable teacher.'

Yupin waited for her to continue, but Sunida had fallen silent. 'Just one, little mouse?'

Again she hesitated. 'Two, honourable teacher.'

Yupin rested a hand casually in the hollow of Sunida's stomach. 'And who was the first to enter your heavenly garden?' Yupin lowered her hand further still and drew her nails gently across the thin down that covered Sunida.

The younger girl tensed. 'It . . . It was the Palat, honourable teacher. The Governor's deputy.'

'And did you know pleasure from him, little mouse?'

Sunida shook her head. 'It was not of my will, honourable teacher.'

'And how often did he enter your heavenly passage?'

'Only a few times, honourable teacher. He left me alone soon after he saw that my reticence would not go away.'

251

'I understand,' said Yupin sympathetically. 'And have you ever known desire, my child?'

Sunida was silent a moment. 'Yes, honourable teacher,' she said, glancing demurely at her feet.

'With the second man?'

Sunida nodded. 'Only with him, honourable teacher.'

'And was it like this, little mouse?' Three soft feathers began to caress Sunida in different places, sending simultaneous waves of delight across her body. Yupin held all three sticks in one hand, dexterously manipulating them like puppets at the end of a string, while her other hand moved up the inside of Sunida's thighs and gently pried her legs open. Instinctively the girl's body tensed again.

'You must learn to relax, little mouse. It is one of the inhibitions that will mar your pleasure – as well as your lover's.'

Sunida relaxed and, as she did so, Yupin deftly inserted two marbles into her heavenly passage. 'Just contract your muscles rhythmically as I talk, little mouse. You will not feel much at first, but soon . . . Now tell me about the second man. Who was he?'

Sunida hesitated. She felt her teacher's roving hands on her breasts now, rubbing a liquid around them and into her nipples. They burnt with a warm tingling while the feathers resumed their tantalizing caresses, distracting her from the burning. The alternating sensation of hot and cold was delicious. She tried to concentrate on Yupin's question.

'He . . . he was a farang, honourable teacher.'

For a brief moment the feathers stopped, and only the heat was in evidence.

'A farang, little mouse?'

'Yes, honourable teacher, I danced for him at the Governor's Palace. And then . . .' Her voice faltered.

'You can tell me another time, if you prefer.' She would save this choice morsel for later. Lord Buddha, they would have plenty to discuss! A farang! Yupin was stunned. Where would a girl like this ever meet a farang? And to think that she was destined for one now. Life was indeed full of surprises!

'Turn over and lie on your stomach, little mouse. And remember to relax.' The feathers started on her back now, deliciously tickling her neck and ears and delving between her buttocks at the same time. As her body alternately contracted and relaxed, the marbles began to have their effect. Sunida groaned and, right on cue, Yupin's practised fingers traversed the young girl's body, tracing the curves of the most sensuous figure – apart from her own – that she had ever known. 'Know that a man and a woman's body are no different in their reaction to touch, little mouse.'

Sunida's head began to move agitatedly from side to side. She glanced round and saw with consternation that her teacher had turned the feathers on herself now. Sunida started to raise her head but a gentle hand pushed her down on to the quilt again and a voice whispered soothingly in her ear. Then she felt her legs pried open once more and a balmy ointment being smoothed around her heavenly garden. Feathers tickled her exquisitely in the most sensitive regions and as they began to explore and titillate her innermost rims, she felt the urge to shout with euphoria.

Suddenly her teacher was lying beside her, her breath warm, her nipples swollen.

'Now, little mouse, we will see how much you have learned. Just imagine I am that same farang you told me about.'

'Yes, honourable teacher.' Sunida closed her eyes and thought of Phaulkon. And everything was wonderful.

Eighteen

'Please be seated, Mr Forcon.' The Barcalon smiled affably and pointed to a plain bamboo chair, the only one in the room, obviously provided for foreign visitors. The solitary, low chair, surrounded by intricately painted Japanese screens, lavish Persian rugs and black and gold cabinets of the early Ayudhya period, stood out incongruously amidst the august prosperity of the panelled audience chamber. The First Minister himself, reclining on an ornate silk couch at the far end of the long room, and partially hidden by a pall of smoke from his hookah, looked very much an integral part of the surroundings.

The summons had come at dawn, just one week after Mestre Phanik's party, and the messenger had waited outside Phanik's house, for his instructions had been to bring the farang in person directly to His Excellency's offices. Phaulkon felt a mixture of fear and relief that the summons had finally come.

Phaulkon ignored the offer to be seated and prostrated himself instead, resting on his knees and elbows with his forehead close to the ground and his hands clasped above his head. He positioned himself so that by squinting upwards through the bottom of his palms he was able to observe the Barcalon without his own face being exposed to the potentate's gaze. Two large windows in one wall of the audience chamber lent light to the proceedings. Phaulkon's every nerve was taut and a queasiness gripped his stomach. He knew that on this interview hinged his fate, that of his companions and the elaborate edifice of years of planning.

The Barcalon leaned over and sucked expansively on the large brass hookah which stood by his side. The Moorish water pipe gurgled pleasantly. He exhaled luxuriously and contemplated Phaulkon through a cloud of blue-grey smoke. He was a portly figure of apparently short stature and his plump, squat legs seemed to disappear into the cushions around him. He wore the traditional cream panung of printed cloth and a splendid coat of beige silk, elaborately embroidered in gold about the mandarin-style collar and the edges of the sleeves. He was of pure Siamese stock with cropped black hair and a sallow brown complexion. His nose, ending in two flared nostrils, dipped in the centre and his dark, alert eyes observed Phaulkon keenly from a distance.

'I see you are well acquainted with our customs, Mr Forcon, but I am told that the Greek way is similar to that of other farangs. We have much to discuss and I am sure your body is not accustomed to long periods of prostration. You had best be seated after your fashion.' Again he gestured to the single bamboo chair.

Phaulkon remained motionless. 'Mighty Lord, I receive your orders. But I, a mere hair, would feel ill at ease in any other position before the great Pra Klang.'

It was the first sentence Phaulkon had uttered, in perfect Siamese, and he squinted up at the Barcalon to gauge its effect. The potentate's eyebrows barely arched as he turned to expectorate the red juices of the betel nut into a copper spittoon that lay to one side of him. At his feet a shadow shuffled forward and a discreet arm reached out to remove the spittoon and replace it with a clean one.

'Your mastery of our language is indeed remarkable, Mr Forcon. Just as the Governor said. Virtually without accent. I must commend you. As you are clearly aware, ours is a tonal language, in which a slight inflection changes the whole meaning of a word. Your missionary priests have unfortunately not fully grasped this subtlety and sometimes make the most comical pronouncements. Our people have been greatly amused by one of your holy men who is always confusing the word for water buffalo with that of the male reproductive organ.' The Barcalon's eyes lit up in merriment and when Phaulkon laughed, he joined in too, apparently pleased that here was a farang who could actually appreciate such nuances.

'But do tell me, Mr Forcon, how did you come to learn our language? After all, you have only been here . . .' he paused, 'a year and eleven days, I believe?'

If Phaulkon had been initially disarmed by the Barcalon's affability, he was reminded sharply of his power by the precision of the man's facts.

'I learned it mostly by ear, Mighty Lord, and with some help from a grammar compiled by the Jesuits.'

'Ah, yes, the Portuguese men of God have been here a long

255

time. They were the first farangs to visit our shores. It seems their nation's power is fading, however, and the Dutch have replaced them.' He smiled. 'Did you know, Mr Forcon, that in my grandfather's day we actually believed the Dutch were sea pirates with no fixed abode? You see, the Portuguese were afraid of losing their influence with us, and persuaded us that the Hollanders were a nomadic tribe. It was not until seventy years ago that our first Siamese delegation set foot on European soil. Imagine their surprise, Mr Forcon, when they discovered that the Dutch actually had a homeland of their own! And that the city of Amsterdam was as large as Ayudhya and a thriving hub of the arts and sciences as well.' He paused and then added, casually: 'With exquisite paintings and finely cast cannon.'

In the silence that followed, Phaulkon wondered whether the pounding of his heart was audible at the other end of the room. Was this a sign that the interrogation had begun? During the long week he had waited for the Barcalon's summons he had gone over every conceivable scenario and rehearsed the answers he would give to a whole gamut of questions.

The Barcalon now turned his gaze on the diamond-encrusted betel box at his feet, and instantly a slave crawled out of the shadows behind him and opened the box, proferring the contents abjectly to His Excellency. For the first time, Phaulkon discerned a whole row of slaves crouching in the far recesses of the room. His Excellency extracted a nut wrapped in a green leaf from the box and began to chew it.

'But you yourself work for the English, I believe, Mr Forcon?'

'Mighty Lord, I, the dust of your feet, have been employed by the English Company since early childhood.'

'And do your loyalties then lie with them or the country of your birth?' Phaulkon sensed that the inquiry went beyond simple curiosity.

'I have lost touch with my country, Your Excellency. I have a new master now.' It was true. Since the age of ten he had been moulded into an Englishman and, twenty years later, his island home was but a distant memory.

'What experience do you have of the Dutch?'

'A great deal, Your Excellency. I was in Bantam for two years. And I speak their language.'

'Ah, Bantam, yes. A sad experience for us and a bitter lesson.'

256

The Barcalon grew pensive and when he spoke again his tone was harsh. 'Not so long ago the Dutch invited a second Siamese delegation to visit Holland. On this new occasion we sent twenty dignitaries to Bantam to be transhipped aboard a Dutch vessel bound for Amsterdam. The Dutch Governor of Bantam who was, shall we say, a frugal man, decided that twenty of us constituted too great an expense for the Dutch government to bear. So, believing it would require unpleasant explanations to send a part of our delegation home, he had seventeen of them executed on the spot. It was not until years later, when the remaining three returned from Holland, that we learned of the truth.'

'How appalling, Your Excellency. I trust you took retaliatory measures.'

'We are not by nature a violent people, Mr Forcon. It is not the Buddhist way. Of course we demanded apologies and compensation – though what sum can compensate for such loss? We were assured that the Governor had since been dismissed. But above all, Mr Forcon, we learned a lesson about farangs.' The Barcalon surveyed Phaulkon carefully. 'Tell me, Mr Forcon, how do the English feel towards the Dutch?'

'We are rivals, Your Excellency. Outwardly we greet each other as friends, but inwardly we strive to outdo one another, and to gain new footholds before the other does.'

The Barcalon inhaled on his hookah and continued to study Phaulkon. 'Such as in Siam?'

Phaulkon's mind raced. Here perhaps was his opening. 'I, a hair, believe the English are concerned mainly with trade, Your Excellency. As to the Dutch, the recent history of the East Indies speaks for itself: Ambon, the Celebes, Bantam, Batavia, Malacca – it is a long list.'

'You are suggesting perhaps,' commented the Barcalon, 'that the English are to be trusted while the Dutch are not?' There was an amused twinkle in his eye.

'Only in so far as the English could form a buffer against Dutch expansion, Your Excellency.'

'In what way?'

'I, the dust of your feet, believe that if Your Excellency continues to grant small concessions to the English, the Dutch will attempt to have them removed. And the English may find

257

the concessions too minor to fight for.' He paused. 'I, an ignorant slave, beg forgiveness for such presumption. But if Your Excellency were to ally himself openly with the English and grant them larger concessions, they in turn would do everything in their power to protect those interests, for the English are essentially traders, Your Excellency. And the Dutch might hesitate to start a war with them that could extend as far as Europe. Thus Your Excellency would have created a buffer.'

'At what cost, though, Mr Forcon? What exactly are these . . . "large concessions" you are talking about?'

'A well-publicized alliance, for one, Your Excellency, and perhaps a base in your country, with a good harbour to careen their ships. Mergui, for instance, on your western seabord. It faces directly across the Bay of Bengal from their headquarters at Madras and would give them great flexibility in the bay.'

'And given such powers, the honourable English Company would itself never, of course, develop aspirations on Siam?' A smile played lightly across the Barcalon's lips.

'Not if the majority of the trading vessels out of Mergui were to fly the flag of Siam and only the captains were English, Your Excellency.'

For a brief moment the Barcalon was taken aback. Then he inquired casually: 'You mean such Siamese trading vessels would be captained by Englishmen in our service?'

'Precisely, Your Excellency. After announcing an alliance, from their base at Madras the English could equip Siam with a new fleet. In return you could offer them the facilities of Mergui from where both you and they could trade in the bay and beyond.' He paused. 'You would not only double your Treasury's profits overnight, but keep the ambitious Dutch at bay.'

The Barcalon drew on his water pipe and then proceeded leisurely to adjust the ends of his panung. To Phaulkon, observing his every movement, they did not appear to need adjusting. It was clear that the Barcalon was engrossed in thought.

'Where would the loyalty of these English captains lie? With Siam or England?'

'First and foremost with themselves, Your Excellency. English seamen in Asia are here to line their pockets. But so long as your purposes were served . . .'

The Barcalon smiled. 'You are a shrewd man, Mr Forcon.

And most persuasive, according to our Governor at Nakhon Si Thammarat. He was in fact quite enchanted by you. By the way, I have not had the opportunity of congratulating you on your award. A rare honour indeed for an outsider.'

'Your Excellency is most gracious.'

'But tell me, Mr Forcon, I understand your colleagues did not accompany you back from the south?' The Barcalon's tone had suddenly changed. 'Are they not well?'

Phaulkon's stomach clutched. He was caught off balance by the abrupt switch. How much did the Barcalon really know? His mind reeled. The original elephant courier had obviously arrived, informing the Barcalon of Phaulkon's award. The white elephant and its procession had not yet reached Ayudhya. The captain of the Governor's ship on which Phaulkon had journeyed had apparently not been carrying any dispatches to the Barcalon, but in the meantime had perhaps a second elephant courier arrived? And if so, how much had the Governor revealed in those new dispatches? It was safer to assume that the Governor had informed the Barcalon of the discovery of the cannon, in which case he would also have explained the detention of Burnaby and Ivatt as a safeguard.

'They stayed behind at the Governor's request, Your Excellency,' replied Phaulkon, noncommittally.

'Was there any particular reason for this in your opinion, Mr Forcon?' The Barcalon toyed casually with the filigree buttons of his silk coat.

The hollow in Phaulkon's stomach seemed to expand. 'I believe His Excellency the Governor was only doing his duty in detaining our chief factor since all our papers had gone down with our ship, Your Excellency.'

'And would you say that you or your colleagues attempted in any way to, shall we say, influence the Governor's way of thinking? With any gifts, for instance?'

This was it, thought Phaulkon. The cannon. He must know about the cannon. What else could he be referring to? Phaulkon's bladder seemed on the point of bursting. With a supreme effort he willed his tone to remain even.

'Gifts, Your Excellency? All our possessions were at the bottom of the ocean.'

'*All* of them, Mr Forcon?'

259

Phaulkon had only one fervent wish, to wake up far away and discover that this was all one dreadful nightmare. He forced himself to concentrate. If he was going to impress the Barcalon with any kind of integrity he would have to take the plunge now.

'All of them, Your Excellency. Unless of course you are referring to the cannon. But I never considered that a gift since the Governor virtually requisitioned it and we had little choice but to present it to him.'

'It, Mr Forcon? There was only one of them?'

Phaulkon hesitated barely a fraction of a second. 'Only one that we presented, Your Excellency. The other four were at the bottom of the ocean.'

The Barcalon's brow furrowed. 'I see. Unfortunately, we do not seem to have any record of the cannon entering our country. A strange circumstance, considering all weapons of war have to be declared on arrival. Perhaps, Mr Forcon, you can throw some light on the matter.'

'With pleasure, Your Excellency.' He paused. 'You see, the cannon were not ours.'

The Barcalon raised his eyebrows in surprise. 'And whose were they then?'

'Mighty Lord, they belonged to Holland. Finely cast in Amsterdam.' Despite the tension, Phaulkon smiled inwardly.

'Indeed? And what were they doing on an English Company ship?'

Phaulkon appeared to hesitate. 'It is a most complex story, Your Excellency. And I, the dust of your feet, am reluctant to reveal the true extent of intrigue between our two farang powers.'

'Proceed anyway.'

'The Dutch paid us handsomely to transport their cannon to Pattani. They did not want to risk being caught carrying them themselves. As Your Excellency pointed out, their entry into Siam was not registered.'

'So you accepted money from the Dutch to transport contraband weapons to Pattani? For a rebel vassal? To be used against Siamese troops?' The Barcalon sounded both incensed and incredulous.

Phaulkon appeared indignant. 'If you will forgive me, Your Excellency, that was not the reality. It was only a ploy. As soon as the cannon had been offloaded in Pattani, our chief, Mr

Burnaby, was to inform Your Excellency, and the Dutch would have been exposed for their support of the rebels. Final, undeniable evidence of their scheme to overthrow Siam.'

The Barcalon looked singularly unconvinced. 'An interesting story, Mr Forcon, but why would the Dutch, your rivals, not foresee this rather obvious conclusion? Surely they must have expected you to double-cross them?'

'Mighty Lord, I believe they gave the cannon to us to transport because they did not think an English ship would be searched so soon after we had graciously been invited back to trade in Siam. And as to any foul play on our part in Pattani, the Dutch would simply have denied any involvement in the scheme.'

'What proof would you have had to the contrary? What proof do you have of their involvement now, Mr Forcon?'

'Mighty Lord, four of the cannon are buried on the ocean floor, but the fifth stands in the forecourt of the Governor of Nakhon Si Thammarat's palace. Its Dutch markings are clear proof of its origin. It was cast by de Groot himself in Amsterdam. His seal is engraved on it. We English have fine cannon of our own. We have no need of Dutch models.'

'Yes, but how would the Dutch themselves have explained these markings, once you had supposedly reported the cannons' arrival in Pattani?'

'They would undoubtedly have claimed we had stolen them, Your Excellency.'

The Barcalon shook his head repeatedly as if to say he had had enough of all this. 'The plot thickens, Mr Forcon, while unfortunately the logic grows thinner. But tell me rather why you told the Governor that it was I who had ordered the whole expedition. You have quite an imagination, I must say.'

'Mighty Lord, I, a speck of dust on the sole of your foot, crave Your Excellency's indulgence. Following the discovery of the cannon the Governor would certainly have imprisoned us if we had not assured him it was Your Excellency who was behind the mission. We needed at all costs to gain time. At least one of us had to be free to return to Ayudhya to lay the whole truth before Your Excellency.' Phaulkon appeared to sink even deeper into the carpet. 'It was a terrible thing to be obliged to say, Your Excellency, and it was prompted only by the direst necessity, I assure you.'

'No, not terrible, Mr Forcon. Criminal.' The Barcalon's tone was icy and in the pause that followed, Phaulkon thought about his execution. Would it be swift and merciful or would he be tortured first to reveal the complete details of the scheme? The Siamese had a well-proven method of extracting information from criminals by tying them naked to a post at dusk in a swampy area. The swarms of bloodthirsty mosquitoes generally took all might to suck the victim's blood dry. In the course of that night there were few who did not ask to confess.

The Barcalon's dour tone interrupted Phaulkon's vision of hell.

'And why, precisely, did you conceal your knowledge of Siamese from the Governor?'

'An instinctive precaution, Your Excellency. The better to learn our position.' Such confessions from time to time, reflected Phaulkon in a last moment of hope, might just serve to make the rest of his story more credible, especially when his admissions were to a certain extent incriminating.

'And why did you learn our language in the first place, Mr Forcon? None of the other traders seem to have made the effort. You are not one of these dedicated missionaries, I am sure.' He smiled wryly. 'If you'll forgive me for saying so, what I know of your life style is hardly compatible.' He stared intently at Phaulkon for a moment. 'You are not, perhaps, a spy?'

Phaulkon's heart stood still. Was this a reference to his purported spying role for the King? He might as well be dead now if the Governor had revealed that part of his story. It would be lese-majesty, punishable by prolonged torture and death. He forced his voice to remain even.

'I learned Siamese, Your Excellency, because I feel drawn to this country as I have to no other before it. And I sincerely hope, some day, to be able to serve it.'

'When already you serve the English?'

'Mighty Lord, only England has asked for my services.'

'In which way do you see yourself serving this country, Mr Forcon?'

'By ensuring that the Siamese flag is known and feared from the Indian Ocean to the China Sea.'

'Even though you are not Siamese yourself?'

'Neither are the Moors, Your Excellency. Yet they serve your country.'

'It is an ancient tradition.'

'One which had its beginnings too, Mighty Lord. And new blood revives. If Your Excellency would but give me a chance, with one shipment I could replenish the coffers of your Treasury beyond anything seen in a year under the Moors.'

'So you, a Greek in the service of England, would build us a new fleet and turn us into a fearsome trading power?' The Barcalon's tone was laced with sarcasm.

Phaulkon ignored the scorn. 'I would sooner do it as a Greek in the service of Siam, Your Excellency.'

'You are indeed liberal with your loyalties, Mr Forcon. First it is Greece, then it is England and now, suddenly, it is Siam.'

'I was nine years old when I left Greece, Your Excellency. It was not a question of loyalties. I wanted to see the world and England had the ships.'

'And what does Siam have today?'

'Great opportunities and a strong hold over my heart, Your Excellency. It is surely possible to esteem another without being branded disloyal.' He paused. 'Does the Lord of Life, His Great Majesty of Siam himself, not hold a special place in his heart for Louis, the French King?'

With trepidation, Phaulkon peered across at the Barcalon. This was sailing very close to the wind, he knew. And this time, unmistakably, he saw the Barcalon flinch.

It was a moment before the potentate spoke again. 'You are a most persuasive man, Mr Forcon. And the truth is I would sooner have you on my side than be obliged to execute you.'

'I . . . do not follow you, Your Excellency.'

The Barcalon examined him in silence. Then slowly he let the words out. 'Before he died, your friend, Captain Alvarez, became very talkative.'

The blood drained from Phaulkon's face. My God, Alvarez! The poor devil! That was one thing he had not reckoned with. Phaulkon had gone to his house only three days ago after he had heard rumours that the captain had escaped from the Queen's clutches in Pattani, but his servants had said the captain had returned only briefly and then disappeared again. They did not know where. Phaulkon had assumed he was in hiding or with some woman again, as he usually was. But if the Siamese had caught and interrogated him . . .

Phaulkon was aware that the Barcalon was watching him like a hawk.

'Before you incriminate yourself further, Mr Forcon, I must advise you that my spies have confirmed Captain Alvarez's recent presence in Pattani. He was, shall we say, living rather intimately at the Queen's palace. On his return to Ayudhya palace guards were sent to interview him at his house. When we had him arrested, he at first denied everything. But under interrogation his tongue soon loosened.

'The sale of the cannon – there were indeed five of them, Mr Forcon – would of course have netted you a small fortune. Well worth the risk of capture, I should say. I am only sorry that our interrogators were . . . over-zealous in their work, and Captain Alvarez succumbed before the interview was quite over. I would like you to have heard the confession from his own lips. Though of course with only the sliver of a tongue left to form the words, his speech was somewhat slurred. My interrogators are now anxious to interview you, Mr Forcon, to complete their files on the subject.'

Phaulkon's stomach turned. Poor Alvarez, he could imagine what they had done to him. He made a final effort to control his voice. It was all or nothing now, because the game was clearly up.

'What your interrogators failed to elicit from Captain Alvarez, Your Excellency – for the simple reason that he did not know it – was that the English Company's only reason for selling the cannon to the rebel Queen was to raise enough money to purchase a consignment of goods from your Treasury. For one full shipment to Persia.' Phaulkon's tone grew unexpectedly aggressive. 'To show Your Excellency how the Moors are robbing you blind.'

The Barcalon flinched. 'Your insolence is unbounded, Mr Forcon. But I must admire your courage in the face of treason.'

'Mighty Lord, you may torture and execute me. But it will not change the truth. It is correct that the Queen was to buy the cannon from us for a large sum. But Alvarez knew nothing about our other motives. To incriminate the Dutch, for instance. He was Portuguese, an outsider as far as the English were concerned.

He was merely collecting a commission from the sale of some cannon.'

Phaulkon thanked his lucky stars that he had taken the precaution of not revealing the whole story to Alvarez. The captain knew nothing of the provenance of the cannon. Only that they were for sale for a large sum.

The Barcalon gazed at Phaulkon. 'Your story, Mr Forcon, began with a delivery of the cannon to Pattani on behalf of the Dutch. Now it has evolved into a sale to Pattani with the proceeds going to the English. I am curious. Where will it go from here?'

'You now have the whole truth, Your Excellency. We planned both to obtain money from the sale *and* to implicate the Dutch.' Mestre Phanik was right, reflected Phaulkon bitterly. This shrewd Barcalon had slowly extracted the truth from him until he had practically turned full circle.

The Barcalon shook his head as one might at an errant pupil.

'Mr Forcon, please. If the Dutch had made prior arrangements with the Queen of Pattani to donate the cannon, why would she pay the English for them?'

Phaulkon had prepared for this during his repeated rehearsals of the interview. 'We had forged a letter from the Dutch Company requesting the Queen to make payment to a third party – Alvarez. He was living . . . he was intimate with the Queen, Your Excellency. She would never have questioned the request. I speak and write Dutch fluently.'

'I am aware of that, Mr Forcon. It is in the Governor's report. How many languages *do* you speak, as a matter of interest?'

'Seven fluently, Your Excellency. And another five reasonably.'

'Do you possess any accounting skills?'

A vague hope surged in Phaulkon again. The Barcalon would hardly need such information to send him to his grave.

'I do, Mighty Lord. I was in charge of keeping accounts for two years at the English factory at Bantam. I have been both storekeeper and inventory clerk.' Why the questions if he was not going to be given a reprieve?

'And could you examine and verify accounts in both Siamese and Malay?'

'Certainly, Mighty Lord, and in five other languages as well.'

Phaulkon's heart sank. Perhaps the Barcalon was playing cat

and mouse with him. Perhaps it was his way of punishing him. He was giving him this last hope only to dash it with the pronouncement of his sentence.

'You see, Mr Forcon, our society is an agricultural one. Our people have neither the head nor the heart for commercial enterprises. That is why we have outsiders, Moors for the most part, filling a number of administrative positions.'

Phaulkon felt himself growing weaker. His mind began to wander and it took a great effort to concentrate on the Barcalon's words.

'But are they loyal servants of His Majesty, your King?' he asked.

The Barcalon's lips parted in a wry smile.

'Let us say they are, in much the same way as the employees of your East India Company are loyal servants of your English King.'

The room began to spin. He must not at all costs allow himself to collapse, thought Phaulkon as a wave of dizziness gripped him.

The Barcalon surveyed Phaulkon at length. The canny farang was still lying prostrate, and he was surviving the interrogation commendably well, with both persistence and self-assurance. A remarkable man, thought the Barcalon. He recalled the salient parts of Phaulkon's dossier: three months in a temple studying not just the scriptures but royal Siamese as well. Amazing! What was he up to? Could Siam harness a force such as this and use it to advantage? The man could, after all, deal in their mother tongue with most of the major trading nations that called at Siam. Providing, always, that his loyalties could be relied upon. That, the Barcalon sensed, was where the problem lay. How far was a man like this to be trusted? He was unquestionably out to enrich himself, but his plans for Siam, with adjustments and supervision, could perhaps succeed. Besides, something had to be done soon. The Dutch menace was real and imminent, and the Moors' heads had become swollen with power.

The Barcalon fancied he saw Phaulkon's prostrate form convulse. Was the man finally breaking down? he wondered. He looked again. No, there was no movement. Perhaps it had been his imagination. It would certainly take a lot to break this man's spirit, reflected the Barcalon. Of course, he could break him

266

now, if he wanted to. All he had to do was read to him a few lines from the farang's own report on his findings in the province of Ligor. And what a brilliant report that was too. He doubted there was more than a handful of his best men who could have written such a report. A royal spy indeed! The audacity of the notion was only matched by the brilliance of its concept. No, decided the Barcalon, he would not destroy this farang. Such wit and energy had somehow to be harnessed – under the strictest control, of course – to the service of Siam. He would not quote the farang's own report to him because to reveal that knowledge would oblige him to execute the man. The Barcalon shuddered inwardly. Not even His Majesty should ever learn that a common farang had dared to lay claim to a direct mandate from the royal lips.

There were many discrepancies in the farang's story, but nothing extreme enough to force him to execute the man. The Barcalon felt a certain relief that the farang had not totally incrimated himself during the interview, because there was no question about it, his services were potentially of great value to Siam.

The Barcalon's mind returned once more to the dossier. Phaulkon's mode of living had been described as Siamese in essence and the Siamese who knew him had all attested to the fact. What farang had ever entered the monkhood and purchased three concubines for life? He was certainly different, and the general evidence pointed to a man genuinely enamoured with Siam and its people.

The Governor of Nakhon clearly thought highly of him. True, the Governor did not have the same experience of farangs as himself, but he was nevertheless a shrewd judge of character. He had given the farang full credit for courage, charm and initiative. Nerves, too, reflected the Barcalon, recalling the Governor's description of the boxing match! The wise Governor had had the forethought to send his niece up to Ayudhya with the last dispatch. The farang was apparently quite taken by her and the Governor had thought she would be the perfect person to infiltrate his house if Ayudhya wanted to observe the farang's movements at first hand. It had been an excellent idea, reflected the Barcalon, and the girl was even now at the palace being trained as a spy.

Also, reflected the Barcalon, the man was obviously adaptable. He had been born in one nation and served another. There seemed no reason why he could not adapt again and serve a third. Perhaps that implied a lack of loyalty, but in reality he had only served one nation: England. He could not truthfully be said to have been disloyal to the country of his birth. For how could a nine-year-old boy be faulted for wanting to see the world? As far as Siam and his loyalties were concerned, well, only time would tell.

It was certainly true what he had said about the Moors. They did rob the Treasury. They had been left too long to their own devices. He had long wanted to look into the matter, but somehow there had never been time, nor had there been anyone to replace them. Could this man, Phaulkon, with his knowledge of accounting, now unearth the true facts? The Barcalon smiled to himself. Perhaps the farangs could be used initially to undermine the power of the Moors. With careful manoeuvring, while they lost their positions, he might be able to direct the anger of the Moors towards the farangs instead of himself. It was certainly worth a try.

He looked across at the prostrate farang once more. If ever the time was ripe to use such a man's services, that time was now. The farang was not sure whether he was to live or die, and his colleagues were held hostage in the south. When his life and that of his friends was hanging in the balance, surely a man would be ready to offer his best efforts.

'Mr Forcon, it is clear to me that your story is a very tenuous one with, no doubt, a moment or two of sincerity. But fortunately for you, we in Siam do not believe in punishing people without absolute proof. I am therefore going to give you a chance to redeem yourelf through hard work and a continuous display of loyalty.' He paused. The figure in front of him did not move.

'You will be put to work in the Ministry of Trade. Your board and lodging will be taken care of. Nothing further. Your assignment will be strictly confidential and you will report to me alone. If you disclose the nature of your work to anyone, you will be executed forthwith. Your colleagues will remain hostage in the south until such time as I am satisfied with both your results and the real nature of your intentions towards this country. Your receipt of the Order of the White Elephant, third class, will remain a closely guarded secret. You may return to your home in the evenings. But you will report to me or my assistants at the ministry first thing every morning.'

Phaulkon remained silent. The room was still racing round and he felt terribly faint. Though he had heard the Barcalon's words and understood them, he felt too dizzy to respond immediately. He remained motionless, willing his equilibrium to return. Slowly, buoyed by the realization of what had just occurred, the blood came back to his face, and his voice, though a distant echo, broke out of its shell as he forced himself to make a final effort.

'Your Excellency's faith in me will be rewarded beyond your furthest expectations.'

The Barcalon inclined his head slightly and Phaulkon, his heart thumping feverishly, crawled slowly backwards, afraid that though his mind was alert his body might fail him before he reached the door.

Nineteen

Sunida tiptoed down the interminable corridors, her heart pounding fiercely. Even after a month at the Grand Palace, the panelled walls, the beautiful porcelains and the legions of slaves still awed her. Though there was no particular reason for silence, she tiptoed anyway, feeling somehow that she was still a trespasser, a temporary visitor who did not really belong. She crouched low, mindful of her height and aware of the palace rules that no one could stand upright within its walls except when walking, even when the Lord of Life was not in residence.

Though her teacher and the two slave girls who had been assigned to her had all been very kind, she missed her dancing terribly and the freedom to behave normally without all the constraints and restrictions of the palace. The novelty of her new situation was wearing off, for she was at heart a country girl, a free spirit whose wings had been clipped. But she would fly again, she resolved, and when she did she would seek out the man she loved. She missed him painfully, and far from casting him out of her mind, he had been with her daily, in the form of Yupin, through all the training and the love-making. If she was as accomplished a courtesan as her teacher said she now was, it was in good measure thanks to him. For it was the image of her farang that had guided her and given her the determination to succeed. One day if she managed to seek him out, he would be the recipient of all her new-found expertise. She smiled. And once she had lain with him again, he would never want to leave her.

The hammering in her heart grew fiercer as she followed the directions Yupin had given her and turned left into a wing of the palace. She had never been here before and the assignment filled her with terror. The thought of it had occupied her mind ceaselessly for a whole day and night, ever since she had been told. Now the moment had actually come. If it had not been a direct command from the Lord of Life himself she would have been tempted not to obey, but her first duty was to His Majesty.

Over the past day she had made as many discreet inquiries as possible and, each time, her apprehensions had only been strengthened. There was no one who had anything kind to say about the man. Why had she been given to him, of all people? Was there no one else who could test her skills? At first she had begged Yupin to be relieved of the ordeal, but her teacher had been adamant. Only if he became brutal was she allowed to resist.

'Little mouse, the Lord of Life, who has taken such a special interest in you, has designated this as your final test. If you pass, you will be ready for your real mission.'

In truth, Yupin herself – unbeknown to Sunida – was just as apprehensive about the whole arrangement, though she could not admit it openly. It would only have frightened Sunida more. But when it came to Sorasak, Yupin knew, the Lord of Life's normally unbiased judgement seemed to cloud. His Majesty was so even-handed and clear-sighted in all other respects that she could only ascribe his attitude towards Sorasak to the guilt he felt at not officially recognizing him. He was, after all, his own flesh and blood, his only son. Sorasak, she felt sure, was the sadist and the rogue he was, at least in part, because of his frustration at not being accepted. For no one, Yupin believed, was by nature wholly evil. She had no sentimental reasons or family ties for justifying Sorasak's behaviour because he was not really her nephew at all, but though she had never discussed the matter with him openly, she was certain that he knew the truth of his own background. How could he not know? It was the palace's worst-kept secret. Sorasak took full advantage of His Majesty's leniency towards him and terrorized the palace harem, enticing the unsuspecting into his lair and abducting those who declined his offers, forcing them to endure the most terrible ordeals. The girls who had returned whimpering from his notorious wing of the palace were generally loathe to talk about what they had undergone, but the welts and scars were proof enough. His Majesty regularly declared himself incensed at the boy's behaviour, but he had only actually punished him once, causing his shoulders to be bastinadoed with a rattan cane. In the privacy of his apartment, Sorasak indulged his perversions with impunity, perversions that would have caused the execution of any other courtier.

271

Yupin herself had never lain with Sorasak, not because she was officially his aunt, for that would certainly not have deterred him, but because he was far too cunning to mix with the favourites of the King. He stayed well clear of them, preying only on those whose existence His Majesty was hardly aware of. The affront to these anonymous victims seemed less personal to His Majesty. Once, when Yupin, outraged at the sight of a girl who had returned with her clothes in shreds and her skin lacerated, had reported the matter to the King, His Majesty had inquired: 'What did you say her name was? Has she been at the palace long?'

Yupin cursed the ill fortune that had brought Sunida to Sorasak's attention. That scheming girl, Kai, who had been hoping to distract Sorasak from his intentions towards herself, had readily answered his queries as to recent additions to the palace harem. She had mentioned the arrival of a girl from the south who was kept virtually hidden and who, it was rumoured, was being trained by Yupin herself for His Majesty's pleasure. Sorasak's curiosity had been aroused, and he had had his pageboy monitor Sunida's movements. Learning that at a certain hour every day she went for a stroll in the gardens with his Aunt Yupin, he had hidden all night in a tree that overlooked that section, and lain in wait for her. Though he had managed to catch only a brief glimpse of her, it had been enough to convince him that he must possess her. It soon became an obsession with him and, relishing this special challenge, he had foregone his usual tactics and had pleaded directly with the King, pestering His Majesty to be allowed to bed with her for just one night. His Majesty, adamant at first, had eventually relented when Sorasak had reminded him of his upcoming birthday and observed how His Majesty always granted him a special favour on that day. Sorasak's birthday, the painful reminder of the birth of his only son, was a particularly sensitive day for His Majesty. The Lord of Life had relented, admonishing Sorasak only that no harm should come to the girl.

Yupin knew all this as she was the one pleading Sunida's case with the King. She knew that His Majesty shunned Sorasak as much on account of his twisted character, which had manifested itself early in his life, as because of his mother's lowly birth. And she could see that His Majesty was in two minds about Sunida.

Yupin felt she would have had her own way if Sorasak had not so deftly used the matter of his birthday. His Majesty, not wishing to reveal the true reason for his acquiescence, had told Yupin that Sunida's tryst with Sorasak would be the ultimate test of her preparedness to meet her mission. If she could please Sorasak, she was ready for anyone. He had further assured Yupin that Sorasak was under strict orders not to harm her in any way.

But Yupin had seen what Sorasak had been able to do, unpunished, in the past and she was far from reassured. She had tried to minimize the danger to Sunida while at the same time putting her on her guard.

'You will not be required to spend more than one night with the man and all you have to do is succeed in pleasing him. And remember what I said: do not resist him. It is only when he is thwarted that he might turn vicious. Just use the skills I have taught you and he will be like a baby in your arms. I know you won't let your teacher down, little mouse.'

Despite Yupin's encouragement, Sunida was terrified. He was after all her teacher's nephew, and she might well be prejudiced in his favour. His reputation in the palace was such that even the two slave girls assigned to her had evinced a dread that they might one day be inducted into his harem. It was rumoured that he practised sodomy and that his sadistic cruelty had been known to mark his victims for life.

All Sunida's former enthusiasm to put her training – the trial sessions with female slaves, the sensuous massages, the culinary preparations, the flower arrangements – into practice, all now vanished and she could think of nothing but the abuse which her mind and body might suffer at the hands of this brute.

He was said to be as strong as an ox, his body honed by constant exercise, especially boxing. She had even heard that he sometimes disappeared into the countryside for weeks at a stretch, following the tournaments and leaping incognito into the ring to challenge a winner. Would he beat her senseless like some boxing opponent, or scar her for life? Once again a vision of her wonderful farang from Ligor rose before her. If only it were he to whom she was going now. With what joy she would sink into his arms and with what zest she would put her new-found

273

skills into practice. Where would she find him again? she wondered sadly.

As she turned into Sorasak's wing of the palace, she encountered several slave girls who stared at her curiously as she passed. Were they already sympathizing with her?

With trembling heart she stood before the door with the black insignia of a bull on it and knocked timorously.

With an effort Sorasak controlled himself. How could his father remain so calm? The bull-necked boxer observed the general through narrowed eyes.

They were in General Petraja's apartments, a few doors away from Sorasak's own quarters in the same wing of the palace. By contrast to the austere furnishings of Sorasak's rooms, the general's walls were cluttered with jewelled swords and daggers, and hung with pictures of war elephants in battle scenes, drawn by court artists. A poem sung to the general's victories was framed in silver in the centre of one wall and gold cabinets in each corner of the room displayed a variety of medals and decorations earned in the Burmese and Cambodian campaigns.

The trim general regarded his adopted son impassively, returning his gaze with restrained impatience. It was after all the boy's birthday today.

'But where will it all end, Father? Now we even have one of these farangs employed in the Ministry of Trade! Have we learned nothing from the Dutch experience, their blockade of the Menam, their conquests in the south?' Seeing that his father continued to stare at him, Sorasak shook his head. 'I still cannot believe that the Pra Klang would have allowed the farangs to infiltrate one of their spies into the ministry. What's more, it could not have been done without His Majesty's approval.'

When he was King, reflected Sorasak, such things would never be allowed to happen. For he would be King one day, he swore it, when his real father had the decency to honour his name and proclaim his rightful parentage. It could only be the King's brothers, he was sure, who were forcing His Majesty to keep the secret of Sorasak's own identity from the world, those false-hearted uncles of his who were terrified to lose their claim. They knew they were no match for him, either in wits or physical strength. They could not hunt or box or outwit the farang invader the way he could. His uncles! He scoffed. The one a freak and a drunkard and the other an effeminate eunuch clinging to Yota-tep's panung in the hope of enhancing his claim. No, when he was King he would kick every last farang out of the country, ridding Siam once and for all of their poisonous influence and their underhand schemes.

'Of course it was done with His Majesty's approval, my son,' confirmed the general. 'The farangs are a threat because they are scientifically more advanced than we are. Though their customs and habits are quite repulsive – they do not wash, they drink spirits till they cannot stand, they eat the bodies of other animals and they have not learned to control their emotions as we did a thousand years ago – yet they are a danger. We must avert that danger by learning from them what they know best, and how better to do that than to keep one of them in our midst and observe his methods?'

'But why can't they stay in their own countries?' demanded Sorasak. 'Is life not pleasant enough there? Do we go meddling in theirs? Do we send our monks to convert their people to the Buddhist faith?'

'No,' replied the general, 'because we are more tolerant. We accept that there are many paths to God while they believe that only theirs can lead to salvation. As I said, they are behind us in matters of the mind. It is only in science that they excel. And that is where we must catch up. In weapons of war, for instance.'

'Precisely,' said Sorasak. 'And look how they operate. First they send their stinking priests and traders to infiltrate the country, and then once they have gauged the strength of our land they signal to their armies that the time is ripe. That is how the festering Dutch achieved their empire in the south. Don't you see that Siam is next, Father?' What a terrible mistake the King was making in receiving these priests so liberally, reflected Sorasak. It would have been much better to close his doors to them altogether. It was still not too late. His Majesty was getting old and if he, Sorasak, the country's rightful heir, were to ascend the throne soon, there might still be time to make the necessary changes.

'Siam may be next in *their* plans, Sorasak, but who says that we on our side will not be ready for them?' More ready than you can know, boy, thought the general. He had been secretly negotiating with Prince Dai, the Macassar ruler of the best fighting force in Siam, who had lost his own nation to the Dutch. Two private Spanish traders had just left for Bantam to buy Dutch cannon ostensibly for the reinforcement of the Spanish garrisons in the Philippines. As soon as the cannon were brought covertly to Siam, the Spaniards would train his best captains to use them. Between the cannon and the fearless Macassars, the Dutch would have quite a surprise in store.

But Sorasak could not be told of such things, even on his twenty-eighth birthday. He was too brash and unpredictable.

'How are we ready for them, Father?' asked Sorasak, barely concealing his scorn. 'With bows and arrows against their cannon?'

'With greater numbers and greater guile, my son,' replied the general patiently. How often Petraja had wished publicly to disown this boy whose notorious rampages reflected poorly on him as a father and would stand him ill in his own quest for the throne. But it was a pledge he had long ago given the King, and it was irreversible.

Sorasak saw the look on the general's face and read his thoughts. Why would His Majesty not recognize him? he wondered again, as he had, obsessively, so many times before. Just because his mother had been a peasant woman? Would His Majesty at least remember his birthday today? The anniversary always seemed to Sorasak like some dark, tainted day, too infamous to be recalled, let alone celebrated. He was overcome by a sudden sadness, a terrible feeling of isolation as he thought of the scores of infants who were received annually into the palace, sent from around the nation by adoring subjects to be brought up under the royal care. All these infants had to do when they first set eyes on His Majesty was to smile, and they would earn the privilege of spending the first seven years of their lives in the palace under the benevolent eye of the royal nurses. Only if their first reaction was to frown or cry were they sent back to their homes. All the birthdays of the lucky ones who had first smiled were celebrated at the palace with enormous fanfare, while his own, the King's very flesh and blood, was a day to be buried and forgotten. One of these children had so captivated the King's heart that His Majesty had not sent him back to his parents like the scores of others at the age of seven, but had kept

276

him on and brought him up as his very own. He was already twenty now. Sorasak clenched his fist at the thought of Pra Piya.

'But tell me,' asked the general pleasantly, 'what you would like as a gift on this auspicious day?'

Sorasak considered a moment. What he would most like just now was to take revenge on those hated farang priests, those conniving spies who, with the excuse of their devil religion, had prevented that pretty Japanese girl from joining his harem. No one had ever dared turn him down before and he would not forget the insult. Her white skin had been exquisite, quite unlike those large-limbed, heavy-framed Circassian dragons with green eyes which had come as a gift to His Majesty from the Shah of Persia. Sorasak had glimpsed them once and had not desired them at all, despite the whiteness of their skin. This Japanese or Portuguese girl, on the other hand, had the normal delicate build of a Siamese, with an added farang fairness that was quite delectable. 'I would like you, Father, to use your influence to have that Portuguese girl I told you about sent to me as a consort. Her name is Maria.'

'You mean Phanik the trader's niece?'

'Yes, Father. I am quite serious about her.'

'But I thought you had written to her and she had turned down your offer?'

'But perhaps if you were to put it . . . strongly to the uncle . . .'

Patraja frowned. 'They are Catholics, Sorasak, that is obviously why she rejected you. Otherwise it would have been an honour for the family, I am sure.' And a terrible tragedy for her, thought the general, recalling the gracious young beauty he had met at Mestre Phanik's reception.

'But if you were to put pressure on her uncle, Father—'

'I cannot force anyone to marry against their religion. Our country has always prided itself on its tolerance of others' beliefs.'

Sorasak felt the frustration mounting. 'But it is only these fanatic priests who have corrupted her into believing that she cannot share a man with other women. I'll soon change her views. After all, she's only a trader's niece while I am the son of . . .' he hesitated, 'the son of the country's most decorated hero. How dare she turn me down? And why do you ask me what I want, Father, if you are not prepared to grant it?'

'Because I expect your requests to be reasonable,' replied Petraja, restraining his anger.

'Reasonable?' burst out Sorasak. 'What is unreasonable about offering a merchant's niece a place in the palace? It is a more than fair offer, I should say, and one well above the girl's station. She should be honoured.'

'If she were not a Catholic, no doubt she would be,' replied Petraja, wondering how much longer he could remain calm.

'But it is my birthday,' persisted Sorasak, his deep voice rising, 'and if you were really my father, you would be more concerned with my happiness.' He looked tauntingly at the general. 'But then you're not my father, are you? Do you think I don't know?'

Rage consumed the general and his hand flew out, striking Sorasak hard across the neck. 'Don't you ever speak to me like that again, you ungrateful cur.'

Sorasak clutched his neck, furious, his muscular frame trembling with suppressed emotion. Then he turned and left the room. Damn his so-called father, he swore, as he headed down the corridor towards his quarters. Damn his hypocrisy. How often had he not heard the general say that if left unchecked the festering priests would soon be telling His Majesty that he could not have more than one wife? He knew that the general considered the farangs a menace that had to be eradicated. He had even told Sorasak that there was a growing faction among the King's courtiers who shared this view. So why wouldn't his so-called father come out into the open with his beliefs? The old man's opinions carried weight enough. What was he waiting for?

Sorasak flexed his muscles and felt his body thirsting for action. At times like these he enjoyed nothing more than disappearing into the countryside to indulge in his favourite sport of boxing. More often than not the ringmaster would pay him two ticals' worth of prize money, without so much as suspecting his identity. He would set off in the morning, he decided, but first he would return to his rooms to see if the King had remembered to send that stunning new concubine to him for his birthday.

Taut and angry, Sorasak pushed open the door of his apartment.

Sunida waited breathlessly in the corner. The room was sparsely furnished, a low rattan table in one corner, bare walls and a quilt

278

of rush mats on the floor. Over the door hung what looked like a priest's robes, the long brown ones she had seen the farang men of God wearing. Could Sorasak be Christian? She had not heard . . .

There was a small window high in one wall but it was closed and the heat was stifling. Outside dusk was falling and two small candles lent little illumination to the room's sinister shadows. Sunida felt distinctly uneasy, the loud beat of her own heart drumming in her ears. She would be glad when this ordeal was over.

Suddenly the door jerked open and her heart froze. Sorasak stood framed in the doorway, his arms folded across his chest. The muscles of his legs and forearms bulged and his large square head sat block-like on his shoulders. A grin spread slowly across his features as his gaze descended on her.

Sunida wai'd to him, smiling bravely.

'So you are the girl from Nakhon,' he said.

'Yes, my Lord.'

He closed the door, bolting it behind him. He saw the Jesuit robe hanging there and unhooked it.

'Take your clothes off,' he ordered, holding the garment towards her, 'and put this on.'

Sunida stared at it apprehensively, instinctively frightened and intimidated at the thought of wearing religious apparel, especially that of the farang priests.

'I said, put it on.' His voice was harsh, his tone menacing.

He watched with interest as she removed first the sash that covered her exquisite breasts and then turned towards the wall to unwind her panung.

'Face this way,' he commanded. She turned gingerly towards him and slipped quickly into the robe. He looked at her appraisingly for a while and his grin broadened. She looked perfect in the brown robe, her long slender fingers protruding from the sleeves, and the line of her sumptuous breasts clearly visible beneath the upper folds. 'Loosen your hair and tighten the cord,' he said.

She undid the bun at the top of her head and let her thick dark hair fall loose across her shoulders. Then she tightened the brown cord round her waist, accentuating the prominent curves of her body.

279

He stared at her admiringly. 'From this moment on you will be a farang priest.' He paused. 'You see, I have come to be baptized, Father. And you must prepare me.'

The combination of heat and fear caused beads of perspiration to form across Sunida's forehead. Her stomach and loins felt wet. She looked up at Sorasak and saw streams of perspiration trickling down his bare chest too, while the flickering candlelight threw shadows across his grinning face. Why was he desecrating the farang priests? She was filled with superstitious anxiety, yet she was in this man's power and judged it best to humour him at this stage.

'You wish to become a Christian, my son?' she asked, unsure of the ritual to follow, and hoping the farang Gods would forgive her.

'Yes, Father. My brother was converted last year. Shall I disrobe now, so you can wash my body in holy water?'

'Lie down on the mat over there.' She improvised, pointing to an area nearest the door. It was best to be close to the exit, Yupin had advised her once. You never knew.

Sorasak removed his panung and lay down on his back on the mat. She took a cloth and immersed it in the large water jar that stood in the bathing area and, using the long sensuous strokes that Yupin had taught her, began to bathe Sorasak's body. It was essential that she remain in control of this brute, she knew, observing that his love lance was growing rapidly erect and that his eyes were now closed.

'You must be a high-ranking priest, Father,' he commented as she worked.

Sunida's mind was awed at how much he must hate the farang priests to defile them so. Once again she asked forgiveness of all the Gods, the farang ones as well as her own.

'I have had many converts, it is true, my son,' she said.

He smiled malevolently. 'My brother told me that your holy book speaks of heaven on earth and that it is the priest's duty to show what that means. Will you initiate me, Father, after I am baptized?'

Sorasak was very excited now, she could see, and the large veins in his bull neck stood out. What kind of initiation did he have in mind?

'Of course,' she replied nervously.

280

'Where is the wine, Father?' he asked. 'Did you bring it?'

She hesitated.

'You are fortunate, Father, because I have some. Over there in the corner.' He pointed to a jug standing on a low table. 'Fetch it.'

Sunida rose, nearly tripping on the heavy robe, and fetched it, wrinkling her nose at the pungent odour.

He sat up and took a gulp from the jug. 'My brother told me that is the blood of our Lord God. You must drink it too, Father.' He handed her the jug.

Sunida was deeply shocked. She held the jug to her lips, determined not to swallow a drop. This was the religion of the man she loved and she would not participate in any blasphemous mockery.

'You are not drinking,' he said, his eyes narrowing.

She pretended to tilt the jug. The wine trickled down her chin.

Now he grew angry. 'What kind of a priest are you?' he shouted. 'Give me that robe. I'll show you.'

He stood up and tore the robe off her, ordering her to kneel naked before him. He put the robe on himself and placed the palms of his hands together in an attitude of prayer. 'I will be the priest now and you will obey me,' he said, standing over her. 'Look at me.'

'Yes, Father,' she said, looking up. She saw the glint of a steel blade on the shelf behind him.

'Have you ever made love to one of us before, my child?'

'No, Father.'

'But you have always longed to, I am sure.' He grinned with pleasure and a trickle of sweat ran down the side of his face. 'You will have your chance, my child. Though we priests are much in demand.'

'I will wait my turn, Father.'

Sorasak's eyes feasted on her tense, voluptuous figure, glistening in the oppressive heat of the room. Then he knelt down beside her.

'Let us pray,' he said, his voice a fervent whisper now. 'Let us pray that your priest may ravage you.'

She judged the distance to the shelf on the wall. 'Take me,' she stammered. 'Make love to me.'

'Louder!' he barked. 'And call me Father.'

281

'Ravish me, Father,' she said louder. 'I beg you.'

Before she could move, he sprang forward and placed his brawny hands round her delicate waist, lifting her off her feet and carrying her over to the quilt of rush mats. She winced at the contact with his callous hands. He saw the reaction and, furious, threw her body roughly down on to the quilt. She fell with a thud and he heard her head bang dully against the floor. Sunida's eyes closed and her body went limp.

'Damn,' he swore, kneeling down and running his hands savagely over her breasts. He slapped her face but there was no reaction. 'And damn you too, Your Majesty,' he muttered. 'You always get the best while I, your only son, am granted but one night with a semi-conscious concubine. May you be dead soon, Your Majesty, that I may assume my rightful place. Because then I'll have anything I want. But meanwhile I'll have your little concubine, unconscious though she is.'

Sunida lay motionless as she listened in shock to the blasphemous words. How dare anyone speak like that of the Lord of Life? She felt a surge of anger as his hot breath caressed her skin and his hard hands explored her body. Her head was swimming from the impact of the fall but it was no more than a jolt and not enough to knock out a trained dancer. She felt his muscular thighs straddle her. He pinched her breasts to see if she was pretending but she gritted her teeth and willed herself to feign unconsciousness.

'Damn,' he swore again. 'I wanted you to remember this night. I will singe your nipples, you little vixen, so when you wake up you will have something to remember me by.'

Sorasak rose to fetch a candle from the corner of the room and Sunida waited till his back was turned. Then, with all the speed she could muster, she sprang up, reaching desperately for the knife on the shelf. He heard the movement and spun round, candle in hand. Sunida abandoned her search and ran desperately for the door, swooping up her panung in the process. Briefly she glimpsed the maniacal expression on his face as the candle crashed to the floor and he dived after her.

'You witch,' he yelled, as he lunged forward.

She felt his hand grab her foot and slip, catching her panung instead. Relinquishing her hold on it Sunida reached the door just ahead of him. She swung the panels open and rushed headlong into the corridor, naked.

Sunida ran, oblivious of direction, while on all sides doors began opening and astonished slaves, attracted by Sorasak's loudly audible ravings, covered their faces at the sight of her. Sorasak hesitated at the door, unsure of whether to follow her. But his own nakedness and his injured pride forced him to suppress his frustration. He slammed the door shut behind him, swearing revenge.

Sunida did not stop until she arrived outside Yupin's door. Naked and exhausted she collapsed into her teacher's arms.

'Honourable teacher,' she gasped, 'keep that man away from me, and let that be my one and only test.'

Twenty

It was early morning. As he entered the bustling market square in the city centre with its mass of colourful umbrellas, shielding people and products alike from the merciless sun, Phaulkon felt a sense of purpose so complete as to be almost tangible. He was piloting his own life's ship now, alone in command, and he knew the course he had to sail. It was up to him to free his friends in Ligor, to work doggedly and unflaggingly in order to earn the Barcalon's favour. For time was fast running out. There were only fifty-one days left before the arrival of Sam's ship. But with luck and perseverence there might just be enough time.

The women were setting up their stalls at this early hour, and as he threaded his way through the noise and flurry, he smiled at the heartwarming sight. He never ceased to be charmed by the peasant women of Siam. With their smiling looks and their contented air, they made one feel glad to be alive. Their movements were elegant and graceful and they had an ease that was lacking in the peasantry of Europe. Even the poorest of them smiled readily and for the most part accepted their lot with pride and dignity. Perhaps the explanation lay in the constantly warm climate and the abundance of fruit and fish and rice, which ensured that the Siamese peasantry was generally better nourished than its starving counterparts in the West.

The markets bulged with every kind of produce, countless varieties of fruit and vegetables, small birds considered great delicacies, dried fish, fresh-water fish, rice, chicken and eggs, while the air was filled with the competing aromas of a dozen different spices: pepper, ginger, cinnamon, cloves, garlic, nutmeg.

Phaulkon wended his way through the jostling crowds past the rows of bare-breasted vendors, squatting on their haunches and puffing on short, fat cigarettes. Their small, well-rounded bosoms were in perfect proportion to their generally slim physiques. He knew that Siamese women's skins wrinkled late in life, and when old age came it was sudden, as if there were no barrier between the long summer of youth and the abrupt winter of decrepitude.

He always enjoyed the marketplace and looked forward to visiting Sri at her stall. A hearty, well-rounded peasant woman with an abundant smile and an infectious laugh, Sri sold fruit and vegetables at the morning market, and enjoyed nothing more than a good bargaining session. Phaulkon was fascinated by her seemingly uncomplicated existence.

Sri was busy roasting locusts, other insects and chestnuts for immediate consumption, and boiling rice inside a hollow coconut shell. She looked up at Phaulkon's approach and smiled broadly, that bright open smile of the Siamese. It was obvious that she was pleased to see him.

'A very great welcome to you, master. But where have you been? The morning market has been destitute without you. How could you abandon us for so long? We had almost forgotten what a farang looks like.' He was one of the few farangs who visited the marketplace, he knew. She grinned widely, displaying a fine set of teeth dyed vermilion by the continuous chewing of betel nut.

'I have been on a journey, mother. What else could have kept me away from you?' He used the affectionate term 'mother' to one who was both older and dear to him.

She threw her plump arms up in the air. 'Do we not have food tasty enough and women pretty enough to satisfy your appetites, that you have to go wandering off to distant shores to seek satisfaction? You look thin and undernourished. Sit down, master, fill your stomach with proper food and let Sri bring you back to life again.'

The stalls on either side were quickly filling. There was nothing quite like the show that Sri and the handsome farang put on together. It had become a staple and much cherished performance, as well-loved as any local puppet show.

'Good mother, I rushed here straight from the ship. Am I in time to be saved?'

She eyed him dubiously. 'I cannot be certain. Though one thing is definite: you will need to buy a large quantity of my foodstuffs to make you whole again.' With a sweep of the arm she indicated her entire stall.

'You recommend then that I eat as much as possible from this particular stall?'

She leaned forward and the neighbours strained their ears.

'Experience has shown that patients have recovered more slowly when eating from other stalls, and some, I am even told,' she lowered her voice further, 'never recovered at all.'

Phaulkon looked appropriately concerned. 'Reserve me the entire stall then.'

'For how many weeks, master? I'll need to put up a sign.' There were muffled giggles all round.

'For one day, mother, or for as long as I can afford your prices. Whichever is the longer.'

'Here, have one of these to start with. There is no charge.' She proferred him a roasted chestnut on a small platter made of banana leaf and sighed contentedly. 'It's good to have you back, master. We've missed you, you know. But I suppose you haven't given us a thought. You men are all the same. Now, what will you really buy this morning? For you, nothing but the best, at prices low enough to ruin a poor old market girl.' She made an attempt at looking destitute.

'I have not come for food so much as for favours,' said Phaulkon, grinning.

Again she threw up her arms. 'Oh, the Lord Buddha save us from these insatiable farangs! Our female population is not safe. Neither is it large enough to keep them contented.' She burst into a raucous laugh. This was a barbed reference to Phaulkon's slave girls, all of whom had been procured by Sri. She had, of course, padded the price a little and taken something off the top for herself, but a small commission on a transaction of that kind was only to be expected, especially as the girls had turned out to be honest and hard-working.

Phaulkon laughed in turn. 'No, no, mother, I am well taken care of in that respect, thanks to you. I have come instead to draw on the immense fount of your knowledge.' He spread his arms to indicate the great scope of her wisdom and she eyed him suspiciously.

'The master mocks me. What can a simple woman like me possibly teach such an experienced lord? And besides, I am too old for that sort of thing,' she added with a great throaty cackle. The neighbouring stalls now abandoned all pretence at discretion and joined in heartily. Phaulkon laughed along with the rest. He found her better company than most of the Europeans he knew. She had been George White's housekeeper and before leaving for England, George had set her up with this little market stall of her own. He had asked Phaulkon to see how she was getting on from time to time, and what had started as a simple courtesy to George had developed into a regular pattern of friendship.

Sri had a prodigious memory for facts and figures and it was that great fund that he needed to tap now. He lowered his voice.

'Mother, say I were a wealthy mandarin and you were an honest vendor, and say I had given a great banquet every week of last year and you had charged me a fair price for every item—'

'You mean,' she interrupted, 'if I had charged you those same fair prices that have crippled me today?'

Phaulkon chuckled. 'That's right, mother, if you had charged me those same ruinous prices, what would they have amounted to for rice and fish, chicken, vegetables, pork, fruit and spices? Can you give me the cost, item by item, over the past year?'

Again she eyed him suspiciously. 'I could do that, master, but if this is a trick of yours to get me to charge you last year's prices for what you buy today—'

'I promise you, it is not, mother,' broke in Phaulkon, laughing. 'But if you make me an accurate list, week by week, remembering every rise and fall in the market, I will be so grateful that I will let you charge me next year's prices for whatever I buy this week.'

'The astrologers predict a terrible crop failure for next year, master, which will have a drastic effect on prices . . .'

He smiled. 'I will accept a limited crop failure, mother, if you will compile my list by tomorrow. I am in a hurry.'

'Hurry, hurry, you farangs are always in a hurry.' She looked up at him with her large, twinkling eyes and focused on the strands of hair that emerged from the neck of his blouse. 'Just look at you. Even your hair grows in a hurry. Why, do you know it takes a Siamese man sometimes a whole lifetime to grow just one hair? Because he is not in any hurry.' There were delighted guffaws from the neighbouring stalls at her remark.

Phaulkon joined in too. 'Ah, but wouldn't you rather own a

whole forest than a single tree?' he asked, opening his shirt to show more of the hair.

'Not when they bear that sort of fruit,' she retorted, wrinkling her nose. The neighbours roared.

She waited for the laughter to die down. 'But is the master serious about this list?' she ventured cautiously.

'Never more serious, mother. And there is no need to tell the whole world about my request. It is strictly between us – and all the neighbouring stalls, of course. Do you understand?'

'As the master commands. But the list will have to be in my head, because I cannot write. And I may have to ask some of the other vendors for prices of foodstuffs I do not deal in. But don't worry, I know who to trust, master.'

'That's all right, as long as you don't give them a reason.'

'I don't know the reason, master, so you're safe there. And they'll never guess who it's for. After all, so many farangs come here asking the same questions every day!'

Phaulkon laughed. 'All right, mother. Let them imagine what they will. As long as you don't tell them in so many words.'

'Not even if they die of curiosity and I have to attend their cremations,' promised Sri. She frowned. 'And even though it will mean no sleep for me tonight, I will have the full list by this same hour tomorrow.'

Phaulkon glanced up at the sun.

'I shall return at that time then, mother. And thank you. You shall be rewarded in your next life for such good deeds.'

'I deserve to come back as a princess and marry a handsome farang.'

'I'll look out for one for you,' said Phaulkon. 'And in the meantime this is for you.'

He extracted a package from his purse and handed it to her. It was a box of cinnamon sweets, a delicacy from the south which he had brought back for her. Clearly delighted, she made quite sure that the gesture was not lost on her neighbours, and as he left he heard her in a loud voice bewailing the circumstances that had allowed such a gallant man to be born a farang on the wrong side of the ocean.

Phaulkon sat at his new place of work. It could hardly be called an office – a small unfurnished room with plywood walls, an earthen floor and a hole for a window. It was set well apart from the mainstream of activity in the Ministry of Trade, evidence of his confidential assignment. He had requested a chair to sit on and a table on which to write, and in deference to such strange farang customs, one of each had been dug up from an old storeroom where unused relics, mostly gifts from the Jesuits, had been left to gather dust. The Siamese squatted on the ground to write.

He had been put to work in the Trade Department of the Treasury, presumably following his acknowledgement of accounting skills, and asked to take an inventory of the King's possessions in the royal storehouses, as well as to examine the maze of entertainment bills presented to the Treasury by the Moors. Whenever a great Asian embassy visited Siam, His Majesty, in accordance with age-old tradition, received the visitors lavishly, sparing no expense. Also by long tradition, the Moors were in charge of the banqueting arrangements.

Spurred by his relentless ambition and aided by a prodigious memory for detail, Phaulkon set to work with a determination that would have done credit to the most dedicated Jesuit, immersing himself single-mindedly in the tasks assigned to him. Spurning all invitations, and working late into the night, he sifted through the mounds of paperwork, putting the bills into chronological order and translating the Muslim dates into those of the Buddhist calendar. He noted the prices of all recurring items and compared them first with each other, then with the dates on which they had been purchased, and finally with the figures he had committed to memory.

It was the end of his fourth week at work. He had visited the marketplace twice more in the meantime, though he had been aware that he was being followed. Each time a different man from the ministry had entered the market not far behind him and pretended to browse around the stalls near Sri's. Others followed him home in the evenings and there was always a figure lurking in the alleyway outside his house when he left for work in the morning. Phaulkon had the impression that no great effort was being made by those trailing him to conceal their purpose, so perhaps the ministry just wanted to let him know that his movements were being observed.

Sri had not let him down. As promised, she had furnished him

289

with a detailed list of food prices – and their frequent fluctuations over the past year – and with quill and rice paper in hand he had spent two lengthy sessions at her side, noting down every figure she had dictated. Then after work he had gone home and committed the list to memory. It would be more impressive when the time came to recite the figures to the Barcalon without having to consult his notes.

The agony of the time passing and the thought of his colleagues held in Ligor was beginning to have a serious effect on his nerves. There was now just over a month left before the rendezvous with Sam White in Mergui. He was sleeping badly, obsessed with thoughts of the discrepancies that lay somewhere hidden in all the paperwork.

Phaulkon contemplated the mound of documents on his desk. It was the twenty-seventh such stack he had laboriously sifted through in as many days – to no avail. There seemed to be no serious discrepancy in the figures. He untied the cord that held the pile of bills together, and with more doggedness than hope began to tackle the latest stack.

Then his heart missed a beat. He went over the figures again, praying that he was not simply overtired. No, the amounts did not tally. Then he noticed a small annotation in the margin of one bill. It was very faint and barely legible but enough to show that it was written in the Malay and not the Siamese script. Although Phaulkon spoke and wrote Malay fluently, the marks were too faded for him to decipher. The annotation was almost opposite the figures which did not match. Spurred on now by a feverish hope, he skimmed the rest of the stack and opened another one. It was several hours before he found the next discrepancy. It had similar annotations in the margin.

A thrill swept over him such as he had not experienced since the day George had placed an arm round his shoulder and pointed across the grey English Channel, with the words: 'Next week, my lad, we sail for Asia.'

The next one he found puzzled him. The amount charged for mangoes did not at first seem unreasonable. He loved that particular fruit and had priced it countless times at the market. But then he spotted the date, 12 December. Mangoes in December? It was a summer fruit that ripened in the hot season, and to his knowledge was never available in December. He would have

290

to make doubly sure with Sri. He would return to the market tomorrow.

After the initial discovery, it was plain – though laborious – sailing. Six days later, working late into each night by candlelight, Phaulkon had amassed enough material to incriminate the Moors beyond any doubt. Meticulously he compiled the evidence and prepared to submit it to the Barcalon at their next bi-weekly meeting, two days hence. That would give him enough time to make quite sure about the mangoes. He could not afford a single flaw in his accusations.

It was close to noon and the broiling sun was at its fiercest. In the marketplace, although the vendors sat safely under their colourful parasols, the air around them was heavy with a humidity that drenched their panungs and sapped their energies. Thank Buddha it was time to pack up the stall and go home to rest, until evening, reflected Sri gratefully. It was already mid-February and the days were becoming increasingly oppressive. There would be three or four more months of this to endure before the rains came to relieve the sultriness and replenish the shrinking waters. But there were compensations at least, reflected Sri, for soon, at the height of this swelter, the earth would give forth its most bounteous fruits – the delicious mangosteens and rambutans, mangoes and lychees from the north – and sales at her little stall would double every day.

She gathered her unsold produce into a basket, smiled to her neighbours, and headed for the river. There she untethered her little canoe and squatted in its stern. Holding the single paddle in both hands she rowed out, staying close to the shore. With a little luck she would sell some of the remaining vegetables on her way home, she thought. Slowly she steered along the river bank in the direction of her compact house on stilts, declaiming her wares as she went and accosting any boats that passed her way.

As she turned the bend that would bring her house into view, she stopped paddling and stared ahead of her in surprise. Her heart began to flutter strangely. Had it been her imagination? she wondered. For the past three or four weeks, ever since that charming farang had come to visit her at the market, she had noticed strangers snooping around her stall. They never asked her the price of anything and none of the other vendors had ever

291

seen them before either. They were certainly not regulars at the market.

Now, in front of her very house, a strange boat was tethered. Unlike any of her friends' boats, it was large and had a grand, swan-like prow. Not the sort of boat that belonged to these parts. In it stood two men. 'Which is the house of Sri, the market vendor?' she heard one of them say. She froze. They were actually asking for her by name! Instinctively she knew that these were the same men she had seen pretending to browse at the market. She felt a growing uneasiness.

She did not like the sound of their voices, as she approached warily, nor did she like the look of their faces. Something about their bearing told her they worked for government. She did not like government officials. They meddled in people's affairs and demanded bribes. Her first instinct was to turn back and hide somewhere until they had gone but that was the one thing that was sure to attract attention. They might think she was guilty of something. She racked her brains to think of what she might have done wrong but nothing came to mind. Gathering her courage, she directed the little boat towards its mooring place at one of the pillars that supported her house.

'Your Excellencies are looking for Sri, the vendor?' she asked brightly, masking her fear. 'I am here, your slave.' She tied her boat to its mooring and wai'd courteously to them. 'Are Your Lordships seekings a special price before the market opens tomorrow?' she inquired, with a nervous giggle. She was convinced now from their austere looks and assured air that they were indeed government officials. Even the white muslin shirts did not seem in place. The men would have looked more natural dressed in the red shirts of palace guards. She shuddered.

'That's exactly what we have come to talk to you about,' replied the more severe-looking of the two, clearly the senior. He had a large wart on the end of his nose that looked as if a well-nourished fly were permanently settled on it. Under any other circumstances she would have found the sight funny. The other man was lean and short and so self-effacing as to be almost nondescript.

'If the poverty of my humble home does not offend you, my Lords, you are welcome to step inside.' Out of the corner of her eye Sri noticed her neighbours pretending to go about their business as if the newcomers had never appeared, but all their doors had somehow remained open and they had discovered a sudden need to sweep the balconies nearest her house. Men wearing fine muslin shirts were hardly a regular feature in this modest community. And one of them even wore brocade slippers on his feet.

'We have come to negotiate a special order for a great nobleman.' It was the stern man, the one with the wart and the slippers, who spoke again, in a voice loud enough to be heard by all the neighbours. 'For reasons I am not at liberty to disclose, our master wishes his purchase to remain anonymous.'

Sri crouched low, almost crawling up the ladder-like steps that led from the water to her entrance door. The walls and door of her house were made of woven bamboo and the six windows were held open by sticks inserted into a groove at their bottom. As she crossed the threshold she was painfully conscious of the simplicity of her surroundings: a crude earthenware jug for washing, a rush mat for bedding and a bamboo screen to hide her modest supply of panungs, all in a single room.

No sooner were they inside than the senior man produced a gold seal from inside his purse and gestured for her to remain silent. It was a superfluous gesture as Sri was rendered speechless. A shudder went through her as she recognized the royal emblem. Merciful Buddha, her worst fears were confirmed. Officials from the palace itself!

She prostrated herself spontaneously, as the man began to speak.

'What I am about to tell you is strictly confidential,' he announced in a hushed tone, 'and if you ever reveal any part of this conversation to anyone, you will incur the severest punishment, by order of His Majesty the King.'

For a brief moment, Sri wondered whether all this was actually happening. But then, out of the corner of her eye, she saw both men prostrating themselves at the mention of the Lord of Life. It was quite real. But how could the paths of the Master of Life and a simple vendor possibly cross? Such things only happened in fables.

'Is that clearly understood then?' The voice of the other man, the nondescript one, speaking for the first time, interrupted her thoughts. It was a rather meek voice, as if surprised to hear itself speak at all.

'My Lords, you may rest assured that if any part of this conversation should ever become known, it will not be from my lips.'

'You are acquainted with one Constantine Phaulkon, a farang, are you not?' inquired the first man, assuming a gentler tone than before.

'I am, my Lord. He comes to the market to buy produce from my stall from time to time.'

'And you have, I believe, procured some slaves for him in the past?'

Sri trembled. Oh Lord Buddha, was there some law against procuring girls for farangs?

'Well . . .' she hesitated, 'I didn't exactly—'

'It's all right. There was no harm in it. On the contrary, we want you to do so again.'

The senior man now nodded to his assistant who produced a small package from inside his shirt and unravelled it on the floor in front of Sri. It was a beautiful batik print cloth from the south, with a green and brown diamond motif, more like a Malay sarong than a panung and certainly unlike anything she or her friends might wear.

'Compliments of the palace,' said the first man. 'You are to wear it to the market tomorrow. If anyone asks you where you got it from, you are to say it was a gift from a cousin in the south. A girl will visit you at your stall tomorrow. She will recognize you by this sarong. She will browse around, examining your produce. You will engage her in conversation and arouse her interest sufficiently to induce her to remain in your company. It must look natural. Your reputation for story-telling is well known, Sri, so you should have no trouble convincing any onlookers that the encounter was a chance one.' He paused. 'You see, we have been making inquiries about you.' He smiled for the first time. 'It is said that you could even sell a saffron robe to a Christian priest.' Both men laughed and even Sri was cautiously amused. It was quite a compliment to her powers of persuasion to suggest that she could induce a farang priest to don the yellow robes of the Buddhist order. Buoyed by the official's flattery, her courage edged back, together with a desire to make the best of this unexpected situation. Perhaps she could turn it to her advantage somehow. 'And how many days do I have to wear the batik cloth, my Lords? People will start talking about the state of my business if I wear the same clothes every day.'

The senior man laughed. 'It is indeed true what they say about her,' he said turning to his assistant. The nondescript man immediately concurred.

In the next instant, the leading official's expression resumed its former austerity. 'The farang called Phaulkon will no doubt visit your stall in the next few days and come across the girl by chance. You will encourage him – if indeed any encouragement should prove necessary – to take her into his household as a permanent fixture. You will, of course, do so casually, and never as though you had been instructed to.'

Sri frowned dubiously. 'But supposing he doesn't take to her? I know this farang. He has a mind of his own.'

'The girl has been carefully chosen to ensure that such an objection does not arise. Just leave that to her. Besides, they already know each other.'

'They know each other? Then why do you need my involvement?' inquired Sri, puzzled.

'Because you are going to be our conduit.'

'Your what, my Lords?' She was not familiar with the word.

'You are going to feed us whatever information this girl passes on to you. On a regular basis. You will become good friends with her and she will visit you frequently at the market. Her name is Sunida. We will visit you here at your home to learn what she has told you.'

Oh Lord Buddha, lamented Sri. She hadn't seen the last of these two. Palace officials, spies, concubines! What a turn her uncomplicated life was suddenly taking. She felt a strange tingling sensation about her stomach. It was hard to tell whether it was excitement or fright. Was it the thought that she might make something out of this? Yet beyond that thought, there was sadness, regret at the idea of having to report back on the activities of her favourite farang, and one who reminded her of Mr George, the master she had loved. He was a fine man this Mr Constant, and she was very fond of him. What kind of trouble had the silly fellow got himself into to merit all of this? she wondered.

295

The authoritative tones of the senior official broke into her thoughts.

'Under no circumstances must the farang suspect your role or that of the girl. Even *she* does not yet know the name of the man she is destined for. Or that he is a farang. I have already informed you what would be the consequences of betrayal on your part. And remember you have been selected by the Lord of Life himself for this most important mission. I need hardly impress upon you the honour that has befallen you.' He paused and puffed himself up impressively. 'Few market vendors, I might add, have been given the opportunity to work for the greater glory of Siam.'

Upon hearing these words, Sri cowered even closer to the floorboards and another slight shiver ran through her. All thoughts of regret vanished. After all, she reflected, there could be no greater calling in this world than to be of service to the Lord of Life himself, the descendant of the very gods.

Sunida made her way breathlessly towards the marketplace, accompanied by a palace guard incognito in civilian dress. Ayudhya! It was the first time she had been outside the double brick walls of the palace in daylight. It had been night when she had first arrived and that seemed so long ago now. She had lived a whole life since then. She looked around her everywhere in awe. What strange and marvellous sights! On the left, near the river's edge, she spied the huge buildings where the five hundred glittering royal barges were housed, and to the right she saw the giant causeway that allowed the people to go across the great river on foot, without having to use boats. She turned almost full circle to gaze after a train of camels winding its way along the banks of a canal. How beautiful were the tree-lined avenues, the humped bridges over the canals, and the wide, open squares of the city. And how exotic its inhabitants: the long-frocked Tonkinese, the fair-skinned Cochin-Chinese, the proud Cambodians, the turbaned Macassars, and the statuesque women from the northern vassal kingdoms of Nanchao and Laos. These nations no longer seemed so remote and inaccessible now. The guard reprimanded her gently, saying she was attracting too much attention, and she faced meekly to the front again, drinking in the wealth of colour out of the corners of her eyes.

She was dressed in a beautiful turquoise panung with a matching sash loosely draped across her breasts and shoulders, and like the rest of the population she walked barefoot. Her hair, oiled and scented as was the fashion, was done up neatly in a bun at the top of her head. She, too, like the northern beauties of Nanchao and Laos, was tall and slim and her month's training with Yupin had left her with a strong physical awareness of herself. She swung her hips beguilingly and noticed with a mixture of pride and modesty that many of the passers-by turned to gaze at her in appreciation.

How exciting and terrifying it all was, she reflected. And now, since that dreadful encounter with Sorasak, her natural optimism had told her the worst was over and that there would be no recurring nightmares like that. Her honourable teacher had assured her that although the vile man had repeatedly inquired after her, His Majesty had strictly forbidden any further encounter. Eunuchs had in fact been placed outside her door with strict orders to report immediately to the Inner Pages should anything untoward occur. No, she reflected, the worst was over. She could look forward to happier days now. Again she wondered, as she had a hundred times before, who the man she was destined for would be, and whether she would find the opportunity to seek out Phaulkon again. The handsome farang still preyed persistently on her mind.

She would meet the man she was destined for in another week, her teacher had finally informed her this morning. A whole week more of wondering! No matter what, she knew she would have to serve that man and reach deep into his heart, for only then could she satisfactorily carry out her duties to the Lord of Life. Of course it would help if he were young and handsome like her farang. She chided herself for such thinking. It could make no difference what he looked like. It was her duty to spy on him and there was nothing more to it.

They turned a corner now into a large tree-lined street, paved in brick and lined on either side with rows of shops. Dozens of artisans, woodcarvers, silversmiths, cabinet-makers, bronze cutters, masons, gilders, jewellers and painters plied their trade; Sunida had never seen such swarms of people as now pressed around the shops, examining the merchandise, clamouring, bartering, arguing and rejecting.

The guard pointed to an open brick archway on the left that led into the large market square and took his leave of her, reminding her to be back no later than sundown. The vendor she would meet had instructions to accompany her back as far as the palace gates.

The guard left and Sunida found herself for the first time alone, jostled by the crowds outside the marketplace – alone to seek out a woman wearing a southern sarong, an unknown woman who would give her further instructions. Her heart quickened and she hovered uncertainly outside the low brick walls that surrounded the market square. She felt terribly abandoned, gazing over the wall in trepidation at the nameless throngs in the marketplace. A wave of nostalgia swept over her and she was suddenly close to tears. How she missed her little room at home and the hours of daily dancing practice, her good friends in the troupe, her uncle, even the familiar face of the Palat. If only Phaulkon at least were here to guide her.

Memories of her childhood returned, and a dim recollection of the abandonment she had felt at her mother's sudden departure. Though her uncle's affection had seemed to increase and the attentions of the courtiers towards her had doubled, she had hated the suspicion that they might be feeling sorry for her. When one day she had watched some village children turn away from her and whisper to each other, 'That's the Governor's niece, the one whose mother ran away,' she had hidden behind a tree and cried for hours.

Tears came to her eyes at the painful memory and she became aware that people were peering at her strangely. A kind old woman came up and asked her if she was feeling all right. She smiled sheepishly, realizing how distraught she must appear, and forced herself to concentrate on the task at hand. She moved forward into the crush, with an effort putting her other world behind her, and focusing resolutely on the new. Before long the amazing variety of produce – some of which she had never set eyes on before – succeeded in distracting her. Meandering wide-eyed from stall to stall, riveted by the assortment of fruits and vegetables, fish and birds, spices and cakes, she was drawn to a small crowd milling around one of the stands, where an animated bargaining session was taking place. The vendor, a plump and effusive woman of middle age who looked and talked like a veteran, was attracting most of the attention, but the customer, a tiny, bird-like creature with a shrill voice, was almost holding her own against the veteran's onslaught. Sunida joined the circle and listened with childish delight to the colourful confrontation.

'You could not find a better bargain in all of China,' the veteran was saying, holding up a ripe cucumber of notable size.

'It would probably cost me less to travel there to buy one,' chirped the bird woman, in her piercing tone.

'Not with the price of transport these days,' countered the veteran. There was general laughter.

'If that's your last price, you'd better give me half a cucumber now, and I'll save up for the rest next year.'

'That's up to you, but the other half will probably have doubled by then.'

Sunida was laughing gaily along with the rest of the crowd when she noticed the colour of the vendor's sarong. It was brown and green with a southern-style pattern. She was considering how best to make herself known when, to her consternation, the vendor turned on her. 'You there, young lady, you look like a person of fair judgement. At half a tical, isn't this cucumber as good as a temple offering?' Temple offerings were, of course, free.

The crowd turned to look at Sunida.

Covered with confusion she started to stammer.

'You see,' cried Sri, 'she's rendered speechless by the insignificance of the price.' The crowd roared with delight as the blood rose in a flood to Sunida's cheeks.

Soon, and much to her surprise, the bird-like creature got a better bargain than she had expected. Sri had guessed Sunida's identity and was anxious to cut the session short.

The crowd dispersed and Sri beckoned to Sunida. 'Come over here, my child. Did I frighten you?' She lowered her voice. 'I didn't recognize you at first. I've been expecting you. My name is Sri. But you can call me anything you like,' she added, smiling.

'Thank you, Pi Sri.'

'I know all about you, so you can be quite open with me, child. Just look around my stall and try to appear natural. This is supposed to be a chance encounter.'

'Is this your own stall, then?' asked Sunida, picking up some very plump radishes.

299

'It is indeed. A farang bought it for me.'

Sunida looked thoughtful. 'Why, did he love you?'

Sri was surprised at the directness of the question. 'Yes, I think he did.' She laughed. 'He was so old that he thought of me as a young girl. It was very flattering.'

Sunida laughed. 'You are very funny, Pi Sri. May I sit down next to you. All these crowds are giving me a headache. And where is your farang now?' she inquired, Phaulkon very much on her mind.

'He went back to his country. They all do in the end. There, drink some hot tea. Five or six strong cups is the best cure I know for a headache. You have to sweat it out.'

'Thank you, Pi Sri.' She paused. 'Do you know the man I am destined for then?' she inquired anxiously.

Sri cleared her throat. 'No, but I understand he will make himself known to us in a week,' she said, smiling conspiratorially. 'We will have become friends, you and I, so we can tackle him together. You can visit me here as often as you like, you know.' She lowered her voice. 'The palace has cleared it.'

'I know. I was told to come to you for further instructions.' Although her first impression of Sri had been a little frightening, Sunida now found herself taking an instinctive liking to the woman. She had a warm, maternal manner and reminded Sunida very much of Prateep, the fat, good-natured housekeeper at the Governor's palace, who had taken Sunida under her wing and been the closest thing to a mother that Sunida had known. Sunida had adored her, especially as Prateep's position did not allow her to scold the child more than cursorily. Only if Sunida had seriously erred was the matter brought to the attention of her uncle. It had been the saddest day of her life when Prateep had died, when Sunida was only fifteen. Perhaps this new friend, who was a part of the King's great design, might become a close confidante.

'That is right, my child. You will come here often and people will get accustomed to seeing us together. This is where you will make your reports and each time you come you can buy your produce at my stall. That way nobody will think twice about it.' She scrutinized her. 'Are you rich?'

'Oh no, Pi, I'm just a dancer.'

'What a pity,' said Sri, with a look of disappointment. 'I was hoping to overcharge you.'

Sunida laughed. 'But perhaps the man I am destined for will be rich and then I can buy lots of your produce. But Pi Sri, if you do not know who the man is, how will I meet him?'

'You will meet him here at the market in a week's time. It will be a chance encounter. All I can tell you is that he is a high-ranking mandarin,' said Sri, following instructions.

'A mandarin?'

'That's right. He will be brought here to my stall. I will know ahead of time and you will be here waiting.'

'And this mandarin knows nothing of all this?'

'Nothing. He will meet you by chance, be charmed by you and ask to see you again. The rest will be up to you.'

'And supposing he doesn't like me? Will the palace blame me for that?' asked Sunida, anxiously.

'He *will* like you, child. Don't worry about that.' It was true, reflected Sri, what they had said. This girl was absolutely stunning. Furthermore she was good-natured and delightfully unspoilt. What man could resist her? As for Phaulkon, with his appetites, he would be the last person to turn her down.

Sunida did not look entirely convinced. 'And I will report everything he says to you here?'

'That's right, my dear. Everything.'

'Pi Sri,' asked Sunida, suddenly exuberant, 'this is my first day out in Ayudhya. Will you come with me and show me around? I'm longing to see it all. It's not the same going on your own. And I'd be sure to get lost.'

Sri was about to explain that she could not afford to lose business by being absent from her stall when the look on Sunida's face stopped her. There was such genuine enthusiasm written all over her that Sri did not have the heart to turn the girl down.

'I'll be glad to, my dear,' said Sri, rising and grudgingly asking a neighbour to keep an eye on her stall for her.

Lost in thought and oblivious to the bustle around him, Phaulkon headed for the marketplace. He had enough evidence now to incriminate the Moors several times over. All he still needed was confirmation from Sri that no mangoes – even imported ones – were to be found anywhere in the marketplaces in December.

301

He walked up to her stall and to his surprise found it empty. It was not like her to leave her stall unattended. She hated losing ground to the competition.

He approached her neighbour, Maew, a good-natured woman, one side of whose face had been ravished by the smallpox. She was lucky to have survived the killer disease. Few who contracted it did. He had often spoken to her during his visits to Sri.

'Where is Pi Sri?' he inquired.

'You just missed her, master, by a moment or two. She left to show a visitor around Ayudhya. A very pretty girl, too.'

Phaulkon smiled, though inwardly disappointed not to find Sri at her stall. He wondered vaguely what Sri was doing showing a pretty girl around town at this hour. Perhaps some relative, the family beauty, had suddenly turned up.

'Tell me, Maew, are there mangoes in December?'

Maew appeared surprised by the question. Surely the master knew better than that. He was so clever. 'In December? Oh no, master, never. Mangoes ripen in the hot season. Not before May.'

Phaulkon thanked her and retraced his steps to the ministry. Tomorrow was his crucial meeting with the Barcalon. He would need to be thoroughly prepared.

Twenty-one

The Barcalon inhaled deeply on his gurgling water pipe and observed Phaulkon from the end of the ministry's long, panelled audience hall. It was early morning and the sun streamed in through two large open windows on one side of the room. Later, when the heat became oppressive, they would be covered by cloths allowing the air but not the sunlight to penetrate. Slaves waving long bamboo fans in each corner kept the breezes circulating.

'Well, what have you to report this morning, Mr Forcon? Something new, I trust?' There was a tinge of sarcasm in the Barcalon's tone. Despite the fact that the farang, as he knew from his spies, had been working till all hours for almost a month now, he had come up with nothing. It would perhaps teach him not to be so sure of himself, or so hasty in his judgements. The Moors would not be easy to incriminate and the farang might now better understand why the Siamese authorities had done little to entrap them all this time.

Phaulkon guessed the Barcalon's thoughts, secretly revelling in the surprise he had in store for him. Nevertheless, in the course of his revelations, he would try to keep any signs of triumph from his voice and belittle his achievements, as good manners required.

'Mighty Lord, this worthless slave begs to present Your Excellency with humble evidence of the Moors' wrongdoing.'

The Barcalon's eyebrows arched. They were naturally high and pointed and when displaced further, rose to a great height on his forehead, almost merging with his hairline.

'Indeed? Please proceed, Mr Forcon.'

'Mighty Lord, this worthless slave craves permission to bring to Your Excellency's attention certain documents I have here.'

'You may approach.'

Phaulkon crawled forward on his knees and elbows, balancing a large stack of papers in the upturned palms of his hands. He had practised the performance at home with the help of his slaves

303

the night before, using a similar-sized bundle. His progress now was slow but adequate. The Barcalon's expression assumed a slight air of amusement at the effort, though without any trace of ridicule.

'I, the dust of your feet, beg to present to Your Most Exalted Excellency, on the one hand a list of the highest prices ever submitted by the Moors for every item of food purchased by them and, on the other, a list of the highest prices ever recorded at the morning market for those same items. In each case the Moors' prices are higher, substantially so. You will notice, Your Excellency, that the bills are inflated at well-spaced intervals, to avoid easy detection, and that the discrepancies furthermore coincide with certain obscure annotations in the margins. Though illegible, they are, it would seem, in the Malay script.'

A slave crawled forward with a golden tray and relieved Phaulkon of his bundle. It would not be seemly for the farang to hand them directly to the great Pra Klang. With head bowed, the slave proferred the tray to His Excellency. The Barcalon picked up the papers and began to peruse them.

'I have taken the liberty, Your Excellency, of inserting slips of paper in the relevant pages,' explained Phaulkon.

The Barcalon studied the documentation scrupulously for some time. Then he demanded a feathered quill and rice paper, and began making copious notes. Finally he set aside in a separate pile those bills in which the prices suggested the greatest discrepancies.

A considerable length of time elapsed before the Barcalon spoke again and all the while Phaulkon remained prostrate at his end of the room, listening to his heartbeat.

Eventually the Barcalon broke the silence.

'I see that the Moors have actually managed to grow mangoes in December,' he said drily. 'Quite a feat.'

He turned and sucked jerkily on his water pipe as if to appease his rising anger. Then he looked steadily across at Phaulkon.

'I must congratulate you, Mr Forcon. I am aware that this is the fruit of countless hours of labour, a tedious undertaking by any standards. You are no doubt expecting some form of reward. And rightly so.'

'I ask nothing more, Your Excellency, than to be of further service to this great nation.'

'And I have no doubt, Mr Forcon, that you have specific areas in mind.'

Phaulkon smiled nervously to himself. Not only was the Barcalon likely to be aware of the nature of his next request, but he would no doubt already have decided on his response to it. Of course, His Excellency could know nothing of Sam White's ship or that there were only twenty-seven anxious days left for Phaulkon to fill its holds with a cargo of goods for Persia. It would take twelve of those days alone to transport the cargo overland from Ayudhya to Mergui, leaving only fifteen. He had to have Burnaby and Ivatt in Ayudhya to run the English Company's affairs while he himself was absent in Persia. It would take ten days alone for an order for their release even to reach Ligor and another ten days for them to sail back, assuming that the Governor lent them his boat and authorized their immediate departure.

He turned to the Barcalon now. 'I, a hair, would beg to show Your Excellency where the Moors are most seriously . . . taking advantage of your government's, er . . . benevolent disposition and indulgence—'

'You mean,' interrupted the Barcalon, 'where they are "robbing us blind"?'

'If you wish to put it that way, Your Excellency.'

'I am only quoting you, Mr Forcon.'

'Indeed, Your Excellency, it is my humble belief that this is the case.'

'And,' coaxed the Barcalon, 'which area of embezzlement are you suggesting to identify next?'

'Your Excellency, I request permission to lead a trade mission to Persia. Needless to say, the entire proceeds would go to the royal Treasury. I ask nothing for myself, but the opportunity to show how much the Moors are profiting.'

The Barcalon observed him quietly. 'Is the English Company then putting in an official request to buy goods from our Treasury?'

'I, a hair, must open my heart to Your Excellency on this matter. There is a small problem. If the goods were to be bought officially by the Company, Madras would expect the proceeds of the sale to enrich its own coffers. Whereas it is my sincere wish

305

that Your Excellency's Treasury alone should benefit from the profits.'

'You mean you wish to purchase the goods personally, Mr Forcon, instead of through the English Company?'

Phaulkon increased the aperture between his cupped hands and peered discreetly up at the Barcalon. A light smile was playing on the potentate's lips and his lively eyes glimmered.

'Your Excellency, I, a hair, am but a modest employee of the Company. As such, I fear I am not in possession of the resources required to effect such an important purchase.'

'It must be cheaper than buying cannon, Mr Forcon, surely?'

'Cannon, Your Excellency? Oh, you mean the Dutch ones? As I humbly explained to Your Excellency, we were given those to transport. It is true we were paid to do so, but the proceeds would not be sufficient to purchase even the smallest part of the cargo needed for a full shipment to Persia.'

'What have you in mind then, Mr Forcon?'

Phaulkon paused. 'I, mere dust on the sole of your feet, would beg Your Excellency to entrust me with the necesssary goods on consignment. Just this one time. If Your Excellency will extend me the credit for one shipment, I will guarantee that three times the purchase value of the goods will end up in the royal Treasury.'

'Three times?' The Barcalon searched him quizzically. 'And what guarantee would you be furnishing us, Mr Forcon?'

'Apart from my word, Your Excellency?' asked Phaulkon, feigning offence. He considered for a moment. 'My colleagues, Messrs Burnaby and Ivatt, would be happy, I am sure, to remain hostage here against the safe return of the ship.'

'I was not aware that their present status was any different to that of hostage now, Mr Forcon.'

'I was hoping that enough time had elapsed for Your Excellency to be sufficiently confident of my intentions to release my colleagues from their present predicament. For every day of absence from their post, the English Company is losing valuable ground to the Dutch.'

The Barcalon ignored the inference. 'But supposing your ship were to get lost in a storm, Mr Forcon, and never find its way back to our shores, filled as it was with our unpaid-for merchandise?'

The Barcalon was being subtle, thought Phaulkon; His Excel-

lency was clearly weighing the possibilities of Phaulkon's selling
the merchandise in Persia and disappearing with the proceeds.

'The English Company would of course insure your Treasury
against such acts of nature, Your Excellency. But for such an
undertaking to be official, the documents would have to be drawn
up and signed by the chief of station, Mr Burnaby.'

'An unfortunate requirement in view of Mr Burnaby's present
indisposition, I would say.'

Phaulkon's heart sank. How much longer did the Barcalon
intend to keep them hostage?

'Perhaps in that case, Your Excellency would prefer to use one
of your own ships, with a crew of your own choosing? I would be
glad to serve as captain and leave the trading matters in the
hands of whomever Your Excellency would care to appoint. My
only objective, as I stated before, is to expose the fraudulent
practices of the Moors.'

The Barcalon smiled openly now. 'You mean, Mr Forcon, you
would like us to supply you with the ship as well as the cargo?'

'Only for your own protection, Your Excellency.'

'But since our crews are composed mostly of Moors, would
that not defeat the whole purpose of the exercise?'

'True enough, Your Excellency.' He paused to consider. 'But
I have a better idea. If Mr Burnaby were to captain one of your
ships and pick his own crew, I would willingly remain here as
hostage against his safe return. I would not be released until Mr
Burnaby had deposited the full proceeds of the expedition into
Your Excellency's Treasury.' If only the Barcalon would put a
ship at his disposal then all was not lost. It was a viable alternative
to Sam White's ship, if the cargo did not reach Mergui on time,
as seemed increasingly likely.

'I was not aware that you too were anything but a hostage
now, Mr Forcon. Is your freedom then yours to bargain?' The
Barcalon smiled amiably and, with a barely perceptible nod,
signalled for his betel box. Instantly a slave slid out of the
shadows to carry out his master's bidding.

The Barcalon extracted a nut from the diamond-encrusted box
and began to chew it pensively. He contemplated the panelled
walls for a while in silence.

He was desperately anxious to put the farang's plan to the test, although he was not going to show any enthusiasm for it. He had a presentiment that Phaulkon's intentions were genuine. It was anyway clearly in Phaulkon's interests that the English captain should return with the proceeds. The Moors would then be exposed beyond any possible reprieve, and someone would have to take their place. But no Siamese ship could be involved in such an exercise. It could not look as if his government had deliberately conspired to expose the Moors. There were too many of them in high places. It had to come about accidentally. Phaulkon would have to be seen to be buying the goods on behalf of the English for export to their trading post at Madras. Never to Persia. It would be the farang's problem to find a ship. If he wanted to proceed with the scheme he would have to use an English ship and explain it away somehow to his Company. And if the Moors discovered that the English were usurping their traditional trading routes, let them fight it out with the English. It would certainly be in the interests of Siam to sit back and watch the Moors' strength being slowly sapped. As for the other farangs detained in Ligor, he had in fact already ordered their return for political reasons. His government after all had invited the English Company to trade again in Siam and it would not seem proper to detain their chief officer without an official accusation. If there were going to be an official accusation, the hearing would have to be in Ayudhya anyway. His gaze descended from the ceiling and focused once more on Phaulkon.

'If I understand you correctly, Mr Forcon, you would like me to release your colleagues and provide you with a ship together with a full cargo of unpaid merchandise for resale in Persia. Is there any further way in which I might be of assistance?' The Barcalon's tone was cutting.

Phaulkon smiled despite himself. 'It does seem like a great deal to ask, Your Excellency, but this slave's audacity is prompted only by his firm resolve to ensure the highest profits for Your Excellency's Treasury.'

The Barcalon continued to study him carefully.

'Mr Forcon, I will agree to provide you with a cargo, on condition that it is to be officially purchased by the English Company for export to Madras. Officially in Siam but not necessarily known to Madras, if you gather my meaning. Furthermore, there can be no official admission of any credit terms. I will also agree to release your colleagues and have them returned to Ayudhya where they will remain under close observation. But under no circumstances will I provide you with a ship.' He paused. 'The Siamese government admits to no part of this transaction, nor is it even aware of its existence.' His dark eyes bored into Phaulkon. 'Do I make myself perfectly clear, Mr Forcon?'

'Perfectly, Your Excellency.' Phaulkon's mind was reeling. Would there be enough time? he wondered. Burnaby would have to get back to Ayudhya to sign the purchase agreement and the guarantees before the merchandise could even leave for Mergui. He would need at least twenty days for that. Then, if all went well, it would take another twelve to transport the goods overland to Mergui. That would already make thirty-two days with no allowance for hitches of any kind. It was too late – unless, of course, Sam White's ship was delayed. But he could hardly count on that. His stomach churned. There might never be another opportunity like this again.

The thought that agonized him most was that Samuel might arrive at Mergui, find no one there and leave after a day or two. There were the tides in the bay to consider and the fact that the ship would have no authority from the English Company to linger there beyond the normal docking time.

Sam was expected to offload his merchandise and turn round. The man would obviously not want to delay a minute longer than he had to.

There was only one solution. Phaulkon had to go to Mergui himself and intercept Samuel. It had been agreed with George that either Phaulkon or one of his men would wait in Mergui a few days before the ship's estimated arrival time. Someone had to be there to meet Samuel. In the absence of Burnaby and Ivatt, it would have to be him. He would have to ask the Barcalon for a few days' rest, feigning over-exertion at the ministry these last weeks.

'Very well then,' said the Barcalon. 'It will be up to you to provide the ship. Once you have, Mr Burnaby will be authorized to captain that ship and the merchandise will be released to you. You yourself will remain in Ayudhya throughout the expedition, under my personal supervision.'

The Barcalon's tone, stern throughout this last oration, suddenly softened and he smiled.

'But, Mr Forcon, I would not want you to think that His Majesty's government does not reward a job well done. You have spent many laborious hours examining complex figures. It is only fitting that you should be appropriately rewarded. I am putting you in charge of the banqueting arrangements for the coming embassy from the Emperor of China. It is due here next month. All catering will be placed under your responsibility. I will explain to Luang Rashid that we are adding some farang specialities to the bill of fare, which may ease the surprise of your sudden involvement. It is a large and important delegation and its preparations will require your full-time attention.'

'Your Excellency is too gracious.' Phaulkon's heart sank. How could he go to Mergui now when the Chinese were due in less than thirty days and it would take twenty just to travel to Mergui and back? He might have known it. There was always method to the Siamese way of thinking. Just as their punishments were related to the nature of their crimes, so were their rewards. He had exposed the fraudulent practices of the Moors in the catering department and now he was being asked to perform in their stead. It was essential that he provide a banquet up to the usual culinary standards, with a conspicuous reduction in cost. He would need a lot of help from old mother Sri again.

At the same time, he had to tread very carefully. He could not afford a confrontation with the Moors at this stage. He was not yet strong enough to risk making enemies of them. Even if Sam White's boat were ever to be filled, its real destination would have to be kept secret, Madras not Persia. The merchandise would have to be discreetly loaded, away from prying eyes. Mergui and the surrounding province of Tenasserim were almost exclusively Moorish preserves. Even the Governor there was a Moor. As to Phaulkon's new banqueting assignment, he would have to find a way of not treading too heavily on Luang Rashid's toes. But how? A nasty thought occurred to him. Were the Siamese trying to get the English to do their dirty work for them, by exposing the Moors but deflecting the anger which would inevitably ensue away from the host nation? He would not put it past them.

'And Mr Forcon,' added the Barcalon courteously. 'General

Petraja has asked me to extend to you his promised invitation to attend the royal elephant hunt at Louvo next week. It will be a grand occasion, held in honour of the imminent arrival of the white elephant which was so fortuitously discovered during your stay at Nakhon Si Thammarat. It has only reached the city environs this week having been delayed often on its journey to the capital. Of couse, its attendants could do nothing to hasten its journey, out of respect.' He paused. 'His Majesty the King himself will be present.'

The royal hunt? Next week? That put paid finally to any plans Phaulkon might have had of going to Mergui. Yet he would set eyes on His Majesty the King for the first time. His heart quickened. And what an honour to be asked to attend a royal hunt. Reiterating profuse thanks, Phaulkon crawled out backwards, his thoughts alternating obsessively between visions of His Majesty at the royal hunt and the sight of Sam's ship pulling slowly away from the harbour at Mergui.

Deep in thought, Phaulkon passed through the great archway that led into the marketplace. It was late morning and the scorching sun was already high in the heavens. Although he had kept as much as possible to the shade of the tree-lined avenues, his shirt and his cotton panung were already drenched. The sultriness of Siam's hot season, he reflected, was hardly conducive to exercise.

He would have ventured out earlier, but the Barcalon had asked him to go first to the ministry and mark out each stack of bills that Phaulkon had already reviewed so that one of His Excellency's most trusted assistants could continue the work, scanning the maze of figures for the annotations. Phaulkon had been granted a little more freedom to move about now, and he did not feel he was being followed as consistently as before, but he had been warned under no circumstances to leave Ayudhya. There was clearly no hope of getting to Mergui and the tragedy was that he had no one to send in his place. Burnaby and Ivatt were still in Ligor and Alvarez was dead. How long would Sam White wait after he had made his first fruitless inquiries? A day, two days, a week at most?

In his desperation, Phaulkon had even considered offering Sri a trip across the isthmus while one of his slaves looked after her stall for her. After all, Samuel was the brother of Sri's former master – and lover, he suspected – so it did make some sense. He could give her a note for Sam, asking him to hold off his departure and explain that he had the merchandise and just needed a little more time. But it was a gruelling ten-day trip each way, and Sri was no longer young. What if she did not survive? He certainly did not want her death on his conscience.

Finally, Phaulkon had considered laying his cards on the table with the Barcalon, in the hope of enlisting his aid in getting a message to Samuel. But that was madness. How could he tell the First Minister of Siam that an East India Company ship was being sequestered by an 'interloper' and diverted to an illegal trade run to Persia, before being blown up to destroy all evidence? How could he tell him even a part of that at a time when Siam itself was making friendly overtures to the English Company. If he were to tell him instead that the mission was officially sanctioned by the Company, why would the Barcalon release the merchandise at all when the major part of the resulting profit would obviously be expected to go to the Company?

There had to be a solution, he kept telling himself, but he was at his wit's end to find it. He had come now to discuss with Sri the question of the banquets that would greet the ambassadors from the Middle Kingdom. The arrangements would have to be lavish and the food second to none. Perhaps Sri—

He stopped dead in his tracks, his thoughts instantly scattering. Was he losing his mind? Had his worries taken their toll of him? He stood staring ahead of him in disbelief at the exquisite creature squatting demurely next to Sri. Sunida! How was that possible? It must be a look-alike. But if it was, he would surely have to fall in love all over again. She was absolutely ravishing in her turquoise panung with matching sash and her radiant black hair done up neatly in a bun. He approached cautiously, staring intently at her as if he expected the vision to disappear and bumping into people as he tried to examine her from every angle. There was no question about it. It really was Sunida. She was chatting volubly to Sri and had not yet spotted him. But how did she know Sri? And what was she doing in Ayudhya in the first place?

He moved closer to the stall now and stood in front of it, his heart beating faster than normal. In that instant Sunida turned round and saw him. Her eyes opened wide as if she had seen a

312

ghost and she stared speechless at him. Then a look of immense tenderness and gratitude came into them. 'My farang.' She wai'd to him deeply, clasping her hands respectfully above her head.

'Sunida!' exclaimed Phaulkon. His first instinct had been that she had come looking for him here, that somehow she had learned of his friendship with Sri. But now, from the expression of absolute amazement on her face, it was clear that this was not the case.

'Sunida!' he repeated. 'What are you doing in Ayudhya? When did you get here?'

Recovering more quickly than he, she smiled, beaming that dazzling smile of hers: 'I have been dreaming of you, my Lord. And now it seems the dream has come true. Is it really you?'

'Don't mind me, master,' interjected Sri, 'I'm just a new type of vegetable for sale.' The vendor feigned indignation that Phaulkon had not even greeted her and that she was being totally ignored.

'Come now, mother. I have just had the surprise of my life. How do you two know each other?'

'We met a moment ago,' replied Sri casually. 'The poor girl was about to buy some fruit from my neighbour. I had to enlighten her, especially as she tells me she's going to be a regular customer.'

'You are?' said Phaulkon, turning to Sunida.

Sunida lowered her head and remained silent.

'Sunida, you haven't answered any of my questions. What are you doing here?'

'I . . . have come to live in Ayudhya, my Lord.' She looked up at him. 'I am so happy to see you again.'

'And I am too, Sunida. But where are you living?'

Sunida hesitated. 'Forgive me, my Lord, but I . . . I cannot say.'

'What do you mean? I don't understand.' He felt suddenly weak to his stomach. What was all this? Could she be spoken for already, so soon after his departure?

'Now, master,' said Sri, coming to Sunida's rescue, 'you really are most indiscreet, throwing awkward questions at a lady like that. Can't you see it's upsetting her?' An overfed customer ambled up to buy some spices from her stall and Sri was forced to turn her attention to the newcomer.

Sunida looked mortified. How could she tell the man she loved that she was destined for another? What an ordeal. Yet she so wanted to be honest with him, and to explain that, no matter what, she loved only him.

'Sunida, what is all this mystery? You should have nothing to hide from me,' said Phaulkon, trying to retain his composure. Just to look at her took his breath away, while the sudden melancholy in her almond eyes tore at his heart. Even in a land where beautiful women were commonplace she was absolutely striking. Why, she could hold her own against any of the beauties in Ayudhya. But had he lost her? Had some terrible tragedy come to keep them apart? The possibility convulsed him.

Ever since leaving Ligor it had been on his mind to send for her or even to fetch her in person as soon as the opportunity presented itself. But time and circumstances had prevented him from acting.

Sunida read the agony in his face. It was best to tell him the truth as far as she knew it, without breaking her promise. Perhaps he would have some suggestions to offer. But here at the marketplace? There was little choice. It had to be here. She could not leave without the palace guard seeing her, and he was waiting just outside the gate. She swallowed hard.

'I am under oath, my Lord, not to reveal my whereabouts. And though I love and dream only of you, I am spoken for by another. He is a . . . a mandarin from Ayudhya.'

Phaulkon was numbed. Another man? A mandarin? Was this really true? He saw from Sunida's expression that it was. His heart and temples began to pound simultaneously. He could not allow this. But how had it ever developed in the first place?

'Who is this man, Sunida? Where did you meet him?'

Sunida lowered her head. 'It was arranged, my Lord. It was my uncle's . . . wishes. I cannot go against them. He brought me up as his own child and I owe him so much. Please try and understand, my Lord.'

'I am trying, Sunida, but you're not helping me. You mean to tell me that immediately after my departure the Governor arranged for you to be betrothed to a mandarin from Ayudhya? Are you married to him now?' He dreaded the answer.

'Not yet, my Lord,' replied Sunida, avoiding further
314

explanation. She did not want to lie to him, but she was under oath never to reveal her mission for the palace.

'And why did your uncle arrange this so suddenly?'

'My Lord, I will tell you the truth. My uncle was aware of my feelings towards you, and mindful of his brother's death at the hands of . . . farangs, he thought it would be an insult to my father's memory if you and I were to . . . further our relationship. He felt we were bound to try and see each other again. So he sent me to Ayudhya for training in etiquette to prepare me for my betrothal to another.' She hesitated, uncertain whether she should repeat her uncle's words: 'To one of my kind.'

Although it was painful to both of them, Sunida was relieved that she had told Phaulkon the truth, word for word as her uncle had spoken. She was entirely ignorant of the fact that this was part of the Governor's plan to make her situation look all the more convincing to Phaulkon.

'But where are you living now?' asked Phaulkon, heartbroken.

'I am under oath, my Lord, not to reveal that. Please do not press me.'

His mind was reeling.

'Come to my house, Sunida. We can speak there in privacy. This is not the right place.' The overfed customer, he could see, had just paid and was preparing to leave.

'I cannot do that, my Lord. I am followed wherever I go.'

'By this mandarin?'

Sunida remained silent, as if in acknowledgement.

'Now, master, you're not harassing this poor girl, are you?' Sri was anxious to resume her place in the conversation.

Phaulkon ignored the question. 'If the main entrance is guarded, we could leave by another exit,' he persisted.

Sunida hesitated, torn between desire and duty. She longed for a few moments alone with Phaulkon, but she could hardly attempt to elude the guard, nor was there any point in asking him if she could go to the home of a farang. He would not have the authority to grant such permission.

But perhaps tomorrow. A wave of hope engulfed her. Perhaps then she could obtain permission. She would ask Yupin for her help, just to visit an old friend.

She sensed it would not help her cause if she was to spend too much time with Phaulkon now. The guard would be checking on

315

her every so often and he would surely report back what he had seen.

'My Lord, I have to leave. They are waiting for me.'

'Just a minute, Sunida. When will I see you again?' Phaulkon's tone was both desperate and determined. 'Tomorrow? Here at the stall? At the same hour?'

'I will try, my Lord.'

'That is not good enough. You must promise.'

'I . . . I promise, my Lord.' It should be possible, she thought. After all, she was allowed to visit Sri, and with help from Yupin she might even have obtained the necessary permission to go to his house then.

'May I visit you again tomorrow, Pi Sri?' she said turning graciously to the vendor. 'You have been so kind.'

'Of course, my dear. And you can even bring the master here, if he promises not to importune you so.'

Sunida left first and a moment later Phaulkon, deeply distracted, returned to the ministry.

Twenty-two

Phaulkon set off for the marketplace well in advance of the appointed hour on the morning following his surprise encounter with Sunida. He wanted to chat with Sri first about the banquet arrangements for the dignitaries from the Middle Kingdom but, above all, he wanted to solicit her help in obtaining Sunida's consent to his plan. He had spent most of the night concocting it and he was more determined than ever now not to lose her, especially as that possibility seemed dangerously imminent.

He had not envisaged or foreseen her uncle's reaction to farangs – and hence to himself – but the more he thought about it the more he understood the Governor's feelings. The man could hardly be expected to be well-disposed towards farangs when the Dutch had murdered his own brother. Given the circumstances, Phaulkon had to admit that His Excellency had behaved with admirable fairness towards him throughout his stay in Ligor. But of course there were limits. To allow his only niece to run off with a farang would be asking a little much. Phaulkon remembered the Governor's hesitation when he had asked him if Sunida could accompany him to Ayudhya. In retrospect he felt that it was not so much that the Governor disliked him personally – the contrary was probably true – but more a question of principle.

Once Sunida was married to this mandarin, whoever he was, it would be difficult, not to say impossible, to try and reverse the situation. Who knew who the mandarin might be? If action were to be taken, it would have to be now. There was unfortunately nothing he could do about the Governor's feelings, but Sunida had unequivocally confirmed her own love for him and that was what counted. He had never felt so strongly about any woman in his life. The thought of her locked away somewhere in this metropolis, with no hope of seeing each other again, was insupportable.

There was now a terrible sense of urgency about the whole matter and he longed for the security of knowing that she was

317

safely ensconced in his house. But how safe would she be there? It would surely be the first place her uncle – and perhaps this other mandarin, too – would send to look for her. He had considered the question at length and he had come up with a plan. He would suggest that she went to Mergui for a month. That would be the last place where anyone would think of looking for her and even if his house were searched regularly over the initial period following her disappearance, her trackers would find no trace of her. By the time she returned to Ayudhya, her pursuers would surely have given up searching his house and she would be able to reside there in relative safety.

At the same time, while she was in Mergui, she could get a message to Samuel. The plan was good from every angle. But would she agree to it? Outwardly submissive though she might appear, he sensed that within that beautiful frame there lurked a strong will that few, if any, could bend. Instinctively he knew that that was in part why he loved her.

Phaulkon recognized that he was obsessed with the fear of losing her; he was determined to make her his at any cost. He knew furthermore that with her Siamese upbringing she would make little attempt to change his life style. His slaves would revert to her control instead of his, but she would never deny them to him. She would not even expect him to marry her officially, as her people were much more liberal in these matters than the Europeans. She would anyway be considered his wife just by virtue of living with him, and if he did not take on a whole series of minor wives, there was no reason for her to require the official status of a major one.

He was still muttering to himself when he arrived in front of Sri's stall. The usual effusive greeting awaited him.

'How delightful to have you all to myself, master. Perhaps you will address a word to me today. Yesterday I was obviously superfluous.' She went through the motions of primping her hair and making herself beautiful.

'I was just surprised to run into an old friend, mother.'

'An old friend, indeed,' pouted Sri. 'If there hadn't been five hundred people around, heaven knows what you might not have done to her. You looked ready to abduct her. Who is this girl anyway?'

318

'You mean you really had never met her before yesterday?' Phaulkon eyed her carefully. He had had his suspicions initially.

'Never, master, upon my word.'

'Her name is Sunida. I met her in the south. What did you think of her, mother?'

'Well, I suppose she was rather beautiful, and graceful and well-mannered and charming and intelligent and,' she smiled, 'clearly besotted with you, master. And I must say, I've never seen you like that either. As lovesick as a tigress for its cubs. What are you going to do about it?'

'Ask for your help, mother.'

Sri frowned. 'Help you? And incur the wrath of some powerful mandarin who'll remove my vendors' licence? No, master, you're on your own there. You heard what the girl said. She's spoken for by a mandarin.'

'I know, mother, but *you* can help her to escape. She seems permitted to visit you.'

Sri eyed him suspiciously. 'No thought for poor old Sri's safety, eh?' She appeared to reconsider. 'What's in it for me, then? And I want more than just gratitude, master. It will be a highly dangerous enterprise.' She might as well squeeze the juice out of this one, reflected Sri.

'Twenty silver taels, mother. That's eighty ticals, to be exact.' Phaulkon gave the words time to sink in. 'What do you say?'

Sri's eyes had grown as wide as a couple of full moons. It was more than she would see in a year. 'But you have to see her safely on her way to Mergui for that,' added Phaulkon, smiling.

'Mergui?' Her eyes resumed their normal size. 'That's on the other side of the world, master. I knew there'd be some trick to it. What are you going to do with her there? Sell her to the pirates? I'll play no part in the destruction of such an angel.'

'On the contrary, you'll be saving her, mother. Saving her from a man she does not love. Besides, she'll be in good hands there. I'll give her a letter for a friend.'

'And what guarantees do I have that you would treat her well?' inquired Sri, feigning concern for the girl's welfare. 'Would she at least be the head of your household? After all, she has the chance now of becoming a mandarin's consort.' Sri was enjoying herself immensely. How wonderful to see the master so besotted!

319

Served him right for all the hearts he had surely broken, her own included.

'Of course I'll treat her well, mother,' replied Phaulkon irritably. 'How can you even ask?'

'Well, let me think about it then. It's not just the money, you see.' She paused. 'How far would I have to travel on the road to Mergui, if I accepted? And who's going to look after my stall in my absence? The competition will leap ahead of me. My neighbours will be thanking you for the rest of their days.'

Phaulkon laughed. 'You wouldn't have to go further than the edge of this town, mother. I just want you to ensure that she's safely on her way. The money will hire guides and porters and a sedan chair and—' He saw her frown. 'Don't worry, mother. There'll be plenty left over for you. Now, will you help me?'

'I'll think it over, master. There's a great deal at stake. And I'd like to find out how *she* feels about it too.'

Phaulkon looked up at the sky. Sunida should have been here by now. What could be keeping her? His very skin tingled at the thought of seeing her again.

He tried to take his mind off her now and launched into the subject of the forthcoming banquets. For the next hour, with Phaulkon becoming more anxious by the minute at Sunida's absence, they listed the various foodstuffs, determining which villages might provide the finest specialities, how long before the banquet they would have to be ordered, which suppliers were the most reliable in the capital and how many quotes should be obtained for each item. They continued the discussion until Phaulkon was no longer able to concentrate.

'But what could have happened to her?' he asked in desperation. 'She promised she would be here.'

'Perhaps the mandarin wouldn't allow her to go out today,' teased Sri.

Phaulkon looked quite desolate. 'But she said she does not live in his house.' It was as much a question as a statement.

'If I recall, she didn't say exactly. She said only that she wasn't married and that she couldn't reveal her whereabouts. But master, you look quite ill,' she said, feigning to feel sorry for him. 'I'm sure she'll drop by another time. I'll tell her you waited.'

Phaulkon gave her a stinging look. 'I can't wait any longer, mother, I must return to the ministry.'

'Well, don't worry, if she comes, I'll give her your message, master. You'd better leave me some money, too, just in case.'

Phaulkon searched in his pocket and handed her five taels. 'That'll be the down payment, mother. The rest will follow when you have put her safely on the road to Mergui.'

'I'll see what I can do, master. If she turns up, that is,' she added mercilessly.

'I'll come and see you first thing in the morning,' said Phaulkon dejectedly, as he rose to leave.

Sri restrained her urge to laugh. The master's face was as long as a ripe cucumber. She had never seen him like that before. He was always so full of verve and enthusiasm, and angry sometimes too, but wretched and lovesick? Never. She smiled. How clever of the palace to have forbidden Sunida to appear this morning. 'Let the farang understand,' the senior official with the Muslim shoes had told her at her home the previous evening, 'that it is not easy for Sunida to get away to see him and that if he does not act soon, he may lose her for ever.'

A fleeting moment of guilt passed over her as she fingered the coins the master had just given her. Twenty whole ticals! A small fortune indeed. But after all, the palace was not paying her for her efforts. It was her duty to oblige. She tried to ease her conscience. She would buy a nice present for the two lovebirds to celebrate their union. There would of course be a little . . . no, rather a lot of change left over . . . But then a poor market girl had to be compensated somehow for her troubles.

Sunida peered cautiously round the first row of stalls. It was difficult to see with so many people in the way. She approached gingerly and peeped again. Thank the Lord Buddha, Sri was alone. Sunida had waited till much later to come, not daring to appear earlier in case Phaulkon was still there. Never had she spent so many excruciatingly long hours waiting. Ever since she had received instructions from the palace that under no circum-stances was she to attend the rendezvous, she had agonized over every minute of the delay. What would he think? That she did not love him? That she did not want to see him any more? How could they make her suffer so? How could they force her to make

321

him suffer so? She prayed that he would surmise that something beyond her control had arisen to prevent her from coming.

She strode up to Sri's stall now, trying not to appear over-wrought. 'Pi Sri, Pi Sri,' she stammered, 'was the master here?'

'Of course he was. Now calm yourself, my dear. You look much too flustered.'

Sunida tried to compose herself. 'And what did he say? Was he angry?' She still looked mortified.

'He wasn't angry, my dear. Desperate rather, I should say.'

'Oh, Pi Sri, I am desperate too. To think that I was the cause of his hurt. I should have come anyway. I should have refused to listen. Will he return?'

Sri took pity on her, such a beautiful, pure child. 'If you will calm yourself, my dear, I will tell you the good news.'

Sunida was instantly attentive.

Sri leaned forward and said in a whisper. 'You know this man you've been trained to spy on? It's someone you already know – and care for.'

Sunida was at first uncomprehending. 'What do you mean?'

'It's the master, child. Your favourite farang. He's the one you're to spy on. There is no mandarin.'

Sunida allowed the words slowly to sink in, repeating them over and over to herself as if to make sure the meaning was the same each time.

'You are not joking with me, Pi Sri?'

'Of course not, my child,' answered the vendor, touched by the girl's rapturous expression. Her whole face had lit up.

'Trained to serve the man I love. To serve my own farang,' Sunida kept murmuring. Then abruptly her features clouded. 'But will I really have to spy on him?'

'I am afraid so, my child. There's always a price to pay for an excess of happiness.'

'Then in my prayers I will implore the Lord Buddha that my master does not oblige me to pass on incriminating evidence to the palace.'

'And I will pray for that too,' concurred Sri with genuine feeling, 'for that information will have to be passed through me.'

'What a dreadful fate to have to spy on one's beloved,' muttered Sunida.

'Yet if he loves our country, my child, we have nothing to fear. Think of it that way.'

Sunida stared hard at Sri. 'You knew all along, didn't you, Pi Sri? That he was the one I was destined for?'

Sri nodded. 'It had to look natural, my dear. You could never have played your part so convincingly if you'd known the truth.' She smiled. 'Even I began to believe in the reality of the mandarin when I saw the anguish in your face.'

Sunida's thoughts were suddenly far away: 'But even my uncle . . .' she began, and then her voice trailed off. No doubt he had good reason, she told herself, perplexed.

Sri surveyed Sunida carefully. 'Your mission begins sooner than you think, my child. I have to send you to Mergui as soon as possible.'

'To Mergui? But that's further even than Nakhn Si Thammarat. Will the master be coming too?'

'I am afraid not, my dear. But you'll be carrying a letter for the master there. The palace, of course, will want to read it first. But take heart, when you return enough time will have elapsed for our mysterious mandarin to have given up looking for you, and you will be able to move straight into the master's house then.'

Sunida cheered up at the thought. 'Will I be able to see him before I leave?'

'It would not be advisable, my dear. Don't forget you're escaping the clutches of a powerful mandarin.'

'I hope there's nothing bad in the letter, Pi Sri.'

'So do I, my dear. But remember, when you return you must never reveal the truth to him, no matter how much you love him.'

'I know, Pi Sri, the Lord of Life has commanded,' she said bravely.

Twenty-three

Captain Samuel White of the East India Company turned and took one last look at the enchanting harbour where for the last two days, without any tangible explanation, he had felt so intuitively at home. Mergui – the greatest port north of Malacca, a jewel on the western shore of the Bay of Bengal, the gateway to India and the West, coveted through history by Burmese, Peguans, Siamese and Portuguese alike and now, once again, firmly in Siamese hands. What would the English not give for a foothold here, he reflected. With Madras to the east and Mergui to the west, the whole bay would virtually be theirs to command.

What a bloody nuisance that no one had been here to greet him. He had waited two whole days now and he could not afford to delay any longer. True, he had arrived more than a week ahead of schedule, but his brother George had led him to believe that someone – either this Greek or one of his henchmen – would be there early, just in case. Any seaman worth his salt knew how impossible it was to gauge precisely the capricious winds of the bay. One thing was certain, however. The tides had their distinctive times and he could not afford to be caught on the wrong side of the bay with the wrong winds prevailing. Nor could he wait in Mergui longer than was absolutely necessary, not if he wanted to cross the bay, round the tip of India, and sail up to the Persian Gulf and back before the onslaught of the monsoons.

He swept the mane of straw-coloured hair away from his forehead and sucked in his breath. How he would have liked to linger a while more in this little corner of paradise, with its Burmese women, its fine cuisine and its breathtaking ocean vistas. But time was of the essence. In the absence of anyone to meet him, he would have to go quickly to Ayudhya to investigate the situation. If Phaulkon was not there or the merchandise not ready, he would turn back and head off without another thought, other than to curse his luck and damn this Greek his brother had spoken so highly of.

So, while his ship was ostensibly in for repairs, Captain White had given his chief officers to understand that he had an important mission to accomplish which might require his absence for as long as three weeks, for that was the least time he had ascertained it would take to hasten to the capital and back. In the meantime, they were to maintain the myth of the ship's overhaul and look busy until his return. The captain had winked in the direction of a lively group of chattering Burmese women and hinted that there should be plenty to keep them occupied. There was also the question of the cargo of opium and fine Indian cloth to be offloaded discreetly and sold on the local market. The men, clearly fond of their devil-may-care skipper, had laughed and promised to deal with both matters in that order.

That morning at dawn, with the thrill he always felt before exploring new territory, Samuel White set off on the eleven-day overland journey to Ayudhya. He had hired four dug-out canoes, several porters to carry crates of gifts, and a half-caste Indian guide who spoke a smattering of English and was for ever prostrating himself in the direction of Mecca, especially when the slightest chore was demanded of him. But at least he could speak to the coolies in their own tongue.

So this, mused Samuel, as they journeyed, was the famous overland route by river and jungle along which most trade from India and Persia travelled to Ayudhya, cutting weeks off an otherwise circuitous sea voyage. The route across the narrow isthmus, often hazardous, linked the Bay of Bengal with the Gulf of Siam, and avoided the long detour round the promontory of Singapura and up the eastern length of the Malay peninsula into the Gulf of Siam and the mouth of the Menam. The saving of two months had the further advantage of avoiding the pirate-plagued waters of the Straits of Malacca.

Although the route ran through seemingly impenetrable forests, malarial swamps, and jungles infested with tiger, elephant and rhinoceros, it was passable during the dry season from November to May. During the rest of the year, however, while the monsoons raged, trade was brought to a virtual standstill. The rivers swelled to furious proportions, the mosquitoes multiplied a hundredfold and legions of leeches came out to suck their fill. The journey at this time was a fight for survival and the few foolhardy travellers who attempted it, desperate traders and overzealous Jesuits for the most part, invariably succumbed to

325

prowling tigers or the deadly bite of the huge meng plu fish that leapt out of the swollen waters and clung mercilessly to the human body.

From Jelinga, a cluster of primitive huts six days upstream from Mergui, the Tenasserim river became unnavigable and the traveller had to hire elephants, bullock carts and sedan chairs to negotiate the bumpy jungle track that led, three days later, to Phriphri on the Gulf of Siam. From there it was possible to find boat service to Ayudhya.

When Samuel set off along the Tenasserim river that morning, he found the current more rapid than he had expected, and whenever the wind allowed them to rest the oars and make use of the small sails with which each canoe was equipped, he was sure they would be dashed against the rocks. But the Siamese oarsmen somehow manoeuvred around them and he soon grew accustomed to the last-minute swerves and the commendable skill with which they suddenly leapt over the side of the boats to wade through the shallower parts and steer the craft round some rock-ridden corner.

Gradually the mangrove swamps along the banks gave way to dense jungle, inhabited by so many tigers and rhinoceros that travellers were unable to venture ashore. The scenery, however, grew more spectacular by the hour, soon alternating between thick forest and sunlit paddy fields which heralded the appearance of walled villages along the shore, interrupting the flow of nature.

They encountered jungle fowl of breathtaking colours, whose majestic plumage shimmered in the sunlight wherever it managed to break through the thick foliage. Entertainment was provided by the endless troops of monkeys that sported along the river's edge, often hanging by a liana from the furthermost branches of the rain trees that reached far out across the water. They too were curious to get a good view of the intruders. Beautiful spotted deer eyed them nervously from the shore and wild boar snorted at them as they passed.

With the approach of nightfall, they anchored in midstream in the shelter of some rocks. The river was to be their home by night as well as by day; they cooked and slept on board the little boats.

As Samuel lay stretched on his back with his arms cradling his

326

head, he stared up at the tropical night sky – an intricate tapestry of brightly shimmering lights – and concentrated on his mission. Soon, even the night chorus of frogs, grasshoppers, crickets and cicadas failed to distract him from his thoughts.

Was this the proverbial chance of a lifetime, the moment he had been waiting for? Everything was ready on his side. The rest would depend on a man he had never met, a Greek in the service of the English at Ayudhya. His brother George, hardly long on compliments, had spoken well enough of the man, so Samuel could only feel optimistic that all might be ready on that side too. But why had nobody been at Mergui to meet him? Perhaps they were on their way there now and he would meet them on this very river. For he had made quite certain that there was only one passable route across the isthmus, and since it was out of the question to journey by night, it was unlikely that two parties travelling in opposite directions should miss each other.

But he had passed no one remotely likely to fit such a description. At one point a beautiful girl, an incongruous enough sight in these jungle surroundings, had passed by in the opposite direction, surrounded by an escort of coolies and guides. They had smiled briefly at each other in passing and his heart had quickened at the thought that there would surely be other such beauties in Ayudhya ready to revive a weary traveller's spirits.

Damn it, he swore again, the goods would *have* to be ready. He could not remain in Ayudhya more than a day or two or his presence there might become known and reported and the Company in Madras might ask awkward questions later on. He was, after all, supposed to be in Mergui and not Ayudhya, overseeing the sale of his cargo of cloth and opium, before returning to base at Madras. His further instructions from headquarters had been to observe conditions at Mergui carefully, especially the facilities of the harbour. Madras, he knew, was cannily playing on Siamese fears of the Dutch and planning some overture to the Siamese government in which concessions at Mergui would seemingly play a part.

After months of propositioning, he had finally assembled a crew that he trusted and a group of officers who were his friends in the Company: if they did travel to Persia and back as planned, they would all swear to the same story – that on leaving Mergui for Madras, the *Cornwall* had been blown off course in the Gulf and forced to seek shelter in the Andaman Islands. That alone should arouse the sympathy of any tribunal of inquiry in Madras, wagered Samuel. The cannibal Andamaners, with their known predilection for white meat, were the fear and scourge of every seafaring man in the bay.

Already his two mates, Jackson and Hayes, who had perished of dysentery on the way to Mergui, had inadvertently provided two deaths he could attribute to the man-eating savages of the Andamans. The rest of the crew would supposedly have hidden in creeks until the storm had abated, and then escaped to sea in lifeboats, abandoning the listing *Cornwall* which had struck a reef. In these primitive surroundings, it was preferable to face the open sea in a rowing boat than risk ending up as the main fare in some native chief's cooking pot. After drifting in two lifeboats for a number of days in a miraculously calm sea and almost depleting their meagre rations, the sixteen surviving officers and crew of the *Cornwall* would be spotted by a Siamese junk and taken aboard.

In reality, reflected Samuel with a growing thrill, if all went according to plan and Phaulkon were ready with the goods in Ayudhya, they would leave immediately for Mergui and load the *Cornwall* up post-haste. She would sail for Persia, sell off her newly acquired cargo and return as quickly as possible to an agreed rendezvous off Mergui. There, in deep waters, with no other shipping in sight, he and the officers would sink the *Cornwall* and board the junk that Phaulkon would have waiting for them.

George had assured his brother that if he timed his arrival in Ayudhya for late February or early March 1680, Phaulkon would have had a whole year to assemble the prized merchandise that the Moors reputedly monopolized: raw silks, teas and porcelains from China, and spices, jewels and aromatic woods from south-east Asia – the kind of cargo that would make them a fortune in Persia. The crew and officers of the *Cornwall* would be given a small share in the proceeds to ensure their loyalty and their confirmation of the Andaman story, and then make their way back to Madras. Samuel would either return with them or join the service of the King of Siam if, as his brother had suggested, the success of the Persian expedition prompted His Siamese Majesty to expand his fleet and take on experienced English skippers to command his vessels. Phaulkon, he supposed, would also have been working on that aspect of things.

Samuel sighed as an owl hooted eerily in the tropical night. It was an exciting moment. He was twenty-eight, filled with a sense of purpose, and his conscience had conveniently been mellowed by two years in the cutthroat trading world of southern Asia. Self-enrichment, at virtually any cost, was the *raison d'être* of the majority of his fellow traders and the object of the game was simply not to get caught. But this was his big chance. Not that he had done badly so far, he mused, though not as well perhaps as some. Not like that blighter Yale, at any rate. The devil was rumoured to be heading for another promotion. Vice-President of the honourable Company's Madras headquarters, this time! And the American quite openly boasted of the fortune he had amassed in private trading, bragging now about some school of higher learning he was going to found in his native New England. No, reflected Samuel, *he* was not going to found another Oxford or Cambridge; all he wanted was to acquire a country estate, a substantial one, mind you, and live the easy life of a gent and a squire in good old England. Because in the end, there was no place like it.

A beautiful moon had now risen, casting a grey sheen over the gurgling waters. He looked around him and saw that the crew had all turned in for the night. He smiled. They were bunched up together in the other three boats while he, Samuel White Esquire of Pottersby Hall, Northamptonshire, Captain (Retired) of His Majesty's East India fleet, had a boat all to himself, as befitted an officer and a gent. Lulled by the constant night sounds of the jungle, he turned over on his side and fell into a deep sleep.

Twenty-four

The tension was almost palpable. The spectators squatted on elevated earthen terraces lining both sides of the extensive field. Two sprawling rain trees shaded the royal enclosure while the rest of the area, but for one venerable old banyan in the final quadrangle, had been denuded of all vegetation. Beyond the large clearing lay forests and jungle on three sides, while on the fourth a broad, mud-baked track led to the nearby town of Louvo, home of His Majesty's summer palace.

In the centre of the field were two gradually narrowing rows of thick wooden posts, planted firmly in the ground and evenly spaced about two feet apart. The alleyway between the posts allowed sufficient room for an elephant to proceed, while the confined spaces between the posts were too narrow for the beast to veer off to either side, should it attempt to escape. Men, however, preferably nimble ones, could slip in between the posts, taunt and goad the elephant and dart out again before the furious beast could stamp the life out of them.

The ever-contracting alleyway led into a square arena the size of a courtyard, bordered by the same tightly spaced posts. The object of the hunt was to entice the elephant, through a series of skilful manoeuvres, into this final enclosure, where succulent sugar cane and soothing female elephants would gradually give it the taste of an easier life and remove all vestiges of intractability. Some of the beasts succumbed more readily than others to such charms while the more obstinate put up a fierce resistance, refusing to yield and challenging their capture for days at a time. Eventually, however, even the most recalcitrant among them emerged chastened and ready to serve King and country. They would work the teak forests and be enlisted in the finest regiments to face the enemy in battle.

Mahouts, heavily camouflaged in jungle foliage and muttering ritual prayers in ancient Khmer spirit language, had already ridden out into the surrounding forests astride tame females, in

330

search of venturesome bulls. The mating calls of their mounts resounded shrilly from the edges of the jungle. The hunt was on.

Out of the corner of his eye, Phaulkon looked in the direction of the royal enclosure. His Majesty's retinue had just reached the edge of the field and all those present had fallen prostrate. Although the distance was too great for Phaulkon to make out the figure of the ruling monarch in any detail, there was no doubt as to which one he was. Towering above his retinue on a huge, richly caparisoned beast, His Majesty glanced regally around him. For a moment his gaze seemed to settle on Phaulkon and then his attention turned to the arena once more.

Phaulkon's heart quickened. Had His Majesty noticed him, even deliberately picked him out of the crowd? It was the first time he had set eyes on the Lord of Life, at any distance. The diamonds on the royal harness and the rubies and sapphires draped about the conical royal hat caught the sunlight and sparkled. The retinue of three hundred mandarins, palace officials and slaves, took their appointed places in order of precedence in the royal enclosure. The Barcalon's place, as the foremost minister in the land, was immediately to His Majesty's right; General Petraja's, as Chairman of the Privy Council, was to His Majesty's left. Phaulkon had heard rumours that His Majesty enjoyed the informality of the relatively small retinue that surrounded him at Louvo, and that his passion for the hunt led him to spend ever more time at his palace here, just six hours upriver from Ayudhya. Here he was even able to exchange a few words with the common man without first having to ennoble him, as etiquette in Ayudhya would have required. It was no doubt tiresome, mused Phaulkon, to have to adhere constantly to the rigid protocol of the capital, where His Majesty had first to get secret word to any commoner he wished to converse with, so that the man could wait at an appointed place and hour for His Majesty to 'come upon' him by chance.

At Louvo, the hunting was unsurpassed, with the number of elephants running wild in the surrounding forests far exceeding that of Ayudhya. Today, the limited crowd of invited guests was to be regaled with a performance of bravado by Luang Sorasak, General Petraja's son. Like his father, Sorasak was reputed to be among the most skilled elephant riders in the kingdom, and one of only a handful who had successfully mounted a 'must'

331

elephant and lived to tell the tale. These 'musts', or wild colossi, were known to go berserk at the indignity of being mounted, and to charge at breakneck speed for the nearest forest, intent on decapitating their rider on the bough of a tree.

In his effort to understand the Siamese, Phaulkon had learned a great deal about elephants, and the deeper he had delved, the more the subject had fascinated him. There was no doubt in his mind that they were creatures of superior intelligence and it had fascinated him to learn how, in battle, a well-trained elephant could pick up his fallen rider with his trunk and hoist him on to his back again, or throw an enemy rider to the ground and trample him to death.

His Majesty, like all his royal predecessors, revered the beasts and often used them in the judgement of criminals, paying tribute to their insight and intuitive powers. An elephant would administer his own justice by trampling the accused to death, or merely tossing him about with his trunk if he felt the crime called for a lighter sentence. When two such judges tossed the accused back and forth between them, gently catching him in the hollow of their tusks, the crime was not considered a serious one. If they ignored the accused altogether, he was given instant freedom.

Phaulkon had journeyed to Louvo with two of the Barcalon's assistants. They had shown him to his appointed place, and intimated that General Petraja, who had invited him to the hunt through the Barcalon, wished to have an informal chat with him after the performance. Phaulkon was in the front row of the commoners' enclosure in the company of some fifty minor courtiers who turned from time to time to eye him curiously. They were all dressed, as he was, in white linen blouses and black panungs, in honour of His Majesty's attendance, though any who had been given a special article of clothing by His Majesty were entitled to wear it on this occasion. As far as he could see he was the only farang present. The royal enclosure took up most of the space on this side of the arena, while the opposite side seemed reserved for peasants and farmers dressed mostly in loincloths, who were invited by roster to attend this revered event. Every man and woman was given the chance at least once in a lifetime to view a royal hunt.

'So we meet again, Heer Phaulkon.' The guttural sounds were strangely familiar and Phaulkon swung round. The crowd made way for two newcomers. The portlier of the two aroused particular interest and the crowd, unaccustomed to farangs altogether, gaped at him with undisguised curiosity.

'Heer van Risling, what an unexpected surprise!' exclaimed Phaulkon in Dutch. 'I did not know you were an aficionado of the hunt.'

The expansive Dutchman, as florid as ever and perspiring under the weight of his European clothing and his own frame, screwed up his face into a distasteful grimace.

'I have come from Ligor to deal with certain matters directly relating to you, Heer Phaulkon.'

Phaulkon ignored the comment. 'And may I ask if you have seen my colleagues Messrs Burnaby and Ivatt?' he inquired.

'We do not mix in the same circles,' replied van Risling, haughtily. 'They are prisoners, I believe.' He turned to his companion, a tall, grey-haired man with elegant, regular features and an easy smile. 'May I present Heer Aarnout Faa, our distinguished director in Ayudhya. Heer Constantine Phaulkon.'

Both men bowed politely and Phaulkon observed with interest the chief of the Verenigde Oostindische Compagnie, known simply as the VOC. He was the highest-ranking Dutchman in Siam, and though Phaulkon had come into contact with other employees of the Dutch East India Company, it was the first time he had met its chief face to face.

Aarnout Faa, the opperhoofd or resident director, employed over forty personnel in organized, clearly defined ranks, including opperkoopmans, koopmans, onderkoopmans, assistant koopmans, full-time surgeons and assistant surgeons, book-keepers, store-keepers, soldiers, sailors and labourers. His headquarters in Ayudhya, a massive brick building on the far side of the river, were the envy of every trader in Siam. Faa, at the apex of it all, and responsible only to the Gouverneur-Generaal in Batavia, Java, was a man to be reckoned with.

'I have been hearing a great deal about you lately, Herr Phaulkon.' His English was perfect. He had obtained a degree in both language and literature at the University of Amsterdam, and though almost twenty years had elapsed since that time, he had had plenty of occasion to keep himself in practice. The trading world of southern Asia was full of English pirates, and the occasional gentleman. 'It seems you have created quite a stir

333

in our little branch at Ligor.' Faa smiled and pointed in the direction of van Risling. 'And you have clearly made an impression on our chief koopman there.'

Van Risling fidgeted uncomfortably. He found it difficult to follow his chief's rapid English.

Phaulkon bowed. 'The impression, I am sure, sir, is entirely mutual.'

'Heer van Risling has just arrived from Ligor,' resumed the director, reverting to Dutch for the sake of his colleague, 'and we were in fact planning on paying you a visit tomorrow in Ayudhya. This fortuitous encounter may obviate the need. I have been particularly anxious to discuss the matter of certain cannon with you.' The director paused. 'I was intrigued to learn that you were transporting weapons of Dutch origin. A peculiar circumstance, Heer Phaulkon, when one considers how proud you English are of your own manufactures.'

'Our trading practices, you will appreciate, Heer Faa, are matters which concern only ourselves.'

'Indeed, Heer Phaulkon. I can well understand your reticence to discuss the subject. Especially if, as I believe, you were attempting to supply Dutch cannon to the rebels at Pattani. I have, of course, expressed my views on the subject to His Excellency the Barcalon. As you know, our Dutch Company has been in operation in this country for almost a century, and we have an excellent relationship with the Siamese government.'

'I am surprised to learn that, Heer Faa. It is not my understanding of the situation at all. Neither is it, I venture to suggest, that of the Siamese government. Perhaps you are a little out of touch, mijn heer. Of course,' added Phaulkon drily, 'not speaking the language must make it difficult to stay in close contact.'

Van Risling drew himself up to his full height and wheezed angrily, as if he had himself been assailed, while the opperhoofd barely flinched and retained his composure.

'As I said before, I am intrigued to learn how you obtained our cannon, Heer Phaulkon. Were you acting on your own, or is this part of some greater English scheme to discredit us?'

'The Siamese and the English are working together to discredit you, Heer Faa. And afterwards to supplant you. That is why the English have been invited back to trade here. It is also why I myself, a member of the English Company, have been given a position in the Ministry of Trade. We are going to undermine you, mijn heer. The goals of the English and the Siamese are now inseparable.'

'Ha, ha! That's a good one!' Van Risling emitted a raucous laugh and every Siamese head within hearing turned towards the source of the uproar. 'So the Siamese are now supplying cannon to their own rebels in Pattani. That's a fine policy. Ha, ha!'

Phaulkon ignored the outburst. If only the opperhoofd would swallow the bait, he thought. Then he, Phaulkon, would be a step closer to realizing his goal.

Sunida was well on her way to Mergui. If she managed to reach Samuel in time and the consequent shipment to Persia was a success, then the Siamese might be better disposed to accept his scheme of a local fleet captained by Englishmen in the service of Siam. And the Dutch could unwittingly hasten the process. The more they antagonized Siam, the sooner he might be called upon to implement his scheme. Phaulkon hoped Aarnout Faa would report his words verbatim in the famous dagh-register, and thus provoke Dutch retaliatory action against the Siamese. The dagh-register, or daily journal, envied symbol of Dutch thoroughness, accompanied every ship returning to Batavia. It contained complete records of trade figures, political and economic trends, transcripts of relevant conversations and every type of information pertaining to a particular branch office. The Dutch did not skimp on detail and none was too small to be entered in the dagh-register. The VOC outposts and factories at Amboina, Banda, the Moluccas, Ceylon, Malacca, Macassar, Cambodia, Formosa, the Cape of Good Hope, Coromandel, Surat, Malabar, Jaffnapatnam and a host of others provided VOC headquarters in Java with voluminous and updated material on every prevailing condition in the area. Dutch supremacy was fuelled by the information contained in the dagh-registers, and the Dutch empire was difficult to challenge on account of it. The Gouverneur-Generaal learned what gifts to make to which officials in which countries and when, and the sheer volume of Dutch shipping which transported the precious journals ensured that Batavia was kept abreast of events well ahead of the competition.

In Ayudhya's case, Batavia was only twenty-five days' sail away and the far-reaching powers entrusted to the Gouverneur-Generaal made him easily the most practical farang ruler to deal with. Both the Siamese monarch and the Pra Klang corresponded with him regularly. Since letters to England and Europe took seven months – when they got through – the VOC in Batavia was itself empowered to make treaties, raise troops, build fortresses and appoint officials in the name of the Dutch government. No new directives had come from the States General, the government of Holland, since 1650, some thirty-odd years ago. The VOC was virtually a kingdom unto itself, with the Gouverneur-Generaal its uncrowned king. Phaulkon smiled to himself. Though Holland was ruled by a States General, the Prince of Orange had been prevailed upon to assume the title of King whenever he received a Siamese delegation or responded to one of their letters. The Gouverneur-Generaal could not allow his country to be diminished in the eyes of the visitors. For to the Siamese it was inconceivable that any self-respecting country could function or call itself a power without a king at its head.

The opperhoofd waited tolerantly for van Risling's laughter to subside. Then he looked hard at Phaulkon.

'In any event, Heer Phaulkon, an express dispatch describing your activities has been sent to His Excellency Heer Rijcklof van Goens, with my comments. The Gouverneur-Generaal usually heeds my advice and since the dagh-register left a month ago, His Excellency will by now no doubt have spoken to the head of your English Company at Bantam.' He paused as the flicker of a smile crossed his lips.

'Your office here is, I believe, subordinate to Bantam? Under the estabished rules of conduct agreed between our two governments, I have strongly recommended the closure of your operations in Siam.' His eyes narrowed as he added, 'Under threat of severe retaliation by us. I am sure, Heer Phaulkon, that in the circumstances we shall, before long, be seeing the last of you.'

Phaulkon scoffed. 'Bantam is not empowered to make such a decision, Heer Faa. The orders come from higher up.'

'From Madras?' Faa asked.

A series of loud mating calls resounded from the adjacent forests. Phaulkon turned in the direction of the sound. 'Do you enjoy the hunt, Heer Faa?' he inquired politely.

'*Godverdorie!*' burst out van Risling, the blood rushing to his face. 'You will answer Heer Faa when he asks a question. His rank is higher than yours.'

336

'I am not a Dutchman, Heer van Risling, so his rank does not affect me.'

'As a matter of fact I do enjoy the hunt,' replied Aarnout Faa, with studied civility, leaving van Risling to mumble angrily to himself. 'Both elephants and tigers, and sometimes,' he smiled wanly, 'even ants who dare to defy the Verenigde Oostindische Compagnie. I enjoy watching them being crushed.'

The Dutch resident director now turned away and concentrated on the arena in front of him. Van Risling was right, he thought. This Phaulkon was impudent and self-assured, though no doubt a man to be reckoned with, far more so than his immediate superior, the spineless Burnaby. But what had this man to be so self-assured about? What could he hope to achieve? South-east Asia was a Dutch enclave. And as for Ayudhya, the VOC exported sapanwood, lumber and lead to Formosa, wax and coconut oil to Malacca, sugar, tin and pepper to India. To Japan, the most lucrative market of all, the VOC had a monopoly – guaranteed by treaty – for the export of deer hides. This gave them control over the single most lucrative commodity in the whole Ayudhya export trade. Although it was true that sapanwood returned a 1500 per cent profit on the purchase price, it was bulky to ship, while the sheer quality of hides, though realizing only 300 per cent, more than made up for the difference. This year alone he expected to ship over 100,000 hides to the Japans for the first time – unless of course the Buddhist clergy requested another suspension in the killing of deer, as they periodically did, or the rumoured presence of a white elephant in the forests put a temporary ban on all hunting in the area.

The opperhoofd sighed inwardly with anticipation. The time had come to make the most of his position and reap the reward for years of dedicated service. Now that the new Gouverneur-Generaal had heeded his advice and reversed the decision to ship the hides first to Batavia, he could export them directly to Japan. He had warned the Gouverneur that storing the hides in the humid climate of Java would leave them open to worming, and sure enough, the first two cargoes had been all but destroyed by worms while awaiting transhipment in Batavia. The Japanese were a discriminating people, and their natural reticence to accept imports made them demanding customers. The hides had to be top quality. Now that he could export directly, reflected

337

the opperhoofd, who would notice a discrepancy of one or two per cent on shipments of 100,000 skins? The Japanese paid in silver too, a much-prized commodity in Ayudhya. His life style would soon be greatly enhanced.

What then were Phaulkon's motives? His knowledge of Dutch and Siamese was impressive. But he or the English could not seriously hope to supplant the VOC. From Batavia the Gouverneur-Generaal regularly supplied the Siamese King with cannoneers, powdermakers, goldsmiths, doctors and carpenters. Even glassblowers and painters. What would His Majesty do without them all? Or without his clocks and telescopes? In addition, he relied on the ready market in Dutch-ruled Java for his surplus rice.

Besides, the local office contributed scrupulously to the cremation ceremonies of key Siamese officials and involved the VOC in all Siamese festivals. They knew how and when to distribute gifts. They were an integral part of the system. The English, on the other hand, were disorganized, preoccupied with their affairs in the sub-continent and, despite their regional headquarters in Madras, pathetically unfamiliar with the area. There were only a few— A great shout interrupted his thoughts. The crowd around him tensed.

A wild trumpeting sound and the crackle of trampled undergrowth preceded the appearance of a male colossus who came roaring out of the forest in pursuit of two females. Ridden by camouflaged mahouts who goaded them desperately with iron staffs, the females appeared miniature in comparison as they headed for the long alleyway of posts. The male was gaining on them with every stride. It was touch and go whether they would reach the alleyway before the giant caught up with them on open ground. The females barely made it through. As the huge male beast entered the narrow lane in hot pursuit and was forced to slow its pace, it threw its trunk in the air and emitted a series of deafening roars. At this point several agile Siamese on foot darted in and out of the alleyway through the narrow spaces between the posts, and attempted to provoke the elephant with sharp sticks.

The beast turned fiercely on one and then another of them, but before it was able to crush the life out of them, they had scampered back through the narrow spaces out of reach of the

338

angry tusks that buried themselves with a thud into the posts. Wrenching its tusks free, the infuriated beast turned and chased yet more of the antagonists as they pursued their strategy of wearing him out.

While some of the men were thus engaged in inciting him, others with commendable skill tossed nooses of thick rope round his hind legs and pulled them fast. But as they could not hold on to the ends of the ropes without themselves being dragged about by the elephant, they were forced to let go and allow the beast to tow the ropes about with him, unmolested.

A great shout now went up from the crowd. The men on foot abruptly dispersed and a camouflaged rider on another female entered the alleyway behind the colossus. It was Sorasak. Although not personally popular, there was a grudging respect for his prowess at the hunt. The crowd waited breathlessly for him to perform. They knew that he had to entice the wild animal into the final enclosure at the end of the alleyway where more agile men on foot would have the precarious task of fastening the loose ropes to the thick trunks of the banyan tree. During this time the rider of the female would attempt to lasso the huge beast and tie both elephants, the wild and the tame one, to each other.

The crowd gasped. Sorasak, taking advantage of a momentary lull when the colossus was stilled by the mating cries of the female, leapt on to the back of the wild beast and hung on to its earflaps. The beast reacted instantly and violently. With a deafening roar it threw up its trunk and reared its front legs in an attempt to shake off the irritant. But Sorasak dug his knees in, leaned over forward and clung to its back until the maddened beast changed tactics and with all its might charged one of the posts lining the alleyway. The post shook to its foundations but held fast; Sorasak held on too and the angry beast backed up and lunged again. This time the post was all but uprooted and with the third assault it leaned to one side, allowing the sheer weight of the elephant to carry it through the opening.

Pandemonium broke out. An enraged bull elephant, abnormally large, was charging straight for the crowd, now a mere fifty yards away. Sorasak was still clinging to the beast's back while digging his sharp goad into its neck in a frantic attempt to make it change course. With only seconds to spare, while the crowd

339

fled in every direction, the beast suddenly veered to the left and headed for the edge of the royal enclosure. For the last twenty yards it maintained a direct line for Phaulkon; it appeared almost as if he were the chosen target.

Phaulkon dived to one side just as two spectators were trampled in front of him. Out of the corner of his eye he saw van Risling hurled headlong to the ground. Two more Siamese, his neighbours during the display, let out a series of screeches before disappearing in a cloud of dust. The ground beneath him shook and Phaulkon felt rather than saw the elephant hurtle by, within inches of his own body.

Killing or maiming everything in its path, the maddened beast charged on recklessly towards the forest. The crowd picked itself up and turned to watch as the rider braced himself for the leap. All knew that it was instant decapitation to ride a charging bull through a forest. Sorasak had to jump clear before reaching the undergrowth, and land with enough skill not to break every bone in his body. He had to time his fall carefully. He waited till the last minute to ensure that, carried by its own momentum, the beast would plunge too far into the forest to turn back and look for him. The crowd gasped as they saw Sorasak leap dramatically in the air and then roll over several times on the ground. Breathlessly they waited to see if the colossus would return. Then they surged forward to examine the damage.

The bold rider was hurt, the blood seeping from a wound in his forehead. A bamboo stretcher was fetched and Sorasak was brought before the King who inquired solicitously after his condition and ordered him delivered immediately into the care of his physicians. People were running in all directions tending to the wounded. Van Risling's corpulent body quivered spasmodically as Faa, shaken but unhurt, tended to him.

Phaulkon half picked himself up and knelt on one knee, his head swimming. Sorasak's stretcher passed almost in front of him. For a moment the eyes of the two men met. In that instant the wounded man's stare fixed itself unwaveringly on Phaulkon. In the cold glowering eyes he saw a familiar and unmistakable look of contempt. He would never forget it. The boxer from Ligor!

Spellbound and gripped by a foreboding that it was not to be their last encounter, Phaulkon followed the stretcher with his

340

gaze until it was out of sight. Then he forced himself to concentrate on van Risling's plight. Obviously Phaulkon's projected meeting with General Petraja would now be postponed. Faa had commandeered another stretcher and together they lifted the bulky man on to it. Van Risling's right leg looked badly broken and he winced with pain as pressure was put on it.

'*Godverdorie!*' he cried, gritting his teeth. For the first time since he had known him, Phaulkon felt sorry for the man. They followed the other stretchers away from the field in the direction of the town.

Twenty-five

The domestic came in to announce the arrival of a farang visitor. The servant, of Indian origin, spoke a smattering of English, enough to obtain for him an immediate post with his master, who was otherwise unable to communicate with the world around him.

Burnaby sat up in the armchair of his English country-style drawing room and requested to know the visitor's name. But that was asking too much. The caller was a farang and as Ananda knew from experience, all farangs had unpronounceable names. Burnaby muttered something under his breath about untrainable natives and told Ananda to show the visitor in.

'Thomas,' called Burnaby, 'we have a visitor. A European. I wonder who that could be?'

'Is Constant back?' exclaimed Ivatt excitedly, running in from the next-door room where he had been practising an old conjuring trick. He had almost mastered it and he was determined to have it ready for his debut at the palace. He might be summoned there at any time now, he reflected nervously. His performances had become a regular feature at the Governor of Ligor's mansion and the children of the mandarin's household had been grief-stricken at his departure. Now, thanks to the Governor's recommendation, he might be summoned to perform before the royal children at the King's palace. 'Who knows,' he had said jokingly to Burnaby, 'I may even meet the King before Constant does and arrange an introduction for him.'

'No, it wouldn't be Constant,' replied Burnaby. 'Even my numbskull of a servant could recognize him, although you never know with Ananda. A two-month absence might have clouded his memory.'

They had arrived from Ligor yesterday on the Governor's boat and had gone straight to Phaulkon's home only to find him absent. Ivatt, who had been studying Siamese with great gusto, had thought he understood the female slave to say that her master was away in Louvo on some elephant hunt. What had

342

Constant been up to? they both wondered. Weren't elephant hunts at Louvo royal occasions? Perhaps Ivatt had misunderstood.

The visitor was now ushered into the sitting room. Both men stared at him curiously. He was the very picture of the Asian adventurer, a gentleman pirate, handsome, in his late twenties, with eyes the colour of a lagoon and a wave of blond hair bleached almost white by the sun. His face was deeply tanned and he had a self-assured, gallant air, verging on the arrogant.

'Samuel White at your service, gentlemen.' He smiled genially at them and from the first instant radiated charm.

Both men rose instantly to greet him.

'I am Richard Burnaby and this is my assistant, Thomas Ivatt. Welcome to Ayudhya, Mr White.'

'Thank you, sir. Your name is known to me. My brother George has often mentioned it in the most flattering terms.' He smiled broadly, displaying a perfect row of teeth rendered more striking by the contrast with his sunbrowned skin.

'Thank you, sir.' Burnaby beamed, but the gratified expression quickly gave way to concern, as he added: 'We have been expecting you.'

The disconsolate tone was not lost on Samuel. His smile contracted and a look of foreboding replaced it.

'I was taken from your factory to Mr Phaulkon's house by one of your staff, but had difficulty in making myself understood. I was eventually brought here. Will you forgive me, sir, if I come straight to the point? My abruptness is prompted only by my poor way with words and by my need to return to Mergui in the shortest possible time.' He barely paused before asking: 'Is the cargo for Persia ready?'

Burnaby hesitated, but his expression said everything. 'We have had some unexpected reversals,' he explained eventually.

A cloud of indignation crossed White's face. Incompetent fools, he seemed to be saying. In a moment his easy charm had switched to disdain and frustration.

'You do not have the merchandise, I take it,' he said coldly.

'Just a minute,' interjected Ivatt, turning to Richard. 'Let's be fair now. We haven't even spoken to Constant yet. I am sure he won't have been lying idle all this time.'

Samuel turned abruptly on the little man. 'Either you have the

343

merchandise or you don't, sir.' Did they not understand that time was of the essence?

'Mr White, we have not seen Mr Phaulkon for over a month,' explained Ivatt. 'Neither have we had any means of communicating with him. We have been away in the south, you see, and I think we should reserve judgement until we have spoken to him.'

'And when will that be, sir?' inquired Samuel, bottling his irritation.

'He is in Louvo, attending the royal hunt,' said Ivatt, stressing the word 'royal'.

White seemed to take heart at the thought that Phaulkon might be moving in the right circles.

'When will he be back, sir?' he asked.

'We're not sure, Mr White,' said Burnaby. 'But much as I'd like to give you – to give us all – hope, it would not be fair to mislead you. We lost the wherewithal to purchase the goods for Persia barely more than a month ago, and I cannot see how even Constant could have reversed the situation in so short a time.'

'You're such a pessimist, Richard,' said Ivatt, annoyed.

Burnaby turned on him. 'I'm not a pessimist, Ivatt. I'm a realist. It is not fair to mislead Mr White or waste his time.'

It was seldom that Burnaby called Ivatt by his surname.

'I am afraid, gentlemen, my time is very short. Unless there is a serious possibility of Mr Phaulkon having the merchandise ready – which does not appear to me to be the case – I cannot linger here. My crew is waiting for me in Mergui and my ship is expected in Madras before the end of the month. I am hardly anxious to leave, considering the rigours of my journey here, but I have little choice.' His expression soured. 'I lost three of my men to tigers on the way up and I was practically eaten alive by mosquitoes myself.' He bent down and scratched his ankles in confirmation. 'So I'd best leave now and get it over with.'

'Would you not wait just one night, Mr White?' pleaded Ivatt. 'I'm sure you could do with the rest. It seems a shame to have come all this way without speaking to Mr Phaulkon. You could spend the night in his house.' Ivatt smiled. 'His quarters provide the best massage in town. You'd be totally invigorated.'

White arched an eyebrow. 'Female masseuses?' he inquired.

'Three of them. They work as a team.' Ivatt winked. 'Devils every one of them, but trained in heaven.'

344

White appeared to vacillate. 'Very well, I will take you up on your offer of a night's rest. I'll leave first thing in the morning. Would one of you be kind enough to accompany me there? Although I know it's not far, I'm not sure I'll recognize the house again.'

'Allow me,' offered Ivatt. He turned to Burnaby. 'With your permission, Richard?'

'Of course. I'll be off to the factory myself. You can join me there, Thomas, as soon as you've deposited Mr White. It's been a pleasure making your acquaintance, Mr White. I'm only sorry the tidings have not been more pleasant.'

'I am too, sir. Frankly, it has been a great disappointment.' He bowed and left with Ivatt.

Phaulkon arrived back in Ayudhya that night after dark. Van Risling had been in too much pain to travel and had remained in Louvo with Faa. He had steadfastly refused to be attended by any of the local surgeons, including those offered by His Majesty the King to the wounded, and had insisted on waiting to see a Dutch physician in Ayudhya. An exasperated Aarnout Faa had finally shrugged his shoulders and agreed to spend the night in Louvo in the hope that van Risling would be up to making the journey in the morning. Phaulkon had been anxious to return to Ayudhya and had caught the last boat that day. It was almost nine o'clock at night when he arrived at his house.

Sorn and Tip were waiting up to greet him at the foot of the steps and told him excitedly that a farang visitor was stretched out on the living room floor having a massage. Tip kept putting her hand in front of her mouth and giggling, as the Siamese normally did to hide their embarrassment, and with a little coaxing Phaulkon learned that the farang was completely naked and greatly enjoying the company of the master's three slaves.

Who was this man? Phaulkon demanded to know. They knew nothing beyond that the little farang had brought him here.

'The little farang?' exclaimed Phaulkon. 'Is he here?'

'Yes, master,' replied Sorn. 'He and the tall farang arrived yesterday.'

'Are you sure?'

'Absolutely, master. They came round to see you and asked where you were.'

345

How extraordinary, thought Phaulkon. How could they have got here so quickly? The Barcalon had only agreed to their release a week ago.

The girls' hands returned to cover their mouths now, and they both giggled like children. The little farang had been learning Siamese, they said, and if they had understood him correctly, he had told them under no circumstances to let this man out of the house. He was to be entertained till he had no desire to leave any more. They had passed the message on to Nid and Ut and Noi, and the farang was still there on the living room floor now. He had been there since before sunset.

'My God, but that was three hours ago!' exclaimed Phaulkon. 'All right, I'll see to it. Tip, go and fetch the little and the tall farang masters and ask them to come here right away.' Tip prostrated herself and crawled out backwards.

'And Sorn, prepare us some food, please. I'm starved. Has the visitor eaten?'

'Not yet, master,' replied Sorn with a twinkle. 'He's been too busy.'

'You'd better prepare enough for four then.'

'Your slave, master,' said Sorn, bending low and retiring.

Phaulkon mounted the steps and stopped at the door of the living room. He could hear the sounds of muffled giggling inside interspersed with a deep stentorian voice. It seemed to be shouting encouragement. He made out a few words in English.

'Go to it, me beauties . . . that's it . . . wonderful . . . don't stop . . . lower now.'

Who the devil was this? Phaulkon threw open the door panels and all activity ceased instantly. The girls prostrated themselves on the ground and Ut quickly threw a panung over the farang to cover him. Samuel White looked around momentarily dazed, then jumped to his feet and strode over to Phaulkon, beaming brightly. He seemed to have forgotten that he was stark naked.

'Now you, sir, must be the acclaimed Mr Phaulkon, of whom my brother George has spoken so warmly.' He bowed. 'Samuel White at your service. It is indeed an honour to meet you, sir.'

'The pleasure is entirely mine, sir,' replied Phaulkon, taken wholly by surprise, and thrilled at the realization of who the visitor was. 'And I am delighted to see that you have already made yourself quite at home, sir.'

346

Samuel looked down somewhat abashedly at his nakedness. The three girls, also naked, were still prostrate on the floor. Samuel smiled sheepishly and moved over to his pile of clothes. 'Your colleague who brought me here suggested I avail myself of the facilities, sir, so I—'

'You did well, Mr White,' said Phaulkon, with a magnanimous sweep of his arms. He would gladly have provided three more such ladies to entertain so welcome a guest, he reflected. 'There is no man I hold in greater esteem than your brother George. Girls,' he said, 'you may leave now.'

Samuel was pulling on his clothes now. He watched in fascination as the three slaves crawled reverently backwards collecting their discarded panungs as they went.

'I was expecting to find you in Mergui, Mr White. I sent an emissary there with a note.'

'I arrived early, sir, so I decided to come up here instead. Especially when I discovered it was only ten days via the overland route.'

Poor Sunida, thought Phaulkon. She would be searching everywhere for him now. They must have passed each other en route.

'You didn't encounter a messenger going the other way, did you?' It was not such a widely travelled route.

'No, sir, though I was on the look-out for one. Was it a large party?'

'The emissary was a young woman, sir, accompanied by half a dozen guides and porters.'

'A female, did you say? No, it couldn't be. I did pass one lady, but she was more like some princess out of a fairy story. What a beauty. I was wondering in fact what she was doing—'

'Your description fits my emissary perfectly,' interjected Phaulkon with a smile. 'She's the one, sir.'

Samuel White whistled through his teeth. This place became more intriguing by the minute. What cursed luck about the cargo. He could do with a little more time in a place like this, what with messengers that looked like goddesses and honey-fingered masseuses that crawled about on all fours and made you jump out of your skin.

'Your emissary won't have much trouble finding the *Cornwall*, sir,' said Samuel. 'She was the only sizeable frigate in port when

347

I left.' He smiled. 'Nor should your messenger have much trouble being received aboard – my officers will be falling over themselves.' He paused and a slight frown crossed his face. 'But I understand the *Cornwall* will be leaving empty-handed, sir?'

'Oh, how is that?'

'I mean, Mr Phaulkon, without the cargo for Persia.'

'And where did you get that information?'

Samuel eyed Phaulkon uncertainly. As if in answer to the question, Tip now reappeared, prostrating herself in the doorway. 'The little and tall farang masters are here, my Lord.'

'Good, show them in.'

Burnaby and Ivatt appeared smiling in the doorway.

'Constant!' they both shouted, coming up eagerly to embrace him. Phaulkon returned their effusive embraces and then addressed himself to White.

'Might this be the impeccable source of your information?'

'It is indeed, sir,' nodded Samuel, a cautious hope creeping into his features.

'Welcome back to Ayudhya then, oh ye of little faith,' said Phaulkon to the other two.

'What do you mean?' asked Burnaby, looking suddenly perturbed.

Phaulkon turned to White. 'Contrary to what you might have heard, sir, I have your cargo. I am only sorry that you should have been greeted with such misleading and distressing news after your arduous journey.'

White was instantly transformed.

'I always knew, sir,' he exclaimed jubilantly, 'that the reputation you enjoy with my brother George was well founded.' He was now quite breathless with excitement. 'You say the cargo is actually ready?'

'Just about, Mr White. I will need two or three days for the final formalities.'

'Call me Samuel, please.'

'Very well. But tell me first, what news do you have of your esteemed brother?'

'I have heard nothing, sir, since he stopped in Madras on his way to England. It was then that he advised me of the purpose and date of my mission to Mergui. He was so confident of your success, sir, that I decided to undertake the voyage without receiving further confirmation. I can see for myself the soundness of my brother's judgement. You must forgive any initial doubts I may have had, sir, but Mr Burnaby here indicated that . . . it was not likely that—'

'No doubt Mr Burnaby obtained his information from the marketplace at Ligor,' interrupted Phaulkon drily. The chief of station was looking remarkably sheepish. Ivatt, too, was noticeably glum but White came quickly to his rescue.

'Fortunately, Mr Ivatt here kept my hopes alive, insisting I should talk to you first, sir,' he said to Phaulkon.

'Call me Constant, please.' He turned to Ivatt. 'Thank you, Thomas. I shall remember that.'

'How . . . how did you obtain the cargo, Constant?' asked Burnaby timidly.

Pretending not to have heard the question, Phaulkon addressed White again.

'When do you have to leave for Mergui, Samuel? I imagine your time is short.'

'Indeed it is, Constant. The *Cornwall* is due to return to Madras as soon as it has sold its cargo of cloth and opium at Mergui. I would not want the prolonged absence of its captain to be noted and reported to the Company. Especially as the Moors down there would be glad of an excuse to discredit anyone attempting to usurp their traditional trading routes. The *Cornwall*'s presence in Mergui seems already to have aroused considerable interest, not to say suspicion, so I have spread the word that she is in for extensive repairs. Now, of course, when my ship does not reach Madras within the appointed time, inquiries will be made, and a search party sent out. It would clearly be fatal for the *Cornwall* to be discovered still in Mergui, when she is in fact supposed to be lost in a storm off the Andamans.' He winked at his audience.

There was a moan from Ivatt. 'Oh no, here comes the next round.'

'Sir?' inquired White.

'Thomas is new to these parts,' explained Phaulkon. 'He is not yet accustomed to the variety of activities we are involved in.'

Thomas turned to White. 'I took a respectable job in the service of His Britannic Majesty's merchant fleet, sir, and the next thing I know I'm mixed up with the biggest bunch of cut-

349

throats east of Dover. I used to be a trapeze artist, Mr White. A relatively safe occupation, I might add.'

White laughed. 'That's a fine comparison, sir. And I can see that while the dangers of the high wire are over swiftly, ours are much more prolonged. Will you be joining our little party to Persia, then, Mr Ivatt?'

'I wasn't aware I'd been asked.'

'I think you certainly qualify for a stake, Thomas, don't you, Richard?'

Burnaby was visibly relieved to be brought back into the conversation. 'Most certainly, Constant. With flying colours, I should say.'

Phaulkon put an arm affectionately round the little man. 'We couldn't have asked for a better comrade-in-arms. Or a more natural rogue. What stake do you want?'

Ivatt paused. 'Given the usual risks, I'd better cover myself with fifty per cent.'

White looked confused. 'Fifty per cent?' he repeated.

Phaulkon laughed. 'Mr Ivatt is judging from what he has seen of Company service so far.'

White quickly joined in the game. 'I would have thought the real danger lay in owning that much stock,' he observed. 'Once my crew found out, Mr Ivatt's life would not be worth that of a shipwrecked sailor in the Andamans.'

'The cannibal Andamans?' inquired Ivatt.

White nodded.

'I'll lower my stake then. And besides, I might have to beg off the journey altogether.' He raised himself to his fullest height. 'I am solidly committed to the palace.'

'What are you talking about?' said Phaulkon, dismissing the suggestion with a laugh. 'What palace?'

'It's true,' confirmed Burnaby. 'You don't know what this lad got up to in Ligor, Constant. The Governor persuaded him to enter the boxing ring in your footsteps. Thomas ran around the arena performing such dexterous acrobatics that his opponent couldn't catch him. The crowd, the Governor included, roared with delight until the bout had finally to be stopped for no contest.'

'Is that how you've been spending your time in Ligor?' said Phaulkon, laughing.

'Not really,' replied Ivatt. 'We spent most of our spare time searching for white elephants.'

'Young Thomas here,' continued Burnaby, 'became a regular feature at the Governor's court, performing daily for the children. I was beginning to despair we'd ever be let out of there. The courtyard was packed every time. And the Governor has given him a recommendation to perform before the palace children here.'

'I know how keen you are on meeting His Majesty, Constant. I'll see if I can put a word in for you,' teased Ivatt.

'How kind, Thomas. But how is your foot, Richard? Mr Burnaby had an accident in the south,' he explained to White.

'Oh, I'm sorry to hear that.'

'It's much better now, thank you, Constant. Almost completely healed. But I'm most anxious to hear about the cargo and your . . . brilliant achievement.'

Phaulkon looked around him. 'I might as well explain the full developments to you as well, Samuel. I am presently employed in the Siamese Ministry of Trade. On probation, I would say. I was interviewed by the Barcalon, who is every bit as shrewd as he is reported to be. I think he has a strong suspicion of our recent activities but he is willing to overlook things if we can be of more use to him alive than dead. I'm counting on that. So far I have exposed the fraudulent banqueting practices of the Moors and extracted an agreement in principle from His Excellency to obtain goods on credit for the trip to Persia. The agreement is conditional on our providing our own ship. Mr White's timely arrival will fill that need. It seems, however, that the Siamese authorities are not anxious to alert the Moors to the fact that they are being investigated. Officially they don't want to have any part in it. That's why they are so anxious for us to use our own ship.'

'And is the Ligor investigation closed yet?' asked Burnaby.

'My feeling is that it will be held over our heads until we have made it worth their while to forget about it.' He turned to White. 'What compensation is your crew getting? Can their silence be relied upon?'

'I had to promise them ten per cent of the profits, to be divided among them.'

'Will they be satisfied with that?' asked Phaulkon.

351

'That's still more than a year's wages, if the returns I have estimated are anywhere near accurate. The Moors must be making a fortune. The crews expect the officers to divide up a further ten per cent of course, and I have explained that the rest has to go back to the investors who loaned the money. I did not specify who.'

'That sounds reasonable. And you think that will ensure their silence?'

'Once the money is in their pockets, they are not likely to blabber, especially when they share the guilt of scuttling one of good King Charles's ships. The only trouble I can foresee is if the profits don't turn out to be as expected.'

'What merchandise do we have ready now, Constant?' inquired Burnaby, as if he had been included in the preparations.

'Tea, Chinese raw silks, satins and damasks, porcelain, sapan-wood, elephant tusks, tin, hides and gumlac. Just as you suggested, Richard,' said Phaulkon drily.

'Excellent,' replied Burnaby, with the gratified air of one whose assistant had performed well in his absence.

'So how soon can we load up?' asked Samuel. 'Time is critical, though I must admit I'm not looking forward to that overland journey again. This time I'm hiring only elephants. The bloody bullocks were a magnet for every tiger in the region.'

'We should be able to have the goods packed in the next two or three days. I'll be talking to the Barcalon first thing in the morning.'

'Mr Phaulkon,' White's tone was notably mellifluous, 'it's been a long time since my brother mentioned this, but once this journey is over, what possibilities would there be of employment here in Siam for the likes of me?'

'Much will depend on the success of this expedition.' He paused. 'I will speak to you openly, more so than I would to a stranger, on account of the great friendship I bear your brother. It shall serve as a bond between us.'

Samuel White bowed. 'And I shall strive to be worthy of your trust, sir.'

'You see, Samuel, it is my ultimate aim to be able to promote Englishmen to positions of power in the western province of Tenasserim, from where they might control the trade routes across the Bay of Bengal.'

352

'The Company has coveted Mergui for years,' said White, with visible excitement.

'It is not the Company I have in mind, but the Siamese crown, with Englishmen in its service, holding positions of power. That is where you might come in, Samuel.'

'Englishmen working for Siam?' repeated Burnaby, startled.

'Yes, Richard, but as allies of their country,' explained Phaulkon.

'That's fine with me,' said White. He whistled. 'I'd give anything to get my hands on the elephant trade for one. There's a fortune in it. Demand completely outstrips supply. You have all the elephants here. I've never seen so many as on my way up from Mergui. And the Siamese know how to catch them. There's an insatiable demand in India. The belligerent princes are always at war with each other and they need beasts for their armies. In peacetime they need them for their weddings and their tiger hunts. And it only takes three weeks to cross the bay. The volume could be staggering.' His excitement was contagious.

'But what about the ships?' asked Burnaby. 'Won't they need special holds?'

'They could be built in Madapollam. They specialize in that sort of thing there. Suitably reinforced, a ship can carry up to twenty of the beasts. I supervised a crossing once. All you have to do is pray for good weather and keep a constant supply of banana trees. Their favourite food distracts the beasts.'

'Are there a lot of accidents?' asked Phaulkon.

'Remarkably few. And mostly due to human error.' Samuel laughed. 'A friend of mine was on a crossing once which ended in disaster when a cup of boiling hot broth was accidentally spilled over an elephant's rump. The infuriated beast drove its tusks clean through the ship's side, drowning its companions and most of the crew.'

Phaulkon laughed. 'We'll put Thomas in charge of the trade. He's had experience in the menagerie.'

'I'll serve them cold cuts only,' retorted Ivatt.

White looked pensive. 'But how are the Moors going to take such blatant incursion into their traditional hunting grounds? They are, after all, in charge of trade out of Mergui.'

'They will certainly not willingly relinquish their hold,' replied Phaulkon. 'But once I can prove the extent of their embezzle-

353

ment – and I am counting on this one shipment to do so – the Siamese may be prepared to contemplate change. That is why it is so important to render the full dues of this expedition to the Treasury. Or as close to them as possible.'

'I understand, and you have my full support.'

'What is the latest situation in Madras?' inquired Burnaby. 'I hear increasing rumours of greater measures against interlopers.'

'Ah,' scoffed White. 'This happens every time a new chief or a new deputy is appointed. They make a big noise and begin by arresting a few scapegoats. But they'll never be able to do away with private trading and they know it. Most of them wouldn't be where they are today without it. Look at Yale, for instance. He's just been appointed Vice-President at headquarters. As blatant an interloper as I ever sailed with. I wouldn't worry about any rumours on that score, Mr Burnaby. The free traders were born the day the first East India charter was signed into law, and that's almost a century ago. And they're still going strong today.'

'For a moment you sounded just like your brother,' observed Phaulkon, with a touch of nostalgia. 'He saw the injustice of creating a royal monopoly and the futility of enforcing such laws in an area two hundred times the size of England. The monopoly simply makes outlaws of private traders.' He looked around him. 'We're outlaws, every one of us.'

'Well, let's make the most of it then, before we're elected vice-presidents,' said Ivatt. They all laughed.

'What I understand the authorities are contemplating,' pursued White, 'which could have more serious implications for us all, is to forbid Company members from entering the service of a foreign potentate, even if they resign their commissions first.'

Phaulkon pricked up his ears at this. 'Which would effectively bar us from working for the King of Siam.'

'Exactly,' said White. 'Not that they could do much about it while we're out here. But,' he continued, his mind very much on his cherished role of country squire, 'a man could be arrested the moment he set foot on British soil again.'

'I suppose I could be persuaded to live out my days in Siam, if you gave me enough slaves,' remarked Ivatt. 'I could always send one or two of them to England to keep me posted.'

'We'll all have to cross that bridge when we come to it,' observed Burnaby. 'For my part I'm happy to settle here.'

354

'If you don't mind my saying so,' added Ivatt, 'you should really learn a bit of the language, Richard. You'll need a mansion just to house your team of interpreters.'

'I'm looking forward to early retirement in England. In the countryside,' said White, pensively. 'What about you, Constant?'

'My destiny lies with Siam, Samuel. I have felt that since the moment I set foot here. And, gentlemen,' he said, looking around him, 'after many reversals, I am convinced that this expedition to Persia is the beginning of the fulfilment of that destiny.' He paused while each man considered his words. 'And now, Samuel, would you mind explaining your plan of action to us?'

'Certainly. After loading up the goods in Mergui, I will sail immediately for Ormuz in Persia. Once out of sight of shore I will hoist the French flag, change the name of my ship to the *Auxerre* and hope not to encounter any French shipping in the area. Fortunately it is still fairly limited. With luck I will sell the merchandise at the port of Ormuz itself without having to journey up to Ispahan. The lavish court of Shah Suleiman and his nobles is, I understand, very partial to Chinese silks and satins and there should be any number of middlemen prepared to pay a substantial price for the complete cargo at Ormuz.'

'Did you hear that, Capitaine Beurnabbé?' said Phaulkon. 'Oh, I almost forgot to tell you, Richard, you've been appointed by the Barcalon to head this expedition. It is my turn to remain behind as hostage.'

'You'd better brush up on your French then, too, Richard,' teased Ivatt. 'It should be at least as good as your Siamese.'

'Mr Burnaby is to be in command of the expedition then?' asked White.

'Yes, Samuel, by order of the Barcalon. He is the First Minister of Siam, as you probably know. He wants it to appear an official English trade mission out of Siam.'

'I understand,' said White.

'Your men will have no trouble accepting the new command, I trust?' said Phaulkon.

'Not when I tell them to, sir,' replied White confidently.

'Good, then,' said Phaulkon. 'I will send Thomas down to Mergui to await your return nearer the appointed time, if he can

355

tear himself away from his palace duties. Shall we say three months?'

White nodded. 'That sounds about right. I'll send a small boat in to advise him. The *Auxerre* will have to stay well out of sight of shore, of course.'

'Understood. Thomas will be in command of a Siamese coastal junk large enough to pick up your whole crew when your ship founders.'

There was a momentary silence as they all digested the plan.

'Well then, gentlemen,' concluded Phaulkon, 'I think that does it. I now propose a toast to the success of the expedition. And then I invite you all to join me in a late dinner.' He walked over to a lacquered cabinet in a corner of the room and produced a bottle of wine and four glasses. Upon the success or failure of this expedition to Persia, he reflected, as he uncorked the bottle, would hang the future course of his life: whether he would abandon once and for all his ties with the Western world and throw in his lot with this wondrous Asian kingdom with which he felt so strangely and strongly linked.

A moment later they were jubilantly raising their glasses of Spanish red wine to the safe return of the *Auxerre* under the command of 'Capitaine Beurnabbé'.

Twenty-six

The Jesuit priest in the flowing brown robe clambered out of the little boat, followed by his servant carrying his baggage. As the priest made his way along the bustling harbour-front towards the little Portuguese mission that stood at the other end of the port, a small distance up the hill, he looked around him and sucked in his breath. How good it was to be back in beautiful Mergui. Pulling the brown cowl closer over his head, his eye travelled from the tall green hills that swept down into the bay to the sparkling waters of the Tenasserim river that washed into it, and finally alighted on the beautiful group of high wooded islands to the west of the magnificent harbour. They were known as the Mergui Archipelago, and many times as a child he had hidden in their turquoise creeks and made friends with the sand crabs and the sea urchins.

As he headed along the noisy waterfront, listening with contentment to the familiar cries of the vendors, he observed several Europeans standing by the wharf and staring out to sea. Following the direction of their gaze he saw a barge approaching the shore, filled with at least a dozen men. He could not tell for certain at that distance, but the reflection of the sun's rays on a number of metallic objects indicated that the crew of the barge was armed. He hurried on.

The boat was now drawing up alongside the wharf. The attention of the bystanders was on its arrival and no one paid the slightest attention to him as he approached. His eyes fixed themselves on the large wooden crates lined up along the wharf and casually he took in the markings. 'Ayudhya – For Export Only' was written in both Siamese and English. Out of the corner of his eye he saw that the men from the barge were indeed heavily armed and that their leader, who stepped ashore first, wore a naval uniform with the insignia of the English Company. Beyond the bay a large three-masted merchantman lay at anchor.

'Good morning, Father,' a voice said. The priest pulled the cowl further across his face and nodded, briefly. Then he turned

357

and continued quickly on his way. He could feel the man's gaze on him, no doubt a perplexed look on his face. Damnation, the last thing he wanted was to attract attention. Without looking back he proceeded at a rapid pace to the far end of the harbour and, climbing a few steps up the hill, reached a small house attached to a chapel. A large wooden cross stood over the roof. He knocked on the door and was granted admittance by a servant. From the far end of the room a portly man of short stature with a round beaming face welcomed him and asked how he could be of service.

'Dom Francisco, I am pleased to see you again,' said the priest, in Siamese.

Dom Francisco craned his neck and looked quizzically at the newcomer, finally removing his glasses to get a better view. He examined him from various angles, still looking perplexed, until finally he uttered a little yelp of surprise, exclaiming, '*Não é possivel, não é possivel*. Luang Aziz! But it can't be. Since when did you join our ranks?'

The visitor removed his cowl and revealed a brown Indian face. The upper lip was lined with a thick black moustache.

'No, Dom Francisco, I have not joined your ranks. But I am here incognito. May we sit down and talk? I have urgent matters to discuss with you.'

The members of the Council of Tenasserim took their places, cross-legged, in the audience hall of the house of their honoured leader, Oc-Ya Mohammed Said. The decor was predominantly Persian, with mosaic inlaid tables, elaborate brass urns and fine prints depicting street scenes of Ispahan. Oc-Ya Mohammed was known better by his title of Oc-Ya Tannaw, or head of the Commission of Tenasserim, than by his given name. The town of Tenasserim, Tannaw to the Siamese, held the rank of city of the second class, an important place in the nation's hierarchy of six orders of cities. Tenasserim was also the name of the province which boasted the great harbour of Mergui, thirty-seven miles downriver from Tenasserim town.

Oc-Ya Tannaw took his place at the head of the Council and looked importantly around him. His uncle had been Governor of Mergui and his fellow Muslims controlled most of the positions of power in the province.

358

One by one he surveyed his fellow members. They were all bearded, all traders, and all Muslim. Officially they owed their allegiance to the Siamese crown and they lived off its land and profited by its trade. But their blood was that of their forefathers across the bay and beyond, the great lands of the Moguls and the Shahs. And in their hearts they knew there was but one God, Allah. So, like the Prophet Mohammed, they wore beards because they were his faithful and because they were not Siamese, who were for the most part unable to grow them.

These were troubled times, reflected Oc-Ya Tannaw. There was change in the air. He felt it and now he needed to be sure.

'Brothers,' he began, you all know why I have summoned you here. I do not like the way events are moving. First this farang, Phaulkon, is given a job in the Ministry of Trade, and the next thing we hear is that our brother, Luang Rashid, is deposed as head of the banqueting department. And who takes over from him? None other than this Phaulkon. Then an English ship arrives from Madras. There is nothing unusual in that except that the captain travels up alone to Ayudhya to see this same farang, Phaulkon. For the last three days, brothers, crates have been arriving at Mergui on the overland route from Ayudhya at an alarming rate. Our spies in the capital were not able to ascertain the contents of these crates. They were packed in such total secrecy and under such heavy guard that our informers were unable to get near them.' He leaned forward. 'The interesting point, my brethren, is that the packing was done in the royal warehouses and not at the English factory and that these same crates are now being loaded on to a large English trading ship at Mergui, once again under armed guard. What does this indicate to you?'

Farouk Radwan, a small, squat man with a thick growth of hair covering his arms, scratched his beard pensively.

'Obviously, Your Honour, these are Treasury goods being shipped out by the English. They could have been purchased from the crown for their factory at Madras or . . .'

'Or?' prompted Oc-Ya Tannaw.

'Or they could be destined elsewhere.'

'Like Persia, for instance?'

'Possibly.' It was Fawzi Ali who replied, removing his mouth from his hookah. 'Though I doubt the Siamese government

359

would do such a thing without informing us first.' He was addicted to tobacco and never travelled anywhere without his pipe. His servant carried it from house to house in case his host did not have one to offer him.

'Why not?' demanded Oc-Ya Tannaw.

Fawzi Ali's lips were already round the hookah again. He removed the pipe nervously. 'Because trade to Persia from this province has been in our hands since anyone can remember. My grandfather traded with Ormuz and Ispahan from the very same house I live in now. What reason would there be to halt the tradition?'

Oc-Ya Tannaw looked unconvinced. 'Royal catering has been in the hands of the Moors ever since anyone can remember too, Fawzi. And look who is preparing the banquet for the Chinese embassy now.'

'The rumour is that His Majesty wants to surprise the ambassador with the insertion of some farang specialities and the intoxicating liquors they need to wash down such offal,' put in Faisal Sidiq, screwing up his nose. His family had been in Siam for almost two centuries and his eyes were less rounded than the rest.

The Oc-Ya dismissed the suggestion with an impatient shrug. 'That's an excuse not a rumour. My impression, brothers, is that we, as a whole, are being investigated. The entire Muslim brotherhood. It is only the beginning, so there is still some attempt at discretion. But there will be more to follow, mark my words. We must find out what is in those crates and above all where they are destined.'

'Aziz left for Mergui this morning, Your Honour. He has gone to enlist the support of the Portuguese mission. He is in disguise, to reduce the possibility of rumours.' Iqbal Sind was the last of the assembled Council to speak. His large hooked nose rose out from his face like the beak of some predatory bird.

'Are the Portuguese to be trusted?' asked Oc-Ya Tannaw aggressively. 'They are farangs too.'

'Yes, Your Honour,' replied Iqbal Sind awkwardly. His timidity belied the ferocious appearance of his face. 'But the Portuguese are Catholic Christians and the English some other sect and they do not see eye to eye. Besides, Your Honour, the fat priest of the Portuguese is desperate to rebuild his church and his

360

superiors in Goa have not been very generous lately. So we authorized Aziz . . .' he lowered his eyes under the scrutiny of the Oc-Ya Tannaw.

'Yes, Iqbal, you authorized . . . ?'

'Aziz to agree . . . to certain . . . contributions, Your Honour. Only, of course, if the priest's information . . . justified our generosity,' stammered Iqbal.

The Oc-Ya Tannaw grunted. 'Muslims contributing to the rennovations of Christian churches?' He looked upwards. 'May Allah forgive us such sins. And may he know at least that it is done only for the protection of his faithful. Allah Akbar.'

'Allah Akbar,' they all intoned in chorus. 'God is Great.'

'Well now, brethren, I have heard your views. I conclude that if this priest of the Christians informs us that the goods are for export to Persia, our traditional domain, and not the English factory at Madras, then this man Phaulkon must be eliminated. I am told he speaks fluent Siamese and Malay, and that he is wily and two-tongued. Such a man in the service of the wrong master could be dangerous. We will have him assassinated by the Macassars. Prince Dai's bodyguards will be only too pleased to carry out the assignment. Do we all agree?'

There was a murmur of approval.

Luang Aziz leaned forward to stress the point. 'As I said, Dom Francisco, your church can be entirely rebuilt on the proceeds.'

A feverish glow lit up the priest's eyes. 'I have your word as a member of the Council?' he asked.

'You do.'

'And all I have to do is ascertain the destination of that ship out there?' He pointed out across the bay where the tall merchantman swayed gently in the breeze.

Aziz nodded unequivocally.

The priest scratched his head. It seemed too easy. 'But what reason would they have for not telling me its destination?'

'They might give you a destination, but not necessarily the true one.'

'And how will I know if it is the true one or not?' He wiped a bead of perspiration from his forehead. How badly he wanted his church rebuilt. He had written twice to Goa and once even to the Bishop at Macau and each time he had been told that the matter was under consideration. He should make do with temporary repairs until approval could be granted. His colleague at Ligor had written to him with the same tale of woe. The church, it seems, was concentrating its efforts – and its funds – on the capital cities and the ruling dynasties, to the detriment of the poor provinces. He shook his head and looked at the Indian before him. The dark eyes stared back at him impassively. How ironical that help should come from the Muslims, of all people.

'You will know, Dom Francisco. You will think of something. You must catch them unawares.' Aziz smiled encouragingly. 'You priests are not without guile.'

'And how will *you* know if the answer is right?'

'I will, Dom Francisco, rest assured. You have only to speak the truth.'

'But why me? Do you not have anyone else who can find out this information for you? Someone more qualified?' He made a final effort to free himself of the assignment. There had to be more to it than this, he was sure. Something he might regret. It was not too late to refuse.

Luang Aziz sensed the hesitation.

'Those men out there are English traders, Dom Francisco. We Muslims too are traders. There is a mutual distrust. But you are a priest, and no rival of theirs. They will tell you what they will not tell us. What harm is there in knowing a ship's destination? It is only a minor trading secret but one which will rebuild your church. No more waiting for another year, or perhaps two or even for ever, for your leaders to send you the funds. You will have it tomorrow, Dom Francisco, in silver, just as soon as we have the answer.'

The priest's reticence vanished. Tomorrow? Tomorrow he could summon the labourers, the carpenters, the masons and the painters and with fifteen taels to spend in a couple of weeks he would have a new church. There might even be some money left over to entice new converts. For how could he convert the natives when the walls of his church were crumbling and the ceilings cracking and the doors and windows were tied in place with cord? The House of God, the only true God, should look neat and clean and holy.

He sprang to his feet with surprising agility for a man of his portly frame. 'I will do it. Leave it to me.'

362

Luang Aziz smiled. 'I knew I could count on you, Dom Francisco. I will be back at the same hour tomorrow.'

'Small boat ahoy!' shouted the lookout. In the absence of Captain White, the lookout went to fetch the first mate and advised him of the arrival of a visitor. It was a lone priest in a rowing boat who requested a few words with the captain privately.

'Well, Simmons, did you tell him the captain was not aboard? The Father will find him ashore.'

'Aye, sir, but begging your pardon, 'e said 'e would talk to any officer what was aboard.'

The first mate leaned over the edge and glanced at the little boat. The priest was hot and perspiring; he had rowed out alone without the help of an oarsman. It was quite a distance from the shore.

'All right, Simmons, send him up.'

'Aye, aye, sir.'

What would one of those Catholic priests want with our captain? wondered John Ferries, the first mate. Still, the English had no particular quarrel with Portugal so he might as well find out.

'Good morning, captain,' said the priest, breathing heavily from the strain of climbing on board. Dark stains of perspiration appeared at intervals on his brown cassock. In his hand he held a small package. 'God be with you, senhor.' He spoke in strongly accented English.

'I am not the captain, Father. But welcome anyway. You look as if you could do with a rest. Here, follow me.' Ferries led him into a small cabin below deck and offered him a seat. The priest looked tired and worn and Ferries felt rather sorry for him. What a God-awful climate to spend one's days in, trying to spread the word of God, he thought. Sooner you than me, Father.

'Well now, what can I do for you, Father?'

'I heard you were going to Madras, senhor. My sister is a nun there. I wondered if you would be kind enough to take this package to her. I didn't know when the next ship for Madras would pass by here, so I took the opportunity . . .'

The first mate was about to tell him that they were not going to Madras at all when he pulled himself short. He took the package. Christ, and I almost told him, he thought. 'I'll be glad

363

to,' he said. The poor nun wasn't likely to see this offering in her lifetime.

'Thank you, senhor, may God's blessings be upon you.' He paused, as if struck by an afterthought. 'Seeing as I've come all this way, senhor, I was wondering whether I shouldn't give the sacraments to any of your Goanese on board. With your permission, of course.' He winked kindly. 'They always do a better job when they've heard the Word of God.' It was a sure bet that there would be some Goanese sailors on board, even if only one or two. Portuguese labour from Goa, almost all half-caste, was cheap and the men made good mariners. They rented themselves out willingly to any nation with which the motherland was not at war.

'Mestizos? We've got a couple. We've also got an Irishman and a couple of Catholic Scots if you want to do the whole lot at once, Padre.' It was the mate's turn to wink.

'The more the merrier, senhor,' said Dom Francisco gaily.

'Wait here then, Father. I'll have them rounded up.'

'Thank you. The senhor officer is most kind.'

Before long there stood before him the motliest crew he had ever laid eyes on. A tall, rib-thin Irishman with a black beard, two freckled Scotsmen, one with red hair and the other blond, and two short, swarthy Portuguese-Indians, Catholics all. They mumbled indistinct greetings in English and Portuguese and then stood, shuffling uneasily, before him. Father Francisco scanned them one by one. They ranged in skin colour from bright pink to almost pitch black and they all looked uncomfortable in the unexpected presence of a man of God.

'I am glad to see you all but I must ask you first to tell me why you did not come to church ashore. I haven't seen one of you there.' He spoke first in Portuguese and then in English, in a voice of gentle reprimand. Their discomfort increased. Then one of the mestizos spoke out, at first haltingly, then gradually seeming to gather courage. All eyes turned towards him.

'We . . . we have not been allowed ashore, Reverend Padre. Otherwise we certainly would have come to church.'

'Not allowed ashore,' said Father Francisco in disbelief. 'But you've been here almost a month!' He leaned forward suspiciously. 'I've seen several men from this ship in town.'

364

'Those are officers, Reverend Padre. The rest of us are confined to ship.'

'What's he saying, Father?' asked the blond Scotsman, a worried look crossing his face.

'He says you haven't been allowed ashore,' repeated Dom Francisco in English.

The Scotsman's face darkened. 'Did he give a reason?' he asked, glancing aggressively at the mestizo. 'Don't listen to him anyway, Father. He's always lying, that one.' He turned to the mestizo. 'You shut your mouth, Rodriguez, do you hear?' He waved a clenched fist at him.

'Hey, Sandy, watch your tongue, for Christ's sake!' said the lanky Irishman. 'You're speaking in front of the holy Father.'

The Scotsman turned shamefaced to the priest. 'Begging your pardon, Father. I got a little carried away. But that blabber-mouth's got us into trouble before. Just so long as you don't listen to him, Father.'

'Have no fear, my son. Whatever is said here will go no further. I am a priest, remember?'

'Is this like a confessional then, Father?' It was the second Scotsman, the red-headed one who spoke this time.

Father Francisco paused. He did not like the question. It was very awkward. If this was not like a confessional, these men were more likely to guard their words, and if it was, he himself would be bound to silence.

'It is not like a confessional, but I am still a priest,' he said ambiguously.

The red-headed Scotsman looked perplexed. The priest switched to Portuguese.

'I will bless you now, my children, for your safe journey to Madras.' One by one they sank to their knees and he made the sign of the cross over them and began reciting prayers in Latin. Out of the corner of his eye he could see one of the mestizos looking noticeably uncomfortable. It was the same one who had spoken out haltingly before. The priest paused now before beginning the Lord's Prayer.

'Reverend Father,' blurted out the mestizo in Portuguese, 'will you say a prayer for all our future journeys, wherever we go?'

'I can do, my son, but when you thank the Lord for your food,

365

do you thank him for all the meals you will ever have or just the one you are about to partake of?'

The mestizo appeared to consider the question.

'Will you bless us then, Reverend Father, for our journey to Madras and to . . .' he hesitated '. . . Persia, in case we go there also before we see you again?'

'Persia?' screamed Sandy, rising to his feet, 'did he say Persia? I'll kill him.'

Dom Francisco looked horrified. 'We are about to recite the Lord's Prayer, my son. Calm yourself or God's wrath will be upon you.'

'Yes, and on all of us, thanks to you, Sandy,' said the Irishman fretfully. 'We're all in this together, you know.' He clasped his hands before him and broke into fervent prayer.

'What's going on here? And who was screaming like that?' The first mate had appeared at the entrance of the cabin. His arm rested on the bulkhead. 'This is a damned rowdy session you've got going here, Father. Doesn't sound much like a mass to me. What's happening?'

'I'm sorry, senhor,' said the priest. 'The men asked to be blessed for their journey to Madras. One of them said something about Persia but the others said they weren't even going there. And a little dispute erupted.'

'Of course they're not going to Persia,' burst out the first mate angrily. 'Who's the fool who said that? Was that you, Sandy?' Sandy was still standing, while the others were on their knees.

'Begging your pardon, sir, it was this half-breed here,' he said, pointing to Rodriguez.

'I think you'd better go ashore now, Father. This is not the kind of blessing I had in mind.'

'I understand, senhor. Please accept my apologies.'

'Will you not hear our confessions, Reverend Father?' asked Rodriguez anxiously. 'Pereira would like you to hear his too.' He pointed to his companion.

'My sons, the officer wants me to leave now. But I will mention you in my prayers. And God will protect you.'

'You are all dismissed,' said the first mate decisively. He forced a smile at the priest. 'Perhaps, Father, after we are back from Madras . . .'

366

The priest made the sign of the cross once more over his ragged flock and departed.

Dom Francisco sat in silence for a long time contemplating the ocean. It was a beautiful view from the open doorway of the little church. What an unpleasant decision, he thought. Again and again he looked to heaven and prayed to God for guidance. He was sure now, almost beyond doubt, that the ship was bound for Persia. But what were these trade secrets that made men so angry? What was the ship carrying that it could not admit to its real destination? Would he cause suffering or violence by revealing what he had heard? Yet even this, he admitted to himself, was not his overriding concern. What bothered him more than anything was the sanctity of the confessional.

Of course, that little cabin could hardly be defined as a confessional, but the red-headed man with the anxious eyes had asked him if it were like one and he had answered equivocally and seen the look of confusion in the man's eyes. He had led him astray. He had led them all astray. He had learned his answers through guile and deception. I am still a priest, he had said. What were they to deduce from that, if not that they could trust him? And who were these poor ruffians to trust, if not a man of God?

A movement to his left distracted him. He shifted his gaze and saw the little figure of Luang Aziz, disguised in his priest's robes, climbing the path towards him. Wistfully he looked around at his ruined church. Another storm like the last one, he thought, and there would be nothing left standing at all. He shuddered. He might even lose his existing converts.

Aziz drew level with the priest and he caught his breath. He looked carefully around him. Seeing they were alone, he removed his cowl.

'Peace be with you, Dom Francisco.'

'And with you, my son,' answered the priest, following the Muslim greeting.

'A beautiful day, is it not? You are enjoying a little rest? I trust it is well earned from the labours you have undertaken.' He raised a small bag in front of him. 'I have brought the money.'

'And I have found out what you want to know, Luang Aziz.'

367

'Indeed? I am pleased to hear that. Are you sure of your information?'

'Quite sure.'

Aziz seated himself cross-legged on the grass in front of the priest and made himself comfortable.

'What is the answer then?'

The priest looked out to sea and pointed towards the great ship. The three masts rose gracefully from the undisturbed ocean like some mythical sea creature from the depths.

'She is bound for Madras.'

'Oh? And how did you reach that conclusion?'

The priest could not tell if there was disappointment or relief in the Moor's voice. 'I went on board early this morning. I rowed there myself.' Aziz looked impressed. 'I delivered a package for my sister in Madras which one of the officers promised to hand over. Then I celebrated mass for the Catholics on board. There were five of them, Scottish, Irish and Goanese. All of them confirmed their destination to me. Both in English and in Portuguese. They are simple people, they would not lie to a priest. And they were alone with me in the room at the time.'

The priest finished speaking and there was a lengthy silence. Finally Aziz spoke.

'You did well, Dom Francisco. Oc-Ya Tannaw will be pleased. You see, we must safeguard our trading interests. Most of the areas across the bay are our monopolies. Madras is not one of them. Here is your money.' He handed over the sack. 'I will not delay as I must carry the news to our leader. We will perhaps be calling upon your services at another time, Father Francisco.' He smiled. 'Your little church will no doubt always be in need of some repair.'

The priest tried to keep the excitement out of his voice. 'No doubt, Luang Aziz. You know where to find me.'

The Moor turned to leave. As he did so, the silhouette of a tall woman came into sight, winding its way up the little footpath towards the church.

'One of your converts, Dom Francisco?' said the Moor, smiling.

The Padre squinted uncertainly at the approaching figure. 'I don't think so, Luang Aziz.'

The newcomer's long strides covered the distance in a short time, and soon she was upon them.

'Good morning, Fathers,' she said in Siamese, smiling graciously at them both. 'Which one of you is Father Francisco?' She was a beautiful young woman, with an open, engaging smile.

'I am, my child,' replied Dom Francisco kindly. 'And how may I be of service to you?'

The girl observed him briefly and then produced a letter from a small cotton purse she was carrying. 'Mr Constantine Phaulkon asked me to bring this to you, Father. He was a friend of Captain Alvarez.'

The second priest pricked up his ears.

'Of course,' said Dom Francisco. 'I have heard of Mr Phaulkon. Welcome, my child. Poor Alvarez,' he added, making the sign of the cross. 'May his soul rest in peace.'

He read the letter and then looked up at the woman, smiling.

'I am to assist you in every way,' he said.

'Thank you, Father. I need to speak with the captain of that ship in the bay,' she said, indicating the large merchantman anchored in the distance. 'I thought perhaps you might know him or that at least you might be able to help me reach him.'

Luang Aziz had been observing her keenly. It was he who now spoke.

'And what might you want with the captain, my child?'

'I have a message to deliver to him, Father.'

'I know the captain,' said Luang Aziz, with a quick warning glance at Dom Francisco. 'Perhaps I can pass the message on to him for you?'

'That is very kind of you, Father. But I must deliver the message myself. It requires an answer, you see.'

'Indeed,' said Luang Aziz. 'In that case allow me to accompany you there.' He observed her solicitously. 'But you must be exhausted, my child. You have probably come all the way from the capital.'

Sunida nodded. 'I have, Father, and I am anxious to complete my mission and return.'

'Of course. It must be important for you to have come so far. A letter, no doubt,' he added, casually.

Dom Francisco had been anxious to speak all the while, but each time he had attempted to open his mouth, the Moor had cut him off with a warning frown.

369

'And I too will accompany you, my child,' Dom Francisco said at last. 'If you—'

'Don't trouble yourself, Dom Francisco,' interrupted the Moor. 'I will look after the lady.' He turned to the girl. 'The Father Superior is so busy,' he explained. Smiling courteously, he beckoned her to follow him.

Sunida hesitated for a moment. There was a conflict of some kind between these two priests, the Indian and the farang one, she could see. But she had her mission to accomplish, and that was paramount. 'Thank you, Father, you are most kind,' she said, turning to go.

Dom Francisco followed them anxiously with his eyes as they disappeared from sight along the pathway that led down to the harbour. He wondered what message the girl could be carrying. Whatever it was, he did not like the way things were turning out. He felt guilty about accepting the money and worried for the safety of the girl. There was no telling what these Moors might do. He decided to follow them at a safe distance.

Twenty-seven

Life for Yupin at the palace had become dreary. She no longer had the erotic instruction of Sunida to occupy her, nor could she risk leaving the palace without the connivance of the Dutch surgeon. She felt truly a prisoner. She had heard bone-chilling accounts of how her lover, Captain Alvarez, had been tortured to death and for a time she had awaited her turn in trepidation, fully expecting to share his fate. To her increasing surprise, however, nothing happened. It was not till some days later that she had learned that his crimes were of a political nature and somehow unrelated to their secret trysts.

For a while she continued to pine for the body of her lover, whom she had by now elevated to the ranks of the martyrs. What a man! Even under extreme torture he had refused to reveal her name. Yupin sighed. She had tired of the concubines of the palace harem who so willingly offered themselves to relieve her melancholy. Things had reached their lowest ebb. No man was allowed inside the women's quarters, apart from the occasional monk and the young prince, Chao Fa Noi. The monks, of course, were sworn to celibacy and whenever she encountered one in the corridors she would fall to her knees, as etiquette required, and place one end of her shawl on the ground so that the monk might walk over it and bless it. As for Chao Fa Noi, the King's youngest brother was, it seemed, blissfully betrothed to His Majesty's daughter, Yotatep. This was thanks, in no small measure, to Yupin's discreet efforts on behalf of Yotatep.

True to her promise to the Princess Queen, Yupin had spoken to the King as soon as a suitable opportunity had arisen. The Lord of Life himself had, in fact, provided the opening when he had mentioned to Yupin his concern about his heir's conduct and health, both of which appeared to be deteriorating rapidly. For the King often summoned his favourite concubine when his mind was burdened. When Yupin intimated that the Princess Queen might consider marriage to Chao Fa Noi, the King's initial shock had quickly given way to careful consideration of the

371

information. If he were forced to appoint his youngest brother his successor through the incapacity or disgrace of Chao Fa Apai Tot, either of which seemed increasingly likely, at least his youngest brother's claim to the throne would be that much more secure if he were married to Yotatep. And if the marriage were proclaimed a love match, as Yupin had hinted it would be, the break with tradition would perhaps be more acceptable.

The Princess Queen had rewarded Yupin handsomely for her service, and now the whole kingdom was waiting for the astrologers to pick an auspicious date for the nuptials. Yet Yupin wondered whether the young prince's bliss was as innocent as it seemed. She felt certain his interest lay more in the throne than in his future wife.

Yupin sighed again. Life was truly bleak. How could she relieve the boredom? In this melancholy state of mind, the image of Chao Fa Noi kept returning to her. Should she throw caution to the winds once again and risk her very life at the hands of the jealous Yotatep? Although her brain signalled her to beware, her body craved the warmth of a man and she longed to read the effect of her prowess on his supplicating countenance.

One day she took a different route along the royal corridors.

Prince Chao Fa Noi was pleased with the way events were unfolding. His eldest brother, the King, had now approved his marriage to his niece, Yotatep, thus greatly strengthening his claim to the throne. His other brother, Apai Tot, though first in line to the succession, had taken increasingly to drink and was now seen frequently in the company of Sorasak, which did not do his reputation any good. The natural ailments that the Gods had inflicted on Apai Tot had developed noticeably in recent weeks, and one half of his face now twitched spasmodically, forcing his left eye to close. And whenever he lost his temper, which was often enough, streams of saliva dribbled from the corners of his mouth and ran repulsively across his chin. No physician could find a remedy for his sudden convulsions and it was generally accepted that he was suffering from the sins of a past life.

The thought of one day ruling this beautiful land pleased Chao Fa Noi greatly. For, once Apai Tot's complete paralysis had set in – as everyone close to the throne, including the chief astrologer, Mahawallah, predicted it would – his claim should be virtually unchallenged. As a woman, Yotatep could not succeed to the throne, and that brute, Sorasak, even if the King were ever to recognize him as his own, did not seem to harbour any ambitions beyond the immediate satisfaction of his lusts.

No, reflected the young prince smugly, the only other claimant to the throne would be himself as Yotatep's husband. He smiled. Why, he might even ascend the throne without the bloodbath that traditionally accompanied the death of any monarch. His brother, Narai, had not been immune to it, and as for his predecessor, Prasat Tong, over three thousand courtiers and noblemen had died in the massacres that had accompanied the struggle for the succession.

Chao Fa Noi was relieved, too, that Sorasak's official father, General Petraja, whom he had at first suspected of harbouring royal ambitions as well, was now openly paying him homage as the rightful heir. The general had no doubt realized that while he, Chao Fa Noi, was prepared to continue the policies of his brother Narai – whose brilliant manoeuvring and self-assurance the young Prince greatly admired – he differed from the present monarch on one major issue, an issue close to Petraja's heart. He would reduce the country's dependency on the Moors and the farangs and train more ethnic Siamese for positions in government. Farangs would be employed only for short spells to pass on their skills before being asked to leave the country. There would be no such thing as farangs employed in the Ministry of Trade, for instance . . .

Engrossed in thought, the Prince headed towards his apartments, situated in the section of the palace just below the Princess Queen's. What sagacious ancestors to have devised such a system, he mused, as he climbed the steps to ever-higher levels. For it was only right that royalty should be at the pinnacle and that everything should be designed to remind one of it. He wondered how many people, outside the women His Majesty had lain with of course, were aware that the King, his brother, was of very short stature. Thanks to the system, his brother was only ever seen in elevated positions – on the tallest elephant, on a balcony addressing his prostrate mandarins, on the raised dais of his royal barge, or borne high in his throne-chair on the shoulders of slaves. And nowhere in the palace precincts was any

373

man allowed to stand and show his full stature – and be compared.

Chao Fa Noi glanced up as he walked, vaguely distracted by the alluring gait of an approaching concubine. Her hips swayed seductively from side to side as she walked, displaying a full, perfectly proportioned figure. Bending respectfully low as she passed, she turned her head in his direction and gave him the most voluptuous smile. The smile was accompanied by a languorous flutter of the eyelids. Yupin! He had seen the famous concubine before in his brother's apartments. What was she up to? He thought about the encounter for a moment and then dismissed it. His betrothed, Yotatep, was always telling him how handsome he was, so it was not unnatural for a woman of the harem to flirt with him thus. He chuckled to himself. If only Yotatep could have seen that little exchange. She was so jealous. She had once confided in him that she was tormented by the thought that he was only marrying her because she was the King's daughter. He had of course quickly assured her to the contrary, but at the slightest provocation her doubts resurfaced and her confidence wavered. She needed constant reassuring. Any woman who so much as looked his way drove Yotatep to a frenzy, and as for himself, if he so much as glanced at one of them . . . He hoped Yotatep would come to her senses once they were married, for she would have to get used to his minor wives. She could hardly object to those. It would be unheard of. Yet he had to admit that her constant questioning on the subject of his love had forced him to ask himself whether he would indeed have married her if she were not the King's daughter? The truth, he had to admit, was that he would not.

It was a torrid, sundrenched day following his encounter with Yupin, but despite the debilitating atmosphere, the Prince was in particularly fine spirits. He had just left the Princess Queen's apartments, where Yotatep had excitedly confided in him the news that the Brahmin astrologers attached to the court had finally settled on an auspicious date for the nuptials. It was to be in just over a month. He was strolling through the spacious, beautifully manicured gardens that surrounded the Princess Queen's apartments, dreaming of his future coronation. How pleasant it was to wander through these well-laid gardens, past

374

the lotus ponds and spouting fountains, along the little pathways shaded by trees and intersected by streams that murmured softly and lent such freshness to the scene.

On the far side of the gardens were the royal stables where the great white elephant from the south had been given pride of place. 'Jewel of the Universe', as the white beast had been officially named in a grand ceremony, had been installed in a luxurious stable nearest the royal apartments. Its proximity to the King and the sixty slaves assigned to keep it were distinctions that placed it above all other members of its species.

Hundreds of courtiers, pages, eunuchs and slaves had already visited the stables to render obeisance to the princely beast, and more were doing so now, including Yupin. She emerged from paying her respects just as the young Prince was passing in the gardens outside. She ogled him so blatantly that there could be no mistaking her intentions this time. She looked quite entrancing. Her hair was sleekly oiled and she had lined her rich lips with white pommade. As she passed him, her pale brown sash came loose as if by chance and exposed one of her breasts. It was firm and upturned and inviting. Before he could stop himself Chao Fa Noi had unwittingly returned her smile. He saw a look of triumph come into her eyes and then she was gone.

That night as he lay on his couch, her smile, that voluptuous smile which promised such infinite pleasures, came back to haunt him. The more he tried to dismiss it, the more it returned to tease him. She knew of course that he was to marry Yotatep. What then did she want? He had heard rumours of Yupin's exploits. Who hadn't? They kept the gossip wheels of the palace turning. It was even said that once caressed by her fingers, a man – or woman – could no longer find satisfaction elsewhere. Could it be true? he wondered. Could there really be such a woman? Would it be so different with someone as experienced as she? He tried to concentrate on other matters but his mind kept returning to the fluttering eyelashes and the uncovered breast. Perhaps if he were to indulge just once . . . He froze. Was that a series of scratches he had just heard at his door? He listened intently but the sound did not repeat itself. All he could hear was the pounding of his heart. Had he imagined it? Were this woman's powers of seduction such that the mind was turned from its normal course?

He listened in silence, hardly daring to breathe. Then the scratching resumed again. It was unmistakable this time. His heart beat feaster. He swung his legs silently off the couch and tiptoed to the door. He put his ear to the panel. The scratching grew louder. He drew the wooden bolt back. How had anyone got past the guards? he wondered. A bribe, no doubt. And if it were her, her face would be known of course. He eased the panels open slightly and peered out between them. Yupin's shapely frame stood in the hallway. Waves of thick dark hair fell loosely about her shoulders, ending just short of her breasts, and her large eyes stared up at him, doe-like in their simulated innocence. He felt a surge of excitement as he edged the panels further apart, glancing nervously down the corridor to either side of him. Never had he beheld such a vision of femininity. She cupped her slender hands and wai'd to him. The trace of a smile that was etched on her lips held endless promise. Unable to take his eyes off her he retreated into the room. She followed him in silence. The panels swung shut behind her and she turned and drew the bolt across them. Then, still without a word, she placed the ends of her fingers on his shoulders and pushed him gently backwards. She laid him down on the low couch and stood over him with a smile of exaltation. He started to speak but she placed a finger across his lips in silence. Kneeling over him, she slowly began to undress him, caressing every part of his body as she exposed it. Her eyes told him not to move, that this was the way she wanted it. She ran her fingers gently over his eyes and closed the lids. Then he felt her swollen perfumed nipples sliding sensuously across his lips and he opened his mouth to receive them one after the other. As he did so, her fingers deliciously explored the inside of his thighs. He lay back and gave himself up to the ecstasy of her touch. She was alternately gentle and rough, savage and sweet, cruel and giving. She turned the fire higher and lower in him, at will. Then, while his excitement tore at him, she produced a small flask from her purse and began to smooth his whole body with perfumed oil. With infinite skill she massaged his genital area and teased his love lance till he thought he would burst. Now her quivering lips and fingers seemed to be darting everywhere at once and he was sure there were two women making love to him instead of one. The young prince had never known such sensations. When, finally, she eased him into

376

her, her sensuous body still poised over him, his palpitating love lance exploded instantly. But she knew and was ready for him and the pleasure on her face was his greatest reward.

Silently she rose and wound her panung on again and at the door she turned and spoke for the first time. 'My Prince, I will return.'

His mind did not find rest for some time. Images of Yupin kept rising before him and he lived again the intoxication of those last moments. Time and again he turned towards the door, straining his ears in the hope of hearing the scratches once more. But there was only the silence of the night. It was not till shortly before dawn that sleep finally came to relieve him.

Yupin was in a joyful mood. She had a lover again, albeit a secret one whose discovery would mean her instant death. She was, after all, the King's concubine and her lover none other than the intended of the jealous Yotatep. Yet she felt alive once more, thriving on the danger and excitement that she always craved. He was handsome too, her young Prince, a child in her hands, ready to be moulded whichever way she chose. She had slipped into his apartments every night for a week now and she was aware that what might have started as a simple curiosity on his part had developed into an all-consuming obsession. It would be more difficult to continue when he was married to the Princess Queen, she reflected with a tremor of excitement, but together they would find a way. After all, he was already beginning to show the initiative. It was now he who had taken to ensuring the guards' silence with bribes.

She traversed the last of the three spacious courtyards that led to the royal apartments. It was a wonderfully balmy evening, unusually cool, and numerous slaves were dressing down the elephants that had been chosen to stand guard in the parade for the visiting embassy from China. For such a grand occasion, there would be as many as one hundred of the beasts thus honoured, some wearing harnesses of gold, others sprinkled with diamonds, pearls, rubies and emeralds. Her lover, too, she reflected, would be resplendent that day in his red brocade vest and his gold filigree buttons.

The guards all knew her by sight and no one questioned her presence as she passed the antechamber that led to His Majesty's apartments. Here, all visitors were stripped to the waist before entering the royal precincts. It was a security measure to ensure that no one carried arms into the King's private quarters. As she approached she recognized her lover's tunic and his conical hat with the circle of gold lying on a rattan shelf. He must be visiting the Lord of Life. She smiled mischievously to herself, and choosing a moment when the guards' heads were turned she grabbed the vest and the hat and thrust them quickly under the folds of her panung. She hurried away, wondering how long it would take the young Prince to guess who had played the prank on him. She imagined he would immediately suspect her and come looking for them in her apartment. She would be waiting for him there . . .

Chao Fa Noi emerged from the royal apartments in a foul mood. His request to sit in the position of honour below His Majesty's right hand during the forthcoming reception for the Chinese delegation had been turned down. He would have to sit to the left while his brother, Apai Tot, as the elder of the two, would hold pride of place. Even if Apai Tot were drunk? he had inquired angrily of his Majesty. He would not be drunk, had come the reply, because no intoxicating beverages would be allowed him before or during the entire ceremonies and he was even now confined to the palace precincts to ensure his early compliance.

Controlling his rage, the young Prince emerged and looked around for his tunic. Where had he left it? He searched the antechamber again. He could have sworn he had left it just there, on the shelf. Perhaps someone had hung it up. 'Guard!' he shouted.

Two guards of His Majesty's elite corps, their hair cropped short and their arms painted with the traditional red band, came running into the antechamber and prostrated themselves.

'Your Royal Highness?'

'Where is my tunic? And my hat? I left them here only a moment ago.'

Both guards glanced around them, puzzled.

'Your Royal Highness, we, two specks of dust, remember seeing Your Highness disrobe and leave them there.'

'Indeed, just here.' He pointed to the shelf. 'Who would dare remove them?' In his mounting fury, the Prince never came near to suspecting the truth. Without further thought he stormed back into His Majesty's apartment. His brother would soon be apprised, if he was not already, that there were thieves in his very antechamber! Whoever had done this would be executed, he swore, as an example to others. It was a disgrace.

Yupin squatted in front of the looking glass and examined herself carefully. A smile spread across her features. There was not a wrinkle in the reflection. Most satisfying at thirty-two she mused. This looking glass would not lie. It had been a gift from His Majesty the King, and he in turn had been given it by the Portuguese holy men. Captain Alvarez had a smaller, less elaborate one in his house. Vaguely she wondered if it was still there now. She applied a little more white pommade to her lips and then glanced out of the window. The light was growing dimmer, it would soon be evening. Whatever was taking the young Prince so long? It had been hours since she had returned to her rooms with his hat and tunic. They were still lying loosely across the bed where she had discarded them. How she longed to see the expression on his face when he entered the room and spied them there. Would he laugh or scold her before falling into her waiting arms? Perhaps he had had many pressing matters to discuss with His Majesty, she reflected. The palace was a veritable hive of activity with the imminent arrival of the Chinese embassy. The Middle Kingdom was the most important kingdom in the world, even greater than Siam, some said, though that was hard to believe. Anyway, the Lord of Life was certainly sparing no effort in the welcome he would extend. She had even heard that some farang dishes were being added to the bill of fare under the supervision of the same farang whom Sunida had been trained to spy on. His name was Forcon or something; at any rate Sunida had sent her secret word that his name meant bird of prey in the farang language. She smiled. How ironic that the bird of prey was himself being preyed upon. Her thoughts were interrupted by a great commotion outside. Quickly applying a final touch of sandalwood perfume to her neck and breasts she stood up to investigate the source of the noise.

She was halfway acros the room when, without ceremony, her door was flung open. Two of His Majesty's guards, the Red

Arms, stood on the threshold and scanned the room. Behind them crouched one of Yupin's slave girls, her eyes wide with terror.

'There they are!' exclaimed the taller of the two guards, his eyes alighting on the bed. His younger companion followed his gaze and then smiled with obvious relief. The Lord of Life would perhaps be quieted now. When his divine rage had abated, the two of them might be rewarded for their find, even though it was one of the slave girls who had actually led them here. The young guard trembled at the recollection of His Majesty's fury. How his voice had thundered! He had dismissed six of his guards on the spot and ordered the culprit located and brought to him before sundown. Otherwise every guard, eunuch and page boy in the palace would be punished. How dare anyone steal his brother's clothes outside his very apartments!

After a fruitless search, His Majesty had ordered the women's quarters to be scoured as well. It was then that this trembling little slave girl attached to the Lady Yupin had come forward and revealed everything. She had been led quickly away for questioning while another girl had directed them to the Lady Yupin's chambers.

'Would you come this way, my Lady?'

'Why? What is happening?' inquired Yupin, a horrible suspicion dawning on her.

'Orders of the Lord of Life, my Lady.'

Proudly she obeyed. As she marched along the corridors to the royal apartments, her head held high against the thousand eyes that stared at her, it seemed to her as if the whole palace were out on duty this day. The corridors all swarmed with people gazing at her; even the slave girls and lesser-ranking pages who prostrated themselves as she passed seemed to be squinting up at her from below.

In His Majesty's antechamber, her lover stood waiting. She read horror and vexation in his eyes while, with a solemn movement, he recovered his tunic and hat from one of the guards, and turned to go. Overcome by a sense of doom, she watched him march off. She turned irresolutely and knocked on His Majesty's door.

*

Yupin awoke screaming. Snarling, ravenous tigers had been leaping at her extremities, devouring first her toes, then her fingers, and finally her breasts and nose. But it was a dream. She had awoken again in the dark, damp dungeon. Despite her exhaustion, she tried to stay awake. Anything to avoid the recurring nightmare. But was it just a nightmare, she wondered, or a prophetic vision of her impending fate? Death by tiger. She shivered and huddled further under the thin, inadequate blanket. How cold it was below the ground. She recalled the long descent down the cold winding stone steps into regions of the palace that had been but a name. Perhaps she would ask for a warmer cover. They were Buddhists, after all, and would not refuse her that. How could so innocent a prank have turned into such a disaster? she asked herself again. Oh Lord Buddha, what a horrible end to suffer for a simple caper. But no, it was not for the prank itself, she told herself, it was for her long list of infidelities to the Lord of Life, for her deception of the master whom she was sworn to honour and obey. What pain she must now be causing that Lord, who had trusted and honoured her and shown her abiding kindness. A tear ran down her cheek. His Majesty might be a tower of strength, but not even he was beyond the suffering of mortals. The enormity of her crime descended upon her with the force of a typhoon. Who would save her now? Would her lover be found guilty too? Would they be roasted together over a slow fire? That whimpering little slave girl would no doubt have revealed everything. Oh, Lord Buddha, would that she could die now, quickly and painlessly.

The bolt slid open and a strapping guard in a red tunic stood encased in the doorway. The light from his flickering torch cast vague shadows across the damp desolate cell with its menacing stone walls. He placed a bowl of rice and soup in front of her.

'What time of day is it, guard, and how long have I been here?'

'It's the evening of your second day, my Lady. You scream a lot in your sleep.' He paused and then added as if by way of consolation: 'It will be over soon.'

'What . . . what is to be my fate then? Have you heard?'

The guard hesitated. Should he tell her what he knew? There were not many secrets in the palace. Though few people were ever permitted to visit the world outside to spread the news, those within its thick walls seemed to make up for it, ensuring that the gossip reached into every corner, always falling on ready ears.

He would tell her, he decided. She was, after all, highly connected, the sister of General Petraja himself, and who knew, if she were ever pardoned, a favour might come in handy.

'His Majesty has declined to pass judgement on his brother, counting himself insufficiently impartial. He has asked His Excellency, General Petraja, to sit in judgement instead. On you as well, my Lady.'

Yupin's heart leapt. Petraja, her own flesh and blood! He would not see his own sister devoured by tigers. And how many times had she not furthered his cause with His Majesty, bringing his name constantly to his attention, until finally he had been appointed Chairman of the Privy Council?

'His Excellency the General has already decreed the death sentence for His Royal Highness.' The guard paused. 'By clubbing of course.' He would be sewn up in a crimson velvet sack, as tradition demanded, and clubbed to death with a sandalwood club. Yupin's hopes crashed. Why had her brother condemned that beautiful young Prince to die? Who would succeed to the throne now? His deformed, drunken brother? Then the same nagging thought she had so often pushed from her mind came forward to taunt her again. He has designs on the throne, that ambitious brother of mine. He must have. Why else would he eliminate the rightful heir? She detested him now. The selfish, power-hungry cur. He would sacrifice his country and his sister to his own ends. For she was as guilty as the Prince. He could not condemn the one without the other; it would be a travesty of justice. She would be executed in a grand and well-publicized ceremony, no doubt, to enable her scheming brother to use his nearest of kin to demonstrate to the world his great loyalty to the crown and his love of justice. In this moment it dawned on her that all along she had protected her brother and closed her mind to his real nature, just as she had done with her wretched nephew Sorasak. Minimizing his faults in the eyes of herself and others, like poor Sunida, whom she had sent into the lion's den knowing full well . . . Yupin burst into tears. The guard glanced awkwardly at her and turned to leave.

'May I have a thicker blanket?' she sobbed, the tears welling in her eyes.

'I'll bring you one, my Lady.' The bolt slid to.

Yupin brushed away her tears with the back of her hand, chiding herself for her weakness. She resolved in this moment to deprive her brother of the satisfaction of seeing her ceremoniously executed. By the time the guard had returned with the blanket, she was ready with a plan. There was one person in the world who might help her, or at least put a quick end to her misery. It was a distant gamble, but it gave her a glimmer of hope.

'I bring you a blanket and more news, my Lady. His Gracious Majesty has commuted his brother's sentence. His Royal Highness is to be publicly flogged by General Petraja in the Grand Courtyard.'

Yupin's heart leapt. 'And what news of my fate?'

The guard hesitated and then glanced at his feet. 'General Petraja, your brother, has condemned you to be devoured by tigers. And Her Royal Highness the Princess Queen has steadfastly refused to commute the sentence. I am authorized to receive your request for the customary last wish of the condemned.'

Once more the door of the cell creaked open, and the guard peered in.

'Well, my Lady, have you considered your last request yet? It will need to be approved.'

Yupin did not answer. She was slumped against the wall and her head drooped heavily to one side. She appeared to be asleep.

The guard bent down to place the bowl of rice, sparsely sprinkled with a few vegetables, by her side. He was straightening up when a hand came to rest on the back of his bare thigh. He stopped, bewildered, as it began gently to stroke him. The fingers played with his skin for a moment and then slipped deftly under his loincloth. He stood still as much from surprise as pleasure. The prisoner's hand felt warm and her butterfly touch was exquisite. In the next instant her fingers were everywhere, deliciously exploring his most secret areas. He stood rooted to the spot, groaning with increasing pleasure.

A dozen thoughts whirled through his mind. Was this famous royal concubine really favouring him – a simple guard – with her charms? His friend and fellow guard Thongchai would never

383

believe this, not in a thousand moons. She had unwound his loincloth now and only the tunic still hung loosely over his genitals. Her searching fingers wrapped themselves deftly round him and she drew him to her and lifted up the tunic. He groaned even more loudly as she wrapped her lips round his swelling love lance. Then, without warning, she withdrew.

'My handsome guard,' she said, staring languidly up at him, 'you know why I am here, don't you? Because I enjoyed the company of real men too much.' Her eyes shone wistfully in the light of the candle as she began again to stroke the muscles of his thighs. 'I never could resist a muscular man.'

She saw the look of suspicion and frustration come into his eyes. She had to convince him quickly. 'I was not good at much in life except giving pleasure,' she continued, 'but in that I excelled. Since I am condemned to die, would you not share a few last moments of pleasure with me?' She smiled. 'Or do you need approval for that?' Her cat-like eyes watched him seductively. 'I am told I have no equal.'

'Why did you stop?' he asked gruffly.

'Because I want you to run a small errand for me first, and when you return I will begin again and never stop even if you beg me to. That is a promise.'

'What errand?' he inquired suspiciously.

'Just deliver a small note for me, my handsome soldier. To a lady in the Portuguese quarter. Nothing that will get you into any trouble. You can read it yourself first. It is my dying request. She was good to me once. The reply you bring me will be proof that you have completed your mission and the ecstasy I will bring you will be proof of my gratitude.' She brushed the skin of his calf tantalizingly. 'And there is something I want you to ask her. Verbally, that is. It will not be in the note.'

He hesitated. 'Let me see the note first.'

'Bring me something to write with then.'

384

Twenty-eight

On the fourth day of the waning moon in the third month of the Year of the Ape, news was brought to the capital of the arrival of the great embassy from China. Two ships awaited permission to enter at the mouth of the Menam. No embassy, not even that of the Emperor of Heaven's court, could enter the capital before the appointed day of the royal audience, nor could it remain in the capital after the audience of leave had taken place.

Only the Pra Klang and a handful of mandarins of the first order were aware that this particular embassy was likely to be granted an early hearing, with a minimum wait to satisfy the pride of the ruler of Siam. For though Siam might hold sway over the vassal princes of the surrounding states, it could not risk offending the greatest kingdom on earth. One of the first duties, in fact, of any ascending Siamese monarch was to send an embassy to the Imperial Court of China. For while Siam was in no way tributary to China, it was necessary to show respect and recognition to the colossus of the north. So while lesser embassies arriving in Siam might have to bide their time at the river's mouth, at the whim of the great monarch, the Chinese could expect a prompt and grandiose reception.

Within hours the resplendent state barges were on their way to the mouth of the river to meet the embassy's ships and escort them up to Ayudhya.

A hundred glittering barges, their prows in the shapes of garuda birds and dragons and sea-horses, carried as many mandarins of the realm to the appointed rendezvous. To either side of each mandarin lay his arms of honour: swords, scimitars and darts.

To the unpractised eye, the procession of state barges might have appeared like a glamorous outing of so many boats of more or less varying shapes and sizes, but to the connoisseur, every one of them told a different tale. Whether they were completely gilded or only half gilded and half painted, whether they were propelled by fifty or by eighty oarsmen, whether their central throne-seat ended in a pyramid or not, to what height the throne's platform was elevated, whether the crew were more or less richly attired, whether the oars were fully gilded or merely streaked with gold – all these and more denoted the specific rank and the precise number of dignity marks of the mandarin that occupied its throne-seat.

Most telling of all was the proximity of each boat to the royal barge in the precise centre of the procession. The royal barge, sent by His Majesty the King, was taller and statelier than the rest, its highly raised prow in the form of a naga snake's head, its elevated pyramidical throne of pure gold, and its hull gilded to the very waterline.

Its gilded throne, shaded by golden umbrellas at each corner, lay empty, the seat reserved for the only item worthy of assuming His Majesty's place: the Emperor of China's letter. For the letter, inscribed on a sheet of gold, was the royal word of the Emperor himself, the object of greater reverence than his ambassador who, in a lesser boat and on a lesser throne, was but his messenger. In the royal boat, four Siamese mandarins of the first rank lay permanently prostrate at each corner of the dais, making obeisance to the letter.

From the leading Chinese junk at the mouth of the river, the letter had been reverently transferred on a platter of gold on to its throne-seat in the royal Siamese barge, while the honoured mandarins who had been assigned the noble task had not dared touch the Emperor's word directly but had borne it, at arm's length and prostrate, at the end of a long golden handle.

Lining both banks of the great Menam Chao Phraya was the prostrate populace, tens of thousands of people with their faces in the mud, honouring the letter as it floated by on its gilded throne, in its gilded barge, driven by one hundred and twenty chanting oarsmen dressed in scarlet. It was as if His Majesty himself were travelling by. As the procession passed, others lay face down in the twenty thousand little canoes that milled about the shore.

Upon arrival in Ayudhya the embassy disembarked for the stately procession to the palace. The letter was placed on a pyramidical gilded throne in the King's own chariot, while the

386

ambassador himself was carried in a chair on the shoulders of the bearers.

Guards carrying blow darts went ahead, shooting peas to clear the way of any stragglers.

The mandarins of the realm, dressed in their finest apparel and joined by their retinues of slaves, preceded the ambassador and led the way towards the royal audience hall.

Armed guards and richly caparisoned elephants lined both sides of the roadway all the way to the main gates of the palace. In the first courtyard were one thousand men armed and seated on the ground, while opposite them three dozen elephants with vermilion harnesses stood in line from one end of the courtyard to the other. In the second courtyard, five dozen bearded Moors sat bolt upright on horseback, their lances held stiffly in their right hands. In the third courtyard, sixty war elephants in golden harnesses and horses with diamond-studded halters lined the perimeters, and two hundred of His Majesty's elite guard, the Red Arms, squatted, holding their swords of gold between their clasped hands.

In the fourth and final courtyard, whose floor was covered in fine Persian carpets and to which only the ambassador and his retinue were now admitted, all the mandarins of the third, fourth and fifth orders lay prostrate; separated from them by a few feet lay those of the second order. Each mandarin wore his conical hat, the number of rings and embellishments designating his rank, and each had a betel box, its size indicating his position in the overall hierarchy.

Beyond the final courtyard lay a stairway, at the bottom of which were two elephants completely covered with gold halters, and two horses whose harnesses were sprinkled with diamonds, pearls and rubies.

Here the ambassador, followed by his interpreter, knelt and placed his hands on top of his head as a sign of respect to the King and awaited the summons to His Majesty's presence. Then, as the Grand Master of Ceremonies announced the summons, the ambassador lifted his flowing black and gold robes above his knees and crawled up the stairway into the pannelled audience chamber beyond. Here he was introduced to the highest dignitaries in the land, the princes, ministers and mandarins of the first order, sixty of them in all, awaiting in profound silence the arrival of the King. They lay prostrate in rows of six to the left and right of the raised balcony at which His Majesty would appear.

The ambassador crawled forward and stopped before a table where the letter from the Emperor his master lay, and where the various gifts brought for His Majesty of Siam were displayed in a huge basin of gold.

At the sound of a trumpet and the clash of cymbals, the Lord of Life appeared on the balcony some ten feet above the floor of the audience hall. No man, not even the ambassador, was permitted to look up at his face.

To either side of him were eight parasols of gold ascending in tiers up to the ceiling. Of one accord the prostrate mandarins lifted themselves to their knees and touched their foreheads to the ground, repeating the process three times. Then the Barcalon's assistant read a Siamese translation of the letter, which had been made beforehand, while His Majesty and the court listened in silence.

The letter spoke of the great friendship the Emperor bore his cousin to the south and warned of the ambitions and evil influence of outsiders who sought to gain a foothold in both their ancient kingdoms. The Emperor pledged his support for his esteemed cousin and enjoined him to stand steadfast in the face of adversity. The Emperor further requested His Majesty of Siam to send emissaries to him with news of developments in his country.

On completion of the reading, His Majesty ordered the letter to be placed in the royal archives and addressed himself to the Barcalon, politely requesting news of the health of the Emperor and of the various members of his family. The Barcalon addressed the King's question to the interpreter who conveyed it to the ambassador. Questions and answers passed through the same chain, ensuring that His Majesty was at no time obliged to address himself to anybody so inferior in rank as an interpreter.

Having completed the full roster of polite inquiries, His Majesty presented the ambassador with a golden betel box and a brocade jacket of the finest quality, to denote the importance of the country he represented. Then, again to the sound of a trumpet and cymbals, the King retired and the assembled mandarins, still facing the balcony where His Majesty had last appeared, crawled reverently backwards and dispersed.

*

The guests were seated cross-legged before small, low tables, each adorned with a silver vessel of flowers. Phaulkon sought out Mestre Phanik who had earlier sent a messenger requesting him to sit by him at the banquet, if he had the chance. Thank God for the Siamese system of sakdina and precise ranks, Phaulkon thought as, bending forward, he traversed the entire courtyard to where Mestre Phanik was sitting with other guests of foreign origin. Imagine otherwise trying to seat two thousand people in their correct places! Fortunately, under the pre-ordained hierarchy, every guest was aware of his appointed place.

Neither His Majesty nor Princess Yotatep, the Princess Queen, were present, the first because kings did not attend public functions where it would be difficult for royalty to eat in an elevated position and equally cumbrous for the guests to eat prostrate, and the second because queens were not seen in public. Chao Fa Apai Tot presided over the banquet, his left eye occasionally twitching and his face contorting into a hideous grimace whenever he attempted a smile. On his right sat the ambassador garlanded with a necklace of mali flowers, and on his left the Pra Klang in full regalia. Then followed the various royal princes of vassal states, Cambodia, Laos, Chiengmai, Kedah, and a host of others, some of whom had voluntarily put themselves under the King's protection and others who had been captured in war and brought back to Ayudhya where they were allowed to enjoy – in exile – the privileges of their royal rank.

Each carried his own cups of gold and silver, presented by the King and denoting the owner's exalted position, and each placed them on the little table before him. Then followed the five grades of mandarins in descending order, the first being nearest to the royal princes and the fifth being the furthest away.

Phaulkon spotted Mestre Phanik glancing over at him, and next to him his niece Maria. She was looking resplendent in a formal Japanese-style kimono of a cheerful azure colour, with her chignon pierced by flowers. Despite the obvious differences in dress, he was once again reminded of Diana the huntress, the favourite statue of his childhood. Apart from the multitude of serving girls, Maria was one of the few women present at the banquet, all of whom were of foreign origin.

The first of sixteen courses, bird's nest soup, a favoured delicacy of the Chinese, was now being placed on each table by bare-breasted slave girls, their hair sleekly oiled and scented for the occasion. There were five hundred of them in attendance.

'What an appropriate choice, my dear friend,' said Mestre Phanik, happily eyeing the soup as he greeted Phaulkon. 'We export so much of the stuff to China, but they never get a chance to sample it fresh from its source. How clever of you. But how are you, my dear friend? Sit down and take a break from your duties. Oh yes,' he babbled on effusively, 'I have heard all about it. In charge of the whole catering department, eh? Mohammed Rashid is hardly pleased, I can tell you.'

Phaulkon smiled and bowed to Maria. 'You look absolutely radiant, my dear.' There was a coldness in her smile and he wondered why.

'You have neglected us, Uncle Constant,' she said, a trace of reprimand in her voice.

'Now, now, my dear, you leave Uncle Constant alone. Do you think this took just a moment to prepare?' He swept an arm across the huge banquet hall. No truer word, thought Phaulkon. He had spent days in the company of Sri, locating the finest, freshest produce at the most reasonable prices, and he had sent to dozens of neighbouring towns for the specialities for which they were renowned. He had spared no expense to ensure quality yet the charge to the Treasury was distinctly lower than for any previous function.

His crowning coup, he hoped, was enlisting the help of Père le Morin, his Jesuit friend who had a passion for God and cuisine and was a dedicated amateur chef; Phaulkon had obtained for him special exemption, as a priest, to enter the royal kitchens. Even Phaulkon himself had not been allowed there. Le Morin had supervised the roasting, Parisian style, of five hundred young partridges from the province of Pitsanuloke, and Phaulkon hoped that this delicacy, though no doubt not to everybody's taste, would add a touch of the exotic to the fifteen other courses and perhaps impress the visitors from China with the cosmopolitan atmosphere of the Siamese court. Besides, he was aware that the Barcalon was anxious to avoid the appearance of any concerted effort to deprive the Moors of their traditional roles, and the farang delicacies might help to justify his appointment.

'You have guessed right, Mestre Phanik,' said Phaulkon as a pair of quail's eggs were placed in little golden bowls in front of

390

each guest. 'You have both been much on my mind but I have returned every evening so exhausted from the day's work that my servants had on occasion to disrobe me while I slept.'

Yet you could surely have found time to visit us just once, however briefly, thought Maria bitterly, wishing she could come out with the question of that Sunida woman and throw it at him. It occurred to her that if her uncle had not been present she probably would have done so.

Phaulkon noticed the frown on her delicate brow. What disturbs her? he wondered again.

'Don't mind Maria, Constant. She is still young and thinks the whole world revolves round her.' He leaned round her back and whispered confidentially in Phaulkon's ear, 'Have you noticed the absence of Chao Fa Noi? I have heard he was flogged almost to death by General Petraja and that it is touch and go whether he will survive. Between you and me, I have always supected the general of harbouring designs on the throne himself. You remember, you met him at my house? After all, if both the Princes were eliminated and the Princess Queen produces no heir, who would succeed to the throne? Apparently Princess Yotatep, who at first demanded the death penalty for the young Prince, is now inconsolable at the thought of his possible demise.'

It was the first Phaulkon had heard of General Petraja's aspirations but Father le Morin had already given him news of Princess Yotatep from the gossip gathered in the royal kitchens. Apparently the Princess had not eaten for three days; and the golden trays sent to her rooms had all been returned untouched to the royal kitchens. The cooks were at their wit's end over what to prepare for her next.

'So, Uncle Constant, now that the banquet will shortly be over and, as I can see, a resounding success, may we expect to see more of you?' asked Maria, turning towards him.

'If you promise to stop calling me uncle, yes. It makes me feel quite old.'

'But you are old, Uncle. At least twice my age, anyway.'

'That will be quite enough, my dear,' said Mestre Phanik, giving her a look of disapproval. 'I don't know what's got into her,' he added, turning apologetically to Phaulkon.

Slaves now filled delicate blue and white cups with Chinese tea and Phaulkon accepted a glass of sparkling red wine.

'She's a woman now, Doutor,' said Phaulkon, 'with a mind of her own.' He too was somewhat taken aback by her unexpected aggressiveness. It seemed quite genuine. Perhaps he *was* getting old, he thought, though he certainly did not feel it. In fact, life was just beginning. He was on the right track now, he felt sure. Burnaby and White had left for Mergui loaded to bursting with the choicest merchandise. The success of the Persian expedition could send him catapulting to prominence. He was counting the days till its return. He was anxious for Sunida's safety too, and praying for her imminent return. Perhaps he looked tired. Still, it was odd that Maria should be so gruff. His thoughts were distracted by the sight of Arnout Faa, the resident director of the Verenigde Oostindische Compagnie, the VOC, sitting near the far wall of the courtyard. Phaulkon caught his eye and bowed. The Dutchman lowered his head in acknowledgement. 'Will you forgive me? I will be back in a moment,' said Phaulkon, rising.

'Bored with our company already, Uncle Constant?' asked Maria.

'Not at all, my dear. Just leaving it momentarily so I can enjoy it the more on my return.'

Phaulkon bowed to Faa and inquired politely as to van Risling's condition. 'He is improving, thank you, Heer Phaulkon. The surgeon has set two broken bones and he is learning slowly to walk again with the help of a stick. I shall inform him, of course, of your concern,' he added with a trace of sarcasm.

'I would appreciate that,' said Phaulkon.

'And I must congratulate you on your handling of the banquet tonight. Expertly done. You are a man of considerable talents, Heer Phaulkon. It is a pity that not all of them are directed towards the right objectives.' He smiled politely as he helped himself to a morsel of sea bass, delicately flavoured with basil.

'Like so many of your plans for Siam, Heer Faa.'

The resident director ignored the jibe. 'How is your new job with the ministry? I trust you are successfully spying for the English?'

'Indeed, Heer Faa. And I am at the same time unearthing valuable information about the Moors. It seems there are surprising similarities between their methods of operation and yours.'

'Oh? How is that? I am curious.'

'The information is unfortunately confidential, mijn heer, but it is all in the reports I have sent to Madras.'

'No doubt those reports will be seen for what they are. An attempt to deflect from our own accusations concerning your conduct, Heer Phaulkon,' replied the VOC chief with a smile.

'You forget that the English Company is hardly prejudiced in your favour, Heer Faa.'

'Ah, but you judge from the junior standpoint of its factors in Siam, Heer Phaulkon. Do not underestimate the finer judgement of your directors in Madras.'

'I do not, Heer Faa, that is why I have no fear.' With a little luck and the success of the Persian expedition, thought Phaulkon, I will not be answerable to those English directors any more. And then, mijn heer, you will have to face me as a Siamese, an implacable antagonist from this very host country. 'But if you will excuse me, I must return to my place now. As always, Heer Faa, it has been a pleasure conversing with you.' Both men bowed to each other.

'My uncle has been reprimanding me for my behaviour towards you, Constant,' said Maria as Phaulkon returned to his seat. 'Should I be asking for forgiveness?'

'You already have, by dropping the uncle. From this moment on I shall never consider you a child again.'

'I am glad. No one else does.'

'As a matter of fact, I have had two requests for her hand since I last saw you, Constant,' complained her uncle. 'It's quite frightening. Because she really *is* still a child.'

'You see, Constant, now that you are converted, my uncle is the only one left to believe that.'

'That is only to be expected, my dear. You will always be his little niece, no matter what age you are. He could never look upon you as anything else.'

'But could you?' she asked coquettishly.

'I wouldn't dare,' replied Phaulkon, teasingly.

'And how mistaken you would be,' she said. It was hard to tell from her tone how far she was speaking in jest. Mestre Phanik, however, appeared noticeably flustered.

'But do tell me, Constant,' she said, suddenly looking him squarely in the eye. 'How is Sunida?'

393

Phaulkon caught his breath. 'Sunida?' he repeated, trying to sound unfamiliar with the name.

Though a voice within Maria told her to stop, some little devil was prompting her. There was no turning back now.

'Oh, come now, Constant, Sunida, the beautiful temptress from the south.' She leaned a little closer to him. 'The one sent by the palace to spy on you.'

Phaulkon was speechless.

Maria watched with satisfaction the effect of her words. What a clever message Yupin had sent, she thought, the more so as it must have appeared unintelligible to the guard. 'The man you asked me about is a bird of prey in your language,' the note had said. It had not taken Maria long to work out the meaning: vultures, hawks, falcons, Phaulkon! So, her beloved Constant was the one Sunida had been trained to spy on. How honourable of Yupin to keep her promise to let Maria know. But when the messenger had asked for poison to kill the rats in Yupin's cell, Maria had been astonished. Yupin's *cell*? What new folly could have caused the beautiful and notorious concubine's disgrace? Aware of the strict rules of the palace and the harsh punishment inflicted on those who transgressed, Maria had sensed that the request for poison was a ploy of Yupin's to take her own life. She had declined the request. As a Christian, she could not condone suicide no matter what hardships Yupin might have to endure. The nervous guard had seemed to cheer up somewhat when Maria had taken the little golden crucifix from her neck and handed it to him, telling him that the prisoner should pray to it and seek strength from it in her hour of need.

Maria's reflections were interrupted by the hitherto speechless Phaulkon, who had found his voice again.

'What are you talking about, Maria?' His voice sounded strangely hollow.

Maria shook her head as if she were dealing with a wayward child. 'How easy it is for a woman to turn a man's head. The beautiful Sunida catering to your every need, so deeply in love with her Constant.' There was a mocking edge to her voice. 'And all the while reporting his every move to the palace.'

Phaulkon was in shock. The roar of the banquet vaguely filled his ears and the figures around him grew blurred. Was this really

394

happening? With an effort he pulled himself together. But before he could think of a reply, Mestre Phanik had interceded for him.

'I don't know what you are talking about, Maria, but your conduct this evening is inexcusable, I am positively ashamed. Will you please explain yourself and apologize to Constant immediately.'

'I will gladly apologize, Uncle, though I have only Constant's interests at heart. The palace has planted a spy in his household and he is apparently unaware of it. Of course the palace has chosen very cleverly,' she added as if to ease his humiliation. 'Her name is Sunida and she has been trained in the arts of love by none other than Yupin whose exploits in our Portuguese quarter are legendary.'

Mestre Phanik looked at her in amazement. He was about to say something to Phaulkon when the expression on Phaulkon's face deterred him. He turned instead to Maria. 'Where did you get this fantastic information? I want to know immediately.'

Maria hesitated, fearful that she might have gone too far.

'May I explain later, Uncle?' she pleaded. 'My main preoccupation at present is to safeguard Constant's interests. He is clearly in danger.'

Phaulkon's face had become quite ashen and he seemed to have abandoned all pretence at dissimulation. He was temporarily distracted by a murmur from the assembled guests as steaming trayloads of beautifully decorated partridge, their colourful plumage arranged round the sides, were brought in by dozens of serving girls. Several heads turned towards Phaulkon in appreciation.

Vaguely he followed the proceedings. His mind was going over every detail of his chance encounter with Sunida at the marketplace. In the light of Maria's astonishing assertions, it was not difficult to replace coincidence with intent. To anyone familiar with Phaulkon's movements, and especially to anyone assigned to follow him, it would not be difficult to ascertain that he frequented the marketplace and that Sri was his friend. Presumably she had been designated the conduit for Sunida's messages. It now seemed an obvious place to deploy anyone the authorities might want him to come upon 'by chance'. He could not help wondering how he could have overlooked the coincidence so lightly at the time. Had he been so overwhelmed at seeing Sunida again? Had he been so jealous at the story of the mandarin – who presumably did not exist at all? He felt the gnawing pain of deception, and the wound of hurt pride. Was her whole act of caring for him a pretence? His stomach felt hollow. He recalled every detail of the story of the important mandarin. It had seemed real enough at the time. But how did Maria know all this?

Maria and Mestre Phanik were now talking to each other in hushed tones, seemingly absorbed in their own conversation. Perhaps they had contrived to leave him alone to his thoughts. Vaguely he heard Mestre Phanik exclaim, 'What! You mean to say that was the same Yupin that came to our house? Meu Deus!'

The delicacies Phaulkon had so painstakingly helped to prepare came and went untouched before him in a splendid procession of golden vessels, porcelain plates and silver bowls.

Then gradually his mood began to change. The natural optimism that had stood by him all his life and that was never far from the surface rose to banish the temporary gloom. He recalled now how the Governor of Ligor had appeared to hesitate when he had first requested that Sunida accompany him to Ayudhya. Had the germ of the idea to implant her as a spy formed even then in the Governor's mind? Had perchance one of the Governor's dispatches to the Barcalon contained the proposal that Sunida might be the perfect spy to plant on him if, as the Governor had surely recommended, he were to enter into government service? If the Barcalon had been impressed with the scheme, he would no doubt have taken it straight to the palace for his Majesty's approval. With the palace's connivance, Sunida could have been whisked up to Ayudhya and put into training there. And what more logical tutor than Yupin, assuredly the only one of the palace females with any experience of farangs? He knew something of Yupin from his friend Captain Alvarez. She was the ultimate seductress, thoroughly versed in the arts of love. He remembered Alvarez telling him once how Yupin often bartered her knowledge with the more voluptuous of the novices in the harem in exchange for their favours.

He put himself for a moment in Sunida's place, a young provincial girl suddenly summoned to be of service to the great court at Ayudhya, possibly even to the Lord of Life himself, whose God-like titles were instilled in every child from birth: He who Guides the Rains of the World and makes the Waters rise and flow, whose Glorious Fame ranges through the World and whose Dignity may be compared with none; a King that is like a God, and shines like the Sun at noonday; a King as righteous as God and of such power that all the world may come and shelter under his Wings; a King who has all Emperors, Princes, and Sovereigns in the Whole World from the rising to the going down of the Sun under Subjection. And such as can obtain His Favour are by him Promoted to great Honour . . .

What an honour indeed to have befallen a young dancer from Ligor. How could she even question her duty, let alone fail to perform it? And, he reflected, feeling already much better, it did not preclude her loving him. But how had Maria found out?

Garlic eels in beds of aquatic chestnuts, fried shrimp in coconut husks, stewed monkey's brains and the cooked stems of seven varieties of lotus flower had all come and gone without impinging on Phaulkon's reverie. But by the time the magnificent assortment of fruits had arrived, a smile had etched itself unmistakably on his face. Gradually it expanded into a broad grin.

The infinite possibilities of feeding desirable information back to the palace through an unsuspecting Sunida had just dawned on him.

Sunida settled more comfortably into the boat's cushions and allowed the quiet, rhythmic splashing of the paddles to soothe her. She was returning to Ayudhya and to her dear Phaulkon, pleased and proud of what she had achieved in Mergui, both for the King and for the man she loved.

Her thoughts returned to the sinister priest who had accompanied her from the church, and the fear she had felt when, without warning, he had stepped in front of her, barring the way. 'Let us talk for a while, my child.' He had led her firmly off the path into a little clearing behind which rose thickly forested slopes.

Sunida had followed him uncertainly, looking around her as they went. They were about halfway down the hill to the harbour. The little church was out of sight above them and the crowds on the bustling waterfront were visible below, but probably out of earshot. The view across the azure bay was breathtaking and from this elevation the sparkling water looked more like a

397

shimmering lake. Only the little islands that dotted the horizon spoke of the endless ocean beyond.

'What is it you wish to discuss, Father?' Sunida asked, eyeing the priest with caution. She sensed a certain nervousness in his behaviour.

'The captain you wish to see is not here,' replied Luang Aziz. 'He has gone to Ayudhya and will not be back for several days. You had better leave the message with me. It will be safe in my hands.'

Sunida was taken aback. Why had he not spoken of the farang captain's absence earlier, in front of the other priest? Why had he offered to accompany her? She looked anxiously around her. And why wait till they were in this isolated spot? This priest seemed a little too anxious to recover the letter.

'I thank you for your offer, Father, but I have strict instructions to deliver the letter in person.'

A hint of anger showed in the priest's eyes. Sunida saw that he was making an effort to control himself. 'And whose instructions are those, my child?'

'I am not at liberty to say, Father. But may I ask what your interest is in the matter?'

Again the dark eyes flared. 'The Governor of this province has asked me to determine the contents of that ship whose captain you seek. We priests are sometimes called upon to serve the nation. You see, we are often able to make inquiries without arousing suspicion. That is why it is important for me to know the contents of that letter.' He held out his hand.

Sunida retreated a step. 'I have already explained to you, Father, that my mission is confidential. Let us proceed to the harbour, please. You offered to accompany me and help me deliver the letter. In the absence of the captain, I will leave it with the officer in charge.'

The priest advanced towards her, his impatience clearly showing. The clearing was surrounded on three sides by steeply rising slopes, thick with bushes and trees and offering little chance of escape. To the front, the priest stood between her and the pathway to the harbour. There was no one else around. If she shouted, perhaps the farang priest in the chapel above might hear her, but then he was most probably involved as well.

'My mission comes from the highest levels,' she said gravely, hoping to impress him, 'and I would have to report any attempt to thwart me.' She could hear the tremor in her voice.

The priest's eyes flashed angrily.

'Give me the letter,' he said, advancing on her and discarding all pretence at civility. She retreated to the edge of the clearing, until she could go no further.

He stood in front of her, a cold, relentless look on his face. To her shock he raised an arm. Was he actually going to strike her? He, a priest!

'All right,' she said, shielding her face with an arm. 'Take the letter then.' She opened her small purse and produced a well-worn sheet of rice paper. The priest took it roughly from her and scanned the contents. 'Damn,' she heard him swear under his breath. It was written in the farang tongue. Perhaps he could not read it, she thought.

'May I have it back now?' pleaded Sunida.

'No, I have already told you I will deliver it to the ship myself. You'd best be on your way now. I have business to attend to.' She stood still, unwilling to move. He pointed to the path leading to the harbour. 'Go, I said. Return to Ayudhya.'

He raised his arm again. Slowly she moved forward, turning every now and then to look at him. She was about to turn down the path towards the harbour when she saw Dom Francisco hurrying towards her from the other direction. But the second priest intercepted him and, taking him roughly by the arm, dragged him back up towards the little chapel on the hill. What strange behaviour, she thought. No doubt this ill-mannered priest needed Dom Francisco to translate the letter for him.

She cast the episode from her mind as she made her way down the winding path to the harbour. Now she would go and deliver the real letter to the ship. If the captain were in fact away, she would leave it with his senior officer as Phaulkon had ordered her to do through Sri.

Sunida was quite delighted with her performance. The various acting roles that had accompanied her dancing career had proved invaluable. She had known how to simulate fear. How many times had she not played Sita being chased through the forest by the evil King. Though she *had* been genuinely frightened just now, she had to admit, especially when the priest raised his hand to strike her.

399

But she was particularly pleased that the idea of the two letters had been her own. She recalled how, prostrate and trembling in the royal audience hall, she had listened as the Jesuit priest had translated Phaulkon's letter into Siamese for the Lord of Life and His Excellency the Pra Klang. How strongly her heart had palpitated at the fear that her lover's letter to the English captain in Mergui might contain damaging suggestions, prejudicial to the welfare of Siam. But the translation had revealed nothing negative. To her intense relief it had merely requested the English captain to remain in Mergui for a few days more so that the necessary arrangements for the trip to Persia might be finalized.

It was then that the deep voice of the Lord of Life had resounded from above, advising that precautions should be taken to ensure the letter did not fall into the wrong hands. She had begged forgiveness for the intrusion and timidly suggested carrying a second letter as a decoy, which could be handed over in case of emergency. To her surprise and pleasure the Lord of Life and the Pra Klang had both enthusiastically approved the idea and she had been dismissed while a second letter was drafted. By the time she was recalled, the Jesuit interpreter had finished writing the letter in English.

His Excellency the Pra Klang had then advised her that if at any time she were accosted by a party trying to recover the letter from her, she was to produce the second one, and that only after strong resistance. This second letter, he explained, also purportedly written by Phaulkon to the English captain, mentioned that though Phaulkon had attempted to buy goods from the Siamese Treasury for export to Persia, the Pra Klang had turned down the request and had only agreed to sell the merchandise to the English Company on condition that it was for export to Madras. The letter proceeded to say that the Lord of Life was apparently much indebted to the Moors for their long and loyal service to the crown and would play no part in assisting the English in whatever schemes they might have to discredit them. This was the letter, reflected Sunida, now in the hands of the rough priest. What did it all mean?

Sunida realized she was beginning to enjoy her new role and her body was suddenly suffused with warmth as she thought of the Lord of Life's words to the Pra Klang after she had brought up the idea of the second letter.

'How fortunate we are to have such a worthy messenger. One who is not only charming and beautiful but wise as well. The farang Forcon had best mind himself.'

She prayed now that Phaulkon would work only for the glory of Siam, for then her happiness would be truly complete.

Twenty-nine

Samuel Potts brushed the dust off the lapel of his black coat, wiped the perspiration from his balding crown and followed the guard into a spacious office, the walls of which were lined with maps and charts indicating trade routes, monsoon trends and flood tides. Red ink dots were spattered widely over the land areas, pinpointing various outposts and factories. Potts was reminded, both by the number of dots and by the ample proportions of the room, of the power and extent of the Dutch trading empire. The flag of the Netherlands stood on the massive, pannelled desk behind which Arnout Faa now rose to greet him.

'Mr Potts, I believe,' he said in English, referring to the letter he had barely finished reading, 'welcome to Ayudhya. I trust you had a pleasant journey.'

'Pleasant enough, thank you, Mr Faa,' replied Samuel Potts, relieved to find the English of his interlocutor so fluent. He himself spoke not five words of Dutch. 'Your representatives at Little Amsterdam at the mouth of the Menam were most obliging. I rested there while they took care of the necessary formalities for me with the Siamese authorities. I am most grateful.'

It was small wonder, reflected Aarnout Faa, that his onder-koopman at Little Amsterdam had jumped to attention. The round Englishman in front of him was carrying a letter from none other than His Excellency Heer Rijcklof van Goens, the Gouverneur-Generaal in Batavia, a copy of which had been sent ahead by express courier to Faa. It directed all Dutch personnel in Siam to lend every assistance possible to Mr Samuel Potts, special emissary from the English East India Company in Bantam. Faa smiled to himself. It was certainly in Dutch interests to co-operate with this man. Mr Potts had been sent with full powers to investigate Dutch allegations, spearheaded by himself here in Ayudhya, that the English factors in Siam were running arms, disposing of stolen Dutch cannon and generally trading for themselves. In a private note attached to the copy of his

402

instructions, van Goens had informed Faa that the English had taken the allegations made by the VOC in Ayudhya seriously enough to instruct their Mr Potts to proceed directly to Madras with the results of his investigation. This was a clear indication that the English wanted to act on his findings with the minimum of delay, and the court of justice at Madras would have complete authority to do so. Though England and Holland were rivals, the two countries were at peace, and certain standards of conduct between them were expected.

'Mr Faa,' said Samuel Potts, seating himself in a chair and gratefully accepting the cup of tea proffered by his host, 'I have taken the liberty of coming directly to see you, before visiting the English factory here. I trust I can count on your discretion to keep this, shall we say, slight lapse of etiquette confidential?'

'Indeed you may, Mr Potts. I am here to give you every assistance possible in your endeavours to learn the truth.'

'The fact is, Mr Faa, that my superiors are concerned by the gravity of the accusations you have made against our representatives in Siam, and though our two nations are in many ways rival, they would like it known that the English in no way condone the kind of activities you describe.'

Faa inclined his head slightly. 'I never doubted that that was the case, Mr Potts.'

'May we go over the facts then, sir, as you see them. Although I have read the translation of your report several times, it would be helpful if we could take the events you describe step by step, so that I can ask questions as we go along.'

'Of course, Mr Potts. In expectation of your arrival I have summoned our representative from Ligor here, so that you may also question him directly concerning the significant events which occurred in his area.' Faa rose and sounded an imposing brass gong which stood beside his desk. 'I am afraid that Heer van Risling's English is far from adequate but I shall be glad to act as interpreter if you wish. I should add that Heer van Risling suffered a small accident recently during the royal elephant hunt at Louvo.'

'I am sorry to hear that. I shall endeavour not to retain him longer than is absolutely necessary.'

'Time is not the problem, Mr Potts. It is Heer van Risling's leg

403

which has suffered.' He smiled. 'His brain, I sincerely hope, is unimpaired.'

In the next moment the portly frame of Joop van Risling was ushered in, hobbling with one hand leaning on a bamboo cane and the other on Pieter, the young Eurasian interpreter who had accompanied him from Ligor. Pieter helped the older man into a chair and retired. For the next few hours the two Dutchmen described in great detail the events that had begun with the shipwreck at Ligor, while the Englishman interrupted with a barrage of questions, frequently taking notes.

There was not more than an hour of daylight left when Potts, in the company of a Siamese guide supplied by the Dutch factory, set off for the English warehouse, a few hundred yards along the bank of the great river.

Samuel Potts pushed the glass away from him and rose to his feet, pacing up and down the room once again. It was the fifth or sixth time he had done so but it did not seem to have the desired effect. The more he tried to calm himself, the more the anger rose in him.

He had been livid when an Indian guard at the gate of the English factory had barred his entrance. He had sworn at the man but his expletives had only served to add to the swine's obstinacy. As if to compound the insult, the heathen devil had muttered enough syllables of broken English to make him understand that there was no one inside the factory anyway. No one inside? Why, the Dutch factory had been teeming with people moments ago when he had left it. Admittedly this caricature of a warehouse was only one-tenth the size of the Dutch one, but nevertheless it was the property of King Charles of England and there were people employed to work in it. Where were the representatives? There were supposed to be two Englishmen and a Greek in the pay of the honourable Company, as well as half a dozen local assistants, and not one of them was on the premises. The one half-witted black guard who was at his post did not even have the sense to understand who he was. Disgraceful. If the Dutch had sought to impress upon him the truth of their allegations, they had certainly got off to a promising start.

Potts poured himself another glass of brandy. He had finally

404

prevailed upon that numbskull of a guard to explain to the guide who had accompanied him where the home of the chief factor, Richard Burnaby, was. Off he had trudged again, only to discover that Burnaby was nowhere to be found. To his increasing ravings the frightened servants had pointed absurdly in the direction of the horizon as if their master had gone to some distant land. Damn the unintelligibility of the language. Damn the ignorance and stupidity of the natives. Damn the heat and the flies. Damn, damn, damn! He banged his glass on the table. The door opened and the same native girl who had served him the brandy peeped in. She was comely for a native, he had to admit. But she was no more intelligible than the rest of them, although she had at least had the sense to bring him a decent bottle of brandy. Probably just mimicking her master's habits anyway. He glanced at the bottle. Good God! Had he drunk that much already? The bottle was half empty. Perhaps it hadn't been full to start with. He tried in vain to remember.

He turned round. The girl was still there, framed in the doorway. 'What time is your master coming home, eh? What time?' he repeated petulantly, realizing as he said it that it was hopeless. She merely smiled at him. Why were these natives constantly smiling? It was damned irritating. Even the black guard at the factory had smiled at first when he had demanded to be let in. It was only when he had raged at him that the imbecile had finally wiped the smile off his face.

From Burnaby's house he had prevailed upon one of the frightened servant girls who had seemed less retarded than the rest to show him the way to the Greek's house. The name Phaulkon seemed to have penetrated their thick skulls because this one girl at least had registered understanding. He had soon discovered that Phaulkon, too, was nowhere to be found but his handsome housekeeper had unexpectedly shown some initiative. She had ushered him into a room and offered him a quilt to lie on, placing her cupped hands against her cheek to indicate that he might want to sleep. But he was not tired. Just frustrated and damned angry. She had seemingly sensed that and shown him instead to a chair in the living room. Then she had left and returned with a cold cloth to smooth his brow, and the bottle of brandy. After washing his face she had called another girl in to massage his neck and shoulders and for a while he had felt better.

405

But then he had poured himself another glass of brandy and set to thinking, and then another and another, and his anger had mounted with every sip. Now it consumed him.

There was a drone about his left ear. A mosquito settled on his face and he slapped his cheek and squashed it. He examined the blood on the tips of his fingers and then wiped them clean on his vest. He heard a gasp from the creature in the doorway and in the next instant she was back with another cloth. She cleansed his hands and then rubbed his vest at the spot where he had wiped the blood off. What was she trying to do? Mother him? Before he could dismiss her she had slipped out. A moment later she returned with half a dozen sticks that burned and smelled sickeningly of incense. She distributed them around the room, placing them in small saucers that were strewn about for the purpose. Damn the mosquitoes. Did she really think these burning sticks would frighten them away? Unless the smell would. What did these natives know of mosquitoes anyway? The insects didn't even deign to bite them. It was only Englishmen's blood that gave them any satisfaction and, in the absence of that, perhaps the Dutch strain would do.

Potts folded his arms across the little table in front of him and rested his head on them for a moment. Within seconds he was snoring loudly. Sunida crept in and placed a cushion against the back of his chair. Then wrinkling her nose at the foulness of his breath she took him by the shoulders and gently pushed him back against the cushions. 'These farangs,' she muttered disdainfully to herself. She recalled how the ship's officers at Mergui had been in the same inebriated state when she had arrived on board unannounced. How ludicrous they had looked trying to show her all those gallantries when they were hardly able to stand. One of the officers had tried for a long while to focus on the letter she had handed him and then given up. She would not be surprised if the letter were still in his pocket now. Thank Buddha her Constant was not like the others. She would have to report the presence of this man to Sri. Then she would have to try and find out who he was and the reason for his visit.

Phaulkon was in a jovial mood as he headed home along the river's edge from the ministry. The banquet for the Chinese ambassador had been a resounding success. At the envoy's farewell audience, almost as elaborate an affair as his welcoming ceremony, the diplomat had gone out of his way to mention his pleasure to His Majesty. Never in his frequent travels as the Emperor of Heaven's representative had he enjoyed a banquet more or observed one in which such attention to detail had been demonstrated. It was diplomatic talk, Phaulkon knew, but the fact that the ambassador had brought it up at all was a feather in Phaulkon's cap.

Since learning of Sunida's spying role he had prepared himself to feed her information always flattering to the Barcalon and ever reverential to His Majesty, and he planned to use every occasion to stress his loyalty and love for Siam and its people. He smiled. Sunida really was the perfect spy. Her lively, inquisitive nature naturally prompted her to ask questions anyway. But he felt sure that she was performing a duty which had been imposed on her and, though she might have hesitated to report any matters damaging to him, she would still have done so, although perhaps with a heavy heart. Even if she was in love with him she was in the service of the King, and the King of Siam was a Chakravatin, a demi-god who came first before all mortals.

How delighted he was to have her back. Never could a man have been more pleased to have a spy in his midst, he reflected. She had returned only the previous day from Mergui, smiling and full of energy despite the long ordeal, pretending reassurance that the mandarin had stopped searching for her, and she had immediately set about relating how a priest had rowed her out to the ship and how the officers had all been drunk when she had arrived on board. Phaulkon had laughed at her description of the ship's officers ogling her and literally falling over one another trying to be pleasant. He had told her then that Captain White had been in Ayudhya all the while and she had teased him saying he had known all along and he was just trying to be rid of her for a while. Then suddenly they had looked at each other and were silent, and driven only by the longing in their eyes they had walked together to his bedroom and lain down on the quilt. They had made love with all the tenderness and hunger of two people who had been apart too long. If any doubts still remained to him that she had not been trained by the top courtesan in the palace, they vanished now. Even the rising emotions they felt for each other could not explain the remarkable evolution in Sunida's sexual technique. She was sensuous, erotic, brilliant and un-bridled – a worthy successor to the famous Yupin. Poor Yupin. For a moment he wondered whether the rumours about her were true. It was said that she had died as she had lived. Unwilling to succumb to the cruel sentence imposed on her by her brother, General Petraja, she was reputed to have first seduced the prison guard, a strapping, well-endowed youth, and then to have deliberately choked herself to death on his prodigious love lance. The poor fellow had suffered the ordeal by tiger in her stead. Sunida had been grief-stricken at the news of Yupin's death.

Phaulkon was glad to be getting home. It had been another protracted day at the ministry. Since the departure of the Chinese delegation he had been set the task of compiling comparative lists of all the prices of goods paid to the Treasury by the Moors for the Persian and Indian markets over the past five years. The Barcalon had assured him that once this task was completed he would be allowed to attend to the backlog of work that had been piling up at the English factory with no one to look after it. Ivatt was now called away with increasing frequency to the palace to entertain the various children of royal adoption. His well-worn conjuring trick of producing a live dove out of the heart of a giant coconut had delighted these children every bit as much as it had the Governor of Ligor's court, and his fame was spreading. Shortly, Phaulkon had told him only half in jest, the English Company would have to advertise for new management, the present directors being permanently employed elsewhere. If Madras only knew!

Sunida was waiting for him at the door. She wai'd to him and though she seemed anxious to tell him something, he insisted on taking her in his arms first and inhaling her cheek deliciously. She closed her eyes happily and inhaled him in turn.

As soon as he released her she told him about the visitor asleep in his living room. She described him as short and round with a curly greying beard and hardly a hair on his head, a pair of spectacles on his nose and a bad odour in his mouth. The description did not fit anyone Phaulkon could immediately think of. She warned him that the visitor had drunk a great deal and that he seemed irascible and petulant.

When Phaulkon cautiously entered the room, Samuel Potts was, in fact, conscious again. He had just jerked himself awake

408

with a particularly loud snore and he was pouring himself a large glass of brandy.

'Ah, the elusive Mr Phaulkon, no doubt,' he said rising precariously to his feet. 'At last. Allow me to raise my glass to the first member of the honourable Company I have managed to encounter since my arrival, despite a massive search. Your health, sir.' He drained his glass and swayed slightly on his feet. Only his voice remained steady.

'Welcome to Ayudhya, sir,' said Phaulkon politely. 'With whom do I have the honour?'

Potts observed him for a while in silence and then hiccuped loudly. He seemed embarrassed at first by his own belch but then shrugged it off. He rose unsteadily to the tips of his toes and hung there for a moment, before tumbling back on to the balls of his feet.

'I am Samuel Potts of the honourable Company's Bantam office. I have been sent to investigate the Company's affairs in Siam.' He swung an arm vaguely through the air. 'Of course that is not an easy task, when you cannot find any of its representatives. But I shall endeavour to get to the bottom of things anyway.'

'I will be delighted to answer any questions you may have, sir.' Phaulkon did not like the look of this man, neither his role nor his present condition. The name Potts rang a bell. He was fairly senior, Phaulkon felt sure; probably one of the Company auditors.

'Burnaby will be the one to answer any questions,' declared Potts. He lurched sideways and rested a hand on the table to steady himself. 'Where is Burnaby?' he demanded.

'Mr Burnaby is in Mergui, sir, on a confidential mission.'

'Confidential, eh? And what might that be?'

'Won't you sit down, Mr Potts. You must have had a tiring journey.'

'Are you suggesting that I am not able to stand, sir?' he asked aggressively.

'I am suggesting nothing of the kind, Mr Potts. I just thought you might be more comfortable sitting down.'

'I am fine as I am,' he answered gruffly. 'Now what is this confidential mission you mentioned?'

409

'My instructions are to discuss it with no one, sir. Unless of course you have a letter authorizing—'

'A letter of authorization?' stammered Potts. 'Why, sir, I have more than that. I have the authority to close down this branch if my findings require it, and to have you all sent to Madras for trial. So don't talk to me about authorizations, young man.'

That's all I needed to know, thought Phaulkon.

'Would you like to spend the night here, sir? We can go to the factory in the morning and—'

'Don't try and distract me from my duty, Mr Phaulkon,' interrupted Potts belligerently, 'or I'll put that in my report too. I'm not spending the night here, incurring favours from you. Your housekeeper has already tried to ply me with drink. I am familiar with such tactics, you know. I have been an auditor for over twenty years.' He rose again on to the tips of his feet. 'You're dealing with Samuel Potts here. Now, where is the other fellow, what's his name?' He strained his memory.

Phaulkon decided not to come to his aid. Let the drunken blighter work it out for himself, he thought. Perhaps he should offer him another drink, and encourage him to pass out completely. He had noticed him eyeing the bottle a moment earlier anyway.

Potts seemed to be racking his brain. 'Where is Irving?' he blurted, noticeably pleased with himself for having remembered.

'Irving is a guest of His Majesty the King,' lied Phaulkon. 'He is attending a dinner at the palace. The honourable Company is in good standing with the highest authorities here, Mr Potts.'

'Maybe here, Mr Phaulkon,' shot back Potts with a knowing look, 'but not in Bantam or Madras, I can assure you. They want your head. And I'm going to help them get it. I'm going to the factory now to examine every one of your books in detail.'

'Now?' asked Phaulkon. 'It's dark outside, Mr Potts.'

'Then why don't you have torches brought? We're going to the factory now.' He looked at Phaulkon suspiciously. 'None of this putting me to rest so you can slip out and alter the books while I'm asleep. I want to audit those books as I find them. And by the way,' he said, recalling the earlier incident with a resurgence of anger, 'why was no one at the factory this afternoon? Not a blithering soul. Except some stupid native guard. Is it King Charles's birthday or something?'

'Not King Charles's birthday, sir, but the heir to the Siamese throne's second cycle,' improvised Phaulkon. 'We try to observe the important holidays of our host country, out of respect.'

Potts grunted. 'The Dutch don't seem to share your attitudes, Mr Phaulkon. They work instead. It's no wonder they're so far ahead.'

'That may be, but they're not popular with the Siamese. One of their former factors, de Jongh, is still talked about today. He used to parade about the streets dressed only in a loincloth and a hat.' Phaulkon observed Potts carefully. 'Most of the time he was drunk. You see, the Siamese abhor any form of lack of control, Mr Potts.'

'Some people cannot hold their liquor,' commented Potts, undaunted. He turned and poured himself another glass. Half of it fell on the wrong side of the rim and formed an expanding pool on the table. He ignored it and drained what was left in the glass. 'So, in the unexplained absence of the chief factor,' he said pointedly, 'will you, Mr Phaulkon, lead the way to the factory?'

'If you insist, Mr Potts, but would it not be preferable to examine the books by daylight? The other staff members would also be there then to answer your questions.'

'I know what you're trying to achieve, Mr Phaulkon, but I will not be deterred. We will proceed now.' Phaulkon appeared to hesitate. Potts looked at him threateningly. 'If you do not co-operate, I shall state in my report that I was refused access. It will look very bad for you.' Phaulkon was beginning to lose his temper, but he nevertheless went to fetch two torches.

It was a dark, moonless night and Phaulkon led the way along a dirt path that followed the river's edge. There were few people about, only the odd fisherman standing knee-deep in water and casting his net into the river; the spirit-conscious Siamese did not venture out after dark unless absolutely necessary. The absence of humans, however, was more than made up for by the chorus of night sounds: the croaking of frogs, the squeaking of crickets, the droning of mosquitoes that settled hungrily on the travellers' wrists and ankles.

The going was not made any easier by Potts who was constantly stumbling and dropping his torch, uttering a series of profanities every time he tripped. At one point he leapt into the air to avoid

411

the attack of a wild animal that turned out to be a stray dog, more frightened even than he was.

The journey, normally a matter of five minutes, took a good half-hour and when finally they reached the factory, Potts, quite out of breath, sat down against the trunk of a tree and would not be moved.

The factory consisted of a large wooden warehouse with a couple of smaller rooms inside, which served as offices. The Dutch factory, by contrast, was an imposing brick building surrounded by a number of lesser ones, also of brick, and it had long been Phaulkon's ambition to upgrade the English factory to the level of its rival.

An Indian guard, armed with a musket, stood watch outside the door and barred the way. He stepped smartly aside as he recognized Phaulkon. With Potts now up and breathing heavily down his neck, Phaulkon inserted a large key into the lock and turned it. He was still considering how best to handle the situation. The books, he knew, were locked in Burnaby's room and though he had a key he had no intention of opening up. Not only were the books far from up to date, but part of the inventory in the storeroom, which consisted of goods amassed by both Burnaby and himself for private trading – and left there since before the Ligor expedition – would not even appear in them. He had planned to put the books in order after all the commotion surounding the Chinese ambassador's visit. Potts' arrival had come at a most inopportune moment. A few more days and . . .

'Where are the books?' demanded Potts, peering round a stack of crates with the aid of his torch. He seemed to have found a second wind.

'In there,' said Phaulkon, pointing to Burnaby's room.

Potts marched up and tried the door. 'It's locked,' he announced.

'Locked?' cried Phaulkon in surprise. 'I can't believe it.' He came up and tried the door himself. 'Damn, and I particularly asked Mr Burnaby to leave it open in case I needed to get anything out during his absence.'

'Why didn't he leave you the key?' asked Potts, suspiciously.

'He never parts with any of his keys,' said Phaulkon, 'but he did promise to leave this door open.'

412

Potts peered at him from behind his torch. 'Call the guard,' he ordered. 'We'll break it down.'

'Mr Potts, I beg you to reconsider. Mr Burnaby is expected back at any moment and locksmiths are hard to come by here. We need one room that closes securely.'

A knowing glint came into Potts' eyes. 'You heard me, Mr Phaulkon. Break it down.'

Phaulkon looked at him. This maniac would stop at nothing, he thought. Yet if the Persian expedition fails, I may still need the English. I'm damned if Potts sees the books and I'm damned if I prevent him from doing so. But of the two, the latter's best. Suspicion is better than certitude.

'I am afraid, Mr Potts, that in the light of Mr Burnaby's imminent return, I consider your request unreasonable. You may quote me in your report if you wish.'

'You are refusing me access?'

'I am refusing to break down a door in the middle of the night which will be difficult to repair, and which needs to be locked for security reasons.'

If Potts had been simmering before, he was visibly boiling now.

'You, a . . . a . . . an upstart Greek, are refusing me, Samuel Potts, senior auditor of the honourable English Company, access? You . . . a bloody foreigner!' he burst out.

'You are drunk, Mr Potts. I hope you won't forget to mention that in your report either. I certainly won't in mine.'

'*Your* report!' exploded Potts. 'Hah! Do you think anyone's going to read *your* report? You . . . a Greek, not even the chief factor here. Why, you bloated little fool . . .' He waved the flaming torch in front of Phaulkon's face.

The guard, hearing Potts' ravings, came running up in time to see him threaten Phaulkon with his torch. He jumped between them, facing Potts and glaring at him. 'Are you all right, master?' he asked Phaulkon in Siamese.

'Get this bloody native out of here,' screamed Potts, beside himself.

'You will go home and sober up, Mr Potts, before you do any damage here.' Phaulkon's voice was firm. 'And stop waving that torch around. This building is made of timber and the wooden crates are highly inflammable.'

413

Potts stood there like a man deranged. 'I dare you to have me removed,' he taunted. 'It's the cannon, isn't it? You don't want me to find the cannon. I know all about them, you see. Where are they?' He started looking around him wildly, peering behind each crate and waving his torch dangerously in the process. The flames brushed precariously against the wood. The guard turned to Phaulkon for guidance. 'I'll deal with this,' said Phaulkon in Siamese. He had to get that torch away from Potts.

'There are no cannon here, Mr Potts. Only highly inflammable crates.'

Potts ignored him, continuing to wave his torch about.

'Give me that torch,' ordered Phaulkon, holding out his hand.

Potts swung round. 'Don't you dare raise your voice at me, you little upstart. I'm the senior man here and I'll have your hide for that.'

Phaulkon started towards him, now barely able to restrain his rage. 'Just give me the torch, Mr Potts, and we'll break the door down as you requested.'

'Stay where you are!' raved Potts, moving the torch frantically from side to side. 'So now you're ready to obey orders, eh? Now that I'm on to the cannon, you're ready to break down the door. Ha!' He grinned insanely. 'It takes more than a junior clerk to fool old Samuel Potts. First we'll find those cannon.'

He retreated, feeling his way backwards with one hand so as not to lose sight of Phaulkon. He shot rapid glances to each side of him as he searched vainly for the cannon. Phaulkon followed him cautiously, preparing to lunge, waiting for a sufficient opening between the crates, which were filled with broadcloth. It would not do for Potts to drop the torch in the middle of them.

Like some cornered animal, the Englishman backed away, staring wild-eyed around him. By the time Phaulkon heard the noise of the guard tripping on a loose plank, it was too late. The Indian had circled round and was trying to sneak up on Potts from behind. When the wood snapped, Potts spun round, losing his balance at the same time. He fell backwards and the torch flew from his hand, landing in the midst of a stack of crates.

The bamboo ignited instantly and the flames spread hungrily through the profusion of dry timbers and merchandise. Ignoring Potts, Phaulkon and the guard dashed towards two earthenware water jars that stood on either side of the entrance. By the time they had dragged the heavy jars over to the flames and begun to scoop the water out with small bowls, the fire had turned into a conflagration. Their efforts scarcely caused the flames to pause.

Potts scrambled to his feet, staring at the flames like one possessed. Then he stumbled out of the building.

Within moments the fire had spread to the walls and roof, and parts of the structure had begun to collapse. Phaulkon hesitated for a moment in front of his office and then, seeing the flames engulf Burnaby's room next door, he ran for the exit, dragging the guard with him. Outside, people were beginning to converge from all directions. Those who arrived first stood watching in helpless fascination as the flames leapt ever higher, until with a roar, the roof caved in. Others, carrying jars of water, began to form a circle round the warehouse to prevent the fire from spreading to the neighbouring houses. But there was enough dust and earth around the warehouse to hinder its onward passage and the flames contented themselves with devouring the victim in hand.

Potts, much sobered, sat motionless against the trunk of a tree, his head buried in his hands.

'What happened?' several people shouted. Each time the question was asked, the guard, who was with Phaulkon, pointed to the figure of Potts by the tree. 'That man over there set fire to the place with his torch,' he told them.

Phaulkon dispatched the guard to the home of the Barcalon's assistant to report the fire. Then he saw two soldiers running up and making inquiries. The people all pointed to Potts. In a city where almost every structure was of wood, it was a criminal offence to be the cause of a fire even accidentally. As to deliberately starting a conflagration . . .

Phaulkon watched in silence as the soldiers arrested Potts and marched him away. The Englishman offered no resistance. Phaulkon took one last look at the charred remains of what had once been the honourable Company's Siam headquarters. In those flames he saw more than the factory burning. He saw his last bridge to the English burning with it. Madras would inevitably defer to Potts' version of events and if the factory were to be rebuilt at all, it would surely not be by Phaulkon and Burnaby, but by their successors, while they themselves faced court martial in Madras. The success of the Persian expedition was now more crucial than ever, he reflected ruefully.

'I understand full well your concern, Mr Faa. But we have laws in this country and these laws must be upheld. As I told you, it is a criminal offence to set fire to a building, whether accidental or not.' The Barcalon puckered his brow. 'The punishment is death. In some rare cases His Majesty may be gracious enough to pardon a subject whose life has otherwise been exemplary, and commute his sentence to life imprisonment. But never in the case of deliberate arson, Mr Faa, as I understand this case to be.'

The Barcalon paused and drew breath. He had not been feeling so well of late, his occasional bouts of asthma occurring more frequently. 'We live in wooden houses, Mr Faa. You can imagine what destruction would result if we did not strictly enforce these laws, or if we were to allow a policy of exceptions. Our subjects would grow more careless than they already are.' The young Siamese interpreter attached to the Dutch Company translated the Barcalon's words. He had just returned from Holland, one of a handful of students sent there to study under the auspices of the Gouverneur-Generaal in Batavia.

'And only His Majesty has the right to commute a sentence, you say?' asked the director of the VOC.

'That is correct, Mr Faa. Only His Majesty has the right of life and death over his subjects. Or over outsiders committing crimes in this country,' he added pointedly.

'But Your Excellency, in view of the fact that Mr Potts is a newcomer here and that the building in question was a foreign outpost, could not the rules be bent a little? Could he not, for instance, be asked to leave the country?'

It was essential, reflected the VOC chief, that this man Potts return to Madras to make his report. With a little luck it would lead to the expulsion of Phaulkon and even the closure of the English branch in Siam. He smiled ingratiatingly. 'We would, of course, be much in your debt, Your Excellency, and you could let us know if there was any way in which we could repay you.'

The Barcalon observed the Dutchman carefully as he listened to the translation. It was the second time this man had come to plead with him in as many days. He was clearly most anxious to get this Englishman out of prison. But why? Why would the

416

Dutch suddenly want to help the English? Who was this Mr Potts and what had he come to Ayudhya for? The key lay no doubt in the answers Phaulkon had given. When questioned about the incident, Phaulkon had replied that Potts was a senior Company official who was being sent round the various offices of the English Company on a routine check of the inventories. On account of the extreme heat, he had imbibed a little too much brandy and tripped over a piece of wood at the warehouse, accidentally dropping his torch. Phaulkon had apologized profusely on behalf of Mr Potts and the Company, and begged that owing to Potts' senior status with the Company and the recent renewal of friendship between the Siamese and English nations, he might be allowed to leave the country. The English Company would gladly indemnify the Siamese crown for any damage caused to the surrounding property.

But privately, Phaulkon had given quite a different explanation. Here, mused the Barcalon, was the crux of the matter. Phaulkon had told Sunida that this Mr Potts was the worst type of drunkard, the kind of farang whose deportment was an embarrassment to his nation and to Anglo-Siamese relations in general. He was furthermore a spy in the pay of the Dutch, the kind of low-life Englishman who would sell his services to the highest bidder. The Barcalon shuddered at the thought of the revelations that Phaulkon had then made to Sunida regarding Potts' utterances. In fact, all the Siamese who had been obliged to repeat the words, from Sunida to Sri the market vendor to Captain Somsak at the palace, had had to swallow hard before speaking. There was not one of them who had not invoked holy dispensation before uttering such blasphemy. Referring to His Majesty as the King of the Crocodiles, indeed! He himself, reflected the Barcalon nervously, had refused to reiterate the outrage to the Lord of Life, thus failing in his sworn duty to repeat every matter to His Majesty; even though withholding information from one's liege was a crime punishable by severe caning of the soles of the feet, even by death if the undisclosed information was in any way treasonous – which this undoubtedly was. Phaulkon himself had apparently been equally outraged when he had revealed to Sunida how Potts had got drunk and insulted the Siamese, calling His Majesty the King of the Crocodiles because his subjects were for ever crawling about on all fours before him like reptiles. The Barcalon tried to blank out

417

the memory. According to Sunida, Phaulkon had been so shocked by the description that he had challenged Potts to take back his words but Potts had only shouted insults back at him. And then, as he had been paid by the Dutch to do, he had set fire to the warehouse, pretending to trip over a piece of wood to make it look like an accident. The Dutch, it seemed, had conveniently omitted to inform Potts, a newcomer to the country, of the laws against arson and had assured him that they would have no trouble obtaining his release. The warehouse guard who had been present throughout had confirmed Phaulkon's story, describing how a great argument had broken out between the two farangs.

The Barcalon forced himself to remain calm and to focus on the issue at hand. The Dutchman was waiting for an answer concerning the release of Potts. But it would never happen, not while he was Barcalon, he swore to himself.

'Mr Faa, I must say that you Dutchmen intrigue me. Only the other day you were asking me to punish the English for stealing your cannon and arming the rebels at Pattani, and today you are asking me to release one of their officials who has just set fire to a building. Forgive me if the Siamese mind is ill equipped to grapple with such logic.' He inclined his head politely.

Faa was in a predicament. It was true that he had reviled all the English and now he was asking for mercy for one of them. But it was essential that Potts reach Madras to make his report. There might never be such an opportunity again. He would undoubtedly incriminate Phaulkon and point to the absence of all the English factors from their posts. Burnaby and Phaulkon would be put on trial and perhaps even hung, and the publicity would be such – he would personally guarantee it – that it was doubtful the English would have the gall to reopen in Ayudhya again. He would be rid of them once and for all and when he had made his role known, his promotion could be impressive. He must somehow obtain Potts' release, even if it meant applying a little pressure on the Siamese . . .

'Your Excellency, Potts is innocent. He has been manipulated by the English. I am prepared to provide a Dutch hostage to replace him until I can prove his innocence.'

The Barcalon observed him quietly.

'You mentioned the very senior rank of this Mr Potts, I

believe. I know of no Dutchman in Ayudhya of a similar rank, unless, of course, Mr Faa . . .' He stared pointedly at the chief of the VOC, a slight smile playing on his lips.

Arnout Faa, normally a composed man, was beginning to feel distinctly uneasy. Damn it, he needed this man Potts on a boat to Madras and not on display in the public square with a board round his neck, as he now was. The dreaded 'cangue', as the Portuguese had named it, rested like a wooden noose round the prisoner's neck, causing his eyes to bulge and his breath to grow short. It was the ultimate public humiliation and the farang Potts had attracted the largest crowd ever seen in the square outside the prisons.

'Your Excellency, in honour of the many years of friendship and co-operation between our two nations, I must humbly ask you to release this man.'

'Mr Faa, though I honour that friendship more than any man, and though I realize that your ardour to have this man released must have reasons beyond my grasp, I repeat that he stands accused of a serious crime in our country and that we cannot create a precedent by sending him unpunished into exile.'

'Your Excellency, I have tried to express the strength of my convictions to you.'

'And I mine to you, Mr Faa.'

Arnout Faa's tone hardened. 'You leave me no choice then but to request my superior, the Gouverneur-Generaal himself, to look into the treaty of 1664 and perhaps delete certain sections which refer to . . . our . . . special protection.'

'Coincidentally, Mr Faa,' replied the Barcalon impassively, 'it has been our intent to bring this treaty to your attention for some time. I am indeed grateful to you for hastening the process. We feel that a number of its clauses may now be obsolete and I must say that in that respect, we have found the English most eager to offer suggestions.'

'Very well, Your Excellency,' said the director icily. 'You will be hearing from us in due course.' He rose to leave.

'It is always a pleasure, Mr Faa.' The Barcalon smiled cordially. Privately, he knew there was not a moment to lose. In the Potts affair, Constantine Phaulkon had proved his mettle: both his talent for diplomacy and his loyalty to Siam. He had pleaded publicly for Potts' release in order to salvage the entente between

419

England and Siam while privately he had challenged Potts for daring to insult the Siamese monarchy. His Majesty himself had concurred with that view. Phaulkon's plans for the defence of Siam would now have to be taken seriously and possibly implemented – without delay.

Thirty

It was on the following Monday that the Barcalon informed Phaulkon that His Majesty the King had graciously summoned him to an audience. Phaulkon was speechless. It was the moment he had dreamed of. The Greek cabin boy ushered into the King of Siam's presence! Yet though he had longed for this moment, and imagined it in a thousand different ways, now that it was at hand, he felt totally unprepared. Apprehension gnawed at his very entrails.

Would this potentate, he wondered, whose power of life and death over millions of his subjects was absolute, be gentle or curt, reasonable or intolerant? Would he allow Phaulkon to speak or would he expect him to listen in silence and subservience? Should Phaulkon express an opinion, or should no hint of contradiction appear to challenge His Majesty's undisputed authority? So little was known about the sovereign that he was alternately described as tall and short, courteous and irritable, magnanimous and petty. No outsider, not even his own courtiers, had ever gazed upon his face; negotiations to allow the visiting French Bishop of Heliopolis – exceptionally – to be seated in His Majesty's presence had alone dragged on for months before permission had eventually been granted. News of the first person to remain upright in His Majesty's presence had sent shockwaves through the Siamese establishment.

On the few occasions when His Majesty left the palace to attend a grand ceremony, presenting alms and robes to the monks or striking the waters of the Menam to command the rains to cease, he was accompanied by a retinue of twenty thousand men. His brightly clad Moorish horseguards led the way in single file, followed by his mandarins, prostrate and silent on their bejewelled elephants, while he himself, ensconced in his golden howdah sprinkled with precious stones, rode on the finest elephant in the centre of the procession. In his hand he held a golden crook to guide the beast, which was said to be so intelligent that it lowered itself of its own accord whenever it saw

421

His Majesty approaching. Prostrate across its voluminous buttocks lay a senior mandarin of short stature who awaited His
Majesty's orders to take over direction of the royal beast, should
the Lord of Life tire of doing so himself. His lesser courtiers and
his legions of slaves strode with lowered eyes in front and behind
their liege, carrying his arms, his betel boxes and his golden
parasols with their thick silver handles; while finally the common
people, forbidden even from a distance to gaze upon the person
of the King, or to utter a sound as he passed, remained
respectfully inside their houses behind closed shutters. Only once
annually was the common populace allowed out in the presence
of their King, on the most colourful ceremony of the year when
thousands of little boats lined the river banks to watch the royal
barge, with one hundred and twenty chanting oarsmen clad in
crimson caps and matching knee pads, streak to victory over its
competitors in the boat race.

Yet however conflicting the rumours surrounding His Majesty
of Siam, Phaulkon had deduced certain likelihoods. The sovereign was surely open-minded, or he would never have allowed so
many religions to be practised freely in his country and, yet more
startling, have permitted their missionaries the freedom to convert his subjects. He smiled. Had the King of Siam fathomed a
truth that had eluded his illustrious brethren in the West, that
the more you forbade a creed, the more you aroused interest in
it? How curious that Siam, where Christian priests could prose-
lytize at will, had rendered so few Christian converts.

At least one side of the King's nature must be generous and
magnanimous, reflected Phaulkon, or he would never have made
gifts of land and money to these foreign creeds that sought to
impose their will upon his people.

Phaulkon rose early on the Wednesday morning of the summons.
The audience was scheduled for eight o'clock. He had been too
excited to sleep, tossing and turning through the night, both
longing for and dreading the dawn. Sunida had stayed awake
with him, comforting him, massaging him, serving as his sounding
board and answering his endless questions as best she could. She
longed to tell him how noble and gracious His Majesty was, but
how could she reveal that she had ever met him? She was
strangely gratified to see that even he, her proud and confident

422

lover, was awed by the thought of coming into the serene presence of the Lord of Life, just as she had been. For that was how it should be.

Phaulkon had agonized over what to wear, debating between European and Siamese clothing, reverting to the one almost as soon as he had decided on the other.

'My Lord, you are worse than a woman,' Sunida had said, teasing him. But uncharacteristically, he had turned on her, and she had kept silent from then on, only answering his questions.

His servants and slaves, too, had been wary of his unusual petulance and had been up most of the night catering to his every need. Never had they seen the master in such a state of nerves; yet they understood, aware of the supreme honour that had befallen him. Twice already he had sent his black breeches back to have a barely visible piece of fluff removed from them and poor Tip had scoured every inch of the material in search of the slightest blemish. His white lace coat had been washed again until the entire household had sworn it glittered like gold.

For he had finally decided on European clothes. Though he was anxious to demonstrate how close he felt to the Siamese and their ways, he thought it might be pretentious for a farang to appear in front of the monarch in Siamese dress. Better to appear in the costume of a farang and let his mastery of the Siamese language and his observance of their etiquette create that much more of an impact.

He had doused himself for a good half-hour and shaved his beard for as long again, ensuring that no single hair came to disrupt the smoothness of the surface. The Siamese had little or no facial hair and he would not display any himself.

Finally, after combing his hair until he deemed it perfectly in place, while Sunida and the staff suppressed their smiles, he declared himself ready and dismissed his household, seeking a few last moments alone.

He sat cross-legged in a corner of the living room and gazed out into the garden. His greatest concern was that the royal audience might be so formal as to exclude any possibility of expressing his views; if he were to do so unsolicited, it might seem out of place or even positively rude. Siamese etiquette was very rigid in all matters, especially where royalty was concerned, and the strict adherence to its forms was synonymous with good manners.

From all he had heard, royal audiences were stylized affairs conducted in set phrases and speech forms; any deviation from the pattern would be frowned upon. However desperate to converse with His Majesty, he certainly did not want to appear uncouth. He had better restrict himself to making only an impression of good manners, he decided. He managed a smile. His command of the royal tongue alone, with its complex ritual, should dumbfound the assembled courtiers. He had kept that little secret up his sleeve all the time, waiting for the moment. There were bound to be other courtiers present, he reflected, especially at a first audience, and he wondered now just how many mandarins would be there. How could he anyway afford to expound his views in front of an assembly that might include Moorish mandarins and their allies already antagonistic to him? Then it occurred to him that His Majesty might not even be able to address him; for etiquette did not permit the ruler to speak directly to anyone he had not first ennobled, a mere commoner. Perhaps an exception would be made in the case of a farang.

On the other hand, might not His Majesty be just as curious about him and wish to delve below the surface of ceremonial formality? After all, this farang had single-handedly exposed the fraudulent practices of the Moors and demonstrated his ability to lay on a banquet more lavish and less costly than any before it. In the Potts affair, had he not further demonstrated his loyalty to Siam by showing outrage at the insult to its ruler? Phaulkon smiled. He was pleased with himself for that little manoeuvre. Through Sunida he had both shown his loyalty to the Siamese crown and ensured the incarceration of the man who would otherwise be on his way to Madras to incriminate him. At least he had gained time – time for the Persian enterprise to bear fruit. If it did, he might be in a position to request a permanent place in the service of Siam. Potts and the English could then jump in the lake. On the other hand, if the Persian expedition failed, he could well be out of favour with the Siamese and unprotected by them at a time when the English would be demanding his extradition to Madras to face trial. Who would he turn to then?

In a few moments he would be prostrate before the man who could seal his fate, the absolute ruler who could make decisions instantly, without reference to anyone. He shuddered at the thought, and instinctively he knew that this audience would be a turning point in his life.

'A messenger from His Excellency the Pra Klang awaits outside, my Lord,' said Sunida timidly, reluctant to break in on his thoughts.

Phaulkon looked up. It seemed almost a relief that it would soon be over. He saw the proud smile on Sunida's face and his heart melted. How difficult he must have been to live with these past few hours. Yet he knew Sunida understood the significance of this day, for he had talked with her so often about his plans and dreams. Indeed, his love for Siam was now inextricably linked with his adoration of her.

He rose and held her tightly to him, inhaling her deeply. 'I love you, Sunida.'

'And I you, my Lord. I am so proud of you.'

She adjusted his collar and smoothed the front of his coat. 'And I know His Majesty will be too.' Gracefully she walked to the door and sank to her knees next to Sorn, Tip and the three slaves. The six of them lay prostrate and motionless as the master descended the steps into the garden where the Barcalon's messenger awaited. It was an infinitely proud moment for them all.

There was still an early-morning freshness in the air as Phaulkon, following behind the Barcalon and his usual retinue of slaves, arrived before the massive gates of the palace, which were always kept shut. Before these hallowed portals every passing rider was required to dismount and show his reverence, and every pedestrian must shut his parasol and incline himself towards the lofty palace spires that loomed majestically above the palace walls. All passers-by knelt a while in reverence here, bowing their heads before proceeding on their way.

Phaulkon's heart pounded as a slave knocked on the massive wooden gate and a guard within inquired after the rank and business of the visitors. On being informed of their identity, the guard immediately advised the Oc-Meuang, the first officer of the forecourt, of the arrival of His Exellency the Pra Klang, with his retinue. Without the Oc-Meuang's permission no one could enter or leave the palace.

One panel of the huge wooden gate creaked open and the

Oc-Meuang, dressed in a collarless red tunic, with matching knee pads and gold bracelets about his arms, emerged and wai'd to the Barcalon. He glanced cursorily at the retinue of slaves and then fixed his gaze on Phaulkon. Approaching him, he felt his body for arms and then smelled his breath for any sign of alcohol. For no armed or drunken man was allowed within the palace walls.

The Oc-Meuang pronounced himself satisfied and the party was ushered through to a first courtyard, covered in grass and graced by a beautiful fountain, and on to a broad terrace surrounded by a low-canopied brick wall. Here the King's guard, 600-strong and known as the Red Arms, squatted on their haunches, no man being allowed to stand upright in the palace except when walking, even in His Majesty's absence. The Red Arms were unarmed except on ceremonial occasions, and their office, much prized, was hereditary. They were skilled rowers, riders and fighters.

The party now passed through shady gardens overhung by trees and dotted with gurgling fountains and small ponds where colourful fish abounded. Sculpted hedges in the forms of animals marked the perimeters and bougainvillaea vines crept up the surrounding walls in an explosion of brilliant colour.

The palace compound, as Phaulkon had discovered through meticulous inquiry, consisted of a walled city, fourteen acres in area, a city within a city, divided into outer and inner sections. In the outer sections, consisting of gardens, stables, courtyards, terraces and audience halls, the King received and entertained visitors and held council with his ministers and mandarins. The inner section, strictly out of bounds to all but a few – eunuchs, pages, royal physicians and an occasional monk – housed the voluminous royal chambers and the quarters of the harem. Even the Barcalon was forbidden access. Little was known about the configuration of the inner sanctum, but rumour had it that a labyrinth of corridors connected several royal apartments which His Majesty used at undisclosed times to foil any attempts at assassination or betrayal.

Emerging from a last spacious courtyard where several mandarins of the third to fifth grades lay prostrate in the hope of receiving their King's summons, the visitors now arrived before a series of steps that led up to the panelled audience chamber

426

where His Majesty had received the ambassador from China. Phaulkon had never been beyond this furthest courtyard where the banquet had taken place. In the distance stretched seven or eight tiers of gently curving roofs, merging into each other in ever-ascending order of height, their golden yellow tiles glistening in the sunlight. This, reflected Phaulkon with a tremor, was the Inner Palace, that den of intrigue where the ascending roofs culminated in the royal apartments.

At the foot of the steps the escort of slaves prostrated itself and would go no further. The Barcalon lowered himself on hands and knees and beckoned Phaulkon to follow. They crawled up the steps one behind the other and emerged at the entrance of a beautiful wood-panelled audience chamber, glittering with gold leaf and lacquer. Here in precise order of rank the privileged mandarins of the first and second grades were assembled, prostrate and silent. Glancing surreptitiously around him as they entered the great hall, Phaulkon was struck by the aura of majesty that surrounded the place and he was suddenly overcome by a sense of his own insignificance. The walls around him were varnished in red lacquer, interspersed with strips of gold leaf, and the floors were covered from wall to wall in the finest Persian carpets.

The Barcalon and Phaulkon prostrated themselves on knees and elbows in the direction of an upper balcony across which a curtain was drawn and over which hung several tiers of golden parasols, the symbol of divine royalty.

They remained thus supine for some moments and Phaulkon could feel the rows of eyes observing him furtively. Was His Majesty going to address him personally before all these dignitaries? he wondered. They were all wearing their conical hats and the special printed panungs that His Majesty had given them, which they were only allowed to wear in his presence. Their betel boxes and ornaments, symbols of their office, lay by their sides.

Suddenly a trumpet sounded and drums rolled. Phaulkon's heart beat faster. Not daring to look up, he heard the noise of the curtain being drawn aside and the voice of the master of ceremonies intoning: 'Since the divine word has seen fit to descend upon the King's slave, who is but filth and dust, that person has the temerity to introduce His Majesty's slave, Kosatanat Forcon.'

427

Phaulkon raised himself on his knees and touched his forehead to the ground three times in the direction of the upper balcony, taking care never to look up. Then he shuffled forward three paces as the Barcalon had instructed him, to enable His Majesty to distinguish the person of the petitioner. Here he made three similar bows and, trembling inside, uttered his first words to the Lord of Life.

'Mighty Lord and Master of Life, your slave craves permission to speak. He implores Your Majesty to suffer his unclean and defiled voice to reach the doors of your divine ears.' The hush that followed was awesome.

'We are pleased to receive you, Mr Forcon,' said the pleasant, courteous, almost reassuring voice from above. 'Our Pra Klang has spoken well of you. Are you comfortable in our kingdom?'

'High and Mighty Lord of me, thy slave, I desire to take thy royal word and put it on my brain and on the top of my head,' continued Phaulkon in the royal ritual. 'This speck of dust beneath the sole of Your Majesty's foot is comfortable and most conscious of the honour of being received into the divine presence.' Phaulkon could sense the astonishment which greeted his further address in the royal tongue. It was some moments before the King spoke again.

'We understand you are a man of many skills, Mr Forcon. We can see for ourselves that your linguistic ability is no mere rumour. We congratulate you on the mastery of our language which we know, from past efforts, does not come easily to outsiders, particularly the Western races. Our minister has praised your skill with figures and we are ourselves keen to learn something of you at first hand. What brings you to our kingdom, and what do you hope to accomplish here?'

Now was the moment to offer his services and assure his loyalty to the Siamese crown, the moment he had dreamed of for so long.

'Mighty Lord and Master, I, a hair of your head, wish only to serve this great nation in whichever way Your Majesty sees fit to command me. The Lord of Life, in his wisdom, has appointed people of other creeds and nations to serve him in government, and this worthless slave begs only the chance to do likewise.'

'We hold no prejudice against race or religion,' replied the King. 'We are all children of the same God. He who serves us

428

well, whatever his origins, will be rewarded according to his merits. We are much gratified by your efforts thus far and distressed to discover that some have not served us so well.'

His Majesty paused and Phaulkon wondered how many of the mandarins assembled might be Moors. 'You must take care, however, as there may be ill feeling towards you on the part of those who have failed in their duty.'

Phaulkon felt instinctively drawn to this monarch. His gracious tone, and his apparent concern, aroused in Phaulkon a desire to throw himself at the mercy of this all-powerful ruler, while at the same time he felt confident he could be of value to him. 'August Lord and Master of Life,' he replied, 'I, who am but filth and dust, do gratefully receive your advice and do place it respectfully on my head.'

'In recognition of your services, Mr Forcon,' intoned the monarch loftily, 'we are pleased to elevate you to the rank of the mandarinate, third class, and we hereby confer upon you the title of Luang Vichaiyen, by which name you will henceforth be known. You will be made Secretary General of the Department of Foreign Trade, responsible to the Pra Klang alone. You will be presented with a silver betel box adorned with one diamond, and with an official court costume, a brocade vest and a conical hat round which you are authorized to place one ring.'

Phaulkon felt the room swim before him, and fearful that he might awaken from some rapturous dream, he dug his nails into his clasped fingers. His Majesty had seen fit to name him Vichaiyen, or 'knowledge of science', and the title of Luang denoted a Lord of the third rank. He was now the Lord of Knowledge! A wave of euphoria swept over him more powerful than anything he had known. In a voice filled with emotion, he poured forth his gratitude to this man who had opened the doors of a new life to him, and honoured him with his trust.

'August Lord, by the power of the dust beneath your feet which covers my head I pledge to work tirelessly for the glory of Siam and to justify the great trust Your Majesty has placed in this your unworthy slave.'

'Vichaiyen, we note your words and are gratified,' replied the King, addressing him by his new name. A slave crawled up to Phaulkon and handed him his betel box, his conical hat, and a beautiful red vest with a brocade of gold.

Phaulkon immediately placed them on his head one after the other, to denote the high esteem in which he held these royal gifts, and then prostrated himself three times as he had done on entering.

'And now, Vichaiyen, you may retire. We will speak with our Pra Klang and our other mandarins alone.'

The audience was over. He had been promoted before the highest mandarins of the court, those of the first and second grades, and he could not help wondering how they felt about this singular honour. Out of the corner of his eye he noticed a scribe taking down every word of the proceedings. They were being recorded for posterity.

Raising himself one last time on his knees and touching his forehead three times to the ground in the direction of the monarch, Luang Vichaiyen crawled reverently backwards without ever looking up or turning his back on His Majesty. Only when he was outside the panelled audience chamber and had crawled down the steps to the courtyard below, did he rise to his feet, and it seemed to him then that he was ten feet tall. His spirits soared and he walked on air. There was no stopping him now, he thought. He placed the conical hat on his head. This was surely the greatest moment of his life. Elevated to the mandarinate, third class! There were five ranks in the mandarinate and he had passed over the lower two ranks completely. He would have to check how many dignity marks went with his new position, but it was surely a few thousand. He was one of the elite now. No European in Siam had ever held such an exalted position, and he was sure to be involved in projects in which the King had a direct interest. If he performed well, the King would be aware of it, and there was no reason why, with extreme diligence, he could not be elevated to the mandarinate second class, and eventually even first class! With power would come riches; in the Orient every official of high rank enriched himself as a matter of course. It was an old tradition, taken for granted. But he must be sure to serve his sovereign's interests well, not just for the wealth and power he might accumulate, or the fulfilment of the ambitions that consumed him, but also because he felt strangely drawn to this ruler. There was something refined and noble about him that went beyond the mere trappings of

430

royalty. With Phaulkon's Western skills and the King's far-sighted attitude, Siam could hold its own against any invader.

As Secretary-General of the Department of Foreign Trade, Phaulkon could really get a grasp on the country's revenues. Every commercial transaction would be brought to his attention. It was a giant step towards the realization of his most ambitious goal.

For the first time he could admit openly to his aspirations now, suddenly they no longer seemed so far-fetched, no longer the impossible dreams that he had had to hide from the world for fear of ridicule. He had nurtured such vague dreams from his earliest days in Siam, and now they were taking shape. He knew trade as well as any man, he was fluent in the major trading languages, he had a ship on its way to Persia that could revolutionize the way of Siamese thinking, he had gained the confidence of the current Barcalon, and now he had even met the King. What was there to stop him? Why should *he* not become Barcalon one day? Barcalon of Siam! He recalled the words, so long ago, of that toothless crone in the smoke-filled, crowded tavern of his Greek island home. 'This lad will one day be a potentate in a distant land . . .'

Phaulkon had been walking slowly, lost in thought, through the maze of gardens and courtyards. He had not even noticed the whispering around him, the furtive glances cast in his direction or even the guard who had been quietly shadowing him at a respectful distance. As he emerged into the final courtyard, Phaulkon was distracted by an excited babble of voices. Catching sight of his conical hat, a group of courtiers prostrated themselves on the ground before him. The full force of his promotion suddenly came home to him. He was now a titled nobleman of the court of Siam.

Thirty-one

Aarnout Faa checked the document in his pocket one last time and ordered the boatmen to wait for him. He climbed the river bank and headed resolutely down the path that led towards the public prisons. He had never visited this quarter of town before but he knew that they were located somewhere on the far side of the evening market. No Dutchman had been imprisoned there during his tenancy as director, he reflected with some satisfaction, though in former times a handful of Dutchmen had been known to languish there, almost always as a result of drinking, he mused. There was that fool Seegfeld who for a bet had stroked the head of a passing monk. His story was repeated as a warning to every newcomer to Siam. The man had apparently been almost too drunk to stand. Though he had won his stupid bet he had paid dearly for it. He had had a sharp sword dropped several times from an ever-increasing height on to the crown of his head until it was sliced almost to the bone; he had also left a festering wound in Siamese-Dutch relations, a wound that had taken years to heal. There were certain beliefs that the Siamese held to be inviolable and the sanctity of the monkhood was one of them. The saffron-robed monks were in fact the only people not required to prostrate themselves before the King.

It had taken Aarnout Faa several visits to the Barcalon to make any kind of progress in the case of Samuel Potts, and though the First Minister had steadfastly refused to listen to any pleas for his release, his persistence had finally been rewarded by a pass to visit him in confinement. He needed Potts' signature urgently on this document. The *Kurfendam* was already two days late departing for Batavia. Faa had held up the vessel while he frantically sought permission to visit the prisoner. The director was a punctual man and every minute of the ship's delay had been an hour of anguish for him.

He strode past the curved wooden roof of the marketplace now and turned the corner into an open square. He stood still. There in front of him a large crowd was gathered to ogle the

432

unusual sight of a farang prisoner. Potts' head was enclosed in what was akin to two rungs of a ladder supported by heavy beams at either end, which prevented any movement of the head and caused extreme discomfort to the victim. There was no necessity to incarcerate such a prisoner or guard him. He was free to move around, for all the good it would do him. Potts' bloodshot eyes registered blank despair, as if the will to struggle had gone out of them. Could this be the same man who less than a week ago had strode confidently into his office? The director shuddered involuntarily as he approached the prisoner.

'Mr Potts, I am most grieved to see you in this condition,' he began with genuine sympathy, 'and I want you to know that, short of a declaration of war, I am doing everything in my power to obtain your release. It seems that the crime you have been wrongly accused of is one which is taken very seriously by the Siamese authorities. They are for the moment hesitant to create a precedent by releasing you.'

Samuel Potts looked blank, staring wearily in front of him. He showed no signs of having heard the Dutchman's words or indeed of having noticed his presence.

'Mr Potts?' There was no response. 'Mr Potts?' repeated Aarnout Faa louder. Potts' eyes shifted slightly in the direction of the sound, then focused vaguely on the speaker. 'Mr Potts, can you hear me?' A distant look of recognition came into Potts' eyes. His lips moved vaguely but no sound emerged. How was a man in his condition going to sign any document? wondered Faa anxiously. His arms might be free but was he even fully conscious?

'How . . . how kind of you to . . . to visit me.' The words emerged haltingly and unexpectedly from the parched lips. Potts' voice was hoarse and the effort of speaking was plain from the agony in his eyes. His head, only sparsely covered by his thinning hair, had erupted in nasty blotches where the tropical sun had beaten down mercilessly on it. A sudden feeling of revulsion at Siamese brutality swept over Faa. He removed his hat and placed it gently on Potts' head. There was a murmur of disapproval from the gaping crowd. Of course, thought Faa, the head again, the sacred extremity of the body. It should never be touched by another person, not even by someone else's hat. He ignored the rising murmur. It was too late to do anything about it now anyway.

433

'Now listen, Mr Potts, we're going to see to it that you're released, do you hear me?' The eyes blinked vaguely in acknowledgement. Faa noticed that the lids, too, were badly sunburned. It was disgraceful. He would speak to the Barcalon about it. Were the Siamese not aware that European skins were more sensitive than theirs? They could not take prolonged periods of exposure, least of all to the harsh sun of the tropics. He would demand emphatically that this man at least be kept indoors.

'Mr Potts, I have drawn up a document describing the events leading up to your unfortunate incarceration. I have explained how on your arrival here you found all the English factors absent and how, when you finally met up with Mr Phaulkon and demanded to examine the Company's books, he set fire to the factory to destroy the evidence of his illegal activities. Do you follow me?'

A vague flicker of understanding again crossed Potts' eyes.

'Mr Potts, it is essential that I have your signature on this document, confirming that the contents are correct. Do you wish me to read it to you?'

Potts lowered his eyelids, as close to a negative as he could achieve.

'Thank you, Mr Potts. You may rest assured that the contents are exactly as I say they are. I have a ship waiting to leave for Batavia just as soon as I take this document on board with your signature. Allow me to help you?'

Faa placed a quill in Potts' hand but there was no strength in the fingers and it fell to the ground. It took five more attempts before Potts finally managed to squiggle something vaguely resembling his name on the document. The effort drained him.

'In my accompanying letter to the document, I have requested His Excellency the Gouverneur-Generaal to send two express dispatches immediately. One to the Barcalon here, demanding your urgent release in the name of continuing friendship between Siam and Holland, and another to the English Company in Madras. Between the two of them we will obtain your release, Mr Potts, I can assure you. So don't despair. And in the meantime I will insist that the Barcalon improve the conditions of your confinement. This man Phaulkon will pay for his crime.'

For a moment Potts' eyes showed more emotion than they had

434

throughout the interview. A look of intense hatred came into them at the mention of Phaulkon's name.

'What's the matter, Joop? You look as if you've just seen a ghost.' Arnout Faa had walked into his office, greatly relieved that his letter was now safely on board the *Kurfendam*. She would be sailing at any moment.

'It's worse than that, sir,' replied van Risling. He looked dolefully across at his boss. 'That swine Phaulkon's been made a mandarin,' he blurted.

'What?' The colour drained from Arnout Faa's face. Van Risling was not usually prone to joking, least of all in matters of this kind. 'Who told you that?' he asked, trying to keep the panic from his voice.

'Cheng, the interpreter. He says the whole town is talking about it.' Van Risling swallowed. 'And there is more, sir. He has apparently been made Secretary General of the Ministry of Trade, second only to the Barcalon.'

Faa was silent for a moment but his expression said everything.

'Perhaps it's just a rumour,' he ventured with false cheer, not really believing his own words.

'That's what I thought too, at first, sir. But I had it checked again and again during your absence. It really is true. What do you think that will mean for us?'

Aarnout Faa's mind was racing. He only vaguely heard Van Risling's question. He had to get another letter off. Would he still be in time to catch the *Kurfendam*? He scribbled a note in Dutch. 'Here, Joop. Have this sent by messenger to Captain Niederbeck of the *Kurfendam*. It must reach him before the ship leaves. He should delay his departure by one more hour. I need time to think.'

But Aarnout Faa already knew what he was going to do. He sat behind his desk and pulled out a stack of stationery from the centre drawer. Then he paused, the end of his quill jiggling nervously against his teeth. The argument had to be forceful and the words just right. It was a disgrace that after eighty years of friendship and co-operation between Holland and Siam, a junior member of the upstart English Company, who trafficked in stolen Dutch arms, should be elevated to the mandarinate, to the most senior position in the Ministry of Trade after the Barcalon, what

435

was more. It was a deliberate slap in the face to Holland, tantamount to an unofficial declaration of war. The Dutch government would have to retaliate, or they would never again be taken seriously. He would suggest an ultimatum for the immediate release of Potts, which he now felt sure the Siamese would refuse. He would stress its importance to Holland as an act of good will. The conditions of Potts' incarceration were demeaning to farangs in general and could be seen as an insult and a threat to the trading community. Failing Potts' release there would be grounds for a confrontation. A dozen warships should show who was in command. Perhaps, he would suggest respectfully to the Gouverneur-Generaal, it was the excuse they had been waiting for. With Siam in Dutch hands, the last piece of the south-east Asian puzzle would be in place. The closest English force was in Madras and the whole thing would be over before they even woke up to the news.

Faa sat thinking a while longer. Then he started putting it all down on paper. When he had finished he reread the letter carefully, sealed it, marked it 'top secret' and summoned Pieter. He was the most reliable and efficient of his staff, a promising young lad – half Dutch to boot.

'Here, Pieter, take this dispatch immediately to the *Kurfendam*. Hand it to no one but the captain. It is highly confidential. That is why I am entrusting it to you.'

'Thank you, sir,' said Pieter bowing and running off.

Arnout Faa looked through the window at the shimmering spires that rose above the great wall surrounding the King's palace. It occurred to him that he would build a similar wall round the Dutch compound. The plaque would read 'Erected in July 1680 by His Excellency Aarnout Faa, Governor.' For who would be a more likely choice for Governor than he? Governor of the new Dutch territories of Siam. He very much hoped the Gouverneur-Generaal in Batavia would see things his way.

'Is His Excellency the Oc-Luang in?' asked Ivatt, beaming broadly. It was one of the words he had learned at the palace that day. 'The farang has been made an Oc-Luang,' the children had shouted delightedly.

He was standing at the gate of Phaulkon's house catching his breath. He was highly excited. The news he had just heard was

436

hard to believe and he was still not certain that he had understood it correctly. He had spent the last two days at the palace doing somersaults and cartwheels and pulling the usual dove out of a coconut shell to the ecstatic shouts of the royal children. It was certainly a novel experience performing in front of one hundred and thirty-eight royally adopted children from all parts of the country. Though he was really a trapeze artist by training, and had learned only one or two conjuring tricks from the theatre magician, the children never seemed to have enough of his limited repertoire. His Siamese vocabulary was expanding fast and the latest words he had learned were '*Eek klang nung, eek klang nung!*' – 'One more time, one more time!' Every day he pointed to ten new objects and the royal children all shouted the Siamese word at once.

But Phaulkon a mandarin? Could it really be true? He giggled impishly. Supposing he had got his Siamese tones mixed up and Phaulkon had been sent to prison instead of being made a mandarin? Where was his lordship, anyway? He hovered impatiently about the gate. Why was the servant taking so long? What a strange country, he reflected. If the royal household ordered him to perform, that was the end of the matter. Their word was law. It did not matter that he was supposed to be employed in the factory of a foreign government. He wondered whether Samuel Potts had been told, upon inquiry, that Thomas Ivatt was unfortunately busy doing handstands at the palace. Phaulkon had sent him a note about Potts' arrival but when he had gone to Phaulkon's house both he and Potts had been absent. Then he had heard rumours about an accident at the factory and he was anxious to ask Phaulkon about it.

He heard muffled giggles now at the top of the steps. The servant was repeating his quip about the Oc-Luang to someone behind the doorway. The figure emerged to inspect him. Sunida! She was looking more radiant than ever. She wai'd to him, smiling brightly and beckoning him to come in. That rogue, Phaulkon, thought Ivatt. How had he managed to lure this enchantress to his den? He was desperately trying to recall the phrase for 'what are you doing here' when Sunida said, giggling all over again: 'His Excellency the Oc-Luang is in his living room. He has been looking for you everywhere.' Ivatt was

437

pleased with his progress. He had understood the first part of the sentence. Sunida ushered him in.

'Thomas!' said Phaulkon rising and embracing him. 'Where have you been? I have sent everywhere to look for you.'

'I have been at the palace these last days, my Lord. It was I who recommended you for the peerage. But tell me quickly,' he asked excitedly, 'is it really true that you are a mandarin?'

'I'm afraid so.'

'What do you mean, afraid? Why, it's brilliant. The possibilities are only just beginning to unfold. Can I obtain credit in the shops by using your name?'

Phaulkon laughed. 'We may well need it. No salary or income comes with the title, you know. Just a pile of honours. Especially the right to serve His Majesty directly and to earn the unbounding respect of the common people. Which includes you, Thomas.'

Thomas pretended to prostrate himself. 'Mighty Lord, I receive your orders. But what do the mandarins live on then?' he asked, a little disappointed.

'Status, money from petitions, gifts from the King, and corruption.'

Ivatt appeared relieved. 'That sounds right up your alley, Constant. You know, when I was a boy, my father was the village schoolmaster. We were poor but we had a lot of books. Every time he put a book down he used to say: "It's a rum world, my boy, a rum world out there, because it's the rogues who have all the luck." And to think that he had never even met you!'

'You stay by me, Thomas. You'll have all the wealth your father never had, I promise you. If all goes well, the Ivatts will never be poor again. I'm sending you to Mergui with an escort in a day or two. Burnaby and White should be back there within a month. You'll need time to get acclimatized.'

'I don't know if the palace will release me, Constant. I am very much in demand. But tell me,' he asked eagerly, 'what is Sunida doing here? Polishing your betel box?'

Phaulkon laughed. 'Among other things. Do you approve?'

'I think she's the most beautiful creature in the world. If I weren't so tied up at the palace myself . . .'

'You'll be seeing more of her, Thomas, don't worry. She's here permanently.'

'The mandarin's consort, eh? Will there be others?'

438

'Perhaps, but that's none of your business. Your business is to prepare for Mergui. Your contact down there will be Father Francisco, a Portuguese priest. You'll find him at the Catholic mission. He was a great friend of Captain Alvarez, God rest his soul. Mention Alvarez's name to the Father, as well as mine. I have never met him, but he'll know who I am. He will help you locate a small junk to pick up White's crew when the time comes. Have the junk ready and waiting. And promise the Father a handsome gift from the Persian profits. Alvarez told me Dom Francisco is always looking for money to do up his little church.'

'What happened at the factory, Constant? I heard rumours—'

'I have been trying to reach you to tell you, Thomas. The factory's been burned down. Potts is in prison for arson. He was drunk at the time.'

'Good God. Does that mean we're out of a job? Am I free to work for Siam, then? I love this place. If there is ever an opening as a mandarin's assistant, Constant, will you let me know?'

'You help Richard to bring back the spoils to Ayudhya first, and we'll see what we can do for you. You're a shareholder, remember? And you can tell White to come up too. I'm in a better position to help him now and I think I'm going to need him. The rest of his crew should stay in Mergui until they can find a ship to take them back to Madras. I wouldn't want them spreading gossip. And say nothing to White or Burnaby about my new honour. At least not until you are out of sight of Mergui. I don't want word to reach Madras faster than it will anyway.'

'What will happen to Potts?'

'We'll have to keep him in prison as long as we can. The more we can delay his return to Madras, the better for us. But come with me to the ministry, Thomas. We can talk along the way.'

Ivatt prostrated himself. 'Mighty Lord, I, a curly hair on your head, receive your orders.'

439

Thirty-two

Père Bartolome Vachet approached the house with definite misgivings. This was, after all, the most important mission he had undertaken in his ten years in Siam. And he had been chosen over all the other Jesuits to perform it. Just how would Constantine Phaulkon, the newly made mandarin, react to his proposals? he wondered. The Father knew Phaulkon to be dogged and self-willed, charming and ambitious. He was a man with a mind of his own and, thought Vachet ruefully, a rather flippant attitude towards religion. Though of course that could be both an advantage and an impediment in this case.

At the gate the priest was greeted by a servant who ushered him inside, where a tall, most becoming Siamese girl accompanied him into the living room. No doubt one of Phaulkon's concubines, he thought. He was said to have a harem like any wealthy Siamese and now that he was a mandarin it would probably grow in accordance with his new-found status. It seemed a question of honour among the mandarins to support several concubines, or minor wives as they preferred to call them, and those who did not were considered to have fallen on hard times. The Father sighed. The Christian insistence on monogamy was the single greatest obstacle to the establishment of the Christian religion in Siam. How many discussions had he not had with his fellow Jesuits at the seminary on how to overcome this problem! Some of the Fathers, though admittedly only a minority, had actually advocated compromise, with perhaps a gradual reduction in the number of wives. But how could you compromise on Christian ideals? There was either monogamy or polygamy. There could be no halfway measure.

The handsome girl showed him to a chair and inquired after his business. He was a Jesuit priest come to see his friend, Lord Phaulkon, he said. She smiled warmly. The master was bathing and would be out shortly, he was informed. In the meantime could she bring him some refreshments? She certainly had a beguiling smile, this one, and she exuded a kind and gentle nature. No doubt she was very attached to Phaulkon. There was a quality about Phaulkon, the Father had noticed, that attracted people. All types of people. And his reputation with the ladies, of course, was well known.

'Thank you, my child,' he said to the girl in Siamese. 'I will gladly take a little tea.' She smiled with delight at his Siamese and gave him a look of innocent surprise. This fine-featured priest with the dancing blue eyes was the second farang she had ever heard speaking her language. Though his pronunciation was a little odd, and not clear like her lover's, she managed to make out the words. Perhaps the priest had not been in Siam as long as her Constant had. What did he want with the master? she wondered. She wai'd to him and went to see about his tea.

Father Vachet sank back in his chair and returned to his thoughts. He had good reasons to be interested in this girl and her relationship with Phaulkon. Would she accept another woman, a major wife, in the household? he asked himself.

She probably would, being brought up to it. But how would he, Phaulkon, react? As a student of human nature, it had constantly amazed the priest that any Siamese woman in love with her husband could calmly accept his sharing his couch with others. Would she not far prefer to be the only wife? Yet these Siamese were somehow different. They could not, for instance, fathom the concept of no divorce. The church had lost more potential converts on account of its inflexibility in this matter than in any other. The idea of being stranded with the ignominy of a bad marriage, without any recourse, sowed terror in the minds of the Siamese – both men and women. So firmly embedded was the concept of legal separation that married women never even assumed the names of their husbands, but retained those of their birth all their lives.

They always listened to him politely, these potential converts, yet it was hard to convince them. Their laws were so strictly defined. At the time of marriage, an independent witness drew up a list of each party's possessions and in the event of divorce these same possessions were returned to their original owners. All the odd-numbered children, the first, third, fifth, went to the mother, while the second, fourth, sixth, and so on went to the father. There was no possible dispute. If there was only one child it went to the mother who had suffered the travail of childbirth.

441

Father Vachet chuckled to himself. They could be cunning as foxes, these gentle Siamese. While generous by nature and remarkably sympathetic to the sufferings of others, when it came to guarding their own possessions, the Siamese became transformed with guile. They were so anxious to conceal their wealth from greedy mandarins or extortionate magistrates – for fear of having it confiscated – that they were always pleading penury, and parents had a difficult time ascertaining the real wealth of their prospective sons- or daughters-in-law.

The tea and the master of the house arrived simultaneously.

'Ah, mon cher Constant,' said the priest rising to greet his host, 'or should I address you now as my Lord Phaulkon? May I be the first to congratulate you?'

'Hardly the first, I am afraid, Father, but a most welcome addition to the list, nonetheless,' replied Phaulkon affably. He had always liked Father Vachet. How clever of the Jesuits to send him to keep up with developments in the changing corridors of power.

'But at least the first from our humble little order, I think? I should be mortified if another brother had beaten me to it.' As well as most surprised, added the priest to himself. The Jesuits had deliberated at some length on how best to approach Phaulkon and though they had differed widely on the manner, they had been unanimous in their decision to send him.

'May I pour you some tea, Father?' Sunida, holding a small silver platter, had sunk to her knees a little distance from him. It would not do for a woman to come too close to a priest.

'Thank you, my child,' he said, his grey-blue eyes contemplating her kindly. He watched her pour a cup and then walk gracefully backwards, crouching as she went. Phaulkon settled into a chair opposite the Jesuit and observed him. He would have made a great buccaneer, he thought. He was handsome, with a shock of dark, wavy hair greying at the temples. Phaulkon could not help thinking that many a lady must have wished he had not found his calling in the priesthood.

'But to what do I owe the honour, Father? I am sure there's more on your mind than mere congratulations.' He smiled artfully. 'I know you Jesuits.'

Vachet laughed. 'You are a mind-reader, mon ami. No wonder

442

they made you a mandarin. Soothsayers are in great demand at court.'

'It doesn't take a soothsayer to see through a Jesuit,' responded Phaulkon, laughing in turn. 'Especially one with clear blue eyes like yours, Father.'

'You save me the trouble, monsieur, of making a great preamble. I will come straight to the point.' The Jesuit's face assumed a serious expression. He looked Phaulkon in the eye. 'Monsieur Constant, I need not conceal from you that our overriding ambition, our very *raison d'être* in this country, is to achieve the eventual conversion of His Majesty, King Narai of Siam.' He paused while Phaulkon gazed at him in silence. He is not actually going to ask me to perform this miracle, surely? thought the newly appointed mandarin.

'You see, mon cher Constant, it is my belief and that of my colleagues at the Seminary that if His Majesty were to adopt the Christian faith, his subjects would follow his lead unquestionably, devoted to him as they are.' The priest's eyes grew wide with zeal. 'And we are talking not of thousands but of untold millions of souls delivered into salvation.' The numbers seemed to intoxicate him. 'Not to mention the vassal states as well. It would be the greatest coup in our history.' He grew suddenly silent, lowering his head as if the suggestion were too awesome even to contemplate.

Phaulkon was about to observe that the Father was dreaming if he thought there was even the remotest possibility of such a conversion, when his instincts stopped him short. His political nose told him to listen. His assistance was obviously going to be requested in some form and any man who needs a favour is usually prepared to give one in return. He had been giving political and military matters a great deal of thought in the last two days since his elevation to the mandarinate, and there was an important task the French Jesuits could perform for him. 'It would indeed be an extraordinary coup,' he said, appearing impressed.

Vachet seemed to be brought back to reality by Phaulkon's remark. 'Yes, mon ami, and one which is not as unlikely as you might think. Not with your help.'

'My help?' asked Phaulkon, feigning surprise.

'There are a few Christian mandarins already. Not many, it is

443

true. Six of them to be precise. You could now become their leader. And with your easy access to other mandarins, there could be more. As to His Majesty . . .'

'But I am not even a Catholic!' protested Phaulkon, as the details of his own plan began to take shape in his head.

'That is not irremediable, is it?' suggested the Father. 'I understand you were born one.'

How does he know that? wondered Phaulkon, impressed. 'Who told you that?' he asked.

'You were born in Cephalonia, were you not, under Venetian rule? It is only reasonable to suppose—'

'I was indeed born a Catholic,' interrupted Phaulkon, 'but I converted twenty years ago.'

'At the instigation of the Protestant English, no doubt.' The priest nodded knowingly. 'You are a practical man, Monsieur Constant.' He smiled. 'And that is one of the reasons we want to enlist your help.'

There was a momentary silence as the two men regarded each other.

'Are you perhaps suggesting I should convert to another religion in order to assist you in your aims, Father?'

'Are they not your aims too?'

'To convert the King of Siam?'

'Yes, to see this whole part of the world Christian. To save millions of souls.'

Phaulkon smiled. 'I've never really considered the matter, Father.' His smile broadened. 'As you say, I'm a practical man.'

'And practical men seek rewards? Is that what you are saying?'

Phaulkon looked at him without answering.

'Greater rewards than that of knowing that you could save millions of heathens from eternal damnation?' pursued Vachet, in a voice that might have thundered from the pulpit.

'Not greater perhaps, Father, but . . . different.'

'How different? Tell me about it.' The Jesuit shifted slightly in his chair.

Phaulkon rose and wandered slowly over to the window, as if contemplating the question. The afternoon sun was streaming in, throwing a blaze of light across the highly polished teak floor. His servants had soon learned how he loved the sight of oiled

444

teak and the floors were scrubbed scrupulously till they shone like mirrors.

The Jesuits were desperate to enlist his help, he thought. Just as he was desperate to enlist the help of France. For France was now the only country powerful enough to give the Dutch reason to pause. He could no longer hope for any assistance – military or otherwise – from the English, and Siam was not strong enough on its own to resist a full military invasion from the Dutch. France – or rather the fear of French intervention – had suddenly become the only possible alternative, the only conceivable weapon to deter the Dutch. Although there was no way in which France could be physically brought into the picture in time, a treaty with Europe's most powerful nation could go a long way towards redressing the balance of power. The Dutch would have to think twice before acting. In the meantime, he would somehow have to obtain Potts' release, just to delay the Dutch until they could find another excuse for war. To his knowledge, they had never blatantly invaded another country without carefully preparing the ground first. They were too methodical for that. They needed the right excuses for the history books.

Pieter, the Eurasian interpreter from Ligor who had accompanied van Risling to Ayudhya, had come secretly to see him at his house only two nights ago and told him that he had intercepted certain dispatches indicating that the Dutch were planning to annex Siam. Young Pieter did not want his country to be invaded, even if he were half Dutch. He had thought Phaulkon was the best person to inform. A dozen warships had been requested from Batavia. Potts' continued detention, against repeated Dutch requests for his release, was to serve as the excuse for war. The news had chilled Phaulkon. All his plans could now blow up in his face. He had held off informing the Barcalon until he could come up with a suitable new plan. The sensitive Siamese might overreact to the news.

'More tea, Father?' he asked, returning to his chair.

You damnable little devil, thought Père Vachet. I wonder sometimes why I even like you. Keeping me waiting all this time.

'Not just for the moment, thank you, Constant,' he replied courteously.

Phaulkon leaned forward. 'The Père de la Chaise is the confessor of King Louis XIV, is he not?'

445

'Indeed he is, monsieur. And you can imagine how proud we are to have such a man as the head of our Jesuit order.'

'The Superior General, I believe you call him?'

Vachet bowed. 'That is so, monsieur.'

'He must be a very powerful man, your Superior General. I mean having the ear of the Sun King . . .'

'Perhaps the most powerful man in France, monsieur, after the King, of course.'

Phaulkon carefully swatted a fly that had settled on his arm. It fell to the floor and buzzed in an agony of death.

'And how aware is the Père de la Chaise of your aspirations in Siam, Father? Is he familiar with the scope and importance of this country?'

'Most certainly, Monsieur Constant. The Superior General is a very well-read man. I might add, in confidence, that he considers Siam potentially our greatest prize. He has discussed the matter frequently with King Louis. It is for that very reason that His Eminence the Bishop of Heliopolis stopped here on his way to China.'

'So the possible conversion of King Narai to the Catholic faith is a matter close to the King of France's heart?'

'It most certainly is, monsieur. You can be sure of that.'

Phaulkon eyed the priest steadily and then announced gravely. 'Perhaps I can be of help, Father.'

The Jesuit leaned forward eagerly: 'You can?'

'I believe so.' He smiled.

Vachet eyed him suspiciously. 'What is your price, then, mon ami?'

'Nothing material, Father, if that is what you are thinking. I have higher considerations in mind.'

'Pray tell, monsieur.'

Phaulkon leaned forward and fixed the priest with a steady gaze. 'I want you to announce a treaty with France.'

Vachet was speechless. 'A treaty with France?' he repeated eventually. 'What . . . what exactly do you mean?'

'A treaty of friendship between Siam and the most powerful country in Europe, sealed with the announcement that His Majesty of France is sending a regiment of soldiers for the exclusive use of his most esteemed and beloved brother, King Narai of Siam.'

446

'But King Louis has done no such thing!'

'Yet he might do when you inform his Father Confessor that millions of souls will be saved from eternal damnation if he persuades his King to enter into such a treaty.'

The Father was awed. 'Possibly,' he said slowly. 'But we Jesuits are not empowered to make such treaties.'

'Not even if it meant achieving your most cherished goal? I thought King Louis was the Defender of the Catholic Faith.'

'Yes but . . . even if . . .' Vachet waved his arms, 'even if we were able to . . . to consider what you are suggesting, how do I know you would be able to achieve the King of Siam's conversion?'

'You cannot be sure of that, Father, neither could I in good faith guarantee it. But I am the best chance you have. Have you ever had a European mandarin working for you before?'

'You would convert?'

'If we were to agree on everything else.'

'But how would I explain this sudden . . . this possible change of heart on the part of the King of Siam? After all, we Jesuits have been here almost twenty years.'

'By the sudden appearance of a Catholic Venetian at the court of Siam. A man of great persuasion.' Phaulkon smiled. 'Let me see now, how many mandarins did you say you had converted? Six in twenty years, that makes one in—'

Vachet cut him short. 'Very well. But you ask a great deal, monsieur.'

'And you seek to achieve a great deal, monsieur.'

'You want me to risk my neck by announcing an unauthorized military pact – for that's what your treaty amounts to – with Europe's most powerful monarch in the vague likelihood that a Greek mandarin at the court of Siam might persuade an Oriental monarch and a few million of his subjects to change their creed. I am not a man who wagers, monsieur, but I would say the odds are against me.'

'I believe you were the one to seek my co-operation in the first place, Father. Remind me again, what did you come to see me about?'

'That was before you gave me your . . . conditions.'

'In what way do my conditions alter the odds?'

The Father was silent for a moment. 'I suppose the odds are

the same whichever way you look at it. But I need more proof, if you will forgive me, monsieur, of your sincerity. I mean no offence, but in the presence of a practical man, it is wise to become practical too, non?' He smiled.

'What proof do you require?' asked Phaulkon.

It was Vachet's turn to rise and walk over to the window. He contemplated the garden in silence for a while and then adjusted the shutters. The sun, which had begun to stream into the corner where the priest's chair was, now sent a blaze of light into the centre of the room instead.

Phaulkon waited in silence, his fingers drumming on the arms of his chair.

Vachet seated himself again. 'I will have some more tea now, if you don't mind, Monsieur Constant.'

Carefully bridling his impatience, Phaulkon rose to strike the gong but Sunida appeared at the threshold before he even had time to lift the hammer. She could hardly be spying on him, he thought. She understood not a word of the language, though perhaps she could tell from the tone of their voices if they were arguing or not. More likely, she was being her usual, helpful self. His conclusions were confirmed when he saw the blue and white porcelain teapot in her hand as she entered. She had been waiting outside the door with a fresh pot.

She filled the priest's cup and smiled sweetly at him. Then she offered some to Phaulkon, which he declined.

'A splendid young lady,' said Vachet appreciatively. 'You can take that as a true compliment coming from a priest. We are not supposed to notice such things.'

'Ah, but it shows you are human, Father.'

The priest waited for the door to close behind Sunida, then he leaned forward slowly in his chair.

'Here is the proof I require.' He gestured around him with a sweep of his arm. 'All of this must go.' Then he pointed in the direction in which Sunida had disappeared.

'All of what?' asked Phaulkon, a nasty suspicion creeping up on him.

'This whole way of life. You cannot be a Catholic and live like this, in sin, with slaves and concubines like any heathen. A Catholic mandarin must set an example.' He paused. 'If I obtain a treaty for you and you fail to obtain the King's conversion, at

448

least my fellow Jesuits and myself will not appear complete fools to have believed that a man who lived the life of a sinner, beyond hope of redemption, would have genuinely adopted our cause and striven to obtain the King's conversion. Why, my order would be the laughing stock of the Christian world. Not to mention the wrath of the Superior General and, least of all, the risk to my own future. No, monsieur, I wish to make myself perfectly clear. In order for me even to consider meeting your conditions, you must demonstrate to me that I am dealing with a Catholic of established piety, happily married to a Catholic woman—'

'Married?' broke in Phaulkon. Throughout the priest's speech, he had become gradually paler. Now he was almost chalk white. 'I suppose you're going to tell me next that you have somebody in mind?'

'As a matter of fact I do. And since I know you have an eye for beauty, I feel sure you will not be disappointed.' He smiled. 'We Jesuits brought her up, and so we know she is capable of keeping you in order. Her name is Maria de Guimar.'

For a moment Phaulkon wondered whether Maria could have had anything to do with this. Then he dismissed the idea as preposterous. Nevertheless he would make absolutely sure.

'And how do you know she would be willing to marry me?'

The Father nodded wisely. 'We know. After all, we brought her up. As an exception, of course. You may know that Jesuits are not allowed to involve themselves in the education of women. But we often inquire after her welfare and when one of my colleagues asked her uncle in jest whether she had found some dashing young man to marry yet, he replied that unfortunately she was quite infatuated with a certain Monsieur Constant and would not look to anyone else.'

'Unfortunately, did you say?' asked Phaulkon.

'Unfortunately, because you were not Catholic, monsieur. For no other reason. Mestre Phanik is a great admirer of yours.' He paused. 'It was Mestre Phanik's remark in fact that gave us the idea.'

'You mean you have been planning this marriage all along?' asked Phaulkon, astounded.

'Planning? No, that would be too strong a word. Let us say, monsieur, that we hoped you would see things our way.'

'Indeed, Father? You amaze me. You mean to say you came here to suggest that I dismiss my . . . staff, change my faith and marry a woman I barely know?'

'It would sound like less of a sacrifice, monsieur, if you measured it against its rewards: the salvation of millions of souls. And those rewards, monsieur, would not only be here on earth, but would extend to Heaven as well.'

'I would need proof of that first, Father. Remember, I am a practical man.'

Vachet sipped his tea and observed Phaulkon slyly.

'But now of course, mon ami, we are no longer talking about sacrifices, but more of expediency. You require a treaty with France, and you want us to obtain it through our Superior General at Versailles—'

Phaulkon cut him off. 'No, Father, that part would come later. I need the treaty now, drafted by you Jesuits here.'

Vachet was speechless. 'Drafted? I thought you said announced, not drafted. You are not asking us to put this in writing?'

Phaulkon stared at him in silence.

'And who would . . . sign this document, monsieur?' pursued the Jesuit, with the look of one who already suspected the answer.

'Whichever among you can best reproduce the royal seal of France and the signature of Monsieur Colbert, the King's Minister.'

Vachet threw up his arms. 'Ah non, monsieur, you jest with me. That is going too far.'

'In that case, Father, we will all be the losers, France, the Jesuits and myself.'

'How is that?'

Phaulkon looked at him hard. 'Because the Dutch are about to invade Siam.'

'Ah, mon Dieu!' he said, aghast. 'You are sure of this?'

'Positive. The only thing I don't know yet is the precise date. But it will be all too soon. Their warships are preparing to leave Batavia now. It would take seven months for a ship to reach France, another three for your Superior General to reach agreement with King Louis and a further seven for a ship to bring a

450

reply. We do not have a year and a half at our disposal, Father. Perhaps three weeks, a month at most.'

Vachet was now moving his head from side to side, his mind filled with thoughts of the fate of the Catholic Jesuits if Protestant Holland took over Siam. He had, of course, heard rumours of Dutch ambitions in the area, but nothing as specific or immediate as this. Yet if anyone should know, it was Phaulkon, working as closely with the Barcalon as he did.

'And what about the English, Monsieur Constant? Can they not do something about it?'

Phaulkon thought about Potts. 'The English, Father, are disorganized and their chief auditor has just been put in prison for arson while under the influence of alcohol. In the circumstances, the English are hardly likely to come to the aid of Siam, even if they were in a position to do so. The Dutch are aware of this.'

Vachet nodded. 'Yes, yes, we know about Monsieur Potts,' he said, sympathetically. 'Le pauvre. One of my colleagues has already been to visit him. We are praying for his soul.'

'So you see, Father, you may yet live to see the King of Siam a Protestant. If the Dutch let you stay that long, that is.'

'But what about the King of Siam? Would he endorse such an alliance with France?' he asked.

'I think he might, Father. It would be my job to ensure that he does. Your job would be to obtain a consensus among the Jesuits for the signing of the treaty. It would have to be announced with a great deal of pomp and fanfare. A magnificent Siamese embassy will have to depart for France in response to King Louis' invitation. All that will be for me to arrange. It is known that His Siamese Majesty is a great admirer of King Louis so the alliance might not appear so far-fetched to the Dutch. But there must be a signed document for them to see.' Phaulkon had a sudden idea. 'There is even a portrait of the Grand Monarque hanging in His Majesty's private apartments. It hangs just next to . . .' He stopped himself as if he were about to speak out of turn.

'You have been there?' asked Father Vachet in awe. No one had access to the King's private apartments. The Jesuits had been trying to reach His Majesty in the privacy of his living quarters for years without success. Perhaps certain mandarins had that privilege . . .

451

'I didn't hear that question, Father,' replied Phaulkon ambiguously. The seed had been planted.

'But even if such an alliance could be announced, would it be sufficient to deter the Dutch?' Vachet's tone was now tense, a permanent note of anxiety in it.

'If they believed the treaty were genuine, yes. Previous correspondence will have to be forged, of course, dating back at least two years.' Vachet looked away. 'Remember, Father, the last thing the Dutch will really want is to risk a confrontation with France on European soil. The conquest of Siam could hardly justify the risk of an invasion of Holland.'

The Jesuit nodded absently: 'Yes, yes, I see what you mean.'

Phaulkon sensed his growing advantage. 'It is very much up to you now, Father. You must impress upon your colleagues the urgency of the situation. There is simply no time to dally. And the Jesuit vote must be unanimous. We cannot have one disgruntled member betraying the whole scheme.'

'I will do what I can. But can I give my colleagues your assurances that you will do all in your power to achieve the King's conversion?'

'You can.'

The Father hesitated. 'Mon cher Constant, there is one other matter on my conscience. It is something close to my colleagues' hearts as well.'

'Pray tell, Father.'

He looked at Phaulkon. 'It concerns Maria. If you were to marry her, would you treat her well?'

'But of course, Father. Who do you take me for? Just because it might be considered a marriage of convenience, does that exclude it being a happy one? Such marriages have occurred throughout the ages, with as good a chance of success as any.'

'I doubt the marriage would take place if Maria even suspected that you looked upon it that way, monsieur. She's very proud, you know.' Vachet looked pensive. 'Too proud sometimes.'

'What she does not know cannot hurt her.'

'Don't underestimate her intelligence.'

'I don't. I have met her. She is sophisticated, lively and beautiful. And she has a mind of her own.'

'But I can tell you one thing, mon ami. She will not accept these others.' He waved his arms in the direction of the door again. 'Any more than I or my colleagues would. Are we agreed on that point, Constant?'

Phaulkon appeared to consider the question.

'Tell me, Father, your Sun King, is he greatly respected?'

Vachet seemed surprised by the question. 'But of course, he is very likely the greatest king France has known.'

'And the Jesuits admire him also?'

'Most certainly. He is the Defender of the Catholic Faith.'

'Even the Père de la Chaise, your Superior General?'

'Our leader is devoted to His Majesty.'

'And we all know His Majesty is married to a good Catholic. Now I was wondering, Father, about Madame de la Vallière, Madame de Maintenon and—'

Vachet raised a hand to cut him short. The list of the King of France's mistresses was long.

'Sunida!' Phaulkon called out. Sunida came in and knelt down respectfully by Phaulkon's side. 'This is my Madame de la Vallière, Father. And I am afraid I cannot do without her.'

'That will have to be between you and God then,' mumbled Vachet. 'I just wanted to register our concern for Maria, that is all.' He rose abruptly, seemingly embarrassed.

'You should register your concern for me instead,' said Phaulkon, smiling. 'She'll probably have me round her little finger within a week or two at most.'

'I sincerely hope so, mon ami; you deserve it.' Vachet walked towards the door. 'I've enjoyed our little exchange. Most enlightening, Constant.'

'It has been very edifying, Father,' said Phaulkon, seeing him out. 'Think it over carefully,' he called after him.

He returned and drew Sunida affectionately to him.

'What was that all about, my Lord?' she asked. 'You two looked so serious.'

'Sunida, I am in trouble. Something terrible has come up.'

'Will you tell me about it, my Lord?'

'I can't, Sunida. It is highly confidential. But I must speak to His Majesty in private and I know that it is forbidden to anyone as humble as myself. I am desperate. The matter is of great urgency.'

'Can you not speak to the Pra Klang, my Lord?'

453

'My respect for the Pra Klang is infinite, but this is a matter only for His Majesty's ears.'

'Oh my Lord,' said Sunida gently smoothing his brow, 'I wish I could help you.'

Thirty-three

Phaulkon walked briskly past the brick archway that marked the entrance to the Portuguese quarter, and headed towards the house of Maria de Guimar. He had decided against wearing his conical hat and Muslim slippers which would have identified him as a mandarin and attracted too much attention in the streets. He needed time to think and he did not want to be distracted. There was so much happening at once, and it was hard to know which way to turn first. He had above all to keep a cool head.

If the Dutch warships were actually ready to leave Batavia they could be here in as little as three weeks. That was all the time he could count on to arrange the treaty with France. And it was not only the Jesuits who had to approve the treaty, but King Narai as well.

It was essential that he speak to His Majesty urgently and privately. Phaulkon could not possibly discuss the finer points of Catholicism in front of five dozen mandarins or in a message via the Barcalon. He had a plan, but it was complex and devious and it required the kind of explanations that could only be made in person.

Most discouraging of all was that even if he managed to juggle the Jesuits and the King successfully and produce a treaty, there was no absolute guarantee that this would deter the Dutch. The warships might well be preparing to leave now and they could reach Siamese waters before they ever heard of any treaty. They would have their orders. Would they carry them out, or would they turn back? Would the commander of their fleet be empowered to make such a decision? Or would he defer to Aarnout Faa? If so, which way would the VOC chief turn? Besides these disturbing considerations it was now essential that Phaulkon somehow obtain Potts' release, in the hope of delaying Dutch action and giving him much-needed time. The return of the Persian expedition was imminent.

Now, as he approached the gate to Maria's house, all these deliberations vanished in the light of a more pressing question, and only one thought occupied his mind. Would Maria accept a proposal of marriage from him? There was no other course of action open to him and he *had* to obtain her consent.

She was proud and headstrong and sure to question his motives. Why was he suddenly proposing to her? she would want to know. He could hardly tell her the truth. He doubted she would accept the idea of a political union anyway, least of all if she knew the real reasons behind it. A treaty with France! He would have to explain his reticence in broaching the subject previously by stressing his shyness over the difference in their ages and the bashfulness he felt on account of his friendship with her uncle. He had kept away from her all this time, the better to think the matter out. But would she be taken in by such explanations? And if by some chance she were, how would he himself feel about deceiving her in this way? Would his conscience trouble him? Not really, he told himself, for a number of reasons. In the first place he had every intention of treating her with the respect he had always felt for her. Secondly, if he considered the alternatives – which for himself would entail no treaty with France, probable incarceration by the Dutch or court martial by the English, and for her, harassment by the Protestant Dutch, the expulsion of her Jesuit tutors and his own unavailability – he felt amply justified in colouring the truth to his convenience. Besides, if she was in love with him, as seemed to be the case, surely it could not be her wish to be separated from him perhaps for ever.

He pulled the bell cord outside Mestre Phanik's house and waited apprehensively for the door to open. A servant appeared and, recognizing him, ushered him in with a low bow. Both Mestre Phanik and the Lady Maria were in, he was informed. Mestre Phanik was in the living room and the Lady Maria was in her room studying.

'Well, well, welcome to our humble home, my Lord Mandarin!' Mestre Phanik's round face beamed with good cheer as he greeted his friend even more effusively than usual. 'What an honour indeed. I hope you got my note of congratulation? I sent it the minute I heard.'

'I did, thank you, Doutor. It was most gracious of you.'

'Not at all, not at all, my dear friend. But you are not wearing your hat!' he exclaimed, looking him up and down. 'Nor your pointed slippers. What is this sudden coyness? A mandarin must live on the trappings of his position. But I want to hear all about the ceremony. What did His Majesty say? Did he address you directly? Could you make any sense of the royal jargon? Who was there?' Mestre Phanik waved his arms in the air. 'But here I am babbling away and completely forgetting my manners. Won't you sit down, and what can I offer you?'

'Tea would be most welcome, thank you, Doutor.'

Mestre Phanik clapped his hands to summon the servant. 'Let us sit down, let us sit down. I am truly honoured that you should find the time to visit us so soon after your promotion.' He glanced down awkwardly. 'I thought that after my niece's unforgivable performance at the banquet, we might never see you again.'

'Oh come now, Doutor. She is just a spirited young lady, that's all. It's part of her abundant charm.'

'And you, Constant, are a born diplomat.'

Phaulkon looked him in the eye. 'I assure you that I mean it. I have nothing but the highest regard for her, Doutor.'

'Well . . .' Mestre Phanik looked suddenly uncomfortable, 'I'm sure . . . that . . . it's reciprocated.'

Phaulkon had seldom seen Mestre Phanik blush before. Should he approach the subject with him first? he wondered. Perhaps fate had willed it that way, since Maria was conveniently out of the room.

'So, my dear friend,' said Mestre Phanik, changing the subject as Phaulkon was about to broach it, 'the accumulation of your services to the nation has earned you great honour. I am so pleased for you . . . and proud too . . . but also a little worried. You see, I have been thinking about these services of yours. Every one of them has exposed the Moors in some way and caused them to lose face. The banquet, by the way, was a resounding success. Everyone who was present has remarked on it. But,' he leaned forward with an air of caution, 'you have unquestionably antagonized the Moors. Mohammed Rashid has been avoiding me. He used to visit me regularly. He has not been here once since you took over his banqueting department. And he is a dangerous man. In fact, I befriended him because I'd rather have him on my side than not. You know his father was once Barcalon, briefly, in the reign of the last King, Prasat Tong. I always thought he had ambitions for the post himself. Being in

457

charge of receiving foreign dignitaries is often a traditional stepping stone to greater heights. Even Barcalon.' He noticed Phaulkon's raised eyebrows and laughed. 'Now, don't you go forming any ideas, Constant!'

'You need have no worries on that score, Doutor,' laughed Phaulkon in turn. 'But tell me, what might this man Rashid do?'

'He is very friendly with Prince Dai. He brought him to my house once. Prince Dai is the hereditary leader of all the Macassars and their loyalty to him is blind. The Macassars are all Mohammedans from the Celebes Islands, traditional fighting men and . . . trained assassins. They're behaving quite peaceably at the moment, since the King gave them due warning when he granted them asylum and offered them their own camp outside the city. But it would not take much . . . If Rashid were to persuade Prince Dai that you needed eliminating . . .' Mestre Phanik drew his hand graphically across his throat. 'And even if you fought back, the Macassars would think nothing of losing a few dozen men to carry out their leader's wishes. I have read chilling accounts of their last stand against the Dutch in defence of their homeland. They swallowed opium, drew their krises and charged into the very mouths of the Dutch cannon. Crazed with opium, they were ready to fight to the last man. I think Prince Dai fled to Siam with the last thousand or so of his people just to save his race from extinction.'

Phaulkon listened with interest, wondering at the same time how to broach the subject of Maria. 'So what do I do to protect myself against a thousand opium-crazed fanatics? Have you any suggestions, Doutor?'

'It's not easy after all you've already done, but . . . why not make an effort to befriend the Muslim mandarins at court? They represent quite a strong faction there. Convince them that you are not after their blood, but only the good of the nation.'

'That's a pretty fine line, isn't it? Especially when they are the ones sucking the nation dry.'

'Perhaps, Constant. But take a lesson from Oriental history. Don't make your move until you are sure of having all the right forces behind you, all the support you need to ensure the success of your coup. If you're going to continue to oust the Moors, you've got to have a powerful faction of your own waiting to replace them – and to defend you against reprisals.'

'As a matter of fact, I'm working on that, Doutor.'

'I might have known it,' said Mestre Phanik slapping his thigh. 'Here I am giving lectures to a natural politician probably shrewder than Machiavelli and Brutus combined.' He leaned forward and patted Phaulkon's knee affectionately. 'I just wanted to warn you to be on your guard. You are in the limelight now, meu amigo.'

'I always value your advice, Doutor, you know that. Only a fool would take it lightly.'

'Thank you. Coming from a mandarin of the royal court that is a true compliment.'

'Is Maria as interested in politics as ever?' asked Phaulkon, steering the subject back to her. 'I recall that her intuitive sense in that area was remarkably developed.'

'Oh yes, she is constantly surprising me. As a matter of fact she told me that the greatest danger to you lay with the Dutch, that they would be stung that one of their own people had not been elevated to the mandarinate when their presence here dates back so far. She thought you should forget about the English and seek an alliance with France.'

Phaulkon swallowed his surprise. 'I am flattered that the two of you should have been discussing my welfare,' he said, smiling warmly.

'Oh yes, of course we . . . naturally . . . you are such an old friend.' Mestre Phanik had started to look uncomfortable again and now he was stammering slightly.

'Doutor, the welfare of this family concerns me too. Which is perhaps why I have hesitated so long before bringing a matter up which is very close to my heart. It concerns Maria.'

'Oh?' Mestre Phanik shifted uneasily in his chair.

'I realize this may come as a surprise to you, Doutor, even a shock, but I have debated the matter at great length before coming to see you.' He paused. The Doutor's gaze swung from a distant point on the wall down to his feet again.

Just at that moment the servant entered carrying a tray with tea and cakes and placed it on the table in front of them. Phaulkon and the Doutor glanced at each other awkwardly.

Mestre Phanik turned to the servant. 'We will pour the tea ourselves, thank you,' he said in Portuguese. The servant, a Portuguese Indian from Goa, bowed and retired.

459

'Would you care for some rice cakes, Constant? They were freshly baked this morning.'

'Thank you, Doutor. I'd love one.' He took a bite out of one, forcing himself to chew it. Under normal circumstances he would have found it quite delicious.

An awkward silence set in, as the two men quietly sipped their tea. Phaulkon chided himself for his cowardice. This would not do. He thought of all the tasks ahead of him; this was only the first. He pulled himself together and gathered his courage.

'Doutor, I am sorry we were interrupted just now. I was about to ask you for the honour of your niece's hand in marriage.'

The Doutor's cup came to a halt halfway between the table and his lips. Meu Deus, he thought. Painfully aware as he was of Maria's feelings it had never occurred to him they might be reciprocated.

The normally verbose Doutor now struggled for words.

'Constant, er, I . . . am indeed honoured. But, have you, er, spoken to Maria on the subject? I mean . . . does she know? And there is of course the question of religion . . . We are, as you know, staunch Catholics . . .' His voice trailed off, as he rebuked himself for unwittingly sounding negative.

'Maria knows nothing of my feelings, Doutor. I have stayed away from her all this time, to be sure of them myself. It was apparent at the banquet that she had misinterpreted my long absence and ascribed it to neglect. It was nothing of the kind. I just needed time to think things over. It was such a big step. I have taken several factors into consideration, not least her youth and religion. As to the former, though I realize there are fifteen years between us, I feel the gap is greatly narrowed – I dare not say by my own youthfulness – but certainly by her maturity. As to the latter, I was born a Catholic and it would be neither inappropriate nor distasteful to me to return to the religion of my youth. I was an impressionable young lad when I embraced the Protestant faith of my English masters.'

Mestre Phanik emitted a long sigh of relief, and it was clear that a great burden had been lifted from his shoulders.

'Then, my Lord Phaulkon, and my dear friend Constant, there remains nothing in the way of my blessing but Maria's own feelings. You must consult with her. She is the final arbiter of

460

her fate. But in the meantime, allow me to embrace you.' He rose and enveloped Phaulkon in a heartfelt embrace.

'Have you then abandoned your policy of neglecting us, my Lord Phaulkon?' asked Maria, as she settled into the armchair that Mestre Phanik had just vacated to attend to urgent matters outside. Her black panung covered her thighs completely, but her pale, delicate legs and her tiny porcelain feet were left alluringly exposed. Though barely an inch over five feet she was perfectly proportioned and it occurred to Phaulkon in that instant that she really was the reincarnation of Diana the Goddess of the Chase. He wondered if the statue still stood in the little square near his childhood home. How long ago and far away it all seemed. Here was that same little boy who had admired the statue, metamorphosed into a potentate of a fabulous Oriental court. Life was indeed unpredictable.

Now that the moment had come, he was decidedly nervous. Not so much because he feared her response – after all, Père Vachet had made Maria's feelings towards him clear and her uncle's nervousness had confirmed them – but because he was not sure how far he was capable of lying to her. Would she expect him to tell her that he loved her? It was quite possible that he might grow to love her, he reflected, because there were certainly enough qualities he admired in her, but he felt strangely shy to tell her to her face that he loved her now. The truth was, and he knew it, that he was enraptured by Sunida.

The irony of it all, he reflected, was that the situation would have been much easier in the land of his birth. There the marriage would have been arranged by the parents, as almost all marriages were, and this one would have had a better chance of success than most, because there was already a mutual respect and even some deeper feelings on the part of one of the betrothed. But here in Siam, women were much freer to make their own choices, and to divorce if the choice did not turn out as expected.

Her voice interrupted his thoughts. 'My Lord, have you come here to dream in silence, or is it the way of mandarins to sit mutely while their subjects bask in the aura of their presence?'

'Forgive me, Maria,' he said, coming sharply out of his reverie. 'I was actually thinking about you.'

'But I am here, Constant. You could honour me with the

461

sound of your voice.' She frowned. 'You have been acting strangely of late. First you don't visit us for weeks and then when you do, you sit in silence with a distant look on your face.'

'If I am silent, Maria, it is because I have been turning something over in my mind. Something which I wish to ask you.'

'Then why don't you ask, Constant? I am listening.'

'Maria, a moment ago I asked your uncle for the honour of your hand.'

Her eyes opened wide. 'Indeed? And what was my uncle's response? You certainly know how to arouse a woman's curiosity, Constant.'

He wondered whether her flippancy was due to nervousness. 'He suggested I refer the question to you.'

'A very wise precaution. And a fair one too.' She contemplated him for a while in silence. 'Because my answer, Constant, must be no.'

Though clearly taken aback, Phaulkon was at first unwilling to believe her. He ascribed it to her pride and no doubt also to the rather gauche and abrupt manner in which he had approached the subject. He was aware even as he spoke that his proposal sounded flat and uninspired, but at the same time he felt strangely relieved that he had not showered her with false declarations of eternal devotion. He could live with gaucherie more readily than outright lies.

'May I ask why?' he inquired.

She observed him again and then spoke in a gentle tone without any trace of bitterness or rancour. 'For a variety of reasons, Constant. Because you are not a Catholic, because I could not accept the life style that you lead and because I do not think you really love me.' She paused. 'As for me, I will not hide the fact that I adore you. But under the circumstances such a union would be too high a price for me to pay.'

It was his turn to be silent. His mind raced. 'Under the circumstances' she had said. Was she leaving a door open? 'And what if the obstacles to this union were eliminated?' he asked eventually. Now that he had heard from her own lips that she cared, there had to be a solution.

'Neither my uncle nor myself could accept a union with a non-believer, no matter how high his rank or worthy his character. Our family has fought long and hard for the right to maintain our

462

beliefs and now that we have found freedom in this tolerant land, we are anxious that those closest to us share in our joy.'

'I have already informed your uncle that I am prepared to return to the faith of my birth. I will gladly become a Catholic again.'

'In name or in soul, my Lord?'

'In both, I trust.'

'The Catholic mandarins find it hard to abandon polygamy. Why should it be any different with you?'

Phaulkon considered for a moment. He could never give up Sunida, but perhaps he could convince Maria of the vital importance, of the indispensability, in fact, of continuing to feed desirable information through Sunida to the palace. It was fortunate in that respect that Maria was already aware of Sunida's spying role. Surely the politically oriented Maria would see the enormous advantage of maintaining this situation? There was no need for her to know that he was in love with Sunida. He would ensure that she never saw them together.

'I can only answer that truthfully after I have tried.'

'I appreciate your honesty, Constant. But I must in turn tell you that I do not believe that any woman could rest happily if she felt that a man had been forced to adopt a religion that was not in his heart, or to forego a way of life which he must hitherto have found agreeable enough. Certainly, I could not.' She stared at him intently. 'Why *do* you want to marry me, Lord Phaulkon?'

'I want a family and companionship and . . .'

'An anchor for your ambitions perhaps?'

'A partner to love and respect and share my life and plans.'

'And what are your plans, might I ask, my Lord?'

He gazed at her unflinchingly. 'To become Barcalon of Siam.' He had never told anyone before.

Her eyebrows arched in surprise and then for the first time during their conversation she broke into a broad smile. 'Meu Deus, but you *will* need my help then.'

He laughed heartily. The ice was broken. 'Dona Maria,' he said, addressing her formally, 'it will not be difficult for me to return to the faith of my childhood, and as to my concubines . . .'

She raised a hand to intercept him. 'Do not make promises you cannot be sure of keeping, my Lord. The loss of your slaves would be a big change of life for you and I would never wish to be the cause of your regrets. There are many Siamese girls, more beautiful and well-born than I, who would be honoured to become the major wife of so distinguished and ambitious a mandarin, and who would have no objection to the number of your consorts.'

'Dona Maria, you are right to question the results, but not the sincerity, of my intentions. Time will prove what words cannot.'

'So be it, my Lord. Let time then decide.' She looked at him gently. 'I notice that you have confronted all my objections but the last one: love. But perhaps you do not wish to be pressed on so delicate a point?' She observed him questioningly.

He hesitated just a moment. Though he had considered the matter often enough, he had not expected her to be so direct.

'Love is such an all-embracing term, Maria. How can I not love the woman who shares my life and plans and . . . joys and sadness and . . . children?' He paused.

'It is not like you to be vague, my Lord. You, who are always so positive and decisive. But in that vagueness you have answered my question.' She forced herself to smile and added flippantly: 'Let me register another objection then.'

'Another one, my Lady? Is there no end to my deficiencies?' She looked at him. He was smiling, the smile that always melted her. However much she might love those strong, prominent features, the lively hazel eyes and the assertive manner, however much she might admire his wit and energy and ambition, it was the smile that enchained her. How much easier it would be to resist him without that smile.

'Your age, my Lord.' She grinned mischievously. 'It must be almost double mine. I am wondering if such a union could even be healthy.'

'Perhaps not to begin with,' he countered, 'but I could strive through good deeds and a pious Catholic existence to keep my age for ever stationary, so that your youth could the more readily catch up with it.'

She laughed and then considered for a moment. 'Did you never have a wife before? I mean in Europe perhaps . . . ?'

'Never, my Lady.' Though almost, he had to admit. He wondered what had become of Vanessa. Her hair had been the colour of the rising Aegean sun and her long peasant skirts had smelled of the freshness of the country hay. They had met when

464

he had gone to spend a few days with George's cousins in Dorset before leaving for Asia. The sun had shone almost constantly for those few days of early summer and he remembered thinking that there could be no two more beautiful things in this world than the verdant English countryside in the sunlight and Vanessa's laughter in the fields. They were deeply in love, she seventeen and he twenty-four. It was George who had pointed to her freckles and to her light English skin. Asia was no place to take an Englishwoman, he had said, and England was no place to leave a wife behind. And so they had cried and he had sworn he would return, and Vanessa that she would wait. Six years had passed since that time. Who knew where she was now?

He looked at Maria. 'You will consider then?'

She nodded slowly. 'I will search my soul. But do not press me. And you, my Lord, will need time to consider if you can adapt to the life of a husband and a Christian.'

He bowed chivalrously. 'I shall search my soul as well, Maria.'

Thirty-four

Phaulkon lay prostrate in the panelled audience hall once more, the Barcalon intoning beside him. Phaulkon had managed, exceptionally, to obtain a private audience with His Majesty in a remarkably short time, though he suspected the impetus had come more from Sunida than from his official pleas to the Barcalon. It felt strange now, lying almost alone in the vast hall without the rows of mandarins and their betel boxes to keep him company.

The usual trumpets and cymbals had announced the arrival of His Majesty and a slight cough from above indicated that the royal presence now stood before the opening of the upper balcony. At his first and only other royal audience, with the mandarins' prying eyes upon him, Phaulkon had not dared to look up. But now, with no one else but the Barcalon present, he dared to risk the offence. He squinted upwards through his fingers to catch a brief glimpse of the royal figure: he saw a bejewelled conical hat, a richly embroidered red coat, and the glitter of precious gems on the royal fingers. The face remained in shadow, however; only the upper torso was visible above the enclosure of the balcony. It was not clear whether His Majesty was standing upright or sitting on some invisible throne behind him, and it was impossible to judge the truth concerning the King's stature. Phaulkon lowered his eyes again, his heart beating faster. The royal voice had begun to speak.

'You asked to see us privately, Vichaiyen? Have you then matters to discuss which are not for the ears of our mandarins?'

For the briefest moment Phaulkon wondered whom exactly His Majesty was addressing by this name when he remembered that he would never be known at court as Phaulkon again. He was Luang Vichaiyen, the Lord of Knowledge, or simply Vichaiyen to His Majesty.

'High and Mighty Lord of me, thy slave, I desire to take thy royal word and put it on my brain and on the top of my head. I, a speck of dust beneath the sole of Your Majesty's feet, humbly

466

requested to see the Lord of Life alone on matters of great political significance.'

'Very well, you may proceed, Vichaiyen.'

'Mighty Lord, I receive your orders. I, a hair of your head, know that Your Majesty is aware of the growing power and ambitions of the Dutch farangs. In your infinite wisdom Your Majesty has seen fit to invite the English farangs here, ostensibly to trade, but ultimately to counter that threat. But now the Englishman Potts has disgraced himself and is paying the penalty. I, the dust of your feet, have many years' experience of the English farangs. They are a proud people and overly conscious of the importance of their nation. When they hear that one of their subjects, a mandarin, has been incarcerated, they will surely send a warship to demand his release. I, a presumptuous hair, beg the Master of Life's forgiveness for suggesting that that warship will point its guns not at the Dutch but at Your Majesty's very own fortifications.'

'This Potts, you say, is a mandarin?'

'My August Lord, I receive your orders. He is a mandarin equivalent to the third grade in their way of reckoning.'

'Have you come to plead for his release, Vichaiyen?'

'August Lord, the hair of your head believes it would be politic to release him, even though he will return to Madras and abuse me, your slave. He will accuse me of setting fire to the factory to hide the evidence of my wrongdoing. And the English mandarins there will believe him because he too is a mandarin and because he will report that I, your slave, was not at my post and neither was my chief, Mr Burnaby.' His Majesty would immediately grasp the gravity of such an accusation, thought Phaulkon. If any of his provincial governors were not found at their posts at any time except during the annual pilgrimage to the capital to drink the water of allegiance, the consequences were dire.

'Your chief is the one who sailed to Persia?'

'August Lord, the same.'

'And if the Englishman Potts is released and returns to Madras to accuse you, what will the English mandarins do?'

Phaulkon was delighted with the question. 'August Lord, they will send a warship to take your slave back to Madras to stand trial. And your slave wishes only to remain here and serve the Master of Life for the rest of his days.'

His Majesty was incensed. 'Abduct one of our mandarins? Never!' There was a pause and the silence in the great hall was awesome. 'It seems to me that these English farangs are not the ones to serve our purpose, as we had once hoped. They set fire to our buildings and insult our subjects. We will find other means to keep the Dutch farangs at bay. What is the view of our Pra Klang?'

'August Lord, I receive your orders,' intoned the Barcalon. 'The English farangs drink too much stupefying beverages and are not to be relied on. They furthermore seem not to be as thorough or as organized as the Dutch farangs. But Vichaiyen has, I believe, another suggestion to put before the Lord of Life.'

'Indeed? We will hear it, Vichaiyen.'

'August Lord, I receive your orders. There is one monarch in Europe powerful enough to instil fear in all others, that is Louis XIV, the great Sun King.'

'The French one?' inquired His Majesty, his curiosity clearly aroused. 'We have heard speak of this King. Tell us about him.' Phaulkon was aware that His Majesty was well-versed in matters concerning King Louis. It was a favourite theme of his, as was evidenced by the accounts of Louis' reign which the Jesuits had been ordered to translate into Siamese.

'August Lord, I receive your orders. King Louis is, like Your Majesty, a ruler of great strength, much honoured by his people. He is an accomplished horseman, fencer and dancer. Outside his country his armies have triumphed and he has recently defeated the Dutch in battle and annexed a part of their territory, called Flanders.' Phaulkon paused to allow the impact of the Dutch defeat to sink in. 'At home he has completed a magnificent palace at Versailles that is the envy of all Europe.'

'Do you suggest an alliance with this great monarch, Vichaiyen?'

'August Lord, the hair of your head believes that a treaty of friendship with such an illustrious sovereign whose love of pageantry and glory is akin to your own would serve as a serious deterrent to Dutch designs. They would think twice before challenging the power of such an alignment.'

'And why should such a distant ruler enter into an alliance with a kingdom so far away as ourselves? What would be the benefit to this accomplished horseman, swordsman and dancer?'

468

'August Lord, the King of France would undoubtedly welcome the opportunity of opening up new areas of trade for France and would see sense in containing the Dutch. Besides, he is a crusader with a great appetite for spreading the glory and culture of France—'

'And the religion, I believe?' interrrupted His Majesty.

'August Lord, the religion too.'

'We are indeed fortunate to be so sought after, are we not?' There was a note of amusement in His Majesty's voice.

'August Lord, it is as you say,' responded the Barcalon.

'The Persian ambassador,' continued His Majesty, 'was recently here with messages from Shah Suleiman extolling the virtues of the Koran, and inviting us to embrace what he would call the true faith. The Jesuits glance hungrily at us like some great prize fish waiting to be hooked, and no doubt the Hollanders will be asking us to denounce the Catholics and follow their Protestant cause.

'We have always tolerated all religions here, Vichaiyen, in the belief that there is more than one path to God. As the good Lord has given different plants and different vegetation to different parts of the world, so has he given us various beliefs. And just as it is hard to say that one plant is better than another, so it is hard to decree that one belief is superior to another.

'We would gladly embrace the King of France's friendship but not his religion. And we sincerely trust that the one is not dependent on the other. But if it is, we strongly urge that the King of France embrace the Buddhist faith which is the older of the two.'

Phaulkon was growing to like this monarch more and more. He was full of wit and wisdom and his views on religion were strangely akin to Phaulkon's own. He could not help smiling at the image of a delegation of Buddhist monks arriving at the court of Versailles in their saffron robes, urging the bewigged aristocrats to renounce their heathen ways and adopt the Buddhist faith.

'August Lord, I receive your orders. Far be it for the hair of your head to suggest that Your Majesty consider another faith. But in the light of the Dutch menace, would it not be expedient for the King of France – by way of his Jesuits here – to hold out hope that Your Majesty's conversion might be brought about in time?'

There was a pause and Phaulkon prayed he had not said anything to offend the King.

'It is a worthy suggestion, Vichaiyen, and if it will serve to procure a treaty with France we will consider it. But we find it hard to believe that so significant an alliance could rest on so unworthy a premise.'

'August Lord, the Sun King is the Defender of the Catholic Faith, a matter he takes very seriously. His confessor, furthermore, is the supreme patriarch of the Jesuit order.'

'His confessor?'

'August Lord, the priest who hears his confessions.'

'The King of France confesses to a priest?' His Majesty sounded incredulous.

'August Lord, he does.'

'What does he confess about, Vichaiyen?'

'August Lord, the dust of your feet believes he confesses that the Master of Life, the great King of Siam, is considering adopting the Christian faith and that it would be wise to enter into an alliance with him, the better to keep an eye on his progress.'

There was a great laugh from above and Phaulkon felt that the first breath of fresh air had been infused into the austere formality of his royal relationship. By his side the Barcalon joined in the mirth, though his voice lacked its usual vitality. Phaulkon knew that he had not been feeling well of late and his appearance showed signs of strain and fatigue.

'Vichaiyen, you put us in good cheer. But though your idea has merit, it will take too long to accomplish. And I fear the Dutch farangs will not give us that much time.'

Phaulkon had deliberated at length whether to inform His Majesty of the impending Dutch invasion but he had finally decided against it. He was not sure how radically His Majesty might react to the news and he was worried that drastic retaliatory measures might not suit his own plans. His Majesty might have Aarnout Faa arrested and the door to any peaceful solution closed. Phaulkon had decided to reveal the planned invasion only if His Majesty flatly refused to accept the concept of a treaty with France.

'August Lord, the hair of your head begs forgiveness for his presumption, but the French Jesuits here are anxious to propose the announcement of a grand alliance with France if Your Gracious Majesty will only assure them of your intentions to convert.'

'You have spoken to them?' the King's voice expressed surprise.

'August Lord, they approached me on the matter, seeking my assistance.'

Father Vachet had only last night informed Phaulkon of the consent of his colleagues on two conditions. First, the Jesuits required satisfactory proof of His Majesty's intentions to convert and, secondly, they wanted the treaty to be drafted by the Siamese authorities and then presented to the Jesuits for their approval. In this way it would appear that the proposal had originated with the Siamese.

'And these priests are able to announce such an alliance without the approval of their King?' His Majesty again sounded incredulous.

'August Lord, they are sure of obtaining their King's consent later on, because the conversion of so illustrious a ruler as yourself would be considered possibly the greatest achievement of the King of France's reign.'

'Even so, the King of France will not punish them for their presumption?'

'August Lord, they are willing to take that risk in view of the urgency of the matter and in the belief that they would be anticipating their sovereign's desires.'

'And what assurances of our intentions will these priests require?'

'August Lord, the hair of your head believes that to convince them of Your Majesty's sincerity it would be sufficient to ask one of them to come to the palace to give Your Majesty religious instruction.' He paused. 'The Lord of Life's interest in matters of scholarship is so celebrated, that if Your Majesty were to treat it merely as an intellectual exercise . . .'

'To listen to another man's version of God is not a heavy price to pay for a treaty that might assure our continued independence, Vichaiyen. We, too, preach the love of our neighbour and denounce stealing and killing and lying. What troubles me rather

471

is that these priests do not wash. Must our nostrils be offended as well as our ears?'

The Barcalon and Phaulkon both laughed. 'Mighty Lord,' said the Barcalon, 'the hair of your head presumes to suggest that as it is Vichaiyen's idea, so let it be his responsibility to ensure that the priest who visits you is always thoroughly scrubbed.'

'An excellent proposal,' said His Majesty. 'We concur. And besides this essential duty, Vichaiyen, you will draw up a treaty in our language and theirs and hand it to our Pra Klang for our perusal. Only then will we decide whether we wish to proceed. But in any case, it will not be before the return of the ship from Persia.'

Phaulkon's heart sank as he listened to these last words. He had not expected this. The *Cornwall* would not be back for at least another month. The Dutch invasion could begin in three weeks.

'August Lord, if the ship were to be delayed for any reason and the Dutch felt that there was nothing to deter them . . .'

'Nothing but our armed forces, Vichaiyen?' There was a hint of sarcasm in the royal tone.

'Mighty Lord, if Your Majesty's forces are indeed prepared, there is no necessity even for a treaty with France.'

There was a momentary pause.

'Naturally, Vichaiyen, we will do everything we can – within reason – to avoid war. But have you had any indications of an early Dutch attack? Any unusual preparations for instance?'

Phaulkon hesitated. It would be best to tell His Majesty now. He could not afford to await the return of the ship from Persia. Why was His Majesty insisting on that point? he wondered.

'August Lord, there are rumours that a large Dutch fleet is assembling in Batavia now. Twelve ships of war, Your Majesty.'

'Twelve ships of war? And did you notify our Pra Klang of this, Vichaiyen?'

'Mighty Lord, this worthless slave has only just heard the news himself.'

'And so you are only just bringing it to our attention,' observed His Majesty drily. 'And where did you hear these rumours then?'

Phaulkon was now kicking himself for not having brought the matter up earlier.

'Mighty Lord, from the interpreter attached to the Dutch

472

factory at Ligor. He . . . intercepted some dispatches sent to Batavia and came to tell me about them.'

'And you trust a *Dutch* official who comes to you with such stories? We are surprised, Vichaiyen.'

'Mighty Lord, the Dutch interpreter, with whom I have had prior dealings, was very much opposed to his country's policy. And this determined him to reveal what he knew.'

'Vichaiyen, you will summon this Dutch interpreter to the ministry immediately upon the close of this audience. Our Pra Klang will interview him and we will judge for ourselves. In the meantime, we will hold off announcing any treaties.'

'Mighty Lord, I receive your orders.'

'But for now,' continued His Majesty, 'we will learn what guidelines these Jesuits are proposing for their desired treaty with us.'

It was a demand Phaulkon had been hoping for, and dreading at the same time. He had somehow to broach the delicate subject of foreign troops on Siamese soil. Such a clause had to be included in the treaty, if the Dutch were to take it seriously. The loss of Flanders to the armies of France would be fresh in their minds. But how would the ruler of Siam react to such a suggestion?

Phaulkon crouched lower on the carpets. 'Mighty Lord and Master, I seek the boldness to tell Your Majesty what I think of the matter that you have deigned to discuss with me who is but your slave. I beg permission to insert a clause in the treaty which allows for the dispatch of a regiment of soldiers as well.'

There was a momentary silence.

'You mean, Vichaiyen, that the King of France needs a regiment of Siamese soldiers for his protection? Such a matter would have to be referred to General Petraja.'

Phaulkon's heart pounded. For a moment he wondered whether the King was serious, until he heard a series of muffled guffaws emanating from the Barcalon. Phaulkon sighed with relief. His Majesty had been speaking in jest. Suddenly he saw the right opening.

'August Lord, what this speck of dust had in mind was more an exchange of troops between Siam and France.'

'Indeed? But how would our noble elephants fare in the wintry

473

climes of Europe? What assurances do we have that enough French slaves would be deployed to take care of their needs?'

Again Phaulkon was not sure whether His Majesty was speaking in jest. The Barcalon was giving him no clue this time.

'Mighty Lord, we could stipulate the number of slaves in the treaty,' ventured Phaulkon warily.

'It would seem to us, Vichaiyen, that the least cumbersome course would be for the treaty to be drafted, displayed for the Dutch to see, and then conveniently lost on the journey to France. It will be your duty to see to that little occurrence, Vichaiyen.'

'August Lord, I receive your orders.'

'In which case, we have no objection if the treaty includes an exchange of troops.'

'Mighty Lord, it is as you command.'

'Very well then, that is settled. We shall await your initial draft with interest, Vichaiyen. And we shall decide on the urgency of this treaty after we have spoken to the Dutch interpreter. Meanwhile, our Pra Klang will take my seal to the public prisons and inform the guards that the farang Potts is to be transferred to the palace dungeons. He will be shipped out of Ayudhya in the dead of night and provided with a competent escort to Mergui and enough silver to buy his passage to Madras. He will be made to understand that it is the members of the English Company of Ayudhya who have pleaded his case, in particular you, Vichaiyen, and that you have pledged yourself hostage against the prisoner's release. We would not want our most recently appointed mandarin to suffer the wrath of the English when we know him to be innocent, would we?'

'Indeed not, August Lord,' said the Barcalon.

'And now, Vichaiyen, we will speak with our Pra Klang alone. Our meeting has been fruitful and you may request to meet with us privately again when the first draft of the treaty is ready.'

'Mighty Lord, I receive your orders. I who am but filth and dust do gratefully thank the Lord of Life for the honour of sharing privately in his divine wit and wisdom.' Raising himself on to his knees, Phaulkon bowed and touched his forehead three times to the ground. Then reverently he crawled out backwards. He would have to find the Eurasian, Pieter, without delay. There was no time to lose.

*

'No doubt you have some questions for us,' said His Majesty to the Barcalon as soon as Phaulkon was out of earshot.

'Indeed, August Lord.'

'Proceed then.'

'Mighty Lord, I, a hair, have to report that Vichaiyen converted yesterday to the Catholic faith. One of our Christian mandarins whose son was placed in a basin of their holy water at the same ceremony came to report the matter to me. I am concerned, August Lord, that Vichaiyen may be working for the Jesuits. He is certainly most anxious to obtain this treaty with France.'

'We have considered that possibility as well. That is why we wish you to interview the Dutch interpreter. If it is confirmed that the Dutch are indeed preparing for war, then Vichaiyen's haste is justified. But if not, we conclude as you do, that he is in the pay of the Jesuits. You may have noticed that he said nothing of any Dutch attack until we informed him that a treaty would first have to await the return of the English ship from Persia.'

'I did notice, Mighty Lord. And it was most astute of Your Majesty to force Vichaiyen to reveal his knowledge.'

'That was not our only motive. For not only do we need to be quite sure of his loyalties, but we are furthermore reticent to announce any treaty with a farang power until it becomes absolutely necessary. The Moors are still smarting from the recent concessions to the farangs and we do not want to exacerbate their already delicate feelings. Too many setbacks at once could force their hand.'

'Indeed, August Lord, yet if there is truth in the rumours of a Dutch attack, will it not be necessary to announce a treaty well in advance of any official knowledge of an invasion, in order not to make it appear like a political necessity?'

'We concur with that view. That is why we must first be quite certain of our ground. And we have every confidence that you will be able to evaluate the Dutch interpreter's evidence correctly. For that will dictate our course of action.'

'Your Majesty is too gracious.' The Barcalon paused and caught his breath. He was having difficulty inhaling and official activities were becoming increasingly strenuous.

'There is more on your mind, we can tell.'

'There is, August Lord. If in fact a treaty with France were to prove necessary, would not the frequent presence of a farang priest at the palace give rise to unfavourable rumours? It would surely not be politic for the courtiers to believe Your Majesty is preparing to convert.'

'Indeed it would not, and we have considered that danger. But the priest who visits here will come as a doctor, as many of them are, and we shall even feign ill health for the purpose. The priest will be told that his real mission must be kept secret until the alliance with France can be confirmed by their monarch himself. And he will be warned that if his mission becomes known, his visits will cease instantly. That should ensure his silence. It should not be difficult to convince these Jesuits that so considerable a matter as our conversion will give rise to unrest in this country, and that we will need to be sure of French protection before we announce such intentions publicly. That will give us almost two years to think of a solution. And Vichaiyen, if his loyalties are in the right place, will not be idle during that time. He is worth ten of their priests and as many of our mandarins. You did well to bring him into our service. It is up to us to watch him and control him and bend this great asset to our will, ensuring that his unquestioned talents and abilities serve the purposes of Siam instead of those of the Jesuits or the English or anyone else.

'And while we're on the subject, make sure, when you release Potts, that the prisoner is told that it is the Dutch and not the English who have pleaded his case and pledged themselves hostage against his release. Potts must remain furious with Vichaiyen, determined to bring him to trial at all costs. When the English Company comes to demand Vichaiyen's extradition to Madras, it will be politic to have him entirely at the mercy of our good will.'

The Barcalon smiled in admiration. 'August Lord, that is most wise.'

'But there is something else you should know.'

'Mighty Lord, I await your wisdom.'

'Despite our uncertainties about the man, we have a certain affection for him. He is . . . how shall we say . . . almost like our first farang son.'

'August Lord, your wisdom is equalled only by your magnanimity.'

*

476

Aarnout Faa sat at his desk, a permanent smile etched on his lips. The timing of the Dutch invasion could not be better. The English were in disarray, the Moors were slighted and ill disposed towards the Siamese King, and the Portuguese were too weak to put up any real resistance. With Potts' incarceration, he had the excuse he needed. There was no one to thwart his plans, no possible impediments on the horizon. Divide and rule, that had been the Dutch policy in the islands of the Indonesian archipelago and it had succeeded. He was increasingly sure that Heer van Goens in Batavia would see things his way. Aarnout Faa's smile broadened. In perhaps three weeks' time, if all went well, a dozen of the finest warships in the world would anchor before the estuary of the Menam and offer the Siamese surrender terms or war. He had just dismissed Joop van Risling that morning and sent him back to Ligor, because he, Aarnout Faa, wanted to be alone to bask in the glory of victory when the flag of the Netherlands was hoisted over the Grand Palace. He, Aarnout Faa, wanted to ensure that only his name was recorded in the roster of history in that moment when the ancient Kingdom of Siam became a protectorate of the mighty Netherlands.

He was sorry to have lost the interpreter, Pieter; he could have done with his services in these momentous times. The boy was hard-working, efficient and full of initiative. But van Risling had insisted on taking the boy with him, saying he was indispensable to his welfare in Ligor, and Aarnout Faa had not pressed the matter. He had felt sorry for his assistant. Joop was, after all, still suffering from periodic bouts of pain from his accident at Louvo and it was only fair to grant him what consolation he could.

There was a knock on the door. 'Excuse me, Excellency,' said the swarthy Indian servant in halting Dutch. 'There is a farang at the gate of the factory requesting to see you. He does not look well at all.'

'All right, send him in.' There was no point in asking these people for names. They never understood them.

A few moments later a macabre apparition stood in the doorway of the VOC chief's office. The face was drawn, the sparse hair dishevelled, there were large pockets under the eyes and deep welts on both sides of the neck. His European clothes, breeches and coat were almost in rags.

477

'Mr Potts!' exclaimed Aarnout Faa, involuntarily stepping backwards from his chair. 'What . . . what are you doing here?' Despite the grotesqueness of the sight, the VOC chief managed a smile. 'Did you escape?'

Samuel Potts sank weakly into a chair.

'Your modesty is most touching, sir, but my captors informed me of the responsibility you bear for my release.' His voice was feeble but distant.

'My responsibility?' echoed Aarnout Faa, unable to conceal his surprise.

'Indeed, sir, and I cannot tell you how grateful I am that you should have offered yourself as hostage against my release. You have my word, sir, that you will soon be relieved of any obligations. As soon as I reach Madras, the necessary letter of apology will be sent to the Siamese authorities together with the compensation that has been requested for the fire.' Potts shook his head slowly. 'You, sir, a Dutchman, have done more for me than all the members of the English factory combined. They will pay dearly for their sins. I will not rest till I have seen them all hanged. Which they will be, mark my words, sir.'

Aarnout Faa's mind was reeling. Who had released Potts? Who had pledged his own substitution as a hostage? It had to be that demon Phaulkon, using his new-found powers as a mandarin. Who else? But why would Phaulkon of all people want Potts' release? Surely it would only hasten his own court martial? And Potts' continued detention, reflected the VOC chief angrily, was the excuse he was to use for his declaration of war. Yet Phaulkon could know nothing of that. So why had he had Potts released? Perhaps the Siamese had simply decided to set him free. But why? There was no point in questioning Potts. Whoever it was had told Potts what he wanted him to believe.

The voice of the slouching figure on the other side of the desk shook Faa from his thoughts.

'Would you mind, sir, if I rested here for a few days before proceeding to Mergui? I need to gather strength for the journey. You may be assured that I will fully repay your kindness including, of course, your generous donation for the expenses of my journey and the return passage to Madras.'

Aarnout Faa composed himself.

'Mr Potts, it is the least I can do for a gentleman in your

478

position, and one who has been so greatly wronged. My physicians will take care of you here and you are welcome to remain in our care for as long as you require. As a matter of fact Heer van Risling vacated our guesthouse only this morning to return to Ligor.'

Whoever it was who had arranged this whole affair had certainly gone to great lengths, reflected the VOC chief. Oh well, he would have to make the most of it and revert to his original plan of sending Potts to Madras. At least the man would incriminate the English factors in Siam once and for all. And at least someone else was paying the bills. Still, it was a damned nuisance not to have the excuse of Potts to declare war. But he would find another one, he swore. There were, after all, three whole weeks to prepare for it.

'I am at a loss for words to thank you for all you have done, sir,' said Potts, making an effort to rise. 'I will not disturb you any longer.'

'Think nothing of it, Mr Potts. I have no doubt you would have done the same for me. I will have you shown to your quarters immediately.' He leaned over and sounded the gong by his desk.

In the next instant a servant appeared. A messenger stood in line behind him waiting to see the VOC chief.

'Show Mr Potts to the guesthouse,' he said to the servant. 'And send for Dr Kornfeldt right away.'

The servant bowed and helped Potts out of the door.

Aarnout Faa beckoned to the messenger. 'Yes? What is it?' he asked curtly in Dutch.

The messenger, a Siamese, did not understand Dutch. He wai'd briefly and produced a letter from his purse. He placed it courteously on the desk. Aarnout Faa reached over and read it. It was written in English and requested the immediate presence at the Ministry of Trade of one Mr Pieter, interpreter at the Dutch factory. Mr Pieter was to accompany the messenger now. The signature was illegible but the note carried the ministry's seal.

'Tell your superiors that he's gone to Ligor,' said Aarnout Faa. 'He left this morning.'

The messenger looked blank. The VOC chief took a quill and wrote in large letters in the space below the seal: 'HE HAS GONE TO LIGOR.'

The messenger wai'd and departed with the note.

479

Thirty-five

'My Lord, I can almost hear your mind thinking.' Sunida turned and put an arm across Phaulkon's chest, inhaling his shoulder tenderly as she did. 'Talk to me if you will, I am awake.'

It was the middle of the night and they were lying on Phaulkon's quilt on the floor. He had not slept. It had been the same for three nights now.

'I thought you were asleep, Sunida. I did not want to wake you.' Phaulkon put his hand affectionately over hers. 'It is true that my mind can find no rest.'

'Sometimes, my Lord, it is better to speak out and exorcize the spirits within you.' She smiled in the darkness. 'You can pass them on to me if you wish. My body would gladly relieve you of the pain, my Lord.'

Phaulkon leaned over and inhaled her cheek. What would he do without this splendid woman? He had never loved anyone so. She never seemed to argue with him and when she was displeased she merely slipped away quietly until her anger had subsided. In the end it made him feel worse than if she had stood before him calling him a thousand names.

She was right, of course. He was terribly distraught. He had finished a draft of the treaty with France, but when he had requested a private audience with the King, His Majesty had suddenly become too busy to see him. The Pra Klang had ordered him to leave the draft at the ministry instead. He would look it over, he had said, discuss it with His Majesty and let Phaulkon know.

Was it because of Pieter? Phaulkon wondered again, as he had countless times. He had been devastated by the discovery that Pieter had left for Ligor the very day he had sent for him. Phaulkon had even considered giving him chase but he was pledged not to leave Ayudhya until the return of the Persian expedition, and those sleek Dutch coastal boats would anyway be too fast to overtake. Pieter would be on the high seas for another ten days, and assuming van Risling would then release

480

him – which was unlikely – it would take Pieter a further ten days to return to Ayudhya. Phaulkon did not have twenty days at his disposal. He cursed his luck and his poor judgement. He should have informed His Majesty immediately about the proposed Dutch invasion, instead of beating about the bush. Without Pieter's testimony it looked as if he had invented the whole invasion to coerce His Majesty into signing the treaty. Even his repeated assertions of sincerity to Sunida, which he assumed were being passed on to the palace through the usual channels, seemed to have achieved nothing. Five days had now passed, almost a whole week out of the precious three that were left to him.

To add to his worries, he had not yet found time to prepare a report on the destruction of the English factory at Ayudhya. He had planned to have a translation of the official Siamese accusations against Potts certified by the Barcalon. Even though Madras would nonetheless believe Potts' version, at least it was a counter-charge, while total silence was tantamount to admitting he was guilty of a serious offence. Madras would assuredly send a ship to arrest him. Phaulkon would need to be firmly entrenched in Siam, in a position of power, when that happened.

But what troubled him perhaps the most was the question of his impending marriage. Maria was coming to visit him that very morning. The note she had sent had stated that she had 'searched into her soul' and was ready to confront him in his 'den of iniquity'.

He had been planning for some time to broach the subject with Sunida, who as yet knew nothing, but his energies had been entirely occupied with trying to communicate with the King. And now Maria would be here in only a few hours.

'Are you thinking about Pieter again, my Lord?' Sunida's gentle voice broke through the darkness.

'Partly.' He had repeatedly told her about Pieter's departure and how distraught he was over it, in the hope that the message would reach the King, but he could not talk to her directly about the treaty with France. It would hardly do for a newly appointed mandarin to be seen discussing such confidential affairs of state with his consort. 'There are other things too,' he said.

'Tell me, my Lord. It will help you to unburden yourself.'

The time was ripe to tell her about the marriage, he decided.

He had put it off long enough. Besides, Sunida should be prepared for Maria's visit in the morning.

'Sunida, there is something I have been meaning to discuss with you.'

'My Lord?'

It was strange, talking in the darkness like this, not seeing a face, just hearing the words.

'Sunida, I'm going to be married.'

There was a pause.

'Have I failed in my duties to you, my Lord?' She started to pull her arm away but he held on to it and put it back across his chest again.

'On the contrary, Sunida. I have never been happier in my life. And I love you more than ever.'

Again there was silence.

'Who is she, my Lord?'

'She is . . . I suppose you would call her a farang. In spirit at least, though she is part Japanese, and a Christian.'

He could feel his heart thumping loudly. He wished he could see the expression on her face.

'But these Christians . . . do they not allow only one wife?'

The anxiety in Sunida's voice wrenched at him.

'Sunida, I have not the slightest intention of letting you go.'

He could feel her relief. The tension went out of her arm.

'She will accept me then, this . . . farang woman?' Despite her apparent acquiescence, there was a note of challenge in Sunida's voice.

'I am not sure about that, Sunida. But we will try to persuade her together. I will need your help.'

'You will certainly have that, my Lord,' she replied. She paused and he could almost feel the agitation in her thoughts. 'It is not that you are tired of eating the same rice every night, is it, my Lord?'

Despite himself, he laughed. He had made love to Sunida every night since her return from Mergui, even when he was tired. His desire for her never seemed to wane. He had neglected his three slave girls totally and not summoned them once since Sunida had moved in with him. It was not that Sunida had any objections to them – simply that he had no desire.

482

'When the rice crop is the best, Sunida, why would a man want to try other varieties?'

'Perhaps farang rice is tastier,' she said.

'Sunida, this marriage is one of convenience and not one of the heart.'

'You mean like our kings marrying the daughters of Burmese kings?'

'That's exactly what it is, Sunida. A political union, for the good of Siam. I will try and explain it to you. But what I am about to tell you is confidential. You see, I converted to the faith of my birth a week ago, the better to serve Siam. I am a Catholic again. You would have laughed, Sunida. The Fathers baptized me in the company of four howling Siamese infants in the little chapel of St Mary.'

'Baptized, my Lord?'

'Yes, that's when they put you naked in a basin full of holy water.'

'They put you in with the other babies, my Lord?' Sunida sounded astonished.

Phaulkon laughed. 'In my case, I was too big, so they just sprinkled holy water over me.'

'And you are of another faith now, my Lord?'

'Not really; it's hard to explain. I am still a Christian, but of a different sect.'

Sunida was silent. He could feel her confusion. He had to explain matters at least partially to her. He wanted her to understand and he needed the King to hear of his motives.

'It is politically expedient just now for Siam to enter into an alliance with a powerful farang country whose King is a staunch Catholic. Such an alliance is important because it may well deter the Dutch farangs from whatever designs they have on Siam. The Lord of Life has been magnanimous enough to give me a small role in these affairs but the Siamese position would be greatly legitimized in the eyes of this powerful farang monarch if I myself were to appear as a Catholic married to a Catholic wife.' He paused. 'Her name is Maria, Sunida. She is a good woman and I respect her. But I cannot love her the way I love you.'

'I am pleased for you, master, and proud of your role and I will receive this lady with all the honours due a major wife.'

Phaulkon was touched. 'I knew you would understand, Sunida.'

'But I will not be dismissed. For I, too, love you, my Lord, and I fear my heart would break from the separation.'

'I will never dismiss you, Sunida. And together we will find a way to convince Maria.'

'What about Ut and Nid and Noi?' she asked, suddenly worried about his three slaves. 'Will the farang lady not want to dismiss them too? They are so happy in this house that I do not see how even the Christian God could be offended.'

'I am afraid I will have to dismiss them, Sunida. Some concessions must be made somewhere.'

Sunida was silent and he sensed her grief on their behalf. 'Poor girls! They were telling me only the other day how fortunate they were to have found such a benevolent master. They hoped they could remain here for life.'

Phaulkon felt saddened. He wished she had not told him that. He had purchased his three slaves and though he had the right to sell them again, he was loathe to do so. Supposing they weren't treated well by their new master? Then a thought struck him and he cheered up. He would give them to Ivatt. Ivatt was becoming increasingly attached to Siam and familiar with its ways. He was learning the language and was very popular with the local people. Phaulkon was sure that not only would Ivatt be delighted by the gift but that he was quite ready for it. Phaulkon had sent him off three days ago to wait for White's arrival in Mergui and as soon as he was back he would present the girls to him.

'But how will you be able to keep *me*, my Lord?' The note of anxiety had returned to Sunida's voice.

He was lying on his back staring into the darkness above him. He pulled Sunida closer to him, nestling her head against his shoulder. He could hardly tell her that he planned to use her spying role as a pretext for retaining her with him. 'I will find a way, Sunida, even if I have to disguise you as a cook. Maria doesn't know what you look like, so it's best if you stay out of the way when she comes.'

'A cook, my Lord?' she said bravely. 'You plan to be the first mandarin to spend time in the kitchens?' He could feel her smile in the darkness. A wave of affection swept over him. Any other woman would have badgered him over the suggestion.

484

'Sunida, if there was even a question of losing you, I would abandon both the alliance and my marriage. That's how much you mean to me.'

'I thank you, my Lord, but I couldn't be responsible for such a decision.'

'You wouldn't be, Sunida. I would.'

She caressed his cheek gently and then closed his eyelids with her fingers. 'Try and sleep now, my Lord. You will need all your strength to fight for me in the morning.'

She began to massage his tired body and to smooth his temples in a monotonous motion until, finally, sleep overcame him. Her duties fulfilled, she fell asleep instantly beside him.

The doorbell rang and Phaulkon felt his stomach turn hollow. That would be Maria. Quickly he sat at the small table in the corner of the living room and began to peruse a stack of papers.

He had not slept more than two hours the night before and it was now mid-morning. He felt tired but nervously alert. More than a week had elapsed since he had proposed to Maria and he wondered what her decision would be. If it were favourable, would there be a whole series of conditions attached?

Maria swept gracefully into the room, ushered in by Tip, who quickly retired. Her hair was done up neatly in a bun and she looked fresh and becoming in a red muslin blouse and a black panung. She smiled pleasantly and wai'd to him.

'Welcome to my den of iniquity,' said Phaulkon in Portuguese, rising to greet her. 'May I send for some refreshments?'

'Not for the moment, thank you, my Lord,' she said, looking around her. 'I must say that on the surface this looks much like any other household. But I must first congratulate you on entering the Kingdom of God. The good tidings have given me and my uncle much pleasure.'

'You know already? News certainly travels quickly,' said Phaulkon.

'My family is very close to the Jesuit Fathers, my Lord.' She smiled. 'I even heard that you did not scream like the other infants.'

'Only because I was too embarassed in front of the Fathers,' he said, offering her a chair.

She laughed and sat down next to a large, stone-studded Indian

485

tea chest, glancing around her as she did at the profusion of Asian artifacts that he had amassed over the years: primitive wood carvings from Borneo, sculpted elephant tusks from India, jewelled krises from Kedah, blow-pipes from Sulawesi and puppet masks from Java. On the walls, several rattan shelves sagged under the weight of books in various stages of disintegration.

'So how does it feel to be reborn, my Lord?' she inquired.

'The better for knowing the pleasure it brings you, Maria.'

She paused and studied him carefully.

'I have missed you, my Lord,' she said, unexpectedly. 'I have given the question of our marriage a great deal of thought, and in coming to a decision I know that my heart has ruled over my mind. Yet the pain of being separated from you outweighs the suspicions I have of your feelings for me and I am reticent to look too deeply into your motives. However, I remain buoyed by the thought that my love may nourish yours and that in time you may grow to reciprocate my feelings. For the present, I ask only that you respect my Catholic upbringing and abide by the tenets of my religion – and yours.'

Phaulkon smiled. 'The bishop himself, madam, may now visit my home without a shudder.'

'May I inquire where all your . . . consorts will be going?'

'I have chosen my colleague, Thomas Ivatt, as my heir, Maria. He will start his own den of iniquity as soon as he returns from Mergui.'

'So that none of your former entourage will remain, my Lord? Not even disguised among the staff? You must forgive my suspicions, but they are those of a woman whose affections do not feel – as yet – wholly reciprocated.'

'Those suspicions are groundless, Maria. Only one element of my past will be present and that for political reasons which I feel sure you will readily understand.'

Maria eyed him suspiciously. 'And who might you be referring to, my Lord? The spy perhaps?'

'Our conduit to the palace, Maria,' he said, carefully including her in the design. 'Think of what an asset she will be to us, feeding whatever information we wish back to the palace. Invaluable.'

He rose, seemingly filled with enthusiasm, and took hold of

her hands. 'What a trump card for a man aspiring one day to rise to Barcalon.'

Her hands felt cold and unresponsive and a frown furrowed her brow. She gazed at him steadily.

'But you are a mandarin now, my Lord. You already have the ear of the King. The spy's purpose is served. What do you need her for?'

'There are things I can suggest to her which are difficult to put outright to His Majesty. Plans and schemes whose seeds I can plant. Ideas His Majesty might secretly adopt while not wishing to acknowledge they came from me. Why, if His Majesty were to like them, he could simply pass them off as his own.' He paused, deep in thought. 'The possibilities, as well as the advantages, Maria, are infinite.'

'Advantages to you politically perhaps, but agonies to me emotionally. How do you think I would feel every time you went to see her to pass your information on?' She shook her head. 'No, my Lord, in this case my heart must take precedence over your ambitions.'

'Even though this arrangement is nothing more than political expediency?'

Maria looked at him sceptically. 'How do you suppose you would explain your sudden abstinence to such a seasoned temptress?' she asked.

'On account of my marriage to you.'

Maria scoffed. 'Oh, come now, my Lord. She is a Buddhist. She could neither understand nor respect such a view. She will seduce you again as she was trained and instructed to do.'

'You don't think I am able to resist her?'

'I do not know, but it would not be wise to put such temptation before so recent a convert. You need time to grow accustomed to the joys of belonging to one woman, my Lord.'

Phaulkon felt the anger rising in him, fed by his lack of sleep. Her obstinacy irritated him. She was coming between him and his plans. Even knowing nothing of his love for Sunida, she was objecting to furthering his career. It was selfish and unreasonable. She was forcing him to resort to subterfuge. It was becoming increasingly clear that she would not accept Sunida on any terms. He cursed his luck. Was this yet another setback in his string of continuing reverses? Would nothing go his way?

487

He would *not* abandon Sunida. The Dutch were about to invade Siam, the King was ignoring his requests, his plans could blow up at any moment in his face and here was this young girl, barely out of convent school, thwarting him and throwing questions of Christian morality at him. Her considerations, in the scheme of things, were petty and trivial. Even if he had not loved Sunida, he told himself, he would have insisted that she remain.

He turned to Maria, a relentless look in his eyes.

'It appears, madam, that you wish to place your moral considerations above the success of my career.'

'I am sorry if you see it that way, my Lord. I was hoping instead that my added energies in the political field would more than compensate you for the loss of your spy. It would be my duty to put all my resources behind your career.'

'I would expect you to do that in any case,' he said haughtily.

'I can see, my Lord, that this discussion is leading to a sad confrontation.'

'These are trying times for me, Maria, and you have chosen a bad moment to stand against me.' For a brief instant, in his mounting frustration, he thought of listing the consequences of her refusal to marry him: no co-operation from the Jesuits, no treaty with France, an invasion by the Dutch and, more than likely, the end of Catholicism in Siam. But then he thought better of it. She would be too proud ever to accept him after that, and he had not yet abandoned hope.

'I had no intention of standing against you, my Lord, only of opening my heart to you. I do not believe my demands have been excessive. They have surely been far outweighed by my concessions. I have accepted to marry you even though I do not feel my love is reciprocated, or that you truly share my faith, or that you will even be faithful to me.' Maria was close to tears, as much of frustration as of grief. 'In truth, my Lord, I am not sure why you want to marry me at all.'

He wanted to say he was not sure himself anymore. He was getting tired. He would soon be saying things he would regret. He could see that she was growing angry now too. This discussion was futile. It was best to postpone it for another day.

'I see that you cannot answer that yourself, my Lord,' pursued Maria, her voice rising. 'I do not understand you. You have just become a Catholic, you have just proposed to a Catholic woman and you can stand there telling her that you wish to keep another woman. Is your whole conversion a charade? Has it meant nothing to you? Is it just a formality to serve some hidden ambition of yours? What about your love of God and—'

'My love of God has nothing to do with my love for another woman,' exploded Phaulkon, unable to contain himself. He stopped, realizing that he was going too far.

'So you do love her,' said Maria, suddenly quiet.

'No, you don't understand what I meant.' He was about to explain further when the door opened and Sunida entered.

Sunida had observed the growing rift between Phaulkon and Maria through a narrow slit between the door panels. Were they arguing over her? she wondered. She hated to be the cause of her lover's grief. Poor Constant. She felt suddenly angry. It had to be this idea of Christian monogamy that was the cause of it all. What a frightening concept. Look at the kind of destruction it generated. Here she was, perfectly content to stay on as a minor wife, taking orders as was customary from the new mistress of the house, obeying her, obliging her, respecting her wishes, not standing in her way, helping her, for Buddha's sake, in performing her task. Constant was no easy man. He was complex and needed careful handling. How selfish of one woman to want to assume all the duties herself and deprive the other girls of their position and their pride. It really was a most uncharitable religion. She would never understand it.

As she listened to the rising voices on the other side of the door, it dawned on her that perhaps this Christian woman did not really believe that she, Sunida, would behave like any self-respecting minor wife. Perhaps this half-farang woman had not fully grasped that Sunida really would defer to her and honour her as the master's major wife. Safe in the knowledge that Phaulkon really loved her, perhaps she should go in there now, reflected Sunida, and tell this girl politely to her face that in no way was she a threat to her, that she had no intention of usurping the major wife's role and that all she wanted was to help. The thought of being disguised as a cook and having perhaps to slink about the house like a thief dismayed Sunida. The more she thought about it the more she refused to be treated with such degradation. She was Sunida, the most accomplished dancer at the court of Ligor, the niece of the Governor of a great province.

Her anger mounted as she thought of the reasonableness of her attitude against the unfairness of this girl's demands. She would confront her, she decided, despite her lover's request that she stay invisible. It would be best in the end for all of them. Before she could change her mind, Sunida had pushed open the door and stood in the threshold, her head held high.

There was instant silence. Phaulkon stared at her in disbelief and the farang girl looked across at her in bewilderment.

Sunida wai'd respectfully to Phaulkon and then slowly walked over to Maria, who had risen to her feet. Sunida stood almost a head taller than Maria. Sunida smiled at her gently and then respectfully wai'd to her. She was certainly pretty and very fair-skinned, thought Sunida, like the white lotus in bloom. It was as if she had stayed out of the sun all her life. She was petite and rather fragile-looking, but well-proportioned for her size, and her Asian blood was visible in the high cheekbones, the somewhat slanted eyes and the jet-black hair. Why do you wish to take away my happiness when I do not seek to take away yours? wondered Sunida.

Maria returned Sunida's gaze, while from the side Sunida could feel Phaulkon's eyes fixed on her. Studiously she avoided his glance. It was too late to turn back now and anyway she had a task to perform.

'I am Sunida, my Lady,' she said, inclining herself again courteously to Maria. 'I have come to pay my respects to the future major wife of the master.'

Maria stared at her for a moment in silence, quietly appraising her. 'I am not the future major wife of the master, madam. If I were married to him, I would simply be his wife.' The tone of her Siamese was polite, but there was a touch of condescension in the voice.

Phaulkon looked on in apprehension. What had come over Sunida? He had told her to stay away. What if Maria were suddenly to reveal her knowledge of Sunida's spying role? He had to separate these two before irreparable damage was done.

'Sunida, I am glad you came in. I was about to order some refreshments. Would you arrange for some tea, please.'

Sunida perceived the urgency in her master's voice. She would

490

not aggravate him further but she would at least say what she had come to say. 'I receive your orders, my Lord. I heard loud voices inside and thought that perhaps you had summoned me.' She turned to Maria. 'I am honoured, madam, to have made your acquaintance, and to have had the opportunity of assuring you of my loyalty and obedience at all times.'

'I thank you,' replied Maria stiffly, 'but I do not think that either will be necessary.'

Crouching low, Sunida walked out backwards, not daring to look up at her master. It was not going to be easy to sway this obdurate girl, she thought, as she closed the door behind her.

Maria turned immediately to Phaulkon. 'What presumption indeed on the part of that girl, my Lord, though I suppose she can know no better. Did you perhaps arrange that little episode to impress upon me your concubine's docility?'

'My betrothal to you, Maria, is no secret. Sunida is not under the impression that she has anything to hide. She was just paying you the traditional respects.'

'The traditional respects of a concubine, my Lord?' inquired Maria bitterly.

'She has been sent to spy on me and it suits my purposes well. That, as I have told you, is the extent of our relationship.'

'Then, my Lord, I am afraid you will have to choose between your career and me.' Maria looked up at him, an angry edge to her voice. 'Even if she were not as devastatingly attractive as she is, I would object to sharing my house with a woman who was openly spying on my husband. Think about it, my Lord.' She turned to leave. 'And now I shall take my leave before she returns with more pledges of her devotion. You should have tea with her in my place, I am sure you will have much to discuss.'

'The subject of your intransigence is unfortunately not a topic she would understand.'

'Then discuss with her the question of her dismissal. Because only then, my Lord, will I ever accept to become your devoted wife.'

'You ask, madam, more than I can give.'

Thirty-six

Samuel Potts reached Mergui shortly before dusk and though he had rested a whole week at the Dutch factory in Ayudhya to gather his strength, his guides had been forced to slacken their pace and the journey had taken a slow fifteen days. The sickening motion of the elephant ride, the terrifying swirl of the rapids, the mosquitoes, and the tigers lurking beyond the fringes of the camp fires to devour what the mosquitoes had left, had taken their toll of him. He could still hear their hungry growls in his ears as he alighted now from the canoe-like boat and stepped ashore. He stretched himself and gently touched his aching neck, feeling the still tender sores where those damned boards had rubbed his skin. Soon he would be in Madras and there would be all hell to pay for the insults he had endured in that native prison. As for Phaulkon . . . Potts would personally bring that devil's treachery to Vice President Yale's attention, and Phaulkon would be arrested for treason. Yale would see to it that the Greek was hung, drawn and quartered, and Potts would have the satisfaction of being present. It had become his one overriding ambition.

Potts paused for a moment on the river bank, where his porters were unloading the limited European clothing that the Dutch had been able to provide for him, and looked across at the bustling harbour. Though he was in no mood to appreciate nature, the sight was so majestic that even his dour spirits were lifted. Great wooded hills swept down to the edges of the bay, and the horizon, now orange in the dying light of day, was dotted with a host of shimmering islands. The ocean was as still as a lake and the evening temperature pleasantly balmy. The tiredness seemed to fall from his shoulders.

The harbour-front teemed with natives in colourful costumes as he made his way past the rows of thatch-roofed stalls where customers squatted on rush mats, eating and chatting. His eye scanned the waterfront and alighted on a group of white men dressed in shirts and breeches, sitting on wooden crates in front of one of the furthest stalls. They seemed in animated

492

conversation. What a stroke of luck, he thought. He would be able to inquire where he might put up for the night but, more important still, they might be able to tell him when a boat was due to leave for Madras. He had not noticed any ocean-going vessels in the harbour, only small native boats and what looked like a coastal junk. He gestured to the porter and headed off in the direction of the Europeans.

As he approached he saw that there were three of them and that they seemed to be toasting each other with great frequency and a good deal of hilarity. Their laughter, however, died suddenly as they caught sight of him and something in the way they signalled to each other and ceased their conversation made him suspicious. He thought he had heard the men speaking English and instinctively he resolved to disclose as little about himself as possible.

'Good afternoon, gentlemen. What an unexpected surprise. I am indeed relieved to find some of my countrymen here. May I join you?'

'Pull up a crate, sir,' replied one of them, with a forced laugh. He was blond and sunburnt with the air of a well-travelled seaman. He had an engaging smile and he looked vaguely familiar. Where had he seen that face before? wondered Potts. The other two were physical opposites. One was tall, thin and balding, and the other was undersized with a mop of curly brown hair.

'Would you care for a drink, sir?' asked the tall man. 'We managed to find a bottle of brandy at the Catholic mission.'

'Most kind of you, sir. I could do with a glass,' replied Potts, noticing from the level of the bottle and the flush on their faces, that they were several drinks ahead of him. The tall man poured him a measure.

'Is there any accommodation to be had here, gentlemen?' asked Potts.

The tall man turned to the diminutive one. 'You know the Father well, Thomas; does he have a spare room?' He jerked his head in the direction of the small church up the hill.

'The visitor might be able to take ours when we leave tomorrow,' replied the little man. He turned to Potts. 'Especially if you're willing to fill the Father's collection box. It's the surest way to his heart.'

493

'Where have you come from?' inquired the blond seaman, glancing suspiciously at the deep welts on the newcomer's throat and neck.

'Macau,' said Potts. 'And before that China.' Macau was a Portuguese preserve, unlikely to be more than a name to the English seaman. As he finished speaking, the face that had seemed vaguely familiar to Potts took on a name. Of course. George White. A younger version of him certainly, but otherwise the spitting image. Perhaps it was his brother. Come to think of it, he had heard that George had a brother working with the honourable Company, in Madras or somewhere.

A comely Burmese woman in a chequered mauve sarong came up holding four banana leaves which served as dishes. Three of them were piled with steaming rice and fried fish, while the fourth bore a thick brown sauce. She smiled and looked inquiringly at Potts, pointing to the dishes. He nodded affirmatively and she returned to her stall to fetch some more. The tall man followed her relentlessly with his gaze.

'You wouldn't fancy that lady by any chance, would you, Richard?' asked the little man, grinning broadly. 'I can't wait to hear you ask the Father for permission to house her in the church tonight with you.' He drained his glass and poured himself another one. 'I must say these Burmese women are freer even with their favours than the Siamese.' Mergui had changed hands so many times between Burma and Siam that its population was by now an even mix of the two. 'We should open a branch office here.'

Richard! exclaimed Potts to himself. That was it. Potts had been racking his brain to remember Burnaby's Christian name. Phaulkon had mentioned that Burnaby was on some confidential mission in Mergui, and the place was not exactly teeming with Europeans. It had to be him. And the little man must be Irving. What were they doing here with George White's brother?

'Where are you gentlemen off to tomorrow?' inquired Potts casually, pretending to make conversation.

'Ayudhya,' replied Burnaby. 'And you, sir?'

'Madras, if I can find a ship going there, that is. Perhaps you gentlemen can help?'

'Madras?' interrupted White, gazing oddly at Potts. 'You've taken a very circuitous route, sir. Why would anyone travelling from Macau to Madras take the overland route through Siam?' He glanced at Potts' scant luggage which the porter was guarding by the stall.

Potts followed his gaze. 'The crew of the junk I was on in Macau robbed me of all my possessions and set me ashore in Siam at the mouth of the Menam. From there I was told this was the fastest route to Madras.'

Samuel White relaxed. 'You're lucky to be alive then, sir,' he sympathized, smiling. 'Very decent of the pirates to put you ashore at all, I should say.'

'We're all lucky to be alive,' said Burnaby, raising his glass. He draped his arm affectionately round the waist of the comely Burmese as she brought another plate for Potts. The newcomer examined the banana leaf gingerly and poked at the thick sauce with his little shell spoon. Then seeing that they had all raised their glasses he lifted his too and drained it in unison.

'Have you also had a narrow escape then?' asked Potts.

'Back from the dead,' answered White. It occurred to him, now that he knew this man was heading for Madras, that he should tell their story. The more people who had heard the tale, the more it would gain credibility. 'Our ship, the *Cornwall*, sank with all its cargo in a storm off the Andamans and we only escaped the savages there by the will of God and the skin of our teeth. We were drifting in two small boats when we were picked up by a Siamese junk and taken into Mergui. We've been drinking to our return from the dead.' He stood up. 'Samuel White's the name, sir, captain in the honourable Company's merchant fleet at Madras. With whom do I have the honour?'

'John Granger, sir,' said Potts, rising and bowing.

'And these here are Messrs Burnaby and Ivatt,' continued White, indicating the others, who had also now risen. 'These gentlemen are from the Company's Ayudhya office. I sent a messenger there to report the loss of our ship and to seek alternative means of transport. They have been most helpful.'

'I am delighted to make your acquaintance, gentlemen,' said Potts bowing again. 'You were not on board this ill-fated ship then, Mr Burnaby?'

'No, no,' replied Burnaby, shifting uneasily on his feet. 'I just came down to make the report. And to help Mr White arrange transport to Madras.'

'I'd be most grateful for a passage, Captain White, if you're going to Madras or anywhere across the bay.'

'My crew will be going to Madras, Mr, er, Granger, I believe you said?' replied Samuel. 'But I myself have some business to attend to first in Ayudhya for a few days. Boats call in frequently enough here though, so I'm sure you'll have no trouble finding passage across the bay; especially if you can pay for it. Demarcora, the Armenian trader based in Pegu, has a number of vessels in the area and his captains are always glad of a little extra pocket money. Oh, but I forgot, you were robbed.' He looked inquiringly at Potts. 'Did the brigands leave you anything at all, sir?'

'Not as they thought, sir, but I had fortunately been warned against pirates in the China Sea and I'd taken the precaution of hiding some Spanish doubloons in the lining of my coat.'

'A very wise precaution,' observed Burnaby. 'Are you a trader then, sir?'

Potts emitted a short laugh. 'You wouldn't know it to look at me now, sir, but I am a special envoy of His Majesty King Charles – long may he reign – to the Emperor of China's court. As soon as I can identify myself in Madras, the honourable Company will assuredly put me on the first ship bound for England. In the meantime, gentlemen, I'd be most grateful for your help.' He looked around him amiably.

'Well, here comes the Father,' announced Ivatt, pointing to the figure of the priest approaching in a long brown robe. 'If you're ready to part with some of your doubloons, sir, we can probably find you some accomodation.'

Father Francisco came up to them, his round face beaming happily, his eyes strangely aglow. He looked quite distracted and he did not at first notice that Potts was not one of the original Englishmen. The ways of the Lord were indeed wonderful, he reflected. Now that the chapel roof had been repaired, he would finally be able to add another wing to serve as a schoolroom. All thanks to these seamen whom, in His infinite wisdom, the Lord had sent to him. They had promised him a percentage of the treasures now concealed in the house of God and these would be more than enough to build the school he had dreamed of.

Father Francisco winked merrily at Samuel. 'Your treasures are safe, my son. God himself is keeping an eye on them. With the assistance, of course, of some of your crew. He . . .' The priest broke off, suddenly noticing Potts for the first time. 'Oh, I see you have another friend with you.'

'John Granger, Father, at your service,' said Potts, rising. What treasure was up there? he wondered. He vowed to find out before the day was out. He smiled to himself. He sensed he was on to something interesting. The activities of this bunch smelled somehow of the hangman's noose.

'Mr Granger has just been in Macau, Father,' said White quickly. 'He was unfortunately robbed there.'

'Macau?' exclaimed the priest excitedly. He had spent five years there before being transferred to Mergui. What a coincidence. The Lord's bounty knew no limits, he mused. Now He was even bringing him news of his beloved Macau.

'Have they repaired the façade of the church of São Paulo?' he inquired eagerly.

'Er, um,' stuttered Potts, taken by surprise, 'frankly, I'm not much of a church-going man, Father.'

'Of course, of course,' replied Father Francisco visibly disappointed. 'You English are all heretics, I had forgotten.' He was suddenly annoyed. But even a heretic might have noticed a thing of such beauty, he thought. How he yearned to hear something of his old home town. 'Where did you stay then, sir?'

Potts hesitated. He was not sure whether there was a representative of the English crown in Macau or not. This was an unfortunate turn of events. He had to get this damned priest off the subject. 'At the inn, Father.'

'The Pousada do Norte?' asked the priest, raptly.

'That's it. Quite charming, too.'

'I once dined there with the Bishop,' said the priest, his face lighting up. 'Are the Ribeira brothers still running it?'

'I never met the owners, Father. But speaking of rooms, I was wondering if you had a spare room to rent here?'

The priest did not hear the question. How strange, he thought, that anyone staying at the Pousada had not met Jorge and Antonio Ribeira. There were only six rooms at the inn and the Ribeira brothers personally received every guest arriving there and made a point of offering them a glass of porto wine. Even English heretics. And how could anyone not have noticed the façade of the church? It dominated the whole harbour. It was to Macau what São Pedro was to Rome or São Vicente to Lisboa.

It suddenly occurred to the Father that this man might never have been to Macau at all.

'And is the bridge across to China still standing?' he inquired.

'Indeed it is, Father, I went across it myself.' This priest was becoming tiresome, thought Potts. He was about to ask him again for a room when he noticed the man staring at him oddly.

'There is no bridge to China, sir. There never has been. Macau is not an island.'

The three Englishmen had been listening with increasing attention to this exchange. A nasty suspicion crept up on Burnaby; and White, very conscious of the need for secrecy concerning their recent mission, now rose to his feet.

The huge hoard of silver, the proceeds of their lucrative sale to the merchants of Persia, was stored in chests lying in the vestry of the little chapel on the hill. Shifts of crewmen from the sunken *Cornwall*, never less than three at a time, were on permanent guard outside the chapel gate while the rest of their mates were enjoying the fruits of their spoils in a bawdy house at the other end of town. Father Francisco had been promised a generous donation for his part, as Ivatt had jokingly put it, in 'temporarily harbouring the treasures of earth in heaven'.

'It seems you have never been to Macau, sir. Who are you?' demanded White with a note of menace in his voice.

Potts felt his knees grow weak and he cursed his luck. He was no match for the athletic seaman in front of him. His brain reeled.

'I . . . I . . . had forgotten, gentlemen, about the bridge.' He looked pleadingly from White to the priest, but finding no sympathy there he turned to Ivatt and Burnaby. 'So much has happened since then, the robbery, that I—'

'But nothing that would cause you to remember crossing a bridge that has never existed,' said White, his tone ugly. 'There are only two ways we can settle this, Mr Granger, if indeed that is your name. Either you tell us of your own free will exactly who you are, or I will drag you into that forest up there and personally beat the information out of you. Now which will it be?'

'Mr White has been known to thrash a man within an inch of his life,' observed Ivatt, graphically.

The priest looked uncomfortable. 'Well, gentlemen, if you will excuse me, I have matters to attend to elsewhere.'

'All right,' said Potts shaking, as White grabbed him roughly by the lapel of his coat, 'I'll tell you who I am.' He glanced around him nervously. The priest was scurrying along the water-front, while a group of natives, close enough to observe the scene, stared curiously at the foreigners. It was almost dark now. Only a few fading blotches of red remained scattered across the horizon.

'I am a senior auditor of the honourable Company,' announced Potts in as imperious a tone as he could command. White hesitated a moment and then relaxed his grip.

'What's your name?' he demanded, less aggressively than before.

'Samuel Potts. I was sent to investigate the Company's affairs in Ayudhya.' He turned to Burnaby. 'I found none of the staff at their posts except for Mr Phaulkon, who treated me abysmally. When I insisted on examining the books, he proceeded to burn down the factory.'

Burnaby stared at Potts in silence. Ivatt waited for Burnaby to speak while White bided his time.

'I was informed, Mr Potts,' said Burnaby, finding his voice, 'that it was you who had set fire to the factory.'

'Me, sir? Don't be ridiculous. Why would I, a senior Company auditor, want to set fire to the very building I was sent to investigate? Come now, sir, where is the logic in that?'

Burnaby watched him shake his head in disbelief. Was it possible that Constant had done as Potts claimed? wondered Burnaby. The Greek did have a nasty temper, he knew, and when roused, there was no telling what he might do . . . he had seen it happen before. Burnaby had heard of Samuel Potts and was aware of his rank. If this man were really he, and Phaulkon had really burned down the factory, they had all come to the end of their careers with the Company, that was certain. They would be summoned to Madras to face a court martial. Potts had to be appeased somehow. But how? Burnaby's brain was spinning.

Potts now turned to White, gaining confidence as he saw the others losing theirs. 'And you, Mr White, I knew your brother George. A fine, if rather unconventional man. May I ask what precisely are those treasures stored in the church up there?' He pointed towards the hill. 'Didn't I hear you say the *Cornwall* went down with all its cargo?'

499

White looked at him. Should he do away with Potts here and now? After all, if a senior auditor of the Company demanded to see the crates, on what grounds could he refuse him? And how would he explain the hoard of silver that filled a score of boxes? Would Potts ever believe it was destined for the Siamese Treasury and not for him? It was a damnable predicament.

'Those crates contain silver, Mr Potts, belonging to the Siamese Treasury,' he replied. 'We have been asked to provide an escort to Ayudhya for them. That is why I have to go up there first. I am sending my men back to Madras to report the fate of the *Cornwall* in the meantime.'

'And who asked you to supply this escort?' demanded Potts, clearly sceptical.

'Mr Burnaby here,' replied White turning to the lanky Englishman, who was again nervously shifting about on his feet.

'That's . . . that's right,' confirmed Burnaby, with a slight stutter. 'When I requested a pass from the Barcalon to travel to Mergui in reply to Mr White's summons, His Excellency asked me to use some of the stranded Englishmen to escort valuable Treasury merchandise back to Ayudhya. It would have been very impolitic to refuse. The Barcalon's requests usually emanate from the King.'

'That's why I decided to separate from my men,' elaborated White, his confidence growing with the story. 'I did not want to refuse a request from the King of Siam when I had heard the honourable Company was seeking better relations with his government. At the same time, I could hardly delay reporting the fate of the *Cornwall*.'

'You mean the powerful King of Siam does not have at his disposal adequate escorts of his own?' demanded Potts incredulously. 'Since when does he have to apply to shipwrecked seamen for his protection?'

'The farangs are better armed, Mr Potts,' said Ivatt. 'Even I, the Company's most junior member, was asked to come along on account of my musket. The Siamese have few muskets of their own and do not use them very competently. I understand that the contents of His Majesty's crates are especially valuable.'

'I will examine them then, gentlemen. Let us proceed up the hill.' Potts' rising confidence was beginning to turn to arrogance as he felt himself gaining the upper hand again.

500

'The crates are sealed, Mr Potts, and furthermore they are the property of the Siamese government,' warned White. 'It would be most improper to break those seals and—'

'I will be the judge of that, Mr White. Follow me, please.'

Potts strode on ahead while White and Burnaby glanced at each other. White made a sign as if to slit Potts' throat but Burnaby shook his head emphatically. Things were bad enough without having a murder on their hands, he reflected. They caught up with Potts and followed him up the hill. Ivatt brought up the rear. They climbed the narrow path in silence and as they approached the little church, White cautioned Potts once more.

'I strongly advise you against unsealing the crates, Mr Potts. The English are responsible for their safe passage and it will not look good if they arrive tampered with.' If Potts opened the wrong crate he would find more than just silver, reflected White bitterly. At least four of the boxes contained items of value salvaged from the *Cornwall*, while the ship's strongbox – hardly something to be salvaged from a sinking ship in a storm – took up the whole of a fifth crate. It would immediately be visible.

'Wait outside here, gentlemen,' said Potts in an imperious tone, as he opened the door of the church and stepped inside. After the harsh sunlight outside, the vestry seemed almost in darkness. The silhouette of a tall seaman barred his passage. 'I'm sorry, sir, but the church is closed today for repairs.'

'I've been sent by Captain White to examine the merchandise,' declared Potts. He looked around him. Lining one wall of the church were the outlines of several large crates. He started towards them.

Two more seamen emerged from the shadows in the corners and stood in front of him. 'I'm sorry, sir, you cannot proceed further.'

'Why not?' demanded Potts, feigning surprise. 'Aren't those boxes the property of the Siamese government?'

'They are Captain White's, sir, and they are not to be touched.'

'It's all right, lads. Let him examine them.' White stood framed in the doorway. 'The contents are all the same so let him take his pick. I don't want more than one box unsealed, though, or the Siamese in Ayudhya'll think we've been helping ourselves.' White had already made up his mind. If Potts opened up the wrong box he was going to die.

Potts started towards the crates. They were piled three high and stacked in rows of four. He pointed to one of the crates at the bottom and the sailors turned to their captain for approval.

White nodded and the three strapping seamen began carefully to remove the crates that lay across it. The load was heavy and it was hard work. The entire crew had had to be brought in the previous day to carry the crates up the hill when they had been offloaded from the junk. White had needed a day or two in Mergui before proceeding to Ayudhya, in order to organize the homeward passage of his crew, and Ivatt had arranged with Father Francisco to store the crates in the church. They had all agreed that it was the safest place.

The crate that Potts had indicated was now standing free. The seamen glanced at their captain for final approval before they broke the seal and prized the crate open with an iron bar. Potts moved forward to examine the contents. 'I'll need more light,' he said. 'Leave the chapel door open.' The small stained-glass windows at the sides provided very little illumination. White was still standing in the doorway, while Burnaby and Ivatt remained outside.

As White stepped inside the church, the light from the open doorway streamed in. Potts bent down to examine the crate. In that instant, like a cloud passing across the sun, the room was once more enveloped in shadow. Potts and White turned towards the door.

A priest stood on the threshold, blocking the light. He stared for a moment at the crates and then at each of the Europeans in turn. It was not Dom Francisco. This priest was smaller and thinner and much too dark for a Portuguese. He looked almost Indian. Bowing slightly to Potts and White, the priest walked past the crates and knelt down at one of the far pews at the front of the chapel. He clasped his hands together in an attitude of prayer and began to chant monotonously in Siamese.

Potts shrugged his shoulders and resumed his examination. The tension in the room increased. White's fists clenched and he looked ready to slit Potts' throat at any minute, whatever the contents of the box.

Potts removed a layer of straw from the top of the crate and then reached down to extract the contents. As he raised the first

502

item, his hands shook with the weight. He put it down and examined it carefully. It was a bar of silver. 'The markings look Persian,' he said, a trace of suspicion in his voice. 'I thought the Moors ran the King of Siam's Persian trade? Why aren't they taking these spoils to Ayudhya themselves?' he inquired.

'How can I answer that, Mr Potts,' replied White, 'when I am not even aware of the contents of the crates? We were asked to perform a service for His Majesty and we are merely carrying it out. John,' he said, turning to the tallest of the seamen, 'you and the boys can reseal the crate now. Try and make it look as if it hasn't been tampered with.'

'Aye, aye, sir.'

'Just a minute,' said Potts. 'I haven't finished yet. I will empty the crate first and then I will examine another one.' White restrained his urge to lunge. Potts pointed to a crate at the end. 'Open that one, please.' The seamen looked at their captain. White's eyes were bulging and his whole body was beginning to shake. They had seen the skipper like this before and it meant trouble.

'Stay where you are,' commanded White. 'I said that I did not want to open more than one crate belonging to the Siamese government, Mr Potts. As it is, one is already too many. I will not allow you to add insult to injury. You have seen what you asked to see.' He turned again to the seamen. 'Seal the open crate and leave the other crates alone.'

'Aye, aye, sir.'

'You will order your men to do as I ask, Captain White, or you will suffer the consequences of my report to Madras. I am a senior auditor of the Company, and as a nautical man, captain, you must be aware of the consequences of refusing to obey a superior officer.'

Potts bent down and picked up the crowbar which the seamen had used to pry open the first crate. Then he walked over to the far end of the stack. He raised the bar and prepared to insert it into another crate. The seamen glanced at their skipper. White's face was flushed and his upper lip had begun to twitch. As Potts proceeded to prise the second crate open, White flew at him and locked his hands around Potts' neck. Potts started to scream as the pressure increased but White ignored the cries, clearly bent on throttling him. The seamen looked on, not daring to intervene.

Drawn by the shrieks, Ivatt and Burnaby rushed in and pounced on White. They struggled to pull him away from Potts, while the seamen looked at each other, uncertain whether to join the contest or not.

Twice Ivatt and Burnaby managed to drag White away and twice he wrenched himself free again and dived back on to Potts. The seamen opted to stay clear and it was several minutes before Ivatt and Burnaby finally pulled White off. Burnaby collapsed, gasping for air, and Potts lay there clutching his throat, while his body twitched spasmodically.

'Have you gone mad?' breathed Burnaby into White's ear. 'Do you want to have us all court martialled? I am responsible for the Company's behaviour here. What will become of us now?'

Ivatt meanwhile was tending to Potts. He had raised the man against his knee and was massaging his chest. Burnaby was too winded to assist him. White lay with his back against the wall muttering incoherently. At this moment the dark-skinned priest came up to him and said something in Siamese. Then he bent over Potts and put his ear to the Englishman's heart.

He knelt by his side and intoned a little prayer. He made the sign of the cross and smiled at the others as if to say that Potts would be all right. After a while he rose, and as he made his way towards the door, he bent down agilely and examined the bar of silver that lay on the floor by the open crate, where Potts had left it. One of the seamen stepped menacingly forward. The priest smiled shyly and put the bar down on the floor again. Then he walked quickly out of the door and disappeared out of sight down the hill.

Luang Aziz rang the bell and was instantly admitted. He removed the cowl from his face and entered the house in his priest's robe. There had been no time to change.

He bowed low to Oc-Ya Tannaw and then even lower to the stiff-backed moustachioed guest of honour immediately to the Oc-Ya's right. 'Your Highness,' he murmured, lowering himself.

'Well?' said Oc-Ya Tannaw. 'What news do you bring us, Aziz?' Five pairs of dark eyes fixed themselves intently on the newcomer. A silence descended on the room.

504

Luang Aziz took his place cross-legged in the only space remaining in the circle and stared for a moment at the prints on the wall. How appropriate, he thought, were these street scenes of Ispahan, particularly the ones depicting a Persian marketplace. Perhaps the farangs had visited the very one.

'I bring bad news, my brothers. The letter I took from the girl was a hoax.'

There was a murmur of disquiet all round.

'But did you not say that she resisted parting with the letter until the last moment?' asked Oc-Ya Tannaw, perplexed.

'She was well trained, Your Honour,' responded Aziz. 'Her deception was convincing.'

He looked around him, worried by the weight of his discoveries but savouring at the same time this moment of glory. It was not often that a man could report such portentous news before so illustrious a company. He glanced at the ruler of the Macassars and saw that he, too, was hanging on his every word. 'The farang ship went to Persia,' he announced. 'It returned with crates full of silver. Persian silver.'

'You saw the markings?' asked the Oc-Ya anxiously.

Aziz nodded. 'I did, Your Honour. Unquestionably Persian. And most interesting is that the farang ship never docked again at Mergui. The crates were offloaded from a Siamese junk. As the junk was too small to have made the trip from Persia, the goods must have been transferred on to it somewhere out at sea. The farang ship clearly did not want to be seen. It must have left straight for home – Madras, no doubt.'

'Did you ascertain who arranged the junk?' asked the Oc-Ya.

'Yes, Your Honour. It was the Jesuit priest, Dom Francisco, and one of the farangs from the English Company piloted it.'

The Oc-Ya Tannaw's dark eyes flashed with anger. 'That priest will pay for his deceit.' He looked around him gravely at the assembled councillors. 'Brothers, we are faced with a Christian conspiracy, spearheaded by this new mandarin, Phaulkon. And the King, it appears, is on their side.'

There was a murmur of shock.

'But why?' asked Iqbal Sind, rubbing a finger nervously over his beak-like nose. 'Why would His Majesty wish to side with the farangs?'

'You will see a pattern, Iqbal, if you look closely. First Rashid is removed as banqueting chief, then Treasury goods are sent secretly to Persia on an English ship, and finally a member of the English trading Company is made a mandarin.'

'It is clear that the position of the Moors is being undermined,' concurred Fawzi Ali, sucking nervously on his water pipe. 'But why? What is the advantage of replacing us with farangs?'

'Perhaps His Majesty is promoting the English infidels to create a buffer against the Dutch.' Farouk Radwan scratched his copious black beard and spat into a copper spittoon by his side.

'Or perhaps,' said the Oc-Ya, looking slowly around him, 'perhaps the Siamese government has discovered the extent of the profits we have been reaping.' He paused. 'Everything points in that direction.'

There was a general hush. The Oc-Ya had put into words the suspicion that had been on everyone's minds. The Siamese government had finally had enough. It was going to break their age-old monopoly.

'We must eliminate the root of the problem – Phaulkon. Eliminate him and you eliminate the source of our troubles. Who replaced Rashid as head of banqueting? Who organized the trading mission to Persia? Who was made a mandarin? Who increasingly has the ear of the King?'

'To eliminate one man is not enough, my brother.' The deep, guttural voice commanded instant attention. All eyes turned to Prince Dai, the hereditary ruler of the Macassars. It was the first time he had spoken. He was tall and regal, the Malay features prominent and strong, the brown cheeks void of hair. Only a moustache covered his upper lip. On one side of his neck he bore the scar of a Dutch bullet wound. He sat straightbacked, his head erect, his eyes devoid of fear. He seemed pensive again and no one dared interrupt him.

When the Prince had first arrived and sought asylum on these shores, the King of Siam had received him and his people graciously and granted them land on which to build their encampment. The Prince and his men had gone to work with feverish zeal and built their village out of virgin forest, as if that might obliterate the shameful loss of their cherished homeland. The wooden huts were simple but adequate and every man had a roof over his head. Prince Dai had admired the generous and

506

warrior-like qualities of this Siamese King who in his youth had ridden staunchly into battle on his royal elephant to confront the Burmese enemy. But now the King was getting old and he had begun to associate himself with white men. As Prince Dai knew only too well, that was the beginning of weakness. How many times had he not seen it happen in his homeland? The Javanese princes that had traded and befriended the heathen Dutch had turned round one day to find the white man sitting on their thrones.

Not a day passed when he did not think of the ignominy he had suffered at the hands of these Dutch as they overran his beloved Celebes, those filthy white cowards who hid behind their guns and did not know how to fight like men. Prince Dai despised modern weapons; he believed only in bodily valour and the skill of the kris. What satisfaction was there in pulling a trigger from afar and seeing a man fall without so much as a contest? The man who fired the gun was as much the loser as the man who fell.

Now, in the west of Siam, the chosen of Allah were already losing their positions and before long the infidel would replace them throughout the nation. It was clear that the days of all Muslims in Siam were numbered unless the Macassars rose to defend the word of Allah. Slowly his eyes travelled round the assembled Moors.

'There is only one way, my brothers.' His lips broke into a thin smile. 'War.' There was silence around him. 'To assassinate Phaulkon would be but a temporary measure. Other farangs would spring up in his place. The whole Muslim brotherhood is threatened. If we are to survive, we must do more than eliminate just one man.'

'But Your Highness, even if we were successful in overthrowing the government of Siam, how long could we rule in its place? The population is almost entirely Buddhist and every last Siamese worships his King.' Once more the Oc-Ya had expressed the precise feelings of his colleagues.

The Prince ran a hand through his thick black hair. 'You are right, of course. But who suggested ruling the country in place of the Siamese?' A smile played on his lips. 'What I am suggesting is replacing one Siamese ruler with another, one who dislikes the farangs and would restore our traditional positions to us and allow us to continue administering the country as before. Such a person has already approached me.'

'May we know who that is, Your Highness?'

'Indeed. Luang Sorasak. He came to see me at my camp just after you requested my presence in Mergui. He told me how there is growing resentment at court over the increasing privileges granted to farangs and especially the appointment of this farang mandarin. We would have a lot of support from within the palace, particularly as there are increasing rumours of an impending alliance with France. It is even said that a treaty is being drafted, with an exchange of troops between the two countries. If this is true it would mean farang soldiers on Siamese soil.' The Prince looked around him, pleased with the effect his words were having. The assembly was in shock. 'Only this morning a secret emissary from General Petraja himself came to see me and indicated that the general too was behind his son. Even the non-Muslim courtiers, it seems, are chafing at the growing power of the white dog, and incensed at the idea of foreign troops. That is why, my brothers, it is time to act now. I pledge my men without hesitation to overthrow the present government, to assassinate Phaulkon and to place Sorasak on the throne of Siam. He in turn is pledged to restore us to our former glory.'

There was a lengthy silence. Then one by one, some hesitantly at first, the members of the Council cast their votes in favour of Prince Dai's plan. The Oc-Ya Tannaw was the last to speak.

'Are your troops then ready, Your Highness?'

The Prince smiled. 'My people have been idle far too long.'

'Very well, then,' said the Oc-Ya, looking around him. 'May Allah bless the revolt of the Macassars.'

Thirty-seven

Phaulkon paced up and down the living room consumed with frustration. Another week had elapsed. The time it would take the Dutch ships to sail from Batavia had passed and if they had left as expected they could be here any day now. Phaulkon had continued exploring every avenue to see His Majesty but the answer was always the same. The Lord of Life was too busy to see him. Even the Barcalon was unavailable, though for genuine reasons, Phaulkon knew. The minister was bedridden now, with recurring bouts of asthma. And there was as yet no word of the return of the Persian expedition.

With his impatience and anxiety stretched to the limit, Phaulkon had determined to take matters into his own hands. If nothing happened today he would visit Aarnout Faa anyway and tell him about the imminent treaty with France. It was hardly his favourite means of procedure but if he could present it graphically enough, perhaps it would give the VOC chief cause to demur. If the invasion could be retarded by even a few days, his Majesty might come round to announcing the treaty in the meantime. It was clumsy, he knew, but it was better than nothing.

He had not seen Maria for a week since she had rejected his offer of marriage on account of Sunida, but there seemed little point in pursuing the matter at this stage, while there was no sign of an impending treaty. Besides, he was quite unwilling to part with Sunida. It was high time his luck changed, he reflected. In a moment of despair he had even been to see the court astrologer, Pra Sarit. The venerable old monk had read the stars and assured Phaulkon that his fortunes would change dramatically in a day or two, and Phaulkon's faith in his destiny, seeking any uplift, had been revived. That was yesterday. Pra Sarit had made some amazing forecasts in his time and Phaulkon determined to wait for the evening of the second day before visiting Aarnout Faa.

It was now midday. Sunida had gone to the marketplace to pass on his latest plea for an audience with the Lord of Life.

He had been sleeping poorly at nights and making up for it with brief naps during the day and he was about to lie down for a rest when he heard voices outside. His heart leapt for the first time in days and he ran to the window.

'These are a few presents for His Excellency the Oc-Luang from his grateful staff,' Ivatt was saying in passable Siamese to Phaulkon's giggling servants. 'Where shall we put them?'

Phaulkon laughed as he saw a score of large crates on the shoulders of twice as many coolies, their faces and torsos soaked in perspiration. Had Pra Sarit predicted right again?

'Stack them up in the living room where I can count them,' said Phaulkon, opening the door. A moment later he was locked in a series of effusive embraces with his comrades Burnaby, Ivatt and White.

'There *is* something in those crates, I presume?' asked Phaulkon jocularly.

'About enough to buy a couple of English counties and a dukedom,' replied Ivatt. 'Sam here has opted for the counties, I'm taking the dukedom, and Richard wants to return to Madras to face trial.'

Phaulkon glanced at Burnaby. Perhaps it was no joke. He certainly did not look as elated as the others.

'How about me?' asked Phaulkon.

Ivatt looked at him awkwardly. 'We all voted on it and concluded that only those who actually participated in the expedition should be rewarded. It's only fair, really. But we have written you a note of appreciation, acknowledging your part in the original idea.'

'I shall frame it,' countered Phaulkon gratefully.

'When we heard the news of your promotion, my Lord Phaulkon, on the Tenasserim river, we almost fell out of our canoes,' said Samuel White laughing. 'Thomas waited till we were in the middle of some rapids to tell us. I think he was trying to drown us.'

'You looked so frightened of the torrent, Samuel,' said Thomas, 'that I thought it was an appropriate moment to distract you.'

They all laughed except Burnaby. They sat down in Phaulkon's living room, chatting volubly. Briefly they related their encounter

510

with Potts, then moved on to more interesting matters. The air was charged with excitement as Samuel described how the merchants of Bandar Abbas and Khoramshar had at first been reticent to buy Siamese goods from European traders. They had been surprised and suspicious not to deal with their traditional Moorish brethren, but the sight of the lucrative cargo of silks and porcelain had soon convinced them otherwise and before long they were haggling and fighting over the entire cargo like vultures over a camel's carcass. It had been like an auction. The bidders had come on board the ship and started by offering a price which was already three times the value the Siamese Treasury had placed on the goods and Burnaby had countered with a request for nine times the cost. The merchants had thrown their hands up in the air but when Burnaby had ordered White to set sail and proceed to the court of the Grand Turk in Istanbul, the merchants had quickly settled for six times the value.

Phaulkon glanced over at the enormous spoils now, stacked neatly in one corner of the living room. Twenty crates of approximately a hundredweight of pure silver. It was a fortune. He would put a small portion of it to use right away.

Only Burnaby seemed morose, not sharing the exuberance of the others. 'It's all very well for you, Constant, being a foreign mandarin and all that,' he said, 'but I am still an Englishman responsible for the Company's behaviour here, and once Potts reaches Madras, what do you think will become of me? I can't see why you two fellows are so sanguine either,' he said, turning to White and Ivatt. 'It's only a matter of time before we're all brought back to face trial, you know.'

'Potts will never reach Madras, Richard,' said White quietly. 'I made sure of that. I obtained passage for him on the same ship as my officers. I gave them an extra cut to ensure that Potts fell violently – and terminally – ill on the voyage.'

Burnaby looked shocked. 'Oh my God! But that is tantamount to murder.'

'Call it what you will, the fact is that Potts is a dangerous drunk and no damned good to the Company anyway. If Potts had opened the wrong box, Richard, not even you could have stopped me from slitting the bastard's throat there and then,' said White heatedly.

'You should have been there, Constant,' said Ivatt, 'when Potts went over to open the first crate. The tension was terrible.

511

We didn't know which one he was going to unseal and Sam here looked as if he was ready to stuff Potts into whichever crate he happened to open anyway.'

'And when he found only silver and insisted on opening another one,' added Burnaby bitterly, 'this madman here rushed up to him and almost throttled him to death. Thomas and I had to pull him off. What do you think he is going to say in his report?'

'If anything, Richard,' said Ivatt, trying to ease the tension, 'you and I should come out as heroes for having saved his life.'

'From the sound of it, Richard,' said Phaulkon, 'Potts is not going to make any report at all. But gentlemen,' he continued, looking gravely around him, 'let us not worry about Potts now. There are more urgent matters to attend to. I have big plans. For all of us.' He turned to Burnaby. 'Richard, the English warehouse is a burned-out shell and there is no merchandise left to sell and no books left to record a sale anyway. So we must all look to our future elsewhere.' He eyed them one by one. 'I congratulate you all, gentlemen, for your part in the success of the Persian expedition, and I give you my solemn word that when Madras comes to get us, we will be ready for them.' His luck had turned and Phaulkon's confidence was back in full force.

'You're sure it was Potts who was responsible for burning down the factory?' asked Burnaby.

'Quite sure,' answered Phaulkon, taken aback by the question. 'Why, did you hear another version?'

'Only the one he's going to tell Madras,' fretted Burnaby. He looked pointedly at White. 'Potts told me himself that he had left his report in the hands of the Dutch.'

'Look, Richard,' said Phaulkon, 'I have no intention of going to Madras to defend myself, but you can if you want to. I've already told you I'll be ready for them when they come, but if you feel you should be there now, then that's your privilege. No one is stopping you.'

Richard looked away.

'Now, gentlemen,' continued Phaulkon, 'I must inform you of pressing developments in your absence.' He paused. 'The Dutch are about to invade Siam.'

There was a gasp all round.

'I want you to round up every able-bodied European you can

512

find,' Phaulkon continued. 'Offer enough silver to get the best men. Tell them it's for a secret mission you can't discuss. We don't want the Dutch or anybody else to get wind of it. I will need a force strong enough to surround the Dutch factory and abduct the VOC chief if necessary. We may have to hold him hostage, if the Dutch declare war. Fifty or sixty good fighting men should do.'

'Oh God,' groaned Ivatt, 'and I thought I had come back to a well-earned rest.'

'Just a moment, Constant,' said Burnaby. 'I was not aware of having approved any of this. I am still chief of station here, you know.'

'Indeed you are, Richard. But as of this moment I am no longer working for the English. You have my official resignation. I am a Siamese mandarin now.' He turned to White. 'You said we had obtained six times the value of the cargo, didn't you, Samuel?'

'Closer to five, Constant, after paying off the officers and crew of the *Cornwall*,' replied White.

Phaulkon smiled. 'His Majesty should be pleased. The most he ever received from the Moors was fifty per cent, not five hundred!'

'Couldn't we put a little aside for a rainy day, Constant?' suggested Ivatt. 'I mean if His Majesty is not expecting that much anyway . . . ?'

'The more we give now the more it will yield later, believe me, Thomas,' assured Phaulkon. 'Our objective is to control Siamese trade to Persia and wrest it from the Moors. We need the Siamese government to finance a fleet and they need us to conduct the trade. So the sooner we deliver the spoils to the Treasury the better. Are the coolies still outside?'

'They are awaiting your orders, Constant,' replied White. 'And by the way,' he added ingratiatingly, 'I'm not overly keen to return to Madras, myself. I was wondering if you had anything for me here?'

'I asked you to come up here for that very reason, Samuel. I have just given you your first assignment anyway – rounding up some good men.' He looked around him. 'As soon as I have obtained an audience with His Majesty we will, I hope, have much to discuss. So, gentlemen, welcome back and congratulations.' He rose to his feet. 'I am off to the ministry now. The sooner they lay eyes on the spoils the sooner I may have my way.'

Like some pasha from the desert, Phaulkon led the way, his forty coolies trailing behind him with his baggage.

'Vichaiyen, we are gratified. You and your men have performed well.' As well as the noted pleasure there was a hint of relief in the royal tone. The prostrate Phaulkon sensed that it was not just the huge spoils that satisfied the King but the vindication of His Majesty's sentiments towards Phaulkon. For some time now Phaulkon had felt he was on trial, a new employee not yet fully trusted, and the return of the ship with everything that Phaulkon had promised had finally turned the tide in his favour.

The sight of the silver had worked wonders at the ministry and the Barcalon's first assistant had made off to the palace as soon as the contents had been unpacked and weighed. The royal summons had come that same evening.

'No doubt you have some requests to make of us.' There was a hint of playfulness in the royal tone.

In the absence of the Barcalon, who was indisposed, Phaulkon was for the first time alone with His Majesty in the audience chamber. It was a singular honour and unprecedented for a farang.

'High and Mighty Lord of me, thy slave, I desire to take thy royal word and put it on my brain and on the top of my head. The only request I make is humbly to continue to serve Your Gracious Majesty.'

'And more specifically, Vichaiyen?' prompted the royal voice.

Phaulkon smiled. 'Mighty Lord, I, a hair, believe that following Your Majesty's gracious release of the criminal Potts, Madras will retaliate as soon as they are given his version of the story. They will demand the return to Madras of your devoted slaves, Burnaby, White and Ivatt, as well as this speck of dust who lies before you now.'

'And you wish to ask for our protection?'

'Mighty Lord, it is so.'

'It shall be granted. The farangs you have mentioned have served us well. However, it does not seem to us politic to await this summons from Madras before bestowing our protection upon them. We do not wish to appear to assist them only *after* a

514

request for their return has been received, in open defiance of their wishes. And it is not our policy to make unnecessary enemies of another nation.

'We shall therefore employ them forthwith and promote them to official positions in our administration from which it will prove inconvenient to release them when requested. Mr Burnaby will be made Governor of Mergui, Mr White, Shahbandar of Mergui, and Mr Ivatt will be our nation's representative on the western seaboard of India. This will represent the auspicious beginning of our new trade policy across the Bay.' His Majesty paused to give Phaulkon time to recover from his astonishment. His dreams were suddenly becoming a reality.

It was a while before he found his words. 'Mighty Lord, your wisdom and generosity know no bounds. The slaves you have mentioned will serve the Lord of Life with the same dedication as this unworthy slave before you, and will strive, as I have, to justify the trust you have placed in them.'

'And you, Vichaiyen, will assume full responsibility for their actions. Any lapse in their behaviour will be a lapse in your own and any error in their judgement will be an error in yours. We find it only fitting that a mandarin of the second grade should assume such added responsibilities.'

Again Phaulkon was speechless. Mandarin of the second grade! This would give him a permanent place in the main audience hall. Now only the thirty most powerful lords in the kingdom, the mandarins of the first grade – members of His Majesty's Privy Council and Governors of His Majesty's provinces – would be senior to him in rank. It would also allow his wife to be admitted to the palace to attend the court of Princess Yotatep, the Princess Queen. What an honour for Maria, if she were ever to accept him. And what a wedding gift.

He felt a surge of emotion. Every time he had distinguished himself, His Majesty had rewarded him. Now if only he could expose and stymie the Dutch invasion, the mandarinate first class could be within his grasp. He was determined to revive the question of the treaty at this audience. As for his assuming full responsibility for his colleagues, it was a small price to pay for such prestige and quite in keeping with Siamese tradition. Under a system of collective responsibility, a father was answerable for the behaviour of his children and a mandarin for the actions of

515

his subordinates. In Siam it was rare for an accused to flee justice when his whole family would be sentenced in his place.

Ivatt, he knew, would be thrilled to enter into the service of Siam, and White could ask for nothing more than to be Shahbandar, master of the port of Mergui. But Burnaby . . . he was not sure how the old man would react. Would he really choose to return to face trial in Madras when the governorship of a Siamese province was his for the taking?

'Mighty Lord, I, a speck of dust on the sole of your foot, thank you from the bottom of my heart for your magnanimity and beg to ask what will become of the present Governor and Shahbandar of Mergui?'

'Those of our subjects who have not served us to our satisfaction must be replaced. They will be brought to Ayudhya to answer for their crimes. Our trade with India and Persia, conducted from our western provinces since time immemorial, has been traditionally in the hands of the Moors and they have failed us. Mr Burnaby will be responsible for order in the Province of Mergui and the collection of our taxes and Mr White will oversee our trading interests in the Bay of Bengal. It will be the Shahbandar's responsibility – and ultimately yours, Vichaiyen – to fit out or build as many ships as the volume of trade may require. Farang captains and officers will assume command of these ships and Siamese crews will be trained under them. The recruiting of such officers and crews will be a priority.' His Majesty paused.

'As a further token of our esteem, Vichaiyen, you will receive ten slaves from ourselves to serve you in your house and accompany you on your travels. As a royal gift they will be expected to remain with you for life.'

What a clever tactic, thought Phaulkon, as the realization of the ploy came home to him. Sunida must have got word to the palace of his impending marriage and her own delicate position. It was not unusual for a mandarin of the second grade to receive such a gift from the King upon his appointment and it would be highly offensive for the recipient to dismiss any of the slaves who were pledged to him for life. The higher a mandarin's rank, the greater the number of slaves who accompanied him whenever he left his house. Were these slaves then to replace Sunida in her role?

516

'But we hear, Vichaiyen, that you are taking a major wife, a Catholic, we understand?'

'Mighty Lord, if it pleases Your Majesty.'

'It would certainly seem to serve our present political purposes, Vichaiyen, but does it satisfy the needs of your farang soul?'

'Mighty Lord, the needs of my soul are as nothing next to the political good of Siam.'

'No doubt, Vichaiyen. But the good of Siam will be better served if your soul is happily disposed.'

'Mighty Lord, in that case this worthless slave must crave the royal favour one more time.'

'We are listening, Vichaiyen.'

'August Lord, my heart is taken by a young consort; her name is Sunida. My Catholic wife-to-be will not tolerate her presence in the house.'

'Indeed?' His Majesty sounded amused.

'Mighty Lord, I, the dust beneath your feet, request to house Sunida at the palace where she will be safe and where, with Your Majesty's gracious permission, I could sometimes visit her.'

'You know, Vichaiyen, we are indeed fortunate that we ourselves did not convert to the Christian religion, or we would now be constrained to turn down your request. As it is, the liberal faith of our ancestors allows us to grant you your wish with a clear conscience.' His Majesty chuckled. 'It does not really make sense, this Catholic business, Vichaiyen, does it? Look at you now, for instance.'

'Mighty Lord, I am but a sinner.'

'So would we all be in your place,' responded His Majesty, tickled. 'And have the astrologers picked an auspicious day for your wedding?'

'August Lord, not yet. My Catholic wife-to-be awaits the departure of Sunida before she will consent to the marriage.'

A great laugh sounded from above.

'Then, Vichaiyen, we had better prepare Sunida's quarters in the palace without delay. As a mandarin of the second grade you will be expected to attend our audiences daily. We think it might be appropriate for you to arrive early to pay your respects to the Lady Sunida first.'

'Your Majesty is too gracious.'

517

'But we are curious on one point, Vichaiyen. Would you yourself wish to see us adopt the Catholic faith?'

'Mighty Lord, I, a speck of dust, wish only that which will bring the greatest happiness to the Master of Life.'

'Which is?' pursued His Majesty.

'Mighty Lord, that which will best satisfy the requirements of Your Majesty's Siamese soul.'

Unseen by Phaulkon, the King smiled. Vichaiyen *was* the perfect diplomat, an invaluable tool in his dealings with the farangs at a difficult time when outside forces had become a serious threat to the survival of his country. Incredibly enough, he sensed, too, that Vichaiyen's loyalties did not lie with those farangs. He had not been certain before but now those doubts had been expelled, ever since the return of the Persian expedition and the return of the royal courier from Nakhon Si Thammarat, almost at the same time. The Governor of the province had interviewed the interpreter Pieter under oath and the boy had confirmed his account to Vichaiyen of the imminent Dutch invasion. It was true enough. The matter was urgent and immediate steps had been taken . . .

'We have examined the draft of your treaty, Vichaiyen, and have approved the majority of its clauses, but we desire a reduction in the number of troops to be exchanged with France. It is to be brought down from one thousand to four hundred. We are anxious to have French soldiers appear as a token of King Louis' esteem and not as an army of occupation.'

'August Lord,' suggested Phaulkon respectfully, 'might not so small a contingent be insufficient to intimidate the Dutch?'

'If the much-heralded treaty is not enough to impress these Hollanders, then it matters little whether there are four hundred or a thousand troops, Vichaiyen.' While to his own courtiers, reflected the Lord of Life, four hundred would appear considerably more palatable.

'In the meantime you may inform the Jesuits that you are pleased with our royal progress and that we have privately intimated favourable prospects for our eventual acceptance of their faith. To coincide, of course, with the arrival of King Louis' troops. Meanwhile, we wish to study the Christian scriptures discreetly so as not to arouse the suspicions of our courtiers. Premature rumours would put a sudden end to the best of intentions. But we need hardly tell *you*, Vichaiyen,' added the King, 'how to conduct matters of such kind in which we have observed your considerable talent. Suffice it to say that you have our approval to feed the Jesuits whatever delicacies they will most readily digest.'

'Mighty Lord, I receive your orders. And I thank you for rendering my task easier. The Jesuits await only this worthless slave's marriage to Maria to ratify the treaty.'

There was another chuckle from above. 'Poor Vichaiyen, you are indeed hounded. We pray that you may return as a Buddhist in your next life, that your problems may be correspondingly reduced. As far as this life is concerned, we shall send an immediate invitation to the Jesuits to attend your wedding, which shall be royally sponsored.'

Royally sponsored, muttered Phaulkon to himself, awed. What an honour! The palace would send out the invitations and His Majesty himself might even attend. The Jesuits could certainly not refuse. He smiled. Neither could Maria. Things were really beginning to—

There was a commotion outside. A flustered first assistant of the Barcalon fell flat on his face accompanied by a breathless messenger. The assistant begged a thousand apologies and offered his head in expiation for the inestimable crime of intruding.

'Mighty Lord, even if these be my last words, I, a hair, have the temerity to report that the Macassars are rising in revolt. They are arming in their camp even now. An advance party has already been to Luang Vichaiyen's house to seek him out. His servants came to tell me.'

'Vichaiyen, you will investigate these matters immediately and if necessary gather together a farang force. They will be liberally compensated. Tawee, you will inform General Petraja this instant. The audience is terminated.'

Vichaiyen and Tawee crawled out backwards to carry out their Lord's instructions.

Thirty-eight

The Macassar camp consisted of a variety of wooden huts of all sizes and stood alongside a small river, a tributary of the great Menam. It was heavily guarded by patrols on the land side while access from the river was less controlled. Just beyond the camp the river wound sharply round a bend and the settlement quickly disappeared from view. Palm and banana trees dotted the landscape and behind the village lay rice paddies, their channels now clogged with water.

It was a moonless night. Sixty little boats moved noiselessly downstream in the direction of the camp, their paddles barely skimming the surface of the water, their presence obscured by the unrelieved darkness. The men crouched low as they passed in front of the vague contours of the Macassar camp, each soldier lying flat in his boat, letting his craft drift silently with the current at a safe distance from shore. An owl hooted in the night and the sounds of armies of cicadas rose in sudden crescendo above the lapping of the water.

In the lead boat Phaulkon strained his eyes. It was like proceeding along a dark tunnel, uncertain of its extremities, with only the merest speck of light for guidance. Kukrit, the trusted slave that His Majesty had sent him that same evening only hours after the audience, squatted by his side, always respectfully lower than Phaulkon, sniffing the wind and listening to every sound. He had grown up in these parts and knew every inlet and bend in the river like a seasoned mahout knew the ways of his favourite elephant.

Royal spies had detected unusual activity in the Macassar camp that morning. The camp was under more or less constant surveillance on account of the warlike reputation of its tribe, and the increased activity had immediately been reported to the palace. It seemed the Macassars were arming. It was fortunate that Phaulkon had been with His Majesty when the Macassar assassins had entered his house that afternoon looking for him. He had been home at that time every other afternoon for the past several days, plotting and brooding over his fate. It was a stroke of fate, too, that he had asked Burnaby, Ivatt and White to look for volunteers that day. Invaluable hours had been gained. His comrades had scoured the farang suburbs and by evening had gathered together as ragged a mob of adventurers as anybody could ever wish to find.

Sixty Europeans, a good half of them armed with muskets, had rallied to Phaulkon's call. They were Portuguese, French and English adventurers for the most part, lured by the promise of lavish rewards and royal favour. There was even an old samurai warrior who had brought with him the remnants of the late King Prasat Tong's Japanese bodyguard whose leader, Captain Yamada, had meddled too freely in court politics and lost his head in the process. The old samurai and five ageing Japanese, fearless of death and anxious to retrieve their long-lost honour, had volunteered to attack the well-guarded camp from the land – almost certain suicide but a manoeuvre that would open up the way for the rest of the troops.

That same evening, aware of the opportunity for further promotion presented by the new developments, Phaulkon had requested permission from His Majesty to lead his own band of warriors against the Macassars and take his revenge. They had, after all, sent their assassins against him. His Majesty, though worried for Phaulkon's safety, was anxious to have the advantage of European firepower and military techniques on his side. No preparations could be too great against the death-defying Macassars. He granted the request, warning Phaulkon to be careful and stipulating that his regiment should remain under the overall command of General Petraja.

The preparations for the surprise attack had begun soon after nightfall and continued through most of the night. Now, shortly before dawn, Phaulkon's boat lay in wait with the others for the assault on the Macassar camp. Surprisingly, his request to remain in the lead boat and to attack the camp from the river had been granted by General Petraja. The general's army was to advance on the village from the land.

Phaulkon felt a light tap on his arm. It was Kukrit. The slave placed a finger across his lips and pointed in the direction of the shore. Phaulkon bent down and the squatting slave whispered into his ear, making sure to keep his head below Phaulkon's and cupping his hands to stop the sound from spreading.

'There are boats, my Lord. Over there. Two dozen of them maybe. With men inside. Macassars, no doubt.'

Amazing, thought Phaulkon. He himself could neither see nor hear anything. But Kukrit was uncanny. He had a sixth sense and the instincts of a wild animal. Phaulkon was glad to have him at this moment, peering into the blackness and distinguishing objects no one else could make out. But what were other manned boats doing on the river at this time of night? There was a good hour left before dawn and even the most dedicated fisherman had long ago retired. Could the Macassars have got wind of his plan?

A large bird shattered the silence as it took off from the water, flapping its wings. Probably a stork. Kukrit was motioning towards the shore now; he took the oar and turned the nose of the boat inland, ready to move. Phaulkon had sat for hours with Kukrit studying the charts and devising the best plan and by now he knew their every move by heart. They would lie hidden in the bend in the river until the signal came just before dawn. The sixty boats under Phaulkon's command contained two men apiece, a Siamese oarsman and a farang soldier. As soon as they heard the signal from shore they would paddle back at full speed to the Macassar camp round the bend. The signal would come from the commander of the one thousand-strong Siamese force, Captain Sukree, who would creep up to the camp overland from the opposite side, overpower the guard and set fire to the houses on the fringes of the village. The Macassars, flushed out of their dwellings by the flames, would head for the river where Phaulkon's boats would be waiting for them.

Ivatt was in the boat next to Phaulkon's and Sam White was just behind him. Burnaby had been dissuaded from participating on account of his age. An English officer, Captain Udall, whose ship had just arrived from England bearing a letter from King Charles II to His Majesty of Siam, had been recruited for the fight, as had been a French aristocrat, the Comte de Plèzes, on his way with dispatches to the court of the Emperor of China. Several dozen cut-throats, some wearing suits of armour and each one boasting greater valour than the next, sat in anxious anticipation of the coming dawn.

If only he could distinguish himself now, thought Phaulkon, it would be another large feather in his cap. Victory could mean the end of any lasting threat from the Moors. The Macassars were the only serious Muslim fighting force. The other Moors were traders and civil servants. Only they—

The sudden cry shattered the silence. The signal appeared premature to Phaulkon. He hesitated a moment. Then an eerie light appeared in the distance and soon flames leapt upwards, slicing the darkness.

'God damn,' exclaimed Phaulkon. 'Come on, let's head for the camp!' The little boats sped forward, each propelled by a single oarsman, no longer worrying about noise now, just speed. In a moment they were rounding the bend in the river beyond which lay the Macassar camp. The distant darkness, invaded by the flames, was less impenetrable than before, and seemed to herald a false dawn, but close up it was still impossible to see beyond the face of one's immediate neighbour. Phaulkon cursed. The land attack had come too early. No doubt those damned Japanese, eager to distinguish themselves, had jumped the signal.

And then all hell suddenly broke loose. A score or so of boats, presumably those whose outlines the farseeing Kukrit had earlier identified, sprang to life and rushed at them as they rounded the bend. Within moments they had rammed Phaulkon's boats, causing chaos and confusion.

Phaulkon cursed. What was going on? How could the Macassars have known about the river attack? He heard shouts and profanities in English, French and Portuguese, and then screams as the attackers found their mark. An arm pulled Phaulkon down and he found himself lying flat in his boat next to Kukrit. 'Sorry, my Lord, there was no time to ask you.'

'Get the farangs! Kill the farangs!' a voice screeched in Siamese above the roar. It was a voice Phaulkon was sure he recognized, and it sent a chill through him.

Confusion reigned as enemy boats of identical sizes and shapes as their own swarmed among them in the darkness, their occupants now straining to see whether they were attacking friend or foe. It was no longer clear after the initial attack. There was the sound of muskets as the farangs retaliated, and in the lead boat Phaulkon crouched low, firing his musket wildly at whatever shadows approached him.

As the flames in the Macassar camp leapt ever higher and spread through the village, instantly igniting the wooden structures in their path, the whole sky was illuminated and the canvas of the river battle was brought eerily to life. Falling corpses and overturned canoes stood out momentarily in the flickering shadows and the cries of the wounded rent the air.

In the camp itself a second battle was raging. Far from fleeing to the river as expected, the infuriated Macassars, crazed with opium, had turned wildly on the advancing Siamese land forces who had flushed them out of their houses. Brandishing their krises and shouting fiercely, the Macassars, though vastly outnumbered, charged into the enemy ranks with no more regard for their own life than a tigress whose cubs had been threatened. For every Macassar who fell, three or four Siamese paid for it with their lives.

At the river, Sorasak, the leader of the ambush, furious at the premature signal that had given Phaulkon the cover of darkness, strained to sight his quarry. Peering through the shadows, he thought he made out Vichaiyen's form standing a short distance away in the front of his canoe. Vichaiyen was facing sideways, shouting directions in the shrill farang tongue. Sorasak took aim. He drew back his bow to its fullest extent and directed the poisoned arrow at Vichaiyen's neck. Though the actual target was small, it was not an impossible shot for an experienced marksman like Sorasak. He let fly but just as he did so a boat rammed into the stern of his, throwing him off balance. He fell back into his own boat swearing. With a cry of frustration he scrambled to his feet again, straining to see where the arrow had gone. A few feet away from him the valiant Comte de Plèzes, an arrow planted between his eyes, toppled forward into the water and died.

Several of the boats had by now overturned and the farangs in the water were grappling with other swimmers, trying to force their heads under water or wrench their hands away from the sides of abandoned boats. Phaulkon shouted encouragement from the stern of his boat while the valiant Kukrit stood guard in the prow. In answer to his exhortations, a huge farang, framed in the growing light of the conflagration, plunged under an enemy boat and lifted it almost clear out of the water, turning it on its side.

Sorasak searched wildly around him, cursing the confusion. It would soon be daylight and he could not afford to be seen or recognized. The plan that had been agreed with his father, General Petraja, had called for Vichaiyen and the farang force to be wiped out before anyone could see that it was not the Macassars who had ambushed them. Timing had been crucial to its success. The attack had to take place in that brief moment of foredawn, with enough darkness for surprise and enough light to identify the enemy. For there could be no survivors, no witnesses to the fact that he was attacking the very troops that had come to punish His Majesty's enemies. But some fool had attacked the Macassar camp prematurely. Sorasak took one last frantic look around him and then lowered himself over the boat into the water, holding on to the side and peering around for any farang faces he could find.

By now, in the camp itself, the wild-eyed Macassars, despite being outnumbered, had devastated the Siamese ranks and dozens of dead and wounded lay waiting for the fires to consume them. Prince Dai was at the forefront of the mêlée and, seeing that his men were clearly gaining the upper hand, he turned his attention to the river. Had Sorasak completed his task? he wondered. Stepping over a mound of bodies he took a circuitous route round the raging fires and made his way towards the river bank.

It was a bewildering scene. Dawn was just breaking and the glow of the sun's first rays competed with the raging flares of the camp. The Prince counted the bodies of several farangs, wondering whether Phaulkon was among them. He had never actually seen the white mandarin before and all farangs seemed alike to him anyway. He was about to commandeer an abandoned boat and paddle into the carnage when he noticed some surviving farangs and several Siamese beginning to regroup and head for shore. So the force had not been obliterated; Sorasak's mission had only partly succeeded.

There did not seem to be many farangs left but perhaps the white mandarin was among the survivors. Sorasak's own force appeared to be decimated, and there was only sporadic fighting now. He had warned Sorasak that the farangs would use firearms but the man had insisted on lying in wait for them at the bend in the river. General Petraja had apparently informed his son that the white mandarin would arrive by that route.

A shot exploded at the Prince's feet and he looked up angrily to see a tall farang in one of the lead boats, his musket still smoking. How dare the man use such cowardly tactics on him. The soldier seemed more elaborately dressed than the rest, in a heavy suit of armour and a ridiculous plumed hat. Perhaps it was the white mandarin, reflected the Prince. Quickly he raised his lance, took aim and flung it with all his strength. It was a powerful thrust and it rammed into the farang's breast plate with deadly accuracy, throwing the man backwards into the river. The figure struggled to stay above water, but, flail as he might, the weight of his armour kept him below the surface. A number of his companions tried to reach him.

Phaulkon was among those who tried too late to rescue Captain Udall. Furious that the emissary of King Charles had died before he could meet his master the King of Siam, Phaulkon whirled round to identify the killer. He spotted the Macassar chief on shore, clearly elated by the success of his shot.

The boats were fast approaching the bank now and he watched as the Prince thrust something into his mouth and turned to face them like a madman. Opium no doubt. The sky was getting lighter by the minute and on the far side of the encampment Phaulkon could see that the Macassars, easily identifiable by their black turbans, were in the majority. They had obviously been victorious and they would soon regroup and head back towards the river.

Twenty yards from shore, Phaulkon dived into the water. He would swim downstream and then ambush the Macassar leader from the land before his victorious troops could rejoin him. If he could only dispose of their leader, the morale of the returning Macassars might falter. There was no time to lose. The muskets which had earlier determined victory in the ambush were for the most part useless now, the powder wet from the river battle, and the Macassars were deadly in hand-to-hand combat.

Phaulkon came up cautiously for air and saw Ivatt dive in behind him. Phaulkon swam off to the side, parallel to the shore, holding his breath underwater as he had done countless times as a child in the waters of the Mediterranean. He wondered whether the voice he had heard in the earlier darkness had really been that of Sorasak, the bull-necked boxer. It was certainly odd that the troops that had attacked them had been Siamese and not Macassars. Damn their treasonous guts, he thought. They had ruined his plan and, worse than that, turned the tide of battle against him. What was General Petraja's role in all of this? he wondered with increasing suspicion.

Feeling he had swum out far enough, he turned towards the shore and came up for air again.

There was a great splash at his side and for a moment he felt a figure swimming alongside him, underwater. Ivatt was certainly a fast swimmer to have caught up with him, he thought. Was he trying to protect him? It would be only a few feet to shore now. An iron hand grabbed his foot. Goddamn Ivatt, what the hell was he doing? This was no time for games. A searing pain pierced his body as a sharp instrument entered his left thigh. He lashed out with his arms and kicked with all his might. The grip round his ankle loosened and a huge square head came up for air. In the same instant that Phaulkon recognized Sorasak, he saw the Macassar Prince running along the bank to intercept them and Ivatt swimming towards shore a few feet to the left, unaware of Sorasak's appearance.

A knife rose out of the water and lunged at Phaulkon, but he threw himself to one side and forced himself downwards with all his weight. The blade scraped his shoulder, tearing at the flesh. His left thigh felt numb from pain. He surfaced for air to find his wild-eyed opponent barely six inches from his face, grinning with determination, his eyes glazed. The arm with the blade rose again, frighteningly close this time, and Phaulkon was about to attempt a last evasive action when a musket exploded and the water around Sorasak was sprayed with shot. The water quickly turned a reddish brown and Sorasak disappeared beneath the surface. Phaulkon looked up to see White frantically paddling towards him.

'Are you all right?' he shouted.

'I think so,' said Phaulkon.

'Lucky I saw what was going on. I had almost reached the shore. I had to turn back to get close enough for a shot.'

Phaulkon heard a movement to his left; a man was swimming just below the surface in the direction of the abandoned canoes. A trail of red marked his progress. As Phaulkon watched, the

527

swimmer hoisted himself with difficulty on to a canoe and began to row away. Sorasak had escaped, wounded though he was. Phaulkon knew him to be a formidable opponent, fired with rage. He knew that one day they must meet again, but for the moment the man was defeated. Phaulkon deliberated whether to follow him; he turned first to shore to see what was happening. The sight that met him decided him instantly. Ivatt was locked in hand-to-hand combat with Prince Dai, and the rest of the Macassar tribe was converging rapidly on them. Confronted and outnumbered by the wild-eyed fanatics charging towards them, the remnants of Phaulkon's army hesitated by the shore with one foot in their canoes and the other in the shallow water.

'Pull back!' yelled Phaulkon in several languages, not knowing the nationality of the various survivors. 'You'll be massacred. They're opium-crazed. Samuel, quick! Get Ivatt out of there!' With an effort Phaulkon swam towards an overturned boat to allow White to get closer to shore in his own.

Samuel took careful aim. It was damned difficult with the two combatants thrusting at each other with swords and krises like maniacs and frequently changing places, but for one brief instant he had the Macassar in his sights and he fired. At the moment of the explosion, the Macassar plunged his dagger into Ivatt's stomach. But the bullet entering the Prince's arm weakened his thrust and the knife stuck in the flesh of Ivatt's belly, quivering violently.

Ivatt staggered back to the river's edge as Samuel's boat beached and the agile captain leapt ashore. He grabbed Ivatt and threw him over his shoulder as the Macassar, clutching his wounded arm, charged after them. White threw Ivatt into the boat and the little man howled as he landed on his stomach and the knife turned in the flesh. Standing with his legs deep in mud, White shoved the boat off into the river and turned to face his charging assailant. The Macassar came at him at full speed, yelling demonically, and White timed his action carefully.

He ducked low, side-stepping at the same time, and in the split second that the Macassar came level with him he threw a powerful uppercut into the side of his jaw and thrust a foot out to trip him. The man toppled over, rolling in the mud.

In the meantime, gasping for breath, Phaulkon had hoisted

himself on to the hump of the upturned boat, and was observing the scene helplessly. His thigh was bleeding profusely.

White looked up in time to see a wave of crazed Macassars converging on him. He turned and dived headlong into his boat and paddled feverishly out into the stream. Several lances were hurled at him but he thrust his oar erratically to one side and then the other, causing the boat to swerve drunkenly, and only two of the lances stuck in the boat while the rest landed harmlessly in the water beside him.

'Come on! Hurry!' yelled Phaulkon hoarsely. Unseen by him, a lone oarsman was heading rapidly in his direction. Several of the Macassars waded into the water in pursuit of White and the remaining farangs but, unable to swim, they were forced to watch in frustration as the boats pulled away.

A boat sneaked up alongside Phaulkon and an arm came from behind and pulled him off his perch into the boat. Phaulkon was too weak to resist.

'I've been looking everywhere for you, master. Thank the Lord Buddha you are safe.' Kukrit smiled and rowed out into the middle of the river.

Breathless with exertion, White followed them. Ivatt was attempting to wrap a strip of torn blouse round the open gash in his belly which was spilling blood at an alarming rate.

With a last effort, Phaulkon raised himself on one elbow and shouted to the remnants of his bedraggled force: 'Head back to Ayudhya. All of you. Now!'

As the least injured among them took charge of the oars, the crisp sound of military trumpets filled the air. They gazed in the direction of the camp to see the Royal Regiment of Elephants converging on the camp. The Macassars turned furiously to face them. General Petraja had arrived with the main body of the army to claim the spoils of victory.

Thirty-nine

Aarnout Faa was jubilant. He had just received advance notification from Batavia that an armada of twelve ships was on its way, under the command of Rear-Admiral Jonas van der Wamsen. It had left Java on 4 May, exactly eighteen days ago, and would reach Siamese waters within three or four days at most. As soon as it had reached the estuary of the Menam, the commander would send a messenger to inform Faa in Ayudhya. The advance courier had confirmed that there were six hundred heavily armed troops on board. In his letter, the Gouverneur-Generaal had expressed outrage at the appointment of Phaulkon to the mandarinate and concern over the political consequences of such a promotion. This Greek had obviously ingratiated himself with the King. It was unconscionable that a member of the rival English Company should thus have the ear of His Majesty of Siam. Where would such inauspicious beginnings lead? Upon the arrival of the Dutch warships, Aarnout Faa was authorized to present Siam with an ultimatum. He was not only to demand the release of Potts but to produce as many other suitable claims as were unlikely to be met – the Gouverneur left the choice of those to Aarnout Faa's discretion – and upon their rejection he was to declare war.

From their position in the middle of the river opposite the capital, reflected Aarnout Faa, the ships' cannon could fire repeatedly into the city for as long as it took to destroy it or to obtain a Siamese surrender, whichever occurred sooner. The few hundred Dutch troops with their muskets would be enough to repel the hordes of soldiers who would swarm around the warships in their little boats, trying in vain to board. With their limited number of firearms, the Siamese fought mostly with spears, harpoons and swords, and the protective chain mail of the Dutch would render their poisoned darts as ineffectual as the trumpeting rows of war elephants that would line the shores in frustration.

For what could hundreds, even thousands of war elephants do

against the cannon of Holland? Everything was relative in battle, reflected Faa. What had a thousand Macassars been able to do against General Petraja's war elephants? And what could a thousand war elephants do now against the cannon of Holland? The Macassars with their short krises had no more been able to reach Petraja's riders on their lofty mounts than these same riders could reach the Dutch cannon in the middle of the river.

Faa smiled. Phaulkon might well be the hero of the moment, but his glory would be shortlived. What would the Gouverneur-Generaal say if he knew that Phaulkon had just been made a mandarin of the first grade, one of the thirty foremost mandarins in the land? Chao Praya Vichaiyen! Heer van Goens had been upset enough to learn of the Greek's appointment to the third rank, but as for the first . . . How ironic, reflected Faa, that these English smugglers and pirates had all been honoured. The little one, the new recruit who had apparently been wounded in the stomach, had been awarded the Order of the White Elephant third class, while that rebel trader White had been confirmed as Shahbandar of Mergui. Harbourmaster general! Incredible! With the head of the English station, Burnaby, named Governor of Mergui, it was a veritable conspiracy. But in these cases, too, reflected Faa, the honour would be fleeting. He glanced down at the Gouverneur-Generaal's missive once more.

Paragraph three confirmed that Madras had now issued a warrant for the immediate arrest of Phaulkon, Burnaby, Ivatt and White to face charges of smuggling, embezzlement, corruption and treason. Their appointments were hereby terminated and they were to return to headquarters immediately. Though the emissaries bearing the warrant were still on the high seas, details of the ruling had already reached Batavia via the English factory at Bantam and authorization was hereby granted to the VOC chief at Ayudhya to act upon it and to ship the accused back to Madras – under armed guard if necessary.

He would wait for the Dutch armada to arrive first, Aarnout Faa decided, and then, with the backing of six hundred Dutch troops, he would make the necessary arrests. With the English out of the way, his cherished takeover of Siam would be unchallenged and he himself, upon the successful completion of the operation, would be eligible for the governorship. A surge of pride ran through him. Paragraph six of the letter had spelled it out: First Governor of the Dutch territories of Siam.

Aarnout Faa looked at his watch and rose. It was time to head for the palace to attend the Barcalon's obsequies. His Majesty himself was to attend. The Barcalon had succumbed only three days earlier, while the Macassar rebellion was in full swing. Dr Kornfeldt had been one of the physicians attending to His Excellency and he had confirmed that it had been too late to save the Barcalon then. The asthma had taken its toll.

Who would the next Barcalon be? wondered Faa. The VOC chief smiled. Whoever it was, the new Dutch Governor would be the one to appoint him.

Maria knelt down beside her uncle. She was clearly distraught.

'What is it, my dear?' inquired Mestre Phanik anxiously.

'Oh uncle, I cannot keep things to myself any longer. I must confide in you.'

'I have been waiting for you to speak, my dear. I just did not want to rush you.'

She hesitated a moment and then the words spilled out. 'I miss Constant so much. I have not seen him since our argument last week. And now he is wounded and suffering and I so want to go to him. But that woman is there, constantly by his side.'

Mestre Phanik observed her in silence for a while. 'You mean Sunida, my dear?' he asked sympathetically.

Maria nodded miserably. 'Yes. And he will not give her up. He told me so.'

'As we know, my dear, she was sent to him as a spy. Think what a useful outlet for him. She must have been chosen by the palace for her . . . skills and it was inevitable that . . . eventually . . . well, you know the customs here, my dear.'

'Uncle, how can you talk like that? And so calmly?'

'Not so much calmly, my dear, as resigned. I tried to tell you about Constant when I found out you had fallen in love with him. But you were so intent . . . You know how drawn he is to the Siamese way of life. You knew he approved of their customs. But he has other qualities.'

'You sound almost as if you were taking his side,' reproached Maria. She had felt such pride on hearing of his heroic part in

532

the Macassar uprising and such relief to learn that he was alive, but it was terrible not to be able to see him now, especially when she knew he was wounded.

'Not at all, my dear. I'm merely being realistic. You knew of his former ménage. I know it hurts, but you really could not have expected him to change completely.'

'But what about you, Uncle? Would you have behaved like that towards your wife?'

Mestre Phanik hesitated.

'One of the reasons I never married was to avoid that kind of problem. I would have missed bringing up a child, of course, if I had not been fortunate enough to have you. I am afraid that the human male is essentially polygamous, my dear, and only the strongest religious beliefs will restrain him. Constant's Christian beliefs are not, I regret to say, that firm.'

'But does that not make him a sinner, Uncle?'

'It does, my dear, but do not be too harsh on him. It is especially difficult in his case, on account of long habit. And as I said, he has other qualities. As long as he treats you well and is a good father to your children, you would do well to accept him. You might be thankful that he is a better husband than most.'

Maria was amazed at her uncle's nonchalance. 'But Uncle, you were always so strict and proper about these things. And now, suddenly . . .'

'We try and bring our offspring up in a world of ideals, my dear, but we have to make certain adjustments when the time comes.' Mestre Phanik put a comforting arm round his niece's shoulder. 'It will be the same with your children one day, you will see.'

Maria observed her uncle intently. Behind the apparent insouciance, something was troubling him, she could see. And he was not showing the sympathy she had expected.

'Uncle, would my father have behaved like that? Would he have dared insist on keeping two women? You always told me so much about my mother and so little about him. I know he was a trader like you and that he died of the plague when I was only two, but you never really elaborated beyond that. It was almost as if you were avoiding my questions.'

Mestre Phanik shifted uncomfortably. He kept silent for a while, seemingly immersed in thought. Then he rose from his chair and paced across the room. Finally he placed his hands on Maria's shoulders and stared solemnly into her face.

'I never told you much about your father, Maria, because I could not find the right words to describe him. You see, he stands before you now.'

Maria was at first uncomprehending as she gazed blankly into the eyes of the man who had just addressed her.

Eventually it was Mestre Phanik who broke the silence. A look of exaltation had gradually come into his eyes, a relief that a long-borne burden had finally been shed.

'Everything I told you about your mother was true, Maria. Except that she was never married to your father. She remained a Buddhist to the end, content in her faith, finding nothing but joy in your birth. She saw no reason to convert. She too died of the plague when you were two. As a Catholic I did not want you . . . the stigma . . . forgive me.'

Mestre Phanik held out his arms to her. He was close to tears.

Maria hesitated at first, then slowly she advanced into his embrace. She held him loosely to begin with but gradually her grip grew tighter until eventually she clasped him with all her strength.

'You see, we are none of us perfect, my dear,' he whispered. 'Take Constant for what he is.'

'You cannot get up, my Lord,' reproached Sunida. It was midday and the sun was streaming through the window of Phaulkon's bedroom at home. 'You heard the physicians' orders. Even the farang doctor agreed.'

Each time Phaulkon had risen on one elbow, Sunida had gently pushed him back on to the cushions again. Both His Majesty's physicians and the Jesuit le Moutier, had been attending to him. He was in danger of losing his leg, they said, if he put any pressure on it, before the wound was properly healed. Sorasak's knife had penetrated deep into the thigh and Phaulkon's whole leg pounded with pain, yet he was desperate to rise. This was no time to lie in bed. There was far too much to attend to: the Dutch invasion, the conviction of the surviving Moors, the alliance with France, his marriage to Maria, Sorasak's betrayal. He had slept only fitfully for three days, awaking in a sweat each time to find himself surrounded by Dutch warships or prostrate

534

before Sorasak who, with a crown on his head, was sentencing him and the other farangs to a slow death.

'I know it was Sorasak on that river,' said Phaulkon. 'I would have recognized him anywhere.'

Sunida looked at him with compassion. How many times had he not repeated the same words? It had become an obsession with him. Constant kept insisting that it was Sorasak who had led the ambush against his farang force at the bend in the river, and that General Petraja had not attacked sooner with the bulk of his army because he did not want to divert the Macassars with Sorasak from slaughtering the farangs first. Twenty-eight farangs had died in the massacre and Constant's blood was boiling. General Petraja had received the Order of the White Elephant first class for his part in quelling the uprising and officially Sorasak had been given an honourable mention when his entire contingent was wiped out after he had sadly mistaken some of the King's fighting force for a Macassar ambush in the uncertain light of dawn.

'You will deal with Sorasak when you are well, my Lord. He will be no match for you then. But for now, you need rest. I will get you some more tea. And by the way,' she added proudly, 'while you were asleep a messenger came from His Majesty to inquire after your health.'

Phaulkon smiled weakly, full of love for her. 'Don't go, Sunida. Stay with me. I need you. How kind of His Majesty to send someone. And what about Maria, has she been to see me?' The need for an alliance with France was pressing. His Majesty had agreed to all the conditions but there still remained the question of his Catholic marriage. The Jesuits were standing firm on that point.

'No, my Lord, but she sent a note while you were asleep. I did not want to wake you.' Sunida went over to the low table by the window and brought a letter to him. He opened it avidly, scanning the Portuguese.

Sunida stroked his forehead gently, trying to draw the tension from his head. How she loved this man. Even though he needed desperately to marry this Christian woman for his alliance with that other farang power, yet he had steadfastly refused to give his Sunida up. There was nothing she would not do for him. She saw a smile of satisfaction come over his face. Had the farang woman capitulated? If the girl wanted Constant, she would be a fool not to, reflected Sunida. She might not get another chance.

'I will read you the note, Sunida.' He translated: 'Hurry up and get well, my Lord. I would rather not be married to a cripple.'

Sunida laughed. 'That is true for me too, my Lord. You would not be able to run to me quickly enough.'

Phaulkon observed her tenderly. 'Sunida, would you prefer to live here or at the palace? I have obtained permission from His Majesty the King to house you there if you wish.'

Sunida considered for a moment. 'Now that you are a mandarin of the first grade, my Lord, I think I would prefer the palace. After all, you will be attending His Majesty's Councils daily.' She smiled. 'Sometimes even twice a day. And I feel that although your farang wife might accept me now because she is anxious to marry you and because she sees that you will not relinquish me, she may change her mind once we are both in the same house together. She may become resentful and even try to turn you against me. And though I know you will not acquiesce, my Lord, I nevertheless would wish to spare you any unpleasantness.' In reality Sunida was thrilled. Once she moved into the palace, the last remaining obstacle to her total happiness would be removed. For then she would no longer have to spy on her Lord. She could speak to him about anything without the everpresent fear that he might incriminate herself. And their love would be whole and unfettered. She leaned over and inhaled his cheek deeply. He closed his eyes.

'Sunida,' he whispered, 'I will be spending more time at the palace than at home.'

'But not too much, my Lord,' she teased. 'I want to have time to miss you.'

Phaulkon laughed. 'Sunida, I want you to go now to the Jesuit mission and show them Maria's note. Tell them the treaty with France must be ratified and proclaimed forthwith. There is no time to lose. Hurry back or I may start walking around in your absence.'

'Don't you dare move, my Lord. I am going to leave Tip and Sorn in here with strict instructions. And you—' she broke off as Tip ushered Burnaby and White into the room. 'Even better,' added Sunida. 'These two will be strong enough to enforce my

536

wishes.' She wai'd to them and pointed to Phaulkon's bed, indicating with signs that he should not leave it. White stared at Sunida entranced, as he did each time he saw her. He followed her with his eyes as she left the room.

Burnaby nodded and walked up to Phaulkon. 'Well, how's the patient?'

'Not bad, thank you, Richard, apart from being frustrated, vindictive and angry. And how is Thomas faring?'

'He's well on the road to recovery,' replied Burnaby. 'You can tell by the improvement in his jokes. They're almost back to normal. The wound in his stomach has been closed now.'

'He said that the fires in his stomach were a good preparation for the spicy Indian food he would have to consume in his new post,' added White.

Phaulkon chuckled weakly. 'And what news of the outside world?'

'There's a lot going on, Constant,' advised Burnaby, 'but nothing that can't await your recovery,' he added quickly, seeing Phaulkon preparing to rise.

'Tell me,' insisted Phaulkon.

'The deputy governor of Tenasserim has been decapitated in the public square. His name was Oc-Ya Tannaw or something. Apparently a surviving member of Prince Dai's inner circle was captured alive and severely tortured. He revealed that the deputy governor had come secretly to Ayudhya to co-ordinate the Muslim takeover once the Macassars had laid the ground for them.' Burnaby paused, looking squeamish. 'The Oc-Ya Tannaw's severed head is now suspended round Prince Dai's neck. The Macassar leader is forced to walk around with it wherever he goes.'

Phaulkon shuddered. It was the traditional punishment for conspirators. Those who plotted together were chastised together. The Prince would probably carry the Oc-Ya's head around with him for three whole days, staring without relief into the dead man's eyes. He would have plenty of leisure to reflect upon their joint guilt, until he too was decapitated.

'And were there any other Macassar survivors?' asked Phaulkon.

It was Samuel who answered this time.

'Only six of them, Constant. The rest were either killed or

took their own lives. Brave as they were, the Macassars were no match for Petraja's elephants.' Even the hardened White lowered his head at this point. 'I attended their executions this morning at dawn. They were sentenced to be devoured by tigers. The famished beasts had been kept all night in a cage. It was an awesome sight. As the beasts gorged themselves on the prisoners' extremities, the French and Portuguese Jesuits present held out their crucifixes to the tortured Macassars, calling upon them to renounce their false gods and be received into the Kingdom of Heaven. But the dying prisoners sneered at them, glorying in the knowledge of their stoicism.'

'All the Moors are being detained for questioning,' observed Burnaby. 'You can see them walking around with their heads shaven while others have had the crowns of their heads sliced with a sharp sword. I was told the elders of the Council of Tenasserim will be stripped of their positions and forbidden to leave their houses, as soon as I am installed as Governor.'

The Moors' power was at an end, reflected Phaulkon. But the Dutch remained, and their threat was the more serious. As soon as Sunida returned he would know more about the alliance.

'Are you resigned to working for Siam then, Richard?' asked Phaulkon. The lanky Englishman's reservations, he knew, had been greatly reduced by his exalted appointment as Governor. It was a special elevation created uniquely so that a farang would be Governor even though not a mandarin.

Burnaby lowered his head. 'It seems that fate has willed it that way, Constant. There's not much waiting for me in Madras.'

'Except a court martial,' commented White drily. 'But speaking of fate, Constant, I witnessed some weird proceedings this morning on my way back from the executions. Some of Captain Udall's men from the *Hubert* came to pay their final respects at the cemetery where the Jesuits had buried the Christian dead. To their astonishment the officers found their captain's grave empty. His body had been exhumed! Searching around them they eventually found it, stripped naked, and propped against a tree. They lifted the body and buried it again, this time covering the grave with a pile of heavy stones. This morning, on my way past the cemetery, I found the same officers there. They had returned, only to find the body leaning up against the same tree

538

again. Horrified, we raised the corpse together and carried it out into the river where we weighed it down with stones and sank it.'

Phaulkon listened with interest. 'I have seen that done before. Siamese necromancers, perturbed by violent events, were probably seeking to read the future. Captain Udall, God rest his soul, was directly involved in these events, and the necromancers – half sorcerers, half spiritualists – must have been using the body as a medium through which to communicate with the world beyond and question the future. The more famous of them will sell their predictions for a fortune. It's interesting that they used the body of a dead farang, though. It must indicate that they believe farangs will have much to do with the course of future events.' Phaulkon paused. His eyes were beginning to droop.

'Are you gentlemen going to the Barcalon's funeral this evening?' he asked in a weak voice.

'We are,' responded Burnaby. 'As future dignitaries of the realm, it is our duty.'

'I wouldn't miss it for anything,' said White. 'Great brass drums have been rolling for the past three days and people with shaven heads are arriving from all parts of the country. There have been fireworks for the last two nights and the entire population is dressed in white. It's the greatest pageant I've ever witnessed.'

'Is there any talk of a new Barcalon?' asked Phaulkon anxiously.

'None that I've heard,' replied Burnaby.

'That's good,' replied Phaulkon. His head fell to one side and his eyes closed. The others glanced at each other and crept stealthily out.

For three days and nights the body of the Barcalon was cleansed and perfumed. Quicksilver was placed on the mouth, ears and eyes of the corpse and priceless aromatics were daubed on the body to ensure it against decay. Saffron-robed monks chanted ceaselessly, day and night, intoning ever louder with each passing night. Drums rolled, cymbals clashed, trumpets blared and masked dancers circled the corpse. Thousands of monks and white-robed nuns, their heads shaven, flocked to the capital from the neighbouring towns and villages to attend the last rites of the great Barcalon.

As a special mark of honour it was announced that the Lord of Life himself would light the funeral pyre, thus ensuring greater help in the world beyond for the deceased, on account of His Majesty's exalted rank.

At dusk on the third day the corpse was placed in a decorated wooden coffin with the Barcalon's finest clothes draped across it. The entire population of Ayudhya, clad in white panungs, the colour of mourning, and with their heads shaven, headed for the river to join the multitude of little boats already converging on the great gilded barges. These were to bear the Barcalon's corpse, his close relatives and the senior mandarins, forming the centre of the cortège.

At the head of the great river procession were several barges bearing alms to be distributed to the monks who had journeyed from afar, and to the poor and needy. There followed the relatives of the deceased with troops of masked dancers hired to keep the corpse entertained. Behind them came the most senior priests and high-ranking mandarins in gilded barges whose prows were in the form of dragons' heads and mythical garuda birds. Directly behind them was the Barcalon's barge with the corpse lying in state on a raised pyramidical platform with a gilded roof. The common people in thousands of little boats lit up by candles brought up the rear and covered the broad river from shore to shore.

The procession, including Burnaby and White, headed down-river until it reached the great temple illuminated by thousands of candles, outside the walls of the Grand Palace. Here the boats turned ashore and the populace disembarked. The corpse was placed in the centre of the lavishly decorated funeral pyre in the courtyard of the great pagoda and the masked dancers began to perform around it while the priests continued to chant.

His Majesty the King, observing the procession from the windows of his palace, now lit the pyre by means of a brimstone fuse which extended from the palace to the temple by the river. The pyre, consisting only of scented woods as a special mark of favour, burst into flame, fireworks were set off, music was played, the dancers went into a frenzy and the chanting of the priests rose to a crescendo and did not cease until the entire corpse had been consumed by flames.

The ashes were gathered with great respect by the senior
540

monks and at midnight they were scattered in the river at a point where the current was swiftest.

It was an occasion of great pomp and circumstance and a time of both mourning and rejoicing. For a great man had passed on to his next life's cycle.

On the morning following the Barcalon's funeral, the assembled courtiers lay eagerly awaiting the arrival of the King. This was no ordinary summons. As the Barcalon's health had deteriorated, His Majesty had recalled every provincial Governor from his post to the capital and now, in silent rows, the sixty foremost mandarins of the realm, and Richard Burnaby, lay prostrate, awaiting their sovereign's command. Most had concluded that His Majesty would be naming the new Barcalon today and few doubted that the honour would fall on General Petraja, the most accomplished courtier among them.

The general himself, spruce as ever with neatly cropped grey hair, his diamond-encrusted betel box by his side, lay in the position of highest honour nearest the balcony where His Majesty would appear. As soon as he was appointed Barcalon, he thought, he would begin his campaign to discredit the farangs and slowly ease them out of power. The Moors had already been dealt a crushing blow. He glanced covertly around him until his eye settled on the only empty place in the assembly. In a back row where the newly appointed mandarins of the first rank lay prostrate, Vichaiyen's space was vacant. The farang was still recovering from his war wounds. You, Vichaiyen, will be the first to go, he thought. You may have escaped the krises of the Macassars and the wrath of my adopted son, but you will not escape me. Your fate is sealed this day. What sacrilege, reflected Petraja, to induct farangs into these hallowed halls. How degrading to the sanctity of the ancient Siamese empire.

The trumpets and cymbals interrupted his thoughts and in the absence of a Barcalon, the King addressed himself directly to the audience.

'Loyal mandarins, we have summoned you here today to speak of important matters. These are trying times for our nation in which outsiders openly covet the wealth of our land. We are no longer living in times of isolation or comfortable seclusion, because the nations of the Western world are travelling ever further afield. The world grows smaller and will continue to do

541

so. These nations of the West are better armed and better equipped than we are and though there might be little else we wish to emulate in them, we must concede that the growing power of their weaponry leaves us ever more vulnerable to attack.

'We have therefore resolved to conclude a treaty with our worthy sovereign brother, the King of France, whose nation has expressed friendly sentiments towards us and with whom we will exchange embassies and gifts on a scale never seen before. It will be the greatest alliance that we as a nation have entered into and will be the first great link between the Eastern and the Western worlds. From the French farangs, from their soldiers and draughtsmen and engineers we will learn matters of science. For, my loyal mandarins, it is in scientific knowledge that the future stability of our ancient land depends.' The King paused to let his words sink in.

'Our next Barcalon will be such a man of science. And we hereby engage you all to solve the following riddle. The one who successfully completes it or, if more than one of you so succeeds, the one who does so by the cleverest means, that man will be our next Barcalon.' The assembly waited in hushed anticipation.

'We command you,' continued His Majesty, 'to ascertain the precise weight of our largest cannon, the one known as Pra Pirun. We require this information as soon as possible and the first man to devise a means of accurately gauging its weight will report to us immediately. The contest will close after one week.'

On receipt of the King's orders, the courtiers all set about finding a solution. One determined mandarin, the Governor of Pitsanuloke, oversaw the construction of a huge-scale with iron chains, but repeated attempts to estimate the giant cannon's weight with anything resembling accuracy failed. At first the cannon could not be raised properly, and when eventually it was, the scales broke. General Petraja, irked by the deferment of his appointment which he had considered certain and worried that one of the mandarins might actually come up with a solution, consulted the astrologers and went to see his friend the Supreme Patriarch. But both the leader of the Buddhist clergy and the nation's most famous astrologer assured him that the task was impossible. No

542

solution would be found because of the sheer size of the cannon. Relieved, the general went home and awaited the end of the seven-day period.

By order of His Majesty, news of the contest was brought to Phaulkon's home by a messenger from the palace. He received the news with a mixture of anxiety and determination. He was not in the best of health but what an opportunity lay before him now, he reflected. This was the chance he had been waiting for. Measure the weight of one cannon and he could be Barcalon! If he were Barcalon he would not need to beg the Jesuits for a treaty, he would *tell* them. And as for Aarnout Faa, he would . . . no, he reflected, he would not do what was expected of him. He would not expel the Dutch from Siam, because it was not in Siam's best interests. Siam needed Batavia for its export revenues and the Dutch had always been prompt and honest payers. No, he would show the Dutch that he was impartial, interested only in the welfare of Siam. He would see to it that the alliance with France deterred any thoughts they might have of conquest. He would use both carrot and stick. But how long did he have? Could he achieve his goal in time to prevent the planned invasion? He ordered Sunida to close the door of his bedroom and gave instructions that under no circumstances was he to be disturbed. For several hours, in total confinement, he pondered the problem of the cannon.

That evening, against the doctors' advice and Sunida's protestations, he asked her to arrange for a sedan chair and ordered the new slaves gifted by His Majesty to carry him down to the river. He stopped on the way to gather an assortment of Europeans and arrived at the spot where the great cannon lay by the river's edge.

Directing operations from his chair he had the cannon hoisted on to a barge which was moored alongside the quay. He marked the ship's exact water line when it sank under the weight of the cannon. Then he had the cannon offloaded and bricks and rocks of equal size placed on board in its place. When the barge eventually sank to the same level as it had when loaded with the cannon, he carefully weighed the bricks and stones and determined with reasonable accuracy the weight of Pra Pirun. The whole process was accomplished in seven hours.

Forty

On the morning following the cannon test, lavish gifts of Chinese porcelain, Japanese screens, silks and handicrafts, sapanwood and sandalwood, rubies, emeralds and diamonds, black and gold lacquered cabinets of the early Ayudhya period, manuscript chests, elaborate wooden door panels with carved figures in bas-relief, and a reproduction of the royal barge's huge garuda bird in gold lacquer, with palms facing outwards and fingers raised upwards, were paraded through the streets of Ayudhya and loaded on the large 200-ton vessel, *Alliance*. These were followed by three elephants in golden harnesses and two rhinoceros sedated with opium and herbs and with necklaces of bronze bells round their necks. The procession caused a sensation in the streets. It was said the three young elephants were destined for the three young Princes of France, the grandsons of Louis XIV, and words of advice were whispered into the elephants' ears as the leading nobles in their conical hats respectfully took their leave of them. The elephants were instructed to depart cheer-fully, and advised that although they would be slaves, they would be in the glorious service of one of the greatest monarchs on earth. Pra Pipat, a sixty-year-old veteran of three Siamese embassies to China, was named the first Siamese ambassador to France. He was accompanied by Father Gayme, a French Jesuit who was to serve as interpreter, two Siamese secretaries of the ambassador and thirty retainers. With much fanfare, the embassy set sail bearing a royal letter extending warm greetings to the French King and congratulating him on the successful conclusion of a treaty of friendship between the two great nations. The entire letter was engraved on a sheet of gold.

On that same morning, a Dutch messenger, Captain Cijfer, was ushered into Aarnout Faa's office.

'Welcome, captain,' said the VOC chief gleefully. 'I have been eagerly awaiting your arrival.' It was an understatement. Faa had been on tenterhooks, counting the minutes. There were rumours of an impending alliance between Siam and France, though he

544

did not see how that was possible. But now, thank God, the warships had arrived.

'I'm sorry that I was so delayed, sir, but I have had a great deal of trouble reaching you. The mouth of the river is entirely clogged with Siamese junks and barges and you have no idea how slow progress upriver has been. There are lavish processions along the entire route from the estuary to the capital. It took me two days to reach here.'

'How strange,' commented Faa, 'the Barcalon's funeral was over two days ago. What could be the cause, I wonder?'

'There is a large Siamese vessel with the name *Alliance* in Roman letters moored at the mouth of the Menam, not far from our ships, sir. Perhaps that has something to do with it. It seems that these great processions which have brought river travel to a virtual standstill are something to do with an embassy travelling to France. I have never seen such lavish gifts or such pomp as I passed on my way here. Do you know what is happening, sir?'

Aarnout Faa felt suddenly uneasy. Great processions, lavish gifts, a large vessel named *Alliance*? Why had nobody informed him? The preparations must have been carried out in great secrecy for his men not to have heard anything. The Siamese did have some ocean-going vessels, though he had never heard of one called *Alliance*. The name was certainly ominous. Perhaps the name of one of the vessels had been changed recently.

As VOC chief, Faa was embarrassed to have to admit to his visitor that he did not know precisely what was happening.

'There are so many processions here, Captain, that I've stopped asking the meaning of them all. But I'll be glad to find out for you.' He leaned over behind his desk and struck a gong.

A servant appeared almost immediately, but before Faa could speak, the man had announced the arrival of a high-ranking mandarin in a sedan chair, accompanied by ten slaves. The head slave had not given the mandarin's name but only his rank. He was of the first order and wished to see the VOC director right away.

'Send him in, then,' said Aarnout Faa complacently. He turned to the captain. 'We will know the answer to your question soon enough.' The captain inclined his head.

A moment later the door opened and a resplendent figure dressed in a gold-embroidered blouse and reclining in an elaborately carved wooden chair borne by six slaves was ushered into the room. At first Faa did not recognize the figure under the conical hat, surrounded by a host of slaves, but the moment it uttered greetings a chill went through him.

'Welcome, Heer Phaulkon,' said the VOC chief, controlling his voice. 'I hear you were wounded in the heroic battle against the Macassars. I trust you are recovering well?'

The slaves lowered the chair and one of them took up a position a few feet in front of it, allowing Phaulkon's leg to rest on his shoulders.

'Quite rapidly, thank you, Heer Faa. There is so much good news to sustain me these days. It seems to aid the body too.'

The captain was staring wide-eyed at the sight of this European dressed in Oriental clothes speaking perfect Dutch and being treated like some prominent local dignitary. Phaulkon's five remaining slaves were lying prostrate and motionless by his side.

'But allow me to introduce you to Captain Cijfer of the Royal Dutch Navy. This is . . . er . . . His Excellency, Lord Phaulkon.' The VOC chief found himself swallowing hard.

'Most honoured, my Lord,' said the captain, bowing. 'But I should wait outside. I am sure you have matters to discuss which—'

'Far from it, Captain,' said Phaulkon, raising his hand. 'Your presence here is most fortuitous. What I have to say is for your ears as well.'

The captain looked at him, confused.

What did he mean? wondered Aarnout Faa. What would he know of this captain or his mission? The Dutch ships would have anchored out to sea and news could hardly have travelled here faster than Captain Cijfer himself. A sense of foreboding gripped him and his stomach felt hollow.

'You intrigue us, Heer Phaulkon,' said the VOC chief, forcing a smile.

'Gentlemen,' began Phaulkon, 'an important alliance is shortly to be announced between two great nations and in view of your own country's long and special relationship with Siam, I wanted you to be the first to know.'

'Indeed, Heer Phaulkon. And which nations would those be?'

Phaulkon took his time and eyed him steadily. He pointed imperceptibly at his diamond-encrusted betel box and a slave

immediately opened it and offered it abjectly up to him. Phaulkon extracted a betel nut wrapped in leaf and proceeded to chew
it. Aarnout Faa's feet shuffled uneasily under his desk while the
captain continued to look on bemused.

'Secret negotiations have for some time been underway
between Their Majesties King Louis of France and King Narai of
Siam,' pursued Phaulkon. 'These negotiations were opened
quietly through the medium of the Jesuits at the time of the visit
of the Bishop of Heliopolis, long before you or I ever set foot in
Siam, mijn heer.' Phaulkon paused and indicated a fan lying by
one of his slaves' feet. Immediately the slave raised it and began
to fan his master. Instinctively Aarnout Faa ran a hand across his
forehead. The expression on the Dutchman's face was grim as
Phaulkon continued to speak.

'These lengthy negotiations have now borne fruit and culminated in a grand alliance between France and Siam to be
announced today. The treaty will coincide with the departure of
a grand embassy – the greatest Siamese mission to leave these
shores – to France at the invitation of King Louis himself. By
prearrangement, an equally great Embassy from the Sun King is
scheduled to depart for Siam at the same time. The Embassy
from France will be accompanied by five thousand troops on
board twenty warships. The troops, sent as a token of King
Louis' esteem for his fellow monarch, will serve as His Siamese
Majesty's personal bodyguard.' Phaulkon paused. 'I am sure you
read French, Heer Faa?'

The Dutchman forced another smile. He could feel Captain
Cijfer's questioning gaze on him. 'Enough to understand the gist,
Heer Phaulkon. Do you have something to show me?'

Phaulkon opened his purse and produced a letter which he
carefully placed on Faa's desk. It was embossed with the royal
seal of France and even Phaulkon had been taken aback when
he had first seen it. It was dated almost a year ago and was the
most perfect forgery – a credit to the ingenuity of the Jesuit
fathers, Père le Moutier in particular, whose years of copying
early biblical manuscripts during his religious studies had paid off
handsomely. The letter was addressed to His Most Esteemed
Friend and Ally the King of Siam and contained Le Grand
Monarque's assurances of his heartfelt satisfaction that the eight
years of negotiations had culminated in so auspicious a treaty.

The very length of time it had taken to conclude was indication enough of its future durability and permanence. It went on to elaborate on the gifts he was sending to His Esteemed Colleague and further explained that the five thousand elite troops were intended as a personal bodyguard 'to protect him at all times and from all enemies, whoever they might be'. The soldiers were instructed to obey his every command.

As he read on, the colour gradually drained from the VOC chief's face.

'But why would a document of this consequence come into your hands, Heer Phaulkon?' he asked. 'I note it is dated eleven months ago. It must have reached Siam some four months ago.'

It was the question Phaulkon had been waiting for. The cue to deliver his *coup de grâce*.

'Because, Heer Faa, all such matters have now been placed in my hands. You see, tomorrow is a most auspicious day for me.' He paused. 'I am to be named Barcalon of Siam.'

Aarnout Faa went white. His first reaction was to scream and shout profanities. But he was a seasoned diplomat, and after only a slight hesitation he said: 'Well, Heer Phaulkon, I must congratulate you on a remarkable career. Your rise to power has certainly been meteoric.' His mind was racing. Could this really be happening? Could it be that the letter was a forgery? Yet would even the diabolical Phaulkon have dared to bluff on so important a matter as his appointment to the post of Barcalon? Lord Jesus, if it were true, where would that leave him? And Holland? But why the devil bluff or forge such a letter? Unless . . . he smiled as a ray of hope invaded him. Unless Phaulkon had somehow found out about the arrival of the Dutch warships. But how? Security was watertight and even he himself had only heard four days ago. The huge preparations that Captain Cijfer had described could never have been concluded in four days, even if there had been a leak. Which was impossible. The advance courier had been a Dutchman, had spoken to no one and had departed immediately. No, cursed Faa, this alliance with France had to be genuine. It was the damndest coincidence and the timing was disastrous. He would have to send an urgent dispatch to Batavia revealing the news and he would have to make an unpleasant decision about these warships now. He could not risk a war with France. It might take a year or two before

King Louis retaliated against Holland, but eventually the finger would be pointed at the VOC chief, and Captain Cijfer was a witness. Faa glanced at the calendar on his desk. If a French fleet were really on its way it could reach Siam by December, only seven months away. How could he take the initiative of risking war with France, not just here but perhaps in Europe as well? He shuddered. No, Heer van Goens in Batavia would have to make that decision. He cursed his luck again and felt suddenly close to tears. If this devil Phaulkon's story were true, how could he now arrest the new Barcalon of Siam and ship him off to Madras? Relations with Siam would be damaged for ever, if they were not already. If Phaulkon had not been sitting in front of him, Aarnout Faa would have buried his head in his hands and cried like a child. His life's ambition, his whole career seemed to be crumbling before him. With a supreme effort he forced himself to look at things from a different angle. It remained to be seen whether this scoundrel Phaulkon was really going to be named Barcalon tomorrow. He would base everything on that, he decided. He would order the fleet to wait another day. If Phaulkon were really installed as Barcalon, he would send the fleet back.

Phaulkon could see from Faa's face what a shattering blow had been dealt him. It was the moment to show a little compassion. The man would be grateful for the least charity now.

'Heer Faa, I came here this afternoon not just to tell you privately of the alliance with France, but to assure you that I, as Barcalon, have every intention of carrying out my duties impartially. I will not favour one nation against another and I will lend my greatest support to those who display a genuine friendship for Siam. You must no longer think of me as attached to the English Company but as a Siamese official in the service of Siam.' He paused and looked meaningfully at Faa. 'I will not hesitate to recommend for an honorary mandarinate any farang or Moor who puts the interests of Siam before his own.'

Captain Cijfer listened in bewilderment to Phaulkon's speech. He had obviously arrived at some momentous point in history. But who was this extraordinary figure who was about to become Barcalon of Siam?

With an effort the VOC chief tried to keep the emotion from his voice. He swallowed his pride.

549

'The treaty granting us a monopoly in hides would remain in force?' he inquired hesitantly.

'Indeed, mijn heer, unless it is either abused or revised by mutual consent.'

'And will the French be given special concessions?'

'No more than anyone else. They will be allowed to build a factory and conduct trade here just as any other foreign power which obeys the laws of this land.'

'And the English?'

'The English, Heer Faa, will be *personae non gratae*, until such time as they can show a marked improvement in their attitudes. The likes of Samuel Potts will not be welcome here so long as I am Barcalon.'

'But Mr Potts was only doing his duty, surely, Heer Phaulkon?'

'By burning down the English factory?'

'Heer Phaulkon, permit me to differ on this point. It was you who destroyed the factory.'

'That is your belief and you are entitled to it, erroneous as it may be. I will overlook it this time, but I do not wish to hear that opinion voiced again in my presence.' Phaulkon's voice was firm. 'And today will be the last day you will be permitted to call me Heer Phaulkon.'

The VOC chief glanced uncomfortably at Captain Cijfer and swallowed hard.

'You were saying, Your Excellency, that relations between Siam and Holland will continue as before?'

'Precisely, and if Holland carries out its duties honourably, I foresee a period of fruitful relations between us. Especially as the English will not be returning here.' Phaulkon turned to the captain. 'Are you on a trading mission here, Captain?'

Cijfer glanced quickly at Faa and then stammered, 'Er, yes, sir, I mean Your Excellency.'

'In that case I should be most gratified if you would remain until tomorrow to attend my investiture.' He smiled graciously. 'The honourable Dutch Company will have a special place reserved for them.'

The captain bowed deeply. 'I should be most honoured, Your Excellency.'

Phaulkon tapped on his chair. As his slaves began to raise it on to their shoulders, he turned to Aarnout Faa.

'May I count on your co-operation, then, during this period of . . . shall we say, transition?'

Faa looked at Phaulkon with grudging respect. 'Sir, you have my word on it.'

The new Barcalon was installed in a grand ceremony at the palace. The Governor of Ligor joined the prostrate Governors of all the other provinces in saluting His Excellency Pra Vichai-yen; Aarnout Faa bowed low with the representatives of the other trading nations in Ayudhya and Père Vachet inclined himself with the rest of the Jesuits who had been instrumental in securing the peace. To the clash of cymbals and the sound of trumpets, His Majesty appeared on the balcony and announced that with his new Barcalon a new era had begun in Siamese politics.

General Petraja gritted his teeth and smiled amiably while Luang Sorasak, his head in a bandage, reluctantly attended the investiture before departing for the distant northern province of Phitsanuloke where he had been named the new Governor.

Phaulkon was married in the second grand ceremony to be held in the main palace courtyard that day, this one conducted by the French Bishop of Ayudhya and attended by the Supreme Patriarch of the Buddhist faith, the first time that the two religious leaders had officiated at the same ceremony. His Majesty sent lavish gifts to the newlyweds, and in a rare gesture of supreme honour made a brief appearance atop his bejewelled elephant, with the white elephant from Ligor at his side.

All the court ladies, resplendent in their ceremonial finery, were present and in the centre of their prostrate ranks, Sunida, enjoying all their recognition and support as the chosen consort of the Lord of Life's favourite minister, gazed admiringly at the handsome Pra Klang in his vermilion brocade coat, presented to him by His Majesty for the occasion. In the furthest row to the back, behind the court ladies and by special invitation, crouched Sri. She wore the southern-style sarong gifted her by the palace and pride in the farang master was written all over her face.

The Lady Maria, radiant in a long white dress of Chinese silk with a matching veil over her head, stood proudly by her husband's side. Glancing at the ladies around her, her eye alighted on Sunida, truly stunning in a turquoise blouse and a black panung, her slender fingers glittering with jewels. The words of Mestre Phanik, her father, came back to her now and it occurred to her that Sunida was no real threat after all. Here, amidst the sea of palace concubines, she was just another Siamese woman behaving according to the precepts of her upbringing.

Maria felt an urge to tell her just how beautiful she was. She caught her eye and smiled at her.

Overcome with joy, Sunida smiled back radiantly. Thank the Lord Buddha, she reflected gratefully, clutching her stomach as she felt the little kick again.